THE KEEP

Also by Roger Taylor from Bladud Books:

The Call of the Sword
The Fall of Fyorlund
The Waking of Orthlund
Into Narsindal
Dream Finder
Farnor
Valderen
Whistler
Ibryen
Arash-Felloren
Caddoran
The Return of the Sword

THE KEEP

Roger Taylor

Published by
Bladud Books

First published in 2011 by Mushroom eBooks

This edition published in 2011 by
Bladud Books, an imprint of Mushroom Publishing,
Bath, BA1 4EB, United Kingdom

www.bladudbooks.com

Cover illustration © Shirley Horton

ISBN 978-1-84319-034-9

CHAPTER 1

Voices were all about him.

Hovering in the moon-hazed darkness they rose and fell like a blustering wind through summer tree-tops. Now near, now far. Now loud, now faint. Now incoherent and wild. Now clear and distinct and full of significance.

Slowly, and almost imperceptibly, a faint but familiar resolve whispered in their wake.

He must listen to them—reach into their urgent susurration—grasp what they were saying. For surely there was meaning to be found in them if he could just touch it?

They had been coming to him since his arrival here, drifting through the half-place between the worlds of waking and sleeping where dreams and reality were inextricably entangled.

Yet with this resolve came the remembrance that his very awareness, his realization that he was, was sufficient to disturb this strange sending. And a too wilful act, a deliberate listening, would end it as abruptly as the fall of an axe.

As it did, yet again.

Slipping intangibly away from him, the voices were already fading into an unknowable distance, dwindling into the soft hiss of his frustrated breath as his eyes flickered open and the dim snow-lit morning world formed about him, solid and real. Now there would be only memories of memories to linger hauntingly through the quieter moments of the day.

Though he knew it would be futile, he could do no other than close his eyes and try to recapture the sounds before they were lost utterly. There was stillness, contentment even, in the waking comfort of his bed and the soft darkness of the early hour. Whatever problems the day might bring— and it would probably bring more than a few, he knew—nothing could be done here either to precipitate or avoid them.

It was good.

But, less than smoke in the wind, the voices and whatever message they were carrying had gone—scattered by his waking and dispersed beyond any retrieval by his seeking after them. The tools of the mind that normally served him so well lurched after them, though half-heartedly. They were too coarse by far to capture and secure so fragile a quarry.

Were the voices the residue of a forgotten dream?

Not an answerable question. He rarely remembered his dreams but, when he did, those fragments that remained with him were, for the most part, prosaic and unthreatening; usually artless patchworks of recent events. They rarely carried either mystery or terror.

Were they an echo of some distant activity in the Keep, carried to him along unseen ways through its ancient stonework? What activity? He glanced at the window. The low snow-filled sky was greying. No one else would be up at this time. Besides, he doubted that anything could echo through this place, so massive was every aspect of its construction. And, too, he was not one to be roused by a mere noise.

Were they no more than the sound of his own breathing intruding into his half-wakened brain?

Possibly, he supposed, though it seemed unlikely. They were too varied, too complex, too full of subtle rhythms to be merely a throttled snore.

He rubbed his eyes and ended the pointless inquiries. They had to have their run, like dogs sniffing about a courtyard—intent and with apparently deep purpose—but they would bring back no prey. Lying back he yawned and stretched extravagantly then pulled a wry face. Whatever the voices were—the word "voices" persisted with him—they at least served to wake him early, a feat which a wide range of mechanical devices and parental and wifely reproaches had never succeeded in doing in the past.

"I sleep well because I've a clear conscience," he would protest.

"You sleep well because you're a lazy sod," was the non-mechanical con-sensus. And, in his clear conscience, he could not wholly deny this. Brisk rising was not one of his stronger virtues.

This was just another puzzle. For though the voices did not wake him sharply, they left him wide-awake and reluctant, perhaps unable, to go back to sleep again. Thinking back over a lifetime of reluctant risings, this was in many ways even stranger than waking him in the first place.

Still, that was how it was. He threw the sheets back and swung out of bed, shivering slightly as the room's cold embraced him.

A tall, stiff-shouldered clock, a relic of the previous occupant of the room, stood by the door. Its intimidating presence made him want to cower when he passed it and his first active decision of the day was the same as it had been the previous day: he really should get round to having the damned thing moved. He squinted peevishly at the ornately decorated face which lowered back at him in its turn like a malevolent and tattooed dacoit. Its fingers, drooping like mustachios, confirmed what the dull sky had already told him. It was early. No bad thing, he conceded reluctantly. Laggard he might be at early rising, but he always enjoyed the feeling of advantage that it gave him. It stretched the day.

Perhaps the voices were nothing more than some self-induced device designed by his deeper—better?—nature to ensure this outcome?

That was a new thought.

He dismissed it. If good intentions had been his saviour he would have been a regular dawn riser long before now.

A spasm of irritation shook him. He had enough to do without wast-ing his time fretting about clocks or, still less, mysterious sounds. Anyway, intriguing though these might be, they must surely be some figment of his imagination, even if he hadn't the imagination to work out what it might be yet. Indeed it would be surprising if working in this place did not stir something in the muddier depths of his minds.

He busied himself with washing and changing but did not turn the main light on. That would have blackened the gradually lightening window and shrunk his world to the confines and comforts of this solitary room which could well have lured him back to the warmth of his bed after all. Better to let the day seep into him.

Better to let the Keep seep into him.

The thought made him pause as he shaved. It was peculiar, he reflected. He had mapped many buildings in his time and some of those that had been acquired during the New Order's recent expansion had been remarkable and unusual. There had been those cities in the east where high soaring, sky-scarring towers sentenced their populations to jostling insignificance in bleak, wind-scoured streets; streets that were shrouded in permanent shadowed twilight except sometimes at the extremities of the day when the sun's blanching touch might sere along them. And in the west there had been those rambling, half-subterranean conurbations of interlinked and ill-defined dwellings. Mapping them had been peculiarly difficult, but their dominant feature was not measurable—the smell, or rather smells. He shook his head at the memory. He did not want to recall too much of that. At least not before he had eaten.

But nothing he had ever seen had been remotely like this great isolated pile. As he had wandered about the place as part of his preliminary study to work out how he might begin this new task, his professional eye had automatically searched for familiar lines and shapes and patterns that would help him order and arrange the building in the catalogue of his experience. But there had been nothing. Not even distant resonances from the sketchbooks and historical texts of his student days. And, so far, that had remained the case, both inside and outside the building. This place was truly unique.

That it was the work of one mind was all too apparent, but whose was beyond any speculation. And what could it have been? When had it been built? Or why? Or, for that matter, how? The rock from which its huge stones had been cut was not to be found in this region and, apart from the seemingly insurmountable difficulty of hauling them through the mountains, it verged on the inconceivable that they had been hewn, slotted, notched, and positioned with such accuracy by brute manual effort. Yet they must have been, for, whatever else this place might prove to be, it was not new, nor even recent. The weathering of those same stones was at least one thing that was familiar—this was an ancient place.

"One step at a time," he said to the puzzling image waving a razor at him from the mirror. There were enough routine technical problems associated with surveying this place without wasting his time turning over questions to which there might well be no answers.

He could always ask, of course...

The image became uneasy. The New Order did not appreciate needless speculation, still less too much active curiosity. He had his allotted task. He must do it efficiently and accurately. That was all he need concern himself with. It was sufficient that this place was theirs now and thus part of their greater intent. It was more than sufficient that they had employed him. It was a mark of their trust in him—an acknowledgement of previous work well done and duties faithfully fulfilled. He should be careful not to jeopardize any of this. True, he was good at his job—very good—but this was not necessarily a guarantee of continued acceptance—and there were always plenty others who would scrabble to replace him if he showed himself to be... unsuitable.

He splashed the remains of the foam from his face with cold water then dried himself briskly. *That* was something that need not be dwelt on. It was not going to happen. He had too shrewd an eye for the reality of his position to risk it with carelessness. He must remain both efficient and inconspicuous.

Do your job. Observe the procedures and all would be well.

Procedures were everything under the New Order.

Keep your curiosity and your speculation to yourself.

He reminded himself again that there were plenty difficult "ordinary" problems associated with this place which would have to be solved if he was indeed to fulfil his instructions.

Some of these were taxing him a little while later as he stood in the fresh-fallen snow by the sole entrance to the Keep.

CHAPTER 2

Although it was on top of a mountain, the Keep was fronted by a deep and steep-sided channel that elsewhere might have become a water-filled moat. As it was, in earlier times, coupled with the cliffs to the rear, it would certainly have been an extremely effective defensive feature, completely isolating the Keep from its surroundings and confining all approaches to the single entrance. This, in its turn, was served by a drawbridge which could be lowered and raised quite easily by one man through an ingenious arrangement of pulleys and levers.

Yet, the moat seemed to be unnecessary. Though he knew little of warfare, ancient or modern, Josyff could see that the very location of the Keep precluded any siege techniques that he had ever heard of other than a patient waiting for its occupants to starve to death. There was nowhere to erect scaling towers or to position artillery, and undermining was out of the question. The place would yield to modern weapons, of course. These could bombard it from the valley far below. But then, who would want such a place, either now or in the past? What conceivable strategic or commercial significance could it have, situated here, far from any great centres of population or important trade routes?

His feet crunching the fresh snow, he stepped out on to the drawbridge and peered cautiously over the edge. This was the only place he had found which offered any view into the gloomy depths of the channel, but even here he could make out only the occasional jagged peak rising out of the darkness. This couldn't be a natural feature, surely? Yet, to be man-made, it represented an achievement every whit as daunting as the building of the Keep itself.

This place held so many questions.

A shiver shook him and, though no wind was blowing, he pulled his coat tight and hunched his shoulders against the cold. He looked up at the snow-covered mountains that surrounded the Keep. This would be a stern and forbidding place at the height of summer but the heavy grey skies, pregnant with yet more snow, added an almost tangible menace to it.

"Still puzzling our problem, Surveyor?"

Josyff started at the sound and turned to see the man who had greeted him on his arrival. One set of eagerly proffered papers had identified him as Badr ak-Herion from the Aggoran province, far to the south. Another set announced him as Josyff's new Chief Assistant. When working in the east, Josyff had had an excellent team and he had recommended that it be kept together for this latest undertaking. However, while no formal reply had come to this, the members of the team had subsequently received instructions that would take them all far from one another.

"The New Order's greater vision," one of them had said flatly as they parted.

"Yes," he had replied in like vein.

"I apologize, Surveyor, I startled you." Badr's hand was extended as though to prevent Josyff from lurching over the edge of the drawbridge, though he was too far away to have done anything should that have happened.

"Yes, Badr," Josyff replied, stepping back awkwardly. "I'm afraid you did. This is a very puzzling building. It's easy to become engrossed."

Badr was a short, heavily-built man with short-cropped hair and a round face that would have been jovial were it not for the small deep-set eyes that pocked it. He gave Josyff the impression of being two people: the one with the rolling gait that could be seen as he pursued his allotted tasks, and one somewhere else, quiet and still, who watched and noted. Still, his manner was affable, and his work—so far as he had been able to do any—had been competent. Josyff reproached himself for his unspoken judgement. Nevertheless, despite the confines of their working circumstances, he felt it would be politic to make no effort to be anything other than pleasantly professional with him.

Badr nodded. "Indeed it is," he said. "What do you think it might have been?"

Josyff's reply was deliberately casual.

"I've no idea. It's enough for the moment that it's going to be no easy job surveying it. It's like nothing I've ever seen before." He met Badr's gaze. "Have *you* had any experience of anything like this?"

The deep eyes blinked slowly and the Chief Assistant turned away to look up at the high curving wall with its narrow windows. "No," he said. His examination moved down into the darkness of the moat and he let out a long misting breath into the cold air. "I suppose we'll have to measure that as well."

There was a ruefulness in his voice which twitched the edges of Josyff's mouth into a faint smile in spite of himself. He abandoned it as Badr turned back to him.

"I haven't had a full brief yet," he said. "Perhaps when it arrives we'll be spared that."

"Perhaps. Perhaps not." Badr gave a resigned shrug and turned back to the gateway.

More than likely, perhaps not, Josyff thought, watching him. The New Order collected information relentlessly. Not a bad thing in itself, he reflected, but there was an indiscriminate quality about it that was unsettling. There seemed to be no judgement of what was being learned, no ordering of it, as if it were being gathered for its own sake rather than illumination—a jumble of words rather than a narrative, a heap of bricks and timber rather than a house.

Then again, who was he to judge the New Order's vision?

Who indeed?

Let it go.

Unconsciously he copied Badr's glance up at the walls of the Keep. Their solidity seemed to anchor him. He had to make an effort to remind himself that it was only three days since he had clambered up the final slope on foot, carrying his fortunately modest baggage.

"We can't ride the horses any further," his guides had told him as the snow started to fall. "And if we walk with you we'll not be able to get back before nightfall." Their leader had taken his arm and pointed. "You'll see the Keep when you reach the top of this rise. There's only one way, and it's quite narrow. You can't get lost." He had looked Josyff up and down as if to satisfy himself on this point. "It'll take you about an hour."

Josyff had had considerable reservations about carrying on alone through the whitening landscape, but there was both a reassurance and a gentle finality in the guide's tone that forbade any serious argument.

He nevertheless voiced his concern. "What if the snow worsens... or a mist comes down?" he asked.

The guide peered up through the falling flakes, dark against the grey sky, and shook his head. "It won't," he said unhesitatingly. Then he looked at Josyff squarely. "You are quite safe, Surveyor. We wouldn't leave you otherwise. But *we* won't be if we don't turn back now." He held out his heavily gloved hand and Josyff shook it automatically. "You'll see the Keep and the way to it from the top," he said again, releasing Josyff's hand and indicating the path ahead once more. "And you're expected. *We* are not."

Josyff tried to look confident. "You'll bring my equipment..."

"As soon as it arrives," the guide replied. He was checking the fastenings on Josyff's pack in an oddly paternal manner. "We must leave now." He patted him on the arm.

And with a final farewell, he and his companions were striding quickly away.

Then they were gone.

Alone, Josyff stood still and awkward in the muffling silence of the deepening snow, looking after his vanished guides. After a moment, an eddy of alarm at his isolation started to whirl in the pit of his stomach and he momentarily considered calling, or even running after them. Then he forced himself to smile at this childlike impulse and the alarm faded. He might not be used to either mountains or snow, but over the past days the grandeur of the landscape he had found himself entering had moved him—awed him, almost—and the silence now descending with the snow brought a peace with it that seemed to enter into the heart of him—quietening him. The guides had been attentive to his needs throughout the journey so far and there had been no hint of concern in their manner as they had left. All would be well.

He hitched his pack needlessly and set off up the winding path.

As the guide had said, the Keep came into view when he reached the top of the rise. Josyff stopped and stared at it for a long, timeless interlude. Even from a distance and with its outline softened by the falling snow, the Keep exuded a massive presence: a sense of timeless patience and resolute purposefulness, an ominous focus. It was as though it were pressing down, perhaps even trying to crush, the mountain vantage on which it stood. Yet, too, it belonged there. It was no arbitrary addition.

Josyff could not have said how long he stood there but when he recollected himself he set off towards the Keep with some urgency, concerned that, notwithstanding the guide's assurance, he could yet be caught by the failing light. As he walked on, he had a sense of the Keep watching him, and of its great weight drawing him forward.

Somewhat to his surprise, it was almost exactly one hour since leaving the guides that, snow-covered and with legs aching and unsteady after the final steep slope, he was standing at the edge of the moat, opposite the closed drawbridge.

"You are expected," the guide leader had said, but Josyff could see no signs of life about the place—no movement on its walls, no lights at its windows. Nor could he see any way of announcing his presence. There was just the Keep, powerful and dominating—and seemingly unreachable.

Looking from the raised drawbridge down into the dark maw of the moat, the fear of abandonment he had felt briefly when the guides left him began to return.

Then, as if in response, and almost noiselessly, the drawbridge had descended.

As he had walked across it, the sound of his heavy tread had seemed intrusive in the mountain stillness.

Badr had been waiting to meet him, standing under a dim light in the shelter of the arched gateway. He thrust his papers forward before speaking.

Josyff recalled the scene vividly as he turned away from his contemplation of the moat and followed Badr back through the gateway.

Only three days ago, he reflected. He felt as though he had been there much longer. Perhaps it was the stillness of the place. He was used to working in bustling places where, after some initial curiosity, people simply moved around him as they went about their various businesses, treating him as though he were little more than part of the buildings he was measuring. Then again it might be the pace at which he was working which was hardly spectacular. Not that this concerned him greatly. The early days of any mapping were invariably spent in wandering about, quietly familiarizing himself with the new challenges and working out the best way to approach the work. And it was obvious from the outset that the Keep was going to be particularly difficult with its seemingly innumerable rooms and halls, and its elaborate winding passages and stairways. Still, initial confusion was usual. It would resolve itself eventually and the building would gradually shrink as he found the order that must lie within it. Then he would need his equipment. It was beginning to trouble him that it had not yet arrived. He looked back over his shoulder at the now obscured track as if the very thought might conjure the guides into being, hauling his paraphernalia through the snow. But there was nothing: just the unchanged white stillness.

He remarked on the delay to Badr as he caught up with him.

"It may not even be at the village yet," the Chief Assistant replied. "I'm not from around here but this snow is both heavy and unseasonal, I believe. Perhaps it's causing problems further afield. At least we've plenty of food."

"The New Order provides," Josyff said stiffly, hesitant to become involved in anything that might imply criticism of his employers.

"Indeed," Badr agreed, tight-lipped, though there was an unmistakeably ironic edge to his voice. Josyff's assessment of the man shifted briefly. He had presumed him to be just another of the New Order's people. Many of the functionaries of the previous government—insofar as it could be called a government—had been either dismissed or, bewilderingly, found themselves with no duties—or salary—without any form of notification. There had been no pattern to this silent purging that Josyff could see, but the equally silent message he received—hovering ever-present in any bureaucracy—was that he should be still and watchful and not draw attention to himself. Whether it was this or his true worth that spared him he could not have said. He was simply grateful that he was still there when it was all over. And, on the whole, like many, he had not been too displeased with what had happened. The Government that the New Order had replaced had been inept to the point of irrationality, and, startling and unexpected though the New Order's emergence had been, even from his comparatively lowly position, and with his disdain for politics and politicians generally, Josyff could see that many of the changes they had brought in were both valuable and necessary.

But that was then. Now, an early intolerance of difference had grown, and with it, brutality. Many good people had gone, he knew. People who had much to offer. And those who were replacing them, particularly those in high office, few though he had met, were... strange... cold and distant.

But then, he reflected, strangeness was not a quality that was confined to the upper echelons of the New Order. Take, for example, the other three who were at the Keep when he arrived.

CHAPTER 3

"Nah, boss, can't move that."

Pursed lips and an unequivocal shake of the head accompanied the statement though they were followed immediately by a flicker of doubt as lean and work roughened hands wrestled with the ornate iron key.

"At least I don't think so."

With a piercing screech of reluctance the key eventually turned. The door, by contrast, opened silently.

"Always a problem, this one." The hands worked the key vigorously, throwing the bolt several times as if to loosen it, but each time it screeched in protest. Wincing, Josyff tapped the owner of the hands to end its torture.

"Can't you oil it?" he asked.

The head shook again, and there was a hint of weariness in the face as one of the hands prodded the now revealed lock.

"Not where it's needed. Riveted you see," came the explanation. "Can't get in it without wrecking it—and the door. Can't think why on a fine old time-piece like this." The other hand slapped the side of the clock affectionately. The sound was transformed into a deep resonant echo that billowed out of the clock's dark interior to fill the room. The lock was prodded again. "Like something off a dungeon, this."

Nyk was one of the three men who tended the Keep. The others were Henk and Qualto. Badr had told Josyff about them shortly after his arrival but had made no effort to seek them out or introduce them formally. Josyff, in his turn, had presumed that details about them and their histories and duties would be in his brief—when it arrived—and had not pressed the matter. They had thus just drifted into his awareness as part of the Keep, his first encounter with Henk and Qualto being a hesitant acknowledging wave across a courtyard while Nyk, grey-haired and overalled, had offered him a nod and a crisp "Boss," as he had passed him, sporting a short ladder on his shoulder and striding along with great purposefulness. It had occurred to him that three people did not seem to be very many to attend to the maintenance of a building of this size, but he had not dwelt on the notion.

This morning however, he had held to his resolve to "do something" about the clock that so dominated his room, and he had sought out Nyk with a view to having it moved. Nyk had a sharp accent that Josyff could not place and a disconcerting habit of craning forward and peering intently into the face of anyone addressing him as though listening to a rather slow child.

"And the door too, for that matter." Nyk's thumb and forefinger were measuring out the thickness of the door. He held them up for Josyff's inspection.

Though he knew little about clocks Josyff could only agree. The lock was indeed massive and the door was thick enough to serve, if not a dungeon, certainly a house.

"It's probably very old," he said weakly.

"Oh, it's old, all right. Everything round here's old. It was old when I started here and I've seen... what...? three squires come and go."

"How long ago was that?" Josyff asked casually

Nyk's head was disappearing into the entrails of the clock and his reply was distant and echoing. It was accompanied by the rattling of chains and some faint and random bell chimes. "We've been here for ever. Me, Henk and Qualto. Henk a year after me, Qualto..." There was a pensive pause. "About two years after Henk."

Nyk emerged from the clock, riffled noisily through a battered box of tools before retrieving an equally battered torch, then disappeared back into it again.

"Thought not."

Josyff found himself being urged to peer into the body of the clock as Nyk reappeared. As he leaned tentatively forward, he saw that the interior was bigger than he had expected and he had a brief impression that the darkness was about to close about him. He felt a twist of claustrophobia but it vanished as the light from Nyk's torch fragmented the darkness. The pendulum swept past his face, startling him. The light flicked about significantly.

"See. Look at those bolts." The light stopped on a large and well rusted bolt head, then moved to indicate several others.

"Well fastened, that." There was a chuckle. "More dungeon work. It makes no sense to put a clock in a case as solid as this and it makes even less to go to such trouble to fasten it down. It's hardly likely to be whisked off by a casual thief, is it? Must've been expecting an earthquake or something."

Nyk's head joined Josyff's in the clock.

"Deep, you see," he continued, fencing with the pendulum to tap one of the bolts with his torch and sending shadows dancing about the interior. "There's lots of them about the place. Somehow they seem to have fastened them direct into the stone. God knows how. I wish I did. This stuff's blunted more than a few of my best drills I can tell you. It's a nightmare to work with." He withdrew from the clock. Josyff joined him. "But they're in to stay. Never moved one of those yet without ruining it. Either the corners go, or the head comes right off." His hands mimicked the wringing of a bird's neck.

Josyff looked up at the clock. Fingers now horizontal, it returned his gaze with one of startled indignation at this unwarranted intrusion.

"Mechanism's beautiful though," Nyk said, looking both to defend his charge and appease his companion. "Really fine work. Keeps excellent time."

Josyff had anticipated a certain degree of muscular endeavour and bad language in the moving of the clock, but not these peculiar complications. "I'm sure," he conceded.

Nyk nodded and fixed an expectant look on Josyff, but held his peace. Uncomfortable, Josyff looked for a way to move away from the subject.

"You must've been concerned that the New Order might reassign you," he said offhandedly, as though he were in reality still pondering what to do about the clock.

Nyk was clattering through his tools again. "Not really," he replied. "Governments come and go, but they're all the same, aren't they? They talk a lot but they always need folks like me to do the real work. And we're not that important, are we? Out here, a long way from anywhere." The clattering rose to an agitated peak. "Besides, they're not really anything to do with us. We're employed by the Estate." He tapped a faded emblem on his overalls. "Like the squires, though the last one used to pretend this was his family place." With a final wrench he produced a long, grim-looking spanner from the box. "Do you want me to try and move one of those?" he asked with a nod towards the clock though with a strong hint of "don't say I didn't warn you," in his voice.

Josyff avoided the renewed gaze as if still undecided, but his curiosity was aroused. He was no bureaucratic schemer but it might be useful to know the fate of those previously responsible for this place.

"What happened to the last... squire?" he asked.

Nyk shrugged. "No idea. Went out on one of his usual jaunts one day, never came back."

Josyff was momentarily silenced by this blunt reply.

"Did *he* work for the government?" he managed eventually.

"Nah, I told you. He worked for the Estate."

Josyff had to ask. "What Estate?"

Nyk gave him a puzzled look. "The one that owns this place," he said slowly and with forced patience.

"But it belongs to the New Order."

Nyk shrugged again. "That's as may be. I told you, it makes no difference out here. We just keep the place going, that's all. And I'm not bothered just so long as my wages are paid, we get supplies, and no one interferes with me." He paused and retreated quickly from this radical position. "To tell the truth I don't think anyone's really interested in this place."

Josyff's mind was now awash with questions. He snatched at one.

"How long has the last squire been gone?"

Nyk puffed out his cheeks and looked up at the clock as if for inspiration. His face became absorbed in a calculation of some kind and his fingers twitched. "About ten years I'd think. Nine or ten. I wouldn't swear to either. It's a long time."

Despite himself, Josyff gaped.

"Ten years! And you don't know what's happened to him?"

Nyk's reply was almost offhand. "He was always wandering off. Visiting relatives, as he used to say, when he said anything. He'd be gone for weeks on end. Never a word." He paused and looked thoughtful. "I must admit I hadn't realized it'd been so long. But no one's ever been to ask about him."

Josyff stammered. "But... but who's been doing his work? And who tells you what to do?"

Nyk replaced the spanner in the box and gave Josyff a knowing, almost paternal grin. "Like I said, we're a long way from anywhere here. In fact, we're even a long way from *here*, here." The grin became a soft chuckle at his own joke. "There was nothing for him to do," he said. "There never has been, for any of the squires that I've seen. They wander about like lost souls. I think the Estate used to send people here when they wanted to get rid of them quietly—out of sight, out of mind, you know. As for us, we know what we have to do. And there's always plenty of it." He faltered and his eyes became briefly distant. "This place is a lot bigger than it looks. Must've taken ten times our number to look after it once." He eyed Josyff. "At least *you've* got something to do. Mind you, not that I know anything about surveying, but I don't think you're going to find this place easy to measure. It's very odd. What do you want doing with this clock?"

Josyff was glad of the sharp lurch back to his original problem.

"You'd better leave it if it's going to be such a problem. It's just not to my taste, that's all. I thought you could just move it into the corridor, but I wouldn't want to destroy it."

"Keeps excellent time." Nyk confirmed again by way of consolation as he closed the door and turned the screeching lock. He picked up his box of tools with a loud grunt and, leaning to one side to accommodate its weight, made for the door. "I suppose I could always cover it up for you," he said over his shoulder.

Josyff risked an informality. "No, it's not that important. I'll learn to love it. Thanks for your help."

Nyk nodded.

When he had left, Josyff sat on the end of his bed, staring at the clock for some time. He had not thought about it before but at least he knew now why its tick was so soft, confined as it was in the substantial casing. But Nyk's observations about the clock were unsettling him for some reason. Why should anyone have built it so massively? And why would they fasten it to the fabric of the building so ferociously? It didn't seem to make any sense. Then again, this whole place was strange. Even to the way its staff was employed, it seemed. There had been no mention of any Estate when he had received his instructions. Still less of any squires. What an odd, archaic word. Some local tradition, perhaps?

But gone for ten years! Just walked away. Josyff shook his head and leaned back on his elbows. Maybe he shouldn't be so surprised, he decided after a little reflection. Nepotism and favouritism were rife in the previous government and greater follies than a few incompetents being put out to grass had been committed in the past. As for Nyk and the others— and whatever this Estate was—even the New Order was entitled to a little vagueness in the handling of its more distant concerns, and, as Nyk had said, this place was a long way from anywhere. It was difficult to see what importance it might have.

Doubtless all would become clear in time.

As he looked at the clock he recalled that its interior had seemed bigger than its exterior. An unusual illusion, especially given the considerable thickness of the casing. On an impulse he stood up and turned the key in the clock door.

The lock opened silently.

CHAPTER 4

Josyff pulled his hand away from the key quickly, taken aback by the ease with which it had turned. Though smaller and lighter than he was, Nyk had given the impression of considerable wiry strength and he had had a determined struggle with the protesting lock.

Probably just because it's not been opened for a long time, Josyff reassured himself. Nyk must have shaken something loose. He would mention it when he saw him again.

He eased the door open very carefully.

It was indeed unusually thick and, as it swung out, it came between the light and the clock, seeming to darken the whole room.

Josyff leaned forward to examine the interior of the clock and once again felt as though the darkness was luring him forward. He had to force himself to smile at his foolishness, but he was nevertheless gripping the edge of the door as he began methodically staring into the gloom. As his eyes adjusted he made out the pendulum, shade within shade, swinging slowly from side to side. A purposeful, loud and resonant click accompanied each passing. And was it his imagination or could he hear a sound like the rushing of a wind as it passed? As though it were infinitely long and heavy and working a vast machine somewhere? It seemed suddenly to be a long way away. He reached out with the intention of stopping it then changed his mind. He might not be able to start it again and he had no desire to make himself foolish in front of Nyk or the others by having to run after him to get it started again. But that was a feeble excuse at the forefront of his mind. Behind it, ill-formed and menacing, was a feeling that he would not be able to stop it, that if his hand closed about it, it would draw him inexorably forward and bind him to its eerie fruitless journey arcing out a measure of the time of this place.

A dangling chain brushed the back of his hand making him jump.

Then he was falling.

Through the darkness.

His hands flailed wildly, snatching at the chains he could feel swaying about him, but they kept slipping away, as though taunting him.

Cold air rushed past him. Faster and faster.

His head was filled with the sound of his own terrified screaming mingling with jangling bells and rattling chains and...

Voices.

Voices chaotic with consternation and fear. Rising and falling with the scything hiss of the pendulum. Louder and louder.

He reached out to them—desperate—appealing.

Even as he did so, light flooded over him painfully and his body was shaken by a racking impact.

Gasping violently for breath and deafened by the pounding of his heart he made no attempt to move for some time.

Slowly he opened his eyes and, as they gradually focused, so the brightness of the light dimmed and both his body and his mind became quiet enough to identify where he was.

He was lying on his bed, staring up at the ceiling of his room.

He put his shaking hand to his face. It was damp with perspiration.

A dream, or, more correctly, a nightmare, he decided, as he cautiously levered himself upright and let out a noisy and unsteady breath. He must have dozed off after Nyk left. He forced himself to stand though it was no slight task—his legs were trembling as much as his hands.

He gave the clock a reproachful look which, with one finger drooping now, it returned.

As the trembling gradually faded he managed a nervous laugh though it sounded oddly flat after the echoing space within the clock. Ironic that only earlier he had been reflecting how rarely he remembered his dreams and how benign they were when he did.

"Enough," he said. Voices, eccentric clocks, squires with nothing to do who just walk away. There was enough to think about here by way of straightforward technical surveying problems without all this nonsense. The words, "mountain madness" drifted into his mind.

No, he thought crossly. There's no madness here. He was just unsettled by this place and its isolation. He was used to busier climes. The enforced idleness did not suit him. If only his brief and his instruments would arrive. Surely the people in the village were used to bringing goods and the like up here through the snow? How else could Nyk and the others survive the winter? With this thought came the unwelcome thought that perhaps the snow was particularly bad. He had no way of telling. Unseasonal, Badr had called it. What if it was so bad that the villagers *couldn't* reach them? What if there was a chance they might run out of food and themselves be unable to reach the village?

He gritted his teeth, straightened up and swore at himself. If that had been a possibility, he was sure, even on his limited acquaintance of the man, that Nyk would have already mentioned it.

He went to the wash basin and splashed cold water on his face. Starting new jobs was always a little ragged and disorganized and this one was proving particularly so. He could ask Nyk about the snow and his equipment in due course. Things would take shape soon enough.

He looked at the clock as he dried his face, then through the window at the snow-covered mountains as though somehow they might have changed. He laughed again, though not as self-consciously as before. A nightmare—he couldn't even remember having such a thing when he was a child—and in the morning too. So much for his early rising. But, in spite of this attempt at dismissiveness, an unease lingered.

As he put on his jacket he moved back to the clock. Gripping the key tightly and not without a hint of trepidation, he made to turn it. It resisted sufficiently for him to bring two hands to bear. Then, with a recognizable screech, it turned. Josyff yanked the door open, though more violently that he had intended. Inside were chains and counter weights and the steadily swinging pendulum with its reassuring and solid tick. The sound of the harsh opening was reverberating distantly.

He closed and locked the door and patted the side of the clock as though it were now an old friend.

Josyff smiled as Badr ushered him into the little room.

"How did you come across this?" he asked.

"Nyk mentioned it," Badr replied. "When I was asking him about your equipment."

"Did he have anything to say about that? About the snow?" He was about to ask, "Are we cut off?" but changed it. "Will the guides be able to bring it through?"

"It shouldn't be too much of a problem, apparently. The snow *is* early but it's not bad enough to block the paths. Presumably the equipment—and the brief—simply haven't arrived."

Josyff was not sure that this was any more reassuring than the news that they were not snowed in. He had done the necessary paperwork before he left and ensured it had been received and acknowledged by the correct departments and that everything was in fact available. Even so, the New Order judged by results and was notoriously indifferent to excuses no matter how legitimate, especially where these might in some way reflect on shortcomings within its own bureaucracy. He had been sent here to measure this place, to prepare plans of it. Failure to do that, for whatever reason, would not be good for him. He might still find himself quietly dismissed from the service like so many others before him.

Still, there was nothing he could do here immediately. Give it a little longer, he decided. One of the advantages of this place was that there were no distractions. Once he was started he should be able to make good progress. Judging from Nyk's attitude towards the New Order it was quite possible that villagers might just be "relaxed" about obeying its instructions—life was reputedly slower away from the cities he had heard. Or they could perhaps be waiting in the hope that the snow might clear. If necessary he could have Nyk take him back to the village to see what was happening.

He opened a box that was lying on the table. In it was a theodolite.

He shook his head and laughed as he examined it. "This is like travelling through time," he said. "These things were old when I was just starting studying." He was about to lift it from the box when an old memory asserted itself. Which way does this damned thing fit? More than once in his early student days irritating time had been lost at the end of a country-slogging exercise as he and his colleagues had struggled in failing light to replace recalcitrant instruments back in their boxes.

One way and one way only.

He noted carefully the marking dots and the position of the levelling screws then gently lifted the instrument out and placed it on the table.

"It's been used a lot," he said, rotating the telescope and running a finger over its scratched frame. "What on earth could it be doing here?"

Badr shrugged. "Perhaps this was a mountain survey station once," he offered. "Or maybe this place has already been measured up."

In the ensuing silence the two men looked at one another with a hint a dry amusement. Josyff was beginning to lose some of his early uncertainty about Badr. Perhaps he too was just another individual considering himself fortunate to have avoided the New Order's "adjusting" of the civic order.

"I think we might perhaps ask Nyk about that," he said conspiratorially. "Just in case he's forgotten to volunteer the information. Even an inaccurate plan would be a great help."

"It would indeed."

Badr was retrieving something from under the table. It was a tripod.

A few minutes later the theodolite was mounted and roughly levelled. Josyff stood back and looked at it, not without some nostalgic pride. "I suppose I should be pleased about this," he said. "Anything's better than nothing. But seeing it makes me want our equipment more than ever. I really don't relish working round this place in the 'good old-fashioned way'."

Badr grimaced in professional agreement.

Josyff gazed around the dusty, windowless room.

"What else is here?"

There was more than he expected. A rummaging search left them both dust-grimed and mildly triumphant. Another theodolite had been unearthed, but it was damaged. There was also a level together with various staffs, rods, chains, tapes, unused recording books, a drawing board and drafting instruments and, prompting a fatalistic in-drawn breath from Josyff, a book of mathematical tables.

"Now we've no excuse at all," he said showing it to Badr in affected horror.

"It would seem so," his Chief Assistant returned in similar vein. The instruments might allow them to measure the place, but calculations would be necessary if the measurements were to be transformed into accurate plans. And those same calculations could be time-consuming, grievously prone to error and generally deeply wearisome when done by hand.

For a moment a hope was held out as the removal of a sheet revealed a chest of long, shallow drawers for the storing of plans. Josyff opened each of the drawers in great anticipation but they proved to be a disappointment. Apart from copious dust-laden cobwebs and more than a few bewildered spiders, they were empty.

"Any use?"

It was Nyk, head peering around the door and his question addressed to the room generally.

"To a museum," Josyff replied.

"Or desperate men," Badr added darkly.

Josyff asked him how the equipment had come to be there and if there were plans already drawn, but was left unenlightened.

No idea where the equipment had come from. Been here as long as he could remember. No *plans* of the place that he knew of, but some very nice pictures in some of the rooms. "No good, then, all this?" Nyk concluded, indicating the spoils of the surveyors' search and wrinkling his nose.

"It might get us started," Josyff conceded, reluctant to seem ungrateful. "We'll have to test it. See what state it's in. But we really need our proper equipment. When..."

"Anything's better than nothing, eh?" Nyk interrupted with an echo of Josyff's own initial response. "That's good." And he was gone.

All eyes turned to the tall figure standing in the doorway of the inn. He returned the collective gaze with an unnerving steadiness then inclined his head slightly in acknowledgement.

His voice was soft and cultured, but everyone heard it very clearly.

"I have to go to the Keep. I am looking for someone to guide me there."

CHAPTER 5

Esyal Wrenith crashed down the steep snowy slope. She rolled over several times at the bottom before coming to a halt, then she lay motionless, face upwards, for a long time. Seen from afar, only the misting in the still, cold air above her told that she had survived the fall.

Nearer, there could have been no doubt. Her breathing was frantic and her face was contorted with effort—the effort needed to stop her from screaming out in a squalling mixture of terror and frustration.

You're still alive, keep quiet, keep quiet, she forced herself to think, over and over, knowing that a hammering repetition was the only discipline that could quell all the other concerns clamouring for attention.

When she had breath enough to speak she allowed the words hiss out softly.

"Concentrate, woman, concentrate. Think what you're doing. One step at a time."

Then she was silent and listening intently.

No sounds of pursuit reached her. Somehow she had managed not to cry out as she had fallen. Either that or her flight had gone unnoticed.

Carefully she began testing her limbs and joints then she levered herself into a sitting position.

Not hurt, she realized. Relief flooded over her though it was followed immediately by the reproach that this had been more by good luck than good management. Next time luck might well not be with her.

There wasn't going to be a next time.

Yet even as the resolution formed, she felt the hollow futility in it. Despair welled up and threatened to sweep her away. They were all lost. Her entire group. *Her* group. Someone had probably betrayed them like all the others though she could not think who. Not that it mattered now.

They had been ambushed and it had only been the untimely snow that had saved her, separating her from the others when it did. She had heard the noise of the encounter but it had echoed all about her and even as she floundered around in circles, desperately trying to determine its direction, it had faded into the swirling white haze.

Had they all been captured? Or, worse, had they all been killed?

She fought back a mounting urge to scream out curses into the silence.

And what had the snow saved her for? Itself? She was hardly equipped for surviving in this weather and this terrain. Her clothes were reasonable but she had no water, no food, and precious little idea where she was.

She was going to die in this place.

Then despair *did* overwhelm her and she dropped down into the snow and sobbed.

The New Order had won. The Rhanen had been defeated utterly. Good men and women who had had the vision to see what others could not and the courage to face it, and who were finally driven to force in an attempt to hold back the New Order's menace. All gone. All scattered, lost. And so many dead. And so many just... no longer there.

She put her arms over her head as though that might hide her from the accusing voices and faces that swam through her mind. They were dispersed in the end only by a violent shiver as the coldness finally impinged on her. She ran still-shaking hands down her tear-stained face and despite the stark desolation of her situation, her despair, as it had done so many times before, began to twist into rage.

She stood up unsteadily and began walking, her thoughts meandering. Why had so few been able to see what the New Order was like?

In some ways it was no mystery. The old government had been a mockery for decades—a shabby remnant of a once great institution. Raised in a sceptical and clear-eyed household, she had learned early that her destiny was largely in her own hands and that nothing was to be gained by looking beyond family and friends for any form of help. It was not the way it was supposed to be, it was not the way it pretended to be, but it was the reality of how things were.

Later she had come to her own conclusion that while government was, at best, a necessary evil, corruption in its many forms—fiscal, intellectual, spiritual—could routinely be expected from those who sought to rule.

Abuse of the power with which the government was supposed to be trusted was accepted as a commonplace and, within depressingly broad limits, was largely shugged off, while their ineptitude was a by-word. In so far as the people prospered reasonably, it was in spite of the government not because of it. And, generally, indifference to and contempt for government outweighed the genuine concern that might have led to a more beneficial drive for change.

It had been a body ripe and ready to fall at the touch of an appropriate wind.

But even so, that did not fully explain how a movement such as the New Order could have swept to power so easily. Many disparate and impromptu groups had arisen over the years as people struggled to fulfil the needs that the government was failing in, but they usually foundered in the thickets of bureaucracy that constantly sprang up to enmesh them. Then, with a suddenness that still bewildered Esyal, they had been displaced by groups of wide-eyed and intense men and women, earnest, powerful and compelling in their speech and manners. Meetings held in local halls one week were held in great stadia the next. Police who had been charged with disbanding them were joining them. Politicians who had condemned them were praising them. Those who looked deeper into their words found only empty rhetoric but their voices went unheard, their arguments and reasons too studied and thoughtful to compete with the tidal wave of simplicity being generated.

And then they were there. Legitimately in power by what seemed to be popular acclaim though, in truth, scarcely a quarter of those entitled to had voted for them.

For a while there was a peculiar silence in the land.

Then...

Where before, there had been debate—inane and unfocused admittedly, but debate nonetheless—there came now only edicts.

And a quiet, seeping menace.

While their words proclaimed openness and freedom, the deeds of the New Order began to recommend silence and obedience. To criticize quite quickly became to defy. Then to defy was to provoke and to provoke was to be presumed guilty of treachery—to be an enemy. The New Order proclaimed both the overwhelming support—and love—of all the people and, at the same time, the presence of *many* enemies, silent, cunning and determined. Enemies of the New Order were, of course, enemies of the people.

And enemies had to be crushed.

And crushed they were. In this regard the New Order was extraordinarily efficient. It helped that it acquired many allies: those who learned quickly when their neighbours were mysteriously missing, and those who looked to secure themselves by *pointing* to their neighbours—and friends—and even kin.

To deal with the apparently increasing number of these enemies, the army and the police became one. Grey-uniformed and sporting the New Order's gentle White Dove insignia they were to be seen in many places. And grey-hearted and anonymous, their unseen aides were everywhere.

A suffocating curtain fell across the land as engulfing and ubiquitous as the snow still falling around Esyal as she came to a halt in the failing light.

For some time she had been wandering aimlessly, her mind too occupied with where she was putting her hands and feet to allow her to dwell too long on her predicament. Now, however, it was becoming too difficult to distract herself with this simple task and she was forced to stop and reflect about what she must do next. Though she knew that she might die in this place, and though despair and guilt still gnawed at her, gone was any semblance of resignation. Without thinking she had quenched her thirst as she walked by eating the occasional handful of snow but now she was both tired and hungry.

Urgently she tried to recall the casual advice she had been given by her cousin as he had led them into the mountains.

What had happened to him...?

Leave it. Leave it! Concentrate!

She cursed herself for not paying more heed. But then they had had equipment and had been making proper and safe camps even though the snow had taken everyone unawares. There had been an air almost of excitement about their expedition. She had spent most of her time thinking how the Rhanen might best be re-formed, how the battle against the New Order might best be continued. She had left the details of their journey to her cousin and his friends—they knew the mountains and where they were supposed to be going. All she and the others had to do was use their commonsense, watch where they were walking and otherwise do as they were told. The possibility that she might have to survive out here on her own never even occurred to her.

Some leader, you, she reproached herself bitterly.

"Don't ask anyone to do anything you're not prepared to do yourself, girl."

"Thank you, father," she whispered softly and not without some pained irony before she returned to her immediate concerns.

Although the snow was falling less heavily now, a wind was beginning to blow, making it dance and swirl, and noticeably colder. It needed no great mountain lore on her part to realize that she must find shelter, and quickly.

It was almost completely dark by the time she wedged herself into a narrow space in a tumbled cluster of rocks. It was sufficient to protect her from both the wind and the falling snow but it was far from comfortable. Nevertheless, it was a considerable relief and she pulled the hood of her coat over her face, wrapped her arms about her, and curled up tightly. Both emotional and physical tiredness came to her aid, sending her almost immediately into a deep sleep, but they did not allow her a trouble-free sleep, and she woke twice in the night full of shaking primitive terrors and with the faint sound of her own cries ringing in her ears.

The third time she woke, it was suddenly and to a brightness that make her screw her eyes tightly after the first shock of opening them. At first she thought she had been discovered, but no violent hands seized her and as she slowly allowed the light to splinter into her consciousness she saw that it was no more than fresh snow under a pale grey sky. As the first shock of this waking passed, so the pain of her night's rest made itself felt and, involuntarily, she cried out as she moved.

It took her some time to extract herself from the gap in the rocks as she carefully tested each limb before moving it, but when she had eased the worst of the discomfort from her back and legs, other needs made themselves felt. She was thirsty and she was hungry. As on the previous day, unsatisfactory though it was, snow had to suffice to quench her thirst, but a painstaking search of her pockets yielded nothing other than a few stale crumbs. Her stomach protested noisily.

"Shut up, damn you," she snarled.

What now, she thought, looking around at snow-covered mountains. Faintly it came to her that at another time they would have been beautiful and she would have gazed at them in awe. But the idea was like a scornful echo. Now, cold, indifferent peaks were just a measure of her desolation.

Downwards, she decided. Downwards towards a river or a stream that she could follow. It would lead her out of the mountains eventually, surely?

And food?

Her stomach rumbled again.

And warmth? And shelter?

Just be careful enough to see that you live to worry about these later, she thought, with grim wilfulness.

And she set off.

CHAPTER 6

"Better than nothing," had been Nyk's assessment of the surveying equipment he had directed Josyff and Badr towards, but Josyff found it difficult to be too rapturous about the discovery.

While the theodolite was not without some mechanical charm, it was very old, intrinsically less accurate than the modern versions, and would be very slow to use. As Badr had remarked, it would look well in a museum, an object perhaps of some nostalgia, a passing tribute to hardier souls who had gone before, but here, in the middle of nowhere, in this mass of convoluted stonework with a difficult job to be done it was as much a taunt as an aid.

Josyff tried to keep the worst of his feelings out of his face as he looked at the instrument. He was not wholly sure about Badr yet. True, the stocky little man had shown one or two unexpected—incautious?—flashes of dark humour which had chimed with his own thinking, but caution was always advisable. Though it seemed unlikely, Josyff knew it was not beyond the bounds of possibility that this whole business was some kind of a test for him, to assess his response to situations where the New Order might appear to be at fault. These were very strange times. And too, less darkly, this *was* his job. Something he was good at. Something that, for the most part, he enjoyed, even though it took him from his wife, home and friends from time to time. The thought of his wife finally cleared his mind. Nothing was to be gained by communicating despondency to those in his charge and that included bemoaning the state of this fortuitously found equipment, or, for that matter, the fate of his own. He must make some kind of progress with what he had. If, after a couple of days, his equipment had still not arrived he would definitely discuss with Nyk the possibility of returning to the village to find out what had happened. That could surely invoke no rebuke.

Nyk had called the room they were in the Great Hall. Unaffected by the heating system that twisted and wound through such of the Keep as Josyff had seen so far, it prompted the two surveyors to wear their coats tightly fastened and to keep moving. However, Josyff was unsettled by more than the temperature. Two tiers of heavy stone balconies fringed three sides of the hall, and high, bleak lighting illuminated a profusion of carved figures protruding from the walls. Long-shadowed, men, women, children, animals, demons, angels, and even wilder creatures of fantasy, all stared intently down into the hall. No two were alike and there was neither consistency in their style nor apparent order or purpose to their arrangement. Except that all of them had their mouths open, as if they were speaking or crying out.

Josyff felt uncomfortable under their collective gaze.

"At least they'll just watch," Badr said as he followed Josyff's uneasy glance. "They won't go measuring their length over one of the tripod legs and wrecking a day's work."

Josyff grunted an appreciative chuckle by way of reply, his tongue protruding slightly as he delved amongst the long-buried memories that he hoped would enable him to set up and use the instrument.

"Well," he announced after a few minutes, slowly rotating the telescope with a gentle forefinger, then clapping his hands briskly. "I've had *worse* trouble setting up one of these in the past. Let's see how it measures."

It did remarkably well, they both decided some time later, although, as they had anticipated, the work proved to be jaw-clenchingly slow, prompting Josyff to remark at one stage that he felt as though he should be carving the readings on to a stone slab. The calculations were even worse as by their nature they were particularly unforgiving, being brought low by the slightest error. At the end, it was clear to both that they could not possibly survey the whole Keep in this way.

Better than nothing the equipment was, but only just.

Normally, Josyff would have quickly established a highly accurate framework of measurements around the outside of the building and then worked inwards from this with subsidiary frameworks from which he would be able to pick up details of the building—from the large to the small, from the simple to the complex. This, however, was not possible here. The terrain, the moat, and the impenetrability of the Keep's walls all conspired to prevent it—well over half the perimeter of the Keep was on the edge of a precipice and the rest of it, save near the path and the drawbridge, was dangerously rugged. Making matters worse, it was quite apparent that it would be difficult to set out even the less desirable alternative to fulfil the same function, namely a convenient framework *within* the Keep. Josyff did not yet know what route he was going to take around the building but it was obvious that the main framework would have many and short sides which meant that the work would require exceptional care and accuracy even with modern equipment.

He confided his intention to go looking for his own equipment, revising the timing of the journey to the next day if Nyk allowed it to be possible at all.

"In the meantime we can set out some internal traverses from here using this," he concluded. "At the worst they'll be useful as a quick check on the work when we come to do it properly."

Badr leaned on the table they had commandeered as a desk and looked down at the large sheet covered with the much corrected calculations that represented their efforts so far. A heavily inscribed pencil ring marked out a closing error—followed by an equally heavy exclamation mark—which they had both agreed was acceptable under the circumstances. Idly he tapped the brown-edged book of mathematical tables.

"Traverse, rather than traverses, I think," he said simply, giving Josyff a significant look.

Josyff conceded the point. "Yes, you're right. Getting more than one done is probably unlikely."

Their discussion was interrupted by the arrival of Henk.

Henk was tall, thin, ponderous in his movements, and with a slouch that gave him the air of a predatory bird, an attribute further enhanced by his long face and bald head. He appeared to be a general labourer for Nyk and Qualto, though from his limited contact with the Keep's tenders so far Josyff had noticed no particular hierarchy of command between them. Eroded by their years together in this place, he presumed.

Henk was also graced with a surly disposition which fitted his physical shape perfectly and when he spoke, which admittedly was not often, it was invariably as though he had just been disturbed in the middle of something particularly important.

He had brought the blessing of the third member of the Keep's triumvirate—Qualto. Hot food and drink steamed appetizingly in the hall's cold air and the sight alone cheered the two men.

It was Qualto who served as the group's cook. In marked contrast to Henk, he was short, round, garrulous and excitable. Food was always one of the small but irksome concerns that troubled Josyff when he moved to a new place and he had been pleasantly surprised by Qualto's efforts. Each time he sat down to eat he promised himself that he would track the scurrying little man back to his kitchen and get to know him a little better than their normal brief encounters permitted. But, like the moving of the clock, it had constantly slipped from his mind. He renewed the promise again as Henk trundled into view.

In anticipation of the arrival of the food, Josyff moved some papers to one side. Henk, however, cleared another part of the table before laying down the tray. As he did so he gave the much amended calculations a dour look then glanced around the hall. The carved multitude returned his inspection.

"These to be measured, too?" he asked with a nod towards the watchers.

"I don't know, I haven't been told yet," Josyff replied, taken off guard by the question. Then, out of a long habit of making friends amongst strangers, he volunteered affably, "I hope not, there are enough problems to deal with here without having to do that."

Henk grunted noncommittally and turned to leave.

Josyff tried again, "Do you know what any of these figures mean? Or who made them? I've never seen anything like them before."

Henk was well on his way now. "No," he replied without looking back.

"Nothing at all?"

"No, Surveyor, I just work here."

Josyff persisted after the slowly retreating figure. "Aren't you curious about them?"

"Not for a long time," Henk replied. He paused and looked at the walls again. "This is a strange place, Surveyor. And full of strange places. No one knows anything about it. It gets tiring, asking. Leave the tray; I'll pick it up later." Then the retreat recommenced, leaving both Josyff and Badr staring after him in silence.

Badr looked at Josyff and mouthed a bewildered, "tiring?"

Josyff shrugged. "My curiosity just doubled the number of questions I had and gave me no answers." He allowed himself some irony. "Perhaps that's what he meant. Maybe his years here have turned him into a subtle philosopher, a spiritual guide for us."

Badr raised doubting eyebrows. "More likely he's just told us not to bother pestering him with any more stupid questions." He mimicked Henk's voice and dismal manner. "He just works here."

This took Josyff a little nearer to Badr and he laughed softly. "While *we* are paid to answer our own questions."

"So it would seem."

They spent the rest of the day doing as Josyff had suggested, setting out and measuring a traverse along a series of corridors that eventually brought them back to the hall again to close off their work. Josyff glanced down at his notebook and shook his head doubtfully.

"Too many short sides and too many wide angles," he said. "I'll be surprised if we don't have a substantial closing error on this." He yawned and snapped the book shut. "I'll work it out later; I'll make too many mistakes if I start now."

Josyff jolted upright. For a moment he was disorientated, thinking that he was in his own private room at home. As the reality of his surroundings established itself about him, he massaged his neck, stretched his arms and legs and snarled at himself. That was the second time he had dozed off. It had been a mistake to tackle these calculations after such a painstaking and annoying day, he realized. They were far too accident prone. And he'd forgotten to speak to Nyk about returning to the village. He swore to himself.

Fresh air, he decided. Fresh air and an early night. He'd do these damned things in the morning then he'd speak to Nyk. He was still far from sanguine about what the day's work would yield, but professional pride would carry him through to the correct conclusion, satisfactory or not.

The cold night air washed over him as he stepped out into the courtyard and he took a deep breath. The snow chill lit up his throat and chest and he savoured it hedonistically before releasing it back into the night noisily. The air was so fresh here, he thought, so free from the dust and stinking fumes of the city. The dragging intensity of the day's work began to slip away from him.

The lighting was fitful, but the snow intensified what there was and Josyff could see quite well. Apart from a few random bird tracks, the courtyard was marked out with well trampled footpaths that betrayed the passage of the Keep's occupants, old and new, through the day. He made a new one of his own towards the main gate.

Passing through the gate he stepped a little way out onto the drawbridge. The light from the courtyard illuminated only a little way ahead and his faint shadow was soon lost. He stopped and stood very still, his eyes searching into the darkness. There was nothing to be seen. No moon, no stars, no mountains, nothing. Just blackness. There would be more light dancing behind his closed eyes, he thought, but he kept them open. He did not want to risk marring this still and silent vision. After a while, he found himself reaching out with this hand as if it might be possible to touch the darkness, so solid did it seem. Then, rather self-consciously, he returned it to his pocket. Part of him was daunted utterly, but another part knew that somehow, like the cold freshness of the air, it was good that there were places like this, where nothing could be seen—where darkness, and silence, were absolute.

He stood for a long time breathing very softly, as though an incautious movement might shift some great equilibrium, and when he turned back to the courtyard it was almost reluctantly.

As he walked along his own new-trampled pathway he wondered idly about Nyk and the others. Where did they all come from? What was this Estate that employed—or used to employ—them? What did they do when they were not working? It was certainly too far to go routinely carousing down to the village. Not that any of them looked like great carousers. Did others relieve them from time to time? Let them get back to their families? *Had* they families? And where in the devil's name was his brief?

He stopped in front of the door. Set deep in a recessed archway it was a stout-timbered affair, liberally studded with bolt heads, and laced about with heavy black ironwork. It was capable of resisting many strong blows, he judged. Yet, as he pulled on the handle, it opened smoothly and silently. A small but telling tribute to Nyk's watchful maintenance, he thought. Slowly he was gaining an interesting measure of this man.

He had noted when he came out that none of the several heavy bolts that backed the door had been thrown. It was the first time he had been outside after dark and he wondered whether this was normal, or an oversight. Then he recalled hearing about how people in the country would leave their doors and windows unlocked without fear of robbery or worse.

It was not so much an unsettling as an alien idea to him, born and brought up as he had been in towns and cities where the strange face rather than the familiar was the norm and where indifference to the affairs of others had been growing apace for as long as he could remember. In the end, too, as the New Order had impressed its will on the community, there had been serious violence on the streets.

Many groups had opposed the New Order in the beginning but, for the most part, they had faded away. Those that had not, however, particularly those who called themselves the Rhanen, had become first disruptive and then increasingly violent and people had been killed before they were finally cowed.

Albeit brief, that had been a bad time, Josyff reflected as he stepped inside and closed the door behind him. Bad and sad, for despite their descent into violence, much that the Rhanen had said about personal freedom and choice had been fine and beyond debate. He reached down out of habit to throw one of the long bolts home, then paused. Perhaps they had been too idealistic, too unwilling to accept that there was harshness in the world and that sometimes all that could be done was to bolt the doors against those who dwelt and thrived in the darkness.

He let go of the bolt and stood up. He should leave it as he found it, he decided. Nyk or one of the others might still be outside.

He did not like to dwell too much on the Rhanen and those similarly inclined. Still less did he like the twinges of sympathy he felt for their cause. If he wanted to keep what he had he must do what was required of him and do it well, leave the running of public affairs to others better suited. Much better suited.

Later, as he lay in bed, he found the unbolted door preying on his mind. It was obviously what was done out here. One bolt left undone was an oversight, but all of them indicated a normal practice. And it was not up to him to interfere. Besides, what could come through that snow-filled blackness to disturb them?

Still, he would mention it to Nyk tomorrow—casually.

He was drifting into sleep when the thought came to him, faint and distant...

...And yet the drawbridge was closed against you when you arrived.

He recalled the sight of it slowly opening and felt again the relief he had felt.

It was almost as if its opening was...

...just for you.

He was dreaming of the darkness beyond the drawbridge. Still and silent. Hiding the mountains. Hiding everything. Everything...

Then he was awake.

And something, somewhere, was screaming.

CHAPTER 7

Josyff did not move. For a moment his mind was flooded with the thoughts that had been occupying him before he went to bed—of doors bolted and unbolted, of the violence that at times had flooded through the city beating against them. Abruptly, he was lying with his arms wrapped tightly about his wife, hoping that her silent trembling would prevent her from feeling his own as noises from the street below reached up and invaded their bedroom. Fearful noises woven into the lights that were flickering through the gap in their once carefully chosen patterned curtains to make a ghastly shifting shadow theatre on the ceiling and walls where there should have been only stillness. Men and women, swearing, screaming, sobbing. Demented anger, clawing fear, desperate, rending pleas, and also brutal laughter that had made him press his hands over his wife's ears, so chilling was it. And other sounds. Footsteps, skittering and frantic, heavy and purposeful. Things being dragged. Dull, sickening thuds whose source he dared not think about.

Then he was at the Keep again, in his room, in his bed, struggling desperately to drive the awful memories from his mind.

But the noise he had wakened to was still with him, though it was intermittent and faint.

It was vaguely familiar.

Josyff's hand was shaking as he reached out to find the lamp that stood on the table by his bedside. It was a clumsy search in the still unfamiliar room and he had to lunge desperately to catch the lamp just as he found it. He was thus wide awake as its soft light dispelled the darkness.

Frowning, he bent his head forward and listened. There *was* a noise. Definitely. High pitched and piercing. It was not the residue of a fading dream that had woken him.

Something inside the clock clunked as it went about its occasional duty, prompting Josyff to get out of bed.

He found that his legs were unsteady as he stood up but he stamped his heels on the hard, thinly-carpeted stone floor to jolt them into submission. As usual, the room was cold.

Picking up the lamp he walked to the door. Nyk might choose to leave the Keep unprotected at night, but as much out of habit as for any other reason, Josyff had used both the bolts on his door. Holding his breath he put his ear by the keyhole.

Whatever was making the sound was not close, he decided, and cautiously he drew the two bolts and opened the door. Lights in the corridor clicked into life as he stepped into it. That was what happened in every part of the Keep he had visited so far, even in those few places that had natural lighting. It was one of many ingenious features he had yet to inquire into.

29

He narrowed his eyes until they adjusted to the sudden brightness then looked up and down the corridor. There was no sign of anything untoward though the noise was now quite clearly audible.

And still it was familiar.

Behind him the clock clunked again, then whirred asthmatically. It was about to chime. Despite his antipathy towards the clock, Josyff was prepared to admit that he found its mellow resonant tone not unpleasant. He stood motionless as a sequence of four phrases rang out. It was the hour.

Three o'clock, he guessed.

He waited for it to strike.

One. The chime echoed softly along the corridor. Strange, Josyff thought, most sounds fell dead in this place.

Two.

Three. There was no terminal whirr and click. Josyff felt a slight frisson of irritation. Four o'clock was too early to be getting up but would almost certainly ensure that he would oversleep.

Four.

Still no click.

Damn!

Then he noticed that the far end of the corridor was darkening.

Five.

Still no click. He glanced at the clock in disbelief though he could see only the side of it from where he was standing.

Six.

The darkness was drawing nearer.

Something must be wrong with the lights.

Seven.

No! Never! Josyff's rapid glance took in the still dark window and, pointlessly, the clock again. It wasn't possible. Something must be wrong with the clock as well.

Eight.

The distant lights were going out with each stroke, he realized. And something was moving in the darkness that they left. Josyff opened his mouth to cry out, but his throat was dry and no sound came. Nor could he move to slam the door as he heard the clock strike again and saw the pulsing darkness draw nearer.

Nine.

Louder now—much louder—and hung about with the sound that had first wakened him, the screaming. Though now he thought he began to recognize what it was. Not that this eased the panic that was beginning to possess him, nor even made any sense.

Ten.

All around him now was the sound of the chimes, tangled in the shrill screaming, and the darkness, moving ever nearer. And in it, ill-focused, as though through a dense fog, he could sense as much as see, flapping wings. Wide and powerful, their beat stirred both the darkness and the echoes of the still chiming clock.

Eleven.

Instinctively he covered his head with his arms. Somewhere, a faint voice urged him back to the safety of his room behind him, but he did not understand it.

Twelve.

The last light vanished and darkness surrounded him. It was the darkness that had enfolded and hidden the mountains. But where, on the drawbridge, he had looked out into calm and stillness, here there was frenzy and terror. Frantic wings beat and buffeted him and, despite the darkness and his protecting arms, he could see, unnaturally large, the gaping maws of a vast flock of sea birds rising and falling on an unfelt wind, their cold black eyes seeking him out.

The sight filled his mind, as did the screeching, disordered chorus, deafening now and laden with an ancient malice. A malice focused on him.

Then he was among them, high in the darkness and chilled by a deep and uncaring cold. He was trying to scream, but no sound came, save the choking pounding of his heart. The beating wings stifled him, filling his nose and his mouth. His arms and legs flailed wildly and then he was falling.

The din changed and a solitary voice rose above it.

One bird loomed before him.

And a body-shaking blow on his forehead ended everything.

"Surveyor."

The word formed itself in the trembling darkness. It was meaningless and it echoed and made something hurt.

The darkness shook gently and he felt himself taking form.

The birds were all about him!

With a cry, Josyff flailed his arms wildly and made to sit up. Voices cried out in alarm and his arms were seized. He was pushed back down. Not that much force was required, for dancing lights welled up to fill his skull with pain.

There was a brief silence.

"Surveyor."

The word made sense now and the sharp accent identified the speaker as Nyk. His voice was urgent and concerned.

Josyff opened his eyes carefully. It was not easy. It was as though they had been sealed against the most searching, dust-laden wind. As the light entered his awareness it was jagged and streaked, but gradually it became coherent and formed itself into Nyk and Badr, looming over him. A third

31

figure, in the form of the watching clock, confirmed that he was in his room. Nyk and Badr looked worried. As Josyff's vision cleared, so did his thoughts and, almost immediately, more prosaic concerns formed alongside the lingering memory of the birds and the darkness. He should not be seen in this condition! It wasn't fitting. He must pull himself together. He must...

Nyk's voice dispelled his scattering thoughts. "You gave us a fright, surveyor."

Something cool touched Josyff's brow and he closed his eyes briefly in acknowledgement of the relief it brought.

"Lie still," Nyk said, needlessly. "It looks worse than it is. Though I imagine you'll have a headache for some time. You must've caught your head on something as you fell, but I can't see what it..."

"Fell?"

Josyff pushed himself upright, setting aside Nyk's restraining hand.

"We were concerned when you didn't come down for breakfast," Nyk said. "You're normally the first up."

"What happened?"

Nyk gave a disclaiming shrug. "We found you lying across the doorway." He glanced back at Badr who nodded but seemed content to let Nyk continue. "Blood all over your face." He offered a bloodstained cloth. "Frightened me half to death." He echoed Josyff's own question. "What happened?"

Josyff shook his head then stopped abruptly and winced. "I've no idea."

"Do you walk in your sleep?" Nyk asked bluntly, prompting a start from Badr.

Josyff remembered just in time not to shake his head again. "No, never," he replied, with a hint of irritation. The sound of the seabirds and the touch of the pounding darkness they had brought had faded, but the memory of them was still clear in his mind. A dream, obviously, like his fall into the depths of the clock. Unsettling, to say the least—frightening, actually, he realized—but he was sufficiently in control of himself to know that he would need time on his own to decide what was happening. Nothing was to be gained by rehearsing such events in front of Nyk and Badr.

He lied. "I seem to remember getting up in the night for a drink." He managed a rueful smile. "I should've turned the lights on. Probably thought I was at home—mistook the door and walked into something."

Nyk glanced at Badr uncertainly. Josyff took the initiative. "Anyway, I'm all right now, just a bit sore. What time is it?"

Both Nyk and Badr looked at the clock and told him. Josyff cleared his throat with gruff reproach and cautiously swung his legs off the bed. He took the damp cloth from Nyk and put it to his head as he stood up. "Thank you, gentlemen. I'm sorry I startled you. Has my equipment arrived yet?"

"Er, no," Nyk stammered, surprised by this unexpected question. "It..."

Josyff held up a hand to interrupt him. "Let me wash and change, we'll talk over breakfast..." He glanced at the clock. "Late breakfast if Qualto can be prevailed on."

The two men left with a mixture of relief and reluctance. Josyff went to the wash basin and stared at himself in the mirror. He could see why Nyk and Badr had been so concerned. His hair was wildly awry and a livid gash ran down the middle of his forehead. It was no longer bleeding, but it looked alarming. He damped the cloth and touched it to the injury gently, drawing in a short breath at the sting of the contact. Around the gash and beneath the immediate pain he could feel the duller ache of bruising. Very soon he knew his forehead would be displaying an interesting array of colours. But what could have done it? There was nothing between the bed and the door for him to fall against that would make such a mark, and hitting the floor or even the edge of the door would not have done it. He winced away from the memory of the gaping maw and the stabbing beak.

For an instant, the face in the mirror became desolate. Missing equipment, premature winter, this bizarre, convoluted place, miles from anywhere, and now dreams—dreams that were walking him about in the middle of the night and injuring him. For the second time, the phrase "mountain madness" came to him, but again he rejected it. He could not reject so easily the feeling that something was wrong, however. Straightforward homesickness, perhaps? He usually had a brief spell of that at some point early in a new job but, unpleasant though it was, he knew it for what it was and this wasn't it. The past fretful year worrying about his job and how he was being perceived by the New Order? He thought he had coped with that, but maybe he hadn't? Perhaps there were doubts and fears gnawing at him deep and unseen...

And the nature of the New Order itself...

"Later," said the face in the mirror sternly. This was no time to pursue that idea. It was coming to him slowly that it was perhaps fortuitous that his equipment had not yet arrived. He and Badr had done reasonably well the previous day but their efforts had merely confirmed that they would be unable to continue much further in the same vein. To measure the Keep and transfer its winding twisting corridors, eccentrically shaped rooms and confusing floor levels on to ordered sheets of paper would be difficult using his own modern equipment, and, realistically, was quite beyond the antiquated instruments they had found, useful though they might be for some preliminary work. It could be deemed culpable of him not to take positive steps to find out where his equipment was, he thought uneasily. He would have to arrange with Nyk to return to the village as soon as possible. The journey would give him ample time to ponder everything that had happened. In fact, it might even put an end to whatever it was that was troubling him. The reflection nodded resolutely.

Josyff's accident resulted in a subtle shift in the relationship between the five men. Though Nyk and Badr had eaten, they sat with him in the small dining room as he ate his breakfast, trying not to look at him too obviously and generally failing to behave as though nothing particularly unusual had happened. Qualto lingered fussily about him instead of bolting out with the plates and scurrying quickly back to his kitchen as he normally did. Even Henk, who normally ate either before them, or elsewhere, made an appearance, sitting at the far end of the long table and resting his long, gloomy face in a cupped hand.

Josyff smiled as he waved Qualto's offer of more food aside.

"It's excellent, but no more, thanks," he said. "I've been meaning to compliment you on your cooking since I arrived, but you're so elusive."

Qualto shrugged vaguely, uncertain how to take the praise. He offered a weak smile and his mouth moved tentatively, but no sound emerged.

"Did you come here originally as a cook?" Josyff asked.

Nyk answered for his colleague. "Yes. The squire had him sent up. I think he thought me and Henk were trying to poison him." He grinned. "Couldn't tell the difference between incompetence and malice."

Josyff motioned Qualto to sit down. "Did you work for the squire?" he asked.

Hesitantly, Qualto succumbed to Josyff's urging and levered himself down on to a chair opposite.

"My whole family did," he replied, somewhat to Josyff's surprise. He had been half expecting Nyk to continue as spokesman. "Well, for the Estate, anyway."

"Do you know what happened to him?" Josyff asked, voicing one of the many puzzles about this place that were refusing to leave him. Qualto's face contorted and, for an alarming moment, Josyff thought he was going to burst into tears. It was, however, merely thoughtfulness.

"He was always odd," Qualto said as his face cleared. His tone was flat, simple and final. He had nothing to add. Josyff sensed Nyk nodding beside him, and there was even a hint of agreement in Henk's unmoving face. If he wanted to know more about the squire it would have to come from another source, or be pieced together slowly over time, from casual remarks. Not that it mattered much. Whoever the squire had been and whatever the Estate was, the Keep was now under the remit of the New Order. And too, they were of no relevance to his present task.

"Do you get many seabirds around here?" he heard himself asking, as if from a distance. His head was hurting.

"Seabirds, boss?" Nyk echoed.

"Seabirds," Josyff confirmed, recovering.

"Nah," Nyk said after a moment's reflection.

"There are always gulls on the high lake." It was Henk, still resting his head on his hand, his mouth barely moving. His eyes rotated to one side and downward to indicate the direction of the lake.

"Oh yes," Nyk agreed. "Up on the lake. A lot of gulls there, but I shouldn't think any of them have ever seen the sea. It's a long way away." He chuckled knowingly. "Are you interested in birds?"

Josyff edged near to the truth. "Not particularly, it was just that I was dreaming about seabirds last night and I wondered what could have brought it on." Abruptly concerned by this almost involuntary revelation, Josyff sought to distance himself from it immediately. "Still, dreams rarely make any sense, do they?" he said, a little too heartily, adding quickly, "Has there been any more snow during the night?"

Nyk leaned back in his chair expansively. "Nah, boss, and it looks as if it's going to be a bright, clear day."

Anxious to continue moving away from his dreams, Josyff frowned. The action hurt his forehead and made him wince.

"Are you all right?" Nyk was leaning forwards, his face concerned.

"Yes," Josyff reassured him, one hand making a reassuring gesture, the other touching his brow cautiously. "The bruising's a little tender, that's all."

"Doesn't look too comfortable," Nyk commiserated.

"It'll improve all the faster when we can make a proper start on what we came here to do," Josyff said, managing a briskness he did not feel. "You say the weather's good?"

Nyk nodded.

"Then I think I'll have to go down to the village to find out what's happened to my equipment. The stuff you found for us isn't good enough unfortunately—particularly not for a place like this. And we're really being held up now."

Nyk pulled a surprised then doubting face. "It's a long way," he said. "A good day and a half for you and me—certainly in this weather—if it's possible at all..."

Josyff knew he must take command. "I... we..." he indicated Badr, "need that equipment. We've done all we can without it. We'll have to make it possible." He became conciliatory. "I wouldn't ask you to put yourself out, especially if it's going to be difficult, but Badr and I are strangers here, we can't go on our own. We need your help."

Nyk looked at his two companions. Qualto shrugged helplessly but Henk made a discreet drinking motion with his free hand. Nyk's eyebrows lifted.

"Well, we do need a few supplies," he said reflectively. "If we can get through we can kill two birds with one stone."

At the word "birds", Josyff felt a cold shiver flutter within him.

CHAPTER 8

Most of the rest of the morning was spent making preparations for the journey back to the village. Though he was not openly hostile, it was apparent by his general demeanour that Nyk was far from happy at the prospect of the long trek through the snow-covered mountains. There was a stiffness about him and an edge to his voice as he spoke to Henk and Qualto which made Josyff reflect that his decision had indeed been rather impulsive. He almost started as the thought came to him, out of nowhere, that he might be running away from this place. He crushed it ruthlessly, allowing less disturbing doubts to occupy him.

Perhaps he should have made the suggestion to go to the village sooner. Would he be able to explain his delay to his superiors? He ordered the past few days in his mind and decided that, yes, he could. He had acted properly throughout. But it would be far better if it did not come to that. Hopeful resolutions began to form. Once they had his equipment, he and Badr should be able to make rapid progress. Unconsciously, he gazed around the room as if examining the entire Keep. It was elaborate but it wasn't that big a place after all, at least judging from the outside, and, for most of the work, they wouldn't have to contend with those age-old problems for surveyors—the weather and unhelpful terrain. He set aside the prospect of dealing with the moat for later consideration. That would depend on his brief anyway.

Then everything was ready and he and Nyk were standing at the main gate making final adjustments to their large packs.

Nyk looked around at the snow-covered mountains, bright and sharp against a clear blue sky. He took a deep breath and let it out in a grey misting cloud which vanished almost immediately. His manner had softened through the morning.

"This'll help clear your head, boss," he said.

Josyff smiled and, less ostentatiously, did the same. The cold air filled him like light. This was a beautiful place. This was a beautiful moment. This was how things should be. But still niggling underneath this exhilaration was the faint and heretical thought that it *was* good to be moving away from the Keep. Josyff gave it no rein, but he hesitated slightly as he turned round to say good-bye to the others. For a moment, it seemed to him that they were not really there, that they were ill-focussed smudges in the bright clarity of the day, and the Keep itself was the shadow of a dark shape in another place. The impression passed almost immediately but the memory lingered like shapeless images dancing behind closed eyelids after an inadvertent glance at the sun.

"Carry on with working out a basic framework for the place," he said to Badr, needlessly repeating a previous instruction.

"I will," Badr replied flatly.

"Better be off, then," Nyk said, looking up into the clear sky and tapping his stick authoritatively on the drawbridge. It echoed hollowly. "Make what we can of the day."

Josyff had half-heartedly protested the need for a stick. "I'm not that old yet."

"You'll need it," Nyk had replied curtly. It was not a matter to be debated.

Nyk took the lead along the narrow path and set a comfortable pace. He proved to be a quiet companion which suited Josyff in his present mood. The start of a new job was always unsettling, but usually fell into a familiar pattern. Virtually every aspect of this job was strange however, not least that he was having to trail through snow-covered mountains to find his equipment after six days. He found himself rehearsing again his excuses to his superiors but a couple of slips and an urgent, "Careful!" from Nyk brought him sharply back to the present.

"Not used to the mountains, are you, boss?" Nyk said, as his supporting hand steadied him. "No disrespect, but it doesn't do to let your mind wander. Especially when it's like this."

A sweeping arm took in a broad sunlit vista of snow-capped mountains.

"Always the same, always different," he went on. "But there's no words for them when they're like this." He shook his head reflectively, then shrugged briskly. "Still, they'll kill you just like that—fair weather or foul—if you don't pay heed." His gloved hand made an ineffectual shift at snapping its fingers. He smiled unexpectedly. "Good for your sense of perspective."

Josyff could only mumble a muffled, "Yes," in reply to this mixture of concern and philosophizing before Nyk was off again, his retreating back inviting only silence.

When they stopped again, a little later, the concern returned as he watched Josyff rubbing his calves ruefully.

"Tell me if I'm going too fast for you, boss," he said. "It's tiring work walking in this stuff."

Josyff nodded reassuringly, but he scarcely noticed the remark. Nyk's comments about his sense of perspective were proving very apt. While watching where he was putting his every step did not make for relaxed walking he realized that all thoughts about the Keep, his work there, the missing equipment, his eerie dreams, had retreated into the distance. Almost as if the hulking presence of the Keep, now long out of sight, had drawn them back to itself. And even as they came back to him, much of their power was gone.

"I'm managing," he said. "Don't worry, I'll let you know if I'm having problems."

Nyk looked at him shrewdly. "We're not doing too badly, but there's a small cave I'd like to reach before nightfall. We'll have to press on."

Josyff straightened and motioned him forwards with a flick of his stick.

As they continued, Josyff tried to note the way they were travelling. He must have come this way with the guides as there had been no dividing of the path that he had seen, but he could not recognize any of it. Then again, he reflected, it hadn't been covered in snow. And too, he had been going the other way. That could be bewildering even in a city full of conspicuous landmarks. But he should take Nyk's advice—he should pay heed. He should not be a witless passenger. Nyk, after all, was only part of the maintenance staff of the Keep, he was not meant to be a guide. What would he do if something happened to the wiry little man—if he slipped and injured himself? Come to that, what would Nyk do if *he* fell. They were alarming thoughts.

"Pay heed," he muttered to himself.

"Pardon?"

"Nothing. Just... missed my foot."

Nevertheless, despite his best endeavours to mark out the route in his mind, Josyff found that just keeping pace with Nyk and watching where he was walking kept him occupied enough. He was glad of the stick.

Late in the afternoon they came to the top of a shallow rise and a cold wind greeted them. Ahead of them lay a slope into a col. Nyk stopped and blew out a noisy breath.

"I thought we'd been having it too easy, boss," he said, pointing down the slope. Josyff could not see the cause of his concern and said so.

"The snow's drifted across this side of the col."

"That's dangerous?"

Nyk looked at him slightly suspiciously and then paternally. "You really don't get much snow where you come from, do you?" he said.

Josyff shook his head.

"It means we're going to have to be even more careful picking our way. And if the snow's soft and deep it'll be really hard walking."

"Is it far to this cave you were talking about?"

"Not very. It's up the other side and over, but..."

Doubt showed on his face. Josyff said nothing.

Nyk looked up at the sky. "Still, not much choice, really," he said. "We can't stay here and it's too late to turn back. Fortunately the light's still with us. And it'll hold."

He hitched his pack. "Come on. Mind how you go. Slow and steady."

The descent into the valley was not particularly steep, but, as Nyk had indicated, it was markedly more demanding than their journey so far. Josyff found the deep, unsupportive snow and the uneven rock-strewn slope that it covered both wearing and alarming. In addition, they were moving in the shadow of the mountains and a cold wind was blowing in their faces.

He was breathless, aching and flushed when they finally reached more even ground.

"Well, it should be easier to find our way back," he said sourly, looking back at the ragged path they had cut.

"Providing it doesn't snow again," Nyk chuckled darkly. Face concentrated, he was rooting deep into one of his pockets.

"Here," he said, eventually, and with difficulty, producing two apples. He proffered one to Josyff. "Eat. We'll rest a little. It's not a good idea to sweat in this weather."

Josyff did not feel particularly hungry, but took the apple out of courtesy. Nevertheless, as he bit into it, its sharp taste seemed to throw off some of his fatigue.

"Sneaks up on you when you're walking," Nyk said, as though sensing this. "Tiredness. It's important to get your pace right. Stop every now and then whether you feel like it or not." He looked with open delight at the apple he had nearly finished. "And eat something."

Josyff had been beginning to feel a little guilty at effectively forcing Nyk into this journey. He was, after all, not a young man, for all his vigour. But the man's brief effusion of pure pleasure set his concerns aside. He had no idea where he was, their situation was one which could easily become desperately dangerous, but he felt remarkably easier in himself.

Running away from the Keep? came the thought again, taunting him, but he set it aside. It *was* good to be away from the Keep but he had no qualms about returning to it—in fact, he was looking forward to it now. For when he did return, he would have everything that he needed to do his work, and the Keep, like many another large and complex building before, would gradually yield its geometrical secrets to his relentless, methodical searching, would gradually have its twisting passages, sweeping arches and elaborate rooms reduced to ordered perspective, to calculation, to lines on paper.

As he gazed around idly at the silent mountains, a hint of recognition formed in his mind.

"I think I remember this place when I was with the guides," he said. He pointed to one of the mountains. It was lower than most of the others and its broad, rounded peak was jagged and broken, quite unlike any of its neighbours.

"Valsen," said Nyk, looking up. "Supposed to have been the highest mountain in the range once. And the site of the First Keep."

Josyff's eyes widened and he waited expectantly for Nyk to continue, but his guide was busily extracting the last from his apple.

"A gift to the mountain," he said as the well-chewed core arced out of his hand. "Better be off, boss. Shouldn't press our luck."

Josyff did not even attempt to rein in his curiosity. "The *First* Keep?" he exclaimed. "The *first*. How many have there been?"

Nyk was moving off. He gave a airy wave. "Only the one," he replied

39

with a slightly embarrassed laugh. "It's just a tale. You know the kind of thing—a mountain has a fancy shape, so a giant used it for a chair... the devil tore it apart... a dragon rested in this cave, lovers in another, and so on. Myths, kids' tales."

Josyff caught up with him. "Are there any "Kids' Tales" about the real Keep?" he asked pointedly. Before Nyk could reply, he pressed on. "Come to that, I know nothing whatsoever about the place, and haven't had time to ask—are there any *grown-up* tales about the Keep. Like, what it was? Who built it? Why? Not to mention, how?"

"Up there's where we're going," Nyk said, pointing with his stick as if to fend off the questions.

"Talk as we walk?" Josyff offered.

CHAPTER 9

The slope up the other side of the col was steeper than the one they had just descended but the snow was thinner and although they still had to use their sticks to test some of the way, it was less demanding.

"I don't know all these old tales," Nyk protested as Josyff pressed his request again for information about the Keep. "You'd be better asking some of the old-timers at the inn when we get to the village. Buy them enough ale and they'll tell you tales to fill a book."

Josyff paused and turned round to look again at the shattered peak of the mountain that Nyk had called Valsen. From his now higher vantage, the mountain looked even more unusual than it had from below. Most of the peaks about them showed the typical signs of ancient glaciation but Valsen was crowned with a peculiarly disordered mass of misshapen and jagged rocks. It looked to Josyff almost as though the mountain top had been shattered by a great force and the remains scattered about in a desperate fury.

His eyes narrowed. Was it his imagination or just the fall of the lengthening shadows deceiving him at this distance, but were the rocks different from those lower down the slopes of the mountain? Were they perhaps like those used to the Keep? And some of them seemed to be bent and twisted, as though sculpted by a wayward child. What natural force could have done that?

"Anything wrong, boss?"

Nyk had continued up the slope and his distant shout cut across Josyff's questions. He almost stumbled as he turned round too quickly.

He was breathing heavily when he caught up with Nyk again.

"Take it easy, boss," came a cautionary greeting. "You're probably getting tired. It's not far now."

"I was just looking at the mountain," Josyff said. "It's different. Looks almost out of place in a way. As if it didn't belong here. And the rock formations along the peak are very unusual."

Nyk nodded. "It *is* a strange place," he said, almost reluctantly. "The locals don't like going near it."

Josyff did not register the reply immediately, then he looked puzzled. "Why would they come out here anyway?" he asked.

"Lost sheep and the like," Nyk replied casually, setting off up the slope again. "And soft city folk climbing—for fun, as they say," he added with a knowing smile.

Josyff allowed him the small jibe. "Do you ever get soft city folk going as far as the Keep?" he asked in the same vein.

Nyk stopped for a moment before replying.

"Nah, now you mention it, we don't. Odd really, I suppose, you can see the place from most of the peaks round here. You'd think someone would drop by now and then." As he walked on, it was obvious that the thought had never occurred to him before.

"It's probably not widely known about. I'd never heard about it until I was sent here," Josyff said, feeling some obligation to reassure. "And it's hardly a welcoming sight, is it? If the first time you see it is after a long hard climb, it's not something that'll send you scurrying back down and rushing along to see it. And it's some way away as well."

Nyk conceded the point and added his own. "It's probably one of those places you mean to look at one day, but never get round to it." He shrugged. "Anyway, we can do without weary travellers cluttering up the place incessantly—wanting this, wanting that. There's enough work to do there without playing inn-keeper to..."

"Soft city folk." Josyff laughed at Nyk's manner as he completed his sentence for him, then a silence developed. "No disrespect, Nyk, but is there all that much work to do?" Josyff asked after a while, as much to break the silence as out of curiosity. "Granted, it's an odd place, but from what I've seen it's very well built."

Nyk paused and stretched.

"You've not been all over it yet, boss. Deceptive, is the Keep. Much bigger than it looks." He frowned slightly, as though at some old problem. "There's parts I've not been to. And a lot more below ground."

Josyff managed to hide his surprise. In his exploration of the building so far he had not come across any basement levels, not that basement really meant anything in that uneven terrain. Nevertheless, the revelation brought back to him vividly how important it was that he find his equipment and get this job under way. Who knew what other surprises this place might have in store for him? What it was, or had been, wasn't really of any significance.

"There's the heating, for instance," Nyk went on, at the same time indicating the top of the rise as their destination and moving off again. "Not to mention the lighting... and the drainage... they work fine, but you generally find a dog's breakfast when you have to work on them, all of them... and all those roofs..."

"Well, fortunately, the heating and lighting aren't part of my job," Josyff said. "Except where they can be seen."

"Think yourself lucky," Nyk rejoined. He reached down to help Josyff up a smooth sloping rock rendered slick with frozen snow which he had clambered up by means of a scrambling rush. Josyff was glad of the strong grip that closed about his arm and hauled him upwards as his own rush was less effective. "I've never fathomed out properly how they work."

"What?" Josyff exclaimed, thinking he had misheard.

"There it is." Nyk was pointing towards a jumble of rocks partially covered with snow. He looked up at the darkening sky. "We've done well. Should get to the village late tomorrow afternoon, after all." He slapped his gloved hands together noisily. "Let's get the stove out and some food on the go." His whole manner was suddenly relaxed and easy. "I'm no Qualto in the kitchen but..."

"After a walk like that, anything will taste good," Josyff interjected, finding Nyk's manner infectious though he could not make out where the cave was that they were supposed to be sheltering in.

It became apparent as Nyk walked to the far side of the rocks.

Josyff was not sure what he had expected, but this was not it. It looked more like the entrance to some animal's lair. It occurred to him ruefully that this job was becoming stranger and stranger.

"It's bigger inside," Nyk said, catching his reaction. Swinging his pack off his back he dropped down onto all fours and briskly brushed a small accumulation of snow aside. "And remarkably dry too, as I recall." He rooted into his pack and produced a torch then crawled into the cave, pushing his pack ahead of him.

Josyff struggled out of his own pack and was about to follow Nyk when an exclamation stopped him.

"Oh!"

It was muffled and surprised.

"Boss."

Surprised and urgent.

Pushing his pack in front of him as Nyk had done, Josyff quickly scrambled through the entrance. It widened almost immediately and, as he straightened up, he had a fleeting impression of a low-ceiling and a narrow space. What caught his attention however, was the focus of Nyk's wavering torch.

Someone else was in the cave.

Josyff felt a mixture of surprise and alarm somewhat incongruously mixed with a pending apology for having barged in on someone already sheltering there, but these faded as he looked at the motionless figure lying on the floor of the cave. Face to the wall and knees drawn up to its chest, it seemed to be unnaturally still. Josyff felt a chill forming in his stomach. Nyk was already kneeling beside the figure.

"Is he...?" Josyff began anxiously, as he took out his own torch and dropped down beside him.

"She," Nyk corrected as he pulled back the figure's hood to reveal thick hair, black in the torchlight and secured by a ribbon around the forehead.

Josyff reached past him and tentatively laid his hand on the woman's cheek. It was very cold. The chill in his stomach intensified in response to the touch. Was she dead? A rush of pointless questions came, his mind racing ahead. Who was she? How did she come to be here, so far from anywhere? Not one of Nyk's soft city folk out climbing, surely? And how was this going to end?

His hand moved from her face to her throat and, unnecessarily, he held up the other for silence. It took him a considerable effort of will to hold his fingers still, shaking as they were with cold and nervousness, but eventually he was able to detect a pulse.

"She's alive anyway," he whispered. "But her pulse feels weak."

He bent down and placed his ear by her mouth, noting as he did so that her lips were dry and painfully cracked. A faint, cold breath touched him. "She's breathing."

He knelt up and shook her gently. "Can you hear me? Wake up!"

After another shake, the woman twitched and made a peculiar whimpering sound. Relief swept over Josyff.

"Wake up!" he said again, more loudly and shaking her harder.

He glanced over his shoulder at Nyk. "Get the stove lit and something cooking," he said. "She'll need something warm inside her." Unusually, Nyk hesitated for a moment before Josyff's "Quickly!" galvanized him.

The woman continued moving in a vague and uncoordinated fashion and making incoherent sounds. Josyff spoke to her soothingly and his shaking became a gentle rocking while Nyk busied himself with the small stove. Soon it was hissing comfortingly and warming the soup they had brought with them. Nyk delved into his pack and retrieved a blanket which he stretched across the cave entrance, securing it with his pack and a few rocks. Despite his concern for the woman, Josyff noted that it was practised procedure and was glad of it. He nodded approvingly. It would keep a little heat in and protect them if the wind rose.

"We should get her off the cold ground, boss," Nyk said as he returned to the stove and made a final adjustment to the height of the flame.

The woman's eyes jerked open as the two men were awkwardly wrapping her in one of their sleeping bags. At first they were unfocused then they widened in alarm. Her mouth opened and a hoarse cry started to emerge but it stopped abruptly as she began shivering violently. Josyff put his arms around her and held her tight. She struggled.

"You're all right. You're safe. No one's going to hurt you," Josyff said, over and over. Eventually she became calmer, though Josyff sensed it was as much through weakness as any reassurance he was offering.

"Here, drink this," Nyk said, proffering a spoonful of soup.

The woman looked at him both fearfully and suspiciously, but then caught sight of the spoon and lunged at it voraciously.

"Slowly, slowly," both men protested, but to no avail. With an unexpected strength the woman levered herself free of Josyff, sat up and reached for the bowl and spoon. Nyk glanced at Josyff who gave a disclaiming shrug and gestured that he hand them over. The woman gulped down the first spoonful then almost dropped the bowl as the warm soup met her chapped lips. Nyk caught it dextrously. For a moment the woman was motionless, her eyes tight shut and the back of her gloved hand pressed against her mouth. Then watering eyes were open and the mouth was determined as she relinquished the spoon, retrieved the bowl and drank the rest of the soup noisily and with an urgency that took the two men aback. Nyk held out a piece of bread as she peered into the empty bowl and she seized it and ate it with the same urgency, pausing only to wipe a squashed portion of it around the bowl.

For some reason the gesture amused Josyff and he smiled.

"Civilization seeping back into your bones?" he said.

The woman, wiping her eyes, looked at him uncertainly and then, with an expression that was a mixture of pleading and shamefacedness, held out the bowl to Nyk who refilled it. This time she used the spoon, though still with some urgency, pausing occasionally to purse her lips.

"I thought I was going to die," she said as she was finishing. Her voice was hoarse.

"What's your name?" Josyff asked, taking the bowl from her.

The woman made to answer then grimaced and wrapped her arms about her stomach.

"Relax," Nyk said. "You've probably eaten too much, too fast. Lean back. And let's get this sleeping bag underneath you properly."

There was an interval of undignified squirming in the comparatively confined space before he was able to ask, "Is that better?"

The woman nodded, tightening the sleeping bag about her. A shiver shook her. "Yes, much," she said. "Thank you." She looked from Nyk and Josyff, her eyes searching and uncertain. "Have you any water?"

"Water, more soup, bread, whatever you want," Nyk replied.

"Just water, please. I'm still thirsty."

Nyk warmed the water a little before he handed it to her.

"How did you get here?" Josyff asked as she drank.

The woman lowered her gaze. "I can't remember," she said after some hesitation. "I just remember walking and walking, getting colder and colder, then crawling into here."

"How long have you been here?"

There was a vague shrug underneath the bulky sleeping bag. "I don't know. I've been asleep, I think... I can't tell... waking... dreaming...

Her face contorted as though she were about to break into tears, but some inner resource took control before either of the two men could offer any consolation.

"You can remember your name?" Nyk taunted gently instead.

His manner provoked a thin smile.

"Esyal Wrenith," she said.

Nyk introduced himself and Josyff. "We're from the Keep." He pointed. "The Boss here's a surveyor and you can thank your good fortune his equipment's been lost otherwise I'd probably have been finding you lying long dead here a few months from now."

Esyal nodded and tightened the sleeping bag about her again, but did not speak.

"Well, you're safe now," Josyff said, trying to soften the effects of Nyk's bleak observation. "Settle down. Have a sleep. There's nothing to be done now. We'll talk in the morning. Decide what we should do."

"Yes," Esyal said softly. "Thank you. I will."

As she lay down on her side, her face away from them, she turned partly and said, "I *am* grateful to you."

But her mind was turning to darker thoughts and even as she spoke, her hand closed about the handle of the knife in her belt.

CHAPTER 10

Even as her hand closed about her knife, Esyal felt a wave of self-reproach. Old habits, she thought. Not that is was an *old* habit. It was a comparatively new one, but like any habit acquired by the need to survive, it was now as deep as though it had been with her all her life.

She felt strange, disorientated. Probably just the sudden change in her circumstances, she decided, not to mention the food and drink she had just consumed so violently. Her stomach rumbled noisily by way of confirmation and for a moment she thought she was going to vomit. She became aware of a pause in the muttered conversation between the two men that was seeping down to her and she found herself holding her breath.

Then it began again, and soon became part of the background to her inner discourse. She had not been lying when she said she did not know how long she had been there. Was it two days since she had become separated from her group—her doomed group? Three? Four? When she tried to remember, all that came was a shifting patchwork of disconnected thoughts and of these she could not tell which were memories of reality and which were memories of dreams and hallucinations. They told her nothing. The only constant, other than the deep, underlying guilt and fear which was with her still, was an aching memory of endlessly placing one foot in front of the other, of knowing she was utterly lost, of a slow chill spreading outward from inside her as she ate snow in a vain attempt to quench her tormenting thirst: a chill that was the vanguard of the deeper one that began to fill her as she slowly realized she was going to die. She shivered as she drove the spectre away, prompting another pause in the conversation above her. She certainly could not remember how she had come to this place. Some primitive instinct must have drawn her here—made her crawl in like a sick animal. It was a humbling, even degrading image, markedly at odds with that of her as a would-be destroyer of the New Order.

Yet now she was saved and safe. A simple bowl of soup and a little warmth and civilization was indeed seeping back into her bones, as Josyff had said. But with civilization came other concerns. Saved, she might have been, but was she in fact safe? Who could say what chance had brought these men here? And who were they? What threat were they to her? The older one—Nyk?—had said something about lost equipment, but it meant nothing—she had not been listening properly. And the other one, Josyff— a surveyor, had Nyk called him? His voice and manner marked him out as educated, professional... but what was a surveyor doing out here? What was there to survey other than mountains?

My group. The thought was stark and frightening, and again she nearly vomited as she was suddenly floundering in the deep snow, listening to her companions' cries coming from all directions through the swirling storm. She was vaguely aware of a soft, whimpering keening threading through the noise.

The murmuring about her stopped again, and she was back in the cave, silent, but with all senses alive as she willed herself to stillness. The keening had been hers. Then the whispered word "dreaming" floated down to her, full of understanding and compassion, and the murmuring continued as though it had not been interrupted.

But Esyal's mind was racing now. Josyff *must* be a spy of some kind, sent by the New Order to seek out the Rhanen's hidden camps. Yet even as the thought came to her, so did others denying it. The New Order wouldn't bother sending spies, they'd just send the army. There'd be no need for even a pretence of subtlety out here, away from any hint of public gaze. Just brute force and killing.

46

She curled her knees up and wrapped her arms about herself more tightly. The knotted cold inside her that had sent out shivers to shake her entire body uncontrollably was gone now, but she still felt tremors as she drifted in and out of consciousness; thoughts of her lost companions mingling confusedly with concerns for her immediate future, and the identity and intentions of the two strangers. She began to think about what she would tell them in the morning and then, almost in spite of herself, about how she could slip back into society to... to what...?

No answer came, but both guilt and relief washed over her as she found herself thanking whatever fortune it had been that had kept her name from the authorities. With care and thought she could pick up her life...

Her mind shied away from the prospect and returned quickly to her immediate concerns. What to tell her two saviours when the inevitable questions came.

"The best way to deceive is to tell as much of the truth and as few lies as possible," someone had said to her in the early days of resistance to the New Order. It seemed now to be almost a lifetime away—some other, quite different time. She tried to remember the face of her adviser, but it refused to come to her. She was still struggling after it as she finally fell asleep. Only then did her grip on her knife slacken.

"Who on earth can she be?" Josyff said to Nyk as they ate their own meal. Nyk had turned down the stove and the cave was lit only by a low yellow flame which flickered occasionally, bouncing misshapen shadows about the uneven walls.

He paused with a spoon halfway to his mouth and looked down into the darkness which hid their new-found companion. "No idea, boss. Looks like—sounds like—a city girl. But how she came out here—no idea." He drank his soup noisily then puffed out his cheeks. "She's damn lucky though." His voice was shaking slightly as if the enormity of the woman's plight had only just impinged on him. "Another day or so and..." He shook his head. "I suppose I might have found her one day, but I don't always camp here. It's dreadful. Could have lain here forever." He shivered.

Josyff saw the older man crawling into the cave, pleasantly tired and looking forward to resting, and encountering the decayed remains of the young woman. A shade of Nyk's shiver reached into him.

"Well, for whatever reason, it didn't happen," he said, with forced heartiness. "And whoever she is, she's safe now. We'll find out more about her tomorrow."

Josyff woke the following morning to light coming through the cave entrance. It took him a few moments to remember where he was and why, but the first really coherent thought that formed was that he had

had a decent night's sleep, free from dreams and mysterious accidents. He reached up and touched his forehead. It was still sore and he could feel the scar.

It was good to be away from the Keep.

He levered himself up quickly at this treacherous thought only to stop immediately as—good night's sleep or no—what seemed to be every joint in his body protested at having been obliged to spend the night huddled on a rock floor. As he carefully stretched out he struck Esyal. She sat up with a cry, one hand raised defensively.

"I'm sorry," Josyff said hastily, holding out his own hands reassuringly. "Don't be afraid. You're safe."

Though he could not see her face properly in the shadows, he caught a glimpse of eyes wide and white. "You're safe," he repeated. "We found you here last night, remember?"

The eyes narrowed and Esyal's posture relaxed.

"Yes," she said, but under the blanket wrapped about her, her hand was clasped around the handle of her knife again. "Thank you," she added flatly. She looked round. "Where's...?"

"Nyk?" Josyff finished the question for her. "Outside, presumably."

The light in the cave dimmed as Nyk confirmed this by crawling in.

He wasted no time on morning greetings.

"Problems," he said.

Outside, the sky was overcast and dark grey. For as far as could be seen, it had that heavy uniformity of texture that indicated, "Snow. And probably a lot of it." Nyk swore softly and his face puckered up in frustration and doubt as he gave this prognosis. Josyff waited. He had nothing to contribute to the older man's thoughts.

Esyal joined them. She was a little unsteady. Looking at her, Nyk reached his conclusion. "We'll get some food in us then we'll have to head back to the Keep."

"But..."

"We're nearer the Keep than the village." Nyk answered Josyff's protest before he spoke it. "You and me might make it to the village if the snow keeps off long enough, but..." He looked at Esyal, who was gazing around, apparently not listening. He lowered his voice nevertheless. "She's too weak. She needs rest and some proper food."

Esyal however, was listening intently. Listening for clues about the two men who had inadvertently saved her life. Too long living with fear had made it difficult for her to trust anyone easily and she had found that silence and inconspicuousness were often her best allies.

The village. What village for mercy's sake? She had no idea where she was and she repeated again the inward cursing at herself for not having paid more attention to her cousin as he had led her and her group through the mountains. And what was this Keep that Nyk was talking about? She'd definitely never heard of that! And was it her imagination or had she seen a hint of reluctance on Josyff's part when Nyk had suggested returning there? It was enough for her to make up her mind.

"I'm all right," she said, straightening up and forcing herself to smile. "Just a little shaky, that's all. I'll be fine when..." She risked an expectant look. "When I've had something to eat?"

Both Josyff and Nyk smiled at this response and the three were soon inside the cave again, eating a hastily prepared but hot breakfast. Under the influence of the simple fare and the spartan conditions, the mood, briefly, became euphoric, as though the three of them had been companions for years.

"I'm Josyff and this is Nyk," Josyff said, as they were finishing. "We're from the Keep. Nyk works there and I'm supposed to be surveying it."

Esyal told them her name but volunteered no other information.

"What's the Keep?" she asked. "I've never heard of it."

"Neither had I, until I was sent here," Josyff replied with a rueful smile. "It's just a building..." He faltered and pointed vaguely with a piece of bread. "An old building... on top of a mountain."

Esyal looked as though she was still waiting for an answer. "And what does 'surveying it' mean?" she asked after a moment.

Taken aback by such an ingenuous question, Josyff floundered a little before replying, "I just... measure... everything and then draw plans of the place."

Esyal nodded, then her forehead creased. "Who would want plans of an old building on top of a mountain miles from anywhere?" Immediately her hand came to her mouth. "I'm sorry, that was rude, wasn't it?"

"Not really," Josyff replied, laughing. "Just... unexpected. And, answering your question, my employers want them."

"Why?"

The question bounced back without pause and Josyff's manner sobered abruptly as caution began to reassert itself. He should be careful, he knew nothing about this woman.

"I've no idea," he said. "I work for the Government as a surveyor and I just do as I'm told. Do my job as well as I can."

He *was* with the New Order, then, Esyal thought, and it was with some difficulty that she restrained her bitter reply: "Too many of you just do as you're told!"

"I'm sorry," she said instead. "That *was* rude. I spoke without thinking."

Less inclined to be forthcoming now, Josyff turned to his own questions. "Anyway, what are *you* doing out here, wandering lost?"

"Wandering, lost," Esyal echoed by way of reply. Before sleeping and since waking, she had arrived at no conclusion about the deceit she should use when these questions arose. She put her hand to her head and made a worried face. "I can't remember how I came here. I just remember walking and walking."

"Was anyone with you?" Nyk asked. "Where do you come from?"

Esyal shrugged her shoulders and made a helpless gesture. "I don't know," she said, hastily adding, "I mean, I don't know if anyone was with me. I live in Dirriol." She held out a hand to stop the expected questions. "I can remember some things but not others, it's..."

Josyff and Nyk exchanged a glance.

"Never mind," Josyff said, as reassuringly as he could manage. "You've had a nasty experience and you're still a bit shaky. Don't worry. The most important thing is that you're safe now. Everything will come back in time, I'm sure."

"And in the meantime we'd better set off back to the Keep before the snow starts," Nyk said, briskly gathering up their plates and the stove.

Once again, Esyal caught a hint of reluctance on Josyff's part.

"I'd like to go to the village," she said quickly. "I want to get back to normal—find out what I'm doing here." She put her hands to her head again. "Get my memory back."

Nyk looked openly anxious. He repeated his earlier concerns. The Keep was nearer than the village, Esyal would still be weak.

"No, I'm well now," she protested. "The rest and the food were all I needed. I'll manage. I won't hold you up." She looked around the cave and quite genuinely said, "I want to get out of these mountains. I don't want to go further into them."

"It's going to be difficult either way if it starts to snow," Josyff offered quietly, as keen to press on to the village as Esyal, but reluctant to force Nyk's judgement.

Nyk wavered.

"If there was anyone with me, they might need help," Esyal said, as a final tilt. "Perhaps they'll know back at the village."

Nyk made to reply but changed his mind and gave a terse nod of acceptance.

Outside, the sky was unchanged.

"We must get as far as we can before the snow comes," Nyk added as a parting shot to no one in particular.

The terrain was easier than that which they had travelled over previously but, despite his sense of urgency, Nyk maintained a cautious pace. Nothing was to be gained and much could be lost by their exhausting themselves walking too fast through the snow or risking injury.

After an hour, snow began to fall.

"Stay close," Nyk commanded. "The way's not too difficult but it *is* long. We mustn't get separated."

Gradually the snow became heavier and the surrounding mountains disappeared into the descending grey sky. None of the three walkers spoke as they trudged along until Nyk stopped them for a brief rest at the top of a slope.

As they halted, silence closed about their small, grey world. A muffled silence, total except for the almost imperceptible hiss of the falling snow.

Josyff looked into the greyness ahead of them, then took Nyk's arm and pointed.

Three figures were approaching them.

CHAPTER 11

Qualto and Henk pressed on with their normal duties while the others were away. Qualto clattering about his kitchen, forgetting occasionally that he was now cooking only for three not five, and Henk, ungraciously devouring the excess and pacing the rooms and corridors of the Keep with his usual slow and relentless gait.

Henk's lanky form appeared in the doorway. Head forward and bent slightly to one side, like a quizzical vulture, he peered intently at Qualto. The cook looked up from his book and returned the gaze expectantly.

"It's snowing," Henk said curtly.

Qualto's mouth tightened in dismay and he closed his eyes briefly, before saying flatly, "Oh dear."

There was a pause.

"Perhaps we should light the beacon," Henk said, half questioningly.

There was another pause as Qualto pondered this. Then he nodded slowly. Carefully he placed a gold patterned leather strip on the open page of his book, closed it gently and put it on the small table his feet had just been resting on.

"Yes. I'll come with you," he said, levering himself out of his chair. "Those steps will be more treacherous than usual if it's snowing."

Lighting the beacon was no great chore, but it did involve climbing an awkward set of wooden steps. Too shallow to be comfortably climbed as a ladder and too steep to be comfortably descended as a stair, they and their builders were casually abused by Nyk every time the beacon had to be lit. On these occasions he also determined to "do something" about them, but as these happened only twice a year—at the summer and winter solstices— his irritation never persisted long enough for him to apply himself to the task. Added to which, given the location of the beacon, he had to concede that the stairs were both well made and ingeniously designed and finding an easier solution to reaching it would be no slight matter.

"Oh my," was Qualto's almost whispered exclamation as he stood in the doorway that opened into the courtyard and looked out at the falling snow. The edges of the trampled pathways that had been made by the casual traffic of the Keep's five residents were already being softened by the new snow and would soon be gentle undulations in a new landscape—small, motionless waves shaped by unseen forces. Qualto looked upwards through the falling snow. Dark against the grey sky, large flakes tumbled purposefully towards him like an invading horde, each following its own erratic, jigging, way. The sight was hypnotic. He smiled as a few selected his kitchen-red face on which to thaw themselves then he pulled his scarf tight, fastened his coat and trotted after Henk.

The stairs to the beacon were in another courtyard but, in common with many of the Keep's outside spaces, this had no door directly into a main building and could only be reached by a meandering open pathway, one of many that were laced around the Keep like a faint echo of its convoluted interior. Some of these were wide and airy avenues, but others were like alleyways, narrow and cramped, and more than a few looked as though they had been formed as much by accident as design. That leading to the beacon was one of the latter and had prompted more than a few discussions amongst the Keep's carers about why the beacon had been placed where it was, or, for that matter, why that particular courtyard had been built.

These questions were running through Qualto's mind once again as he walked along the alley with his hands stretched out tentatively to touch the walls on each side of him, as though to prevent them closing in on him. He glanced upwards at the strip of grey sky high above. Only a few snowflakes could be seen, all impetus seemingly lost as they wandered their way to the damp stone floor.

He tripped and swore.

The least Nyk could do is put some lights in here, he thought reproachfully, he's been threatening to long enough.

Then he was emerging into the comparative brightness at the end of this chasm and his thoughts turned towards...

These damned steps. Always make my legs ache.

Henk was already by the beacon as Qualto reached the top of the first flight of stairs. He waited with his usual watchful and, at times, irritating patience as Qualto edged his way along a narrow platform and clambered up the second flight of stairs. Only when Qualto was standing beside him did he turn his attention towards the beacon.

"Better give it a clean while we're here," he said, taking some cloths from a small cupboard in the base of the plinth on which the beacon stood and handing one to Qualto.

Not that it needed much cleaning. The polished glass facets glinted even in the dull light and offered little for the snow, or even occasional bird droppings, to cling to, while the air around the Keep was free from the dust and fumes to be found in the towns and cities. Nevertheless, the two men were thorough. Although neither Nyk, Henk, nor Qualto knew why the beacon had to be lit every solstice, they took a peculiar pride in always ensuring that it was, and in keeping it bright and clear. Perhaps their attentiveness came from the hint of perfection that lay in the beacon's straight and clean-cut edges which contrasted so vividly with the coarse rounded stonework of the Keep. Or perhaps it came from the rich rainbow images buried deep in its lenses that shifted even as they were observed. Or perhaps it was just because it was beautiful; diamond-like in its clarity and definition—another contrast to the ponderous weightiness of the Keep. Whatever the reason, the pride in maintaining the beacon was there and, despite the inconvenience involving in reaching it, the two men polished it with both zeal and some affection.

Eventually, satisfied with their work, both of them stepped, almost reverently, into the narrow interior of the beacon. After unnecessarily checking that there was oil in the reservoir, Henk lit the broad circular wick and carefully adjusted its height. The mantle was already beginning to glow white when they gently closed the door and began their journey back.

As the beacon's light reached out through the quiet storm, changing the dark snowflakes into bright and confusing whiteness, a little of its light bounced off the outer wall of the Keep and down into the alley where it softened the gloom for the two retreating figures.

"They'll be glad of that if they've turned back," Qualto said, banging his feet against the wall by the doorway to dislodge the snow that had accumulated on them.

Henk gave a non-committal grunt.

"They *will* have turned back, won't they?" Qualto asked with some anxiety. "They wouldn't carry on to the village through this?"

Henk gave a disclaiming shrug, coupled with another grunt.

Qualto blew out a noisy breath as he threw up a small snowstorm of his own by vigorously shaking his coat before hanging it up. "Then again, it mightn't have reached them. Maybe it's just local. It *is* unusual. Very early this year."

"A lot of things are unusual... out of joint... this year," Henk replied. "Strangers wandering about the place. Getting in our way. Disturbing things."

"We could use a little disturbing from time to time," Qualto rebutted. "And they're hardly in our way." He made an airy gesture. "An army wouldn't get in our way in this place."

"You know what I mean."

"No, I don't actually. Badr's all right—keeps himself to himself a bit, but he's a souther, you expect that kind of thing. And that surveyor seems pleasant enough."

"When he's not dreaming and falling out of bed or pestering Nyk about his clock."

"Well, he's not pestering you, is he?" Qualto felt a little indignant. Whatever else the two newcomers were, they were guests—and the man had taken pains to compliment him on his cooking—something he had not experienced for a long time. "Besides, he's from the city. The mountains unsettle people like that. He's used to crowds and noise. And anyway, this place takes some getting used to." Henk looked set to reply but Qualto pressed on. "And it doesn't help that his... equipment or whatever it is... hasn't arrived. He's probably as keen to be away from here as you are to see him go, and he can't even start his work." He concluded this observation with a challenging look as he returned to his chair and reached for his book.

Henk became defensive. "I didn't say I wanted them to go," he protested, his voice coming as near to plaintive as it could. "It's just that..." He hesitated and looked around, almost as though someone might be listening. "It's just that the place... feels different."

"What, do you mean *it* doesn't want them here?" Qualto's voice edged towards sarcasm.

Henk gave him a half-concerned, half reproachful look. "You don't know this place like I do," he said.

Qualto toyed briefly with an unequivocally sarcastic response—in his opinion, Henk spent too much of his time brooding in distant parts of the Keep, parts where he had no particular reason to be—but he relented. "Well, there's no denying that," he said, resting his unopened book on his knee. "There's places here I've never had call to go to. And it's a big, brooding old pile at the best of times."

Henk made a sound that approximated to a chuckle. "It's big, certainly. There's places *I've* never been to, let alone you."

"Really?" Qualto was genuinely surprised at this revelation. He was also surprised at Henk's talkativeness and, for a moment, he had an impression of things moving that had not moved for a long time, of things recently disturbed and uncertain. He shook it off. "I just took it for granted that you and Nyk knew the place backwards," he said. "You're always pottering about here and there."

Henk had sat down on a couch facing the dull fire. Lounging back and spreading himself across it diagonally, he occupied almost the whole of it. The room was one that the three men used as a kind of common room. Like most of the rooms in the Keep no one knew what its original purpose had been or even how it had come to be used as it was. It bore the signs of orderly but male occupancy: it was functionally clean and tidy but such few pictures and ornaments as decorated it had obviously been there for ever.

"We go where we're needed. Keep things working," Henk conceded. "Like we're supposed to. It's a job."

"It's a *good* job," Qualto reminded him firmly. "Damned sight better than working in the fields or dancing to someone else's whims in a factory, day in, day out."

"We're all dancing to someone else's whim," Henk said sourly.

Qualto puffed out his cheeks. Henk could find the dark side of anything at times. "Well, at least it's a nice leisurely dance, not a crazy non-stop jig like the last place I worked," he said after a short pause. "And I haven't noticed you rushing off to the village looking for a new job recently."

Henk grunted softly and looked around the room. "I think you might, soon," he said.

"What!" Qualto was wide-eyed. He abandoned his attempt to start reading again.

"I said, I think it might be time to move on." Henk was still gazing about the room.

"What's got into you?" Qualto demanded.

"I don't know," Henk replied simply.

"Something to do with Badr and the surveyor?" Qualto offered, now genuinely perplexed. "Upsetting our routines?"

"I don't know," Henk repeated. "It might be. But..." He stopped.

"But?" Qualto prompted. The sense of uncertainty, of things moving, that he had experienced a few moments ago, returned. He stared intently at Henk's long and gloomy face but, as usual, there was nothing he could read there that would help him.

Henk made to speak.

"Don't say 'I don't know' again," Qualto anticipated. "You started this hare running. You follow it."

"Do you ever feel this building, Qualto?"

Qualto's bewilderment began to turn into concern.

"What do you mean, feel it?"

Henk made an uncharacteristic gesture, waving his hands awkwardly. "Feel that it's almost..." He hesitated. "Alive?"

CHAPTER 12

"Alive?"

Qualto looked at Henk uncomfortably as he softly echoed him. He did not know how to answer. He, Nyk and Henk did not talk very much and such conversations as they had were usually confined to everyday matters. They had worked together long enough to know most of one another's histories, tales and foibles, to form clear conclusions about each other, and to have these same conclusions both mellow and harden with time. They got on together quite well and their silences were, for the most part, companionable. But now Henk was breaching an unspoken pact. For in their shared silence, as well as their having little new to say, save when one of them returned from a trip home, there lay a deeper silence. The silence that the Keep had bred in generations of caretakers and helpers long before Nyk, Henk and Qualto. The Keep was a strange place: certain things about it were not spoken of.

Henk was avoiding Qualto's gaze, looking around the room with its familiar, well-worn furniture and decor which, like the stairs to the Beacon, and an equally well-worn list of non-urgent matters, was going to be "seen to" in the near but seemingly never arriving future. Qualto was embarrassed by what he took to be his companion's embarrassment. But he was concerned also. He resorted to the obvious.

"I don't understand what you mean," he said. "The Keep's the Keep—a building like any other—stone, timber..."

He stopped as he found himself the focus of Henk's unexpectedly challenging gaze.

"Well, all right," he conceded reluctantly. "It can be creepy, at times—unsettling—I'll grant you that. But it's old... and big... and empty, and..." His voice tailed off.

"Empty it isn't," Henk said flatly into the ensuing silence. "It's full of things."

Qualto held out a hand to stop him. "Enough, Henk," he said sharply. "I don't know if you're developing a sense of humour in your old age, but if you are, I don't like it. What's the matter with...?"

A knock on the door made him start violently. It opened tentatively and Badr's head appeared. "Am I interrupting anything?" he asked.

"Not at all," Qualto replied, grateful for the intrusion. "Come in." He pointed to a chair by the fire. Badr entered and sat down rather self-consciously.

"Do you need anything?" Qualto asked.

"No," Badr replied hastily. "I don't mean to impose. I was just..." He shrugged. "Tired of my own company."

Qualto smiled. "Not much more you can do without your equipment?"

"Not really. I've worked out a plan for what I think we should do next, but it's clearer than ever that the instruments Nyk found just aren't good enough. They're very old. I was impressed by the way surveyor Josyff used the one that was still working, but it was... too slow, too inaccurate. And this place is so very... convoluted... bewildering."

Qualto glanced at Henk who was casually prodding the fire with a long poker.

"I've just been outside—it's snowing again," Badr went on.

"Yes, we lit the Beacon," Qualto said. "It'll help them if they've turned back."

Badr's eyes widened in realization. "I could see a light catching part of the wall and the snow, but I couldn't see where it was coming from."

"It's a little bit awkward to get to. You'll come across it soon enough when you start finding your way about properly. It's normally only lit at the solstices but, under the circumstances, we thought it might be needed."

"Yes," Badr agreed. His brow furrowed. "I hope they're safe. I'm not used to mountains myself. Just how dangerous is it, walking in this kind of weather?"

"Very." It was Henk. "And there's nothing we can do here except wait." He added emphasis to his words by making a series of vigorous jabs at the unresponsive fire.

Badr opened his mouth to speak but nothing came.

"Henk can be a great comfort," Qualto intruded, glowering at the tall figure ineffectively assaulting the fire. "What he meant to say was: it *can* be dangerous if you don't know what you're doing. Fortunately, Nyk does know what he's doing. Don't worry, he won't be taking any unnecessary risks."

Badr ran his hand nervously through his short-cropped hair. It was a gesture that spoke of bubbling anxieties barely contained. Qualto had a momentary impression of the man's loneliness, far from the flat lands of the south and trapped in this difficult building and this alien landscape.

"You really mustn't worry," he said, as reassuringly as he could. "Nyk *does* know what he's doing. And your surveyor's sensible enough to listen, isn't he?"

"Yes, yes, I'm sorry," Badr said forcing his hands to be still by resting them heavily on the arms of the chair.

"The mountains and this place must be very unsettling for you," Qualto offered, before Badr could say anything further.

"They are," Badr admitted, apparently with some relief. "Not that I'm not used to being in unfamiliar places. But I think not being able to do anything doesn't help."

"Well, Henk's right there. I'm afraid we can't go chasing off through the snow to see if they're all right. For one thing, we can't leave the Keep empty. And for another, we might well miss them; then we'd all be in trouble. We'll just have to wait—they're not due back for a couple of days anyway—and they might have to wait at the village if this snow's widespread. There's nothing to be gained by fretting—at least they're not out there battling against a blizzard. It's difficult, I know, but try to... take it easy."

Badr nodded, though seemingly it was a reluctant acquiescence. "I understand," he said. "But it's not in my nature to take things easy. I like to be working—planning, solving problems, thinking."

"And there are plenty of problems here?" Qualto asked.

"More than you know," Henk muttered, unheard by Badr as he replied, "Yes, I've never seen anything like it before. It's fascinating—very interesting—at a casual glance it seems to be much bigger inside than out. Just an illusion, of course—some clever trickery by the builders. Do you know when it was built?"

"No," Qualto replied, adding, in anticipation of the next question, "Nor why. No one seems to know anything about it. The Estate owns it—or owned it, anyway—and we keep it in good order as best we can. Been like that for generations—unchanging. Except we haven't had a Squire since the last one left—*that's* different."

Badr glanced around, as though sensing the building all about them. Then he shrugged and smiled ironically. "You tend it and we're here to measure it—all just doing our jobs without knowing why."

"Maybe this New Order's got plans for it," Qualto suggested.

"I'm sure they have," Badr replied flatly. "They've usually got plenty of plans." He gave the word, plans, a cynical twist, but stiffened immediately as though to call the reaction back. He pressed on hastily. "But I don't know what they are, and I can't imagine. This is such an odd place and so far from anywhere."

"It's the Keep that's got the plans," Henk said, giving up on the fire and stretching his long frame across the couch again.

"I'm sorry," Badr said, as though he had not heard.

"Henk's a bit out of sorts," Qualto intervened hastily and with some forced joviality. "He doesn't like having his routine messed about."

Badr looked nervous, as though expecting to be caught in the middle of a private quarrel, but Henk's voice was level and dull as he spoke.

"It's nothing to do with routines. It's to do with this place waking up. It's been going on for weeks now."

"Henk!" Qualto hissed urgently with a placating look towards Badr. "Our guest will think he's locked up here with lunatics."

Badr's eyes flicked from Henk to Qualto several times as if in confirmation of Qualto's concern, then he seemed to reach a decision.

"That's an odd thing to say, Henk," he said simply, though he glanced at Qualto almost as if for permission to continue. "You don't mean it's haunted, do you?"

Henk slowly turned and stared at him. "Do I look like a child?" he said starkly.

Badr flinched momentarily but held Henk's gaze.

"Not at all," he said, his tone part defiant, part conciliatory. "I've known people who do, that's all. It's not something I believe in personally, but I've been in plenty of buildings that have an atmosphere about them."

"Damp," Henk sniffed dismissively, turning back to the fire.

Badr's round face cracked into an unexpected smile and he chuckled, his deep set eyes sparkling. "Yes, it usually is. Or the plumbing."

Qualto looked relieved.

"But what did you mean," Badr persisted gently. "The Keep has plans?"

"You don't know the New Order's, I don't know the Keep's," Henk replied tersely. "But I'll be glad to be away from here at the end of this tour. And I don't think I'll be coming back."

Briefly, Qualto's expression became anxious, then irritable. "What's that supposed to mean? You can't just walk away from your bond, end of tour or not."

Henk hunched his shoulders sulkily by way of reply.

Uncomfortable at this exchange, Badr stayed silent.

Qualto tapped the arm of his chair fretfully. "You might at least tell us what's bothering you," he said sharply after a long pause. "We're all stuck here, tour or no, ghosts or no, and you behaving like a cross between a doomsday soothsayer and a long streak of cold water's going to take some putting up with."

Badr looked down and casually covered his mouth to hide his involuntary smile at Qualto's outburst.

There was another silence.

"Well...?" Qualto insisted.

Henk turned and fixed him with a long, gloomy stare.

"Come with me," he said, standing up.

Qualto gave Badr a conspiratorial nod of invitation and held out an arm towards the door for Henk's guidance.

Badr soon lost his bearings as he trooped along behind Qualto and Henk. His surveyor's habit of noting junctions, turnings and small landmarks while wandering about a strange place served him for a while longer, then that too had to be abandoned.

They were moving generally downwards, he knew, but beyond that he had to settle for not losing sight of his guides.

None of them spoke and the air was filled with their slightly misting breath and the sound of their marching feet. The cold had started at the Great Hall. Its high lighting had winked into life as they entered, making it seem as if the protruding carvings were turning to examine the cause of the disturbance. After that, the cold had stayed with the trio as they moved along corridor after corridor, and staircase after staircase.

"Is it much further?" Qualto panted eventually. "You might have told us to bring our coats."

"It's always cold here. We'll go back past the kitchens. You can rustle us up something warm," Henk replied dourly.

"How nice for me," Qualto retorted softly, to no one in particular. The exchange gave Badr momentary relief as he too had been silently pondering the reproach that Qualto had given voice to. He kept glancing over his shoulder. Oddly enough, he had not been struck by any atmosphere about the Keep when he had arrived. Possibly it was because the place was so unusual—his curiosity and wonder might have over-ridden any subtler responses. But he could sense something now. Not that it was particularly mysterious. It was just the way the lighting worked. That had disconcerted him from the beginning. Once he had become used to it, it did not disturb him that lights would click on as he entered a room, although the slight pause could be annoying and often left him groping for a sometimes non-existent switch. Nor did it disturb him too much that the same happened when he walked into a corridor. But what *did* disturb him was the illuminating of a length of corridor as he walked along it, for the lights behind him would be extinguished after he had passed, giving him the impression that he was being pursued by a silent darkness. Like something from a nightmare. It did not help him that very little of the Keep received light from the outside and when the lights went out, the darkness was total. Now, as he followed Henk and Qualto down seemingly interminable corridors, all new to him, the sensation became almost oppressive and he had to make a conscious effort to fight off a feeling of claustrophobia.

His hand kept opening and closing about the torch which he had been in the habit of carrying since shortly after his arrival.

Then Henk had stopped. They were at a junction. He was looking around, as if uncertain where he was. Badr did not find the action reassuring. Qualto was doing an impromptu jig, stamping his feet and rubbing his hands.

Henk reached a decision. As he stepped forward, the corridor ahead of him lit up. It was quite short. At the end of it was a door.

He motioned the others forward.

CHAPTER 13

As the three figures drew nearer, Nyk and Josyff moved forwards to greet them. Esyal however, remained where she was and pulled the hood of her coat further forward so that it completely concealed her face.

"Jonal, Aryck," Nyk called out as the grey silhouettes became recognizable. There was a brief flurry of confusion as Nyk and the two men greeted the other and asked and answered the same question.

"What are you doing out here?"

"We were coming to see what had happened to the Surveyor's equipment," Nyk explained.

"And to get some extra... supplies," one of the new arrivals laughed. Nyk gave a disclaiming shrug.

"Do you have the equipment?" he asked.

"We do, and you're welcome to it."

Without further comment, the two men began unhitching their substantial back packs. Nyk pulled a rueful face. "Aren't you coming back to the Keep?"

Jonal gave Nyk a discreet and knowing look, his eyes indicating the third figure who was standing, like Josyff and Esyal, a little way back from this meeting.

"No. The going was worse than we thought before we set out—much worse—really slowed us down. We don't have enough supplies."

Nyk looked both surprised and concerned. He leaned forward urgently but Jonal replied to his question before he asked it.

"The gentleman was very... insistent... we come out." His manner asked that the matter not be pursued.

Nyk glanced quickly at the silent figure standing nearby. As though taking the scrutiny as an invitation, the figure stepped forward. He was the tallest there and, like Esyal, his face was hidden by the hood of his coat.

"I am Adroyan Sirthied," he said, extending his hand to Nyk. His voice was soft and cultured but full of quiet assurance—oddly powerful. "You are Nyk, I presume?" he went on as Nyk uncertainly took his hand.

"Yes, yes," Nyk replied unsteadily.

"I've come to..." Adroyan paused. "To... help the surveyor." He turned to Josyff, who instinctively straightened.

"The Keep is important to us," Adroyan said, taking Josyff's hand. "You must do your work well."

Josyff felt a swirl of indignation begin to flare up at this high-handed and unnecessary injunction, not least as it was uttered without even a greeting, but Adroyan was speaking again before it could find voice.

"But then, you always do, don't you? That's why you were chosen."

The seeming compliment aggravated rather than calmed Josyff's reaction but he remained silent. Adroyan turned to his guides. "We must continue; I need to reach the Keep."

Jonal gave him an enigmatic but far from friendly look.

"You can go on with Nyk and the surveyor now, sir. We didn't expect the conditions we ran into. Never known this much snow so early. It's not good." His thumb pointed over his shoulder and he spoke to Nyk as if in appeal before turning back to Adroyan. "It's bad back there. We haven't the supplies to go on to the Keep and get back. Even if we leave now it's going to be difficult to get back to the village." Though he spoke quietly, his tone was a mixture of fearful defiance and anger. Josyff sensed irritation in the listening figure of Adroyan. The tentative dislike he had taken to this stranger hardened, but so did a resolve to be cautious: the man exuded New Order. And he was no underling—no mere "helper". Who was he?

Why was he here? What did he want? Questions he knew he could only wait to have answered.

As if in confirmation of Josyff's conclusion, Adroyan said, "You are needed here," his voice still quiet, but full of command.

Jonal faltered momentarily, almost as though he had been struck, then he seemed to gather courage from somewhere. "With respect, we're needed more at the village, sir. We've families and jobs to tend. If we go on to the Keep in this weather we could be stranded there for weeks. It's going to be dangerous getting back as it is. You'll recall I advised you against this trip."

There was a tense silence. Josyff half expected a conceding nod from Adroyan, but it was Jonal who took the initiative. He held out his hand to Nyk.

"Sorry we can't stand and chat, Nyk, but you'll have to be moving quickly yourself if you're going to get to the Keep today. You can manage all this?" He nodded towards the packs that he and Aryck had been carrying.

Nyk looked set to talk further but settled for a shrug and, "We'll be all right. You get along—and take care. Regards to your family."

Jonal bowed towards Josyff and nodded towards Adroyan, then he and Aryck turned about and set off back the way they had come.

"Wait!"

It was Esyal. She was moving after them. "I must go with you," she said, her voice urgent.

Jonal looked at Nyk inquiringly.

"We found her in the cave," Nyk explained, almost apologetically. "She seems well enough but she can't remember where she's from or how she came here. Perhaps someone in the village might know who she is or who she was with."

Jonal put his hand to his head and looked quickly at the still motionless and watching Adroyan then at the way back to the village.

"We can't take her," he said urgently to Nyk. "It's going to be hard enough for us on our own without dragging some passenger along."

"I'll be no passenger. I can manage," Esyal said forcefully.

Jonal looked back to Nyk who gave an almost imperceptible shrug. It was enough.

"No!" Jonal's tone was final but he snatched at an excuse. "If your memory's gone you might have a head injury—it's too risky. I'm sorry." Then, as if offended by his own abruptness, "What's your name? I'll ask about you in the village. But for now you'll have to go to the Keep. You'll be safe there."

"Esyal Wrenith," Nyk answered on Esyal's behalf. "We'll be all right for supplies for a few weeks, but send someone out as soon as you can."

Jonal and Aryck were walking away. Jonal raised an acknowledging hand.

"No, wait!" Esyal shouted again.

"Too dangerous, girl," Jonal called back over his shoulder. "Go to the Keep. It's a safer journey. But not if you waste time arguing."

Esyal made to move after them but Nyk caught her arm.

"No," he said. "If Jonal and Aryck say it's safer to go on to the Keep then that's what you should do. They know the mountains, the paths and the weather—better than I do, for sure. They'd have taken you if they could."

"They can't stop me following them, though—nor can you," Esyal said defiantly.

Nyk released her arm and took a step backwards, partly extending his arm as if to encourage her on her way. "That's true. But you'll die if you do. Look at them."

Esyal followed his gaze. Jonal and Aryck were already almost lost in the swirling snow.

"I'll follow their footsteps," Esyal protested. Then her shoulders slumped. "They're going too fast, aren't they? I..." She was clenching her fists and her voice was angry and bitter. As it faded, a soft, hissed oath drifted into the dead greyness.

With tentative paternalism, Nyk patted her arm, then he addressed the whole group briskly. "Come on. We've no time for debating. Let's get moving."

There was a brief, bustling interlude as he attended to the distribution of the packs that Jonal and Aryck had brought. Josyff took a relish in Adroyan's unspoken but obvious reluctance to carry anything, though he was careful not to let it show.

"I know this stuff's important to you, boss," Nyk said to Josyff with apologetic firmness. "But if things get bad, we'll have to stow it somewhere—come back for it another time. The cold won't hurt it, will it?"

"It shouldn't do," Josyff replied. "I don't relish leaving it after waiting for it for so long, but I understand."

"The measuring of the Keep is important," Adroyan announced sternly.

Only a long misty breath out betrayed Nyk's wilful patience.

"No disrespect sir, but the choice might be ourselves and the equipment buried in the snow out here 'til Spring, or the Keep unmeasured but us alive ready to measure it another day."

Somewhat to Josyff's surprise, Adroyan appeared to be debating this point with himself before he eventually gave an imperious wave of his hand to indicate that they could all move forward.

Nyk took the lead, with Esyal walking by his side whenever she could.

"Stay easy but stay alert," he told them. "Just put one foot in front of the other and we'll get there. Don't fret about how far we've come or how far we've got to go—it won't make any difference to either of them, but it'll wear you out." He chuckled softly to himself, "Like life."

They walked on for the most part in silence. Despite Nyk's instruction that they stay alert, Josyff found his mind wandering, lured into a sense of isolation by his own slow and steady footsteps, the silence of his companions and the deeper silence of the snow-streaked greyness enclosing them all.

Images of the past days came and went, sharing only their dreamlike strangeness. The clock, the darkness rushing along the corridor, the seagulls, the blow to his head, all mingled eerily with the mundane realities of his profession—how he had come to be chosen for this job, how his equipment had been sent separately, how his team had been scattered. And what, for pity's sake, *was* the Keep and why did anyone want to know anything about it, a bizarre and ancient building out here in the wilds? He pursued none of these as he knew he had no answers and they wove themselves into a web which pulsed with the steady rhythm of his walking and his breathing.

A cry and a push snapped him awake. Instinctively he reached out and grabbed the stumbling Adroyan. As the big man righted himself, Josyff felt the arm he was holding briefly tense as though to snatch itself free. Then it relaxed and he released it.

"Thank you," said Adroyan quietly, his voice flat. Josyff nodded, uncertain what to say.

"You two all right?" came Nyk's voice.

"Yes," said Adroyan casually, brushing his arm where Josyff had gripped it as if to remove a blemish.

"We'll take a little rest at the top of the next rise," Nyk said.

When they halted, Josyff realized, somewhat to his embarrassment, that he did not know where he was. Engrossed in his own thoughts, he had lost track of the slopes they had climbed and descended. Although it was not snowing as hard now, visibility was still poor and he could see none of the peaks that he had carefully selected as suitable landmarks on his outward journey.

"Not much further now," Adroyan said, interrupting Josyff's silent self-reproach.

It sounded like a categorical statement and Nyk looked at him in surprise. "I'm afraid not," he said. "It's quite a way, yet. We shouldn't stop for long."

Adroyan was staring up into the greyness. Though his face was hidden, his posture indicated an inclination to argue the point.

"Are you sure?" he asked, still gazing upwards.

"Certain," Nyk replied.

"Strange," Adroyan said softly, and patently to himself. "I could have sworn..." His voice tailed off.

"Have you been here before, sir?" Nyk asked.

Adroyan shook his head absently but did not reply. Josyff had the impression of a predator scenting the wind.

Nyk glanced at Josyff, his expression a mixture of bewilderment, concern and irritation.

"Where are we?" Josyff asked him discreetly.

"By the Valsen," Nyk replied, equally softly. He nodded towards Adroyan, still looking upwards. "Maybe he's smelt the First Keep," he muttered caustically. Then, to Josyff's alarm, he voiced the idea directly to Adroyan.

"There's an old tale saying that the First Keep was up there, sir. Though there's only ever been the one that we know of," he said briskly, but with the manner of a confident underling testing his bounds. "Maybe you're psychic," he added jovially.

Adroyan looked at him for a moment, his face hidden in the depths of his hood, then he looked upwards again and nodded his head once, very slowly, very slightly. Josyff found the movement unsettling. Nyk however, seemed unconcerned. He was rooting through his pockets.

"Do you have any food, sir?" he asked Adroyan.

Before any reply came, Nyk handed an apple each to Josyff and Esyal and held one out to Adroyan. He stepped forward and took it with a quiet, "Thank you."

"They're the last," Nyk said, setting off. "We'll eat as we walk. If we can keep a steady pace, we should be there before nightfall."

"And if we can't?" Esyal asked.

"We hobble through the dark," Nyk replied, biting into his apple noisily. "I don't want to camp if we can avoid it."

Esyal fell in beside him as she had before.

She felt oddly disorientated. Her anger and disappointment at not being able to go with Jonal and Aryck to the village had been unable to sustain itself through Nyk's steady but unremitting pace and had faded. Or, more correctly, like the mountains around her, they had been overlain. Nameless concerns permeated her thoughts, smothering her attempts to work out a clear strategy for what she must do when they reached the Keep. Ideas came with great clarity only to slip away as soon as she began to pursue them. Trains of thought took mysterious and unnoticed directions as they might in a dream—seemingly logical at the time but then rambling and incoherent.

"Just keep walking."

Nyk's voice dispelled her latest foray. She looked at him vaguely.

"You're tired and weak from everything that's happened," he volunteered. "Don't fight yourself, or the mountains, or the snow. Just keep your eye on me, and walk."

Even as she was nodding in response to this, Esyal felt her knees weakening and the greyness sweeping in upon her.

CHAPTER 14

"Well?" said Qualto.

Henk extended an arm towards the door, inviting him to open it.

"If this is a surprise party I have to tell you it's not my birthday," Qualto said caustically as he pushed past Henk.

The door was no different from many that could be found about the Keep: close fitting timbers shaped to the arched doorway, heavy iron hinges and a simple pivoting latch. Qualto lifted the latch and pulled at the door. Expecting some resistance from a door in such an unused part of the Keep, Qualto staggered slightly as it opened with ease. Henk reached out and steadied him. Badr, who had been watching the exchange between the two men with some amusement, stepped back as cold air wafted over his face and a sound like a low sigh filled the passageway.

"What the devil was that?" Qualto exclaimed, stepping back. He shivered noisily, provoking the same response in Badr, though he managed to disguise the movement.

"What was what?" Henk asked, watching Qualto intently.

"That noise, of course," Qualto replied, angrily. "Like someone... like someone..."

"Someone in despair?" Henk finished the sentence as Qualto stumbled into an awkward silence.

Badr found his mouth was dry. He cleared his throat noisily and affected a cheerfulness he did not feel.

"It's probably an outside door or a window open somewhere," he said. "You can get all manner of draughts and noises in a great pile like this."

"No." Qualto and Henk spoke simultaneously.

"The only unlocked doors are those we use, and they're all shut," Henk added. "And none of the windows open." He looked down at Badr. "And there's no wind today."

Badr felt that he should say more, but he knew enough of the Keep to know that Henk was correct. Both the sound and the chilling waft of air had faded but they hung in his memory as though the cold stones about him were softly whispering to him. He fought down another urge to shiver.

Qualto, however, appeared to have recovered from his initial alarm. "Is this what you dragged us all this way for?" he asked, irritably. "A draughty corridor?" Henk did not reply but swung the door to and fro a few times: it moved silently and easily.

Qualto eyed him. "You've been down here oiling the hinges haven't you?" he said suspiciously. "Most of these old doors haven't been opened in years and screech like crushed cats."

Henk remained silent but once again held out his arm, this time motioning Qualto through the doorway.

"Where does it go?" Qualto asked.

"Where does anything go to in this place?" Henk retorted. "Up, down, round—rooms and more rooms."

"After you, then," Qualto insisted.

Henk ducked unnecessarily as he walked through the doorway, Qualto following him. Badr paused to secure the door open with a hook in the wall that dropped into a ring in the latch. He'd been trapped in strange rooms before now by ill-hung doors slamming, and when it hadn't been embarrassing it had been alarming, not to say downright dangerous—as it could be here.

He noticed that the wall was unusually thick as he passed through the doorway, making it almost like a short tunnel. And indeed, as he stepped into the passage beyond the door he felt as though he had ended a journey. Something had changed. He paused and gazed around.

He was aware of Henk watching him silently.

"Feels different," Qualto voiced his own response bluntly.

Yes, Badr thought, but *where* is the difference? He looked back through the door. It stood open and the passage beyond stretched off to end in darkness in the characteristic manner of the Keep. And the passage they had entered looked no different. Typical of many such in the Keep, it was generously wide with a low rise arched ceiling, a smooth, tight-jointed stone floor and equally smooth, undecorated walls. He took in a slow breath. There was no smell that he could detect. Not even the stale odour of long unmoved air, for unmoved it must be as there was no hint of the breeze that had greeted them when the door was first opened. Then again, he reflected, the way air moved about this convoluted building was a mystery in its own right—nothing ever smelled of stagnancy yet there was no apparent ventilation. He brought himself back to the present. There was no apparent change in the temperature to indicate they had moved into a deeper and older part of the Keep, but there was change enough to mist the breath and keep one from loitering.

"It's in your head."

Badr started. The voice sounded unnaturally loud.

"What?"

"It's in your head." It was Henk and he was speaking normally. "What you can feel. Everything looks the same, but it's different."

His manner was that of someone stating a straightforward fact, quite free from the combative justification that had coloured his exchanges with Qualto previously. Badr half expected Qualto to rebut the comment but the cook was silent.

"I don't understand. What do you mean?" he said reluctantly and after a long pause. Just as Henk's voice had sounded louder than it was, now his own felt hollow and detached.

Henk shrugged and tapped his head. "Voices," he said. "Or things that would be voices. Like something trying to talk to us."

Both Qualto and Badr stared at him. Badr alarmed, Qualto both alarmed and concerned. He took his friend's arm and spoke to him softly and urgently.

"What's the matter with you, Henk? You're making a fool of yourself in front of our guest."

Henk shook off Qualto's hand, almost angrily. "Just listen!" he said, an unexpected passion lighting his face. Badr took a step backwards, abruptly all too aware of the fact that he had no idea where he was in this maze of a building or what these two people were really like. He took some comfort from the fact that Qualto seemed to be as surprised and concerned as he was.

"Maybe we should get back," he said, in an attempt to restore a sense of normality.

"Just listen!" Henk said again, with even more force but with a note of entreaty. "It's been like this for months."

"You've been coming down here for *months*?" Qualto exclaimed, ignoring the plea. "What in God's name for? There's nothing needs doing down here, is there?"

"There's work needed everywhere, all the time," Henk retorted, more his normal self again, somewhat to Badr's relief.

Qualto gazed up and down the passage with slow and wilful deliberation. "Well, I can't see anything."

Henk came the nearest he could to straightening up indignantly as he aped Qualto's inspection of the passage. "That's because you're the *cook*," he said definitively, snapping out the final word.

Qualto's eyes narrowed and he seemed set on continuing the discussion in like terms, until a quick sidelong glance at Badr reminded him to be more circumspect. He raised his hands apologetically. "All right, all right, I'm sorry. It's not for me to tell you and Nyk your jobs. But this *is* a long way from anywhere you normally go, isn't it?"

Henk was silent, though it was obvious from his expression that he was struggling with something. Slowly he wilted back to his normal posture.

"I like to wander about," he said, half reluctantly, half with relief. He became self-consciously comradely. "You know how it is. We grumble about the place but we're part of it and it's part of us."

Qualto shuffled his feet uncomfortably but did not speak. Henk became defensive. "And it *is* our job to keep an eye on all of it, whether there's work to do or not."

Qualto gave a conciliatory nod, increasingly anxious to have this matter ended and to get back to his kitchen and normality, not to say warmth.

"But..."

"Just listen." Henk was insistent. "Please."

It was not a request that could be refused. Silence enfolded the group. Henk beckoned to them and began walking along the passage. Badr cast another nervous glance back at the open door then followed him, as did Qualto, conspicuously tightening his mouth to indicate he had a great deal to say, but wouldn't.

All three moved like guilty late-night revellers returning to a darkened household, placing their feet carefully as if the least sound might bring retribution down upon them.

Badr noticed that the passage ahead of them was lit for a greater length than he had seen elsewhere in the Keep. He was paying particular attention to it, not relishing the moment when the lights behind them would go out and the door become invisible.

Why such concern about the door? he thought. It was securely held open—he had made certain of that. It had no bolts to tumble accidentally into place should another mysterious draught catch it, and it hadn't been jammed into its frame with damp and age. They had passed through many other doors to which he had not given the least thought, yet it would not go from his mind, constantly enticing him to look over his shoulder. It was as though he had passed through a border into another land and the door was the only way back. In fact, it was almost as though he were no longer in the Keep.

"Where are we going?" he said in an attempt to gather his rambling thoughts. He found that he was whispering.

"Just a little further," Henk replied, also whispering.

Badr and Qualto exchanged a glance in which they agreed to continue for the moment.

Henk was leaning forward slightly, as though listening to something. Badr peered ahead. The scene before him was unchanged—a typical Keep passage, albeit again lit more extensively than others he had seen. He frowned and narrowed his eyes. The feeling of strangeness would not leave him and its cause was like a familiar name slipped suddenly from memory and being buried deeper the more it was striven after.

Let it go, he thought. But he could not.

Something was wrong with what he was looking at—something subtle... and disconcerting... like a cunningly crafted optical illusion—lines meeting that could not meet—lines not meeting that could only meet.

What was it? Where was it?

He shook his head and the impression was gone.

Too long staring at the same thing, he decided.

But it returned after he had walked only a few steps further, like a reflection returning to a momentarily disturbed pool, but, unlike a reflection, it remained elusive—a shadow in the corner of the eye.

He looked at Henk, head craned forward. Could Henk actually be hearing something?

Well, even if he could, it would be no more than some freakish reverberation from another part of the Keep. Probably from outside, for all that the doors and windows were supposed to be closed. There were many openings into a building other than doors and windows. Badr realized abruptly that his thoughts were harsh and noisy as if, like a child, he were trying to shout down a growing unease.

He cleared his throat and wilfully forced his body to be silent and his mind to be still.

Whatever Henk might be listening for, Badr could not hear it. There was no sound except the rustling of their clothes, and their soft footfalls and breathing. And Qualto's breathing was patently the overture to an impatient outburst.

Well, whatever's troubling Henk—and me, for that matter—Qualto seems to be oblivious to it.

They reached a junction. The passage had widened and the three men stood facing two seemingly identical passages, one to the left, one to the right. Both were lit for quite a distance and appeared to be sloping slightly downwards and curving away from one another. Badr was startled. The lights had been coming on well ahead of them as they walked along but he could not remember seeing the approach of this quite distinct feature.

You're walking about in a dream, he reproached himself, blinking deliberately and shaking his shoulders loose. Walking these long, monotonous passages with their damned retreating lights can be hypnotic. And this cold doesn't help. Get a hold of yourself. But, despite this rationalization, the shock of the sudden appearance of the junction was reluctant to leave him and he was aware that his breathing was shallow and his pulse was fast. Qualto's voice came both as a relief and a focus.

"Enough, Henk," the cook said. "Are you going to show us something, or are you just going to walk us to death."

Henk was looking doubtfully from one passage to the next.

"You don't know where we are, do you?" Qualto exclaimed heatedly.

Henk did not reply but maintained his inspection of the two passages.

"I don't remember this," he said finally, just as Qualto was moving determinedly to face him.

"What do you mean?" Qualto asked, obviously taken aback by this admission.

Henk looked down at him. "I mean, I don't remember this," he said. "I was along here a week ago and these passages weren't here."

Qualto's eyes narrowed and he leaned forward, looking intently at his friend. Badr risked an intrusion before Qualto could speak.

"Are you very familiar with this part of the Keep?" he asked. "These passages are all very similar—and it's difficult to judge distance—especially with these lights..."

"They weren't here," Henk insisted, though his posture and expression gave the lie to this certainty.

Badr's concern about what he had been seeing—or not seeing—finally dwindled into nothingness before his natural pragmatism.

"I think we should get back," he said bluntly, taking Henk's arm. "It's cold and we've walked a long way, and these passages are disorientating at the best. Come on." He made to turn Henk around gently, but the tall man did not move.

Qualto sided with Badr. He became conciliatory. "He's right, Henk. Let's get back. I'll rustle something warm up and you can tell us what's bothering you. It doesn't matter if you can't find it now. It's not going to go anywhere, is it?"

Henk was shaking his head. "No, this is new," he said, though apparently to himself. "It wasn't here."

"Henk, you've just made a mistake, that's all," Qualto said, his voice now a mixture of concern and irritation. He paused and, briefly, the latter prevailed. "I don't know why you want to go wandering about this place. There's nothing down here that needs attention."

"It wasn't here," Henk said again, oblivious to Qualto's outburst.

Then he was striding off down the left hand passage.

CHAPTER 15

Nyk swore as he caught Esyal. The impact almost over-balanced him but he recovered before Josyff could reach him. There was a brief swirl of confusion until Nyk lowered her gently to the ground and knelt down beside her. Josyff dropped down next to him, but Adroyan remained standing, motionless.

"Esyal, Esyal," Nyk said purposefully, supporting her head and slapping her face lightly. There was no response. Then, in an echo of Josyff's actions when they had first found her, he felt for a pulse in her neck and, satisfied with that, bent forward attentively to see if she was still breathing.

"What is the matter with her?" It was Adroyan. There was a hint of irritation in his voice.

"I don't know," Nyk replied. His manner was icily polite and Josyff saw his jaw stiffen momentarily. "She's alive. She may just be exhausted—we've no idea how long she's been out here or what she's been through..." He fell silent.

"Or?" Adroyan prompted tersely, noting Nyk's uncertainty.

"Or it may be some kind of head injury." Anger surfaced briefly in Nyk's voice. "Whatever's made her lose her memory may be serious."

"Is there any sign of a head injury?" Adroyan's tone was neutral now.

"No, but that doesn't mean anything."

Nyk's brow furrowed and he looked back the way they had come.

"Should we go back after Jonal and Aryck?" Josyff said, anticipating Nyk's thinking. "If it is a head injury she'll need proper help—a doctor."

Nyk looked intently at Esyal for a moment and then back once more into the greyness before replying. "No. We've no choice. Whether she needs a doctor or not, we can only go back to the Keep from here." He looked at Josyff with both concern and resignation. "We're going to have to carry her."

"We can leave the equipment," Josyff said, slightly surprised at his own lack of hesitation. "Mark the place and..."

"No!"

It was Adroyan.

"The Keep must be measured. It is important—very important."

Josyff spoke quickly as he sensed Nyk's temper slipping from his control.

"With respect, sir, I know precious little about travelling in the mountains but even I can see that while a moment ago our position was risky, it's now become dangerous. The girl will have to be carried. We can come back for the equipment first thing tomorrow. It won't suffer for a night out here."

Adroyan inclined his head as though he were listening for something, then he looked slowly round.

"The weather might worsen," he said, adding softly, as if to himself, "The Keep must be measured." He stepped forward. "I'll carry the girl."

Before anyone could protest, he crouched down and picked up Esyal, seemingly with little effort. "She is light. She'll be no great burden."

Nyk looked openly confused at this unexpected development but recovered quickly.

"You're sure?" he asked, peering into the darkness of the hood hiding Adroyan's face.

"Yes."

"Speak if she becomes too heavy," Nyk said, abruptly authoritative. "If *you* collapse we'll be in *real* trouble and it'll be more than the equipment that's lost." He did not wait for a reply. "We must get on."

He set off again and Adroyan followed him. Josyff hitched his pack until it was comfortable, picked up his share of the equipment, then took up the rear. More and more questions were demanding attention as he looked at the tall new arrival but he thrust them away. The next few hours were going to be grim enough without him taking a tumble because he wasn't looking what he was doing.

The three figures moved on through the falling snow, maintaining the same steady pace that Nyk had set since they left the two guides. He seemed to be unaffected by the extra weight he was carrying, as too did Adroyan, and Josyff could not avoid feeling a twinge of inadequacy as his legs eventually began to protest and his packs began to grow heavier. He was more than relieved when Nyk stopped at the top of a slope.

"A few minutes," he said. "Get our breaths back."

Adroyan carefully leaned the still unconscious Esyal against a rock, stretched himself and rolled his shoulders to ease the strain in them. His hand went into the hood to wipe his brow.

Well, whoever you are, you're certainly strong, Josyff thought, as he crouched down in front of the young woman. He leaned forward and placed his ear close to her mouth, then he checked her pulse.

"She's still breathing and her heart seems to be beating strongly," he said, "In as much as I know anything about such things."

Nyk shook his head. "I've no idea what we're going to do with her if she's really hurt," he said, looking worried. "Still..." He glanced around into the greyness. "One thing at a time, I suppose. Let's concentrate on getting all of us back safely."

"I can carry her for a while," Josyff volunteered to Adroyan.

"She is too heavy for you," came the unhesitating reply. "We can stop again if the effort becomes too much."

Both what he said and the way he said it left Josyff unable to do anything other than grunt an acknowledgement which was both wordless and graceless.

"It's not too far now," Nyk said briskly into the awkward silence, and as if to atone for a momentary doubt. "It'll be dark early, unfortunately, but, barring accidents, we should be back at the Keep before we have to start using lights."

Adroyan's head went back and once again Josyff had the sense of a predator scenting the air.

"Good," Adroyan said, picking up Esyal. He nodded to Nyk to continue.

The snow shifted and changed as they walked: sometimes it fell thick and discouraging, making them lower their eyes and lean forward; sometimes it almost stopped, leaving stray flakes dancing in the air, but only as if bracing itself for further onslaught. The sky remained unbroken but grew slowly darker. Nyk's pace increased perceptibly and he kept glancing back at his charges. Josyff was beginning to feel very tired and he was increasingly grateful for the stick that Nyk had thrust on him. He noticed that Adroyan's posture was less confident than it had been and allowed himself a small hint of satisfaction. It was followed almost immediately by a reproach. The arrival of this stranger was fortuitous. He and Nyk on their own would not have been able to carry the girl and all the equipment. In fact, he reflected, they would have been hard pressed to carry her and *any* of it.

The thought of the equipment brought with it thoughts of his work and in turn an unexpected longing to be home with his wife, to see this strange, unsettling job finished—filed away—reduced to the safety of an old memory. He shook his head and echoed Nyk's earlier advice—"Just put one foot in front of the other and we'll get there."

"Ah."

It was Nyk. He had stopped and was pointing.

"Splendid," he said. "They've lit the beacon."

Josyff followed Nyk's hand. It took his eyes a little time to adjust but gradually a faint glow in the distance took form. "The beacon?" he queried.

"That'll be Henk's idea," Nyk said, not answering the inquiry. "Can be quite thoughtful at times."

"Not much further, then?" Josyff said.

"Further than it looks," Nyk replied pitilessly. "But the beacon'll help. It's going to be dark before we get there."

And, after a further brief check on Esyal, they were moving again. Josyff tried to keep his mind off his own increasing discomfort by thinking about the others. Nyk was older than he was and Adroyan was carrying a greater burden and both were walking on without complaint. After a while however, he stopped looking for solace of any kind and his mind became like the dark, impenetrable sky above, filled with the monotonous instruction, "one step at a time".

His aching legs and shoulders stopped his thoughts from wandering as he followed the others through the deepening gloom, though with each step he thought he could sense the present of the Keep weighing down on him.

Just tiredness, he managed to think, after a while. Be better when I've had a good sleep and got started on this job properly.

But the thought had the ring of a rationalization and it offered no consolation.

As Nyk had said, the beacon proved to be a considerable help. Though it shone high above their heads, its light bounced off a myriad snow-covered surfaces and lit their way like a soft moonlight.

Then the Keep, or more correctly, the bright star of the beacon, came into view.

"Don't look at the beacon, you won't be able to see your feet when you look down," Nyk warned. "There's still plenty of places to take a tumble."

Adroyan either did not hear, or chose to ignore the advice. He stopped sharply, almost causing Josyff to bump into him, then stood staring at the Keep. He threw his hood back. Josyff took the opportunity to lean on his stick while Nyk turned his back on the Keep and waited. Josyff could not see his face but judged it to be full of wilful patience. By contrast, Adroyan's face was all too visible now. Josyff glanced at it then turned away quickly. Deep shadows gave the man's face the appearance of having been carved and there was a look in his eyes—bright and predatory—that was disconcerting to the point of being frightening. Cradled in his arms, Esyal should have looked like a tired child being carried by loving parent, but to Josyff she looked more like unconscious prey—the prize of the day's hunt.

He flinched. Adroyan was speaking to him. "This is indeed the place. It must be measured—you must measure it well, surveyor."

A frisson of anger suffused Josyff—I always measure things well, it said—but he was both too tired and too instinctively cautious to let it catch fire.

"Tomorrow we'll start," he replied.

"Let's get there first," Nyk intruded sourly, and he set off again.

As they trudged up the final slope, Josyff began to make out the shadowy form of the Keep at the edges of the light. In addition to a growing sense of oppression, something seemed to be wrong, although he could not make it out.

Until they reached the top.

The dark chasm of the moat greeted them. The drawbridge had been lifted.

CHAPTER 16

Qualto swore and ran after Henk's retreating form. With an effort—the big man was striding out—he overtook him and turned to stand in his path.

"Enough! Enough! Enough!" he shouted, each exclamation louder than the previous and each accompanied by a determined sweep of the hands. "I'm not going another step further. I'm cold and we've got a devil of a way to go back. Let's get back to the common room—have a drink—a warm one—and a chat."

Hesitantly Badr moved to his side in silent support.

Henk moved forward, almost as though to brush Qualto to one side, but Qualto's hand shot out to rest squarely on the taller man's chest.

"Henk, what are you doing?" Qualto's voice rose in volume and pitch so that the last word had an incongruous squeak to it. The sound echoed a little, tremulously, and Henk started visibly. Qualto pressed home his advantage. "I said, enough! Turn round, right now, and take us back. Whatever's bothering you can wait for another time."

He pointed at Badr and moved to conciliation before Henk could reply.

"When the surveyor gets back with his equipment, our guest..." he laid emphasis on the last word and indicated Badr again, "...and he will be all over the place. They'll get down here as a matter of course..."

"That's right, Henk," Badr intervened. "We have to measure everything— everything." He too became conciliatory. "Quite possibly you'll be able to help us. There'll be nothing untoward here, you'll see. A building's a building—this one's probably going to be more awkward than usual, but we'll soon have it down on paper."

Badr could see that Henk was almost leaning on Qualto's hand and the little man was having to exert some force to prevent himself from being moved backwards. Then Henk relaxed and his expression changed.

"Down on paper," he echoed, looking around him. There was a long silence. "No, I don't think so."

Badr decided not to argue the point. He had no idea what was bothering Henk or where they were and he had the distinct impression that Qualto was little wiser. All that mattered now was that Henk had to be turned about.

As if responding to the thought, Qualto's other hand gently took Henk's elbow and made to ease him round. For a moment there was a silent deadlock.

"I really would prefer to get back," Badr said, a slight plea in his voice. "This isn't exactly my idea of an evening stroll. It's cold and we've come a long way, and it *is* getting late."

"Suppose Nyk and the surveyor have come back," Qualto added. "They'll be wondering where..."

"They won't be back until late tomorrow at the earliest." Henk dismissed Qualto's remark irritably, but at the same time responded to the pressure on his arm and to Badr's solid presence planted firmly but discreetly in front of him. He looked round then gave a slight nod. "This wasn't here," he said, as a resigned parting shot, and turned back towards the junction. The others followed him. Badr felt reluctant to look back as he sensed the darkness reclaiming the passage behind them.

When they reached the junction, Badr found himself running his hand over the cold stonework as though to satisfy himself that it was not some bizarre illusion. He reproached himself for his folly, but admitted that he would be much happier when they were back to somewhere that he recognized.

They walked for what seemed to Badr to be a long time. Probably because it's uphill, he thought, though he felt a considerable sense of relief when the lights in the passage ahead flickered into life to show the door, still standing open. Qualto too, straightened up at the sight and held out his hands as though to clap them, but the gesture faltered into an uncertain dither. Nevertheless, he strode out more purposefully.

As when he had passed through it before, Badr noted that the dark recess of the door was unusually long—far longer than any wall thickness he had so far encountered in the Keep. What could be above this? he thought, as he lifted the hook from the latch and closed the door gently. At the last, there was a resistance and as he overcame it there came again a faint sound like a distant moan, and a waft of cold air.

He was about to make some remark about stiff hinges, but decided not to. No one else spoke, and Qualto motioned Henk forward again with a nod.

As they walked along, Badr did his best to ignore Henk's odd behaviour by thinking about the problems that surveying this building was going to present. For one thing, he mused, this little escapade showed that it was very much bigger than it appeared to be from the outside and with these maze-like passages there was a real possibility of getting dangerously lost. He must discuss this with the surveyor when he returned. A few simple safety precautions would be advisable.

He was still in this mood when they eventually came back to the Great Hall. It seemed to Badr that the gaping figures protruding from the wall had the look of having fallen suddenly silent at some unwelcome intrusion. He scowled at the unwanted image and glowered briefly at Henk's back.

Damn the man and his antics, giving everyone the creeps—doors and corridors appearing from nowhere! He was surprised, on reflection, that he hadn't laughed outright. Probably just good manners, he mused. Or perhaps taking on protective coloration amongst strangers—Henk's manner had not invited mirth and he *was* the only one who knew where they were. He abandoned his reflections. He knew where he was now—some food and a warm drink as Qualto had suggested and the whole venture would be seen with a different perspective. Maybe even Henk could be softened into some degree of geniality. Even so, the sooner he and the surveyor were striding through this place, doing their job, the better. Marking, measuring, re-capturing the patterns and shapes that the original designers and builders had laid down. Rooting into its nooks and crannies, ferreting out its puzzles and seeming anomalies—generally disentangling it. The thought raised his spirits. He had been impressed by Josyff's work the other day—they'd work well together. Whatever surprises this place had in store for them—and doubtless there'd be plenty—they'd yield to the combined persistence and professionalism of the two of them.

Then they were back in the common room. Qualto began immediately laying into the dull fire but merely succeeded in reducing it to further sullenness. Before he could destroy it utterly, Henk gently wrested the poker from him.

"Food?" he said, his eyes indicating the door.

Qualto held his gaze uncertainly for a moment, then grunted and left.

Badr sat down without comment and pulled his chair nearer to the fire.

"I'll soon have it going," Henk said, rooting in a carved wooden box by the side of the hearth and taking out some coals and kindling timbers. "Qualto's a first class cook, but when it comes to fires..." He pursed his lips and shook his head. "He has a way with them—rather like a bucket of water has."

Badr chuckled. Henk's recent strangeness seemed to be visibly falling away from him as his long hands coaxed dull redness into flames.

"An ancient solace, the fire," Badr ventured as the fire began to blaze up.

Henk nodded but did not reply.

Qualto returned, carefully carrying a tray on which was a large bowl, three smaller ones and a loaf. An aroma filled the room which, had the two waiting men not already been hungry, would have made them so.

"Just some soup left over," Qualto disclaimed, deftly wielding a serving ladle. "I keep making for five instead of three."

They ate in silence.

Badr finished first. He had not realized how hungry he had become. He thanked Qualto, then leaning back in his chair, idly picked up the book that Qualto had been reading earlier. He did not recognize either the title or the author.

"It's very interesting," Qualto volunteered. "You like to read? There are quite a few more by the same man in the book room."

"Book room?" Badr queried.

Qualto made vague navigational gestures with his steaming spoon. "Didn't you and the surveyor come across it the other day?"

"No," Badr replied. "It was slow going with those old instruments, we didn't get a great deal done and what we did wasn't particularly satisfactory."

"Oh, there's a wealth of stuff in the book room. Shall I show you where it is?"

The comfort of the chair and Qualto's soup were spreading a pleasant lethargy through Badr and his immediate reaction was to decline the offer. Some brightness in Qualto's manner however, prevented him. He held out an acquiescing hand and smiled conditionally.

"Providing it's not too far."

Qualto was finishing his soup. "Neither far nor cold," he said. "Come on."

The book room was indeed not far, though it was at the end of one of the many passages that Badr had noted but not yet ventured along. As they entered through tall double doors, the lights came on, revealing a large rectangular room. Book-filled shelves lined all four walls. Badr let out a small exclamation. The room was unlike any he had encountered in the Keep so far, not least because it was thickly carpeted and had a silence that was noticeably different to the echoing silences he had become familiar with. The lighting was also brighter.

The shelves extended to at least twice his own height, Badr judged, and they were served by sloping ladders mounted on rails. He reached out and touched one curiously. It moved silently and smoothly.

"Nyk makes sure they work properly," Qualto said. "Even more partial to this place than I am, Nyk is. Any sign of stiffness, or a squeak, and he'll drop whatever he's doing to put it right."

Badr nodded casually. "It's very... calm," he said, unconsciously lowering his voice. "Where did all these books come from?"

"Most of them have been here for ever," Qualto replied. "But every now and then a batch will come up from the village. We catalogue them, put them on the shelves." He indicated an elegant wooden cabinet of small drawers in the middle of a wide table at the centre of the room.

"The Estate sends them?" Badr asked.

Qualto shrugged. "They just arrive," he said.

There were eight large tables, each with six chairs, placed symmetrically about the room.

"There must have been a lot of people here once."

Qualto shrugged again but did not reply.

"May I?" Badr inquired, indicating the waiting shelves.

"Certainly," Qualto replied.

"I'll put them back where I found them," Badr said, anticipating a plea.

Qualto raised his hands in mock urgency. "No—that's the way we lose them. Just leave them on the tables. We'll put them back. I'll leave you to have a look around—see if there's anything you fancy reading. You know your way back?"

Badr acknowledged the mixture of concern and gentle taunt with a soft laugh. "Yes, I think I can manage that. If not, I'll just shout."

Qualto smiled broadly. "I'll be listening."

Then he left. The doors made only a muffled click as he closed them.

So different, Badr mused, as he strolled around the room. Quiet, bright, clean, warm, and yet, though there were no windows, with a freshness in the air. He might have been in part of a large city library. It seemed that the Keep was going to keep presenting ever new revelations and questions. Plenty of time for that, though. For the moment he could just browse.

The drawers in the cabinet on the central table all bore labels, each marked in a neat, clear handwriting. He opened the one marked "K" and began fingering through the cards headed "Keep, The".

There were a great many. He drew out the first one part way, anxious not to risk jeopardizing whatever filing system Qualto and the others used by removing it and putting it back in the wrong place. His concern proved to be unnecessary; the card would only move so far. Badr's forehead creased in curiosity. How the devil had they contrived to do that? Was this place going to be nothing but puzzles and mysteries? Still, he could read it—there was the title and the author and...

What? The card bore no identifying letter or number to indicate where the book could be found. Nor, for that matter, did any of the shelves, he noted, glancing round. He looked at the card again. Underneath the title was a rectangle with sides divided and sub-divided into smaller rectangles, one of which was black. It took him a moment, some counting of the banks of shelves and a glance at some other cards to work out that this was a representation of the shelves, the black rectangle presumably being the book in question.

As proved to be the case.

Badr was smiling to himself at both the ingenuity and the strangeness of the system as he located the book. It was almost as if it had been prepared for people who could not read, he thought ironically as he sat down at one of the tables. He also allowed himself a brief smugness at having fathomed out so quickly how the card worked.

A Brief History of the Keep by S Airthieid, said the spine of the book.

Not that brief, Badr reflected, hefting it.

He turned immediately to the back of the book.

Splendid, he growled inwardly. No index.

Then he riffled quickly though it, searching idly for plans or sketches. Somewhat to his surprise there were quite a few. He stared down at one, picked at random. Like the layout of the book as a whole, it was in an elaborate style that gave away its age. The current fashion was for simplicity, the avoidance of unnecessary decoration or commentary. He saw the logic of that—indeed, agreed with it—but there was still a slight frisson of concern for worthwhile things lost: care, attention to detail in the execution of the drawings, drafting skills that were useful in their day but were no more.

The quietness of another age, he mused, running his fingers gently over the drawing. Then again, it had been a harder age and such skills were as much a product of fear for one's job as pride in one's skills. The present closed about him again. He wouldn't be so sentimental about times gone if he had to survey this place with those old instruments! Still, someone must have done something.

He turned to the front of the book, and gave an audible grunt of surprise. Just as there was no index so there was no information about the author or how the book had come to be written.

He leaned back, shaking his head. The chair was very comfortable and he could feel the effects of Henk's tour and Qualto's soup starting to wash over him. He stifled a yawn and began to read, at the same time warning himself not to go to sleep. He read the same line twice—three times...

Then he was wide awake and sitting upright.

The ladders that served the shelves were all moving.

CHAPTER 17

For the first time since he had met him, Josyff saw Nyk agitated. It was peculiarly upsetting; more so even than the sight of the closed drawbridge. Despite Josyff's position as the most senior employee of the New Order, Nyk was the group's natural leader—the Keep and its environs were unequivocally *his* domain. Josyff felt the need to intervene.

"It was closed when I first arrived," he said, to no one in particular.

Nyk cast a quick glance at him, but before he could speak, Adroyan, still carrying Esyal, moved forward towards the edge of the moat. Dark against the scattered light of the Beacon high above them, he looked slowly from side to side as though imposing his will on a line of surly underlings.

The snow started to fall thickly again, swathes of it caught bright white and dancing as they passed in front of the Beacon.

"That was just routine maintenance," Nyk said. "There's no reason why it should be shut now."

"Can you... signal... the others in some way?" Josyff asked, tentatively, his voice low as though he did not want Adroyan to hear.

Nyk had no such concerns. "No," he replied bluntly.

He answered the next question before it was asked. "There's nothing we can do. This is the only way in and out. That's why we keep it well maintained."

"Ho, the Keep!"

Adroyan's voice was powerful even in the snow-deadened air. Both Josyff and Nyk jumped at the violent rupturing of the silence and, for a moment, Josyff thought he felt a stirring in the air, as though a whispering crowd had suddenly become still and was turning towards this disturbance. He half raised his hand as if to prevent Adroyan shouting again.

"Ho, the Keep! You've arrivals at your door."

"Why would they shut it?" Nyk said, as much to himself as anyone else.

"Whatever the reason, it wasn't long ago," Josyff said, pointing to the broad notch cut in the rock that served as a bearing for the drawbridge. There was the merest skim of snow on it. "In fact, it might have been closed as we were coming up the hill."

"We should not be opposed thus."

It was Adroyan. He looked grim.

"What?" Josyff said, not without some irritation. "No one's opposing us. They've just pulled up the drawbridge for some reason. I've no doubt there'll be a sensible explanation for it."

"Can't think what it could be," Nyk muttered. "But we'd better make preparations for spending the night out here before we waste too much effort trying to rouse them. They're not expecting us back so soon"

Josyff was about to remonstrate with him, but the older man's logic was impeccable. Whatever had happened, they might well be destined for another night outside and they could perish from exposure a few paces away from shelter just as easily as a day's walk away.

"How is the girl?" Nyk asked.

When Adroyan did not reply, Josyff went up to him and gently checked Esyal's pulse. Adroyan seemed not to notice him but continued staring fixedly at the dark mass of the Keep.

"Well, she's still alive," Josyff said. "But..." He shrugged. "And I've still no idea what's the matter with her. I suppose we'll have to..."

"This is not a good sign." Adroyan cut across him. "This place must be measured—contained—as a matter of urgency."

Despite his concerns about the status of this newcomer, Josyff answered sharply.

"The only matter of urgency, not to mention the condition of the girl, is our getting into the Keep or making safe shelter out here for the night. Without one or the other, any... measuring... is going to be irrelevant."

Adroyan inclined his head slightly but did not turn to him.

"You are right, surveyor," he said after a long pause. "It's just..."

There was no plaint in these word—just anger—but his intended sentence died in the cold air. Once again he looked from side to side along the frontage of the Keep, as though this further inspection might reveal an entrance somewhere, then he turned to Nyk.

"Shout again," Nyk offered. "No harm in it. And if they're in the courtyard, they might hear." He shook his head and muttered, "I just can't think why..." Then he gave a resigned wave of his hand. "Shout."

It was a collective command and, for a little while, the three of them bellowed at the unyielding face of the Keep.

"Any caves around here?" Josyff asked, as they eventually lapsed into silence.

Nyk shook his head. "No. We can camp here if we must. Just think ourselves lucky it isn't blowing." He was still patently unsettled by what had happened.

"We'll be all right," Josyff said, endeavouring to be optimistic. "There'll be a reason for what they've done."

Nyk grunted doubtingly and began unfastening his pack. "Going to be a squeeze," he said.

"Wait. Listen!"

Adroyan was craning forward, his head inclined, and though his voice was low and urgent, its tone commanded silence and Josyff found himself holding his breath. After a moment, he made to speak, but Adroyan's hand urgently motioned silence before he could. The big man leaned further forward. Josyff unconsciously emulated him while Nyk just watched, his face uncertain and his hands frozen in the act of undoing the straps on his pack.

Then Josyff sensed something—something at the very edges of his awareness...

But slowly growing.

Something familiar.

Disturbingly familiar.

Voices.

Rising and falling, faint in an unknown distance.

Voices like those he had been waking to since he arrived at the Keep!

He felt a chill pervading him far colder than the falling snow but some instinct advised him to give no outward sign. Yet despite this his eyes closed in concentration and his senses reached out.

In the name of pity, what was happening here?

Hearing strange voices during the first moments of waking was patently a manifestation from his dreams and, doubtless, some response to this bizarre and isolated building. But out here... in the snow... when he was wide awake...?

Some kind of mountain sickness? Or just plain tiredness... alarm? Or maybe Adroyan bringing reminders of the New Order and that went with it?

No. He might be tired but he *was* wide awake and clear-headed. The trek of the last hours had ensured that. Whatever the voices were, they were there.

Adroyan must have heard them.

And Nyk?

Discreetly, Josyff opened his eyes and glanced at Nyk, but even as he did so, Nyk was asking, "Listen to what?"

Adroyan hissed him silent. Nyk turned a bewildered face to Josyff and conspiratorially mouthed the same question accompanied by a disclaiming shrug.

Josyff closed his eyes but made no reply. How could this noise not be heard?

He had no time for consideration however, as the voices were abruptly all around him, clamouring for his attention: incoherent yet full of meaning, if he had but the wit to understand. What were they saying? What were they asking?

Was that fear?

Or a warning?

He was almost on the point of crying out in rage and frustration when a realization filled him.

"Help!"

For the briefest of moments the voices swirled and kaleidoscoped into order and the word rang through him. Then, like a climber's fingers slipping from a tentative hold, they were just as quickly gone, and all that remained was the soft hiss of the falling snow.

"What did it say?"

Adroyan's voice, booming and coarse, jerked Josyff's eyes open. The big man was scarcely a pace in front of him, still bearing the unconscious Esyal. Josyff took a pace back.

Tell him nothing, came a message from somewhere. Nothing!

"Y... you startled me," he stammered. He was blinking. Even though they were lit only by the reflected light of the Beacon, it seemed abnormally bright after the darkness in which he had heard the voices. And though he could not see Adroyan's eyes in this artificial gloaming, he could sense a commanding gaze searching his face.

"What did what say?" he managed. "I didn't hear anything." He turned immediately to Nyk both for support and to avoid Adroyan's scrutiny.

Obviously reluctant to take sides, but unable not to, Nyk looked from one to the other. Then, with another shrug, apologetic this time, he said to Adroyan: "I heard nothing, sir." Adding quickly: "Then, my hearing's not what it was."

Adroyan's teeth flashed white for an instant in the gloom.

Whatever that was, it was no smile, Josyff thought, but before he could pursue the thought, Nyk shouted, "Look!"

He was pointing.

The drawbridge was moving. The black rectangle was slowly tilting forward.

No sound was being made by whatever mechanism operated the bridge and as Josyff focused on it, it seemed for a moment that it was quite still and that it was he and everything around him that was moving. It did not help that the bridge's progress was peculiarly uneven, as though the act of opening were being opposed in some way. Momentarily disorientated, Josyff swayed, and took an unsteady step backwards.

Nyk caught his arm.

"Careful, boss!"

"I'm fine," Josyff said. "It just surprised me."

Unexpectedly, Nyk grinned. "We should be getting used to surprises on this trip by now," he said.

Josyff's tension vanished. Here was safety, warmth, food, small tales to tell. And, as a slightly guilty afterthought, help for the girl.

"Indeed we should," he replied cheerfully.

The drawbridge dropped into its rocky bearing as silently as it had descended. Nyk and the others did indeed keep it well maintained, Josyff reflected, as he picked up his packs and began walking across. Nyk joined him.

Halfway across he turned casually to see where Adroyan was, but their new companion had not moved.

Josyff beckoned him forward.

But Adroyan still did not move. His head was turning slowly from side to side as though he was still examining the silent frontage of the Keep and could not see the road that had opened in front of him.

"Come on, sir" Josyff called.

Adroyan stopped his search and stared along the drawbridge.

"Can I enter?" he asked.

Josyff was unable to keep the surprise from his face.

"Of course," he replied, with a smile and a broad, inviting gesture. "Though it's scarcely my place to allow it. This is more your property than mine. I just work here."

Adroyan looked at him. "This place belongs to no one, surveyor, and my question was rhetorical." There was irritation, if not outright disdain in his voice.

"I'm sorry, I don't understand..." Josyff began.

"No."

The exchange was ended. Josyff did not know whether to feel embarrassed, indignant, or afraid that he had committed some folly before this disconcerting new arrival. He had little time for reflection however, as Adroyan began walking forward. It was apparent from his first step that he was having difficulty—he looked as though he were moving against a powerful wind or struggling through a busy crowd. Josyff took it to be fatigue due to the burden he had been carrying.

"Can I help?" he asked.

"Measure this building, surveyor—measure this building."

It was a curt dismissal.

I *don't* understand, Josyff thought desperately, though he did not speak this time. I *do not* understand. He turned away. Hang him. If he's going to be so objectionable he can go to hell. Tells me I was specially chosen for the job then has the gall to tell me to do it well! Too high and mighty to ask for help when he needs it!

At the same time he reminded himself who Adroyan was. Where in the New Order's hierarchy he might lie, there was little point conjecturing. Few had any understanding of it. It was sufficient that he was in it and that he was no workaday underling. He would have to be treated with the utmost circumspection, not to say, suspicion, at all times, and no indication of this should be shown in either his, Josyff's, or Badr's conduct.

It was no new game. He had been playing it since the New Order came to power—as had many of his ilk—those whose concern it was to deal with matters practical—to get things done and who used reason as their currency. It had been a learning driven by sinister, if intangible necessity. And still it continued—there was always the feeling that such as he were merely tolerated as just so many useful tools—at any time expendable. It was both alarming and bewildering.

Then again, Josyff reflected cautiously, out here, isolated, who knew what might come of being closely confined with the likes of Adroyan? And how would he deal with Nyk, Qualto and Henk—so used to independence in their work?

Josyff turned back to look at his possible nemesis.

For a moment, Adroyan looked as though he were far away, at the end of a long tunnel—stretched and distant. The vision passed as quickly as it had come but Adroyan still seemed to be having difficulty. Almost in spite of himself, Josyff felt a twinge of compassion. Esyal was quite slight in build but she was also a dead weight and Adroyan had carried her a long way. He must be exhausted.

Josyff put down his packs and walked back to help him. This time he made no offer of help, he simply voiced his conclusion.

"You're exhausted, man. Give her to me." Before Adroyan could reply, Josyff was summoning aid.

"Nyk!"

Adroyan's face looked strained and his eyes were unfocussed.

Then the drawbridge started to rise again.

CHAPTER 18

Momentarily disorientated, Badr half rose from his chair, though he saw immediately that he would not be able to prevent any of the ladders either colliding into one another or into their end stops. He dropped back into his chair heavily and involuntarily tensed himself against the pending collisions, noticing as he did so that he was gripping the edge of the table. But no collisions came—or none of any damaging magnitude at least. As the ladders drew closer, so they slowed and gently came to a halt together. Badr felt his hands releasing the table. Carefully, he stood up.

What the devil had just happened? An earth tremor? Surely not. They were things that happened in other countries, not here. And he had not heard any rumbling nor felt any shaking. Nor were there any other signs of such an event—no books dislodged from the shelves, no chairs tumbled over. Yet something must have set the ladders in motion. And too, something must have slowed them.

He walked over to one and pushed it gently. It moved as had the one he touched when he entered the book room—smoothly, effortlessly. Crouching down, he looked to see if there was any braking device to prevent accidental collisions, but there was nothing. Simple, elegant and, he noted, very well made, the ladders were just metal frames on wheels running on rails set into the floor.

"Everything all right?"

Badr almost tumbled over.

"I'm so sorry. I'm so sorry." Badr found himself looking up at an advancing Qualto waving his arms in frantic apology. "I didn't mean to startle you..." He reached out needlessly to help Badr to his feet. "I thought you'd heard me coming in."

Badr made a reassuring gesture. "I was just looking at this." He patted the ladder but for some reason he felt reluctant to touch on what had just happened.

"Nicely made. Did you want me?"

"No... I... we... Henk... thought you shouted." Qualto looked decidedly uncomfortable.

Badr shook his head and, to change the subject, indicated the book on the table. "I've just deciphered your storage system. I was trying to find something out about this place."

Qualto's manner became apologetic again. "I must admit I didn't hear anything. But Henk was very insistent." He glanced at the book. "I'm afraid all you'll find is the same tales over and over. Wouldn't like to say where they've all come from but there's precious little either original or informative."

"You've read them all?" Despite himself, Badr could not keep the challenge from his voice.

Qualto either did not hear it or chose to ignore it.

"Quite a few. I like reading. And sometimes there's not much to do here." He pursed his lips pensively and like a moon drawn inexorably to its planet, returned to his original purpose. "Henk swore he heard you shouting."

Badr was drawn after him. He asked the hovering question.

"Did anything... strange just happen?"

"Strange?"

Badr continued on his trajectory. He shrugged. "I was looking through that book and I nodded off. Then, all of a sudden, I was awake and..." He hesitated. "The ladders were moving... running along their rails... all of them."

"Moving?" Qualto echoed, gesticulating vaguely.

Badr pushed the ladder by way of demonstration and watched it as it slid off silently.

"All of them," he confirmed.

Qualto watched the ladder roll to a halt then looked at Badr.

"You were dreaming, perhaps?" he offered, after a moment.

Badr was definite. He spoke as to an old and trusted friend. "No. I was awake—*wide* awake." Then he voiced the thought as it came to him, as much to himself as to Qualto. "Almost as though something dangerous was going to happen."

Qualto opted for humour. "You *must* have been dreaming. There's nothing dangerous here." His arm encompassed the silent shelves by way of demonstrating their harmlessness. "Except knowledge, of course," he chuckled. "Following Henk into the bowels of the Keep now, that's a different matter." The chuckle became an uneasy laugh.

Badr joined him, self-deprecatingly. Qualto was being perfectly reasonable. There could be no danger here and there was certainly nothing that he could see that would move the ladders. Yet, he hadn't been dreaming, he knew. He had woken, clear-eyed and clear-headed—*very* alert. The ladders had been moving—all of them.

The word "danger" hung in his mind, reluctant to leave.

"Are you sure nothing happened?" he pressed, apologetically. "No shaking... tremors... do you get avalanches—rock falls—anything?"

"Rarely," Qualto conceded. "And I've never felt one shake the Keep. This place is *very* solid. Sometimes when I look at it from the outside it looks as though it's so heavy it'd crush the mountain itself." He nodded as if to mark the end of this diversion and returned to Badr's concerns. "Henk was fiddling with the fire again, the way he does—he can never leave it alone—always has to... anyway, it flared up." He waved his arms. "Gave him a bit of a shock, I think." He chuckled to himself. "Then he cocks his head on one side and says 'the surveyor's calling.'"

"The *surveyor's* calling?" Badr queried.

Qualto paused and reflected for a moment. "I didn't give it a thought, now you mention it. I just presumed he meant you. It could hardly be Mr Josyff, could it?"

"Well, it *wasn't* me."

Badr smiled. The strangeness of the past few minutes had faded, to be followed by at least a semblance of a rational explanation. The fire flaring indicated a draught from somewhere. Possibly the wind outside had picked up and, buffeting around the Keep's eaves and ridges, had reached in through whatever ventilated the book room to disturb the ladders. They *were* very light to move.

It was far from being a wholly convincing argument but...

"Still, no harm done. You've probably spared me an uncomfortable awakening in the middle of the night—sprawled across that table." He stretched and motioned Qualto towards the door. "That said, I think I'll go to bed—it's been a long day."

"Do you want to take the book with you?" Qualto asked.

Badr shook his head. "I'll come back tomorrow and have a good root around. There were plans and sketches in that, and there may be others. They could be helpful. I might be able work out how best to set about this job before the surveyor gets back. That'll be useful."

As Badr was closing the door, the book room lights blinked out, and he felt a momentary return of his unease as he watched the narrow strip of light in the door frame darken, dwindle and vanish.

"What's happened?"

Henk's voice banished the feeling. His stooping form was craning towards Badr like a watchful fishing bird, as he came along the passage.

"Nothing, thanks, Henk," Badr replied.

"I came as soon as I quietened the fire."

"I'm fine," Badr assured him. "I didn't call out. I think you must have misheard something. Gust of wind in the chimney flues probably—it was enough to move the ladders in the book room and wake me up. It's probably blowing quite hard outside."

He spilled out his reasoning quickly as if unwilling to consider it further, but Henk did not let it by. His forehead wrinkled.

"Ladders moving? Wind?" His voice was a mixture of scorn and concern. He looked to Qualto, but his colleague was in no mood to pursue the matter.

"I'm going to wash the dishes and get to bed. I've had enough mysteries for one day—not to mention exercise!"

Badr intercepted the pending interrogation written across Henk's face. "Well, whatever it was, I'm sure there's a sensible explanation somewhere— as there will be for your mysterious passageway once we get round to looking for it. In fact, just a night's sleep will probably work wonders."

He then engineered a quick flurry of good night's and the trio parted.

Not for long however. Badr had gone scarcely twenty paces when he felt a cold draught on his face. It must have brought with it some subtle perfume, for he found himself returned vividly to the deep doorway through which Henk had led them on his strange exploration. And too, faintly, there was the hint of sound carried on it.

"Listen!" Henk's voice rolled over it briefly but it emerged again as both Badr and Qualto stopped and turned.

It seemed to Badr that the sound was striving to be coherent, but it was echoing and distant and flitted away from his examination like a vague shadow in the corner of the eye.

And then it was gone, and with it the chilling draught.

Badr had to take a small step forward to catch his balance as, craning after the sound, he had closed his eyes and leaned forward. The lights in the passage seemed unnaturally bright.

"The main door must be open," Qualto said hastily. "I could've sworn I shut it. I'll go and check."

"It *is* shut," Henk said. "That wasn't from the outside."

"I'll check!" Qualto's slightly irritable tone chimed with Badr's thinking. Neither of them had any desire to be drawn further into Henk's peculiar mood.

Hope of this vanished almost as soon as they reached the door, however, for it was indeed closed. Worse, it was bolted.

Qualto stretched up on his toes and tapped the handle of the top bolt, though as much to reassure himself he was seeing what he was seeing as to draw it, Badr thought. This time it was he who ventured into humour. "It's having us staying with you," he said, affecting a lightness he did not really feel. "We've infected you with our city habits."

Qualto did not reply but continued staring at the bolt handle. "I didn't bolt it," he said. "Definitely didn't bolt it." He turned to Badr, his face fretful. "No one ever bolts doors here."

Badr had little to offer. "Perhaps you did it without thinking. There *has* been quite an upheaval to your normal lives recently—us arriving—the surveyor hurting himself—the fuss about the equipment—and now him and Nyk leaving and the snow coming..."

But Qualto was shaking his head. "No. I didn't bolt it. Look, I can barely reach it. I certainly wouldn't throw it without thinking about it."

Badr could do little but share his bewilderment.

"Just another little mystery to sleep on," he said, before quickly becoming practical. "Can I help you with that?"

"Yes please." Qualto was putting some unsuccessful effort into drawing the bolt. "That's odd. We mightn't use these things, but Nyk does keep them clean and oiled." He relinquished the handle to Badr.

A little taller and quite a lot stronger than Qualto, Badr took a firm grip and pulled. For a moment, the bolt did not move, though its resistance gave Badr the impression that he was contending not with a rusted or ill-fitting bolt but with a contrary will. When finally it yielded, there was no jarring jerk or scrape of protest, but the effort opposing Badr persisted until the bolt was completely clear of its housing. As it finally dropped free, a pounding on the door made him jump. Qualto moved back rapidly, his face alarmed. Before either could speak, muffled voices made their way through the knocking. Without thinking, Badr drew the lower bolt quickly and dragged the door open.

CHAPTER 19

Even as he opened the door it occurred to Badr that this was perhaps not the wisest of actions. Yet he sensed no danger in the knocking, urgent though it was.

"What the devil's going on?"

It was Nyk, pushing the door as Badr pulled it, to their mutual surprise.

"Why was the drawbridge up? What were you thinking about? And why did you start raising it again while we were still on it?"

Nyk's questions burst out angrily as the restraining tension of leading this motley group evaporated abruptly in the warmth of familiar surroundings.

Qualto gaped.

Josyff moved forward, gently easing the gesticulating Nyk to one side. He spoke to Qualto quietly but urgently.

"We've a sick woman and a new guest," adding softly, "an important guest." He indicated Adroyan carrying the still motionless body of Esyal. "Could you and Henk find quarters for them. And then perhaps some food and warmth for us."

"And a place for the Surveyor's equipment," Adroyan intervened.

Josyff's jaw tightened and his hand flicked out towards a nearby alcove. "Just put it over there for now. It won't come to any harm."

He slammed the door shut by way of emphasis.

Qualto dithered briefly then nodded and trotted off.

"I'll get Henk," Badr said. "Good to see you back safe."

"Good to *be* back," Josyff said, with a smile.

There followed a bustling interval which saw Esyal laid out on the long couch in the common room, rooms quickly found and allocated, layers of chilled clothing discarded, packs emptied, and Josyff's equipment stacked by a narrow-eyed Nyk, under Adroyan's supervision. Qualto was clattering busily about his kitchen.

"What's the matter with her?" Henk asked when the flurry had subsided and all, save Qualto, were gathered in the common room.

Josyff briefly recounted their journey but concluded with an unhappy shrug.

"I have no idea. She has a steady pulse, she's breathing, even her colour's good considering the cold." He scowled. "I can only think that it's some kind of head injury, although there's no sign of any outward damage." He ran his hand carefully through her hair as though yet another examination might give him the lie, but there was nothing. He looked round at the others but found no answers there either. "I think all we can do is perhaps take turns to sit with her in case she wakes up or... her condition changes in some way... until we can get a doctor from the village."

No one disagreed, or laboured the point that at the best it would be several days before a doctor could be brought. Nor did anyone touch on the fact that they might all have no choice but to stand by helpless in their ignorance while this young woman died.

Josyff pulled a chair up to the couch and sat down. He glanced at Adroyan. The big man was sitting by the fireplace, staring into the blaze that Henk had conjured. He had the hunched air of someone carrying a burden and Josyff felt an unexpected twinge of sympathy for him.

"You must be exhausted," he said. "You carried her a long way."

Adroyan tilted his head slightly as if he had been woken from a reverie, then turned to look at Josyff and stared at him as though momentarily not recognizing him. Eventually he said, "Yes, yes," offhandedly. "I was the best suited. To have left her would have distracted you from your work."

Josyff had made his remark partly out of a habit of courtesy and partly to establish some relationship with this unanticipated new arrival, to draw him into—to welcome him to—this "family" that circumstances—a degree of common adversity—had formed. Insofar as he had expected anything, this reply was not it. The placing of his work before Esyal's life was peculiarly shocking and he could not keep it from his face.

"Who are you?" he asked, his normal caution forgotten.

Adroyan was looking into the fire again. "Your superior," he replied. "The person who chose you for this task."

Though Adroyan's voice was flat and emotionless, Josyff's mouth went dry. What the devil was happening here, and what, in the name of pity, *was* this place? The thought of his wife came unbidden and, for an instant, he wished he were with her—far away from the Keep, the mountains, the New Order, everything.

The awkward silence that followed was broken by Qualto bustling in with food and drink. As the atmosphere eased, Nyk's original complaint re-surfaced, though less irritably.

"Why did you shut the drawbridge?" he asked Henk.

"I... we... didn't," Henk replied, adding, with just a hint of injury, "I didn't know it was shut until you told me. What would I do that for?"

"It couldn't have shut itself."

Henk floundered visibly, concluding, reluctantly, "It must have... somehow. No one here's been outside since we lit the Beacon, and then that's all we did."

"That's true," Badr intervened. "Most of the time we've all been prowling around the bowels of the building looking at something Henk wanted to show us."

"It's counter-balanced, isn't it?" Josyff said.

Nyk seemed glad of the intervention.

"It is," he replied, adding thoughtfully, "Very finely balanced, actually."

"Something odd happened only a few minutes before you arrived," Badr said. "I dozed off in the book room and when I woke up, all the shelf ladders were moving." He wafted his hand sideways in demonstration and offered, hesitantly, "Perhaps there *was* some kind of earth tremor... a slight one... or something."

"I never heard anything," Henk said, a touch sulkily.

"You heard someone call out, though, didn't you?" Qualto said, part in accusation, part in conciliation. "Or thought you did."

"We were shouting on the other side of the moat," Josyff said. "Perhaps our voices carried into chimney stacks. But we didn't feel any kind of earth tremor, or hear anything."

He looked at Nyk for confirmation but his erstwhile guide was still fretting about his unwarranted exclusion from the Keep. "It might be counter-balanced but I can't think of anything that would make it move on its own—least of all three times."

"Three times?" Qualto queried, showing a hint of Nyk's concern.

"Three times," Nyk echoed. "It's shut now. I told you, the damn thing started shutting while we were standing on it." He looked half inclined to leave the room to investigate the problem immediately. "It makes no sense—it's solid equipment and in good order. And I checked it only the other day."

"Look at it tomorrow," Josyff urged. "It's been a long, tiring day and you've been carrying the responsibility for us all. You've done more than enough just getting us back. Given that we're all safe..." He hesitated and glanced at Esyal. "There's nothing that needs emergency attention."

"The surveyor is correct."

It was Adroyan. He was standing.

"You've done well," he said to Nyk. "The only thing that is urgent is the measuring of the Keep..."

"And the girl," Qualto said pointedly.

Adroyan paused and Josyff thought he saw a brief touch of irritation pass over his face as he looked down at Esyal. "Yes, and the girl," he said, his voice flat again. "But nothing can be done now. It's late and we're all tired. Rest, now, all of you, rest."

There was a quiet command in his voice that brought Josyff to his feet before he could think about it. He stopped himself as he was about to move to the door. "I'll sleep here," he said. "Keep on eye on the girl—on Esyal. We can't leave her."

Only Adroyan demurred. "You have much to do. You must rest."

Josyff managed to keep the anger out of his response. "If she wakes in the night, she might need help—someone has to be here. And the least she'll need is a face she recognizes—that's me or Nyk." He did not allow Adroyan any interruption. "Nyk needs a decent night's sleep in his own bed. He's done more than enough these past days and he has plenty routine work to catch up on as a result, I'm sure—not least the drawbridge, which sounds as if it needs looking at urgently. Plus or minus a few hours won't make any difference to what Badr and I have to do."

Adroyan looked set to dispute this but said simply. "As you wish, surveyor," and turned to leave.

"Can you remember the way to your room, sir?" Henk asked.

"I can... thank you. Good night."

When he had gone Josyff looked round at the others. They were all looking back at him and he knew that a careless remark now could make him the unspoken leader of a faction against this... intruder. It was tempting and it took him a considerable effort not to show his real feelings. Compared to Adroyan, they felt like old friends. But whatever might transpire here, Adroyan had the authority. Tomorrow he could quietly speak to him and formally confirm that he was who he said he was but even that would only be to show Adroyan that he was being watchful of the New Order's concerns. There could be little doubt that the man was indeed who he claimed to be—his whole manner radiated it. And if he was here—out in the middle of nowhere, in a bizarre and seemingly useless building—then something important was afoot and it would be a foolish man indeed who risked antagonizing him. There were other surveyors as capable as he.

He declined the leadership being offered him by opting for the mundane.

"Can you find me a couple of blankets, Henk? One for me and one for Esyal. It might get cold in here once the fire drops."

It broke the conspiracy, Josyff thought—though it would arise again, he knew. Mistrust and obsessive watchfulness were hallmarks of the New Order's way even though they served no worthwhile civic end. They merely bred their own kind and, Josyff had long concluded, would ultimately destroy themselves as the State became progressively unable to function. What he had not concluded and which coloured his daily working life was how long this would take and what harm would be involved, save that the longer it took the greater the harm would be. His task was no longer surveying, it was surveying and doing whatever was necessary to retain his position in the old hierarchy that now found itself serving the New Order.

Bad though he considered this to be, there was lurking beneath it the unfounded but persistent suspicion that not only did the New Order not care about the society it had gained power over, it even intended it to deteriorate, the better to control it. This, when it came to him, he chose not to ponder.

Henk glanced at the fire and almost chuckled. "It'll be some time before that drops, but I'll get you something."

"I'll get you some water, as well," Qualto added. "She'll be thirsty for sure if she wakes up."

Conspicuously, none of them discussed Adroyan, and after Henk and Qualto were satisfied with Josyff's comfort for the night, they all left.

Josyff pulled two chairs together so that he could stretch out between them. It was remarkably comfortable, and despite being in his walking clothes and feeling the need for a wash, the exertions of the day together with Qualto's food began to make themselves felt and he soon became drowsy.

As he drifted between waking and sleeping however, frissons of unease made him restless. Walking away from the Keep he had felt an indefinable tension slipping away from him, as though he were gradually shedding a burden. He had not noticed any return of this tension on the journey back, but then his mind had been on other matters, not least, putting one foot in front of the other safely. He opened his eyes and turned over to gaze up at the ceiling. Shadows danced across it as the firelight flickered and bounced through the iron-barred frontage of the fire and Henk's array of fire irons.

Though he could not have said why, the thought filling his mind was simple and familiar—from somewhere deep inside him came the knowledge that he did not want to be in this place. He clenched his teeth and swore under his breath, his professional pride remonstrating with this unasked for and unwanted visceral intrusion. It had been a fraught few days, that was all. No equipment, trekking through the mountains, finding Esyal, meeting Adroyan. Fraught indeed. Do the job, he reminded himself, almost viciously. Check it thoroughly—very thoroughly—so that no return visit would be required, and leave. Badr would be fine, he was sure, Nyk and the others were helpful and pleasant—even Henk in his own way— better than many he had met, for sure—and whoever Adroyan was, he would, presumably, have nothing to gain by slowing progress in any way. Indeed, a few days living in this place with him might in fact prove useful. It was an unexpectedly positive thought.

His eyes beginning to close, he turned on to his side.

Esyal had done the same. She was staring at him.

CHAPTER 20

Eyes widening, both Josyff and Esyal sat up quickly; he in surprise and concern, she in response to his sudden movement. She reached automatically for her knife, but disguised the gesture as an adjustment of her clothes as soon as she realized what she was doing. There was no danger from Josyff, she knew.

"Are you all right?" Josyff asked, leaning forward.

Esyal feigned confusion.

"Yes," she replied. "I think so. Where am I? We were... out in the mountains... in the snow..."

"This place is called the Keep," Josyff said. "Still in the mountains and the snow, I'm afraid, but warm and safe... and well stocked..."

"The Keep. I remember. The man with you... Nyk... he mentioned it. You're Josyff, the surveyor, aren't you?" She did not wait for an answer. "How did I get here?"

"What do you remember?"

"I remember the cave... and you and Nyk finding me... and some other people..."

"Nothing else? No idea where you're from or how you came to be in the mountains... anything?"

Esyal shook her head.

"You... fainted," Josyff said with an uncertain shrug. He moved his chair closer and looked at her intently. "Or something. You wanted to go after the men from the village but couldn't. You were very upset. You walked with us for quite a while then you just collapsed. Are you *sure* you're all right?"

Esyal ignored the question. "So you carried me here?"

"No. It was Adroyan. I don't know what would have happened had it just been me and Nyk. He must be remarkably strong." For some reason he found this overt admission disturbed him.

Esyal was silent for a moment. She knew that Adroyan was strong as she had woken as they were climbing the final slope up to the Keep. Then it had been not so much her instinct for self-protection that kept her silent and listening, as a feeling of security and comfort such as she had not felt since she was a child. It puzzled her now that she had felt no alarm or confusion at finding herself where she was. It puzzled her too that she awoke as from a long and refreshing sleep. And with a faint echoing of distant voices surrounding her.

Although the sureness of Adroyan's cradling arms had not faltered, the security she felt was soon replaced by the habits that opposing the New Order had developed and hardened. And, she recalled, from his behaviour at their meeting, this person carrying her was New Order, without doubt. The thought chilled her and further prompted her to silence and stillness. What was he doing out here? Was he one of those who had attacked her group?

There would be no answers to these questions, she knew. All she could do was wait and listen. In the meantime, let him work, she had concluded. Better him exhausted than her.

Now, sitting opposite Josyff, she had no doubt that this decision had been correct and that she must maintain the charade of her forgotten memory. Against all expectation she was safe—she had survived. All reason dictated that she should have died, alone and wandering the mountains, but chance had not only rescued her, it had placed her in close proximity to one of her enemy. Briefly she wondered if some deep unknowable force were at work—something that others might call destiny, perhaps? But she was, above all, pragmatic. Such a question could not be answered and to pursue it needlessly was to risk losing the opportunity that had been presented. Deal with what is, she reminded herself. The work of the Rhanen was not yet finished. Here she could learn and, as appropriate, scheme. And to that end it was important that she gain the confidence of Josyff and the others. She had heard enough already to know that they were just ordinary people, effectively pressed into the service of the New Order and that Adroyan was an outsider to the group. That should prove useful.

Yet something was unsettling her.

"I'm trying to remember what happened when I... fainted," she said, to break an awkward silence. "But I..."

Her voice faded.

Her fainting puzzled her as much as her unflustered awakening. She did not faint! She had never fainted. She was strong and determined—she supported others—she was good at that. What had happened?

Nyk had been setting a stern pace, but not one that she could not accommodate despite being tired from the previous days' wandering. She hadn't been hungry. Her clothes were adequate for the conditions; she was not cold or wet. Granted she had been angry and frustrated by her inability to return to the village and, if she were honest, fearful about what lay ahead. Yet...

Then from nowhere came the thought that she had been taken away. Taken away and then returned.

It floated into her mind through the quiet hiss of Henk's fire.

She managed not to react outwardly to it. It made no sense, yet it shocked her. Shocked her because it felt not like a random thought, one of many to be sifted and considered on the way to a solution, but a categorical statement: this is what happened.

Despite her restraint, Josyff sensed some change in her and voiced his main concern as discreetly as he could. "You've no... headache... or anything?" he asked.

"No. I feel fine."

"We thought perhaps you'd fallen—banged your head—just passing out like that. We were very worried."

Esyal was shaking her head even as she ran testing hands through her hair.

"No, I feel fine," she repeated. "No headaches, no bumps and bruises that I can feel—nothing. Maybe I was just more tired than I thought."

Silence descended between them again. Josyff was relieved that Esyal had awoken, both for her sake and for his own, because he was not going to be an impotent witness to some tragedy. Esyal too was relieved to have one less pretence to maintain. All she had to do now was remember that she had no memory and that she must find out what was happening here. It was obviously something important and thus potentially useful.

Already ideas were forming. If they were all trapped in this place then a degree of community would inevitably develop between them and, New Order or not, Adroyan would be a part of it.

"What is this place?" she asked.

"Other than that it's the Keep, I'm little wiser than you are," Josyff replied unhelpfully. "I'd never heard of it before I was sent here."

"Yes, you told me. You're here to survey it or something, aren't you?"

She stretched luxuriously and looked around. "Well, whatever it is, I'm glad it's here," she said. Then she looked straight at Josyff. "And that you and Nyk found me." She shuddered involuntarily as she was momentarily alone and desperate, huddled in the chill of the cave.

Josyff leaned forward anxiously.

"I'm fine," Esyal said, with as reassuring a smile as she could manage. "Just remembering how I nearly died."

"You were very lucky."

"Yes I was—very." She looked squarely at Josyff. "Have I thanked you and Nyk?"

Josyff smiled. "You might have. I'm not sure. It's been a long day. But it's of no consequence. We could hardly have left you. It's really Adroyan you need to thank. He's the one who carried you."

"Yes. I will... in the morning," Esyal said flatly, briefly guilty at her judgement of Adroyan. Whatever he was, he *had* carried her.

Still, he *was* New Order.

"Do you remember anything?" Josyff asked.

"No. Only wandering in the snow."

"And your name."

"And my name."

She stammered and waved her arms vaguely. "I don't understand any of this."

Josyff decided not to press the matter. He became avuncular. "Well, now you're safe. And once you're properly rested and fed, I'm sure your memory will start coming back."

Esyal was anxious that her "condition" not be subjected to too much scrutiny. She became casual.

"Oddly enough, it doesn't seem to be bothering me," she said.

"I noticed," Josyff replied. Abruptly, he yawned.

"I'm sorry," he said ruefully.

"I'm keeping you awake," Esyal said, with genuine regret. "I *am* all right now, truly. Go back to sleep, I won't disturb you any more."

Josyff settled back into the chair and pulled the blanket over himself. "I have to admit, I feel much easier now that you're awake," he said. "And I *will* have to get started on this job properly tomorrow—we've lost a lot of time." His eyes were closing as he added a final injunction. "If you feel unwell, you must wake me... straight away."

"I will."

As he finally drifted into sleep, Josyff felt a brief spasm of alarm. What strangeness would the Keep visit on him tonight? The thought seemed to stretch on forever, like a rope trying to draw him back to wakefulness and flight, but it could not sustain itself against the demands of his body now that his mind was free of immediate concern for Esyal.

She, on the other hand, was wide awake, though she chose to continue lying motionless on the couch—nothing was to be gained by wandering about in the middle of the night. She was going to be here for a few days at least. There would be plenty of time to discover what was happening.

She frowned. She was now so awake that her mind was racing to and fro, searching for something to cling to, to find its bearings, to rest a moment while it quietly weighed and considered everything that had happened. She looked at Josyff, his face relaxed but alive with the flickering firelight. He was no New Order creature, she had already decided, nor were Nyk and the other two, from what she had heard of their conversation. They were working for them certainly, but what choice would they have had? They were just ordinary men getting on with their lives, doing their jobs. Part of her coiled in anger at this supine acceptance of the New Order—why didn't these people see what she saw? Why didn't they speak out? Do something, instead of dumbly bending the knee and lowering the head, acquiescing in their own imprisonment? But a quieter part of her held it in check. Had she herself more than once not wanted to quit this fight against such seemingly overwhelming odds? And she had no family responsibilities that might act as hostages against such passion. Then, too, a colder part now, honed by bitter experience: had she not learned long ago that railing against the apathy of others both wasted her own energies and, worse, antagonized those she wished to persuade to her way, driving them into further apathy or active opposition, doing the enemy's work?

The tumbling thoughts slowly became calmer, allowing two to rise up and dominate. She was alive! Where, scarcely a day before, she had been facing a bleak and lonely death, now she was facing a future, and with it, opportunity. The prospect washed over her—exhilarating—almost overwhelming...

And with this came hunger!

Feigning unconsciousness while the others were eating had been surprisingly easy, so intent had she been on maintaining her deceit. But now, freed from that, the remaining savoury smell of Qualto's cooking began to make itself felt.

Briefly she considered waking Josyff, but dismissed the thought as she looked at him, breathing heavily and completely relaxed on his makeshift bed.

Let him rest, came an unexpectedly compassionate thought. It was followed by a more calculating one: she now had a legitimate excuse for prowling about the place should she be discovered.

Quietly, she swung her legs off the couch and went to the door. It opened noiselessly on to a darkened passage. Tentatively, she stepped out. As she did, the lights came on, making her step back, alarmed. Nothing else happening however, she pondered which way to go. In both directions the passage ran straight for some way until it reached a junction, but what caught her eye was a door in the wall opposite, slightly ajar, and about halfway to the junction.

It proved to be the kitchen. The lights came on as she entered, startling her again, though less so than before. It was very clean and very orderly. Not that she had thought about it particularly, but she had imagined that Qualto's cooking would be rooted in disorder and that a group of men alone must necessarily descend into squalor. She did not dwell on the revelation however; the proximity of food was increasing her hunger pangs dramatically. It took her only a moment to locate the remains of the impromptu meal that Qualto had prepared and only a few more to heat it, find a bowl, and begin eating.

"Simple pleasures," she murmured, echoing what her father would have said.

"You are recovered, then?"

Esyal nearly knocked over the bowl as she jumped up.

Standing in the doorway was Adroyan.

CHAPTER 21

"I'm sorry. I startled you," Adroyan said. His hand extended as if to help but he did not move forward.

Esyal mimicked the gesture, her hand waving as if to indicate both that he should come no nearer and that she needed no help.

"You did," she gasped, spitting food. "I thought I was the only one awake."

Adroyan's face was expressionless though he was staring at her intently.

As she had mimicked his gesture, so Esyal returned his gaze.

What dark eyes he has, she thought. Almost as though the irises are black.

"I see you're recovered," Adroyan said.

"Yes. I just... woke up. I don't know what happened, but I'm fine. Josyff said you carried me all the way here after I... collapsed," she said, starting to eat again.

"The surveyor," Adroyan said, as if momentarily uncertain who Josyff was. "Yes, I carried you. I was the best suited."

"Thank you," Esyal said simply and genuinely, natural courtesy briefly setting aside her reservations about this man. "You must be very tired."

Adroyan seemed to shrink a little and he moved into the room and sat down at the table, partly opposite Esyal, the open door at his back. He looked around Qualto's kitchen and echoed Esyal's first impression. "He is an orderly man, our cook." Then, without pause. "Yes, I am tired."

"I'm sorry if I disturbed you, walking about," Esyal said. "I tried to be quiet."

"You did not disturb me."

A look flashed across his face that made Esyal start. Was it anger? Hate? Fear, even? It was gone before she could determine, but her hand had casually dropped into her lap to be near her knife.

"This place disturbs me," Adroyan went on, though seemingly to himself. "It is dangerous. It binds. It must be measured, encompassed, so that..."

His voice faded.

"I don't understand," Esyal said awkwardly. "What do you mean, 'dangerous'. It's not going to fall down, is it, surely?" She reached out, slapped the wall, and smiled. "I don't know anything about buildings but it feels solid enough to me." Then the other words he had used impinged on her and the question blurted out before she could stop it.

"And how can a *building* bind anything?" she asked.

She was watching him carefully now, uncertain whether to be alarmed or amused.

"Many things can bind," Adroyan said. "And this place is one such." His gaze became less distant and he looked at her. She had the feeling that she was being studied as though she was an unusual specimen of some kind.

"But such matters are of no concern to the likes of you—an attractive young woman..."

'The likes of' grated on Esyal more than the clumsy compliment, but she gave no outward sign. Adroyan continued.

"I am sure you have far more interesting things to occupy your life. What is your work?"

Esyal gave an insincere smile to acknowledge the flattery and shrugged her shoulders. "I've no idea. I still can't remember."

"You remember your name." There was a hint of accusation in Adroyan's voice. Esyal ignored it and shrugged her shoulders again.

"Yes, I do," she replied. "It's all very odd. I can remember some things and not others—I can walk—and eat—and talk, but... how I come to be here, where I live... all gone."

"You do not seem to be concerned."

Esyal looked suitably bewildered. "No. I don't know why that is, either. Josyff thinks it's probably a good sign... shows that my memory will start coming back bit by bit."

Adroyan nodded slowly, still looking at her intently. "Yes, the surveyor," he said again, for no apparent reason.

"I'm surprised you're having difficulty sleeping after carrying me all that way," Esyal said, looking to deflect his questioning. "Josyff went to sleep as soon as he saw I was all right. Perhaps it's just being in a strange place. Or perhaps you're over-tired, as my mother used to say."

"Your mother?"

Esyal put her hand to her mouth in hastily feigned surprise, and turned away in case her eyes might reveal the reality of her slip to this searcher.

"My mother, yes... I can see her... tall, blonde... But that's all." Her brow furrowed and she stood up, gesticulating earnestly. "I mustn't be afraid," she said, apparently earnestly admonishing herself. "I'm safe here. I might have died, but I didn't. I'm safe. Whatever's happened to me, my memory *will* come back, I'm sure. I mustn't try to force anything, must I?" She looked at Adroyan as if for support.

"I am not a doctor," he replied after a moment. Esyal noted, with some satisfaction, the hesitation in his manner. "But if you feel well and are apparently uninjured, I suppose time and rest will... resolve the matter."

"Yes," Esyal said. She sat down again and began toying with the dish she had been eating from. "Yes, it will. In any event, with all this snow, I suppose that's all I'll be able to do. It'll probably be some time before I can get back to the village." Then, abruptly, "Do you want something to eat? Perhaps you can't sleep because you're hungry."

"No thank you, I ate with the others."

Having gained the initiative, Esyal pursued her questioning, affecting naiveté.

"Do you know what this place is?"

"This is the Keep," came the unhelpful reply.

"Yes, but what is it, out here in the middle of nowhere? And why would anyone want to survey it?"

"It must be measured..."

Esyal interrupted. "You said that before. And encompassed, you said. I didn't understand then and I still don't. What do you mean?"

For a moment she thought he was about to get up and leave, but instead he turned his gaze back to her, almost schoolmasterly now.

"We cannot determine what this... place... is, or what to do with it until we know its size, its shape, exactly. When we have that, then... we can put the place to some... good use... for the benefit of the public."

You're lying!

The thought struck Esyal so forcefully that she almost cried out. She had no idea where this revelation had come from save that it hung in his last phrase. The New Order always prefaced its intrusions into the freedom of the people with declamations about the public good—particularly the greater good.

Be still. Be calm. Listen. Show nothing. Think.

"How can such a place benefit anyone except the few who like to climb and walk in the mountains?" She allowed a touch of scorn into her voice.

Abruptly, Adroyan leaned forward and spoke urgently.

"Do not concern yourself, young woman. Rest and mend your mind. These are matters beyond you."

It took Esyal a considerable effort of will to remain silent, but she could not prevent her jaw stiffening and her eyes narrowing.

Adroyan gave no sign that he had noticed this and he pressed on. "There are forces in this land which you cannot understand. Forces that will spread far beyond our borders. Forces that will bring order and security to the disordered lives of peoples across the world."

Esyal's caution immediately became fear. Questions tumbled into her mind. What was this man talking about? And who was he? Then, more pressingly, was he dangerous? He was certainly peculiar. And he was between her and the door. Her hand dropped to her lap again, to be near her knife, as her mouth went dry and she began to tremble.

"What are you talking about? Forces! Forces? What forces?" Her voice was hoarse and she gave a grating cough to clear it. "You mean an army? Is this place some kind of fortress?"

Adroyan hesitated and looked around Qualto's immaculate kitchen. "A war," he said, though to himself rather than Esyal. "It could be. It could be a war. Yes."

"Who are you?" Esyal could scarcely believe she had asked the question as it blurted out. She had heard the reply he had given to Josyff. It had been an unequivocal statement of authority. What was he going to say to her now?

"I am Adroyan Sirthied. I am responsible for... the Keep. And for its measuring. It is an important task. That is why I chose the surveyor, Josyff, and his assistant. They are both very able." He glanced around the kitchen again, almost anxiously, Esyal thought. "And this will need able men."

Receiving no rebuke, Esyal took a chance. "If they're able men—competent professionals—why are you here? I wouldn't imagine they'll work any harder or better with their boss breathing down their necks. It might even slow them down."

"This is an important task," Adroyan said again. "It must be supervised. No detail must be missed."

Esyal was inclined to pursue her point but sounder judgement prevailed. She shrugged. "As you say, it's *your* responsibility. I don't know anything about surveying."

"And there may be aspects to this task that are beyond them."

What's he justifying himself to me for? Esyal thought.

"Ah, you're a surveyor too? A senior surveyor?" She smiled to bring a slight taunt into the question. "Three heads are better than two."

Adroyan blinked and grimaced slightly as though he were being distracted by a slight but persistent pain.

"Are you unwell?" Esyal ventured.

"No," Adroyan replied. "It's just that this place is deeply disturbing."

"You said that before," Esyal said. "And I still don't understand what you mean."

Adroyan stood up, though Esyal sensed no threat in the movement. "Yes, I did." He looked at her. "I mean you no discourtesy, but it is a measure of how disturbing this place is that I find myself discussing it with you when I know that you cannot help."

"Knowledge lies in the strangest places," Esyal said, echoing her father.

"Not this knowledge," Adroyan replied. "You may be assured that the nature of this... building... is something that you could never understand."

Esyal's voice became cold. "Possibly. But while I might have lost my memory for the moment, I don't think I'm particularly stupid." She tapped her head. "There seems to be quite a lot up here. Perhaps if you explained yourself better..."

Adroyan put his hands on the table and leaned forward.

"Did you hear the voices?" he asked, quietly, almost as if he were afraid someone might overhear him. "The voices—all around us—when we were outside and the drawbridge was closed against us—did you hear them?"

Esyal's mind went back immediately to waking in Adroyan's arms and hearing—or perhaps, just sensing—voices fading into the distance. Was this some trick he was playing on her? Did he know she had been awake for some time? Worse, did he in some way know that she had not lost her memory? She lied without hesitation.

"I don't remember anything between walking through the mountains with you all and waking up here." She gestured towards the still open door. "In that room along the way—on the couch." Then, almost in spite of herself, "You're talking in riddles. This building disturbs you—it... binds... whatever that means—you talk about 'forces' and wars, for heaven's sake— now you're telling me you heard voices in the middle of the mountains." Committed, she decided to play the helpless female. "I'm truly grateful for what you did for me—I'd probably have died without your help—but you're beginning to frighten me."

Adroyan studied her thoughtfully for a moment, but as he opened his mouth to speak, a sharp cry rang out.

CHAPTER 22

The cry came from the passage outside. It was not loud but it was distinct and it was full of fear.

Esyal stiffened and drew in a sharp breath. Adroyan, by contrast, turned his head slightly and raised his hand a little as if demanding silence.

"You heard *that*," he said, without looking at her.

Despite her immediate alarm, Esyal was oddly heartened by the hints of both sarcasm and reproach in his voice. They gave him an unexpected humanity.

"Yes," she said simply, disarming both. But even as she was speaking she was snatching a large knife from a serried rank of Qualto's edges and points that glittered in a nearby rack. She moved past Adroyan to the door. As she did so, Adroyan seemed to wake as if from a reverie. He seized her arm. Instinctively, Esyal transferred the knife to her unhindered hand. Equally instinctively she made no attempt to struggle free from the grip, but turned on her captor.

"Let go!" she demanded before he could speak.

"Where are you going... with that?" Adroyan nodded towards the knife.

"Let go," Esyal said with great deliberation, her voice and her gaze menacing.

Adroyan's black eyes stared at her intently for a moment, then his grip slipped away.

"Where are you going with that?" he repeated, though his voice now was that merely of a concerned friend.

Esyal cursed herself inwardly. Her time with the Rhanen had given her fighting reflexes that were not those of an ordinary young woman. She had been too quick to seize the knife, and shifting it to her free hand and effectively threatening Adroyan had said a lot about her. Perhaps he hadn't noticed, or, at least, understood what her actions implied, but it had not been wise.

Should she apologize—try to make excuses?

No. That would merely draw attention to something that might indeed not have been noticed.

The cry came again. Though wordless, its appeal for help was unmistakeable.

For a moment, Esyal hesitated. Her confrontation with Adroyan had broken the momentum of her initial response and she found herself asking Adroyan's question—where *was* she going?

She had no good answer. In a strange place far from anywhere and surrounded by people she did not know save that one of them was New Order, rushing around, knife in hand, towards who knew what, was reckless to say the least. Then she realized she just wanted to be away from Adroyan, or away from his direct interrogation.

Still, there was one piece of damage she could at least mitigate. She looked at the knife as if she did not know how it had come there, then threw it casually on to a nearby worktop. Discarding a weapon was not her idea of wisdom, but the gesture might prove useful in future dealings with Adroyan and, rightly or wrongly, having committed herself now to going to the aid of whoever was calling, if the worst came to the worst, she still had her own knife in her belt.

That done, she stepped out into the passage, without speaking further to Adroyan.

But there was only silence there as the lights bloomed into life. Glancing in both directions, she ran across to the common room with the intention of waking Josyff.

Pushing open the door, she paused. She could see Henk's fire, lower and redder, though still hissing contentedly as he had prophesied, but Josyff was not there. Esyal glanced quickly about the room to see if he had merely moved to a more comfortable chair, but she knew he had not: the blanket that had covered him lay discarded and crumpled on the floor.

She stepped back into the passage slightly on tiptoe as if she were afraid of waking someone—or something.

"What's the matter?"

It was Adroyan.

"I don't know," Esyal replied. "But the surveyor's not here."

Adroyan pushed past her, none too gently. He strode purposefully around the room, his eyes everywhere.

"I told you, he's not there," Esyal said.

Adroyan turned to her, his face unreadable.

Even as she held his gaze, Esyal caught a shadowy movement at the edge of her vision. At the same time, and from the other side, the cry reached her—still wordless but still full of fear. She was aware of her heart beating rapidly as her legs carried her backwards until she was pressing hard against the far wall of the passage. Turning to face the movement, she saw a tall thin figure approaching. Stooped and dishevelled he was obviously straight from his bed, and his expression was one of both irritation and concern though this became surprise as he saw Esyal.

"Oh, you're awake," he told her.

"Yes," she said, eyeing him uncertainly. "Was it you shouting just now?"

"No, of course not," came Henk's testy reply. "Was it you?"

"No."

Henk looked at her attentively for a moment.

"Are you sure?" He rubbed his head.

"Yes!"

Henk scrutinized her a little longer before turning to Adroyan.

"It's not the surveyor again, is it?" he asked.

"Again?" queried Adroyan.

"He's had... accidents," Henk said, hesitating. "I think he... walks in his sleep... or the building..." He stopped and lifted his hand in a futile attempt to flatten his hair.

"Or the building?" Adroyan pressed.

"I think he walks in his sleep," Henk repeated definitively. "Bumps into things, hurts himself. This place affects some people oddly."

He motioned his listeners in the direction from which the call had come, and set off, his head craning forward. Esyal and Adroyan fell in behind him.

At the end of the passage, another crossed it at right angles. It ran for some way in both directions before curving out of sight. Several doors opened on to it and it was well lit. The three did not speak as they came to a halt. Henk cast from side to side listening for some indication of which way he should turn. Finally, with a shrug, he turned left.

"Shall we go the other way?" Esyal asked.

"If you want to get lost," Henk replied.

Esyal bridled slightly at this offhand response, and considered for a moment setting off in the opposite direction regardless. However, the passage looked very much like the one they had just come along and it needed no great feat of imagination to appreciate that she would perhaps not have to travel far before being completely disorientated. A vivid image of endless passages interweaving and shifting like the threads of a terrible knot rushed into her mind. Involuntarily she tightened her arms about herself, catching Adroyan's eye as she did.

"Just the thought of getting lost in this place," she said hesitantly. "Is it very big?"

"It has yet—"

"—to be measured." The interruption and her caustic tone spilled out before she could stop them but they dispelled her disturbing vision. "Yes," she added, pointlessly but half-apologetically.

"Best stay with me," Henk said, also more conciliatory. "The Keep's been in an odd mood lately."

Esyal shot an inquiring look towards Adroyan but his face was again unreadable.

She transferred the inquiry to its cause: Henk.

"An odd mood?"

"Yes. It's been like it for some time, now." He stopped and straightened up and his voice became thoughtful. "But it's been worse since the surveyor arrived."

"It?" Esyal probed.

Henk turned to her. "The mood, the changes. The place is changing—no one believes me—Qualto, Nyk—going round with their eyes shut—don't like to see it—but it's changing all right. Something's unsettling it."

Esyal was about to demand an explanation when Adroyan forestalled her. "Precisely what is changing?" he demanded.

They came to another junction. Only one passage from it was lit. Henk nodded. "The main hall," he said, as if confirming an earlier conclusion.

"The main hall is changing?" Adroyan echoed.

"That's where the surveyor's gone—if it is the surveyor," Henk replied. "Thought it would be."

"Explain what you mean by changes," Adroyan insisted.

Henk replied without looking at him.

"You'll see," he said.

The passage was widening.

"When you start your... measuring. You'll see."

Before Adroyan could pursue Henk's enigmatic remark, they were walking on to one of the balconies that overlooked the Great Hall.

Esyal let out a soft cry of surprise and ran forward to lean on the stone balustrade, her eyes scanning the carvings staring from the walls all around her. Below her, standing motionless in the middle of the hall, was Josyff.

He looked up and raised his hand in surprised greeting before any of them could speak.

"Oh, it's you. Did you hear it too?" he called. "I was beginning to think I was dreaming again."

"Are you unwell?" Adroyan shouted, his long body looking like one of the protruding carvings as he leaned precariously over the balustrade.

"I'm fine," came the reply. "Just puzzled."

"This way, sir." Henk, almost deferential now, touched Adroyan's arm and indicated a doorway at the end of the balcony. It led them down a narrow, spiral staircase between walls which were randomly decorated with carvings similar to those in the Great Hall except that they were set into the stonework. As Esyal looked at these, she felt that many of them were set ready to spring out at her, like wild creatures protecting their lairs— or waiting in predatory ambush. Paradoxically this impression was even worse with those where the openings were sealed with glass. Flaws, if they *were* flaws, in the glass, resulted in the figures being lit peculiarly and shifting shadows made them seem to move. She was quietly relieved to emerge into the broader confines of the Great Hall, though for a moment she thought that all the carvings were turning to examined her.

She focused immediately on Josyff who was advancing to meet them. He was smiling as he spoke to her.

"I thought it was *you* shouting when I woke up," he said. "I thought, perhaps you couldn't sleep after your... experience... wandered off to explore and lost your bearings." He shrugged. "It's easily done. This is no ordinary building. And the way the lights work can be downright alarming until you get used to them."

Esyal was apologetic. "I'd just gone for something to eat. I... we..." She indicated the others, "thought it was you. I'm sorry if I alarmed you."

Josyff was dismissive. "It's all right. I knew it wasn't you when I heard it the second time. It wasn't a woman's voice." Then his smile faded and his face became uncertain.

Adroyan cut through the exchange. "But who *was* calling out, then?" he said.

As if by common agreement, all three turned to Henk who was looking around at the watching carvings. He met their combined gaze with a dour indifference.

"It's no good asking me. I told you; this place is changing. Something's disturbed it. I don't know what's going on, but I'm leaving at the first chance. I want no part of it." Though his demeanour was unchanged, there was just enough harshness in his tone to indicate an underlying fear.

Josyff was about to speak, but Adroyan forestalled him.

"You'll leave when your tour is ended. You have a bond."

Henk looked at him directly. "You think this place cares for my bond?"

Adroyan did not reply.

"I will leave when I can," Henk continued flatly. "You should do the same—all of you."

Unsettled by Henk's remarks and wanting to end the uncomfortable tension that Adroyan's intrusion had caused, Josyff became conciliatory.

"Well, it's an academic debate at the moment. We're all here until the snow eases whether we like it or not. More to the point, someone was calling out for help and we still don't know who it was."

His voice faded into the silence of the Great Hall as the four stood motionless, listening, waiting.

Not for the first time, Josyff wished himself far from this place. The sense of release he had felt as he had moved away from the Keep tugged at him pitilessly. That he was not dreaming, that he had heard someone calling—for help—was confirmed by the presence of the others. That the voice had not belonged to Nyk, Qualto or Badr, he was certain.

"It's gone." It was Henk.

"It?" Josyff queried.

"It," Henk confirmed, without amplification. "We may as well all go back to bed." He turned towards the stairs. Esyal caught his arm.

"But someone called out for help," she said urgently. "We can't just..."

"It's gone," Henk repeated.

Esyal released him and looked at the others in exasperation and confusion. Adroyan was looking at the carvings, his head turning slowly as though he were doing a delicate exercise. Josyff could do little other than shrug.

"Henk knows the building," he said, weakly. "It might have been some freak of the weather. This *is* a very unusual building."

"That was no draught, no creaking door," Esyal protested angrily. "It was a..."

Josyff stepped closer to her and lowered his voice. "Well, whatever it was, it's stopped now. And besides, we can't search this place without Henk's help. Let's take his advice—it's desperately late and I for one am tired. Plus this place is bitterly cold. We can talk in the morning."

Reluctantly, Esyal agreed and within a few minutes she was back on the couch in the common room staring up at the ceiling. Henk had said nothing as they walked back but had become almost cheerful as he descended on the fire and stirred it into vigorous life again.

Josyff tossed and turned for a few minutes, but the fatigue of the day's efforts once again overrode his concerns about what had just happened and the returned unease of being back in the Keep, and he was soon asleep.

Esyal turned and looked at him. It was difficult to ignore the countless questions that kept vying for attention. But none of them were answerable, she knew, least of all now. She must watch and listen—and, too, if Henk made good his intention of leaving the place, she must be with him. She could do nothing out here, and there was always a chance that whoever had attacked her party would find their way here. Whatever else it is, this place is a rat trap, she concluded before drifting off. She must get away.

Through the passages curled a vague and tremulous whisper. Briefly it filled the Great Hall, like the wind in distant trees, then it was gone.

"They can... hear... us."

CHAPTER 23

The following day Qualto roused everyone with hand-rubbing expectation.

The previous evening had been occupied with concerns for Esyal and the drawbridge and Badr's experience in the book room. Now he would be able to wring from Nyk and Josyff what he hoped would be a more enjoyable account of their trip. He made a great fuss of Esyal.

"Raiding my kitchen, using my knives, eh?" he said with mock severity and a fencing gesture.

"I'm sorry, I was hungry," Esyal confessed. "And I just grabbed the knife when I heard that cry. It startled me."

"It seems then that your more knowledgeable self is prepared to defend itself," Adroyan said.

Esyal cursed inwardly, a young woman rescued from certain death in the snow should perhaps have fluttered nervously at hearing such a sound, rather than seize the nearest lethal weapon to hand. She gave a guilty shrug and a self-deprecating grimace of feminine helplessness to gloss over the momentary break in the general conversation that Adroyan's remark had caused.

Nyk, Qualto and Badr had not heard the cry and pressed the others for details. Josyff was their chief witness, though he could do little other than recite the events as they had happened. Mindful that he was a stranger amongst old friends, he refrained from mentioning Henk's peculiar remarks about the building. Henk himself, like Adroyan and Esyal, sat silent, listening, and, as if by some long-developed alchemy of understanding, his friends chose not to press him for his version of events. There was a brief, uninspired discussion as to what the cry might have been but it soon dwindled into an awkward silence.

Esyal broke it briskly. "Well, I'm sure there'll be an explanation for it somewhere. It certainly wasn't a dream and I don't believe in ghosts, so..." She waved her hands vaguely and addressed Josyff and Badr. "You'll find it when you're doing your work." Then, to no one in particular, "What time is it? Does this building have any windows? I haven't seen one so far. I *suppose* it's daylight out there—what's the weather doing? Will we be able to get to the village, do you think?"

"It's about half past nine, it's a bright sunny day, but I doubt anyone will be going to the village for some time," Qualto replied comprehensively, adding, "And there are windows in the kitchen."

Hearing the time, Josyff pulled an unhappy face but Qualto forestalled his complaint.

"You needed to sleep—all of you. You'd had a long tiring day—two days. And, it seems, a disturbed night." He became authoritative. "I shouldn't imagine a few hours here or there is going to make any difference to your work, but being half-asleep may well." He turned to Esyal before anyone could dispute with him.

"I'll show you round afterwards. And find a room for you—one with a window." He smiled. "I have one in mind right now—beautiful view—especially today."

"I'll help you clear up," Esyal said, still anxious to distance herself in Adroyan's mind from her knife-wielding behaviour.

"I'd better get started as well," Nyk said, scraping his chair back. "I want to find out what the devil's the matter with the drawbridge. We could've been out there yet and no one any the wiser."

"Never touched it," Qualto proclaimed, raising his hands. "Neither of us."

"I never said you did," Nyk replied unconvincingly. "But machines don't start and stop on their own."

"You've left something loose," Qualto said with heavy but not malicious scorn. "You know how finely balanced it is."

"I don't leave things loose!" Nyk protested and, provoked, voiced his suspicion. "Are you *sure* you haven't touched anything—maybe looking for something when you went to light the Beacon?" He faltered guiltily. "Thanks for that, incidentally. It was a godsend."

Qualto was magnanimous in his victory. He started stacking the plates.

"What would we go in the gatehouse for? I didn't touch anything, Henk didn't touch anything. You know me—I'd no more mess about with any of the machinery around here than you'd help with the cooking."

A brief smile flitted across Henk's face.

Nyk became apologetic. "I'm sorry. As you say, it's been a difficult two days and it was... upsetting, to put it mildly... to see the bridge closed against us when we finally got here. I can't think what..."

"Go on—shoo—get it sorted out," Qualto decreed. "I've plenty to do, as has Henk—and I'm sure our surveyors have too."

After a brief flurry of activity, Josyff, Badr and Adroyan were left alone in the common room. Adroyan was looking absently at the grey remains of Henk's fire. Josyff gave Badr as conspiratorial a look as he dared before speaking.

He cleared his throat uncomfortably.

"You told us last night that you're responsible for this project, sir..." Adroyan was reaching into his jacket. "I've no reason to doubt you, but procedure is procedure, as you know, and I... we... will need confirmation of this if we're..."

Adroyan held out a letter to him.

Josyff took it with a nod of thanks, then laid it on the table so that he and Badr could read it together.

"You are correct to ask," Adroyan said, returning to his study of the dead fire. "Does that answer your queries?"

The letter could hardly have been simpler: "Adroyan is decreed Master of the Keep."

Not knowing what the duties or authority of the Master of the Keep were, the letter left Josyff no wiser as to Adroyan's place in this venture, but that was of no concern now. All that he was concerned about was the heading and the signature. The heading was that of the Ordrans, the supreme governing body of the New Order, and the signature, illegible, but identified in print and countersigned by Josyff's immediate superior, was that of its First Member, the rarely seen leader and instigator of the New Order. He noted a shakiness in his superior's signature—and that his own hands were trembling slightly too, despite his best efforts to give no outward sign of what he was feeling.

Badr's response was more open. He cast a quick glance at Adroyan's back and silently puffed out his cheeks. Then he slid the letter back to Josyff as if the very act of touching it might draw attention to him in some way. Josyff could do no other than give him a curt nod of understanding. There was no saying who Adroyan was. That he was of the New Order, Josyff had surmised from the start, but that he was there at the direct command of the Ordrans—that he might even *be* one of the Ordrans—was deeply unsettling. Whatever the formal duties of the Master of the Keep might be, the letter ensured that his authority here was effectively absolute, and also that every word would have to be watched.

All of which prompted more questions about what this building was to be used for and why this survey was so important. And why had he and Badr been selected? He was good at his job, he knew that, though that had been no protection for many of his erstwhile colleagues. Briefly it came to him that perhaps even Badr was there to watch and study him, report on him. But it faded. From his limited experience of him, he knew that Badr was at least able and competent, and skill in a practical profession was not a hallmark of the New Order's creatures. He was no chatterbox, for sure, but then they had not had too much opportunity for conversation, and cautious silence *was* a hallmark of most of those who worked for the New Order.

But underlying these concerns was the chilling thought that he had been at the focus of the silent watching eye of the Ordrans. How long had that been going on? What did they know about him? What files, what tales, what gossip about him had moved through the rarefied upper reaches of the new Order?

His stomach felt like lead.

Damn their eyes! They foul everything they touch, these people.

This brief and inner spasm of stark rebellion took Josyff by surprise. He reproached himself, took a surreptitious deep breath and ordered himself to forget such thoughts. Do your job, get it over with, get back to your wife, away from the New Order's gaze. The thought of his wife focused his mind. Watch your tongue—keeping a rein on it has got you this far and it'll get you through this. And just watch Adroyan closely—very closely.

Carefully re-folding the letter, he returned it to Adroyan and, despite his resolution, took a risk.

"Thank you, sir. This must be a particularly important building to have brought you all this way." There was no response. "Do you have any specific orders for us? Do you wish to see...?"

A leisurely gesture from Adroyan stopped him. Without moving his gaze from the fire, he shook his head slowly. "You have your instructions. This place is to be measured—thoroughly and well measured—and you and Badr are the best suited to do it. I am here to oversee the work and..." He hesitated. "And to make such decisions as may be needed." Then, as an afterthought, "and to advise should you encounter difficulties."

"*You're* a surveyor, sir?" The remark was out before Josyff could stop it. He sent a silent oath after it.

Adroyan turned very slowly and looked at him. Josyff redoubled his inner cursing as he tried to avoid the black-eyed stare without looking guilty.

"*You* are the surveyor, Josyff."

"Yes, sir," Josyff nodded, over-eagerly, anxious to be away. "Now the equipment's here we should be able to make good progress."

He motioned Badr towards the door.

"We'll have to check and calibrate everything before we can get started properly, but it shouldn't take too long. Shall I keep you advised of progress?"

There was a long silence. Josyff was about to ask the question again when an indifferent "yes" reached him.

As they walked along the passage towards the main door, Josyff took another risk.

"It seems the New Order have been watching us, Badr."

"Yes," Badr replied, noncommittally. "I just do my job."

Josyff stopped. The revelation about Adroyan's status had disconcerted him more than he had thought and for a moment he felt physically unable to walk. He put his hand to his head.

"Do you want to sit down a moment?" Badr asked.

"No," Josyff replied after a long pause. He took a deep breath. "I'm fine. It's just that so many odd things have happened these past few days, I... can't make out what's going on."

Badr looked round at the blank walls of the passage as if for inspiration. "No, neither can I. Getting posted here in the first place made little sense, so far from home and all my usual work contacts. Then a high ranking official turns up—never known the like of that before. And that girl—so lucky—such a chance being found like that—alone in the mountains—no memory. The drawbridge opens and shuts itself, the ladders in the book room move on their own, and even Henk thinks that doors and passages are appearing out of nowhere." His round face wrinkled, halfway between a shamefaced laugh and desperation.

Badr's last remark seemed to release Josyff.

"What?"

Badr composed himself and they set off again. As they walked, Badr recounted his and Qualto's long trail after Henk the previous evening.

"I got quite alarmed at one stage. He's an odd one, Henk," he concluded. "I think even Qualto was bothered, though he didn't say anything."

Josyff was shaking his head. "Doorways and passages coming and going! I can *believe* he didn't say anything—what *could* he say? They're old friends—or old colleagues anyway."

They came to the room where the equipment had eventually been stored the previous night. Josyff found the sight of it heartening.

"I think the best we can do is leave Henk to Nyk and Qualto and get on with our work as quickly as possible. The sooner we're done, the sooner we're away. And we'll soon find out if doorways and passages are moving."

Badr chuckled. He was already setting up a tripod and carefully extracting one of the instruments from its box. When he had finished mounting it, he patted it and gave a theatrical sigh of relief.

"Working with those old instruments the other day was... interesting," he said. "Not to say salutary. It reminded me just how much time and effort these save."

"Indeed," Josyff agreed. "It does no harm to get such a lesson from time to time. Appreciate how lucky we are. I'm too near to "the good old days" to be deeply drawn to them."

It took them the rest of the morning to check the equipment thoroughly. With the aid of Henk in locating some chairs and tables, they set about establishing their main working area in a large well-lit room off the Great Hall. Tall windows offered a view of the snow-covered mountains.

"How long are you going to be?" Henk had been silent for most of the time, not disagreeably, but communicating with nods and grunts, and the question took Josyff unawares.

"I really don't know," he replied. "Even from what I've seen so far, the building's deceptively big and very complicated..." He was tempted to make some comment about passages and doors moving but resisted it. Instead, he decided on an attempt to make Henk an ally, though against what or whom, he could not have said. "But you can rest assured, Badr and I will be working as quickly as we can. No disrespect to you and the others but I've a good home I'm missing and I'd like to be away before the winter really sets in."

Henk looked out at the mountains. "Yes... odd, the weather. Couldn't hazard what it's going to do next. Maybe it's an early winter, maybe..." He shrugged. "But lots of things are out of sorts at the moment. I don't like your boss."

Startled, Josyff caught Badr's eye. Of the many responses that offered themselves, he opted for one that he hoped was both tactful and cautionary.

"He's like me and Badr—new to the mountains. City ways. Probably seems unusual to you. I'm sure we'll all get along when everyone's settled in. He's..."

Henk was shaking his head. "No. He's not good. I don't like him. There'll be trouble, too—the building doesn't like him."

Before either Josyff or Badr could respond to this they were interrupted by Nyk. He knocked on the open door and leaned into the room. He looked both embarrassed and concerned. Josyff felt a frisson of alarm.

"Sorry to interrupt," Nyk said. "But we have a problem."

"What's the matter?" Josyff asked.

Nyk cleared his throat. "The drawbridge. It's shut again." He paused awkwardly. "And I can't get it open. We're shut in."

CHAPTER 24

"Shut in?" Josyff echoed. "What do you mean?"

"Just that," Nyk said, with an uneasy mixture of irritation and helplessness in his voice that unsettled Josyff. "I can't lower the drawbridge. We're shut in."

"I thought you said it was easy to move—counter-balanced in some way," Josyff said.

"It is—was," Nyk replied. "And it should be. But it won't move."

Unexpectedly, Josyff felt a powerful anger rising up. Couldn't these people manage their own equipment, do their own work? They'd been here long enough! What in God's name could he do about anything, if the man whose job it was couldn't? He'd more than enough to do with this place without wasting time nursemaiding incompetents.

That such a response was unjust, he knew, but that barely mitigated it. Fortunately, he still had sufficient composure to keep silent and turn his face away from Nyk as this passion surged through him, so that it manifested itself simply in a tightening of his grip about the leg of the tripod he was holding, and a tensing of his jaw.

"Well, we're surveyors, not engineers," Badr said, almost jovially, as if sensing Josyff's reaction. "I can't imagine what we can do, but we can have a look at it with you, if you want."

Josyff's anger vanished as quickly as it had come, but it left him unsettled. He was not prone to such outbursts nor ever had been. It was completely out of character. Something was wrong.

But what...?

Both Badr and Nyk were looking at him as if for permission. He forced himself to smile and, with an effort, released his grip on the tripod leg.

"Of course," he said.

The machinery for opening and closing the drawbridge was housed in a room that completely surrounded the gateway. Its existence was not immediately apparent however, as it was built within the thickness of the Keep wall. Only two nondescript doors, one on each side, indicated its presence.

Nyk led Badr and Josyff across the snow-covered courtyard, bright and cold under the clear blue sky. The Keep walls hid most of the mountains and Josyff found his eyes turning immediately to the gateway in anticipation of the light and openness it normally offered. The sight of the opening, now sealed, dark and ominous, felt like a blow and briefly he felt as though the whole Keep were closing about him.

Nyk opened the door on the right hand side of the gateway and held it as Josyff and Badr entered. They all paused for a moment after Nyk had closed the door. They were in an echoing and high arching chamber which, though well lit, seemed at first gloomy and oppressive after the sunlit brightness of the courtyard.

"Bigger than it looks," Josyff remarked as his vision cleared.

"Up here," Nyk said, setting off up a wide flight of stairs. The others followed. The stairs led directly on to the floor which spanned across the top of the gateway. Nyk pointed to a machine at the far side of the room— chains and pulley wheels defined it as lifting equipment. "That's to raise and lower the drawbridge," he said. He shook his head. "None of this makes any sense," he muttered, largely to himself. "But this," louder and to Josyff and Badr, "is what we usually use."

He took hold of a large hand-wheel protruding from the wall and made to turn it. It did not move, even though he was applying a conspicuous effort.

"Normally, you can turn this with little more than the weight of your hand. Now..." He gave it a final frustrated push. "It's solid—absolutely solid." He stepped aside and extended a hand, inviting his listeners to test this for themselves, which, out of a mixture of curiosity and courtesy, they did.

"There's no give in it at all," Josyff remarked needlessly.

"Rock solid," Nyk confirmed.

"Could it be the sudden cold?" Badr offered. "Something frozen somewhere?"

Nyk shook his head. "We get colder than this every year and it's always worked as smooth as silk. Apart from the fact that I keep the main pivots lubricated, they're actually heated. Whoever built this place really knew what they were doing. Far ahead of their time."

"And the machine?" Josyff asked.

"Trips out immediately."

Nyk walked over to the machine and pressed a button. There was a low hum and a soft thud and then silence.

"That's what it's meant to do—stop if the bridge is jammed," Nyk explained. "It's very sensitive, and it's working fine. Never known the like of it before. I check everything out regularly. Not only because it's in the Procedures but..." He left the sentence uncompleted.

Josyff looked at Badr and then back at Nyk before making a vague hand gesture.

"Is it possible part of the machine itself has failed—broken—and lodged in the mechanism?"

"Nah, look." Nyk motioned them towards a descending flight of steps to one side of the machine. It led them down some way below the level of the courtyard. At the bottom he clambered over a guard rail and began pointing out the working parts of the drawbridge and the lifting equipment.

"Simple and straightforward," he concluded. "And all in good order—nothing wrong with it—nothing jamming it, blocking it... nothing... but the whole thing is solid as a rock."

Josyff felt for Nyk's muted anger. Even in his limited acquaintance of the man he had come to respect both his ability and his conscientious commitment to his job. But he was at a loss. Though he could certainly bring a rational mind to Nyk's problem he had no practical experience of dealing with such machines. He tried to ease the sense of urgency that Nyk was patently feeling.

"Exactly what does it mean?" he asked. "The gateway being sealed? What does it mean to us, here, now?"

"Right now—not much," Nyk replied after a brief pause. "We've plenty food, water and such fuel as we need. But if we can't get it open, then we're trapped. Whatever this place is, or was, no one can get in or out except over the drawbridge."

Josyff felt again as though the walls and ceiling of the chamber were closing about him, but the sensation vanished almost as if it had been ripped away by an unseen hand.

"Does anyone ever come up from the village?" he asked, grasping for support at the ordinary, though he knew the answer even as he spoke.

"No one comes here... except those with business here. And that's usually only Henk, Qualto and myself. It'll be spring before anyone even thinks about us." He gave an odd shrug, half optimistic, half fatalistic. "Unless, of course, there are more surveyors and their superiors on the way." He laid an unexpected and slightly caustic emphasis on 'superiors'. Josyff noted it but wilfully set it aside, marking it as something that might possibly be of use in the future. "Still," Nyk continued. "Even if there were, they'd be in bigger trouble than we are. As I said, there's only one way in and out—they'd be locked out!"

"There'll be a way out somewhere," Badr said, speaking for the first time. "If between us we can't find a way across that moat, I'd be very surprised."

Nyk pulled a wry face. "You may be right," he said, though it was a dismissal, not a concession. "But I doubt it. There's certainly nothing here that'll reach across the moat that I can think of. And you'll need to be a rare climber if you're thinking about going down into the moat."

Badr was about to remonstrate with him, but Josyff interceded. "Either way, let's not get too far ahead of ourselves. If we're not going to starve to death in the near future then we've plenty time to find a solution." He turned to Nyk. "We've not really started on our survey yet. Let's the three

118

of us look over everything here again. There may be something right under your nose that you just can't see—it's happened to me often enough. The last few days have been a major upheaval for you—upsetting your entire work schedule, I'm sure—plus it's been tiring as well. Perhaps going through it all with us might just bring something to light."

"No harm in trying," Nyk conceded.

Badr was looking down at where the counterweight to the drawbridge seated against a cross wall.

"Have you got a crowbar?" he asked Nyk, who looked at him nervously. "What for?"

Badr pointed at the counterweight. "Thought I'd try a little brute force. And a bit of impact—might just shake something loose. Have you got a hammer as well?" He held out his arms to indicate the size he had in mind.

Nyk did not seem to be over-enthusiastic about the idea, but receiving only a "why not?" shrug from Josyff, disappeared into the further reaches of the underground chamber. When he returned he was carrying a long crowbar and a heavy hammer.

"Excellent," Badr said, climbing over the guard rail and taking them from him. Hefting the hammer proprietorially he walked along the length of the counterweight, eyes cast down, looking for a suitable place to implement his idea.

"This is a remarkable piece of work," he announced after the second tour. "It'd be difficult to get a knife in here, let alone a crowbar."

Then he had put down the tools and was kneeling and scratching at something. He produced a small knife from somewhere to help him.

"Well I'm damned," he said as he crouched low and blew the remnants of dust from the small hole that he had exposed. "Look at this."

"This" was a notch cut into the heavy metal edging that formed the seating for the counterweight.

"It looks as if it might be a leverage point," Badr said.

"I've never seen that before," Nyk said.

"You've never had cause to look before, have you?" Badr replied. "Besides, it was full of dust and grease. I only spotted it by chance."

"It's not a very neat job, is it?" Josyff said.

"Just what I was thinking," Nyk agreed. He was examining Badr's discovery closely. "And there are marks on the counterweight here." He stood up. "It's not part of the original manufacture—that's all good workmanship— very good. This looks as if it's been cut with a knife and fork." Josyff smiled at the remark, glad of the momentary easing of the tension, but Nyk was thoughtful again.

"I wonder if this has happened before," he said, vaguely indicating the closed bridge. He made a beckoning motion towards the crowbar. Badr handed it to him. "Let's see if this will do the trick."

The notch was wide enough to take the broad end of the crowbar and after satisfying himself that it was not likely to slip, Nyk heaved on it. Nothing happened. He shook his head. "We should be able to push this by hand from down here," he said, running his sleeve across his brow.

"Let me try," Badr said. "I'm stronger than you."

Nyk relinquished the crowbar without demur.

"Are there any more notches we can use?" Josyff asked as Badr began pulling on the crowbar.

Before anyone could answer, Badr, his face reddening with effort, exclaimed, "It's moving!"

Josyff looked down and saw that the line between the counterweight and the metal edging was slowly widening. Abruptly, he felt disorientated—he was part of a vast, silent emptiness and the gap, indeed the whole floor, seemed suddenly to be far far below him. Instinctively, he reached out to steady himself, but the impression vanished even as he touched the counterweight. He became aware of a commotion about him.

"What was that?" Nyk was saying; he too was steadying himself against the face of the counterweight, and there was the ringing clatter of the falling crowbar suffused all around by the fading echoes of a large impact.

Badr was staggering back. "God knows," he gasped, his eyes wide. "The damn thing just... slammed shut." He looked at his hands ruefully. "It just tore it out of my hands."

"Are you hurt?" Josyff asked, anxiously.

Badr examined his hands again. "Just a little... and shaken."

"What did you mean, slammed shut?" Nyk asked.

"Just that," Badr replied. "It felt as though I was working against a great spring—some force that increased as I put more effort into it." He became explanatory. "It didn't have that unyielding feeling of something jammed solid—and it didn't feel as though some obstacle was being broken or crushed. Very strange."

A look of determination came into his eyes and he picked up the crowbar. "Let's try again."

Something deep inside Josyff said, "no!" but it was over-ridden by Badr's sense of challenge, and he ignored it, compromising a little by repeating his earlier question. "Are there any more notches like this we can use?"

After some scratching and poking, they found another—cut rough and unfinished into the metal. Nyk said nothing, but his nose wrinkled as if in distaste and he looked little happier when, at Badr's further urging, he returned with a second crowbar.

"I don't use *one* of these once in a blue moon—now we're using two..."

"You don't see this jamming itself shut once in a blue moon either," Badr retorted, obviously relishing the prospect of a battle with the recalcitrant drawbridge.

Though a reluctant volunteer, Nyk looked set to take charge of the second notch, but Josyff stopped him.

"I'll do that," he said. "You know this place better than we do. Watch what's happening and call out if it looks as if we're... doing damage to anything."

Nyk handed him the crowbar with a grunt of acknowledgement and Josyff braced himself. At Badr's command he began heaving.

"It's opening again," he heard Nyk saying, but he sensed too what Badr had spoken of. The resistance he was meeting had indeed an almost wilful quality to it. The more he pulled, the greater it became. Then it happened.

CHAPTER 25

After breakfast, Esyal followed Qualto out of the common room ostensibly to help him in the kitchen, but her primary motive was to avoid further contact with Adroyan—her knife-wielding of the previous evening still being large in her memory, she assumed it was in his too.

She had determined to win as many allies as possible in this place, not least because she knew she could be there for some time.

"It pays to have friends in low places," her father used to say about dealing with civic officials. "They're the ones who can make your life a misery if they want, and little's to be gained by fighting them anyway. They're only infantry—there's always plenty more to take their place when you've bayoneted them to death. It's the generals you have to go for."

Esyal had seen him at work often enough to learn that this was sterling advice and she followed it whenever she could. Not that it could be followed so easily since the coming of the New Order. Fear pervaded the 'infantry' now—fear at many levels, but which universally overwhelmed any instinct to help and oblige—fear that, at its most trivial, insisted on the grim observance of the minutiae of the innumerable regulations that now flowed out of the Government, however inane or contradictory—fear that turned officials into mere survival machines, and informers.

Esyal had noted from the outset that Nyk, Henk and Qualto were seemingly unaffected by this. They were a small island still in an easier past. Not surprising really, she concluded. It was simply a matter of distance. This place was too far from anywhere to interest the New Order. Until now, of course. Which brought her thoughts full circle: until such time as she could safely leave she must find out why Adroyan was here. But first came survival—and allies.

Qualto's kitchen was largely as she and Adroyan had left it the previous night, save that the dish she had been eating from was gone and the knife she had thrown aside was back in its rack.

Qualto had bustled in ahead of her and was now busy at the sink, clattering the breakfast dishes purposefully and whistling softly to himself.

"Shall I dry those?" she asked hesitantly.

Qualto paused uncertainly. "They'll drain," he said eventually.

It took Esyal little insight to diagnose the problem and she met it head on.

"I'm in the way, aren't I?"

Qualto placed the last plate in a rack, wiped his hands and placed the towel neatly back on its rail. He smiled apologetically. "No," he said unconvincingly. "It's a big kitchen, but... I'm not sure there's much you can do to help, though the offer's appreciated. I'm very... organized."

Esyal returned the smile with a winning one of her own. "I can see that," she replied, looking around. "But for three, not seven. There's going to be a lot more to do and I suppose you've got duties other than cooking, haven't you?" She did not wait for an answer. "I'll not get under your feet—truly. Anyway, you can brush me aside with them if I do. I've got to do *something*. I'm not here on official business like the others, I'm just a stray who's wandered in and can't get out. I can't take your food and hospitality without making some kind of a contribution. And I don't want to spend the days doing nothing—I'll go crazy."

The combination of logic, charm and plaintive appeal routed Qualto's already none-too-strong resistance. He yielded.

"You're probably right. I suppose all three of us will have to get used to our staid old habits being disrupted until this survey is finished and everyone's gone."

"And that could be some time," Esyal said.

"It could indeed," Qualto agreed. "This snow is early, but it looks very... set. It could well be spring before the way back to the village is clear again. I imagine they'll have finished their survey by then, but, that said, this place is much bigger than it looks—and *very* complicated." The memory of his and Badr's journey with Henk the previous night returned, disturbingly. "I've worked here for a long time and I wouldn't pretend to have seen every part of it."

"It *must* be big," Esyal said.

Qualto shrugged. "Maybe I'm just not curious enough."

"Or adventurous enough," Esyal teased.

"Hmm, maybe. Look where being adventurous got you, young lady." He continued before Esyal could reply. "And talking of adventures, what was one of my knives doing on the worktop this morning." He raised his eyebrows quizzically like a patient but all-knowing schoolmaster.

His look surprised Esyal. Don't underestimate this man—he could well be more than just a plump and jolly cook. In fact, she decided, he is! She had speculated in assuming he had other duties here, but he had not denied it. She must find out what they were. And she must not underestimate Nyk or Henk either. It took unusual people—special people—to man an obscure outpost like this.

Heeding the warning, she remembered her thoughts when Nyk and Josyff discovered her in the cave: the best way to deceive is to tell as much of the truth and as few lies as possible.

"I didn't do any damage to it, did I?"

"No," Qualto replied. "But you might have done—to yourself. All my knives are very sharp. You could cut yourself badly and not even feel it." He was not to be deflected from his question however, which he repeated not in words but in an inclination of his head.

"I... er... just grabbed it when I heard that shout," Esyal confessed.

"It was *that* frightening—a cry for help? It *was* a cry for help, wasn't it?"

"It sounded like one when it came again, but not at first—it frightened me to death, coming out of nowhere like that. Adroyan jumped as well."

"He didn't grab one of my best knives."

"He's a big man," Esyal protested, raising her voice. "And I'm..." She faltered, then shrugged. "Maybe... I'm just used to looking after myself."

Qualto's lips pursed thoughtfully, then he was the cook again. "A good trait," he said, starting to wipe down a working surface. "Especially in a woman—I admire it." He became mockingly stern. "But make sure you clean my knives and put them back properly in future. And *do* be careful."

"I hope I won't need to be—other than for helping you with the cooking." Before Qualto could dispute this ambition, she pressed on. "What do you think it was? It *sounded* like a voice."

"Not hearing it, couldn't say," Qualto replied, as casually as he could. "Echoes, wind, some stray animal out in the snow?" Esyal was shaking her head. Qualto wanted to give her an easy assurance, but somehow he could not. The reports of the voices in the night conspired with Henk's odd behaviour and Badr's experience in the book room to unsettle him. Nor could he drift lightly into casual conversation with this new arrival. He reverted to the previous subject.

"I notice you've a knife in your belt," he said, pointing. "You seem to be very... martial... for a young lady."

Esyal stopped an involuntary movement to close her jacket and cover the knife. She managed to look mildly surprised.

"Yes, I noticed. I imagine it's part of whatever I brought into the mountains. Survival stuff. I suppose there's a pack full of clothes and food somewhere out there."

"May I?" Qualto made a beckoning gesture for the knife.

Esyal, wilfully awkward, drew the knife and handed it to him. He turned it over a few times, squinted along it and tested the edge then wrinkled his nose slightly.

"What's the matter?" Esyal asked.

"Nothing. It's a good knife. Very good, actually. But I think we can get a better edge on it, though. Shall I?"

"Yes, I suppose so," Esyal replied, vaguely. "Does it matter—being a bit blunt?"

Qualto chuckled and became fatherly. He waved the knife at her like an admonishing finger. "Well, it doesn't *matter* in the great scheme of things, I suppose, and I'll confess to being... over-fussy... about such matters, but whatever you're going to use it for, a knife's no good if it doesn't cut properly, is it?" Without waiting for the permission he had sought, he took down a sharpening steel from a rack and engaged it in a deft and very rapid series of strokes and counter strokes with the knife. "Not only that," he continued above the noise. "It can be downright dangerous—uncontrollable, you see." The steel was back in its rack and Qualto was wafting the blade up and down a leather strop. Esyal watched this effortless workmanship with the quiet and slightly envious wonder of any intelligent person watching a skilled craftsman at work.

"There we are," he said eventually, handing the knife back to her. "That will do what you ask it to now, not jerk and stick and generally do what *it* feels like. Just treat it with respect."

Esyal took the knife gingerly. "I will," she said, carefully sheathing it. "In fact I think I'll leave it just where it is."

"Well, I doubt you'll be needing any 'survival stuff' while you're here," Qualto said, with a smile. "Fork, spoon, and an *ordinary* knife should be all that's necessary. And there are plenty of books to read if the boredom looks like proving fatal."

"Maybe I'll be able to help the surveyors," Esyal mused.

"Maybe," came the reply. "They seem pleasant enough. I'm sure there'll be able to find something for you to do. I think the job's going to be bigger than they thought—this place is very deceptive. And they got off to a rather shaky start, their equipment not being here." He pulled a wry face. "Josyff put a brave face on it but I don't think he was too impressed by the stuff that Nyk found for him—very old-fashioned, even to my eyes."

"And will *you* find something for me to do as well?" Esyal pressed.

Qualto surrendered. "Well, as you carefully pointed out to me, there are seven of us now, so I suppose there'll be more than twice as much cooking to do."

Qualto's arithmetic brought an uncomfortable thought to Esyal.

"Is there enough food here for so many if we're liable to be here for a long time?"

Qualto looked pensive. "How long's a long time?" he asked rhetorically. "We have a great deal down in the cold rooms, but I'd better check—just in case. A little discreet eking out now might spare us hungrier times later."

He smiled. "You can help me with that." Then he clapped his hands. "But first—your room. I think I have the very thing for you—come. It's right above the surveyor's." Taking her arm he gently propelled Esyal out into the passage and after a short walk, towards a flight of stairs.

Qualto trotted up them with unexpected agility, though he was a little flushed and breathless when they reached the top. He paused at the top and, leaning over the stone balustrade, pointed down the well.

"You know where you are?" he asked. "Turn right at the bottom, right at the end of the passage and you're straight back to the kitchen or the common room."

"Yes, thank you. I'm learning to watch where I walk around here. Could you show me where the book room is, as well?"

"Certainly. Want to see if there are any cookery books?"

Qualto was chuckling again.

"No," Esyal replied, with some mild indignation. "I just like reading... I think. You're very cheerful all of a sudden."

"Here we are."

Qualto threw open a door and motioned Esyal through it.

"What do you think of that?"

The room was large and airy and filled with bright sunlight. Through a large window could be seen snow-covered peaks sharp against the blue sky. It was furnished simply but adequately: a large bed, four chairs, and a chest of drawers, carved with figures similar to those in the Great Hall, Esyal noticed.

"You can put your clothes in there," Qualto said. "And there are washing facilities there." He indicated two identical doors.

"Clothes?" Esyal queried with a knowing look and a downward sweep of her hands. "I'm wearing them."

Qualto dithered. "Ah, yes. Of course. I'd forgotten... er..." He turned left and right a few times, distractedly patting his hands together until he found a solution. "There are clothes in the stores—plenty of them. I imagine there'll be something to fit you down there. We'll have a look right now, if you're happy with this room."

"It's splendid," Esyal said. She went over to the window and saw that the room was slightly higher than the walls of the Keep. Below was the courtyard, footprints criss-crossing the snow.

"Is that the drawbridge?" Esyal asked, pointing.

Qualto joined her. "It is, yes. Odd though, it's not normally closed. It's probably Nyk, poking and prying, trying to find out what happened last night. Nothing he likes better than a good problem to get his teeth into—though he'd never admit it." He turned away. "It'll be something to do with this weather, for sure. We'll get the full story at tea time. Be prepared to be regaled with tales of gears, levers and lubrication—probably more than once."

Despite his soft humour, Esyal sensed a hint of anxiety in his manner, though she chose not to pursue it.

"Clothes, bedding," he proclaimed. "Come on."

"And books?"

"And books."

After he had helped her unearth sheets and blankets for her room, Qualto spent what was left of the morning showing Esyal around those parts of the Keep where he and the others lived and worked. He larded his tour with ample warnings about "wandering off".

"I don't want to frighten you, but it *is* a big and confusing place. You could very easily get lost and it won't be easy to find you. Do be careful."

In the book room, he discreetly pushed one of the ladders. It rolled away quietly and easily and he almost convinced himself that Badr had been dreaming about his experience the previous night.

Finally, and with several repeated instructions about how to return to the common room, he left Esyal in a room not dissimilar to the book room but lined with racks of clothes.

Despite herself, Esyal gaped when she entered.

"Who do these belong to?" she asked.

Qualto shrugged. "The Keep—the Estate—or the New Order now, I imagine. There are all manner of odd things in this place—we just do our jobs—keep everything in order. They may even be for guests. Anyway, I doubt anyone's going to be upset if you use some of these. Have a wander round. I'll be in the kitchen for a while if you need me."

Just as he was about to close the door, he paused and cocked his head on one side as though listening to something.

Then, soft, but growing rapidly and relentlessly, came a low rumbling.

CHAPTER 26

The gap between the counterweight and the edging began to widen as Josyff and Badr levered together.

"It's opening!" Nyk shouted, excitedly. He was leaning with his shoulder against the counterweight, pushing, reluctant to leave the remedying of this—*his*—problem to outsiders.

But even as his cry echoed around the chamber, Josyff felt a deep sense of the wrongness of what he was doing rising through him, and a deep fear, although in some way, the fear did not seem to be his. He had scarcely time to reflect on these unbidden sensations, when the sense of disorientation he had felt before returned, not only in full force, but magnified many times. Like the fear, his limbs, his whole body, seemed no longer to be his. He was being stretched and flattened, made both infinitely heavy, yet dispersed, intangible. He was many things at many times in many places. Strange images, giddying, distorted perspectives overwhelmed him.

And as abruptly as they had come, they were gone and he was in the drawbridge chamber again—breathtakingly snapped back into normality. All around him was noise and confusion. The crowbar was being torn from his grasp and he was...

Falling?

A reflex—far faster than his lumbering and bewildered mind—turned his head to one side and brought a hand up to protect it as he crashed forward into the counterweight. For an instant it seemed as though he was being crushed into it—great weights pushing him mercilessly.

Then he was staggering backwards violently under the impetus of his own protective reaction. After several uncontrolled paces, his legs finally buckled and he landed gracelessly but relatively painlessly on his behind.

The chamber was ringing with the remains of a loud noise, though he could not immediately recall having heard one. It was both screechingly high—the memory of gulls he had dreamt of flickered briefly into his consciousness—and profoundly low, shaking him deep within, as though the mountain itself were trying to speak. As it faded, Josyff thought he saw the upper reaches of the chamber walls bending and buckling, like waves at a shore edge.

He blinked, and the impression was gone, as was the noise. It was replaced by the sound of his own gasping breath and by the exclamations of Badr and Nyk.

Badr was stamping his foot and shaking his hand violently. Nyk was leaning against the counterweight with his head in his hands.

Josyff stood up, unsteadily.

"What happened?" he asked Badr.

"God knows," Badr replied, through gritted teeth. "The crowbar just slammed into that damn thing and took me with it. I don't know how I avoided getting my fingers broken. As it was, it just caught the end of my fingers." He paused to grimace and blow on his fingertips. "I'll be all right in a moment. See how Nyk is."

Nyk, too, was now standing, gingerly massaging one side of his face.

"Banged my face," Nyk said, before he was asked. "It's nothing. What the devil happened? It was opening, then..." His voice faded and he gave a helpless gesture.

"It's *your* drawbridge, you tell *us*." Badr was forcing words out in a continuing attempt to take his mind off the pain in his fingers.

"I don't know, I don't know," Nyk said, as if the repetition might inspire him in some way. He put his hand hesitantly against the face of the counterweight. "This, I can push by hand..." Once again the sentence was left hanging. He took his hand away, stepped back and looked at the unyielding surface. His voice was steadier when he spoke, though with a hint of desperation in it. "I know this machinery inside out. I look after it, I understand it. It's clever, reliable, simple, it works, it... There's nothing—*nothing*—that could make this happen. If some part had somehow... fallen off... which isn't possible—we'd be able to see it. No, it can't do it, not jam shut like this. And as for slamming like that..."

"Well, jammed it is, and slammed it did," Josyff said. "And with enough force to knock all three of us over."

An uncomfortable silence fell on the trio.

"We *have* to get it open," Nyk said eventually.

"If what you say about getting out of here is true, then indeed we have," Josyff said. "But we're not going to do it this way." He nudged one of the crowbars with his foot. "That's perfectly clear. You two were hurt and I was lucky—just dumped on my backside. Who's to say *what* might happen if we try again? Are you all right, now?"

This last was addressed to Badr, who was still pacing up and down nursing and shaking his hand, but whose foot stamping had stopped.

"Yes," he replied with a rueful smile. "It's down to unbearable pain now. I'm just waiting for the time when I can look back on this."

Josyff chuckled at this unexpected humour, and turned to Nyk.

"And your face?"

Nyk's fingers tested his cheek. "I think it'll be tender for a day or so, but no harm done. It was the shock, mainly. It was as though someone pushed me. Just couldn't stop myself."

Josyff took unequivocal charge.

"Gentlemen, this is obviously serious, but it's not yet urgent. I suggest we retreat and regroup in the face of superior force. Let's find Qualto and reflect on this over a little food."

They did not have to find Qualto however. He and Esyal were heading hurriedly across the courtyard as the three of them emerged into the bright snowlight.

"Did you feel that?" Qualto asked, obviously agitated. "What was it?"

"What was what?" Josyff asked.

Qualto's arms fluttered. "That rumbling, that shaking. Surely you heard it—felt it. I thought the place was going to fall down. Very alarming."

Josyff forestalled an open-air discussion. "Let's get into the warm and talk there," he said, pointing towards the open door. Qualto turned about as one of his busy hands made a signal of agreement. Nevertheless, regardless of Josyff's injunction, he continued with his tale as they walked the short distance.

"I'd just taken Esyal to find some clothes in the stores when everything started to shake—even the walls and the floors—you could feel it..." He shuddered. "And a deep rumbling sound—like someone rolling a huge boulder. All the clothes were jigging about on the racks—they looked like things possessed. The room seemed to be going round and round. I thought I was going to be sick."

The warmth of the Keep closed about them as Nyk closed the door and Josyff glanced as Esyal. She was pale, and patently exerting control over herself but, catching his look, she nodded to confirm what Qualto had said.

They came to the common room and by some unspoken consent all sat down around the table, rather than in the more comfortable chairs ringed about the fire.

"When did this happen?" Nyk asked.

"Just now," Qualto replied. "As long as it takes to get from the stores to the courtyard."

Josyff and Badr looked at Nyk. He nodded but did not speak.

"Everything was shaking, you say?" Badr asked Qualto. "Floors, walls?"

"Everything," Qualto confirmed.

"It's been an earth tremor—a slight earthquake—I'll wager," Badr said. "It must have happened just as we were struggling with the drawbridge. We were just too preoccupied to notice any noises and shaking. It was probably something similar that moved the ladders in the book room last night."

"There was no noise last night," Qualto objected. "And the walls and floors weren't shaking."

Badr gave an airy wave. "Well, *something* woke me. I wouldn't pretend to be an expert on earthquakes, but I remember one from when I was a boy, travelling with my father—only a small one, but it made *everything* shake—very frightening—feeling the ground you're standing on moving. And they come in clusters—big shocks and little ones—little ones could have been happening for days. Why you didn't notice anything last night, I don't know, but there's no saying how a massive building like this would respond to vibrations."

"That's true," Josyff agreed. "And it's as good an explanation as any. It was no small thing that slammed that drawbridge on us, just now." He turned to Nyk. "If it's balanced so delicately, perhaps, like Badr's ladders, it was responding to smaller tremors when it was opening and closing of its own accord."

Nyk nodded appreciatively, more than a little relieved to have a mystery reduced to a problem. "I suppose it'd account for what's been happening—and if there's been movement of the ground itself, maybe the pivots have been misaligned. That could jam it badly. I'll have a look afterwards." He drifted into practical considerations. "Mind you, I don't know how we can fix it if that's happened."

Qualto was still doubtful. "We've never had anything like that before."

"They're rare," Badr said, matter of fact. "Very rare in this country."

"Do you think there'll be any more?" Qualto asked.

Badr waved a hasty disclaimer and repeated his claim not to be an expert.

"Perhaps even that... voice... we heard last night was something to do with it," Josyff said. "Parts of the building... moving... creaking, maybe. And I seem to remember reading somewhere that all manner of odd things happen before an earthquake—mysterious lights appearing, animals being agitated—picking up things that we can't feel."

The prospect of a rational, albeit unusual, explanation to the events of the past few days was alluring, but even as he spoke, Josyff knew that this was wrong. His voice rang in his head with the echoing urgency of a frightened child shouting in the dark. With a certainty that defied reason, he knew that there had been no earthquake—no new cracks would be found in the building, Nyk would not find the drawbridge pivots damaged—there had been a will behind the closing of the drawbridge—an intent.

"You've gone quite pale."

Esyal's voice made him jump.

Josyff forced a smile and unearthed a hasty excuse. "I'm fine, thanks. Probably just a bit of reaction to that fall."

"It certainly sent you staggering," Badr confirmed.

Josyff shrugged and somehow managed to force aside his unwelcome revelation. "No harm's been done—except to my dignity. As I said, I think a slight earth tremor's as good an explanation as we can manage at the moment. Unless you need any special help, Nyk, Badr and I will get back to our work."

"I'll look in the old logs," Qualto said. "See if there's ever been anything like this before."

"Logs?" queried Josyff.

"The records of the work we do," Qualto explained. "Keeping them isn't the most favourite job for some of us." He looked significantly at Nyk, who studiously avoided his gaze. "But I quite enjoy it." He became enthusiastic. "They go back for I don't know how many years. I keep threatening to dig out the really old volumes and study the place properly, but..."

"You never get round to it." Nyk completed the sentence, a note of satisfaction in his voice indicating that this was no new boast.

"Well, now your routine's been thoroughly disturbed, this might be the opportunity," Josyff said. "Do you think they go back to the time when this place was built?"

Qualto became pensive. "I wouldn't imagine so," he said. "But to tell the truth I don't know. The older logs are a little... disordered."

"They're a mess," Nyk intruded. "Looking after them's not on the Duty Orders so they've been neglected for years."

"Even so, I'd be interested to look at them, if it's no problem," Josyff said.

"It's no problem, providing you don't mind dust," Nyk replied.

"Maybe I could start tidying them up."

It was Esyal. She looked at Qualto.

"I shouldn't think helping you is going to take all day and I've got to do something useful while I'm here."

Qualto looked at Nyk who gave a moue of indifference. "No harm in it," he said. Then the moue became a slight grin. "Though you'd better have a look at them before you volunteer for too much."

"They *are* bad," Qualto agreed.

"I'm growing more intrigued by the moment," Josyff said. "Can we have a quick look now, before we start work again?"

"Certainly," Nyk said. "They're kept by the book room. They..."

He stopped abruptly.

Standing in the doorway was Henk, his arms around the apparently unconscious form of Adroyan.

CHAPTER 27

There was momentary silence and then confusion as everyone stood up quickly, Qualto knocking over his chair in his haste.

Badr was the first to reach Henk, who was struggling under the weight of the big man, and then Adroyan was lying on the couch that Esyal had occupied the previous night. Henk dropped gratefully into his usual chair. He was breathing heavily.

"Are you all right?" Nyk asked him, bending forward and looking anxiously into his face.

"I will be as soon as I get my breath back." The reply was accompanied by a wave of the hand that was both reassuring and dismissive. After a brief hesitation, Nyk appeared to be satisfied and, without leaving his friend, he turned to look at the others, gathered around the motionless figure of Adroyan.

"What happened?" he asked, still speaking to Henk.

"No idea," Henk replied. "There was this rumbling and roaring... everything was shaking. I thought the place was falling down. Frightened me to death. I was running for the door when I found him—in the Great Hall." He extended his arms sideways. "Flat out on his back, gawping up at the ceiling, mouth open, eyes wide. Thought maybe something had come loose and hit him, but he was in the middle of the Hall—nothing near him."

Nyk swung back to him. "You carried him all the way from the Great Hall!" he exclaimed. "You could have killed yourself. Why didn't you come

131

and get us? You're no Spring chicken..." He was raising his hands in apology even as he spoke. "I'm sorry. That... earthquake... or whatever, has shaken us all up." He indicated Josyff and Badr with a floundering gesture. "We were in the... oh, never mind, never mind. How is he?"

"Well, he's breathing, and his pulse seems fine—just like Esyal the other day," Josyff replied.

"There's no head injury that I can find," Badr added.

Henk levered himself up out of his chair. "What earthquake?" he demanded of the group.

"That's what we think it was," Badr said. "And what moved the ladders in the book room last night."

"We don't get earthquakes round here," Henk declared with contemptuous certainty.

"We've no other explanation," Nyk intervened. "It knocked us three scattering." A gesture swept over Josyff and Badr. "Qualto and Esyal felt it, you felt it, and something knocked this one out. What else could shake a building like that?"

Before Henk could reply, the sound of a sharp intake of breath intruded and Adroyan was sitting upright, his eyes wide and his arms extended to the side as though he were trying to keep two opposing forces apart.

The watching circle widened briefly before closing about him again, concerned.

"How are you, sir?" Josyff asked.

Adroyan's black eyes focused on him sharply. "What happened?"

"We don't know, sir. We think there's been an earthquake. Henk found you unconscious in the Great Hall and brought you here. Perhaps you slipped and fell."

"The Great Hall..." Adroyan echoed. Then alarm lit his face and his hands came up again, though this time as if to protect himself. Almost immediately however, an icy control took over and he swung his legs off the couch and made to stand up.

Josyff laid a restraining hand on him. "Give yourself a moment, sir. You may be injured."

Adroyan hesitated then stood up, making Josyff step back. "I recall. I was overwhelmed," he said, as though that answered a question. He looked round the room, his eyes distant. "But I am awakening now." Then he seemed to recollect something and his gaze turned back to Josyff.

"Why are you not working? This... place... must be measured... *must* be measured... as soon as possible."

Josyff fought down a spasm of anger sufficiently to control his voice.

"It will be, sir. And if you're sure you're well, Badr and I will get back to our work right away. But *someone* will have to help Nyk with the drawbridge. If the quake has actually moved its bearings we may not be able to open it."

"What do you mean?"

"The drawbridge, sir. It's jammed—jammed shut. Nyk, Badr and I were trying to free it when the quake happened. We..."

"Jammed *shut*, you say?"

"Yes, sir. And according to Nyk, it's going to be no easy task getting out of here if we can't free it." Though he had asked no question, he deliberately adopted the manner of someone waiting for instructions from a superior.

Adroyan did not reply at once and, it seemed to Josyff that, albeit only slightly, his head bowed and his shoulders lifted, as though for a moment he was contemplating a defeat of some kind. When he spoke, however, his voice betrayed no such thought, and his posture was straight and tall again.

"Yes, that must be attended to. We must not allow this place to bind us here." He looked at Nyk. "Find out exactly what has happened and report to me."

"He won't find anything."

It was Henk. He was standing in the doorway, as though about to leave.

"That was no earthquake—I told you, they don't happen around here. It was the building. It's waking. It's changing. It's..."

"Henk!" hissed Qualto, stepping forward, his hands flapping his colleague to silence. "Enough! Enough foolishness. What's got into you lately?" Embarrassed irritation put an edge in his voice. "You spend too much time wandering about in places where you've no need to be. You'll go... melancholy mad." Qualto managed to inject a little humour into this faltering conclusion, making it with a smile and a conciliatory gesture. His voice returned to normal. "Badr says there might have been lots of little earthquakes moving the place, shaking it, for days now. Too small for us to notice them. Who knows what effect they might have had on us?" He turned to Josyff. "They might have been responsible for your own disturbed nights, mightn't they?"

The thought had not occurred to Josyff, but he felt an unexpected sense of relief. Maybe, indeed, there had been subtle tensions building within the fabric of the Keep that had affected him... and Henk. But the relief faded as quickly as it had come, driven out by the same inner, if unreasoned, certainty he had felt before. Whatever was happening, it was something other than earthquakes.

Nevertheless, he replied, "Quite possibly."

Henk was shaking his head.

"Think whatever you want," he said, with an air of finality. "I'm leaving as soon as I can."

Nyk and Qualto exchanged an exasperated glance.

"Well, regardless of the fact that you've got your tour to finish, none of us are going anywhere while the drawbridge is jammed shut," Nyk said bluntly.

Henk gaped at him, uncomprehending.

"It can't jam—it's balanced," he said, part statement, part question.

"It's jammed," Nyk announced definitively. "Three of us couldn't lever it open just now." He rubbed his face. "Go and see for yourself."

Henk turned from side to side a couple of times before stepping back into the room. He looked round at each of the others. Josyff was unable to meet his gaze and turned away.

Qualto had no such difficulty. He gave a brief grimace of distress and pity, and stepping forward, took Henk's arm.

"Henk, you fret too much. This place is only bricks and mortar..."

"Stone," Henk interrupted.

"Stone, then," Qualto conceded with a soft, explosive laugh. "*Stone* and mortar. But that's all. It's a queer place, but it's still just a heap of carefully arranged rocks. It can't think, it can't move... or change itself... can it?" Henk made to reply, but Qualto pressed on. "You keep yourself too much to yourself at times—let the place get on top of you—and wander into places where we've no need to go. Your memory probably plays tricks on you—all these endless passages and rooms." He flicked a thumb towards Josyff and Badr. "Just wait until they've been working for a few days— they'll tie it down in ink and paper, then see if it can move."

Henk cast a doubtful glance towards the surveyors. "You mean well, Qualto," he said. "But you're wrong. Something's grievously amiss with this place..." This time it was he who pressed on as Qualto tried to speak. "But I'll say no more about it. Time will tell." He turned to Josyff. "I doubt your work is going to be what you think, surveyor, but..." He touched his hand to his mouth in a token of intended silence.

Nyk intervened. "It'll be easier for all of us if we keep to simple practicalities—and the only real problem we have at the moment is that, for whatever reason, the drawbridge is jammed shut and we're trapped here. It's nothing desperate for now, none of us have anywhere to go anyway, but sooner or later we'll have to get it open... or find another way out of here, and I don't relish that!" He spoke directly to Henk. "Come and help me find out what's happened."

Henk grunted a cursory agreement and Nyk spoke to Josyff.

"I'm *assuming* none of us have anywhere to go—will this problem with the drawbridge interfere with your work?"

"Not for some while," Josyff replied. "Later on we might need to do some confirmatory work on the outside, but the real work's here and there's plenty of it. That said, let me know if the problem proves intractable. If we have to find some other way out of here I think it's going to need all our best efforts."

Nyk was confident. "We'll sort it out all right, I'm sure. Are you fully recovered, sir?"

This last was addressed to Adroyan, who was standing by the fire, seemingly aloof from this debate.

"I am," Adroyan replied. He turned to Henk. "Your concern was unnecessary. Take me to where you found me."

Adroyan's tone overrode Nyk's request for help but Henk looked between the two of them.

Nyk nodded. "Come to the gatehouse when... the gentleman... has finished with you," he said. Adroyan did not seem to notice the hint of sarcasm in Nyk's wilful hesitation, and left the room without further remark. With a half-apologetic shrug to Nyk and the others, Henk followed him.

"Well, as the patient seems to be fully recovered and the cause of all our mysteries has been found, I'll get back to the gatehouse myself. See if I can find out exactly what's happened." Nyk raised a caustic eyebrow, implicitly enlisting the others as co-conspirators.

Josyff had been taken aback by Adroyan's brusque manner and he was glad he had gone. The prospect of being confined in this place with such an individual for any length of time cast an unpleasant shadow across his thoughts, but he did not respond to Nyk's unspoken offer.

"I'd like to have a look at these logs you keep, if I may," he said to Qualto. "Can you spare a few minutes to show me where they are?"

Adroyan seemed almost to be scenting the air as he and Henk emerged into the Great Hall.

"You were over there," Henk said, pointing.

"Show me. Show me precisely." Adroyan's tone was authoritative.

Henk shot him a surly glance and made no attempt to disguise a sigh of irritation as he strode out towards the middle of the Hall. Frowning, he turned round a few times, looking alternately at the floor and then at the watching statues.

"You'll understand, sir, that I was... agitated... when I found you—the place was shaking and rumbling—never known the likes. I just picked you up and dragged you out. Didn't think to take out a tape to measure where you'd fallen."

This sarcasm, Adroyan *did* notice, and he turned sharply to its source. Henk, however, head craning forward, met his gaze with an unyielding one of his own.

There was silence.

"Yes," Adroyan said eventually, his voice flat and without any concession. "Show me as closely as you can."

Henk tapped a foot, grunted, "Here," and then moved to one side.

Adroyan slowly circled the spot, mimicking Henk's movement, his gaze intent and shifting from the floor to the statues. Then, apparently satisfied, he straightened and turned to face the statues squarely. Henk took a pace backwards as if expecting some strange, perhaps violent, event.

But nothing happened.

Until, that is, he became aware of a soft and distant whispering filling the Hall.

CHAPTER 28

Henk could not have said when the sound began—merely that he realized it was there. Vague and hesitant at first, with the uneasy quality of an image hovering in the corner of the eye which would vanish on direct inspection, it changed, somewhere beyond Henk's perception, becoming not so much louder as more distinct. Yet still indefinable.

A wind, softly moaning through unseen chimney stacks?

Waves breaking on a distant shore?

Countless voices, rising and falling, carried by an unhelpful and shifting wind?

All these things and none of them.

Henk's head craned even further forward than usual as he found himself drawn into listening intently. But part of him wanted to flee, as he had fled the rumbling and shaking that had led him to this place and the unconscious Adroyan but a little while before. For though the sound was indistinct, there was a fearful quality to it: an urgency? A striving?

War! Henk realized. Desperate, horrific, and total. It was as though he was suddenly on the fringes of some grim and awful arena: an inadvertent witness.

Yet what truly chilled him was not the bloodstained rage and madness of battlefield slaughter, but a cold and alien strangeness—a quality beyond anything he had ever known. And too, a vastness. Amid the swirling turmoil, he was the least of things. His destruction, his complete annihilation, would be both effortless and unnoticed.

"What is this?"

He heard his own voice echoing distantly.

There was no reply.

Adroyan was standing motionless, his arms extended, his head thrown back, and his eyes closed. Henk fancied he could see a shimmering about him, like the air dancing above a sun-baked horizon. He blinked wilfully and slowly, trying to still the disturbance, bring the man into focus. But to no avail. Adroyan was both near and far away, and it seemed that the shimmering was not merely about him, but passing through him, almost as he might appear beneath fast and turbulent water.

Henk realized that he was trembling; the shaking of his body resonating to this rippling distortion. He felt his legs beginning to buckle and, for a moment, a surge of panic that threatened to unman him completely. But some other resource intervened and, with a teeth-gritting effort, he stamped his foot and clenched his fists to force himself back in control of his body. The impact steadied him a little and gave him his voice again. He repeated his question.

"What is this?"

The noise took his words and twisted and spun them so that they danced and whirled like dead leaves in a blustering autumn breeze before being scattered and lost.

His alarm abruptly became an unreasoning anger and, without thinking, he was stepping towards Adroyan—the apparent cause, or the focus, of this disturbance. Washing about him, the whispering rose and fell, insistently urging him forward. Only as he came within arm's reach did he realize that his fists were still clenched and that he was possessed by an intention to strike Adroyan down. Well used to the isolation of the Keep and to living in close proximity to only two companions for long periods at a time, Henk had no easy inclination to violence and the realization jolted him, jolted him sufficiently to halt his purposeful advance and deny this intention. As he stopped, the sound wavered, as too did Adroyan's near-ecstatic posture.

A thought closer to his true self came into Henk's mind.

"Is anything wrong, sir?"

As if foundering on the concern in his voice, the sound changed; the conflict within it intensified until it became a screeching, like fingernails down glass. Henk's hands came to his ears, but even as he did so, the sound seemed to fold in on itself—at once both triumphing and destroying itself.

The Great Hall was silent.

Not even an echo of the disturbance lingered.

Henk lurched forward a pace to catch his balance, but Adroyan staggered backwards some distance before he recovered. Briefly his face was riven with confusion, wavering between despair and revelation. Henk stared at him, wide-eyed, despite some instinct telling him to look away.

"Yes, yes, yes." Adroyan was murmuring softly to himself. "This *is* the place. The nexus—the knot—the great knot, which bound the Powers and denied us victory."

He looked directly at Henk and this time Henk *did* turn his face away from what he saw there.

"But the time is near, we—*we*—will fathom the mysteries of this place—unfurl the binding hurt—mend time—release the..."

He stopped, and his eyes, hitherto focused on some unknown distance, became clearer. He straightened, and, his voice normal again, asked, "What did you hear?"

Henk found this abrupt reversion to normality just as unsettling as the unexpected passion he had just witnessed and he had to fight down a powerful urge to turn and run.

"A noise," he said after a long moment under Adroyan's now coldly indifferent gaze. There being no immediate response, he felt the need to elaborate. "Very odd—never heard anything like it before... even with a gale blowing outside. Something to do with this... earthquake, maybe?" He was about to ask, "Did you hear it before—when I found you?" but thought better of it.

Adroyan glanced around the hall. "Probably," he said casually, neither answering the question nor furthering the exchange. But Henk saw the brief look in his eyes. The triumph and defeat that he had heard in the noise were there too, but mingled with doubt and anxiety.

"Probably," he echoed, dully, to end the conversation. He had no desire to stay longer than he had to in the Great Hall, especially with Adroyan.

"Do you need me any more?" he asked. "Nyk might be needing help with the drawbridge."

"Yes, the drawbridge," Adroyan said, attentive now. He made an urgent gesture. "It must be released. We must not be held here. There are things to be done—important. Go and help."

Henk needed no further encouragement and, after an awkward shuffle, was striding away with an untypical vigour in his step. He did not look back as he reached the archway that led from the hall. He would have seen little had he done so, for Adroyan was standing motionless, his head inclined slightly, as if listening to something.

"I did tell you they were a little disordered," Qualto said, apologetically.

The room where the Keep's logs were kept was reached from the book room and they had spent a few minutes in there first. Badr had demonstrated his knowledge of the cataloguing system, carefully echoing Qualto's injunction, "leave the books on the tables," and then shown Josyff the ease with which the ladders moved.

"It *must* have been some kind of an earth tremor," Josyff concluded again, though more for want of something to say than from any conviction.

"We call this the Archive," Qualto said. "A bit pompous, I suppose, but..." He left the sentence unfinished.

Josyff, Badr and Esyal gazed round at the room. It was small compared with most of the rooms in the Keep they had encountered so far; smaller even than the common room. And it was indeed disordered. The shelves lining four of its five walls were filled with books, stacks of papers, boxes and parcels. Randomly distributed amongst these were jars of pens and pencils, disordered heaps of writing paper, several small clocks, a variety of dust-covered and sorry-looking ornaments, and a liberal dispersion of less readily-identifiable objects. A battered desk at the centre of the room was similarly decorated, and the floor was little better—cluttered as it was with boxes too large for the shelves, and lumpy, anonymous sacks between which isolated stashes of brushes and brooms rose, sentinel-like. Only a hasty intervention by Qualto prevented Josyff from tripping over a bucket.

He gave a guilty smile as he balanced the bucket precariously on an already unsteady box.

"Perhaps junk room might be more appropriate," he said.

Josyff searched briefly for a kinder description to ease his host's awkwardness, but found none. So he laughed.

"I'll have to play the bureaucrat," he said. "'Not my department'—but I'm sure you know where everything is."

"I doubt it," Qualto confessed. "Not in here. I've no idea why we've let this place get into such a state—it's not as if we were short of space. I really must get round to..." Again he left the sentence unfinished.

Esyal intervened. "I can tidy this up, if you want. Perhaps start sorting out your old records—your logs."

"As well as helping with the cooking, and helping the surveyors?" Qualto said, giving her a wry look.

Esyal's hands fluttered momentarily, before she reaffirmed firmly. "I have to do something."

Qualto gave a shrug of acceptance. "Well, it *does* need doing. I suppose you might as well. With all that's happened these past few days, everything's upside down. I'm sure we'll all end up doing all manner of unfamiliar things. I certainly can't see our daily routines getting back to normal for a long time."

"Until you're finally pulling up the drawbridge behind us all, eh?" Josyff said, with a chuckle.

Qualto responded in kind. "No disrespect intended, surveyor. It's just that we're not used to change around here. The odd little calamity now and then—something leaking, something squeaking, something not working, but..."

"I sympathize. I don't imagine you choose to work in a place like this for the excitement."

Qualto let out what might almost have been a sigh. "No indeed. Though I'm not sure whether the Keep needs us or whether we need the Keep." He was silent and thoughtful for a moment then he clapped his hands sharply and became brisk. "Anyway. Anyway. Change is change. Heaven knows, no two days out here in the mountains are ever really the same. And you're all here, and most welcome. Esyal—thank you for your offer—set to—tidy this place up—bring order to our disordered records—and you'll be most welcome in my kitchen any time, as well." He took Esyal by the arm and led her to a set of shelves by the door. Josyff and Badr drifted behind them, caught up in the backwash of this sudden activity.

In contrast to the rest of the room, these shelves were comparatively tidy; serried ranks of stout books faced the advancing group resolutely. They were set out in groups, each with a different coloured binding, though all were embossed in gold with the same design on their spines. Qualto picked one and riffled through the pages for the others to see.

"There doesn't seem to be much written in it," Josyff said, looking over his shoulder.

Qualto stopped and placed his hand palm down on the page, to hold it open. There was a date and then three or four lines of clear but not particularly neat handwriting.

"One page per day it says in the Duty Orders, and one page per day it is," he said.

"And yours not to reason why, eh?"

"Indeed," Qualto confirmed with a knowing smile.

Josyff followed his mood. "What happens if you have a busy day?"

Qualto's smile broadened. "Oh, we're allowed a degree of literary discretion to cope with the likes of the last few days," he replied. "And it's not as if we're short of new books." He indicated the lower shelves, also full of the same kind of books. Josyff bent down and picked one at random. Every page was blank. He could not help expressing his surprise as he replaced it and scanned the other waiting volumes that filled the shelves.

"Good grief, even at one page a day these'll last you forever."

Qualto answered his next question before he asked it.

"The Estate sent them years ago." He made a disowning gesture. "Maybe someone bought a job lot for a good price."

"I can't see them being cheap however good the price." It was Badr. He was idly thumbing through one of the empty books. It had a pale blue cover. "It's good paper and this binding looks expensive to me." He took another and compared it with the first. "And look at these covers. Is this design the same on all of them? It's very elaborate—here..." He offered the books to Josyff who took them after a brief hesitation. He turned them towards the light to examine the covers.

"I haven't really looked at them," Qualto said. "I think they're all the same. That kind of... scrolling pattern is common on Estate documents. I don't know if it's just a traditional style or if it has some special significance."

But Josyff scarcely heard him. He was looking intently at the design neatly scored into the soft cover. Lines of varying thickness and depth wound their way from the spine to fill both covers. Sharp-edged and clear, they twisted and wove themselves into a myriad elaborate patterns and intricate knots.

Or...

Was it perhaps just one line?

He turned the book over several times, and brought it closer to his face.

It *was* one line, he decided—one single thread. Innumerable short branches deceived the eye into seeing multiplicity where there was none, but there was definitely only one line threading its way through the seeming confusion. He felt a small frisson of triumph at this discovery and something prompted him to bring the other book closer to compare the two. He noticed as he did so that all the branches tapered delicately and appeared not so much to end as to plunge into the depths of the book.

Scanning from one book to the other and moving them back and forth, he was about to remark that the patterns were not quite the same, that there were subtle differences between them, when his eyes began to shift their focus. Before he could respond to this, the two patterns were dancing and wavering, moving to a rhythm which was suddenly pulsing through his mind.

The images came together.

He was falling...

...falling...

Into pale blue depths, with golden lines singing all about him.

CHAPTER 29

The singing touched him, passed through him, rising and falling to a pulse that he could not hear but which he sensed and which pervaded everything.

A meaning came to him, though he heard no words...

"This is one that hears... (reaches? touches?)... us."

Somehow it stilled his mind's screaming denial of what his senses were telling him. Instead, it became a mixture of both curiosity and anger.

He was no longer falling—if he had ever been. He was floating—hovering in the pale blueness, watching the golden lines gently twisting and turning as though caught in a soft breeze that only they could feel. He reached out to touch one as it came nearby, but his hand closed about nothing. Had it moved away from him? Had his hand passed through it? Or was it actually some vast object in the far distance? He could not tell, he realized. Near and far seemed to have no meaning in this place.

"What is happening?" he heard himself asking—demanding. "Who are you? What are you? What are you doing to me?"

The lines danced and jigged in response, as did the singing. He had an impression of incredible fragility; of someone—something—handling a precious object of great value and great delicacy, at once exhilarated and fearful, lest ignorance or awkwardness might allow it to slip away, perhaps even shatter it beyond repair.

"Don't be afraid," he said, quite aware of the incongruity of the advice.

"*Don't be afraid.*" The message echoed back to him. Laced about it were emotions that for a moment threatened to overwhelm him: he was salvation, he was doom; hope and doubt mingled in equal proportions. Then he was pervaded by a terrible weariness—a battlefield weariness, a deep longing for rest, for peace, for all this to be over. Yet, at the same time there was the knowledge that this could never truly be—the battle must continue—there was no choice—not to fight was to be overwhelmed. The starkness of the certainty chilled him and some part of him started to reach into this knowledge. But even as it did, so the fear, the sense of fragility, returned—a tenuous grip was failing; fingers were slowly losing their purchase on a narrow lip of rock.

"*Another. There is another. Do not... let...*"

The plea was clear, as was the desperate effort behind it, but after a brief hesitation, the words, if words they were, ended abruptly, as though a door had been slammed shut—or straining fingertips had finally lost their hold.

"Any insights, Surveyor?"

Qualto's question jolted Josyff as it filled the space left by the sudden departure of...

Of what...?

He was in the Archive again, staring intently at the two books.

"I'm so sorry," Qualto exclaimed guiltily. "I didn't realize you were so engrossed."

Having become almost instinctively used to concealing his feelings under the New Order, Josyff managed to disguise his agitation in a theatrical shrug and a conceding laugh. This also gave him the chance to note his companions and it needed little perceptiveness to see that whatever had just happened to him—and it had felt like many minutes—had apparently passed unnoticed. It must have happened in an instant! Terrible questions that had begun on the previous nights began to reassert themselves, but while he was struggling silently to regain his mental balance he found himself giving voice to the thought that had immediately preceded his disturbing translation.

"They *are* slightly different."

He carefully cleared a space on the desk and laid out the books purposefully.

"No great insights though, but see."

He willed his hand steady as his finger slowly marked out a line on one cover and then its equivalent on the other. Qualto leaned forward, his forehead furrowed with concentration. Badr joined him.

"You're right," Qualto said. "It's not much, but they *are* different. You've keen eyes to spot that. Being a surveyor, I suppose." Josyff made no answer.

Badr picked up two more books, then a further two and, after a quick but intense inspection, announced, "They're *all* different." He shook his head in disbelief. "Amazing—the changes are quite slight but they seem to progress from volume to volume. Very odd. Very impressive too. I wonder how they did it—these can't be hand-worked, surely?"

"More likely a fault on the printing machine," Josyff offered.

Badr looked doubtful, but returned the books to the shelves without pursuing the matter.

Josyff clapped his hands softly. "Anyway, you and I had better get back to work while there's some of the day left to us. I'm sure Nyk'll let us know if he wants any more help." He looked around the room, raised his eyebrows in mock despair and said to Qualto, "We'll leave you and Esyal to get on with your... reorganizing."

He did not feel the lightness he affected however, and he threw himself into his work with considerable vigour for the rest of that day. Not only out of a sense of too much time already having been lost, but to prevent the questions that were now clamouring for attention from rising to dominate his thoughts. Concentration on the familiar professional routine, with its constant decision-making, checking, re-checking and meticulous record-ing of information, kept these largely at bay and helped him to put time between the present and what had happened in the Archive. He sensed a need to reassure himself of the solidity and reality of this place and, more disturbingly, of his own sanity. For that was threatening to become his greatest concern. All the strange things that had happened to him since his arrival at the Keep—the voices, the clock, the gulls, and finally the eerie blue world he had found himself in, seemed to have no rational explana-tion, other than that his mind was fevered in some way—he was either ill or... slipping into insanity.

Could it be a reaction to the strain of silently struggling to survive under the enigmatic will of the New Order for so long? Or was it due to working high in the mountains, or perhaps nothing more that tiredness due to all the trekking through them he had done recently?

None of these conclusions rang true. Physically, he felt fine—the clear air and silence of the mountains refreshed rather than enervated, despite events. Mentally, he was having no difficulty with his work—indeed, he was pleased with the rapport he had quickly established with Badr.

As for insanity, he consoled himself with the idea that it would be the very last thought to occur to him if his mind was actually failing. And some of the happenings had been witnessed by others: Badr's experience in the book room the previous evening, the voice calling out during the night, the drawbridge, the rumbling and shaking. The rest could reasona-bly be attributed to dreams, with the conspicuous exception of the incident in the Archive. That was particularly disturbing. Not least because none of the others present had noticed anything—whatever had happened, had, for them, passed in an instant.

"Do you want to plot this?" Badr asked as they finished a section of work towards the end of the day.

Josyff was stretching and he havered for a moment before deciding. "No, leave it for tomorrow. Come to it fresh. It's been a... peculiar... day. Not to say a peculiar *few* days. We've done well. It's a joy to be working with decent equipment at last. We'll soon get this place sown up and be on our way back to..."

"Civilization?"

"Normality," Josyff suggested, more diplomatically.

"Always assuming the drawbridge is open," Badr pointed out.

"Thanks for reminding me," Josyff said sourly.

Unexpectedly, Badr chuckled. "Maybe we should start working on some way to get out of here."

"Maybe we should," Josyff retorted. "And maybe we will." He closed the lid of one of the instrument boxes and tapped it significantly. "But only when *this* job's properly finished."

"It could prove to be serious," Badr went on, more anxiously. "Counterbalanced, the whole thing might be light as light, but out of balance it'll be a devil of a weight. Way beyond us to move. And we *are* in the middle of nowhere surrounded by sheer cliffs and a very deep moat."

Josyff was more phlegmatic. "Serious or not, there's nothing we can do about it at the moment. Let's wait and see what Nyk has to say. We could be wasting our time just talking about it. He might have sorted it out already—panic over."

"And if he hasn't?"

"Tomorrow's tomorrow." He lowered his voice. "Besides, I'd be very surprised if someone somewhere wasn't looking out for the interests of our representative of the Ordrans. I'm sure resources will become available, as required."

Badr bowed his head in acknowledgement.

A little later, washed and changed, Josyff lowered himself luxuriously into an armchair in his room.

He allowed the questions to return that he had largely kept at bay during the day. They were less insistent. A good day's work had done much to calm what he now saw as a tension that had been steadily mounting since he arrived. Even while working he had managed to allay most of his concerns, at least for the time being, and now he wilfully brought old problem-solving habits to bear on the incident in the Archive—the only one that was still really unsettling him. Somewhere he sensed that he had the answer to this and that it would doubtless emerge if he gave it the opportunity. All he had to do was allow ideas to wander into his thoughts without comment or analysis. However preposterous or improbable they might be, something would emerge, even if he did not recognize it at the time.

Had it been an hallucination? Something peculiar in the material of the book covers? No. The notion made him smile but he let it run. They had had an odd smell, for sure, but only the smell of old books. Had it been a waking dream? He had heard of such things in people deprived of sleep for long periods, but that was not the case here. Despite the trek through the mountains and the disruption of the previous night, he was far from tired. Had the others noticed him drifting off and simply not spoken out of embarrassment? Unlikely, he decided. Badr and Qualto might possibly have behaved like that, but Esyal wouldn't, for sure. Apart from the fact that the conversation had continued unbroken, he had been... wherever he had been... for several minutes.

Occasionally his thoughts wandered away from the Keep—to the Valsen and Adroyan's almost haunted response as they had passed it—to the fortuitous finding of Esyal, who could so easily have died—to Adroyan's guides who were so anxious to return to the village—to the early winter—to his wife. He did not dwell long on any of them, especially his wife. That he missed her he needed no reminding of, and he knew from experience that fretting to be with her again would not make that moment arrive any sooner. Indeed, in marring his concentration it could delay their reunion even longer.

He leaned forward in the chair and rested his head on his hand thoughtfully.

Well, if there was an answer lurking somewhere in his mind, *he* certainly couldn't see it immediately. Not that that really mattered. Just sitting, thinking, would have 'shaken something loose', as he liked to say. He had great faith in the ability of his unconscious mind to solve intractable problems—it had done it often enough before, after all. All he could do, for the moment, he had done. He looked down at his hands, almost expecting them to be shaking, facing as he did two equally unsettling options: that his mind was playing tricks on him—the most likely possibility, he thought— or that something real had happened—which was absurd, of course...

Wasn't it?

But his hands were steady. And his mind was clear. Further, he needed no answers to those questions right now. Do what you're here to do. Do your job. Concern yourself about the reality or otherwise of what had happened as and when it interfered with that!

At Qualto's urging, not to say his insistence, mealtimes were specific and unvarying and the group had already developed the habit of eating together. Nyk, Henk and Badr were already in the common room when Josyff entered. They were looking pensive.

"No solution to our problem, I presume," Josyff said as he sat down.

145

"No," Nyk confirmed. "And it's snowing again."

For some reason he could not have explained, the remark struck Josyff as funny.

"Never snows but it pours, eh?" His chuckle rolled into a laugh which proved to be infectious. Both Badr and Nyk smiled and Henk almost did. Josyff continued. "All of which prompts the question, what's holding us here?—the drawbridge, the snow, or our professional obligations?"

"I'll have another look tomorrow," Nyk said. "But I doubt I—we," he nodded an acknowledgement towards Henk, "will find anything. It's not exactly a complicated piece of equipment. Everything seems to be fine—nothing cracked, displaced, out of level, bent, buckled, twisted..." He splayed his hands then dropped them into his lap. "It's just... immovable. A complete mystery. It's almost as though it was being held to the wall by a magnet or some such force—invisible, but real enough."

"That's an odd thought."

"Yes, it is. But I had it all the same." This time Nyk chuckled.

"You seem easier about it," Josyff said.

"I am and I'm not," Nyk replied. "As you just pointed out, drawbridge or no, we're all stuck here until the snow clears and our jobs are finished, so there's no immediate urgency and certainly nothing to be gained by worrying. Still... I mightn't be so 'easy' if I've not come up with an answer long before then."

He raised a finger as if to mark a change of direction. "That said, I'm sure it came free for a moment—just before Henk arrived. I'd swear I could hear something happening to it. The place seemed to... quiver... and..." His brow furrowed as he tried to recapture the moment. "The bridge seemed to move when I put my hand on it—as it should. At least, I thought it did. Then it was gone. There was a soft thud... and everything was the same again."

"Maybe another tremor," Badr suggested.

"When was it?" Josyff asked, not really knowing why.

Nyk told him. As far as Josyff could judge, the event coincided with his own strange experience in the Archive. "I didn't notice anything," he said, to avoid having to say anything else. There was general head-shaking around the table and the entrance of Esyal ended the exchange. She was carrying a battered scroll.

CHAPTER 30

"Look at this," Esyal said.

She hovered about the table briefly before deciding there was not enough room to spread out the scroll, then retreated to the couch, signalling the others to follow.

"I hope you know where that came from," Badr said, half-jokingly. "Qualto's very fussy about his filing systems."

Esyal raised her eyebrows. "In the book room, maybe, but not in that Archive." She blew some dust off the scroll and then, with an expression of distaste, brushed some from her sleeves. "Some of this dust must be as old as the building."

Kneeling down by the couch, Esyal began carefully unrolling the scroll, using a heavy cushion to hold down the top edge. The others gathered round her.

"I was just browsing to see if I could find out whether there was *some* kind of order to all the scrolls in there—looking to see where I could start—when this slipped off the top of a pile. Set off a small avalanche. Tricky things to stack, scrolls."

The paper was thick and very reluctant to stay flat. It had an aged, yellowish tint which became darker towards the edges. As Esyal unrolled it, small but neat writing was revealed to which marginal notes had been added in a less steady hand. The text was interspersed with small sketches, also neatly drawn and augmented with less tidy notes.

"This caught my eye," Esyal said.

She pointed to a series of sketches of the drawbridge. They showed different views of a scaffolding frame which encased the drawbridge and passed above the wall to overhang the moat. Several men were pulling on an elaborate system of ropes and pulley blocks. More were watching.

"Food, gentlemen, lady."

It was Qualto, entering carrying, with no slight deftness, a large and heavily laden tray.

"What's that?" he inquired as he floated his burden on to the table.

"Perhaps *you* can tell us," Josyff said, as the group dispersed and retreated towards the food.

The scroll rewound itself determinedly and Esyal handed it to Qualto as she passed him. After a brief struggle he opened it and held it up to the light.

"Fine draughtsmanship. Fine penmanship," he said sagely. "From the Archive, is it?"

"It is," Esyal confirmed, as she helped herself to food. "Just came across it. I thought it looked interesting. I haven't read any of it, but it looks to me from those pictures as though they're trying to open the drawbridge."

"It does indeed."

Qualto put the scroll in the middle of the table.

"Any idea how old it is?" Josyff asked.

"None at all," Qualto replied. "Maybe there's a date on it somewhere. It's got to be very old to be written like that, though."

"That kind of handwriting isn't a 'tradition of the Keep', then? Not part of the Duty Orders?" Josyff said, half-teasing.

Qualto took the gentle jibe in good part and returned it in like vein.

"No. Just keeping the records is, that's all—no marks for neatness." He glanced around and spoke to Henk. "By the way, where's Adroyan?"

"Left him in the Great Hall," came an offhand reply. "Shooed me off to help Nyk." He shook his head. "Odd fella, that..."

Josyff intervened quickly before Henk had an opportunity to say anything that might prove injudicious.

"Adroyan has authority signed by the First member of the Ordrans," he said, as casually as he could. "He may even *be* one of the Ordrans."

There was a momentary silence around the table. The Keep and its regular occupants might be far from the centres of political activity but not so far as not to appreciate that this information was not trivial.

"Glad you told us," Nyk said significantly. "I did wonder about him. It didn't seem to me that you and Badr needed any kind of supervision. And Jonal and Aryck weren't too keen on him, I could see that when we met them—and they're an easy-going pair."

"What do you think it means?" Qualto asked no one in particular.

"Probably nothing for you," Josyff replied. "Directly, anyway. It'll be something to do with our work, though I can't think what—he doesn't pretend to know anything about surveying. He probably has to make some kind of assessment about what they've got in mind for the place."

"Which *will* affect us," Qualto said.

Josyff grimaced at the failure of his attempted reassurance. "Maybe. Maybe not," he said. "Whatever they want to do, you're here—you know the place—you've the experience in dealing with it..." His voice tailed off— he had had enough experience of the often arbitrary ways of the New Order to know that such logic was pointless.

Nyk rescued him by expressing the thought that he had voiced to Badr just a little earlier. "Well, if he's so important, then somebody will be waiting to hear from him, I'm sure. Our jammed drawbridge may not be the problem we're envisaging." He smiled mischievously. "It'll be interesting to see how they cope with the moat."

"Yes, indeed," Josyff agreed.

"He's still odd," Henk grumbled and he began recounting the incident in the Great Hall. Josyff could find no opportunity to stop him and finally gave up looking for one—Henk was a grown man, if he wanted to gossip to comparative strangers about someone who could be one of the Ordrans, then he'd have to take his chance. Besides which, he was being unusually loquacious—every detail of what had happened was being related as if he needed to be rid of it, and it was unlikely any interruption would stop him. And the tale was indeed hauntingly strange. He had no reason to doubt that Henk was telling the truth of what he had heard and, given that, it raised yet more unsettling questions about what was happening here.

Henk said Adroyan had called the Keep a nexus, a knot, a binding hurt to be unfurled—to release the Powers. The words meant nothing to Josyff, but they conjured images that, like the voices he had heard, seemed to have meaning even though they were unintelligible. The word "resonance" came to him—a stirring involuntarily invoked by a note sounded elsewhere.

Almost in spite of himself, he asked, "You say you heard voices?"

"'Probably something to do with the earthquake,' he said," Henk mimicked—surprisingly accurately. "I just agreed with him. Seemed the wisest. But it sounded like voices to me. And *he* was listening to them."

"What did they say?" Josyff asked.

"Maybe it *was* something to do with our earthquake," Nyk said, trying to keep the conversation commonplace and before Henk could reply. "It must have happened the same time as the drawbridge came loose."

And the same time as what happened to me in the Archive, Josyff thought. He kept all sign of it from his face but his stomach tightened.

"Well, whatever. Voices, earthquakes, jammed drawbridges, his food's going cold," Qualto protested in a tone that indicated he would be making no special meals for the latecomer, Ordrans or no. "Where did you say you left him?"

"The Great Hall," Henk replied impatiently. "And I didn't leave him, he chased me off. Maybe he wanted a secret word with his voices."

Josyff raised an eyebrow at the unexpected sarcasm. Qualto ignored it.

"You don't think he's wandered off and got lost, do you?" he said.

Nyk's expression became one of exasperation and, his fork hovering uncertainly, he muttered something under his breath. He made to stand up then thought better of it.

"If he's not turned up when we've finished I suppose we'd better go and look for him," he decided.

"He'll be along when he catches a whiff of Qualto's cooking," Esyal said, pushing an empty plate away and puffing out her cheeks to indicate satiety. "That was excellent."

"Thank you, Esyal," Qualto said with heavy emphasis and an inclination of his head. "It's always pleasant to be appreciated."

"I mightn't know who I am, but I know good food, and I seem to remember some manners. Thank *you*."

"Yes indeed," Josyff added. "A fine end to a long and... interesting... day."

"It's not over yet," Nyk said, pushing his chair back. "We have to find our other guest."

"I wouldn't worry," Esyal said with a grin. "If we all get woken up by someone shouting tonight, at least we'll know who it is. Besides, he can't have gone far, can he?"

The three residents replied almost as one.

"Yes, he can."

Josyff looked at Badr and held up a beaker in a mock toast. "Here's to tomorrow. Maybe we'll get a good clean run at this job." Then, turning to Nyk: "We'll help you."

"Thank you, but unfortunately you can't," came the immediate reply. "No disrespect, but you'll probably only get yourselves lost if you go too far. We'll try his room first—and the Great Hall—he may still be there—just forgotten it was meal time—or not hungry. After that..." He gave a resigned shrug followed by a grimace of annoyance. "It's difficult. We just take this place for granted—forget how complicated—and big—it is. And you've not been here long enough yet to realize it. We'll have to work out some kind of a... procedure... when we find him. Just to make sure we've some idea where you all are at any time."

"Good idea," Badr said, remembering his disconcertingly long trek with Henk and Qualto.

"We'll produce plans and lay down markers routinely, as we work," Josyff said. "That should help."

Nyk nodded. "In the meantime, we'd better find our guest." He motioned to Henk and Qualto.

"We'll clear this up for you then," Josyff said to Qualto who was hesitating with a pile of plates in his hand. "We can find the kitchen without getting lost."

"I'll look after them," Esyal intervened proprietorially, seeing Qualto becoming even more uncertain at the prospect of the newcomers invading his kitchen. He did not seem to be completely reassured by this promise, but accepted it with a reasonable grace.

When Nyk, Qualto and Henk had gone, Esyal became even more proprietorial, supervising Josyff and Badr's collecting of the dishes, and directing them towards the kitchen.

As she ushered them in she began opening drawers and cupboards and examining their contents in a manner she would not even have considered had Qualto been there.

"I think I know where everything goes," she claimed. "But he's very tidy, Qualto—*very* tidy." This she said as much to herself as the others, abruptly feeling nervous.

"I think we can manage," Josyff said, turning on the tap and clattering the dishes into the sink. Esyal jumped at the noise and mouthed an edgy, "be careful!"

Josyff looked at her keenly. It occurred to him that for someone who had lost her memory, she seemed to be remarkably unconcerned. He broached the subject directly.

"How's your memory? Has anything come back to you—who you are, where you're from, what you were doing in the mountains?"

On the pretext of continuing to search Qualto's cupboards, Esyal turned away from him as he was speaking.

"No, nothing," she replied. "It's very odd." Composed now, she turned and addressed Josyff's unspoken question. "You'd think I'd be more upset, wouldn't you?" She paused. "Then again, I've never lost my memory before... I think..." She grinned. "So I don't know how I'm supposed to feel. Still, for whatever reason, I'm *not* upset. In fact, I feel fine." She became more serious. "Perhaps it's something to do with being trapped in this place. It doesn't matter who any of us are here, does it? Or what we do. Not while we can't leave. We'll all do what we can to... get along... survive. Later on, when we're back in the real world..." She hesitated. "The outside world, that is, maybe..." She shrugged.

"I hadn't thought about it like that," Josyff said. "As you say, surveyors, Ordrans, resident staff, lost young women—the labels don't really matter at the moment—we're all prisoners in effect."

"And dishwashers," Badr added, precariously waving a plate he was drying, to the horror of the watching Esyal.

"And dishwashers," Josyff agreed, with a laugh. Then he changed the subject abruptly.

"What do you make of Henk's tale about Adroyan and the... voices... in the Great Hall?"

Badr exhaled noisily to indicate he was at a loss. "Well, I've no doubt Henk heard *something*, for sure. But then he was seeing passageways come and go the other night, so..." He shook his head. "Maybe this place gets to you eventually. That said, he seems rational enough—a bit surly, but I've met worse."

"A lot of peculiar things have happened these past few days," Josyff said.

"Well, an earth tremor seems to be the best candidate," Badr said, though without any great conviction. "There'd have been some kind of a build-up to what we all felt and a massive old building like this is going to make some strange noises if it's being twisted and turned."

Scepticism hung in the air.

"That was a voice I heard last night," Esyal said insistently. "It was no creaking floorboard." Remembering the incident, she looked unconsciously towards the rack of knives. "And Adroyan heard it clear enough—as did you."

Josyff attempted no denial. "Which leaves us where?" he said. "If everything that's happened isn't some natural phenomenon—what is it? Ghosts?"

Uncertainty replaced the scepticism.

"We'll have to settle for a mystery," Esyal decided, with a flourish. "Wait and see what else happens. I'm sure, as you said, you'll find a lot of answers as you go about the place. In the meantime we all just carry on doing what we can. You survey, Nyk'll try to open the drawbridge and I'll help Badr and carry on sorting out the Archive."

A little later, Qualto's kitchen tidied to Esyal's satisfaction, they returned to the common room. It was deserted.

"I suppose we'd better take Nyk's advice and stay here," Josyff said. "He's got enough on his hands without having to look for us as well."

There was no dispute. Badr picked up a book from the mantle shelf and settled himself into an armchair by the fire. As if by common consent, Josyff and Esyal made for the scroll still lying on the table. Carefully they unrolled it to reveal the sketches that had first attracted Esyal's attention, then weighing it down with a few ornaments, they sat down to study it.

Then Qualto was at the door, flushed and breathless.

"Something's happened," he said. "Can you come and help?"

CHAPTER 31

As Nyk, Qualto and Henk left the common room in search of Adroyan, Nyk turned to the others irritably.

"We've got enough problems with that damned drawbridge, without one of this lot wandering off and getting lost. There's no saying where he could be." He looked at Henk who shrugged.

"I told you—he just shooed me off—told me to come and help you, which I did, for what it was worth. All of a sudden it was important we opened the drawbridge."

Nyk conceded. "Well, I suppose we'd better look in the obvious place first. If he's not there we'll try his room. Could be he just wasn't hungry. And he doesn't strike me as the kind to bother telling anyone what he's doing."

"Gives me the creeps," Henk muttered as they set off. "Looks right through you."

Nyk made a disparaging noise. "Bigwigs—they're all the same. 'Do this, do that'—not the faintest idea how to do anything themselves, of course, and nary a word of thanks when you do it for them. Or worse, a condescending pat on the head and a 'well done'" he snapped his fingers and made a haughty gesture, "'whatever your name is.'"

Henk said nothing but Qualto chuckled. "Still, better keep your thoughts to yourself," he said. "You heard the surveyor, he might be one of the Ordrans—not someone to take lightly. They certainly didn't—the surveyors—and they seem level enough folk."

"Yes," Nyk agreed. "Don't worry, I've wit enough to keep my mouth shut." He turned to Henk again. "Which is something you could do to practice."

Henk made to reply but Nyk continued. "We might be at the back of beyond but times are changing and, from what I hear, this New Order gets its interfering fingers into everything sooner or later. I don't need to tell you that this is a good posting—suits us all—we get on, we work well together. Wouldn't do to make ourselves too conspicuous—like one of us going on about wanting to leave, for example. You understand?"

Henk gave a reluctant nod.

"Ordrans or not, this fellow's from somewhere *very* high up," Nyk went on. "And Qualto's right. We should do what the surveyors do—they know how to behave with these people, and if they're staying quiet and respectful, we should do the same."

"I'm not arguing," Henk managed.

"You're always arguing," Nyk insisted. "You mightn't say much, but when you do it's contrary and you walk round looking like a question mark if you can't be bothered speaking."

Though Nyk's tone was light and he was speaking as only a friend could, Qualto intervened to silence him and what he could see was Henk's pending rebuttal.

"Later," he hissed. "You want to walk straight into the Great Hall bellowing that kind of stuff?"

Nyk grunted and fell silent as they entered the Great Hall. It was empty. As the echoes of their footsteps faded, the silence of the place folded about them and they stood motionless for a moment.

"Marvellous," Nyk muttered eventually.

"Adroyan... sir!"

Henk's unexpected shout made the others jump.

"For Heaven's sake, you frightened me to death!" Qualto exclaimed at the same time as Nyk protested in similar vein that Adroyan wasn't a dog!

"No. He'd have come for his food if he had been," Henk replied tersely.

"Let's try his room, then," Nyk said.

"If he's not there we could try the gatehouse," Qualto offered. He looked to Henk for support. "He *was* particularly worried about the drawbridge all of a sudden, you said."

"Yes. I'll go and look," Henk said.

"No!" Nyk said. "We'll stay together until we've looked in the obvious places, then we'll work out a plan of campaign if we have to."

"*I'm* not going to get lost," Henk objected.

"And if you find him, and he says 'come with me', and he's off on some other jaunt, what then?" Nyk looked at him for a moment, eyebrows raised, then added, "Come on," before Henk could protest.

But Adroyan's room was empty too. After some hesitant and tactful knocking, the three entered.

"He's very tidy," Qualto remarked as he looked round the room.

"Hmm." Nyk seemed less impressed. "Bit too tidy for my taste. Everything's laid out as if it had one place and one place only. Feels... obsessive... to me. Look at that bed—looks as if it's been ironed, for crying out."

"It would look obsessive to you, you're a slob," Qualto said. It was one of many well-worn insults that the three companions had developed over the years and it provoked no response.

"Gatehouse?" Henk queried.

"Gatehouse," Nyk agreed.

"This has been an interminably long day," Qualto remarked as he opened the main door. Light streamed out into the mountain darkness to reveal that it was snowing again and the courtyard lights blinked into life as though keen to spread the news. The air was alive with dancing snowflakes and the way to the gatehouse was smooth with fresh snow.

"Doesn't look as if he's been here," Henk said.

"This lot would cover his tracks in minutes," Nyk retorted. "He could've been there since before we ate. Come on, we'll have to check."

Hunched against the falling snow, they scuttled across the courtyard and through the door into the Gatehouse. The lights came on as they entered.

"He can't be here, then," Qualto said.

"We'll have to check," Nyk replied, heading up the stairs, two at a time. "He might have had an accident."

The others toiled up after him with markedly less enthusiasm, Henk muttering to himself and Qualto hanging heavily on the handrail. By the time they reached the top, Nyk was already descending the stairs on the other side of the room.

"Is he down there?" Qualto shouted after him.

"Nah," came the reply after a brief silence.

As Nyk turned to come back up the stairs he paused and looked at the blank wall of the counterweight. Almost as if drawn to it he walked over and, after a slight hesitation, pushed it gently.

It moved. He stepped back with a cry of surprise, followed by an oath.

"What's the matter?" Qualto shouted, leaning precariously over the handrail.

Nyk was clattering up the stairs.

"The damn thing's free again. It moved—I just touched it—and it moved..." He swore again. "What the hell is happening here?"

Qualto and Henk glanced at one another. Nyk was not given to agitation, still less swearing. He pushed past them and strode across to the hand-wheel that operated the drawbridge. It turned easily and silently. An indicator at the side of the wheel swung smoothly round to show that the drawbridge was almost completely open.

"That's just snow on the bearing pad," Nyk said dismissively, though his face was riven with irritation and bewilderment. He opened and closed the drawbridge several times, finally leaving it open before he abandoned the wheel. His expression did not change.

"It makes no sense," he said, largely to himself.

"Do you think perhaps we should... wedge it open... lock it in some way?" Qualto asked tentatively. He had to ask twice before Nyk indicated that he had heard him.

Qualto pressed on. "Whatever's happened, the way's open *now*. If it shuts again..." He gave a fatalistic shrug.

"Yes, yes, you're probably right," Nyk agreed distractedly. "I was just..." Silence descended on the group.

"Well?" Qualto asked after a while.

"Well what?" Nyk retorted.

"How do we lock it open?" Qualto replied, raising his voice, his eyebrows and his arms simultaneously.

Nyk abandoned his reverie and became practical.

"I don't know," he said. "I've never even thought about it—no need to." He looked around the chamber as though seeking inspiration.

"Maybe the weight of the snow will help keep it open," Henk suggested.

Nyk nodded. "Normally it doesn't need 'keeping open'. But Qualto's right—there's no saying it won't shut again—or when it'll open if it does. We'd better rig something to keep it open while we can."

Qualto and Henk looked at him expectantly and he returned to looking around the chamber to avoid their gaze. Then he pointed to the underside of the now horizontal counterweight. "We'll prop that. Then it can't swing down. We've got plenty big timbers in the yard. That'll be a more solid job than trying to fasten the other end down."

Henk nodded appreciatively but Qualto looked unhappy.

"You mean bring the timbers from the yard? Now?"

Nyk just looked at him by way of answer and Qualto's expression became one of reluctant resignation. Nyk chuckled. "You can always stand on the end of the bridge while Henk and I go for them."

Qualto scowled at him before conceding sourly, "Let's get some coats and gloves, and get on with it, then."

Nyk was already rooting in a cupboard and producing working clothes. "Go and get the others," he said over his shoulder to Qualto. "Ask them if they'll help. Me and Henk'll get across to the yard."

"What about Adroyan?" Henk asked.

"What about him?" Nyk retorted offhandedly.

"We're supposed to be looking for him, that's what. He might be lost."

"And he might not be—he could be sitting in the book room—or wandering about the kitchen looking for food by now. Either way, I'm sure he'll be in the warm somewhere." He relented slightly. "Besides, he's the one who's suddenly keen to get the bridge open, isn't he? He's going to be less than pleased if we tell him it opened and then closed again while we were wandering about looking for him."

Even with Josyff, Badr, and Esyal, drawn from the comfort of the common room by a breathless Qualto, it took them some time to haul Nyk's painstakingly selected timbers through the rambling open ways of the Keep, not least because, in some of them, the snow, dancing to the will of unfelt breezes, was drifting. And getting them into the gatehouse proved particularly tiring, there being no other way than to manoeuvre them up the stairs, across the building and then down the opposite stairs.

When the last piece was lowered down, a collective relaxation spread instantly through the group and there was much comradely puffing out of cheeks and wiping of brows.

"Well, at least the bridge didn't close while we were collecting that lot," Badr said.

"You're right, you're right," Nyk said, with unexpected urgency. "Help me lean a couple of these against the back wall, just in case it decides to move while I'm thinking how to do the job properly."

There was a brief spell of confused activity and, the temporary safeguard installed, they each returned with added enthusiasm to their relaxing.

Nyk turned to his guests. "Thank you. I appreciate that was work over and above the call of duty but it would've been difficult for just the three of us."

With a nod of acknowledgement towards Esyal, Josyff echoed her words in the kitchen. "Right now, it doesn't matter who we are or what we do. The drawbridge might be open again, but while the snow's so thick, we can't leave. We're still... prisoners, I suppose... and we'll have to do whatever's necessary to get along."

Nyk nodded and looked at Henk.

"You still set on leaving right away?" he asked caustically.

"I certainly am," Henk replied, though he looked torn. "I know you think I'm cracked, but all this business has nothing to do with any earthquake. It's the Keep—it's... waking up... It's been coming for a long time, now I think about it, and I don't want to be here—just don't want to be here."

"Henk... I..." Nyk began, but Henk pressed on.

"Still, the surveyor's right. We're stuck here until the snows go. Unless, maybe, we get a long frost—we should be able to get through then." He looked round as if inspecting the weather outside. "But it doesn't feel like it at the moment."

Nyk's face filled with a mixture of dismay and distress. He made a series of vague gestures before admitting, "I don't know what to think, Henk. You certainly *sound* cracked. What you're saying doesn't make any sense. But..." His voice faded into silence.

"I know it doesn't make sense," Henk said. "But I'm right. This is a bad place to be." He turned to Josyff and Badr, awkward witnesses to this conversation between old friends. "It's drawn you two here—reached out and drawn you here."

Josyff was at a loss but Badr almost snorted.

"I wasn't *drawn* here. I was *sent* here—like all of us—by my employers—plain old-fashioned civic authorities—bureaucrats—shinies—seat polishers—using orders—forms—bits of paper with signatures and instructions on them. 'Go and do this,' they said. 'Help the Surveyor.' So here I am. No distant siren call from the mountains."

Despite his obvious impatience, he managed to inject just enough good humour in this outburst to forestall too angry a response. Nevertheless, Josyff prepared to intervene.

It was unnecessary. Henk's reply was immediate but, though quiet, was far from subdued.

"And who told your 'civic authorities' what to do?"

"The New Order," Esyal answered for him.

Henk assumed the look of a successful interrogating lawyer.

"One of whom has been drawn here along with the rest of you."

Badr made to reply but Henk simply said, "You didn't hear those voices in the Great Hall—and you didn't see *him* when he heard them."

Badr opted to retreat from his denunciation by changing the subject. He indicated Esyal.

"And I suppose she's been drawn here as well."

Head craned forward, Henk gazed at Esyal unnervingly.

"She'll be here for a reason, for sure," he said eventually. "We all are."

This time Josyff *did* intervene. "Well, it doesn't matter. For whatever reasons, we're all here and we're all stuck here. At least the drawbridge is open now so that's one less problem to worry about."

Anxious to draw Henk away from his uneasy concerns, Nyk cast a final look of reserved approval at the timbers supporting the counterweight and agreed. "Yes it is. I wasn't relishing trying to find some other way out of here. This lot will do for the time being. I suppose we'd better move to our next problem—finding our other guest."

"Can we help in any way?" Josyff asked.

Nyk was about to refuse when he changed his mind.

"We'd better go back and try the common room again—and the book room. We'll decide what to do next if he isn't there."

The snow was already obliterating their earlier footprints as they trekked in single file across the courtyard, their silence amplified by its muffling stillness.

Before they reached the door, it was thrown open. Framed in it was Adroyan

CHAPTER 32

Adroyan gesticulated to Josyff but then had to step back to allow the group to pass out of the falling snow and into the building.

"You've plotted today's work—drawn it?" he demanded of Josyff without any preamble.

Qualto closed the door noisily, making the bolts rattle, though he did not throw them. It gave Josyff the opportunity to control his irritation. Nevertheless, it was somewhat to his own surprise that his voice was quite level when he replied: "No, sir." Old reflexes moved him immediately to forestall any rebuke. "We've done good work today." He indicated Badr. "Useful progress. But it's been a long and peculiar day, we're both tired, and I know from past experience that doing this kind of work when I'm tired merely leads to mistakes and the need to re-do work. It's inefficient and time-wasting."

He noticed as he spoke that Adroyan, normally a solid, rather static presence, was strangely mobile. One hand was tapping his leg and his eyes were restless.

Excitement? Nervousness?

Josyff could not decide, though he could quite clearly discern impatience. Adroyan looked inclined to pursue his inquiry, but Josyff's explanation, both neutral and straightforward, left him no avenue open.

Qualto and Nyk moved simultaneously into the subsequent silence, siding naturally with Josyff who, particularly in the presence of Adroyan, they were beginning to perceive as "one of them".

"You missed the mealtime, sir," Qualto said. "You must be hungry by now. I can make you something, if you wish." There was just a hint of a school-teacherly, "be on time in future," in his voice.

"And the drawbridge is open again," Nyk said, before Adroyan could reply. He clapped his hands with satisfaction. "No idea how or why, but it's open. We wedged it temporarily while I work out a better way of stopping it happening again."

Adroyan twitched edgily under this joint assault, looking from Qualto to Nyk and back again two or three times.

"Open again," he echoed. "Good—yes, good. I was concerned."

"We all were, sir," Nyk said. "But whatever caused it, it's open now so it's only the snow that's keeping us here."

"Snow?"

"Very heavy now, sir."

"Can we leave?"

Nyk was unequivocal. "Too dangerous, sir. I'd hopes the other day that this was just a spell of bad weather, but it's really settling in. Looks as if the winter's here early this year. And I'm afraid it could be a long one."

"I'll do a full inventory of our supplies," Qualto interjected reassuringly. "I'm fairly certain that food's not going to be a problem, but I'll check anyway. If necessary we can work out a little rationing scheme."

"Yes, yes," Adroyan waved him silent. "Do whatever is necessary. But this is the place... it..." He stopped abruptly as though recollecting where he was and turned back to Nyk. "The measuring of this place is most urgent—I can't emphasize *how* urgent—we need more people here—more surveyors. I must get back to the village."

Nyk returned his gaze squarely. "It's not possible, sir. If you remember, Aryck and Jonal—your guides from the village—they wanted to get back as quickly as possible then and it's worse now—they wouldn't even take Esyal for fear she'd slow them down. And they're experienced guides. No disrespect, sir, but you're city-bred. Mountains might make fine scenery, but they're always dangerous and at times like this even more so."

Seeing that Adroyan was not responding well to this advice, Nyk became both blunt and conciliatory.

"I don't know what's especially important about this place but I think you'll have to take some comfort from the fact that at least these surveyors got here and can get on with their work—a few days later and neither they nor their equipment would have got through. In fact, just a *day* later and the equipment wouldn't and they'd have been stuck here for the winter with nothing to do. Even I could see that that old stuff I found for them wasn't up to the job." He smiled. "Though they were polite about it."

"Nyk's right, I'm afraid, sir," Josyff said, reluctant to see Nyk fighting unaided. "We did some work with it, but it wasn't really suitable—a building like this needs modern, accurate equipment. If it hadn't arrived we'd have been very badly delayed, if not lost, but now it's here we'll be able to make good progress. You're the judge of the urgency, of course, but I'd be very surprised if we didn't end up with the job finished and nothing for us to do except wait for the snow to clear. I'm sure you'll have plenty of time to study the results and..." He hesitated. "Make whatever decisions it is you need to make."

Adroyan looked from side to side several times as though thoughts were washing to and fro about his mind. Gradually the movement slowed and then stopped.

"It seems that circumstances conspire both for and against me," he said. "I must accept the realities of our position. But..." He frowned impatiently, then quite suddenly he was calm—and smiling—something that none of them had seen him do before. "Yes, I'm sure all will be well. It may just be a testing time—for me—but everything that is needed is here." He turned to Qualto. "My apologies for missing the meal you prepared; if you can find me a few scraps to get me through the night, that would be most welcome."

"Of course, sir."

Qualto surged into action, taking Adroyan by the elbow and whisking him off in the direction of the kitchen.

The others watched them leave in silence. Adroyan's departure had left a peculiar quietness in the hallway.

Nyk ended it. "Nice to see him smile," he said.

"Yes," Josyff agreed, half-heartedly.

Yes, I think it's a mask, too, Esyal thought. A mask on a mask—the man was impossible to read anyway.

"I wonder what it is about this place the New Order's got him so bothered about," she said.

"Maybe he doesn't know," Nyk speculated. "Maybe, like Josyff and Badr here, he's just been sent out here to do a job."

Josyff shook his head. "People carrying the signed authority of the First Member of the Ordrans aren't just sent out to do jobs."

Nyk, however, was in no mood for dark conjectures—the drawbridge was open again and wedged, and he had satisfied himself that, if needs be, he could handle this newcomer, whatever bits of paper he might have.

"Well, it's none of my concern and he can be as urgent and fretful as he wants, it won't clear the snow. In the meantime, I've a couple of little jobs to do then I'm for an early night." He glanced at a nearby clock as he was leaving. "Before it's too late."

At the mention of an early night, Josyff felt the quiet pressures of this long and strange day close about him. "A wise decision. I think I'll do the same. I need to draw a line under these past days. We'll be able to get stuck into this job properly tomorrow."

The mood spread. Henk grunted a terse, "good night," and left, and Badr stifled a yawn. Only Esyal appeared to be unaffected.

"Come and look at that scroll before you go," she said.

Josyff was inclined to refuse but he had to pass the common room on the way to his own room and Esyal's tone had more of command in it than request.

He pointed towards the main door and made a token resistance. "The drawbridge is *open* again, you know..."

"Yes, yes, but this might tell us why it happened," Esyal insisted. "Surely you're curious?"

"No, I'm not."

"Yes, you are. Come on."

The scroll lay on the table where they had left it, the ornaments they had used to hold it open standing like patient sentries. Badr headed for the fireside armchair and the book he had been reading. "I'll leave you two to it," he said, adjusting the cushion and leaning back luxuriously. "I'll be doing as the natives do just as soon as I've finished this chapter."

Josyff smiled. "I don't think you're going to get that far, but we'll wake you when we leave."

Badr opened his book with heavy disdain.

From the kitchen, the faint sound of Qualto's voice attempting what was apparently a one-sided conversation drifted in through the open door as Josyff and Esyal turned their attention to the scroll.

"A different time," Josyff mused to himself as he looked at the sketches. "More leisurely than today, for sure—look at the draughtsmanship in these."

"A different time, maybe," Esyal said. "But the people don't seem to be much different. Look at their faces."

Josyff bent forward to examine the particular sketch she was pointing at. The detail was remarkable. There was... fear... in many of the faces. And other things. Still staring at the sketch, Josyff sat back, as though he could not quite believe what he was seeing. But it was there, he realized: fear, and anger, and determination. And the whole sweep of the drawing gave the impression of urgent movement everywhere.

If this was just a working drawing showing what was done to the drawbridge, why would anyone take such pains? He voiced the thought.

"Perhaps he was just a naturally good artist," Esyal offered.

"Damn good," Josyff replied. He looked quickly at some of the other sketches. They were all obviously by the same hand and they all had the same quality. A thought occurred to him. "These look like dignitaries or officials of some kind, here." He tapped the scroll lightly.

"The ones doing the watching?" Esyal asked acidly.

A laugh bubbled up in Josyff at her tone but he managed to reduce it to a knowing smile as he pressed on.

"Maybe... maybe they had some kind of... official artist... to record special events. Did you see any other sketches?"

Esyal looked at him wide-eyed. "I've only had the job an hour," she exclaimed indignantly.

This time Josyff could not contain his laughter. "Yes, of course," he conceded. "Sorry."

"Let's spread this thing right out and see if there are any more," Esyal said, implementing her suggestion even as she spoke. More ornaments were drafted into service, a slowly drowsing Badr being prodded into confused wakefulness in the process.

"Excuse me," Esyal said insincerely as she stepped over his extended legs.

Badr shook his head violently and levered himself out of his chair. He looked ruefully at the book, closed it carefully and put it on a nearby table.

Josyff commiserated. "Henk's fires are too comfortable to read in front of."

"I should've known better," Badr admitted. "Especially after a day like today." He drifted across to the table. "Have you found anything interesting?"

Before anyone could reply, there was a brief scuffle and a near-disaster with two of the ornaments as the scroll strove to return to the tight-rolled condition that it had been kept in, presumably since its creation. Badr gathered up some of the books that were lying about the room and ended its struggle.

"Longer than it looked," Esyal said, as a still-rolled portion of the scroll stuck out over the end of the table, resolutely refusing the lure of gravity.

"These *are* impressive, aren't they?" Badr said, doing as Josyff had done before, and bending forward to study the sketches more closely.

"No ordinary draughtsman, this," he proclaimed after a little while.

"My thoughts, too," Josyff said. "I was speculating that they might have had some kind of official artist to record special events."

"Possible, I suppose," Badr said, still engrossed. "It certainly looks like a special event, judging by the number of people there."

"More an emergency than an event, judging by the state they all seem to be in," Esyal said, with a hint of a taunt in her voice. The two men nodded in agreement and continued their study of the sketches.

"They're a bizarre mixture of drawings of record, working drawings and works of art," Josyff muttered as he carefully unrolled the remains of the scroll. "Oh!"

His soft exclamation drew the others to him.

"Nasty," he said.

The sketch he was pointing to—the last one on the scroll—showed the scaffolding surrounding the drawbridge lying in ruins. Where many of the previous sketches had reflected a sense of movement and activity, this one radiated stillness, as though the collapse had happened very quickly and stunned both watchers and workers into a shocked silence.

"There are people under this," Josyff said. "Look." He indicated an arm extending from the wreckage—then a foot—and a hint of a coloured shirt in the darkness.

There followed a swift comparison of the sketches to identify the different characters portrayed there.

"Four," they concluded, eventually.

"And probably killed," Badr added. "Certainly badly hurt at least. Those are big timbers, and those chains and pulley blocks will be very heavy too."

"I notice none of the dignitaries are hurt—just further away, and looking helpless," Esyal said, overtly acidic this time.

Josyff ignored the comment. "I wonder what it was all about," he said, before giving an immediate and self-deprecating shake of his head. "Of course, we could do the obvious and read the text."

Badr cast a dubious eye along the length of the extended scroll with its sketches and its close lines of meticulous script.

"Some other time," he said, through another stifled yawn. This one proved to be infectious, and spread rapidly through the ranks of his allies. It ended the study of the scroll which was relieved of its restraints and allowed to roll back into its long-stored shape.

"I'll see if there are any more like it tomorrow," Esyal said, as she placed it carefully behind a heavy ornament.

A little later, Josyff sank into his bed with hedonistic relish.

"Good night, my love," he said to his absent, yet ever-present, wife. "Good night. It's been another bizarre day. But a good one—I think. At least the job's under way. And the door's open again—we're free to leave—apart from miles of snow-filled valleys, that is."

His thoughts meandered as sleep slowly took over him: he reviewed the day's work and planned tomorrow's; puzzled about the drawbridge and the mysterious echo of what was perhaps a similar event in the past shown on Esyal's scroll. And then there was Adroyan. One of the Ordrans, perhaps? What to make of him and his being here? These were not considerations conducive to sleep but they could not impinge on the momentum of Josyff's fatigue and he was soon asleep.

Then, seemingly without the passage of any time, his eyes were wide and he was surrounded by shouting and hammering.

CHAPTER 33

Amid the noise and commotion, a voice was whispering urgently, very close to his ear.

"Draw this as it is, measurer. As it is. As accurately as you know. On your life, make no error, miss no detail. This will need great study. We *must* prevail."

The voice was insistent and Josyff knew he must obey its commands without question. It was also familiar...

"I shall, lord," he said, to his unseen overseer.

A hand was laid briefly on his shoulder, at once encouraging and intimidating.

Immediately in front of him, stretched on a specially built frame, was a scroll, across which a hand—thinner, longer and more delicate than his own, yet his for all that—was moving. It held a fine charcoal and was drawing faint lines with great sureness and speed. Later, he would ink these in more firmly and he sensed his mind registering this and many other things, locking them firmly into his memory for later recall. He must not be distracted by the turmoil and confusion now filling the courtyard; he must capture the essence of what was happening. Not that he understood what was happening—no one did—not even the lord it seemed, though the very thought, near-heretical, made him uneasy. Yet for the lord to address him as directly as he had just done indicated a quite untypical emotion in him, even though his stern and cold exterior seemed to be unaffected.

As well as he could, he set the idea aside. It was not for the likes of him to ponder the ways of the lord. He was here to serve. He would do as he had been ordered. Somewhere in his drawings perhaps the lord might find what he was looking for.

Raised voices lifted his attention from the scroll to the scene in front of him. The general clamour faded abruptly and the sounds of a quarrel reached him: this was not the way, this was dangerous, unstable, it would collapse, people would be hurt, more time should be taken, more thought given. The plaint was over-topped by a younger, more strident voice, full of anger and impatience. He recognized both voices. Aggravated by what had happened, long-held tensions, inevitable in an isolated community like this, had risen to a peak and were now fracturing into outright enmity.

He paused, his hand hovering unsteadily above the scroll and, as if emulating him, the whole courtyard became still. All were watching, frozen in their tasks, awaiting the outcome of this confrontation.

Then the lord was striding towards the two men. He did not appear to be hurrying, but his normal leisurely gait seemed now unnervingly urgent. The quarrel stopped and the measurer saw the two angry faces turning and facing their master, approaching like a black wind. The older man was leaning back, his face taut, almost wincing in anticipation of a blow. The younger, wide-eyed and reckless, was about to compound his folly by speaking to the lord before he was spoken to.

"Get on with your tasks."

The lord's voice hissed across the courtyard before he reached the two protagonists and before such an outrage could occur. The measurer's hand started to move again, and the watching crowd was moving again as though there had been no interruption. Only the two men remained motionless, and only the lord and the measurer were watching them. All other eyes were wilfully turned away.

Then another sound filled the courtyard. It needed no great wisdom to identify it as being bad. A loud, jagged creaking, rising in pitch and intensity, brought the hubbub to a halt once again, but only briefly. Josyff felt the measurer's terror and he had a fleeting impression of ropes snapping and whistling lethally free, of equipment being dropped, and of people scattering to the extremities of the courtyard as the elaborate structure they had built around the drawbridge became grotesquely fluid and mobile. Like a wounded creature making a last effort to avoid its death, the framework seemed to rear up and then hover interminably on a point of balance.

Josyff felt himself hurtling backwards, the scene in front of him shrinking rapidly as it descended into chaos and horror. As it shrank, so the noise of the collapse and the screaming of the crowd became attenuated: first a nerve-jarring grinding and then a shrieking like fingernails down glass, increasing in pitch until it was barely audible. Then there was blackness.

Josyff sat up sharply, wide awake and trembling. The high distant sound was all about him but it was carried away by the fleeing darkness as the bedroom light clicked softly into life.

So vivid had been the vision of the courtyard and his role as measurer that it took him a few moments to recollect where he was. When he did so he lay back with an unexpected sense of relief.

Well, there was no doubt about that, he thought. *That* was a dream, not some inexplicable happening like hearing voices, or tumbling into the clock. The memory drew his eyes to the offending timepiece. It was the middle of the night—a long way to dawn and the next day's work. The clock's innards clucked dyspeptically as if replying to an unasked question. It must have just struck the hour, he decided. That would account for the dying reverberations hanging about him were he woke.

He chuckled. Maybe he was getting used to the place, maybe having Adroyan about—a watching official—made the job feel more like his everyday routine. Or maybe it was just that he and Badr had managed to do a decent amount of work—had made a start at reducing this place to numbers—to lines on paper.

The lights dimmed and went out and his thoughts turned back to his dream. Obviously the source of the images in it had come from Esyal's scroll. And it would have taken little imagination to re-enact the crash portrayed there. He realized now, too, that though he had not seen his face, the "lord" who so dominated the scene had been Adroyan.

Still, it had been extraordinarily intense and compelling. When he had finished work tomorrow, he must have another look at the scroll—study the text—find out what it had all been about. It could well be that this dream had given him insights into the event that he was as yet unaware of. It was an article of faith with him that the deeper reaches of his mind would often solve problems while he was sleeping that his conscious mind was struggling desperately with. And perhaps Esyal might have found some more scrolls continuing the tale.

His thoughts were drifting as sleep began to return. Esyal—odd girl... What had she been doing in the mountains, so far away from anywhere? And why was she so unconcerned about her loss of memory—surely a terrifying experience? And Henk. What was troubling him? It seemed unlikely that after years of working here he'd suddenly develop such an aversion to the place—and when escape was impossible. Then again, perhaps it was precisely that that had done it. Being trapped here had brought some old problem to a head. Josyff yawned noisily. Anyway, it didn't matter. The man might be a bit morose, but he was helpful enough—and he lit a good fire. Josyff smiled into his pillow.

Then, without any seeming intermission, he was back in the courtyard looking at the wreckage of the collapsed framework, though he was seeing it this time not through the eyes of the measurer, but as himself. Noise and uproar reigned, but there was also something oddly different about the scene.

Dust, he noted, irrelevantly. It was summer—and the courtyard was hard-packed earth...

He looked down. No—it was paved—hard smooth stone slabs. No lawns here.

But that wasn't the difference...

"This is a very vivid dream."

He turned. The speaker was Esyal. She was staring at him, but speaking to herself, her eyes wide with surprise. He returned her gaze. Someone bumped into her, knocking her away from him and out of his immediate view.

"The lord, the lord!"

The cry, uttered by many voices, rose to dominate the scene, and, as if touched by an overseeing will, the milling spectators began to converge on the tangle of ropes and timbers that was the remains of the framework.

Josyff moved with them, partly because he had little choice in the press, but also because he knew people were trapped under the wreckage. Quite possibly they might be dead, but equally, they might only be injured and the need for rescue was urgent. He found himself struggling with others to move a large baulk of timber. There was no order to what was happening around him, just frantic people dragging out timbers and ropes. Part of him knew that this was dangerous foolishness—that it might do more harm than good—but he was too taken up by the mood of the crowd to heed it.

And then, with terrible clarity, he could sense the pinioned helplessness of those who were trapped. Held motionless and impotent by restraints beyond their strength.

"*Listen!*"

The word seemed to form in Josyff's mind rather than be spoken within his hearing. It was hedged about by tenuous, elusive meanings—some commonplace—bewilderment, disbelief—others alien and disturbing—beyond anything that he had words to describe. But the command was not addressed to him! He was an inadvertent eavesdropper.

"*He... (it, they?)... are there. They exist. They can hear us.*"

Images of a shared territory, distant and tenuous, of dubious reality, perhaps even mythical, flitted through Josyff's mind.

"*There lies the Destroyer. We* must *be freed.*"

Though doubt and uncertainty permeated the words, Josyff sensed dispute, debate.

"*It is the only way.*"

Josyff could feel the rough texture of the timber hard against his face as he braced his shoulder underneath it and began to push. He felt others around him striving to the same end, but then the niggling doubts about the wisdom of what he was doing found voice.

"No! This is wrong," he shouted across the courtyard.

The clock clucked again as he found himself sitting upright and staring at it, wide awake. He swore. Was he not going to have *one* undisturbed night in this place? The clock began its chimes for the hour by way of reply. Josyff gave it an arch look.

"Enough is enough. No more scroll, courtyard, dreams, voices—anything—nothing! Just sleep. Sleep! I've work to do here," he growled as he turned over, closed his eyes and pulled the blankets up so that they almost covered him entirely. "Work to do. Work to do. Just sleep. Just..." His voice became an incoherent mumble as the light clicked out.

When he woke again, it was to the knowledge that his last injunction had been observed. Bright snowlight lit his room and the clock was striking a comfortable hour. Better still, he felt refreshed and relaxed. Today he and Badr could really get this job under way. Whatever the drawbridge did, whatever Adroyan did, whatever mysteries hung about Esyal... anything short of a *real* earthquake—he was not going to be deflected.

And so it proved. Although Adroyan was late and silently aloof, breakfast was quiet and companionable. Nyk chatted earnestly, as much to himself as anyone else, about how he was going to strengthen the props that were holding the drawbridge open, making points with significant gestures and jabs with his cutlery and co-opting a hunched Henk who, along with the others, grunted appropriately. And, with a token offer of help should it be needed, Josyff and Badr left to continue their own work.

"Esyal was a bit... quiet this morning," Badr remarked. "Kept giving you strange looks."

"Can't say I noticed," Josyff lied. "Maybe her loss of memory is starting to take its toll."

"Could be, I suppose," Badr said. "She did seem to be remarkably unconcerned about it, I thought. Then again, there's a lot been going on these past days—kept her occupied."

"Anyway, she's Qualto's problem for the day," Josyff went on. "Sorting out his old documents. Let's just be thankful she didn't attach herself to us by way of wanting to be helpful."

And so the day passed—free from inexplicable happenings of any kind—routine, insofar as such a word could be applied to so convoluted a building as the Keep. Apart from a single casual sighting of Qualto, they saw no one until Henk appeared to advise them that their meal was ready.

"Excellent timing," Josyff announced, clapping his hands loudly and rubbing them together. "We'd just decided to finish for the day."

Henk nodded and sniffed.

The meal was a little more lively than breakfast. Nyk recounted his work on the drawbridge. "Any earthquake strong enough to close it now will have to bring the walls down," he concluded.

"What if *we* want to close it for some reason?" Badr asked, wilfully provocative.

Nyk gave him a long look to test the remark for humour.

"It won't be a problem," he declared firmly, though with some knowing irony and without elaborating.

"How are you getting on with the Archives?" Josyff asked Esyal, who, as at breakfast, was quite preoccupied. "Found any more scrolls?"

"Yes," Esyal replied after a brief hesitation and with a tense smile. "Three. I've spread them out in the book room if you want to look at them."

"Splendid," Josyff said enthusiastically. "I'll have a look right after..." He caught a subtle shift in Adroyan's posture. "A little later on, maybe. I'd like to make a start plotting the work we've done today and planning out what we can do tomorrow."

Esyal did not reply. She had other things on her mind. She wanted to look at the scrolls again; then there was the killing of Adroyan.

CHAPTER 34

Esyal had gone straight from breakfast to the Archive. For the moment she did not want to think about the dream she had had. It had been extraordinarily vivid...

And it had obviously been brought about by her study of the scrolls...

Later, later...

She looked around at the dusty disorder of the Archive and dismay set in.

She thought of Qualto's meticulous, well-ordered kitchen. How could someone like that let this place get into such a state? She ran a distasteful finger over one of the volumes then silently cursed her enthusiasm in volunteering for this job. Qualto's own enthusiasm for her to do it might have proved a warning of what she was letting herself in for. Then again, she doubted Qualto was much of a conspirator. He was far too open and straightforward—as far as she could see.

She, on the other hand...

However long she had to stay here, it would end eventually and she still had work to do. The Rhanen might be in outright retreat at the moment but some destiny had rescued her and brought her to safety when she had seen only death ahead. Whether it had been chance or some other power she did not care, nor, for that matter, even considered. A new resolve had slowly grown in her—or, more correctly, an old resolve had been re-awakened. The New Order was unequivocally an evil thing; its watching eyes, and dead, controlling hands stifled all they touched, forcing people and events into an expression of their will. While mouthing the words of freedom, it was the antithesis of it. In time, of course, it would wither and die, like any rigid, inflexible thing. But how long would that take? How much hurt would be done while she waited? And how much longer would it take for the people to recover from the New Order's corrosive overlordship? Might there not come in its wake merely a different tyranny?

No—she could not do nothing—she must renew her fight.

And here was opportunity. The same events that had preserved her had brought her into the presence of someone near the very heart of the New Order—perhaps even one of the Ordrans. The very least she would gain from Adroyan was knowledge—about him, and maybe the inner circles of the New Order...

The prospect warmed her. As did her offer to help Qualto. Her sense of natural fairness and her low cunning had both told her it was unfair and unwise for her to sit around, being fed and housed while others were working—particularly as it seemed that Adroyan had no such qualms. He was already showing the signs of someone who was not part of the group. If she too had opted to do nothing then she would be outside the group also—and inevitably be perceived as his ally, whatever that might come to mean. *Now*, she could be part of the group and also a friendly face for Adroyan—a peace maker—a builder of bridges. She would make herself quietly useful to him as the subtle effects of his self-imposed isolation made themselves felt—and they would. She smiled at the thought.

"You might be New Order, but somewhere you're human like the rest of us, you bastard," she muttered very softly, as though she did not want even the dusty documents around her to hear.

For now though, she must get on with her immediate work. She must draw the others about her. And quickly, she decided sharply. Apart from any long-term plans she might have, there was still the matter of the men who had attacked and routed her party. That had only been a few days ago and presumably they were still out there, unless the intensity of the snowfall had sent them scurrying. Maybe having the drawbridge jammed shut was not such a bad thing after all, she reflected, with some irony. Then again, if a troop of New Order soldiers arrived to find one of their leaders trapped inside—and Adroyan *would* identify himself to them, undoubtedly—who could say what resources they might bring to bear to rescue him—and her!

Her mind made up, she turned to the task in hand.

Where, in the name of pity, was she to start?

She stopped herself on the verge of a sigh and her eyes narrowed determinedly.

When you don't know where to start—start.

Probably backwards from these, she thought, looking at the ordered volumes on the shelves by the door. But first she needed space.

Some time later, it was beginning to emerge. The door to the Archive was held open by two boxes and the general clutter from the Archive floor had been carried into the book room where it lay in rows with the disconsolate air of conscripted soldiers on first parade. Esyal looked round at the Archive. The carpet was now strangely patterned, with oases of ancient cleanliness between marginally younger paths of grime and dust.

Not bad, she decided, although a glance down at herself told her that she must look in the store room to see if there were any clothes more appropriate for this kind of work.

After another flurry of activity, the contents of the desk had advanced into the book room to form a flank guard to the conscripts.

A chair had emerged during the clearing of the floor. Esyal pulled it up to the desk and sat down with a proprietorial air.

Henk appeared in the doorway.

"I thought you were helping Nyk," she said.

"I was—I am—I was just passing—going to pick up something."

Esyal smiled and extended an arm to indicate her achievement—and to invite praise. The invitation was unsuccessful but his eyes took in the room and she thought she detected a faint hint of approval. She opted for a little less subtlety.

"Looking better already, isn't it?" she insisted.

Henk's gaze drifted to the exiled documents now lingering in the book room.

"Looking different," he said.

Esyal was about to engage in some banter but when she spoke she heard herself asking, "Why do you want to leave, Henk?"

The question surprised her almost as much as it did Henk, who looked for an instant as though he was going to run away. Instead, he looked at her intently.

Esyal pressed on, then retreated a little. "You've been here a long time, haven't you? Nyk and Qualto are your friends. I'm sorry, it's none of my business, is it? But..."

She left the sentence unfinished, terminating it with a hasty, "I shouldn't have asked."

Henk, however, seemed unconcerned. He ignored the apology and simply answered the questions. "Yes, I have, and yes, they are," he said. "I don't *want* to leave—it's a good job, and it suits me—I just have to. We should all leave."

"In *this* weather?" Esyal's incredulity at the sincerity—the fear?—in his voice was genuine.

Henk's head drooped forward even more than normal and his cheeks puffed out as though he were wrestling with some great problem.

"I don't know. It'd be dangerous, I suppose, but..."

"It'd be more dangerous to stay?"

Henk ignored the words she put into his mouth. "Did you find any more scrolls like the other one?" he asked.

"No... no..." Esyal stammered, taken unawares by this sudden change of subject. "I haven't looked yet. I've just been making some space to work in."

"Remembered who you are, yet?" This second question, as unexpected as the first, was delivered like a fast and subtle sword thrust, and was accompanied by a shrewd, piercing gaze. Esyal could not meet it. She pushed her chair back and stood up slowly so that she could disguise her avoidance.

"I know who I am," she corrected. "Well, my name, anyway. I just don't know why I'm out here, or where I come from. Maybe later it'll bother me, but right now I'm just glad to be alive—very glad." She shrugged. "It doesn't even matter that we're all trapped here. Still, thanks for asking, but nothing's come back at all. Perhaps if I keep myself occupied, it'll sneak up on me."

"Hmm."

Esyal levered the questioning back to her own advantage. "You still haven't told me why you want to leave—why you want *all* of us to leave. I know some... odd... things have happened these past few days, but Badr said it was probably an earthquake—or something. And nothing dangerous has happened, has it?"

Henk's lip curled.

"It's no earthquake," he said, almost sneering. "You don't get earthquakes in this country. Everyone knows that. Did you feel the ground shaking?"

"No, but Nyk and..."

Henk answered his own question. "No. Of course you didn't. And Nyk's not going to argue with the surveyors—but he'll tell you—there was no sign of damage to the drawbridge—not anywhere. Nothing had moved. It wasn't jammed, it was held tight shut just as though something was holding it. And you didn't hear those voices in the Great Hall—or see Adroyan listening to them."

Esyal made a vague gesture of admission. "I don't know what to make of any of it, Henk—drawbridges, voices. I just can't see that anything bad enough has happened to make you want to leave so urgently—still less the rest of us—and in this weather! Maybe it's just all the upheaval. I suppose we're an awkward bunch to be suddenly dropped into your daily routine." She lowered her voice. "And if Adroyan's close to the Ordrans—or maybe even one of them—he'll be particularly... unusual."

"Oh, he's unusual, all right," came the immediate response. "He's near the heart of what's going on. The surveyor's arrival seemed to unsettle things, but since *he* arrived..." Henk's lip curled.

Part of Esyal wanted to get on with her work and was inclined to shut him off with as polite a "did you want something, I'm busy," intrusion as she could manage, but there was a momentum to their discussion that would not allow it voice.

"You still haven't said why you want to leave so urgently," she said, inwardly reproaching herself for allowing this to continue.

Henk stared at her. "No, I haven't, have I?" He paused. "Then, I don't think I've got words for it. Hairs on the neck go up..." He rubbed his hands together nervously. "Your insides go heavy and tight. I feel like a rabbit that's just seen a fox heading towards it. Doesn't know what's going to happen—just that it'll be bad."

Esyal had lived too long on her wits to hold the analogy to scorn. Indeed, what Henk described, she was herself experiencing as she listened to him. Naturally taciturn and self-sufficient, it had cost him a price of some kind to speak like that to someone who was really a complete stranger—a brief interruption to his long service to the Keep. Much as she would have preferred to, she could not idly ignore either Henk's admission, or her response to it.

She was silent for some time, uncertain what to say.

Henk spared her. "You think I'm cracked, don't you?"

The incongruity of the plea snapped the unease between them and brought a smile to Esyal's face.

"No, I don't," she replied without hesitation and looking at him squarely. "I think maybe you're worrying about nothing—but then I could be wrong—you live here. Either way, if we don't know what we're looking for, we're going to have to wait and see what happens."

Henk pondered the logic of this. "And if it's a fox? Something bad?"

Esyal shrugged. "Well, I can't imagine what it might be, but we still have to wait—see what it is. Running's like whimpering—it attracts predators. Maybe we'd be better standing our ground." Then, retreating discreetly from this heroic posture: "Anyway, don't forget, Nyk's wedged the drawbridge open. At least we can't be trapped here now." She leaned forward earnestly, speaking as the thoughts came to her. "Perhaps you could get some things ready for a hasty exit—food, clothes, travelling equipment. Stack it all near the door—then if the... fox... arrives and we do have to run for it, we'll be ready."

The simple practicality of the idea obviously appealed to Henk. His dour face brightened and he even drew himself up a little taller.

"Yes," he muttered softly to himself. Then with a brusque, "I'd better get back to Nyk," he was gone, leaving Esyal at the beginning of a sentence and off-balance—mouth gaping. She shook her head as if the brief exchange might have been a daydream. Then Henk's initial question returned to her. "Did you find any more scrolls?"

She glanced back at the waiting shelves. She'd done the hard part—she'd started. The scrolls would be as good a place to continue as any, she decided.

Some little while later, and more than a little dust-smeared, she had located three scrolls which appeared to be of the same type as the one she had first found. After a brief and irritating attempt to examine them on the desk, she took them into the book room and laid them out side by side on the floor, using heavy books to pin down their curling corners. Numbers at the head of each, carefully drawn, but in a different hand to the rest of the writing, enabled her to put them in the correct sequence.

As she had laid them out it had been her intention to study them, but as she looked again at the drawings on the first one, the memory of her dream of the previous night, held at bay so far, rushed in upon her.

CHAPTER 35

It was the vividness of the dream that unsettled her more than its content. She did not normally remember dreams and on the rare occasions she did, they invariably slipped away very quickly after waking even if she did not want them to.

But as she stared down at the pictures, this one was still with her—all of it—no part missing or quivering as though it were about to slip into whatever inner recesses of the mind shelter forgotten dreams.

She had been in the courtyard. No preamble, no sense of journey, not even a sense of dislocation—just there, as she should be. It was not the present courtyard, with its snow-covered lawns, but the one in the drawings on the scroll. The ground was hard under her feet—paved, she noticed—and the dry tang of summer dust in the air caught her throat. All around her was uproar and, directly ahead, in front of the drawbridge, was a ruinous tangle of ropes and chains, all swinging wildly, wrapping and unwrapping themselves about a mass of broken and splintered timbers. Some of the timbers were also moving—creaking into final resting places—high-pitched and protesting, like some grotesque creature searching for a comfortable position in which to die.

Her gaze was drawn to a man nearby. He had his back to her but seemed to be oddly out of place, almost motionless in the confusion, save that he was sketching on a scroll.

It was Josyff, she realized!

This must be a dream, she thought. She had heard of people being aware of their dreams when they were in them, even being able to manipulate them, but it had never happened to her. It had always sounded like fun but although she felt a small frisson of excitement, it was fear that seemed to be rising to the fore.

"This is a very vivid dream," she said out loud, as if for reassurance that it *was* a dream and in the vague hope that perhaps the sound of her own voice might awaken her. Nothing happened however, except that Josyff turned and looked at her, his expression startled and bewildered. He seemed to recognize her, but then someone bumped into her and she was carried away by the press of the crowd. She made a brief futile attempt to get back to him but soon had to concentrate on keeping her feet in the crush. Then, like so much flotsam, she was thrust out of the melee and in the lee of an abutment. Her thoughts were whirling. This *was* a dream, wasn't it—her sleeping mind weaving its own tale from the happenings of the day and the drawings on the scroll? She clung to the thought.

Yet everything was so real...

"The lord! The lord!"

The cry made her look out at the crowd again. Its chaotic movement was becoming almost dance-like as it surged towards the shattered structure.

There must be someone important under that lot, she thought. Then to force herself to remember that this was a dream she tried to recall which of the figures in the drawings might have been this "lord". She frowned. None of the four figures that she and Josyff had identified as being under the collapse had been dressed in the manner that had made Josyff identify them as dignitaries and had prompted her own sarcastic rejoinder. And the 'lord' must surely be a dignitary.

Even as she reached this conclusion, some impulse made her look away from the crowd and across the courtyard. There, quite still amidst the confusion, stood a solitary figure. He, if it was a man, was dressed in a simple black robe, like a monk's habit, with the hood pulled well forward. There was a strange presence about him that held Esyal's gaze.

Then, as if hearing something, the figure turned its head slightly and looked directly at her. Her hand tightened about the edge of the abutment and she fought an urge to move back behind the shelter of it. Standing now in the book room, looking down at the scroll, Esyal became aware that her fist was clenching as she recalled the moment, but the memory of the dream moved on relentlessly. The blackness within the hood was darker than the robe itself, as though it were a deep void—an opening into another place. But she could feel a searching gaze peering through it...

"Look!"

The word echoed through her mind, carrying with it a haze of nuances of meaning—listen? touch? or was it, feel? know this? sense this? be aware? And it brought with it a peculiar disorientation—as in a picture she had once seen of a stairway with flights that descended and turned repeatedly until, quite seamlessly, the lowest step had become the highest. Esyal put her hand to her ear, partly to steady herself and partly to determine where the voice was coming from. But even as she did so she knew there was no sound save that of the crowd—no voice had issued that injunction. Yet she knew that it had come from the watching figure. Abruptly, though she could have offered no reason for her certainty, she realized that the figure was not part of the dream, but the cause of it! She was here because it had brought her here.

"They are here. They can see (hear? sense? know?) us."

The words, if they could be called words, cut across this unsettling revelation. In sharp contrast to her own, albeit unfounded, certainty, these seemed to be riddled with doubt. They carried with them a feeling of intense argument. Someone—something?—somewhere, was persuading, was struggling against the scepticism—indeed the outright disbelief—and scorn!—of others.

And she was the object of the doubt!

Confused questions, unvoiced, but quite real, unfolded in the cloud of meanings that hung about the words, like waves rippling outwards from a stone thrown into a lake.

"Was she (it?) or was she not real, this... disturbing... creation? And the others here, what are they?"

A twinge of annoyance began to form within Esyal at the idea that she was being viewed like an oddity found by the wayside. But it had no time to manifest itself. More words, this time seething with urgency and a long, angry frustration, swept through her.

"It is here—the...(demon ?)... that caused this—that bound us thus—we must be freed—and the way is here."

Esyal felt more than words now—she felt a will—a will, alien and dark, turning its attention to her. She also felt her lip curling in a snarl of defiance that came unbidden from something feral deep within her. Then a voice, vaguely familiar, rose above the din of the crowd, shouting denial, and she was awake—wide awake, lying on her bed in the Keep, holding her breath, she realized, and slightly giddy from the unsettling images that pervaded the words.

And even now, hours later, she felt a hint of her visceral response to the searching will within the dream tugging at her lips. It was quite unlike anything she had ever known before—even during the most violent of events. It was the response of an animal.

Like the rabbit? she wondered.

No, she decided. That was no rabbit's response. More like fox vying with fox.

And yet it was more even than that—it had a quality that seemed to arc back through time to some ancient darkness.

It was an unsettling image, but it was dispelled almost immediately as, for no apparent reason, she realized that the shouting voice that had awoken her had been Josyff's.

Drawing in a deep, hissing breath she crouched down and, balancing on tiptoe, looked intently at the drawing. She did not remember dreams, she kept telling herself, in the hope that her insistence might offer her some revelation. But this must have been a dream—what else could it have been?

But so real...

Reaching no conclusion, her thoughts ground to a halt and she gave a snort of disdain. "I'm turning into Henk," she said, looking round and speaking to the silent books. "It must be something about this place. Pull yourself together girl—get on with your work."

Esyal was nothing if not pragmatic.

And for some time, bustling about the Archive, seeking to bring some kind of order to the chaos there, she was able to forget the dream.

Until Adroyan arrived.

He arrived as unexpectedly and as silently as Henk. She had clasped an ill-formed and too-large stack of books at the top and bottom and it had promptly opted to avoid her grip by bellying out in the middle.

Her rising "Oooo," ended in a sharp squeak of surprise as Adroyan stepped into the Archive and with an extended hand forestalled the collapse.

"Thank you," Esyal said automatically, after a silent negotiation took the books safely to the desk. Adroyan merely nodded and looked around the room.

"You are making progress?" he asked

Esyal gave a disclaiming shrug. "I'm not sure what progress means here," she replied. "I'm just trying to find out what there is, then I might be able to put it in some form of order." She smiled and counter-attacked. "Were you looking for something?"

Adroyan's black eyes flickered briefly in surprise and he looked at her as though he were trying to recall something. Esyal felt again the faint stirring of the ancient response she had experienced in her dream. Then Adroyan's inspection was gone.

"I'm just... learning... about this place," he said, though he avoided her gaze and his expression gave a hint of both surprise and regret that he had answered thus—or at all.

Esyal noted it. "I didn't mean to pry," she lied by way of apology.

Then she probed further, with heavily feigned naivety.

"What do the Ordrans want with this place? It's so odd and out of the way."

Seeing that the question disconcerted Adroyan, she prevented him recovering his balance by changing the subject before he could reply.

"I found some more scrolls," she said, pointing through the door. "Those are they—laid out next door."

"Yes, I noticed," Adroyan replied.

"Have you any idea what they mean?" Esyal pressed, walking past him and into the book room. Dance around him for a while—see what turns up.

Adroyan was drawn after her. "They're just a record. Presumably they mean what they say. Have you read them?"

Esyal gave a winning smile and made an airy gesture to show her dusty hands. "No, I'm still at the floundering stage in here."

Adroyan looked at the scrolls. "Continue with your work," he said curtly. "I will look at these. They may be helpful."

Esyal drifted towards the Archive. "We think there were four people buried under that collapse. Maybe it'll tell you what happened to them."

"Why they were doing what they were doing is more important," Adroyan replied, his manner a peculiar mixture of condescension to an underling and surprise that he had taken the effort. And again Esyal noted it.

Keep dancing, she thought.

"Yes, I can see your superiors wouldn't be pleased to find the place locking people in and out at its own fancy."

Adroyan paused in his study of the scrolls and turned his head slowly towards her. His black eyes held her. She felt the insincerity of her smile showing through but she did not seem to be able to move. He asked the same question as Henk.

"Have you remembered who you are yet?"

She gave the same reply, though with a stammer.

"I... I know who I am—my name, anyway. I know all sorts of things. I just don't know where I'm from or why I'm here."

Adroyan's gaze did not leave her.

"Do you remember the Rhanen?"

Esyal felt her insides shaking and hoped that none of it showed. She wanted to tear herself away from his inspection, but a wiser part of her told her to stand her ground. Rabbit and fox—whimpering attracts the predators. That same part also reminded her of her knife and made her keep her hand away from it.

"Weren't they people who preferred freedom to the New Order?" she said, her voice much steadier than she had anticipated.

177

"The New Order *is* freedom," Adroyan responded. "There can be no freedom in a society without order and stability. And obedience to the greater good."

It took Esyal no small effort to resist the temptation to argue the point.

Adroyan continued, as if uneasy about her silence. "The Rhanen were a handful of malcontents, opposed to the authority of the majority—harbingers of anarchy. They did much harm."

There was barely-hidden passion in his voice. It was as disturbing as it was unexpected. Full of hate and anger, Esyal judged, but, ironically, it reassured her—at least it was a human quality, unlike his cold distance and authoritativeness.

Did much harm, did we, she thought. That was interesting—and a revelation. However it had come to be, the New Order had gained such a peculiarly strong grip on the many institutions of government that it had always been difficult to know what effect the Rhanen were having—a sense of futility had always threatened to overwhelm them.

Her renewed resolve asserted itself. If I get the chance here, I'll do more, she thought. Then she managed a moue of indifference.

"I'm not really interested in politics—it's boring," she said, turning away from his gaze by easing closer to the Archive door as though anxious to get back to work. "Besides, weren't the Rhanen all killed or arrested?"

"Most of them, yes," Adroyan answered, flatly. "A force is pursuing the remnants of them through these very mountains even now."

"Ah. Is that why you're here? To see if this place can be used as a barracks or something? I imagine your soldiers would be glad of it given the way the weather's changed. Are you expecting them?"

"No, I'm here on another matter."

"Something more important?"

Adroyan's attention returned briefly to the scrolls, then he straightened up and looked around the room as if examining the entire Keep.

"Yes," he replied. "Far more important." Passion was again seeping into his tone, though it was triumphant this time. It seemed to Esyal that it was forcing words from him where a colder part of his mind would have urged silence. The reluctance, torment almost, at this conflict, flitted briefly across his face. Esyal could not avert her gaze without conceding she had seen it, so she willed her eyes to blank unresponsiveness.

"This is an ancient place—a Place of Great Power," Adroyan pressed on. "With each hour I become more certain. When it is fully measured and understood, there will be such knowledge here that not only will the Rhanen be eradicated once and for all, but the very flaw in people's nature which turns them to the Rhanen will dwindle into insignificance. And not only in this country, but far beyond—far beyond. We will bring order to all things, all places."

Even as he was speaking, the ancient, feral snarl that had come to Esyal in her dream returned again, tugging urgently at her. With it, as though it had come from some place far beyond herself, came a realization that this man—*this creature*—would bring about terrible harm if he were not stopped.

"*He (it?) must be made no more.*"

The words formed in her mind as they had in her dream.

Made no more?

The images that hung about the phrase were confused and unsteady, as if those who spoke (?) them were struggling with a concept they did not understand. Yet to Esyal, the heart of their intent was brutally clear. Adroyan would have to be killed.

And the urgency in the words told her that it must be soon.

Very soon.

CHAPTER 36

As he had announced, Josyff went straight from his evening meal to the room off the Great Hall that he and Badr had commandeered as an office, to plot some of the day's work. It went well, though there was a small closing error at the end which left him puzzled.

Sort it out tomorrow, he concluded after a brief consideration. The scheme was young yet and the routine duplication and cross-checking inherent in the work would root out any discrepancies soon enough. He was almost jaunty as he walked into the book room.

To his surprise, both Esyal and Adroyan were there and it took no great sensitivity to detect the uneasiness hovering in their silence.

He broke it with a brisk greeting and a question to Esyal.

"Is this the full story?" he asked, indicating the scrolls.

Esyal gave him a strange look as though she wanted to ask him something in return, but was too unsure about how it might be received. "I don't know. The writing's very odd—what I've read of it. A mixture of technical bits and pieces about what they were building, a diary of some kind, and what seem to be bits of... myth... legend. And there's a lot of it."

Josyff chuckled. "Well, you've plenty of time." Esyal's eye narrowed but before she could reply, Josyff pointed again to the scrolls. "What about the pictures, then? Do they show who was hurt—what happened afterwards—did they get the drawbridge open?"

"Have you plotted today's work?"

It was Adroyan, though he did not look up from the scrolls as he spoke.

"Yes, sir," Josyff replied. He was about to expand on the progress he and

Badr might well make from now on, but experience told him to stay silent. People like Adroyan had a gift for latching on to the least remark and using it like a weapon. Stick to the truth and say as little as possible was the axiom that had helped Josyff keep his position throughout the coming of the New Order. To be either ingratiating or rebellious was to court disaster just as effectively as incompetence. Quiet conformity seemed to be the way. Obedience?

He waited.

"I will look at it," Adroyan said.

Josyff swore inwardly. He needed no urging to get this job done as soon as possible. He wanted to be away from the place and back with his wife and he neither needed nor wanted an interfering superior breathing down his neck incessantly, expecting him to work twenty four hours a day.

"As you wish, sir," he replied. "Though there's not much to see at the moment—just a start on some baselines. Unspectacular but very important. We're using a room off the Great Hall." He extended an arm towards the door by way of invitation. Adroyan straightened.

"Oh, the Keep'll keep." It was Esyal. "It's been here long enough and it'll be here tomorrow, measured or not. Let's sort out these scrolls—see if we can find out what happened—and when." She spoke directly to Adroyan. "It could be important if you want to use this place. A permanently wedged open front door isn't particularly desirable, I imagine."

Josyff remained silent, his eyes moving between his two companions. Esyal continued to surprise him. Whoever, whatever, she had been before she lost her memory, no residual respect for the Ordrans—or even caution—seemed to have been left with her. He felt a frisson of both alarm and dark amusement as he waited for Adroyan to reply.

Just as Adroyan was about to speak, Esyal added, "It'd be out of place, wouldn't it? A kind of... distortion." She did not know where the word had come from, it just felt appropriate.

Adroyan faltered, either disturbed by the word or simply because he was unused to such freely given comments. Josyff remained stonily silent—if Adroyan were to respond badly to this small onslaught, it would be he, the nearest available underling, who would doubtless bear the brunt of it.

But no reproach came. Adroyan cleared his throat softly and said: "You are satisfied with the work you have done? The equipment is good?"

"Yes, I am, and yes, it is, sir," Josyff replied, again wilfully avoiding any amplification.

Esyal stepped forward quickly and knelt down at the end of the last scroll. The small flurry of movement precluded any continuation of Josyff's interrogation.

"Look at these," she said. She was peering intently at a series of pictures running down the scroll. Josyff joined her.

"Same artist as the first ones," he said after a brief inspection. "What's so special?"

"I don't know," Esyal replied. "Just..."

Her voice tailed off and she stood up and began prowling the narrow avenues between the scrolls.

"There's the collapse, here—lots of people milling about. Then nothing much seems to happen after that. All these pictures just show what seems to be general tidying up. There doesn't seem to be any further attempt to open the drawbridge. And the number of people gets smaller and smaller. At the end, there are just two. One leaning on part of the wreckage, the other standing by this abutment."

"It's a woman, too," Josyff said. "And the drawbridge is still shut. Strange they didn't record the whole incident. Presumably they got the drawbridge moving again—or it started working of its own accord, like now. Maybe there are more scrolls."

"None like this," Esyal said. "And there doesn't seem to be any way to date it, so I won't even know where to look when I get started properly—assuming most of the other documents are dated, that is. They *are* supposed to be a record of events."

"And the lord was slain."

Adroyan's voice was flat and indifferent, as though he was talking to himself, but both Josyff and Esyal looked at him sharply.

Josyff was the first to recover. "Lord...?" he queried uncertainly, caught by the coincidence of the word with his dream. Esyal, similarly disturbed, watched him narrowly but said nothing.

Adroyan, crouching, ran his finger along a line of the text. Josyff and Esyal read it over his shoulder.

Compelled, for reasons she could not begin to explain, but with what she hoped was a casual tone, Esyal voiced the question she had clung to in her dream.

"We worked out last night that there were four people under that wreckage, but, as I recall, they all seemed to be wearing some kind of livery—like workers, or servants. None of them looked like this lot over here—the dignitaries."

She pointed to a group of figures in one of the earlier pictures, and invested the word "dignitaries" with the same mild contempt she had used the previous evening.

"It probably doesn't mean anything," Josyff said after an awkward silence. "We might have counted wrong—or maybe the artist wasn't as meticulous as we give him credit for." Even as he spoke, he recalled the lord's voice whispering urgently to him.

"Draw this as it is, measurer. As it is. As accurately as you know. On your life, make no error, miss no detail."

The lord, to whom he had given the identity of Adroyan. Nothing unusual in that, of course. Adroyan was a figure of authority over him—an unwanted figure—who would necessarily loom high in his thoughts. But...

"Then again," he managed. "I don't know... perhaps it wasn't considered respectful to make images of your..."

"Master." Esyal's completion of his sentence carried the same contempt as before.

"You do not believe in showing respect to those given authority over you?"

It was Adroyan.

Esyal felt the searching challenge in the remark and knew she should best avoid it. But in spite of herself, she engaged.

"Who gives anyone the authority to give someone authority over me?"

Adroyan's expression was unreadable.

"Such permission is not needed," he said. "It is the way of things. Some—a few—lead—have authority. The rest follow—they accept that authority."

Rage filled Esyal but she managed to avoid further entanglement. "Well, as I said, I'm not interested in politics. It's not only boring, it's complicated." A flick of her hands affected a dismissal of the subject. She addressed Josyff: "Anyway, why would it be disrespectful to draw your boss?"

Josyff floundered. In his mind it was Adroyan who was under the wreckage—drawn in to end the dispute between two of the workers—dominating the scene, all eyes turned towards him, long black cloak—habit?—billowing softly behind him. He saw again the measurer's hand, beginning to move, just as the structure collapsed and he had been hurled from the dream. Yet there was no figure so dressed in any of the pictures.

He shrugged. "Different times, different ideas. Some people think that making an image of someone is to gain power over them. Or perhaps the artist never got chance to draw the man—perhaps this... lord... only dropped by briefly to see how things were going before the measurer..." He corrected himself hastily, "the artist... had chance to draw him."

"Still," Esyal said. "It's odd that something as serious as this lord being killed isn't even referred to in these pictures."

"I agree, but... oh!"

The exclamation was due to Adroyan passing roughly between them making them both step back in surprise. By the time they had recovered, he was striding purposefully towards the door, seemingly oblivious to the small stir he had just caused.

Josyff saw the portent of an acid comment in Esyal's expression and quickly raised a hand to signal her to silence; he had caught a glance of a darkly angry face as Adroyan had passed. He lowered his hand only when Adroyan had left and, almost in spite of himself, voiced his immediate concerns.

"Esyal, I know it's none of my business, but you really should be more... circumspect. Don't risk provoking people like Adroyan. I don't know who he is, I've never met him before, or even heard of him, but I do know the authority he has here is from the highest office in the Government. People like that are best avoided if possible, and treated very warily if it's not— *very* warily. Certainly don't let our peculiar circumstances here lure you into a false sense of familiarity."

Esyal looked set to be defiant, but Josyff did not give her chance to speak. "I said it was none of my business, but just think for a moment. It doesn't seem to be bothering you, but you don't even know who or what you are— or what relatives and friends you have. It'll cost you nothing to be a little careful. Antagonizing someone like Adroyan is... risky, not to say downright dangerous. You mightn't mind what happens to you but there could be serious consequences for other people as well."

Esyal pouted briefly then nodded. "Yes," she conceded, reluctantly. "I suppose you're right. I'll try to remember to think before I speak." To deflect the conversation away from her feigned memory loss, she affected a lighter tone. "But whatever I am, I don't think I've much to do with people like him. Or even like you. I'll be a nonentity somewhere—doing something innocuous—one of those who accept authority." Josyff gave her a cautionary look as the defiance returned briefly to the surface again in this last remark. She dispelled it with an airy gesture. "Still, he didn't have to barge between us like that—not even an 'excuse me.'"

"No. But he did. And we both survived the ordeal, didn't we?"

But *he* won't, Esyal thought viciously. Just as soon as I've decided how to deal with him. And our "peculiar" circumstances will be ideal for that.

"I wonder what made him scuttle off like that," she said, as much out of genuine curiosity as to keep the thought from her face.

"He was reading this, I think."

Josyff was crouching at the end of one of the scrolls. Esyal joined him.

"This writing's very small." She removed the books restraining the corners of the scroll and brought it close to her face. "And it's a different hand."

She read. *And thus was the evil from those beyond—the many-faced— defeated. The danger had been terrible but at the very point of their victory the Way was sealed against them by the death of their own creature, the one risen from nowhere, the one called the lord. There is a dark justice in that—a balancing.* She paused and read on in silence for a moment, then frowned.

"What's the matter?" Josyff asked.

"The last part's awful."

She was obviously distressed. Josyff took the scroll from her gently. The writing had become weak and unsteady.

I am failing now—as are the others. We will not escape. The changes have stopped—presumably the great danger is passed. But still they are holding the gate closed—I do not think they understand what they are doing to us—time, death, seem to have little meaning to them—they are deeply strange. Certainly I do not understand them or their conflict—or how it has spilled down into our world. There is no more water now—it will not be long. To those who find us—be warned—be warned. The like of the lord—channels for great evil—must surely be drawn here again, now that those beyond know of us—and can reach us. We are pawns. The Keep will ever be a danger—its Heart must be destroyed. I have tried to find it but it eludes me—perhaps it has gone again—folded away—I am too wea... The script tailed off into an illegible scrawl.

"You're right, it *is* awful," Josyff said after a long silence. "Trapped here—dying of thirst—all those people." He shuddered involuntarily. For a moment he felt as though the entire Keep were closing about him, gripping him, holding him, binding him to its service. "Thank God Nyk's got the drawbridge wedged open," he muttered, making a note at the same time to check on the work. The final feeble writing at the end of the scroll disturbed him beyond his natural feelings for the suffering of the author—beyond the simple human touch across the ages.

CHAPTER 37

"What on earth does all that mean?" Esyal asked. "Many-faced, channels for evil, the Heart of the Keep must be destroyed?" Her voice was unsteady and she was playing nervously with the scroll—briefly, a little girl. She looked down at her hands.

"Hello, what's this?"

Josyff was pointing to writing on the back of the scroll. Neat and confident, it was in marked contrast to the writing they had just been looking at.

"It's almost like a copying exercise," Josyff said. "Looks like a poem of some kind."

He read:

And the silence was sundered...
Movement, and darkness and light...
And the pain of parting and difference...
And conflict in the Ways unknowable...
For each would be the whole.
Yet in striving, the whole could not be made.
And in not striving all would become again silence.
Which must not be.

Must not be...
Conflict...
Into the darkness, into the light...
Arcing to and fro...
Searching. Reaching...
For that which was not silence would know itself...

"Oh," Esyal said incongruously after a brief pause. "Doesn't rhyme very well, does it?"

The plaintive note in her voice exploded a low chuckle out of Josyff.

"No, it doesn't," he agreed, a little too quickly.

"Don't patronize," Esyal retorted, fixing his arch look with a narrow one of her own.

"Sorry."

"I wonder why someone would write a poem on the back of the scroll? It's not as if it's any old piece of scrap paper—it's some kind of official document, isn't it?"

"It seems like it," Josyff agreed again. He peered narrowly at the writing, then, with a little awkward scrabbling, compared it with that on the other side. "But it looks to me as though it's been written by the same person who made this... final... record. Look. Here, before the writing started to deteriorate."

Esyal took the scroll from him.

"You're right," she decided unhappily after some scrutiny. "Everything's questions, questions, questions and no answers." She stood up and jerked an angry thumb towards the door then began counting on her fingers. "What got into him, rushing off like that? What's this poem mean? What happened to these people, and what's this writer burbling on about—those "beyond", many-faced, channels of evil, Ways unknowable? It's creepy." Then, violently: "Damn! This whole place is creepy. Suddenly I can see why Henk wants to leave. It's like a grotesque asylum—where the inmates are sane and the building's mad!"

Josyff quailed before this unexpected passion, at the same time smiling uncertainly at her image of the building.

"Well, at least the door's open," he offered.

Esyal's jaw set as she turned to him but, before she could speak, the floor began to shake and a low rumbling filled the room. Esyal staggered and let out a startled cry and, even though he was kneeling, Josyff had to put a hand on the floor to steady himself. The ladders which served the shelves began moving alarmingly. The shaking grew in intensity, as did the rumbling, and Josyff found himself holding his breath and clutching fruitlessly at the carpeted floor. There was a final jarring thud, then silence and stillness returned.

Josyff's breath burst out of him as though he had been dropped on the floor and, for a moment, he could not move. His heart was pounding and his stomach churning. He was vaguely aware of the sound of the ladders bumping into their stops, but it was muffled and distant as though stifled by the weight of the silence that had flooded back into the room. Gradually he levered himself to his feet—his legs were trembling.

Esyal, white-faced and wide-eyed, was clinging to one of the tables.

"Are you all right?" he heard himself asking.

"Yes," came a shaky reply, followed by, "No, yes—yes—I'm not hurt, anyway—what the devil was that?"

Josyff did not reply. He was willing his reluctant legs to carry him to a nearby chair where he slumped down gratefully, put his head in his hands and waited for his body's responses to grow quieter.

"Are *you* all right?" Esyal asked him as she too sat down.

"Like you, yes and no," Josyff managed. "But a little better than I was a moment ago—I think." He answered her previous question. "That *must* have been an earthquake, for sure. Terrifying."

As his composure slowly returned, Josyff looked around the room. Despite what had seemed to be an extremely violent upheaval, little appeared to have been disturbed. A few books at the ends of rows had tumbled to lie flat on the shelves and that was all. The ladders appeared to be none the worse for their impromptu journeys. Irrelevantly it came to Josyff that they had probably been designed to withstand far worse abuse from ordinary users.

"No harm done here, by the look of it," he said, standing up and taking a deep breath. "Except to our nerves and our dignity. We'd better see how everyone else is."

Heading back towards the common room, they encountered a flustered Qualto—towel in one hand, large knife in the other.

"Are you expecting rain or attackers?" Esyal asked.

Qualto let out an incoherent noise, part squeal, part growl. "Rattled every pot and pan in my kitchen. Never heard such a racket. Thought the whole place was going to come crashing down."

"Any damage?" Josyff asked.

"Just one plate slipped off the table," Qualto said. "Otherwise nothing, as far as I could see. Surprisingly. What...?"

Josyff anticipated the question. "No idea. Probably an earthquake. No harm done in the book room. We were just coming to see if you and the others were all right."

The common room proved to be deserted, but as they were leaving it, Nyk appeared at the end of the corridor. He was steadying himself against the wall and seemed to be in a distressed condition. They ran up to him.

"What's happened?" Josyff asked, concerned, and taking his arm to support him.

"Broken," Nyk replied. His eyes were wide and his expression shocked. "Just broken. Like so many matchsticks."

"What's broken?" Josyff pressed.

Nyk gesticulated vaguely. "The timbers—holding open the drawbridge. Broken." He was shaking. Josyff ushered him towards the common room and motioned to Qualto. "Go and get him something to drink." Qualto scurried off, towel flapping and knife glinting.

Josyff led Nyk to a chair and sat him down gently. As he did so, Badr and Henk appeared in the doorway. Even the impassive Henk's face was alive with questions, but Josyff held up a quietening hand and they both remained silent where they were. He crouched by Nyk. It upset him to see this bright, resilient and likeable man—his unobtrusive but unstinting support since his arrival—in such a state. He glanced round the room.

"We're all here—bar Adroyan—and none of us are hurt..."

Qualto arrived, pushing his way between Badr and Henk. He handed a mug to Josyff who sniffed it and then offered it to Nyk.

"Drink this," he said quietly. "It'll help settle you down. Then you can tell us what's happened to upset you like this."

Nyk took the mug hesitantly—his hands were still shaking—then nodded.

"Thanks. I'll be fine. I'll be fine," he said, unconvincingly. "Just give me a moment."

"None of us are leaving," Josyff said, affecting a light-heartedness he did not feel.

In as much as he had expected any response to this, it was not the one he received. Nyk looked at him, took a purposeful drink, bent down to put the mug on the floor and said flatly, "Damned right we're not. Not now."

"What?"

"We're not leaving. The drawbridge's closed again—just like before. Tight shut." He pressed the palms of his hands together with a strain that made his shoulders shake, as though the effort alone could crush the present back into a safer past.

For an instant, Josyff felt himself in two places at once: in his dream, struggling with a heavy timber in the din of the dusty courtyard, and at the same time poring over the scrolls in the book room with Esyal. For reasons which he could not have identified, the first question which rushed out of the confusion and found voice was, "How much water do we have here?"

It seemed to surprise Nyk as much as it did Josyff. The wide-eyed anxiety slipped away as he turned again to his questioner.

"A lot, a lot," he stammered before becoming matter-of-fact host answering the needs of his guest. "Constantly topped up by the rains and the snow—there are enormous storage tanks—this place is meant to house a lot of people—a lot. Why?"

"Oh, nothing important," Josyff flustered. "Just something... unpleasant... that Esyal and I were reading about. I'm sorry. Finish your tale first. What's happened?"

"What's happened? You tell me, because I don't know." Nyk's face became fretful again. "I went back after dinner to tidy up some bits and pieces. Nothing special—just so that I'd be able to get back to normal right away tomorrow. I was up a ladder lifting some tools down when all of a sudden the place shook. Just shook. Not much, I don't think, looking back, but it frightened the life out of me. I was down that ladder and up the stairs before I knew what I was doing. Didn't realize I could move so fast."

He blew out a noisy breath and took another drink.

"Just as well, though. The place seemed to tilt over. I... fell... it felt like falling... against the wall and something held me there. Then there was this noise. Things... tearing, breaking... dreadful sounds. Probably didn't last very long but it seemed to go on forever. Then..." He snapped his fingers. "It was gone. I could move. The place was quiet and still—just a bit of dust coming up from below."

He fell silent.

"And?" Josyff prompted.

Nyk hesitated. "I grabbed a handrail and just stood there until my legs stopped shaking—or at least stopped enough for me to stand on them." He looked down. His feet were tapping nervously. He pressed his hands on his knees to stop them. "Then I went back down the stairs—very slowly, and holding tight to that rail, I can tell you." He shook his head. "I couldn't believe it. All those timbers we put in—and those I'd put in today—and the fastenings—all smashed—just snapped like dry kindling—and scattered everywhere. And the counterweight upright again—tight shut just like it was before. I didn't even need to touch it to know that—it looked as though it were rooted to the wall."

Unwanted images from the scrolls and his dream filled Josyff's mind, and it was to still these rather than offer Nyk any reproach that he asked, "Didn't you say that anything that tried to close the bridge would have to take the walls down?" His tone was harsher than he had intended.

"I did," Nyk replied. "That's what I thought. And the walls *have* been damaged. Not enough to bring anything down, but anchors and bolts have been torn out. I'd never have thought it possible. What the devil's happening?"

An uneasy silence filled the room.

Josyff glanced around. Everyone was visibly shaken but they were all looking at him. He forced himself to be matter-of-fact.

"So much for getting back to normal," he said, as lightly as he could, patting Nyk on the shoulder. He addressed the others. "It's late, and I'm open to suggestions, but I can't see any of us getting any sleep after this so we'd better go and see the damage for ourselves."

"And if that drawbridge has shut again, we need to give some serious thought to getting out of here, bad weather or no," Badr added. "There's no saying what might happen next."

"No." Adroyan's voice filled the room. He was framed in the doorway, his eyes alive. "The measuring must be finished—it is more urgent than ever, now." He looked squarely at Badr who had turned round when he spoke. "When that is done we can consider leaving."

Josyff noticed Badr's jaw stiffening, and Esyal, notwithstanding his earlier advice, was obviously about to enter into violent disagreement.

"Very well," he said briskly. "Leaving we'll have to leave 'til later, anyway, but we still need to find out what's happened. Let's go and see what's happened."

CHAPTER 38

As the group emerged from the main door the courtyard lights came on to reveal that it was snowing again. And quite heavily—the signs of Nyk's unsteady flight from the Gatehouse were already beginning to disappear. Nyk and Josyff leading, they scurried across the courtyard, heads bowed. Adroyan came last, like a sheepdog watching for any spirited individuals that might try to bolt.

Josyff glanced up at the heavy bulk of the Gatehouse ahead. Despite the light it was difficult to see clearly through the falling snow but, as far as he could see, the looming structure seemed to have suffered no damage. He remarked on it as they entered the building and began climbing the stairs.

"Nor in here," Badr said, looking around.

As they passed the hand-wheel that controlled the drawbridge, Josyff took hold of it in the faint hope that perhaps Nyk had in some way been mistaken about what had happened. He released it almost immediately with a sharp intake of breath.

"What's the matter?" Badr asked.

Josyff did not reply straight away but tentatively touched the wheel again before taking hold of it. "It's locked solid, but it's shaking," he said, confidently tightening his grip. "Feel it."

Badr took hold in turn, his head inclined in concentration. "It is," he said. He gripped the wheel with his other hand. "It's picking up vibrations from somewhere." His knuckles whitened. "And my grip's not stopping it—not even changing it. What, in the name of sanity, is there around here that would cause vibrations like that?" He turned to Nyk who was just about to descend the stairs to the counterweight chamber. "Is their any machinery nearby?"

"Not nearby, no," Nyk called back. "It's all quite a way away—and there's nothing that shakes." He disappeared from view, Josyff following him. Badr released the wheel, flexed his hands a couple of times then ran them down his jacket as though to wipe something off.

Down in the counterweight chamber, Josyff found that Nyk's description had been woefully accurate. The timbers that he and the others had struggled to bring there and erect had been scattered about like the unwanted toys of a wilful child: several of them were broken.

"Mind where you're walking," Nyk said, catching Josyff's arm as he missed his footing and staggered. He looked down at what he had trodden on. It was an anchor bolt, bent but still solidly embedded in a large piece of stone.

The wall was pockmarked with damage where others had similarly been torn out and with the remnants of shattered wood where timber had yielded before bolt.

"Good bolts," Nyk said, following his gaze.

"Indeed they are," Josyff said. He frowned and gave voice to his thoughts as they came to him. "The forces needed to do all this are enormous, but the damage is too..." He struggled briefly to find the word. "Too localised... too much in one place for it to be done just by the ground shaking."

Nyk gazed around. "I hadn't thought about it—but you're right. And, come to that, how could the drawbridge do this? It's finely balanced—you can move it with little more than a push of your hand. Which means..."

"It can't exert any force greater than a push of the hand," Josyff said. "It should just... clatter up and down if it's shaken."

"Unless something's levering on one end of it."

The conclusion did nothing to clarify what had happened and they fell silent.

The others had joined them and were wandering about aimlessly. Adroyan, still the last, remained at the foot of the stairs, again as though to prevent anyone leaving.

"Ye gods," Badr muttered softly. "What the devil did this?"

"Devil indeed," Adroyan echoed from his watch post.

Badr went straight over to the counterweight and put his hands against it.

"You won't move it," Nyk said.

Badr nodded by way of reply then motioned Nyk and Josyff to come closer. "Feel this," he said.

The two men did as they were asked, but both touched the face of the counterweight cautiously at first, as they might test something hot.

"It's vibrating," Josyff said after a moment.

"Just like the wheel upstairs," Badr responded.

"Which means what?"

"I don't know." Badr turned to Nyk. "You're sure there's no machinery nearby that would do this?"

Nyk was mimicking Badr's earlier gesture, looking at his hand as if expecting to find it stained in some way. "Yes, I'm sure," he replied, with a hint of impatience sufficient to make Badr apologize.

"I'm sorry. I meant..."

"I told you, there's nothing in the whole Keep that would cause this kind of shaking," Nyk said definitively. "Everything runs—is running—smooth and well." He waved an arm across the entire scene. "And there's nothing here that could do anything like this." The hand spiralled in to smack his chest. "Ask me what *did* do it—*I've no idea.* But it wasn't anything here—and it wasn't any earthquake either. Anything powerful enough to do this just by shaking the ground would have done damage all through the building—surely?" There was a small cadence of doubt in this last word, but it evoked no response from anyone.

Something prompted Josyff to take a chance. He looked across at Adroyan. "Do you have any thoughts about this, sir? It's very like the pictures on the scrolls—the drawbridge jammed shut and destruction all around—and you managed to read more than we did."

Adroyan looked around uneasily. Josyff watched him keenly. For a moment it seemed to him that the man's authority had evaporated, leaving behind a hesitant and timorous shell.

Like a hunted animal, he thought. He's afraid. What's he afraid of?

Then, more alarmingly, the thought, what should *I* be afraid of?

"*This is the Destroyer.*"

As if in answer to his unexpected question, the words whispered through his mind like the sound of a distant crowd carried on a dying wind. Instantly he was back in his dream, struggling with the timbers in the dusty courtyard. But as quickly as it had come, the illusion was gone, as was the impression of Adroyan's weakness.

Adroyan was looking at him strangely, his head craning forward slightly as if listening to something far away. "What did you say?"

"I asked if you'd any thoughts on this, sir," Josyff repeated. "The scene here's not unlike that shown on the scrolls."

Adroyan looked distracted again for a moment then said, flatly, "No." He turned and began walking quickly up the stairs.

"*Destroyer, Destroyer, Destroyer...*"

The voices returned to Josyff. Though echoing and fading they wrapped themselves around the sound of Adroyan's footsteps and Josyff found himself clenching his fists to prevent his hands lifting to cover his ears. At the top of the stairs Adroyan stopped. Gripping the handrail—his knuckles were white with effort, Josyff noted—he addressed the watching group.

"Waste no more time on the why's and wherefore's of this, it is beyond you," he said. "Surveyor, your work is more urgent than ever now. I can brook no further delay—this place must be measured—its Heart must be found as quickly as possible."

And he was gone.

There was silence after his footsteps died away.

"What the devil was all that about?" Esyal was the first to speak. "Beyond us!" she mimicked, "Why's and wherefore's!" then looked at Josyff. "There was something about the Heart of the building in that scroll, wasn't there?"

"The Heart of the Keep must be destroyed," Josyff recalled.

Esyal waved her arms vaguely. "I don't want to seem stupid, but is that some kind of technical term that builders—surveyors—use? Heart of the building?"

"Not that I've ever heard," Josyff replied. "It made no sense in the scroll and it makes no sense now." Noting that he was once again the focus of attention, he told the others briefly about the collapse of the framework around the drawbridge that he and Esyal had read of in the scrolls.

"All of which means what?" Badr asked.

"I've no idea," Josyff said, resisting the temptation to kick a nearby piece of rubble angrily across the floor. "None at all—save coincidence. This place is nothing but questions and mysteries." It took him a further effort to control the frustration that was on the verge of bursting out.

"I suppose you and I'd better do what we're here for—get this place measured and down on paper, as soon as we can. That should keep..." He hesitated. "...our employer satisfied. And the sooner it's done the sooner we can *all* bend our minds to getting out of here."

Badr shifted from one foot to the other uncomfortably. "Do you think the place is safe to... be in?" he asked eventually. "Shaking like this."

"I don't know what to think," Josyff replied. "But Nyk's right, whatever caused this seems to be confined to this part of the building. A few ornaments and the like might be rattling in the Keep proper but no damage's been done—that we know of. Besides, safe or no, we can't get out!"

Henk intervened, seeing the opportunity to pursue the suggestion that Esyal had made to him earlier. "I'll put some food and outdoor clothes by the main door—and maybe bag some up and leave it out in the court-yard. We've got plenty. Then if anything bad happens, at least we won't be stranded helpless in the snow."

Josyff nodded appreciatively. "And water too," he said. "Don't forget the water."

"And water," Henk confirmed.

Nyk's expression lightened. "That unpleasantness in the scrolls seems to have made a substantial impression on you."

Josyff dithered briefly. "It did. I didn't mention before but it seems that all the people involved in that incident died there—and died of thirst."

Nyk's face darkened. "Unpleasant indeed," he said. "But at least *that* won't happen to us."

"Are you happy with Henk's idea?" Josyff asked Badr.

"Yes, it's good."

"Right!" Josyff's foot could be restrained no longer and it sent a piece of rubble skittering noisily across the floor. He felt better. "There's nothing we can do here except mope around and ask unanswerable questions. I'm off to bed. It's been a long and bizarre day." He drew out the word 'bizarre'. "Here's hoping tomorrow will be a little better."

Even as he closed the door to his room behind him, Josyff's forced enthusiasm slithered away. He slumped down on the bed. Were it not for the responses of the all-too-real people about him to everything that was happening, he would truly have begun to doubt his sanity. Dreams and unaccountable noises, even his experience in the Archive, he could, with some effort, attribute to his imagination and its response to this peculiar place—not to say, this whole peculiar project! But the damage done to the timbers that had wedged the drawbridge could not be set aside as some transient personal aberration, nor to the previously favoured explanation, an earthquake. This might perhaps have accounted for the earlier incidents but, as he himself had said, the damage was too massive and too localized for it have been done merely by the ground shaking.

All of which meant what?

He swung his legs up on to the bed, lay down and covered his face with his hands. For a while he neither moved nor thought much. So many strange things had happened in so short a time that his mind temporarily gave up all attempts to rationalize them. There was a childlike element in his stillness: if he did not move, nothing would happen, he would be safe. The insight made him smile a little. Quite deliberately, he was refusing to pursue the unresolvable aspects of recent events, knowing that it would be both futile and wearing. He would let them sink into the deeper recesses of his mind whence, if undisturbed by conscious ramblings and argument, would come either more inspired answers, or at least a more resigned attitude towards the insoluble.

His faith in the ability of his inner mind to deal with difficult problems was profound: it was tried, tested and reliable and, whenever he had paused to reflect on this part of his nature which, unseen and unheard, guided his thoughts, he had reasoned that, whatever it might be, it was on his side—it would work always in his best interests. How could it profit by doing otherwise? To work against his interests would be ultimately to destroy itself.

Still, it was intriguing, posing as it did the question, "who's in charge?" Did he do something because of his conscious will or because he had been silently prompted by his inner self?

It didn't matter of course. Many things happened in his body about which he knew nothing and it did not bother him. Indeed he was glad to have this not inconsiderable intellectual resource available to him, albeit not directly controllable. But then, he supposed, perhaps it was controllable to some degree. Was he not controlling it right now by abandoning his conscious concerns and effectively telling it to take over?

But maybe it prompted you to do just that.

Josyff laughed softly as the circling thought occurred to him.

"Enough," he said, out loud. He felt oddly relaxed. "Sleep, then work. Let's keep things simple. Let's get this place dealt with and get back home." Whatever Adroyan's anxieties about, and ambitions for, this project were, he would keep away from them—they were none of his concern and he would be risking more than he cared to think about if he went out of his way to pry into them. He would do as he was told, then leave. The man could well be Ordrans, for mercy's sake, he reminded himself finally and with some force—you got this far without attracting the adverse attention of the New Order by keeping away from such people and their antics, just keep on doing it!

What if sleep brings more dreams?

The question was as unwelcome as it was unexpected. Josyff growled at it, stood up and began preparing to go to bed.

But it was still there a few minutes later, when the room was dark, the pillow soft and restful on his face, and the empty part of the bed where his wife should have been had been patted ruefully.

Let them come, he decided. So much had happened since he came here that verged on the fantastic, that another dream would hardly be a momentous event. And, apart from some alarm and a bump on the head through sleep-walking, they had caused him no harm. Gradually he drifted into sleep, recent events occasionally bubbling to the surface as if to catch his attention and each time being dispatched into the depths. This much I do control, he thought fuzzily, down you go to where you can best be dealt with.

The image of another place, another world even, mysterious and alien, part of him and not part of him, affecting him and being affected by him, yet profoundly unknowable, was suddenly all about him, vivid with realization.

But the image was not his...

CHAPTER 39

With the image came words. Inaudible yet intelligible they filled Josyff's mind like those that had come to him when he had been in the Archive and when he had dreamt he was in the courtyard. They shifted and changed, now seemingly from one speaker, if speaker were the appropriate word for such a phenomenon, now from many. And there were so many meanings hovering about them: some straightforward and commonplace, others deeply alien, so much so that he was utterly disorientated when they touched him. Part of him reached out to steady himself...

"Be still, measurer."

The words were reassuring and calm, reaching deep inside him, but underneath them he could sense a nervousness, fear even, which knew that a mistake—a misjudgement—here would lose something precious.

Just as it had been in the Archive, he thought. It was a human quality and it both intrigued and reassured him.

As did the blankets and the soft comfort of the bed he could feel about him.

Am I awake? Am I drea...

The words intruded.

"You are... elusive, measurer. Now here, now gone, now simple and clear, now tangled beyond all undoing. It is the strangeness you carry with you— you, who should not be—who are so much (smaller? inadequate? incomplete?). You go beyond—to places I (we?) cannot touch (see? hear? know?). It is... unexpected. You... bewilder..."

Josyff had a sensation of complex patterns built from simple shapes repeating over and over and diminishing endlessly, but shifting through impossible geometries. It was gone almost before he could register it. A phrase from the scroll came in its wake and hung there enigmatically— many-faced—but it was almost immediately displaced by an frisson of fear out of which came:

"This is a frightening place you are in (of?), this... nexus... this... knot..."

Nexus, knot—these were the words that Henk said Adroyan had used when the two of them had heard noises—voices?—in the Great Hall. The great knot that bound the Powers!

Josyff felt the fear in the words but it did not affect him—it was as though he were both observing events from some mysterious vantage while at the same time lying safe in his room. What he did feel was a powerful curios- ity—a need to question, to inquire into everything that was happening. It tore at him—and he could sense the same urgency hovering about him. Reflection, resonance—the words fluttered about his mind like trapped moths.

Nexus!

"Do you mean the Keep?" Josyff heard his voice speaking softly into the darkness. It stilled the moths.

"How could it come about, this... creation? (monstrosity? impossibil- ity?). How could such a thing be drawn even from the strangeness that the Destroyer carried? So small a thing to bind so much."

195

The words were musing, not talking to him.

"Do you mean the Keep?" Josyff pressed. "This building?" Deliberately he visualized such of the Keep as he was familiar with—winding corridors, echoing halls, empty rooms. He thought he sensed a sigh.

"The merest shadow. You cannot see it as it is. It is beyond you."

Josyff felt challenged. "Show me, then."

"I (we?) will lose you. You are..."

"Elusive, yes." Though part of him still felt itself outside and separate from this exchange, another part felt almost excited. "Do not end this. It is important," it told him.

"Very well," Josyff conceded. "But tell me who you are."

There was a long stillness which eventually filled again with disorientating images. They stopped almost immediately, as though sensing his disturbance, leaving only a lingering, *"We are."*

Josyff did not pursue his question. Do not end this, it is important!

"What do you want?" he asked instead.

"To be released."

"What binds you?" Josyff heard himself asking.

He was falling through the dark innards of the clock, grasping at chains which constantly eluded him; he was floating in the blue world with golden threads dancing all about him. But were they chains and threads, or were they... edges? And, pervading all, he could feel the beating of wings reverberating through and around him—a great energy, struggling...

Then all was still and silent.

"This binds us."

"I don't understand."

"No. You are... elusive (small? inadequate?)... it is difficult."

Unexpectedly, Josyff felt impatient. His years of facing and solving practical problems took over. "It is you who comes to me, distressing me, making me fear for my sanity. I do not know who or what you are, *I* cannot reach *you*. Maybe you *are* no more than a figment of my imagination but if you are not and if you need something from me, explain yourself! Find a way to make it easy!"

Before any reply could be made he grasped for something that was unequivocally real.

"Is it you who've closed the drawbridge—trapped us here? Have you done it before?"

"Before? Trapped—bound—yes—the Destroyer—the one whose strangeness had made (shaped?) this impossibility. Bound him as he bound us. Now he is free again."

"No. He must have died, long ago—as did many others—very unpleasantly—you killed them all when you sealed this place."

"Died? This is to... be... no more?"

"Yes."

There was a long silence during which Josyff thought he could sense a debate going on beyond his awareness.

"It is difficult. Even your... existence... is difficult (doubtful?). We (I?) draw from the nearer parts of your strangeness to talk (touch? measure? reach?) you. To be no more is as bad for you as for us? Much feared?"

"Yes."

"And killed is to make no more?"

"Yes."

"But the Destroyer is here again."

"No—he is dead—you killed him—made him no more." Adroyan's name came to him. "But perhaps there is one here who might be like him."

"Another?"

"Perhaps."

There was another silence; shorter this time, but deep and very still.

"Aah. The spiralling ways of your strangeness—shapes within shapes—ever beyond us. They build. So dangerous."

"Why did you kill him—and all those others?"

Without pause, the words formed about him with an awful clarity.

"Such is the nature of war."

Josyff shuddered at their touch, they were so laden with emotions: from bitter regret to cold and ruthless determination; from impotent anguish to screaming vengeance. They burned through him.

"War?" he said, suddenly both frightened and furious. "What war? Whose war?"

"The war. The war we fight to defend ourselves from those who would seize all—bind us to their will—take us into the darkness."

Josyff felt a fear echoing his own.

"In war, you... you kill your own kind. You don't kill people who have nothing to do with it! Are you intending to do the same again? Kill us all?"

"We must be released."

"Yes, you've told me that, now answer my question."

"The Destroyer must be made no more—killed—or terrible harm will come to all."

"And you would kill me—and the others, for this?"

"The Destroyer must be..."

"Enough! Answer my questions. Explain yourselves properly."

An uneasy silence formed about him. Abruptly, his rage over-mastered his fear and he burst out, "Know this, whoever or whatever you are, if you threaten me—and my companions here—we *will* resist—we *will* fight you." Something in the silence thrust the next into his head. "We will ally ourselves with the one you call the Destroyer. If you drag us into your war you must take the consequences."

197

The silence seemed to curl through his mind until it formed the word, *"Wait."*

Slowly, in the wake of this... command? request?... awareness of his surroundings seeped back to Josyff—the comfort of his bed, the muffled clucking of the clock.

What was happening? What was he doing, holding this bizarre debate with... who?... what?... himself?

He must be dreaming. Perhaps his inner mind, prompted by his very thoughts about it as he had clambered into bed and abandoned tasks to it, was showing him some manifestation of its efforts. He felt an unexpected twinge of amusement. The circularity of the idea appealed to him.

Carry on, he thought. It's entertaining if nothing else. The rage he had vented at the unknown... speaker... had felt good. It had been a release—something that the ordinary circumstances of his life did not readily allow, particularly in recent times. It had surprised him too. He thought of himself as being easy-going and practical—dealing with things the way they were rather than fretting about the way they "ought" to be, and he was certainly not given to angry outbursts. But then, he reflected, how was it possible not to be angry at the New Order and its secretive, repressive ways? It took neither paranoia nor great political insight to see that under an insidious aura of subtle fear and deceit they were quietly corroding ancient freedoms, slowly binding the people to the will of the State, relentlessly gathering more and more power to themselves...

Why?

Like his unexpected anger, the question took him by surprise. Either because of an indifference to politics or because he had been too occupied keeping his position—surviving—it had never really occurred to him before. Perhaps he had realized intuitively that it was a dangerous question—not wisely asked and definitely not to be discussed in public. But now, engaged in this silent debate with himself, it *had* been asked. Why *would* the New Order—anyone—seek to hold such power? For control of some kind, presumably; but what kind?

Over the years, he had worked with enough people to know that they—like himself—were not easily controlled. Indeed, people in general were downright slippery, with a consummate flare for getting and going their own way, all too readily avoiding, forgetting, postponing, lying, 'misunderstanding', ignoring, when put to a task they did not want to do. So much so that those with the skill to manage such control—true leaders—were both rare and memorable.

Yet even as these thoughts paraded themselves he realized that this must be precisely why the New Order behaved the way it did. It was not interested in the subtleties of civilized leadership, it was sufficient for its need that people obeyed, and fear in turn was sufficient to ensure this. It was a bleak and disturbing conclusion. Not least because the question "why?" remained unanswered. What were the needs of the New Order?

"Power."

The words were about him again, as though they had never left.

"It is an end in itself for the likes of the Destroyer—its roots are beyond us—deep in their—your—strangeness."

Unsettled by both the reply and the implications of eavesdropping, Josyff threw the accusation back immediately. "And it is not for you, also? Why do *you* fight? Come to that, *who* do you fight? Who would you have power over?"

There was a hint of defensiveness in the reply.

"We fight to survive. We seek no power over others."

Still angry, Josyff felt the urge to pursue. "And your enemies? Would they say the same if I asked them?"

"Yes."

The lack of any hesitation somehow diffused Josyff's anger. It felt like a good omen.

"And who should I believe?"

"Your belief is irrelevant..." Doubt and fear flooded through the words. *"Perhaps you are only a creation of our (my?) own desperation—it is difficult. Your very existence—your reality—is doubtful. But if you are as you seem—and I believe it so—you are but an aspect of us—a shadow—an echo. We are different (complex?) beyond your imagining, measurer—we touch (share? coincide?) only by virtue of this..."* Josyff caught again a confusion of words—impossibility, monstrosity, obscenity—mingled with his own images of the Keep. *"...but we are as you. Judge us and our enemies as you judge yourself and yours."*

"Well, you needn't doubt my existence. I am here and real. It is you who are the hallucination—the mirage—part of me talking to myself. As for judging people..."

The doubt and fear were gone, replaced by impatience and a commanding determination.

"The Destroyer is with you, you must make him no more. The harm he will do is truly appalling."

"What do mean, for mercy's sake?" Josyff replied, in similar vein. "The only person here who might be this... Destroyer... or his kin, is Adroyan, and..."

Before he could finish, the words reached into him and drew out the image that formed around Adroyan's name.

"Yes, it is he."

The fear returned, this time almost palpable, and the impatience became a desperate urgency. *"He must be made no more."*

For the first time, Josyff felt afraid. Whatever this conversation was, and it could only be one of his own making... surely...? it was going in a disconcerting direction.

But still he followed it...

"This is nonsense—blistering nonsense. What am I supposed to do? I mightn't like the man, but I can't... make him no more—kill him! Even with good cause, I doubt I could do it. I'm no fighter... soldier. I don't have it in me."

"*It is... in... you, measurer—it is... in... us all.*"

"You know nothing about me," Josyff blasted angrily. "And besides, it's not my war. Why don't you do it?" An idea came to him. "Crush him with whatever that... force... was that you used to close the drawbridge."

A weary feeling washed over him like that of an elderly teacher struggling to explain the inexplicable to a persistent but not very bright child.

"*To act thus is too dangerous—it could destroy us all—he, like you, carries strangeness and the consequences would be beyond calculation. Your world (plane? dimension?) is bound (made whole? held together?) by the merest reflection of the force that sustains ourselves. It is truly beyond your comprehension, but such of it as we use to seal you—and the Destroyer—within the... nexus... should not be possible. It is only the existence of the nexus itself that makes it so.*"

"I've no idea what you're talking about," Josyff said. "Nexus, nexus! This is just a building—a heap of bricks and mortar—well, stone and mortar, anyway—and some bits of wood and metal. It's unusual and it's in a god-forsaken place but that's still all it is. Are you sure you've got the right place? Besides, I can't do anything about it other than survey it—measure it. And Adroyan's just my superior—my boss—I can't do anything about him, either, least of all murder him. I have to do as he tells me. And it's still not my war!" He was still unhappy about the turn of the conversation but somehow unable to disentangle himself.

"*It is the nexus, measurer, and it is your war. Your kind made it and bound us thus, only you can release us. If you do not...*"

Something changed.

"*There is another with us...*"

CHAPTER 40

After Josyff had left the Gatehouse, the others drifted in his wake without debate, Nyk summarizing their thoughts with a weary, "The surveyor's right. It's been a long and bizarre day and there's nothing any of us can do right now. I'm off to bed as well. Can't see me sleeping much, but..." He shrugged.

They had walked across the snow-covered courtyard in silence and parted with nothing more than a few cursory 'Good night's before each lighting their own ways along the Keep's corridors.

Esyal bolted her door then caught sight of herself in the night-blackened windows. For some reason the image staring back at her was unsettling, as was the thought of the mountains beyond—beautiful and majestic in the sunlight, but ominous when hidden in the darkness. She drew the curtains then lay back on the bed and gazed at the ceiling. She was there for some time before finally forcing herself to change and get into the bed. Then she continued gazing at the ceiling. She was tired but could not get to sleep— did not want to go to sleep.

What the devil is this place? And what the devil is going on?

Though she knew the questions were unanswerable she could do nothing to stop herself asking them.

So much had happened in so short a time. She had gone from being lost, alone and beaten, and from facing a lonely and cold death, to being warm and safe and in a position to destroy a member of the Ordrans—for member of the Ordrans she was increasingly sure that Adroyan was. And not only that, but destroying him at the cusp of some important New Order project—something that might perhaps do them real harm!

Yet she remained unsettled. Life in the Rhanen had schooled her to violence, but it had come neither easily nor happily and her abrupt, cold-blooded even, decision that Adroyan should die, when she reflected on it, was like nothing she had experienced before—like the silent mountains beyond the windows, it was a dark, forbidding presence.

Killing Adroyan was the right thing to do, of course. She knew that. Whatever the outcome, she doubted she could bear the self-reproach that would surely follow later if she missed such an opportunity. And time was not on her side. Although they were all locked in this place at the moment, they would be free sooner or later. Worse, if the men who had scattered her party out in the mountains were still about, caught by this snow, they might arrive at any time and begin asking questions she would find difficult to answer convincingly. Already her "loss of memory" story was proving awkward, especially in the absence of any form on injury to sustain it. She would have to consider how she could discreetly abandon it before some slip brought it crashing down on her.

"Just think—think," she murmured to herself fretfully. It was, after all, only going to be a choice of deceits. She just needed to take a little time to work them out in detail, then she could choose the best.

She turned on to her side with a grunt. This could all be dealt with later—it *was* only a matter of details—important ones, admittedly, but details nevertheless—she must not be distracted by that part of her that did not want to look too closely at her sudden decision to kill Adroyan.

It had not been simply the logic of the situation, though that was sound enough. It had been visceral—completely unexpected—almost like a revelation. But even as she reluctantly returned to it, the exertions of the day began to make themselves felt—drowsiness seeping through her, clouding her thinking and urging her to forget the problem. She resisted the lure—now was an ideal time for this—alone and quiet—safe...

Twice she jerked back into partial wakefulness...

"...almost as if someone had put the idea of killing him into my mind," she was murmuring the second time, apparently continuing a conversation with someone.

Stay awake, she commanded herself. Sort this out, it's important...

But someone was speaking somewhere—there were voices, vague and distant, like a buzzing in her head. For a moment she thought it might be outside her door and although this was not quite enough to bring her fully awake, her hand slithered from beneath the blankets towards her belt knife, strategically placed on a chair by the bed. It fell limp before it reached its goal. The door was locked and bolted. There was no risk of surprise attack. Still, she should get up and find out where the noise was coming from, but...

She listened.

The voices rose and fell, now distinct, now nearly inaudible.

There were two. One was familiar—very familiar—though the name of the speaker frustratingly refused to declare itself. The other was deeply strange—now like one person, now like several, even a crowd, speaking at once. And it was no idle chit-chat—they were debating something.

Am I dreaming? she thought...

Then images were forming around the words, dancing with them as though caught in their buffeting backwash.

And she was part of it... riding the words... to and fro... echoing about the complex, winding corridors of the Keep, now bright and shimmering with colours she had never seen before. Beautiful sweeping shapes arced into places that could not be. Cascading lights fell down and down giddyingly through twisting perspectives until, quite seamlessly, quite naturally, they were at their own beginning—round and round impossibly.

But there was something hovering beneath the beauty, something about the Keep, something dangerous—a sense of intrusion—distortion—a fabric strained beyond its tolerance—a knife-edged equilibrium...

"There is another with us..."

The words folded around this revelation were clear and sure.

Esyal found herself holding her breath, as if the least movement might set in train the irrevocable shattering of this illusion... or draw some danger down on her.

"Do not be afraid... listener..."

As the words touched her they stopped sharply. Everything became silent and still save for a faint and high pitched trembling at the edge of her awareness.

"*Warrior...?*"

The word was filled with many emotions, but dominant amongst them was fear—not fear of Esyal but the fear of daring suddenly to hope. Esyal winced away from the pain she sensed and it faded, gradually being replaced by curiosity... and excitement.

"*You do not see us as the measurer sees us. You are the same yet different— different aspects (views? facets?) of the same. Wait... wait... I see...*"

Then, set in a confusion of shifting and changing patterns, there was a figure. Part of Esyal noted distantly that her eyes were closed but it held little sway against the patent reality of what she was seeing. Yet, what *was* she seeing? It *was* a figure, surely? But where it was, or even what it looked like, she could not truly have said. At times it stood distinct and sharp, while at others it seemed to be just part of the frenzied background, being scattered and re-formed in bright, scurrying colours or submerged in a foaming tide of grim shadows.

"Who are you?" she asked, almost shouting, as though a great wind were blowing. "What's happening? Am I dreaming?"

There was wide-eyed realization in the words when they came again, but they did not answer her questions.

"*You* can *reach into the darkness and the light!*"

"What? Answer me! Who are you? What's happening?"

The lights buzzed and whirled about her, more frenziedly than ever, but the figure at their heart became clearer, more solid. Another formed by its side, fainter and less certain.

"*That is the measurer,*" came an answer before she had asked the question. "*Through you, many joinings (junctions? paths? ways?) are possible. You are truly unique (alone?) in your strangeness. Truly a warrior. A rare find...*" The hesitant sense of hope returned briefly.

"I don't know what the devil you're talking about," Esyal burst out. "Answer my question, damn you! Who are you? And who's the measurer?"

There was a pause.

"*We have no name you would know us by, warrior. We are before (beyond? above?) you. We are the... First Comers... Because of us, you are.*"

"Because of us, you are?" Esyal echoed quizzically. "What does that mean? *You* made us?" The rebel in her began to bridle. "Gods, are you?" she sneered, safe in her locked room and her dream, despite what she was seeing and hearing.

"*Gods?*" There was another pause. "*Creators. No. We are just the First Comers—born, it is said, when the Great Silence was sundered. You are, because we are. You, the measurer, the Destroyer, are a part of us—shadows (echoes? reflections?)—lesser aspects of ourselves.*"

"The Great Silence was sundered" sounded familiar to Esyal, but before she could pursue it the word "lesser" made her bridle again, only to be deflected by immediate curiosity when, "...and full of strangeness," followed.

"Strangeness?"

"Dark depths of... confusion... where we cannot (dare not?) go, save only sufficiently to draw this so that we can reach you."

The figure made a slow sweeping gesture. Colours swirled turbulently about his hands and Esyal was swept up in a kaleidoscopic vision of innumerable tumbling scenes—all manner of people, places, incidents—every one of which, she realized abruptly, was from her own memory. And not only actual events but events from her imagination—childhood dreams, adult aspirations, fantasies.

"They're mine! My thoughts."

"They are from the very edges of your strangeness, warrior. It is a fearful place for us—beyond all control (calculation?)."

"I don't understand."

"No, you cannot. It lies at the very limits of what we know and it is beyond you, just by virtue of what you are. But still you are more than you know."

Then the words were impatient, anxious to move on.

"We need your help. And the measurer's. You must make the Destroyer no more."

Esyal wilfully ignored the urgency. "I still don't know what you're talking about, or who you are. And what are you doing meddling with my thoughts? And who's this... measurer... hovering in the background? Come to that, what am I doing talking to you. You're a figment of my imagination—old bits and pieces of my life mixed in with what's happened the last few days."

"No, Esyal."

The voice was different. It came from the second figure and she recognized it as Josyff's straight away.

"The imagination is mine." There was a hint of uncertain amusement in it. "And I think enough is enough. I didn't like the direction this was going in moments ago. Now I'm imagining you imagining me—time to wake up, I think."

"Yes," Esyal agreed.

"No! Do not leave! Such a joining may not come again."

Although the "No!" had been authoritative and commanding, the remainder was a plea, full of desperation. Esyal hesitated and the words hurried on. Behind and within them Esyal could feel some kind of urgent activity. Even as she noted this, the figure became clearer, as did that of the measurer.

"Warrior, measurer, we hear (see? feel?) your doubt. You are not where you *normally are—we understand... we think. You have come again to the fringes of your strangeness, as is your way, and you think us a product of it. But we are not. We have been reaching (hoping? searching?) for you since the nexus was formed—since the Destroyer—in great doubt (pain? confusion?). Now you are found—the measurer drawing after him the warrior. Such alignments are almost beyond calculation. We need your help."*

Esyal felt it easier to continue talking than to seek some way of waking herself. "You've said that before," she said, continuing acidly, "You want me and the measurer to make the Destroyer no more. Can you rephrase that so that it makes sense?"

"He—they—whatever, wants us to kill Adroyan."

It was Josyff's voice again but before Esyal could reply she heard a sharply drawn breath.

"Ye gods! You were going to do it anyway! Your memory's fine. You're... you're one of the Rhanen..."

Esyal started violently and she could feel her whole body trembling as much as if this revelation had been shouted through all the corridors of the Keep. She saw the figure of the measurer twitch and fade. Josyff's voice was continuing.

"No, no, no, this is insane. I must wake up—get away from this. I..."

"There is little time, measurer." The voice was tense now, as though restraining panic or despair. *"You are drifting away from the strangeness. We cannot hold you. You and the warrior must make the Destroyer no more. The Enemy has found him and touched him and he is seeking the Heart. Great harm will come to everyone—everything—should he find it. You..."*

And like a candle flame caught in the wintry gust from a suddenly opened window, the voice was gone.

Esyal jerked upright, wide awake, heart racing. The light came on. It took her a moment to realize that someone was banging on her bedroom door.

CHAPTER 41

Josyff woke sharply but did not move. Throughout his discourse he had somehow known himself to be safe in his bed at the Keep and dreaming, but now it took him some time to remember where he was. As he slowly recovered, he levered himself upright and glowered at the clock.

Too early to get up, but he did not feel inclined to go to sleep again.

Time to think, he decided, and lay back again.

He was oddly relaxed. His discussion with—whatever it was—had been deeply strange, but there had been far less of the disturbing disorientation that he had experienced in his previous dreams and in the Archive. And, remarkably, all of it was still there, as clear in his memory as if it had been a routine business meeting—clearer indeed, than many real meetings he'd been to, he reflected ruefully.

What *had* been a little disturbing was the manifestation of Esyal in the dream. Not her presence—she was, after all, someone currently impinging on his daily life—but the peculiar, not to say downright frightening insight he seemed to have had into her mind: the vivid revelation of an intention to kill Adroyan, the falsity of her lost memory story, her membership of the Rhanen. That must all have been his imagination, of course, he presumed, but this self-reassurance lacked conviction. Perhaps having wilfully invoked his inner problem-solving resources as he went to bed, they were also telling him the meaning of subtle signs he might have picked up from her. All of which left him none the wiser.

For a moment he contemplated telling Esyal he had dreamt of her, but the very prospect of such an admission made him feel like a gawky adolescent and he abandoned it immediately. Nevertheless, whatever the source of his thoughts about her and the reason for them, he *would* watch her more carefully—there *were* many questions about her which no one had seriously pursued: how did she come to be wandering alone in the mountains? how could she lose her memory when she showed no signs of injury?

Something made him glance uneasily around the room. Like a shadow in the corner of his eye, there seemed to be something hovering about the edges of his awareness. It was almost as though the figure in his dream was still there, listening, watching... scheming... plotting?

He frowned. The whole thing might have been his own fabrication, but why should he be thinking of a war of all things? The New Order was many things, but it was neither threatened by, nor, as far as he knew, a threat to any neighbouring countries. And even if it were, he would not be able to do anything about it.

"It is the nexus, measurer, and it is your war. Your kind made it and bound us thus, only you can release us. If you do not..."

Your war, your kind—your, plural. Yet the "only you can release us" had been addressed to him personally, he was sure.

The statement had been unfinished, interrupted by the "discovery" of Esyal. Then the voice had turned from him, effectively reducing him to an eavesdropper, while it pursued its conversation with Esyal. Josyff recalled the contained excitement that pervaded everything as Esyal was identified as a warrior. What could it have meant? Even from his limited acquaintance of her, Josyff had little doubt that Esyal would be a problem for anyone who picked on her—but a warrior, a soldier, a fighter? It made no sense.

But what did around here?

The clock clucked at him.

Images of war...

"You and the warrior must make the Destroyer no more. The Enemy has found him and touched him and he is seeking the Focus. Great harm will come to everyone—everything—should he find it."

Josyff turned over with a growl of irritation as the words reiterated themselves unbidden. Still they made no sense. Then he resorted to what had become his usual solution to the mysteries of this place: do your work, do it well—and quickly—get away from here—back to the city, your wife, even the New Order bureaucrats you have to work with...

Suddenly the room was filled with an intense brightness. Josyff swore violently. His immediate thought was that yet another thing was going wrong with the Keep's peculiar equipment. Instinctively he turned away, covering his face and head with his arms in anticipation of some form of explosion as whatever was apparently overloading the room's lamp took its inevitable toll.

But it did not come.

After a moment he cautiously opened his eyes and peered out around his protective arm. The brightness was still there, all around him, throwing deep black shadows into those parts of the room that it could not reach. But it was not emanating from the room's solitary lamp, which looked dull and grey by comparison, it was floating uncertainly in mid-air between the bed and the door.

Eyes screwed tight and with a shielding hand raised, Josyff peered into it in an attempt to see its source. Is this another dream? he thought, noting, somewhat to his own surprise that he was more curious than afraid.

But the fear was being restrained only temporarily. It began to reassert itself almost immediately, for the light had a baleful, unhealthy tint to it.

Like something rising from some ancient burial swamp, he thought.

His stomach began churning at the sight alone, but worse, far worse, he sensed images forming at the fringes of his mind—foul images. He found himself gritting his teeth and breathing deeply in an attempt to hold them at bay, for he knew that, like vomit, once they began to move they could not be stopped. He knew, too, that his effort would be futile and, like a dark, boiling cloud, they were overwhelming him—sweeping both over and through him. At once fleeting and timeless they possessed him utterly: feral eyes full of cruel knowledge and purposeful malevolence; lank-fingered hands like talons, searching, prying, lusting; black mouths, foetid with decay and necklaced with tearing teeth. But, perhaps worst of all, ancient and primeval desires, scurrying and boiling like maggots on a newly exposed corpse...

His desires, he realized.

He tried to cry out in denial, but could not.

A voice—voices?—like nails down glass rose to mock his denial, hissing out of the horror, cold, venomous and scornful. Josyff felt his skin crawling and then all control leaving him as the words touched him.

{"...measurer..."}

His hands came up again, protectively, as blackness closed about him. Only as it finally engulfed him did he catch a distant note of shrieking frustration in the voice...

...When he opened his eyes, the light was normal again and the room was silent and still, save for the soft steady march of the clock—oddly comforting now.

His mind, though, was still full of echoes of the grasping darkness and, for a moment, he thought he was going to be violently sick. He swung himself upright and round on to the edge of the bed in preparation. The sharp movement made him dizzy and he closed his eyes and pressed his hands down into the bed to steady himself. Again he breathed heavily and deliberately and this time both the nausea and the dizziness passed.

But not the memories...

He glanced at the clock. Scarcely any time had passed since the last time he had looked. Leaning forward he put his head in his hands. He was reluctant to think about what had just happened for fear it might release some other nightmare.

"*Measurer.*"

Josyff jumped as the voice filled his mind. Before he could speak however, he was once again in the eerie world of shifting perspectives where he had watched the... the speaker... the First Comer...? debating with Esyal. As he looked around, the figure he had seen before slowly appeared from the confusion. It was clearer than before but still he could make not out any details save that, at times, it seemed to be an old man, robed, perhaps like a monk.

"*You are safe, measurer. As yet they can scarcely reach you.*"

Though there was reassurance in the voice, there was a tension beneath it which effectively negated it.

"Scarcely?" Josyff echoed back. He felt his words twisting into the tension as if they had to be reshaped before they could be understood. He thought he sensed a resigned sigh precursing the reply.

"*Many things are coming together that should not. The Nexus makes possible what should not be. It is truly an abomination.*"

"In the name of sanity, who are you? And what was that that called my name before?" Josyff burst out, before asking the question he knew could not be answered. "Are you real or are you just... imagination...?"

"*We are real, measurer. And, we think, so are you, though we cannot understand how that can be, so diminished must you be. But things are as they are and you are as you are. We cannot know what you perceive (see? think?*

hear? feel?—so many meanings!) but as we can touch you only through your strangeness so it can only be of your own creating."

"That voice—that awful voice. And those... things... I saw, were nothing of my making," Josyff exclaimed angrily. But even as he spoke he knew that he was merely blustering and that what he had seen and heard had indeed emerged from some dark, atavistic part of his own being—grotesque fears and fantasies from... childhood? perhaps even earlier—something that was an integral part of him—of everyone. He was appalled. Suddenly it was as though the innumerable tiny bonds that held his life, his whole self, together, were untying themselves, slipping apart to leave... to leave, what?

He made to cry out but the figure, as if sensing his mounting distress, spoke again.

"We are learning—we are all learning. As the chaos mounts so we find the courage—and the skill—to ride it. So must you."

The voice was clearer, as was the figure, though it was still predominantly a silhouette. It moved immediately from encouragement to instruction.

"You must seek out the Heart of the Nexus and destroy it." There was a sense of urgency in both the words and the movement of the figure.

Josyff recovered himself enough to say, "I don't know what you're talking about."

"You will. You are the only one that can find it. The warrior can protect you."

"Protect? Protect? From what?"

"From the Destroyer."

"I don't..."

"Listen, measurer. Listen, learn—know!" The urgency was greater now. *"With the drawing to the Nexus of your strangeness—and the warrior's—and the Destroyer's—our world will open into yours, the place that hides the Heart will be unfolded and the Destroyer will gain great power, power that does not belong there. The balance there will be disturbed beyond recall and with it the balance here."*

Part of Josyff was screaming, "Wake up! Wake up!" but as though it had heard the cry, the figure leaned forward, extending its hand in denial. So unexpected was the purposeful movement against the swirling and twisting background that Josyff merely gaped and blinked as the hand continued its movement and came to rest on his shoulder.

"Your confusion, your doubts, are understandable. You have not chosen this way. But nor have we. Chance—or some instrument beyond any of our knowing—has made you as you are and circumstance (alignment? congruence? coincidence?) has brought you—and us—here."

The figure's touch was oddly gentle and seemed to suffuse through him, filling the words with complex and subtle meanings. Josyff had an almost overpowering sense of a vast, elaborate structure balanced on the slightest of supports and in such delicate equilibrium that the least breath might bring it down. And too, a sense that such a collapse would send repercussions echoing out and out across unknown and unknowable places and times. That it made no sense to him did not lessen the appalling impact of the impression.

He reached up to touch the hand on his shoulder as if for help.

But it was gone.

As was the figure and everything about it. There had been no hiatus, no fading or diminishing, or even a sense of abrupt change. Josyff was simply sat on the edge of his bed, his hand frozen in its journey to his shoulder. He looked round the room slowly. The experience with the figure had been so clear and intense that it seemed to him for a moment that it was the room and the Keep and everything about his being here that was a dream.

The sensation took some time to pass, but even when his sense of present reality had fully returned, Josyff found himself unable to resort to what had become his normal rationalization of such events; it had been a peculiar dream—a mere reaction to his unusual circumstances. Quickly, but thoroughly and more calmly than he might have expected, he rehearsed the events of the past few days. His mind was remarkably clear. Too many things had been observed by others, not least the smashing of the supports to the drawbridge, for him to attribute them to a personal aberration or some form of mass hysteria. But then, what were the implications of such a conclusion? That somewhere, in a place that was... here yet not here... there were sentient creatures waging a great war—a war that the very existence of the Keep had drawn unnaturally into this world—a war in which Adroyan, Esyal and himself played some pivotal role. It defied all logic, but...

Still he could not reject what had just happened. Literally could not. It refused to leave him—refused to be denied.

He put his hands to his head.

What to do...?

For a little while he was motionless, both physically and mentally. Then the momentum of his practical nature carried him forward.

Either all this was true, real and happening, or it was not. If it was not, then he was definitely in the throes of some kind of mental breakdown. If it *was*, however, then something appalling was happening... somewhere—he shuddered briefly as he recalled the dreadful voice and the fearful images that had briefly come to him—and he might be caught up in it whether he liked it or not.

Given that he had felt no precursors to any kind of mental distress—indeed, despite the unwanted separation from his wife, he had taken his selection for this job as a reassurance that he was as well established with the New Order as anyone could expect to be—it seemed that he must at least accept the possibility that the manifestations he had witnessed were from... outside himself.

Still, whatever the truth, he decided, he could not do nothing. He began to dress, at the same time mulling over how he might learn more about what had happened without drawing ridicule down on himself, or causing the others alarm. It did not take him long to realize that he would have to find some way of broaching the subject with the only other person who might have experienced the same—Esyal.

CHAPTER 42

Heart racing and scarcely aware of what she was doing, Esyal swung out of bed and began dressing quickly, both her female and her fighting instincts ensuring that whatever was about to happen she would not face it half naked.

The banging continued with increased urgency and now the latch was rattling.

She pulled her belt tight and comforting then drew her knife. Hiding it behind her back, she moved to the door.

"Who is it? Who's there?"

There was no reply, just more banging.

She put a hand on the door. Then, leaning forward cautiously, she brought her ear close to it.

"Who is it?" she demanded again.

A vaguely familiar voice seeped faintly through the thick timber.

"For pity's sake, let me in!"

Henk? she mouthed silently as the familiarity became recognition. Curiosity began to vie with her alarm. What the devil was he doing?

Not trying to make a silent romantic tryst, for sure. Despite the circumstances, she smiled at the thought. But wasn't there desperation, if not outright fear, in his voice, muffled as it was?

It was not in her nature to do anything gratuitously reckless, but neither was it in her nature to stand by and do nothing. She sheathed her knife and seized a chair—a good blow to the legs would be unavoidable and would almost certainly bring Henk down, if necessary. Safer, on the whole, than using her knife—it was unlikely to do as much serious injury, she wouldn't have to close with him and it should give her an opportunity to escape.

She took a deep breath, reminded herself grimly that no plan survives first contact with the enemy, then quietly unlocked the door and eased the bolt.

Stepping to on side she shouted, "It's not locked."

It was needless information. The door crashed open and Henk tumbled into the room.

Esyal, chair drawn back to strike, quickly positioned herself between the staggering man and the door with a view to fleeing and seeking help if she had to. All such thoughts left her however, as she glanced down the passage. For some way she could see the stone walls and ceiling typical of the Keep, but beyond this was a bubbling confusion of movement and light. She hesitated, momentarily fearful that a fire had broken out. But almost immediately came her own scornful reassurance—not in a stone building!—and the realization that this... apparition... was not smoke but something else...

Something unspeakable...

Then, without seeming to move, it was directly in front of her, filling the doorway, a swirling mass, livid and tormented, like a long stagnant river suddenly in spate, and lit from the inside by a flickering, baleful light. And with it came a foul stench and a high-pitched chorus of jibbering voices— part animal, part human and part something she could not begin to identify, save that it was manic and menacing—and directed towards her!

As she stared into it, aghast, the voices faltered.

Am I still dreaming?

And, as though drawn by the thought itself and carried on a scream-ing wind, the voices rose up again, full of recognition and intent. The only thing that stopped Esyal moving backwards, away from this horror, was the fact that her legs would not move—not move purposefully, that is— they were trembling violently, as was the rest of her.

The voices swirled and shrieked triumphantly and chattering fragments of them began to merge and become coherent until, amid the din, she heard:

{"Warrior..."}

Slithering through her mind, the voice, if voice it could be called, was acid with scorn and contempt. And it was vile. It shrivelled Esyal's stern intention to defend herself and involuntarily she flinched away from it. As she did so, and again as if drawn by her very thoughts, reaching hands shaped themselves out of the tumult and stretched towards her, at once both beckoning and grasping.

{"Warrior..."}

Esyal felt the hands and the voice closing about her... luring her forward...

All sense and feeling was draining from her.

She could do nothing... nothing...

She must... she must go with this...

She swayed unsteadily and ancient reflexes closed her hand about the back of the chair to restore her balance.

The touch of the smooth polished wood—crafted, solid, real—formed a sharp and clear focus for her.

She gasped, like a long-submerged swimmer breaching the surface, as she was drawn abruptly back to who she was and where she was.

Then, scarcely realizing what she was doing, she was swinging the chair, one-handed, at the swirling confusion now seemingly surrounding her.

She felt no physical impact as the impromptu weapon passed through the shimmering mass but she sensed a change, and what had been the voice became a venomous hiss of... anger? fear?

It made no difference. Whichever it was, the response provoked a renewed effort from Esyal and she began swinging the chair in a wide arcing figure-of-eight while her other hand drew her knife.

Then there was a frenzied interlude, not measurable in normal time, as chair and slashing knife swung to and fro wildly, powered by Esyal's dark will.

...it seemed to her that she was in some other place—some other time?—the chair a hard-edged shield, the knife a sword, enemies about her, pressing and dying...

Slowly, through the chaos, like a rock gathering pace down a mountainside, a low note began to rise. It increased in intensity until it was a booming roar, over-topping all else and filling Esyal's entire world.

And it was over...

Esyal was staggering backwards, her legs buckling. She landed incongruously on her backside, still clutching the chair and the knife. In front of her, leaning with his back to the door, was Henk, wide-eyed and deathly pale, his face alive with fear. In her heightened awareness, Esyal could hear the dying reverberations of the slamming of the door still echoing about the room. All semblance of the disturbance had gone and Esyal knew that she could safely open the door and that she would see only the passageway.

She opened her mouth to speak, but for a moment her rasping breath and pounding heart would not allow her.

Her legs still shaking, she levered herself upright using the chair for support.

"What was that?" she managed eventually, waving her knife at Henk like an admonishing finger.

Henk's eyes widened further and he extended a hand fearfully as if to protect himself.

"I'm sorry, I'm sorry," Esyal said hastily as she realized what she was doing. The apology was sincere, but a small, cold part of her noted that Henk was not a threat before she sheathed the knife. It gave her a brief frisson of unease.

"What was that?" she repeated.

But Henk was in no state to reply. He was slowly sliding down the door. Esyal quickly pulled him forward and managed to swing the chair underneath him before he collapsed completely. Then she put her hands on his shoulders both to support herself and to prevent him from slumping forward, and looked earnestly into his face.

"Henk—it's gone. Whatever it was, it's gone. We're... safe."

She hesitated over the last word, far from certain whether she was correct or not, and not even clear about what she meant.

Recognition slowly spread over Henk's face. He struck straight to her doubt.

"You're sure?"

Ironically, his doubt dispelled Esyal's. "Yes I am," she replied. "There's nothing in here and there's nothing on the other side of that door. I told you, it's gone."

"It'll be back," Henk said.

With a bravado she did not truly feel, Esyal announced, "And we'll see it off again," before bursting out, "What the hell is happening, Henk?"

Henk quailed and Esyal was briefly torn between cradling the man's head and furiously boxing his ears. She did neither, but took her hands away from him and sat down on the end of the bed.

More quietly she repeated her question. "What was that, Henk? What's happening?"

Henk too was gradually regaining control but his voice was unsteady as he replied. "It's the Keep. It's waking up. We should've left—snow or no snow. We should go now."

But he made no move to leave.

Still quietly, Esyal said, "I don't know what you're talking about, Henk. How can a building wake up, for pity's sake? Anyway, what we should and shouldn't have done is irrelevant now—we're trapped in this place, if you recall."

"I recall well enough," Henk replied, briefly his surly self again. "But I can't answer your questions. I don't know how a building can wake up—but it is. It's always been an odd place. Now things are moving, changing... have been for a while." His eyes widened again as he spoke and he pointed a nervous finger over his shoulder at the door. Esyal leaned forward and laid a hand on his arm, repeating her assurance.

"It's gone. It's truly gone." She wanted to question him further, not least about how he had come to be pursued by... whatever it was... but she judged it might only plunge him back into stark terror. She glanced at the window. "It'll be dawn soon. We can stay here until then. Things are never as bad in the daylight. We can go and find the others. See if they saw or felt anything."

Henk followed her gaze towards the greying window, but did not reply.

They both sat silent for some time; Henk, motionless, staring at his feet, Esyal, subtly restless, her mind buzzing with ever more questions...

And concerns. The memory of Josyff's outburst in her dream returned to trouble her.

"Ye gods! You were going to do it anyway! Your memory's fine. You're... you're one of the Rhanen..."

That couldn't really have happened, surely. It was just a reflection of her own fears bubbling to the surface...

Wasn't it?

But it had not felt like that then, nor did it now. It had felt real—very real. No less real than the clutching monstrosity she had just taken a chair to.

"You looked like something else when you were fighting that... thing... just now."

Esyal was snapped out of her reverie by Henk's announcement.

"What!"

"I said, you looked like something else just now—when you were fighting that thing."

"Something else? What do you mean?"

"Some*one* else, then. Like someone out of an old book, a soldier, surrounded on the battlefield—swinging a sword and shield."

Esyal just grunted and ran her hands through her hair to disguise any outward response she might have made to this peculiar revelation. Her imagining such a thing in the heat of the moment was odd enough, but Henk actually seeing it brought even more questions, none of which seemed to be remotely answerable.

"Just your imagination, probably. You were very agitated when you arrived."

This time Henk grunted. "You needn't spare my feelings," he said. "I wasn't agitated, I was scared to death—and still am. But I saw what I saw, just like we both saw what was chasing me."

Esyal decided to risk pressing him. If nothing else it would give her own tumbling thoughts something to occupy them.

"Can you tell me exactly what happened? How did this all... come about? When did it start? Where were you? And why did it come after you?"

Even as she was speaking, Henk was shaking his head. For a moment Esyal thought her earlier fears were about to be fulfilled and that he was about to lapse into terrified incoherence. But he was merely answering her questions.

"I don't know. After that business in the Gatehouse, I was wide awake." He digressed briefly. "I don't sleep well when my routine's disturbed at the best of times, and... there's been a lot lately... disturbance..." He looked at Esyal, but she made no response and he continued. "Anyway, I thought I'd start getting some things together—our emergency store, start putting them by the..."

There was a knock on the door.

CHAPTER 43

Both Esyal and Henk were on their feet immediately, Henk hastily putting the chair between himself and the door. Esyal drew her knife again. Seeing this, Henk tentatively lifted the chair to change it from a shelter to a weapon.

There was another knock. Esyal felt herself twitch slightly, but both her mind and her instincts were already regaining control. The knock had none of the Henk's pounding urgency that had woken her before. Indeed, it was quite discreet. Whoever was out there was making no assault. And too, Henk was there in the event of trouble, although, she reflected, with some dark amusement, he could well be more of a hindrance than a help judging by the way he was dithering with that chair.

"Mind you don't hit me with that," she instructed him before calling out, "The door's not locked. Come in."

The latch clicked and the door opened slowly. Henk's fingers tightened nervously around the chair while Esyal's shoulders relaxed as she slowly breathed out.

A head appeared hesitantly around the door. It was Josyff.

He knows!

The thought, certain and clear, flashed into Esyal's mind, overwhelming all else. But it was gone almost before she registered it and she neither reacted to it nor questioned it. Some part of her had told her something she needed to know—it was enough for the moment. She tried to read Josyff's face but it was alive with such a gamut of emotions that it defied her. Rapidly rising to dominate however, was embarrassment—embarrassment that re-doubled as his glance took in Henk.

"Come in," Esyal repeated, sheathing her knife and motioning to Henk to put down the chair.

Uncharacteristically, Josyff stammered, and stammered badly.

"I... I... er..." His gaze was to all parts of the room except Esyal and Henk.

His manner began to render Esyal almost as tongue-tied but the blank bewilderment on his face served to draw together for her the alarming confusion of everything that had happened since she arrived here, not least the burden of maintaining her feigned loss of memory and her conflict with whatever had just pursued Henk. Events that were as convoluted as the corridors and passages of the Keep itself merged into a tangled whole— still enigmatic, but somehow clearer. She cut through Josyff's floundering. No preamble, just explanation and question.

"We've had a... visitation, for want of a better word. Something's just attacked Henk—frightened the living daylights out of him. I don't know what it was but it frightened the living daylights out of me, too, and it's something to do with this place and everything that's been happening here." Then, "Did you share the dream I just had?"

Josyff gaped as if he had been struck. As he met Esyal's testing gaze, the word "warrior" came into his mind—and without any of the incongruity that should have hung about her light frame and half a head difference in height. He recognized the solution she had chosen—she had slashed through confusion, scattering crowding doubts, to end what was perhaps an almost paralysing uncertainty. Whether she had done it intuitively or rationally did not matter. She had set her own will on circumstances and was prepared to move now as change dictated.

She had also dashed aside the fumbling approaches to the subject he had been practising since he left his room, and given him the opportunity, if not to end his own confusion, to at least bring it to a head. He took the same leap and answered her question.

"Yes, I did." He glanced briefly at Henk. "I know... much more than I did before."

"And?"

Momentarily, Josyff realized that this girl—this woman—sharp-eyed and watching—could draw her knife and be on him before he could move. In the confines of this all-too-real room, it was a revelation even more alarming than the one he had received about her in his dream... or whatever it had been.

How had he not seen such dark purpose and strength in her before?

Because she had chosen to hide it and you do not look for such things, came the reassuring reply, though in its wake came the more unnerving realization that now she had chosen to reveal it...

Whatever "warrior" meant, she was undoubtedly dangerous.

"And nothing," he replied. "Your business."

The aptitude for avoiding contention that had protected him from the New Order spoke immediately, but, almost in spite of himself, he took another leap.

"Besides, I think I'm with you."

He turned hastily to Henk who was staring straight ahead, fixedly, and who seemed scarcely to have noticed this terse exchange. He reached for the commonplace to anchor himself.

"I can see you've had a fright," he said to him. "I suggest you sit on that." He indicated the chair. "And tell me what happened."

He had to repeat himself before Henk's eyes focused on him and his suggestion was accepted.

"We have to leave," Henk said, sitting down clumsily.

"Not possible." Both Josyff and Esyal spoke at the same time, provoking an uneasy smile.

"Tell me what happened," Josyff pressed.

Henk nodded towards Esyal. "She'll tell you. I don't want to talk about it."

A little reluctantly Josyff turned back to Esyal.

"Never mind you don't want to talk about it," Esyal exclaimed angrily. "I don't know what the devil it was—I just had a go at it with a chair—you're the one it was after."

"No," Henk said, suddenly agitated. "Not when I got here, it wasn't—it was you it wanted."

Josyff cut across Esyal's pending reply.

"Will one of you just tell me what 'it' is, because I didn't see or hear anything on my way here."

This time it was Henk and Esyal who exchanged looks. Esyal shrugged.

"He woke me up, banging on the door. When I opened it, he... fell in and there was this... thing... filling the passage—like a... sick cloud." She grimaced at the memory. "I don't know. I can't describe it. Diseased, bloated, utterly foul." She hesitated, searching for words. "Something... distorted... something that just didn't belong. Anyway, I just swung the chair at it a few times until he slammed the door—I think. And it just... vanished."

"This was just now?"

"A few minutes ago."

Josyff repeated himself. "I saw nothing, heard nothing and my room's not that far away."

An uncomfortable silence fell on the group.

As much out of desperation as in the hope of obtaining an answer, Josyff spoke to Henk: "You've never seen anything like this before?"

Henk gave an irritated snort and stood up, scraping the chair along the floor. "Of course not. You'd think I'd still be here if I had? I'm going."

"Going! Going where?" Esyal said, exasperated and, somewhat to her own surprise, concerned about this surly individual.

"Back to my room then away from here, before I go completely crazy."

"For pity's sake, Henk, how?" Esyal's voice reflected Henk's own frustration. "Whatever's going on, we're locked in, remember?—Unless you know something we don't. And you're not crazy. I saw what you saw clear enough—I've no idea what it was, but I saw it!" She jabbed her fingers towards her eyes. "And..." She glanced at Josyff. "Other... odd things... have been happening as well."

Henk ignored the attempted reassurance and became defensive. "I'll find a way out, somehow."

Esyal raised her hands in a gesture of defeat. Josyff made to speak, but, with unexpected speed, Henk was on his feet and out through the door.

"Henk..." Josyff called out, but he was gone.

"Leave him," Esyal said, as the sound of his rapid footsteps faded. Josyff became aware of her standing very close to him.

"You and I have things to discuss," she said. "You know much more, you said. Tell me—exactly—it's important."

There was a mixture of menace and pleading in the voice that unsettled Josyff and his reply blurted out almost like a startled animal.

"You haven't lost your memory, you're part of the Rhanen and you're intending to kill Adroyan."

The startled animal froze as Esyal's eyes widened and her mouth began to work silently. At the least he would hear a vehement denial. At the worst...

But...

"It did all happen then. You *did* share that... dream. And all this is real." She gesticulated vaguely. "I don't know whether to be relieved or..."

"Afraid?" Josyff offered, more than relieved himself at not having to contend with this new-found and violent Esyal. "I'm both, I think. It *is* a relief—a considerable relief—to know this isn't some trick of the mind, but if it's not that, then what is it? Who are these people, these creatures? Where are they? And what do they want with us?"

"They want us—or, specifically, me, to kill Adroyan."

"Which you were going to do anyway."

Part of Josyff was aghast at the things he was saying, but the release brought on by the realization that his "dreams" had at least some element of objective reality, however bizarre and improbable, had swept aside his normal caution.

"Yes," admitted Esyal, equally incautious now. "He's Ordrans, for sure." She leaned forward and her voice fell as though there might be eavesdroppers. "He might even be the First Member."

"That had occurred to me," Josyff replied, equally softly. "But..." His day to day normality was beginning to seep back into him. "You can't just kill him. It's insane."

Esyal felt a political rant of justification forming, but it faltered and died. Somehow, everything now was different. The New Order, the Rhanen, their bitter conflict, all seemed to have changed. There had been a silent shift in perspective.

"Do you have an alternative?" she asked.

This time is was Josyff whose eyes widened.

Esyal pressed him and part of her rant emerged unbidden. "What then? Carry on doing what you've always done? What everyone else is doing? Dodging, ducking, going along with everything, for a quiet life? Let the New Order take more and more power to itself? Until what?"

"It's not that simple," Josyff protested. "I work for the Government—always have. I'm nearer to them than you—more vulnerable. And I've a wife to think of. I did what I had to do to survive—to get through what was happening. Like you, presumably." He bared his teeth. "Anyway, what the hell's it got to do with you? And why am I discussing this with you?"

Esyal's reply was brutally simple.

"You did what you did because you were where you were. We all do. Now you're somewhere else. You're taking sides."

"No, I..."

"Yes you are. Everything's changed—I've no idea how or why, but changed it has and you've no choice but to change with it."

"No." Josyff was definite. He glanced at the brightening window. "This will all fade with the sun—and over breakfast. I'll get on with my work, finish it and get out of here as soon as I can."

"You're forgetting the drawbridge," Esyal taunted.

"That's just a... problem—a technical problem. I'll solve it when I have to."

Esyal waved dismissively and shook her head.

"No choice," she said, slowly and emphatically. "Believe me, it's better to accept this now than later—a lot less painful—I've learned that the hard way. However insane all this seems, it's real, and we've been dragged into it whether we like it or not. One way or another we'll have to see it through."

Josyff sat down on Henk's chair and put his head in his hands.

"Wishing's not going to make it go away," Esyal said, her voice almost sympathetic. She knelt down in front of him. "Look, I'm as bewildered as you are but we've all seen too much to hide under the blankets. We've got to be practical. Work out how to deal with it." She glanced towards the open door. "Henk'll probably set the pace. He'll tell Nyk and Qualto what he's seen and what he's going to do. That'll stir the whole thing up—maybe they've all been having 'dreams' and been too scared to talk about them. And it'll be interesting to see what Adroyan's response will be."

Josyff looked up and met her gaze searchingly.

"You won't betray me, will you?" she asked, again part menace, part plea.

"And you won't kill Adroyan, will you?" he replied.

Briefly Esyal's face stiffened. Her eyes became first hard and then shrewd. "Not for the moment—that's a promise."

"It's not good enough. You say this is all real—and I can't deny that it feels that way—but what if it's something... in the food, the water, the mountain air, anything that's affecting us? Adroyan might just be another Government officer stuck out here like the rest of us—away from his friends and family and wanting to get back home."

There was a hint of impatience in Esyal's expression but it did not appear in her voice. "You don't believe that for a moment," she said. "You're a civilized man—every bit of you wants to avoid this and you're snatching at the least excuse." Josyff made to speak, but Esyal continued. "I can understand that—I was the same once—perhaps will be again one day. What I *will* do is keep talking to you—talking honestly. We can be allies without being conspirators. And I won't do anything against Adroyan without telling you."

She paused. "Besides, I've a feeling that things are going to become even stranger, and very quickly, and Adroyan will be near the heart of it all."

Josyff wished he could disagree. "I've not much choice, have I? Besides, what proof have I of your intention that makes any kind of sense? 'We shared a dream, I read her mind'! I think not. No, I won't betray you, and yes, I'll be your ally." He levelled a finger at her. "But do nothing to…"

Esyal's hand flicked out and struck him in the chest in a gesture at once discreet and urgent. She was staring over his shoulder.

He turned to find himself looking up at Adroyan.

CHAPTER 44

Josyff stood up hastily, almost knocking the chair over. Esyal, by contrast, rose from her kneeling position quite slowly, at the same time moving away from him so that he did not stand between her and Adroyan. By not resting her hands on her knees for support she seemed almost to rise up out of the floor and was balanced and steady throughout.

Josyff was tongue-tied again.

A welter of half-formed explanations for his presence in Esyal's room were tumbling through his mind. They were vying for attention not only with each other but with those asking what Adroyan was doing here.

None prevailed. Partly because his own excuses would be lies and, he knew from experience, difficult to sustain, and partly because that same experience had taught him the value of saying as little as possible as a means of avoiding certain problems, particularly where his superiors were concerned.

His eventual "Good morning, sir," was mainly a reflex, though it enabled him to snatch the nearest thought and take the initiative.

"Are *you* having difficulty sleeping, as well?"

Adroyan did not reply.

"Did Henk wake you? He left in quite a hurry just now."

Josyff managed to maintain a semblance of a welcoming smile, but it was difficult. Adroyan was standing like someone held motionless by a great wind. A shadow from the doorway was falling across his face, giving the impression that the darkness had flooded into his eyes and turned them into dead, black pits. Josyff felt a twinge of almost superstitious fear—that they would still be thus if Adroyan came into the room.

The reality was little better than this disturbing image as Adroyan, apparently with some difficulty, took a small step forward. His eyes were alive with fury.

Josyff quailed inwardly. "Is anything wrong, sir?" he asked, affecting a concern he was far from feeling, and more than a little surprised that his voice was not trembling. But even as he spoke he saw that the look was being replaced by Adroyan's normal cold gaze. Nevertheless, it radiated an angry frustration.

"I woke early," Adroyan replied flatly.

As he did not seem inclined to offer any further explanation, Josyff took the risk of offering one.

"I think we all did, sir. I don't think the recent happenings are conducive to a good night's sleep."

The cold gaze turned to him, focused now. "I told you to waste no more time thinking about these events. Your work is more urgent than ever now, delay could be... very bad. This place must be measured and its Heart found quickly."

"Yes sir," Josyff said. "As you said last night. I understand your urgency but I'm uncertain what you mean by the Heart of the building. Is it..."

"*That*, I will attend to. But I can only do so when your work is completed," Adroyan interrupted.

"It's just that it's an expression I'm not familiar with and there was a reference to the Heart of the place in the scroll we were looking at yesterday—something about it having to be destroyed but having been... folded away..."

"Waste no more time on this—it is not your concern."

Adroyan's tone was final, almost menacing, and Josyff retreated with a simple, "Sir."

"Did you want to see me?"

Josyff was so engrossed in this near confrontation with Adroyan that Esyal's inquiry made him start. She was standing very straight and with an open smile on her face. Adroyan, by contrast, had hunched his shoulders, after the manner of Henk, giving the impression of a hulking animal debating whether to charge and crush some unwanted intruder.

Don't flinch, Esyal, Josyff thought, his mind suddenly filled with images of a thundering avalanche unleashed by the tumbling of a tiny pebble.

But Esyal seemed to be both frail and strong, at once conspicuously weaker than this man, yet at the same time stronger—quite capable of doing him great harm. It was a bewildering impression and it held Josyff motionless.

Then Esyal did move. But she neither flinched nor retreated. Instead she took a small purposeful step forward, her head tilted slightly to emphasize her question. Adroyan swayed as though he had been pushed but he disguised the movement by taking a small step backwards and turning again to Josyff.

"No, it was the measu... the surveyor, I came to see." Then to Josyff. "You fully understand the urgency?"

"Yes sir. We'll make good progress now," Josyff replied automatically. But Adroyan was not listening. He continued the turn that Esyal's advance had evoked and was walking out of the room.

"What the devil was all that about?" Josyff exclaimed when Adroyan's footsteps had faded. As he turned to Esyal to pursue this question he saw that the assured young woman was gone. In her place was an Esyal, pale and uncertain. She was sitting on the end of the bed, looking down at her hands. They were shaking.

"Are you all right?" he asked anxiously.

She nodded. "Yes... no... yes. I'm just..." Her voice faltered. "He was going to kill me. He came here to kill me." She covered her face with her hands and bent forward.

"What? Don't be ridiculous." He heard the words ringing emptily in his head even as spoke them. "He was..." Josyff floundered.

"He was what? Looking for you? In *my* room at this time of the night? Now who's being ridiculous?" Esyal's contempt made Josyff wince.

"All right. That was stupid. But..."

Esyal extended a hand for silence, then wrapped her arms tightly about herself and bent forward again. Josyff hovered impotently until, abruptly, she drew in a deep breath and stood up, apparently fully herself again. "Don't ask me how I know, I just do," she said, before Josyff could speak. "It was written in every inch of him. Only you being here stopped him—or stopped him trying, anyway." Her brow furrowed and she looked at Josyff intently, her expression calculating. "You worry him in some way—unsettle him. I'd say he's almost... afraid of you."

Her searching gaze was disconcerting, prompting a nervous laugh from Josyff. "I don't think so. I doubt anyone's ever been afraid of me, least of all someone like Adroyan. Why should they be?"

"Why indeed?" Esyal agreed. "But it's so—trust me—I know something about fear. He came to kill me and you stopped him. And he certainly *needs* you."

"*That* may be so," Josyff conceded, happy to avoid Esyal's repeated assertion. "But that's hardly a great mystery. This job has suddenly become urgent and I'm the only surveyor here."

"Measurer, he called you—nearly called you, anyway." Esyal said. "Like in the scroll—and what that... person... called you. And where has this sudden urgency come from?"

"I don't know," Josyff said, irritably. "People like Adroyan are always wanting things yesterday even if they don't need them for months. That's normal. You don't argue. But one thing I *do* know for certain in the middle of all this... confusion, is that 'Destroyer' or not, Ordrans or not, he's my boss, my superior, and I do what he says."

Esyal was still looking at him. "That's as maybe, but he *is* afraid of you.

And he did come to kill me." Before Josyff could denounce this again she leaned forward, earnest. "Listen, Josyff. I understand you want to cling to what used to be normality, God knows so do I, but it's not going to do you any good." She gesticulated towards the door. "That man—that whatever he is—and you and me are caught up in something very... strange. I've no idea what it is except that it's dangerous. We didn't ask for it—no rights, no wrongs, no justice and fairness—it just happened—that's the way with dangerous things—they just happen. What you need to grasp is you've no choice but to accept it and start working out what to do. I told you before, easier sooner than later."

Josyff desperately wanted to dismiss her remarks but found he could not. Yet what was to be done? For pity's sake, he couldn't even seriously accept that Adroyan had come to kill Esyal, let alone that he was in the middle of a war of some kind! Yet...

He shook his head. "I don't know. I don't know. We're not getting anywhere talking about it over and over." He looked at the window. The sky was lightening now. "Let's go and see if any of the others are up and about. Maybe find Henk. See if he's told them anything."

"Oh, he will have," Esyal said. "You didn't see that thing that came after him. He's got one thought and only one thought in his head—how to get out of here and how to get out quickly."

"Haven't you?"

Esyal paused, then let out a soft murmur of surprised resignation. "Oddly enough, no, now you mention it. Though it's the obvious course." She stammered. "I... I... couldn't do it. I've spent too long fighting these people—I can't just run away now this chance has come."

"To kill Adroyan?"

She frowned, puzzled. "No. There's something more. I can't grasp it. It's as though something has been woken up in me—as though everything I've ever done was just to bring me here." She blew out a noisy breath. "I'm feeling afraid and excited at the same time. It's very unsettling. You ask *some* questions, Measurer." Then she was matter-of-fact again. "Besides, I've a feeling Henk's going to find it harder than he thinks to get out of here."

Josyff pulled a wry face. "Badr was telling me how he walked him and Qualto all through the bowels of the place the other night, claiming that doors and corridors had been changed. He's an odd character for sure."

Esyal did not join in this subtle condemnation. "Maybe not so odd. Whatever's doing this can move things—inanimate objects—we've seen that. And maybe it's been trying to reach someone—anyone—here for a long time. Working with whatever it could find..."

"Our 'strangeness,'" Josyff said, raising an eyebrow.

Esyal tapped her forehead. "That's here," she said with certainty. "Our minds, our thoughts, all the stuff we've got in here. I've never thought about it before, but we don't know where it goes when we're not using it, do we? Or how it comes back when we need it. Our whole life's experience. It must be somewhere where these... people... can pick it up and use it somehow."

"You seem very sure about that."

"I am," came the immediate reply. She motioned to him impatiently. "Come on—let's do as you said, find the others."

Josyff had to trot to catch up with her as she strode off along the corridor. When he did, she continued.

"Some of the stuff I saw was mine, I know that, definitely. Old thoughts—some of them I haven't remembered in years. They were just... rearranged... and twisted into odd perspectives. Shapes that seemed normal at first glance but which couldn't be—impossible landscapes."

"I saw things like that too. Peculiar optical illusions."

Esyal narrowed her eyes and shook her head as though trying to clear her vision.

"Problem?"

"No. Still... adjusting."

"Well, that's more than I seem to be able to do at the moment. How can you be so certain that this isn't all some bizarre nightmare?"

She turned and smacked him sharply on the chest with the back of her hand. "Does that feel like anything you've ever had in a dream? Or this." She slapped the wall. Josyff flinched, not least because she was surprisingly strong.

"No, I..."

"No, I, nothing," Esyal snorted. She was becoming agitated. "Just because everything that's happened is like nothing we've ever known doesn't mean it's not real."

"You'll concede it's a probability we're dreaming." Josyff was unexpectedly defensive.

They were clattering down the stairs and Esyal stopped sharply. She looked around, her head thrown back, like an animal scenting for prey—or predators.

"No. I won't concede it," she said. "Not now. Not now. That would make me doubt and hesitate and this isn't the time for hesitation. We can't afford it." Then she seemed to relent a little. "Besides, if it is a dream—*my* dream—then I must be testing myself in some way—am I going to keep on until I win, or am I just going to curl up and die in a cold, dark cave—wondering whether I'll freeze before I starve?"

Josyff could not meet the conflict in her gaze. He ventured a little humour. "Well, if it's anyone's dream, it's mine."

She responded with a soft chuckle, and another vigorous slap, this time on his arm.

"You can have it," she declared, and she was off down the stairs, her momentary doubt gone. Josyff rubbed his arm ruefully and made a note not to do anything that might provoke Esyal into hitting him again, companionably or otherwise.

The passage lights flared into life as they reached the bottom of the stairs, and the sound of voices reached them. Angry voices.

CHAPTER 45

Esyal stopped and listened then pulled a rye face.

"It's Henk and Nyk," she said. "I'd have preferred to be met by the smell of cooking than what that sounds like."

Josyff raised his eyebrows. "You can think of food after everything that's happened?"

"Well, this particular "warrior" marches on her stomach without a doubt," Esyal replied. "Come on, we'd better see what's going on."

The kitchen was lit and showed signs of cooking under way, but the voices were coming from the Common Room. When they reached it, the door was partly open. Josyff rapped it sharply with his knuckles before he pushed it open and entered. Esyal followed him.

Henk, Nyk and Qualto were standing in front of the fire. Henk had the poker in his hand and was jabbing fitfully at the fire, as though he might find some kind of steadiness in one of his routine chores. Nyk, his grey hair awry, was patently fresh from his bed and looked decidedly irritated, while Qualto, hands raised in a placatory manner, was obviously trying to act as peacemaker.

They fell silent as Josyff and Esyal entered. Qualto looked embarrassed and Nyk made a conspicuous but unsuccessful attempt to present a pleasant face to their guests. Henk, by contrast, looked up from the fire and immediately levelled the poker at Esyal.

"She saw it. Tell them. Just tell them—what you saw."

Now it was Nyk who looked embarrassed. "I'm sorry. I don't know what's got into him. He..."

"Nothing's got into him," Esyal said, her voice forceful but matter-of-fact. "Something chased him into my room. I've no idea what it was, but we managed to beat it off."

A peculiar silence followed this blunt and simple revelation. The poker twitched as Henk tightened his grip on it in a combination of relief and triumph. Nyk's face creased into despairing confusion, but Qualto's mouth dropped and his eyes widened.

"Something?" he echoed. "Some *thing*?"

"Some *thing*," Esyal confirmed.

"Like... a creature... an animal?" Qualto indicated Henk. "He said it was like a... cloud."

"Probably smoke from the kitchen," Nyk grumbled.

Qualto's expression became briefly indignant. "I don't burn things," he snapped, before once again becoming nervous.

"It was more like a cloud than an animal," Esyal agreed. "And it wasn't smoke, nor a dream, nor an optical illusion. But it *was* foul."

Nyk turned to Josyff in search of a rational arbiter, but Josyff could only shrug his shoulders.

"I didn't see anything—or hear it. Whatever it was, it was gone by the time I got there. But I believe these two. They're not lying and they're not deluded. Something very odd is happening here and I think it's going to get worse."

Nyk had the air of a man surrounded. "We're all... unsettled. There's been some rattling and shaking, that's all—probably an earthquake, like Badr said. And it's an old building..."

His voice tailed off, and he seemed to sag. Josyff felt a pang of sympathy for this capable and conscientious man who suddenly found the long-established familiarities and supports of his life shifting and yielding. At the same time it made him realize how far he too had moved from what he would have regarded as the normal byways of his life. He was mildly surprised to find how little this concerned him.

You get used to most things, I suppose, he was thinking as he said to Nyk, "It's no earthquake, for sure." Abruptly, he became aware that everyone was watching and listening to him intently, even Esyal.

"*Measurer.*"

The voice—or was it the memory of the voice—made him pause. Like the slow tick of the clock in his room, he felt his life change. These people, even the "warrior" had turned to him as leader. Helplessness rose up through him, but so did the realization that if he did not accept their verdict, if he did nothing, something *really* bad would happen—something chaotic and uncontrollable.

Are you tinkering with my thoughts—my "strangeness"—using me for your own ends? he thought.

It was an unanswerable question. If he received a reply he would be none the wiser. It might be from those beyond who were creating this, and it might be either lie or truth, or it might be just his own imagination.

And, like a small light piercing through a dark night, he remembered.

Our thoughts, our strangeness, disturb them. We are beyond their calculation. They are struggling to communicate, not trying to manipulate. Granted, if they learned to communicate effectively—and they probably would, given that they were apparently fighting for survival—then they might well try to manipulate, but he could do nothing about that, save... save what? Save trust his judgement. His pragmatism asserted itself. Besides, if I cannot see the bars of my cage then I must consider myself free.

He sat down in a chair by the side of the fire.

Badr entered.

"Everyone sleeping badly, then?" he asked. He was smiling, but his expression became uneasy even as he was speaking. "Is something wrong? Has something else happened?"

"In a manner of speaking," Josyff replied. He indicated a chair. "Sit down, please. In fact, sit down, all of you, we need to talk. And put that poker down please, Henk, the fire's fine."

Henk hesitated, then did as he was asked, hanging the poker on the firedog with uncharacteristic gentleness. It swung slightly and struck the highly polished shovel hanging next to it.

The brief glint of bright light and soft chime made Josyff aware of the silence in the room and, again, of the scrutiny of the others.

When you don't know where to start—start.

"Badr, what did you think of my work today—yesterday, rather?"

Badr looked somewhat at a loss.

"Fine," he replied. "What can I say? It was just an ordinary day's work. There was that closing error at the end, but that'll come out in the wash, I'm sure." He cleared his throat uncomfortably. "You obviously know your job and we seemed to get on well enough. Is there problem?"

"No, no problem—not with work anyway. It's just that you were with me all day and, given that we... newcomers... are all strangers, both here and to one another, I suppose you've known me..." He shrugged. "...the longest."

Badr smiled broadly. "I suppose I have," he said, with a soft chuckle. "Though I can't say I'd have thought of it in those terms. What's the significance?"

"The significance is that you can confirm that, as far as you can tell, I'm sane and rational."

Badr's brow furrowed. "I can, certainly, but why would I need to?"

"Why indeed? Listen."

Briefly, Josyff outlined his experiences since he had arrived at the Keep. He avoided his revelation about Esyal and her intentions and also made no direct reference to their conclusion that Adroyan was the Destroyer. It proved to be an easier telling then he had expected, the tale emerging as though anxious to escape.

He concluded. "Taken one at a time, I can attribute things like the seagulls, the clock—to being dreams. I don't normally dream—or remember them, anyway—but a long journey, new place, problems with the equipment, it was a possibility, as was my being... unwell. Even what happened in the Archive I could perhaps pass off as some kind of waking dream. But all of us have heard things, felt things, seen the drawbridge behaving as though it had a mind of its own or was under the control of something beyond us. It's too much. However fantastic it might seem, I've got to think that someone, somewhere—some power, if you like—*is* reaching through to us, and that it's asking for help."

He sat back and examined his audience with the same intensity they had previously been subjecting him to. Henk was nodding his head and looking even more triumphant than before. Qualto looked more bewildered and nervous. Nyk had leaned forward halfway through the tale and, with his elbows on his knees, was looking steadfastly down at the floor. Badr was staring fixedly at Josyff, his expression unreadable.

"Still think I'm sane?" Josyff asked him directly.

Badr was a long time answering and at one point seemed inclined to turn round and leave. "You put me in a difficult position. You're my superior, I..."

"No," Josyff interrupted. "We're trapped here. In this matter we're all just men—men and a woman—people—facing a common problem. You're like me, you're practically minded, speak as you find—be honest. There'll be no reproach. Do you still think I'm sane?"

The blunt repetition of his question jerked a reply out of Badr.

"You seem sane enough to me, but what you're saying is..." He shrugged. "Isn't. Isn't sane. I don't doubt you believe what you're saying, and we've seen what we've seen, but you can understand how it sounds."

"I can indeed," Josyff said. "And you can understand my reluctance to speak about it—as you just pointed out, I'm your superior here. Now, has anything happened to you that you've chosen to keep silent about for fear of seeming foolish?" He looked round and included the others in this question.

"It's certainly been an odd few days, for sure, and I've had a little trouble sleeping," Badr replied. "And that long walk that Henk took us on the other night was a bit... unsettling." He paused. "And while I'm reasonably content to explain all the rumblings and shakings to some kind of earth movement, even the noises we heard, I've got to admit I've no idea what's happening with the drawbridge. It's... it's quite unfathomable. It *is* almost as though something's holding it shut."

Josyff was turning to Nyk and Qualto when Esyal said, "Tell them about me."

He looked at her, concerned, but she nodded in confirmation.

"All of it?" he asked.

Esyal wavered for a moment then gritted her teeth. "Yes, all of it. Something's telling me we haven't begun to grasp the danger we're in. And I don't think we've much time. Yes, tell them."

"Very well."

Josyff sat back so that he could see everyone in the room at the same time. He took a deep breath.

"When Esyal and I shared our dream—our contact with these... people... beyond, I found I knew what she was thinking. She's not suffering from memory loss, nor has been from the outset. She's hiding. She's part of the Rhanen. She got separated from a group trying to escape through the mountains when they were attacked by a New Order force. She thinks Adroyan is not merely Ordrans, but might even be the First Member. She wants... she's..." He faltered and looked at her for further confirmation. She cut across his hesitation.

"I'm certain he's the Destroyer that these... others... are so concerned about and I *do* think he's the First Member. Apart from being the focus of the New Order and all that means for us, he's also a focus for one side in this war, wherever it is—the bad side. I think we've no choice but to... deal with him. I think if we don't, their war will tilt over into this world and terrible things will happen."

Nyk's face had begun changing while Josyff was speaking. Now it twisted into an expression of desperate irritation. "This is *ridiculous*! People from 'somewhere else', coming into dreams to tell us there's a war going on— and that we're part of it. I've never heard such... Is this some kind of a joke you're playing... some kind of city joke to play on the yokels?" He levelled an unsteady finger at Esyal as his thoughts bounced in another direction. "I don't know anything about politics. We all just get on with our jobs here. But I know enough to know that joke or not, you shouldn't be joking about being one of the Rhanen. You'll get us all arrested."

"By whom?" Esyal retorted forcefully, leaning forward and holding his gaze. "Who's going to be out in these mountains now? And who could get in here even if they wanted to?"

"We're shut in *now*," Nyk said angrily. "But the drawbridge could open itself again any moment—it did it before. It's only something mechanical— we'll find out what it is if we look hard enough. It doesn't need..." He waved his arms. "...creatures from another world, for crying out loud. I've never heard anything so stupid in all my life. It's..."

"It's not just 'something mechanical.'" Henk's voice stopped Nyk in full flow. "And it's nothing new. There's been something going on here for months— it just got worse when this lot arrived." He waved his hand across the new arrivals. Abruptly he was very calm. "I know you think I'm a bit weird. Maybe I am. Maybe we all are—working out here in the middle of nowhere. But you've known me long enough to know I'm not barmy. I've seen what I've seen and felt what I've felt and this girl's right—something bad's happening. I can't close my eyes without seeing that... thing... that... apparition... rushing after me. It was like something out of the bowels of Hell." He shuddered. "God knows when I'm going to be able to sleep again."

"Damn you!" Nyk muttered, his face riven with mixed emotions in response to this. "I don't doubt you believe what you say, Henk—or the surveyor here, but..." He opted for simplicity. "It just makes no sense. Any of it."

"That's as maybe," Henk said. "But it makes enough sense for me to get out of here right now. I'll make a bridge across the moat myself if I have to." He picked up the poker and jabbed it into the fire in emphasis. A shower of sparks rushed up the chimney as if they too were fleeing from an unseen enemy.

Nyk made a vague, frustrated gesture and Josyff once again found himself the focus of attention in the room.

"Very well," he said. "This is what we'll do."

CHAPTER 46

Josyff looked at each of the others in turn as his mind raced to find a way to bridge the gap between the new normality that he was beginning to accept and the rational, commonsense one that Nyk, Badr and Qualto remained in.

The question, why are they looking to me and not Adroyan, the most senior person here? came to him, but he did not pursue it.

In its wake he began speaking, scarcely knowing what he was going to say: "That something very peculiar is happening here isn't open to debate, is it?" Somewhat to his surprise his voice was quite measured and he kept the question rhetorical by continuing immediately.

"But in addition to everything we've all seen and heard, other things have happened to me, Esyal, and Henk. These are forcing me—us—to a conclusion that I can see is... difficult, to put it mildly... for the rest of you. In your place I'd be looking at me askance too, but until I start foaming at the mouth or showing *clear* signs of insanity, can we agree to take things at their face value and just work out what we ought to do?"

Again he did not wait for any reply.

"Nyk, Henk, I think you should start looking into how we can get out of here as a matter of urgency. Sooner or later that's going to have to be done anyway. And that moat's wide and deep. A way over it is going to need some serious thought."

"I've been thinking about it already..." Henk announced earnestly.

"I'm sure you have," Josyff said, holding up a hand to stop him before he could continue.

"Nyk?" he asked.

Nyk frowned. "There are things to do round here, you know. We can't just drop all our jobs and..." His protest faded.

"The jobs will still be there if we get out of here, and a day or two's delay won't make much difference to anything, I imagine." He leaned forward. "But if we don't get out of here, the jobs are irrelevant. And I think we'd be foolish to assume that the drawbridge will suddenly open of its own accord again. Besides, your routine's been destroyed already, hasn't it?"

Nyk closed his eyes and growled. "Yes, it has," he admitted reluctantly. "I suppose it would be a mistake to do nothing and there's no saying how long it'll take us to work something out. It doesn't help that we're not exactly overwhelmed with labourers to do the work either." Then he levelled a sharp finger at Josyff. "But this business about people from... somewhere else... and a war going on, and something chasing Henk through the corridors. You're an intelligent man, a professional surveyor, and I've got to accept you've seen or heard something very odd, but not all that nonsense, it's—"

"—not necessary that you believe us." Josyff concluded his sentence quickly. "Just try to keep as open a mind about it as you can. We *can* agree on that, can't we? And, at the least, if something unusual happens to you, it won't be a complete surprise."

Nyk gave a grudging gesture of acceptance but looked uneasily at Esyal.

Josyff anticipated. "Esyal will be keeping her political intentions to herself until we're free from here," he said, adding, with a significant look at Esyal, "Won't you?"

"Yes," she said, without hesitation. "There are more important things going on here than the New Order and the Rhanen. But you don't need to believe that either, any of you." She returned Nyk's stare. "And that said, I'm as keen as everyone else to be away from here—tell me if there's anything I can do help you and Henk. I'm not stupid and I'm not afraid of hard work."

Nyk raised an eyebrow at this unexpected offer, but before he could speak, Henk accepted it: "We will."

Nyk looked as though he was going to say something, but thought better of it.

"This is all very well." Badr's face was concerned, and his voice burst loudly into the brief silence. "But what about Adroyan? No disrespect, Josyff, but he's the one with responsibility and authority here—he might have other ideas about all this."

"Indeed," Josyff replied. "And, in my estimation, nothing's to be gained by waving it all in front of him. So you and I will get on with our jobs, quietly and quickly. Get this place surveyed and down on paper as soon as possible. He'll have no complaint to find about us, trust me. And I doubt he's remotely interested in what Nyk and the others get up to. Besides, if he *does* ask them, they can tell the truth—they're trying to find a way out of here. This place—and our welfare, I suppose—is their responsibility, and getting us out safely is important."

"And all this other stuff—this... war. These creatures. And..." Badr gestured awkwardly towards Esyal.

"As I said, nothing's to be gained by raising any of that," Josyff said. "Let's keep things as simple as possible: do our work, get out of here—and these mountains, don't forget—and worry about 'all this other stuff' later."

"If we're allowed to get out," Esyal said.

"Let's deal with one thing at a time. You help where you can. And keep away from Adroyan."

"If he keeps away from me."

Josyff's look darkened. "Keep away from him," he insisted. "Run away if you have to. Better still, don't wander off anywhere alone. Keep company with someone all the time."

"Would you like to help me make some breakfast?" Qualto offered, nervously searching for solid ground amid the general uneasiness.

Josyff was grateful. "Sounds like a good idea, though I don't know whether I'm hungry or not at the moment."

"Then you are," Qualto told him, firmly. "And whatever's the truth of what's happening here, it's better faced on a full stomach, I'm sure of that. It won't take long." He motioned Esyal to follow him as he left.

In the kitchen, Qualto was uncomfortably businesslike, moving about with his usual easy efficiency but avoiding looking directly at Esyal, even as he allocated some fetching and carrying to her.

"I wondered about that knife of yours," he said, eventually, the words tumbling out hastily. "Not that you were carrying it—that's reasonable, out here—but the way you handled it. No fumbling, no awkwardness—most of all when you sheathed it after I'd sharpened it. You didn't even look what you were doing."

Esyal waited.

"It's *very* sharp now," he said. "As a knife should be. Take care how you use it." He was speaking more calmly now and looking directly at her. This time it was she who had difficulty meeting his gaze.

"I will," she replied, flatly.

Qualto returned to his work.

He became explanatory.

"Nyk and Henk and me—we've worked together here for a long time—we're used to one another. We all have our ways. Henk's not very talkative, and he can be a bit... morose at times. But he's solid... practical, down-to-earth... not given to idle fancy. I doubt he's got the imagination, to be honest. If he says he's seen something, then he's seen it and I believe him. As for what it might be, that's a different matter. The tale you and the surveyor are telling takes some swallowing, you'll admit, but again, even though *you're* a bit... relaxed... with the truth, the surveyor seems straightforward enough. I don't know." He paused and looked upwards reflectively.

"Thinking about it, something's been troubling Henk for a while now. Since before you all arrived." Then he was both practical and concerned. "I've never seen him agitated like this. And if he wants to get out of here, in the middle of winter and the middle of a tour of duty, then whatever he's seen has frightened the wits out of him."

He was looking at her again, questioning.

"It frightened the wits out of me," Esyal said. "I don't know what it was. Shapes, sounds, colours, things I couldn't begin to imagine, things that looked, felt, as though they shouldn't even be able to exist. Yet they were real, for sure. It was like a..." She searched for a phrase. "Like an optical illusion... but for *all* my senses. And there was some kind of consciousness in it—something bad—*very* bad—malevolent." She shuddered as her words brought back the memory. "It was foul."

Qualto shook his head anxiously, as if disputing within himself. "Where would such a thing come from? And why would it chase Henk?"

"I don't know. It makes no sense to me and I was there! But whatever it might be and however it came here I know one thing about it, for sure: it's a predator, a hunter. It has that much in common with you and me."

Qualto muttered "predator" to himself with a soft, self-mocking chuckle. "How do you know that?" he said. "Your instinct?" His tone was gently taunting, but Esyal ignored it and answered him simply.

"I didn't need instinct. I told you, it was foul, awful, and when I flinched away from it, it... reached out towards me—my fear drew it after me. That's a predator."

"But you attacked it, nevertheless?"

Esyal gave a rueful grunt and her eyes were briefly sad. "Yes. The only reason you don't think you're a predator, is that you haven't learned about it yet. I learned quite a time ago that I'm one, whether I like it or not. Though I'll admit, I don't know what I thought hitting that thing with a chair would do. It was just the nearest weapon to hand."

"Well, it seems you drove it away."

"I don't know how. The chair didn't seem to hit anything—there was no impact. It just passed through it," Esyal reflected. "And so did my knife." Qualto looked up from his work and stared at her, intently.

"I thought I was teasing you when I said "instinct" before—but maybe I wasn't. Perhaps it wasn't what you hit it with but something in you—some intent. You seem different."

"Well, I'm not lying and hiding any more, am I?"

Qualto continued his scrutiny. "No, I think it's more than that. Can't put my finger on it, but you've changed."

Esyal made to deny the charge, but found she could not. She *had* changed. She remembered the impression she had had of fighting with sword and shield—hacking down an enemy without pity. But as she tried to recollect details, she could put no face to the enemy, nor a landscape for the battlefield, nor any reason why she was there.

What she did remember was the hatred and scorn in the word, {"Warrior..."}

And then the fear she had felt clinging about it when she attacked. *That*, she had relished—and relished now. It was vulnerable.

"Yes, you're right," she said, reluctantly. "I have. It's as though something in me is... waking up."

Qualto was still staring at her.

"Of course, it might all be no more than some kind of delayed shock," he said. "A few days ago you were alone and shivering in a mountain cave, expecting to die, I imagine. Now, by the slenderest of chances, you're alive and safe—a change like that, let alone everything else that's happened, is bound to have some effect."

"That's true," Esyal conceded. "But it's more than that, I'm sure." Her earlier conversation with Josyff returned. "I'm certain now, the more I think about it, these... people, creatures, whatever they are, are using our own thoughts to reach through to us." She placed her fingertips against her temples. "They're some kind of common ground between us—I think they root through them to find things they can use..."

Qualto's eyes were widening.

"I know, I know," Esyal said. "It sounds insane, but it makes an odd kind of sense."

"*Very* odd," Qualto retorted with heavy irony.

Esyal leaned forward. "Wait until something happens to you before you get too sure of yourself." She tapped her forehead and posed the question she had asked of Josyff. "Where does all our knowledge exist, Qualto? Where do all our thoughts come from and go to? We only keep a couple of things in our mind at once, but we can unearth things from years ago like that." She snapped her fingers.

Qualto returned to his work and signalled to Esyal to pass him a tray.

"I wasn't being dismissive—or sarcastic, or anything else," he said defensively, clattering dishes. "I'm just trying to make some sense of everything." He paused. "And how the devil should I know where my thoughts go? What a question. And all this talk of rooting and unearthing—you make my mind sound like an old garden shed."

A laugh spluttered out of Esyal, provoking a snorting chuckle from Qualto. Esyal's response caught her by surprise, as did the sensation of relief and lightness that followed it.

"You're not going to ask me where I keep my sense of humour, are you?" Qualto asked archly. He handed a loaded tray to her.

"It might be useful to know," she replied. "Maybe if these creatures used that they'd be less inclined to go to war."

Qualto gave her a quizzical look. "Was that serious or was it a joke?" he asked.

Esyal pursed her lips. "I really don't know," she said. "And right now, I don't particularly care. Let's eat."

The common room was silent when they entered it carrying the food. Adroyan was sitting at the table.

CHAPTER 47

"Qualto, you do us all proud. I for one am most grateful for your efforts. Out here, to be frank, I had expected the worst."

Josyff found Adroyan's avuncular tone even more disturbing than his usual authoritative brusqueness. He was still unsettled by Adroyan's arrival in the common room when he had greeted everyone with an unexpected affability. It had plunged the room into a brief and awkward silence which was scarcely eased when it was eventually broken by a series of stuttered "good mornings". Adroyan had ignored the hesitant response and had gestured towards the table.

"I apologize for interrupting your conversation, gentlemen, but let's be seated." He became confidential. "I took the liberty of peeping into the kitchen on the way past and I think our meal will be here very shortly."

As it was.

Josyff noted Esyal stiffen as she entered and saw Adroyan and, for an instant, he thought she was going to attack him then and there. He had a fearful image of flashing mayhem and spraying blood and he kept his eyes on her as though his gaze alone might remind her of her promise not to harm Adroyan—for the time being.

It was unnecessary however. Esyal was too seasoned a conspirator to act so impetuously, but, more significantly, she had sensed a change in Adroyan as soon as she saw him and every part of her cried out "danger!". Following this came the realization that she would have to learn a great deal more about this man before she attempted to destroy him. Whatever had happened to *him* during the night, he was stronger.

But then, she reflected, so was she.

She gave him a cheery greeting as she distributed the plates, though her manner did little to relieve Josyff's sense of unease. He forced himself to take a discreet deep breath and it took him some effort to stop his hands shaking.

Two of a kind, he thought. Treacherous, deceitful—and murderous. Both edging for position. For all their pleasant manners, they're fighting this damned war, he concluded, and ultimately they would fight it regardless of anything that got in their way.

Or anyone.

Laughter brought him back to the present.

"I said, I hope that's work you're thinking about, Surveyor."

It was Adroyan. He was chuckling. The sound seeped seductively into Josyff's mind. "I'm sorry," he said hastily. "I was..."

"Miles away." Adroyan finished his sentence with an outright laugh.

"Indeed I was," Josyff admitted with an embarrassed laugh of his own. "At home, actually. No disrespect to our hosts here, but home is home, and thinking about getting out of here took me there..." He snapped his fingers, then found himself plunging on. "I've taken the liberty of asking Nyk and the others to pursue the matter of getting out of here as a matter of urgency. It's work that's got to be done sooner or later and, in my opinion, the sooner the better. I think it's going to be very difficult."

Adroyan appeared to mull the idea over, though his eyes were indifferent.

"I don't share your various worries about this," he said to the entire table. "I think it will resolve itself as soon..." His voice tailed off but returned quickly to close the matter. "I think it will resolve itself. But I see no harm in your recommendation." His attention returned to Josyff. "So long as it does not affect *your* work. That remains urgent and must remain your first concern."

"We understand that," Josyff replied, surreptitiously drawing Badr into the exchange.

"Will this interfere with *your* normal work?" Adroyan asked, turning to Nyk.

"No more than it's been interfered with already, sir," Nyk replied, with a good-natured laugh and a disclaiming shrug. "But our routines are quite flexible. What has to be done always gets done and nothing important will go untended. And, with all due respect, sir, thinking about this, I think the surveyor's right. I'm far from certain that the drawbridge will suddenly come loose again. In fact, I don't think it will." He warmed to his conclusion. "And if it did, what then? We couldn't wedge it open last time so presumably we wouldn't be able to again. That means we'd all have to leave immediately we got the chance—regardless of the weather, preparations..." He indicated Josyff. "...the surveyor's work, anything."

Adroyan inclined his head to indicate acceptance of Nyk's point. "It's of no great import," he said, a hint of boredom in his voice. "If I'm right, then you'll have lost some time and labour, and if I'm wrong, then thanks to your efforts and foresight we'll all be able to leave when *we* decide. Do what you see fit. I've complete faith in your judgement."

The rest of the meal felt surreal to Josyff. At one moment, Adroyan was just one of a group of casual acquaintances chatting idly as they ate. At another, he was something monstrous skulking behind a mask—watching, waiting. His impressions of Esyal were no less confused. She was smiling and talkative, but there was something watching and waiting in her as well, though not so much hiding as being icily controlled.

I suppose we're all the same, he thought, glancing around the table. Everyone affecting to be relaxed and easy, but resolutely avoiding mentioning what must be uppermost in their minds: the tale that he and Esyal had just told; a tale at best bewildering, at worst, terrifying.

Then the meal was over and the group was breaking up. At Qualto's request, Esyal was helping him clear the table, while Nyk departed with Henk, the latter having almost a spring in his step as he left.

Josyff could not help smiling as he too made to leave. "I think Henk's more than a little relieved that you raised no objection to my suggestion, sir," he said to Adroyan. "He looks almost enthusiastic at the prospect of working on a way out of here."

Adroyan ignored the remark. He motioned Josyff towards a chair by the fireplace.

"A word with you before you go, Surveyor," he said.

Josyff indicated Badr, but Adroyan shook his head and gave a small but unequivocal gesture of dismissal. Its coldness made Josyff wince inwardly and he could not help giving Badr a discreet nod of apology.

"I'll start setting up the equipment," Badr said, with an equally discreet nod of acceptance.

As Badr left, Josyff perched himself bolt upright on the edge of the chair. Adroyan, by contrast, sank back into his. A partial shadow falling across his face made his eyes black and unreadable—just as they had been when he entered Esyal's bedroom, Josyff noted . He sat silent, scrutinizing Josyff intently.

Despite Henk's fire, Josyff felt cold, as though the presence he had sensed watching and waiting within Adroyan was assessing him—judging him. For a terrifying moment he thought that Adroyan might suddenly metamorphose into the monstrous creation that Esyal and Henk had described...

"These are delicate times, Surveyor."

Adroyan's voice cut through the fantasy.

"In what respect, sir?" Josyff managed, stammering a little and cursing himself for it.

Adroyan's hand moved slightly, left then right, an oddly refined gesture. "Just delicate, Surveyor, just delicate. A feather's weight here—ruination and chaos. A feather's weight there—order, progress."

"I'm not sure I understand what you mean, sir." Josyff felt his composure returning.

"No, of course not. Why should you? You're a loyal servant of the New Order. Your work is excellent, and you do it... without question."

Josyff thought he sensed a reproach in this last.

"I'm a professional surveyor, sir," making an effort not to seem defensive. "I measure and record things—buildings, landscapes—and commit them to paper as well as I'm able. I make sure that my employers—the State—through yourself in this case, have what they need to make *their* decisions—the political decisions. Technical matters aside, there's rarely anything to question."

"But you question this particular venture."

The comment caught Josyff by surprise and it showed on his face. "No," he protested softly and quite genuinely. "I'm curious about it, quite naturally. Very curious. Even without the peculiar happenings of the last few days, this is an odd place, and very isolated. It's difficult to see what anyone would want with it, but, no, I don't question my instructions." He leaned forward a little, gathering momentum. "And even part of my curiosity is professional. If I know why a place is being surveyed it can sometimes help me present the work in its most useful form."

"You pre-judge the requirements of your superiors?"

Part of Josyff cowered at this conclusion, but another felt a frisson of anger. The one restrained the other and his manner was quite calm when he replied.

"I use my professional judgement, sir. My training and experience have given me skills beyond that of just measuring and I put all of these at the service of my superiors—as I presume they would wish me to. I study their needs and, if appropriate, make observations on their... practicability, or on alternatives that they might not have considered..."

"Yes, you do," Adroyan said, before he could continue. "As I said, your work is good. That is why you are here."

He fell silent but continued his steady scrutiny of Josyff.

"Is there some unusual aspect of this scheme that you feel I might be able to help with?" Josyff asked, uneasy at the protracted silence.

Unexpectedly, Adroyan's face filled with doubt. Josyff realized that it was the first time he had seen him show any real emotion.

"What do you know of the present Government, Surveyor—the so-called New Order?"

Taken aback, Josyff's thoughts floundered. In the end he did what he usually did, he told the truth.

"I know very little, sir. I've no interest in politics. I've no desire for power and, to be honest, I've difficulty understanding those who have. I do my job, pay my taxes and try not to break any laws."

"That was not my question," Adroyan said, though in a tone of quiet explanation rather than rebuke. "Tell me what you *do* know. It is important."

Josyff involuntarily glanced from side to side, like a trapped animal looking for escape.

"As I said, sir, I know very little. Whatever the failings of the old

Government, and there were many, by all accounts, it let people get on with their daily lives without too much problem so I'd no real cause to take an interest. I've heard it said that there's a peculiar alchemy in the will of the people that gives us the Government we need, but that said, I'm far from clear in my mind how the New Order came to power so quickly and so totally..." Something about Adroyan seemed to be drawing him towards indiscretion. "And I'm not... fully at ease... with the its... secrecy and its apparent desire to... interfere with people's lives so much."

No sooner had the words left him than he felt like a suddenly-wakened sleepwalker swaying on the edge of a sheer precipice.

Adroyan frowned and Josyff's mind began frantically searching for ways to unsay what he had just said. Then his mouth went dry for another reason. The monstrous presence he had sensed watching and waiting in Adroyan throughout breakfast, was in front of him.

CHAPTER 48

But nothing had changed. The room looked the same, the fire was burning gently, a faint, homely clatter of activity from the kitchen was still drifting in through the open door, and Adroyan looked the same, leaning back in his chair. Yet he was not the same. He had been transformed utterly. What was sitting in front of Josyff now radiated a presence identical to that which had visited him after his contact with Esyal and the figure. He felt his stomach begin to churn and his skin to crawl as had happened before, but, also as before, he could not move.

"Aah."

The sound was like a nest of disturbed snakes and Josyff tensed himself in anticipation of that nerve-tearing voice—{"...measurer..."}

And indeed there was a distant, echoing hint of it when Adroyan spoke.

"This will be difficult for you, Surveyor," he said.

Mimicking the voice of your masters.

The thought sprang unexpectedly into Josyff's mind from somewhere. There was a deriding sneer in it...

But was there also a warning?

Be alert.

It came to Josyff that perhaps, in this changed and unchanged figure in front of him, Adroyan's masters might have found their way into this world, might be watching, might be guiding the shell they were occupying.

He forced the thought to one side urgently before its endless interweaving implications could overwhelm him. At the same time he forced himself to speak.

"What will, sir?" he asked, his voice more casual than he had expected.

Adroyan flinched slightly, as though he had not anticipated a reply. Then he leaned forward and it seemed to Josyff that a great shadow rose behind him, filling the room, enclosing him in a dark place where only he and Adroyan existed.

"This is necessary. Do not be afraid, no harm will come to you—you above all are valued—but do not resist."

Before Josyff could respond, Adroyan was reaching out towards him. He felt his own hand moving to prevent this but it was too slow. Then he was aware of a pressure on his forehead, on the scar that his dream—if dream it had been—about the seagulls had left. Somewhat to his surprise it had not troubled him and he had thought about it only when he had cause to look in a mirror. Even there, though it was still sore to the touch, it had healed well and had not discoloured as he had anticipated.

Now it seemed that it was opening and Adroyan's hand was passing through it and into the depths of his mind. Before either inquiry or fear could properly form, a giddying black tide of confusion swept up his thoughts and carried them away.

Then it was gone. All was still and silent and he was no-thing and no-one, floating in the blackness, waiting...

Yet part of him, tiny binding strings, stretched out, searching for familiarities—the fire, the noises from the kitchen, the edge of the chair hard against his legs.

But there was nothing.

Nothing except Adroyan's presence...

...which felt somehow protective now...

...keeping many things at bay.

And with that realization came another: this was no place to be. Wherever it was—*whatever* it was—it was *their* place—a place of evil—ancient evil—a place of unfettered destruction and distortion—an unequivocal confirmation of the events he had been drawn into.

Free yourself!

{Do not resist.}

Adroyan's words formed about and through him, inaudible, but carrying with them the tone of the foul presence that he had encountered in his room.

{"You are protected. You are valued. No harm can befall you."}

Josyff quailed before their awfulness—the more so because of the concern and reassurance they were labouring to impart. His brief rebellion hesitated, then died under the weight of stark terror and his hard-learned talent for silent watchfulness in the face of overwhelming odds.

Then around and through him, possessing him totally, was the light that had filled his room only hours earlier. It was baleful and ominous, and with it were the same terrible images, though this time they were worse by far. As before he tried to cry out in denial but again could not. There was no denying what they were—manifestations of something deep within him—something ancient and primitive, even inhuman. Then he recalled Esyal's fancy: "Our minds, our thoughts. All the stuff we've got in there. These people can pick it up and use it somehow."

The memory helped him. These images might indeed be his, but whatever was directing them, guiding, reshaping their malevolence, was *not* his. That was the work of another mind—or minds. Left to their own devices, he knew such thoughts would wither and die in the light of his conscious revulsion, sinking back, unwanted and unneeded, into the depths where they belonged. These creatures used them to communicate their own peculiar horror. It was all they had. He qualified the conclusion—to reach us safely, that is. To use the force they had used to close the drawbridge seemingly unnerved them, he recalled—for some reason it was too dangerous—*it could destroy us all—the merest reflection of it binds your world—it should not even be possible—only the existence of the nexus makes it so.*

But he had little time to ponder these scurrying thoughts. It seemed to him that every least part of him was being dispersed—spread into and through some unknowable place, curving and re-curving, twisting into perspectives that could not be. And examined! All the time, examined. Greedy eyes that were as cold as they were wild squinted and peered into him; clawing hands sifted, probed, searched. And throughout, ravening mouths hissed and rasped at one another in some unholy communion, from which he could discern only the descant, *{"Measurer! Measurer!"}* Josyff could hear them echoing to and fro throughout this demented world, chilling voices crying out in a disordered chorus. They were full of triumph and loathsome expectation.

Despair filled him.

But even as it did he sensed a change—slight and subtle, but quite distinct.

The triumph was faltering. Angry shards of doubt were crystallizing in it, jagged and destructive.

Josyff's despair began to turn to fear. What had these creatures found in him and what would they do next? His mind cried out to him to struggle but he was without form. Then the doubt was becoming certainty and the triumph was disappearing under a welter of fury.

Yet despite his mounting terror, another hint of hope came to Josyff through the turmoil.

Whatever had brought about this frightening change, it was not *his* doing. The fury was clearly focused elsewhere.

And the hold the creatures had on him was faltering.

Like a falling man wildly snatching for support at whatever is nearest, Josyff found again his resolution.

He would be free of these obscenities!

Free!

Even as the word formed, the many images and sensations pervading him were changing. Slowly they were losing their coherence and beginning to rotate. As though caught in an irresistible tidal force they began to accelerate, the noise rising in pitch at the same time. Josyff felt himself being drawn into it, though something was resisting.

The movement continued to accelerate until it became a blur and the accompanying sound an intolerable screech.

Josyff's fear rose in parallel with this mounting disintegration until it threatened to overwhelm him, then suddenly a blood-red flash gashed across his mind like a blow from a flailing weapon, and he was in the common room again, thrust hard back into his chair as if he had fallen back there in reaction to the disappearance of a sustaining force. Faintly he could hear the remains of the screech, an insect buzz, fading into the distance.

Something buffeted him, and a voice, blurred and unintelligible, mingled with the sound of his pounding heart and gasping breath. It repeated itself several times until he heard, "What were you shown?"

Josyff struggled to make his eyes focus on the questioner. The final whirling movement of the vortex into which the creatures and their world had vanished still lingered in both his awareness and his vision and it seemed as though the room itself was moving, making him grip the arms of the chair tightly.

"What were you shown?"

The question came again and simultaneously brought the room to a halt and Adroyan's face into clear focus. Josyff stared wildly. It seemed that Adroyan's eyes were wholly black—as though the pupils had expanded to fill the entire orb. It was a deeply disturbing image and Josyff heard the rasping sound of his own breath being drawn in. Instinctively he tried to turn away but something was preventing his head from moving. Denied flight, he closed his eyes tightly...

"Surveyor!"

Realization of what he was doing, and to whom, rushed in on him and he opened his eyes immediately. Adroyan's face was close to his, but the eyes, though searching, were quite normal.

"What were you shown?" he was asking again.

Josyff reached up to discover that it was Adroyan who was preventing him from moving, holding his head as one might hold a wilful child's. As Josyff's hands touched his, Adroyan released him and slowly sat back. Josyff had a momentary illusion of Adroyan's face, unnaturally bright, retreating along a dark tunnel.

Uncertain about the question he was being asked, he asked one of his own.

"What just happened? Did I fall asleep? I'm sor..."

But Adroyan cut through his attempted distraction.

"You were spoken to. That much I could feel. Tell me what you were shown, what you were told."

His voice carried a power that commanded Josyff at a level he felt unable to resist. He heard himself describing what he had just seen and heard, though somehow he managed to omit his appalled reaction to the foulness and outright evil he had sensed.

Adroyan listened, rapt, almost awe-struck, his eyes searching Josyff's face relentlessly, as if their intense focus might draw further meaning from the words.

As Josyff finished, so his self-control began to return. He repeated his question.

"What just happened, sir? Was it a... dream?"

He narrowly avoided saying "nightmare" and was sufficiently in control of himself now not to ask, "and why do you want to know about it?" The answer to that would presumably come in its own time and he was far from sure he wanted to hear it.

Adroyan closed his eyes as though he were praying.

"You are blessed indeed, surveyor," he said after a moment. "Even I, who have served them for so long have never been touched as you were."

Alarmed by this pronouncement, Josyff clung wilfully to a show of confusion and bewilderment.

"I'm sorry, sir. I don't understand. What just happened and who are you talking about?"

Adroyan opened his eyes. They seemed to be staring into the far distance, but when they returned to Josyff's face there was an almost paternal look in them.

"I said this would be difficult for you, surveyor, but you have seen what you have seen, and heard what you have heard. Answering your question, what has happened is that you have been looked upon, weighed in the balance, and found to be whole." Once again his eyes became distant. "Blessed indeed," he repeated softly to himself before returning again to Josyff. This time his expression was full of proprietorial pride. "I knew I was right to choose you. Such is their guidance. You are not a man to deny or disregard such evidence. You have such... remarkable... clarity of thought."

Josyff snatched at the remark, his anxiety to be away from all this outweighing his curiosity. "That's kind of you to say so, sir, but I'm just a surveyor. Good at my job, I know, but nothing special."

"In that you're wrong, surveyor," Adroyan said.

He leaned forward quickly and tapped Josyff on the forehead. Josyff could not help flinching but this time nothing happened.

"In here, such mysteries lie. Barely more than a handful of all too fragile flesh, yet in its tangle of threads and pathways it holds and conjures up all that we are. All our subtleties and complexities. All here." He leaned further forward and his voice fell almost to a whisper. "And more, surveyor, much more. Far down, in its distant reaches, it touches on a great commonality, a commonality which joins us to many things, things not only beyond our everyday understanding but beyond out wildest imaginings."

Josyff could do no more than repeat himself. "I'm sorry, sir, I... I don't understand."

"Of course not," Adroyan replied. "Even I do not understand much of such matters. But that is of no concern. It is sufficient that it is the way it is. It is sufficient that *they* understand it and can speak to us and that we serve them truly."

Josyff felt part of him grow very cold.

But it was not the cold of fear, it was the glacial coldness of a predator, long hungry, that has just seen rich prey and knows it must watch and wait now as never before, for no other chance will come its way and a long slow death is already beckoning.

CHAPTER 49

Josyff became very still, both inwardly and outwardly, some ancient instinct knowing that the least inappropriate movement or thought might send his prey flying. Though he had never felt anything like this before, and was, in part, appalled by it, it seemed to be deeply familiar.

Softly, like a gently thrown lure, he spoke the words as they formed in his mind,

"They, sir?"

The prey did not bolt. Rather, it relaxed. Josyff continued his vigil.

"Those who made themselves known to you—spoke to you—judged you."

"Yes, sir. But who are they? How...?"

Adroyan stopped him with a gesture and became part teacher, part preacher.

"The 'how?' is beyond us, surveyor. As for who they are..." He paused as though searching for an answer to a question he had never been asked before. "In less enlightened times they were worshipped as gods. Later they were sometimes referred to as The Ancients, The Old Ones..."

The First Comers, Josyff nearly said, but something would not allow the words voice.

"Both fitting enough titles for the ignorance of the times." Adroyan was continuing. "But 'ancient' does not begin to measure their age. Indeed, age has no meaning for them. As for divinity..." He became dismissive. "This world could not contain such godhood. They both pervade and are... outside... time and the narrow, constraining confines of this world. This world that in our arrogance we think is the totality of all things, of all reality." He paused, and seemed to be suppressing a great passion. "But the true reality is that we, and everything we know, are merely the backwash of their world—an inadvertent consequence, a shadow, if you will, of their existence. So far as their language can be understood by us, they call themselves the Diirredyn—'those who have been forever'."

Josyff found he was copying Adroyan's movements and tone. "This is indeed very strange, sir," he said. "And hard to believe, not to say impossible, had I not seen what I've seen. But I have to ask, what would such... beings... want with us if we are so... inconsequential?"

For a moment he thought he had let his prey slip, for there was brief conflict on Adroyan's face. It found partial voice. "We do not question, surveyor. We accept. We obey. We have faith. That is our role." He gave an almost imperceptible sigh which reminded Josyff to exercise the utmost caution with this man at all times. "But though you are not one of us, you are their choice and you are what you are, so I must make due allowance."

He gestured around the room. "There is something about this place that has reached across the bounds of time and space and into their world. It has done great harm. It has bound them in some way and they look to us here, now, to release them."

Carefully, Josyff eased back into his chair, the predator inside him still watching. He shook his head.

"Sir, I appreciate your patience, but this is still difficult for me. I'm a simple man—not stupid, but quite ordinary. I measure things. Things that I can see, touch. I transfer their likeness to paper. The evidence of my eyes and ears obliges me to accept what you are saying about other worlds, worlds that somehow can't be seen or felt but which are all around us. But..."

A raised hand silenced him. "Do not concern yourself with understanding this as you would understand anything in *this* world," Adroyan said. "Few have that kind of knowledge. It is sufficient for you to know that you have been judged and found fitting. That final test of you was necessary and I have told you what I have told you to reassure you about your... sanity, for want of a better word. All you must concern yourself with now is that you do your work and do it well. Study this place intently, *fix it in your mind*, clearly, strongly. And do it with the utmost urgency—there are tides moving here which come but rarely. They must not be missed."

Josyff chose not to question this last remark, sensing another rebuff, though he did risk another question. "I will, sir," he said. "But might I ask how it is that we're involved in such an... extraordinary matter?" It was as near as he dared come to the question, "What do you and the New Order want from these creatures?" He knew that the true answer would be to do with the accruing of more power to themselves and he knew, too, that he would not be told this. But any lie he heard by way of reply might be revealing in itself.

Again, a flicker of conflict passed over Adroyan's face and he paused for some time before replying.

"It is not relevant to your work, but we are... repairing a great wrong—correcting a mistake made a long time ago." He looked round the room, his face briefly a bizarre mixture of fury and plaintiveness. His words seemed to force their way out. "No harm was intended in the making of this place, but harm was done and we... we have a moral duty to make it right." Then, as if sensing that this pious declaration would inevitably ring false, Adroyan abruptly became avuncular and down-to-earth. He sat back and affected a shrewd worldly look. "And too, we have extensive and important plans for this place in our own here and now, so your work serves more than one end."

And it was over, Josyff realized. There was going to be no amplification of either of these statements. Adroyan's manner was dismissing him. Whatever the Diirredyn had wanted from him they had presumably found, though he still had no idea what it was. Nor did he particularly wish to know. The recollection of them and his helplessness before them, which he had been managing to hold at bay, began to push through his resistance. His stomach hardened and his skin crawled and he was hard pressed not to wrap his arms about himself in a scurrying embrace to slough off the sensation.

That these creatures were profoundly malevolent needed no great insight—they had not even attempted to disguise themselves from him in their gloating examination. It followed that Adroyan and the New Order must thus be kindred spirits or, at best, had been woefully deluded into supping with this particular devil. Not that that particularly mattered. Whatever their motivation, as far as Josyff was concerned, they were now irrevocably tainted by the corruption of their masters. Though perhaps corruption was the wrong word. The New Order might well be ruthless and cruel in their acquisition of power, but it was at least understandable, it was human. The immediate sense of evil that Josyff had had of the Diirredyn, by contrast, seemed to be oddly superficial: a manifestation drawn, presumably, from the depths of his own darker nature but covering a reality that was utterly and chillingly alien—quite beyond all human understanding. They cared less about the pain and horror they could inflict on humanity than battling armies did about the ants beneath their feet except, Josyff sensed, except perhaps that inflicting such pain might occasionally give them a transient pleasure.

And I'm working for them, doing their bidding, he thought. It was a numbing and awful thought, not least because he had no idea what he was doing that was so important to them and thus no idea how not to do it.

"Do your work and do it well," Adroyan had said.

"Fix this place in your mind, clearly and strongly," Josyff mouthed silently.

Why?

"I'll leave you now."

Adroyan's voice broke through his reverie, making him jump. Looking up at the figure now standing towering over him, he began to splutter out an apology.

Adroyan continued. "I see you are thinking about what has just happened. I suppose that is understandable, but do not spend too long in this, it will yield you nothing, and you have important and urgent work to do. Faith will sustain you and that will come in time. You do not know how blessed you are."

Josyff nodded vaguely and began mumbling something he hoped sounded appropriate, but Adroyan was leaving even as he spoke. There was a brief impression of him silhouetted in the doorway then he was gone.

The room seemed to brighten, become more spacious, and Josyff found he was taking in deep breaths. It was as though he had been holding his breath since Adroyan began this grim interview. He covered his face with his hands.

What, in the name of pity, was happening here? Adroyan was right, he could not deny what he had seen and heard—and felt—even though it was unlike anything he had ever experienced before and the explanation for it he had been offered ran counter to all reason.

His hands came down and gripped the arms of the chair and he blew out a noisy breath. Put it aside, he instructed himself. He had no doubt that Adroyan's observation that thinking would yield him nothing was correct, though he was damned if he was going to have 'faith' in these creatures no matter how 'blessed' he was.

Do your work, get away. The solution he had determined previously asserted itself again.

But you'll be doing *their* work, said something inside him as he was halfway out of his chair.

And ours. Do it!

The whisper was faint, and Josyff had a momentary sensation of something leaving him, though it was gone before he could properly register it, like misting breath in the cold winter air. He recognized it clearly enough however. It was the voice of the figure—the First Comer—who had spoken to him during the night.

Unknown to him and, presumably to the Diirredyn, this... individual... this consciousness, whatever it was, had been lying silent somewhere within him throughout his 'judgement'. Spying perhaps? Or observing his reactions?

Unexpectedly, a surge of rage welled up inside him.

If the Diirredyn and the First Comers were indeed at war, and if he was being drawn inexorably into it, he had no doubts about whose side he would be on. His experience of the First Comers might be limited but it had been markedly more benign than his experience with the Diirredyn.

But to use him thus... unknowing...

Then a doubt.

Could it be that the First Comers were in fact no better than the Diirredyn? That this was a war between two equally vile antagonists and that their differing appearances to him were mere artefacts of the way they were using his mind?

The question cut across his anger and dropped him back into his chair heavily.

No, no. He had too many unknown factors to deal with as it was, there was no need to fabricate more. They would be endless—and all unanswerable. He would trust his instinct. If he was truly trapped in this, then he would oppose the Diirredyn as far as he was able—oppose them until a conclusion was reached or until the First Comers proved themselves to be other than they appeared. Then...? Who could say?

But he must be a willing participant, he must know what was happening and why. Even Adroyan had sensed the need for that and partly yielded to it, though it was not insignificant that he had made no mention of the war.

This brief inner debate left Josyff feeling quieter, more resolved, even though it left him no wiser. The only real clarification he had received was that, insane though the whole of this was, *he* was not losing his mind. On the other hand, he thought, automatically weighing and balancing as was his way, here he was, seemingly rationally contemplating becoming a soldier in an unseen war against an unseen enemy in a snowbound building in the middle of nowhere.

A soft, self-deprecating laugh spluttered out of him.

It released him.

Come on, Nyk, get us out of here! he growled inwardly and, overriding all other considerations, there came a determination to take the utmost possible interest in what Nyk and Henk were doing to escape this place. Notwithstanding the commands of Adroyan and the antics of the Diirredyn and the First Comers, he would be away from here at the first opportunity—snowbound mountains or not.

Badr was leaning idly on a window sill. He made no pretence of industry when Josyff arrived—he had unboxed the equipment and set them up and could do nothing else. The sight of the instruments, so everyday, so familiar, jolted Josyff unexpectedly. He had an almost overwhelming urge to get on with his work—to immerse himself totally in something he knew and understood. But he could see Badr eyeing him uncertainly and he knew that his unasked questions would be hovering between them constantly if they were not dealt with. He must continue as he had before Adroyan had arrived in the Common Room. The only hope of bringing some semblance of reason to what was happening was to have everything visible. To hide things would be to invite them to fester.

He shouldered a tripod, picked up his documents and set off in the direction of where they had finished the previous day. Badr followed without speaking.

"I appreciate your not asking about what Adroyan wanted," Josyff said as they walked along. Their footsteps came together and echoed along the passage. As usual, the lights ahead of them bloomed into life while those behind went out so that the darkness followed them like a watching shadow. "But there are things you need to know. Time, perhaps, to take sides."

CHAPTER 50

As they walked, Josyff told Badr all that had happened during his meeting with Adroyan. He told it simply, without either drama or embellishment.

And without pause.

He concluded: "Whatever all this is about, and it's utterly beyond me, two things are uppermost in my mind. Firstly, I will finish this job—for several reasons, not the least of which is that working will help keep me sane. But as well as that, I'm a professional surveyor and it's what I've been sent to do, and, in any event, it seems that this is what everyone—Adroyan, First Comers and the Diirredyn—want me to do."

Badr spoke for the first time. "Maybe that's a good reason for not doing the work."

Josyff stopped abruptly. Silence enfolded the two men.

If he had expected any response from Badr, this was not it.

"You believe all this?" he said, his voice wavering between incredulity and relief.

Badr looked along the passage in both directions. It was long and straight and both ends of it disappeared into darkness.

"I don't think I'm alone here with a lunatic, if that helps," he said, with a weak smile. "Although it would make things easier if I thought I was, oddly enough. Something deeply strange is happening in this place without a doubt, but what it is, God knows. If it's as you say, however insane, maybe we shouldn't do this work—shouldn't give them what they want. But if it's just some peculiar phenomenon, something about the building, the altitude, the isolation, that's affecting us all, and we abandon the brief, then we'll both not only be out of a job, but unlikely to work again—or worse. Either way it's not a prospect I relish. The New Order can be more than difficult if you get on the wrong side of it." He paused then said briskly, "You said you had two things on your mind."

Josyff stammered slightly as he gathered his thoughts again. "Er... yes... notwithstanding finishing this work, I intend to do everything I can to help Nyk and Henk find a way out of here."

Badr pondered this for a moment then nodded. "Yes, I agree with you," he said. "Whatever the truth of all this, whatever the rights and wrongs, I don't think we've much choice."

And he set off walking again as if all that was to be done now was the implementation of their agreed decision. Josyff followed him. The lights ahead came on.

The day went well. In fact, it went exceptionally well. The two men became a remarkably efficient team. They talked little and then only about the work in hand, but their silence was companionable and on the occasions when his thoughts drifted back to the Diirredyn and the First Comers, Josyff found it reassuring. He had been right to speak out and draw Badr openly into this mystery.

Methodically, painstakingly, checking and double-checking, they moved through rooms and halls and passages, some lit only by the Keep's own enigmatic lighting, autonomous and alert, others bright with snow-reflected sunlight surging in prodigally through windows and skylights. As they marked and measured and recorded, the building slowly began to take shape in Josyff's mind. It was a good sign, a familiar sign, and he felt the tensions of the past few days easing a little—now the job was truly under way. His ability to remember and manipulate shapes had been a natural trait he had taken for granted in his youth, but he had refined and developed it over the years into an invaluable professional asset. It not only gave him a template to protect him from any gross mistakes he might make when plotting the work, it enabled him to walk through a building while sitting at his desk or relaxing in a chair or even lying in bed. He would do this when some unusual problem presented itself, though sometimes he did it just to enjoy a particularly interesting or beautiful building.

Towards the end of the day they were tracked down by Esyal who, in an oddly matronly manner that made the two men exchange a discreet smile, advised them that their meal was ready.

Adroyan was in the common room when they arrived. He was standing and his posture was restless. He looked at Josyff significantly.

251

Josyff forced himself to smile. "It's been a good day, sir," he said, anticipating the man's query and risking a slightly knowing look. "We've done well. I'll plot it after we've eaten. It's a deceptively big place but with a few days like this it'll soon take shape—on paper *and* up here." He tapped his temple.

Adroyan was about to speak when Nyk and Henk entered. They were talking quite loudly—or rather, Henk was. Josyff raised an eyebrow in surprise. Nyk was his usual purposeful self, though looking mildly harassed, but Henk was using his hands and arms to emphasize the points he was making. His face was a little flushed and his overall manner markedly more agitated than Josyff had ever seen before. He fell immediately silent however, when he saw Adroyan, who made to speak again. This time, Qualto and Esyal bustled in noisily, carrying steaming plates. In the flurry of movement that followed this entrance, Adroyan abandoned whatever he was going to say, curtly advised Qualto that he would "eat later," and left.

"I'll keep it warm for you, sir," Qualto half-shouted after the retreating figure, but there was neither reply nor any other form of acknowledgement. Josyff thought he detected in Qualto's manner an inclination to throw the dinner after him but decided that he was probably attributing his own wishes to him.

Nyk was rubbing his hands in anticipation of the meal.

"Just the thing," he announced. "Qualto, there are times when you achieve perfection."

"I gather we're not on short commons yet," Josyff said, indicating the plate in front of him.

Qualto gave an insincerely guilty shrug. "Oh, we can start tomorrow," he pronounced airily. "To be honest, after all the confusion this morning, I forgot. Besides, Nyk and Henk have been in and out all day, and it's cold out there."

"It certainly is," Nyk said. "Winter's definitely here."

"Which means what, if you manage to make a way out of here?" Josyff asked, speaking with his mouth full.

"It means it'll be extremely dangerous for anyone who tries to get back to the village," Nyk said flatly. He was looking deliberately at Henk who, equally deliberately, was ignoring him. "And your day was good, I gather, Surveyor."

"It was indeed. Very good."

"And no... developments... about what we were discussing this morning?"

Josyff reminded himself of his resolution to keep the others as informed as he could, no matter how strange the tales he would have to tell. He stopped eating and looked at Nyk. "Yes and no," he replied. "Yes, in that Adroyan spoke to me at some length and confirmed that he *is* aware of what's happening here and he is part of it, though, I suspect, no more in control than the rest of us. No, in that nothing he said has made me want to change what we all agreed this morning. I'll tell you the details after I've plotted today's work but right now I'd like to go through whatever you and Henk have been doing." He indicated Badr. "Four heads are better than two. And if we carry on like today, this job's not going to take all that long and I... we... want to be away the instant we're finished—dangerous or not."

Nyk made no demur. "We've done a lot and nothing," he said. "Mainly gathering materials and getting them out into the courtyard." He looked rueful. "We lost some good stuff when the bridge closed. Still, some of it will probably be salvageable. And there are all sorts of bits and pieces in the stores and various other places which I'm sure we'll be able to use. The *real* difficulty's going to be fastenings—bolts, nails, screws and so on. It wouldn't surprise me if we ended up making dowels."

Badr gave a low, snorting chuckle. "Dowels?" he echoed. "What about rope and string?"

Nyk looked at him like a worldly-wise schoolmaster dealing with a testing pupil. "That as well," he replied. "Almost certainly."

Badr's eyes widened. "You're serious, aren't you?" he said, needlessly.

Nyk maintained his pedagogic look. "We've nothing long enough to go across the moat in one piece, and even if we had, we probably wouldn't be able to handle it. So that means bits and pieces tied together—which means joints, fastenings—a lot of them." He let Badr go. "As I said, bolts and the like we don't have too many of—rope, oddly enough, we do. Don't know why, but that's the Keep for you."

"Maybe they used to climb a lot," Esyal suggested casually.

Nyk shrugged.

"Talking of which, is there any chance of getting out of here by dropping down the back and moving around?" Badr asked.

The three residents all stopped what they were doing and looked fixedly at him. Nyk grinned at his discomfiture.

"You haven't got that far in your work, have you?" he said. "Firstly, there are only a couple of small windows on that side and secondly it's a sheer, smooth drop for a long way down. I think even an experienced climber would baulk at it."

"Just a thought," Badr said.

"Why don't you look at the scrolls we found in the Archive?" Esyal said into the ensuing silence. "Someone's tried to do this before..."

"And come to grief, as I recall," Nyk said.

"Even so, it's worth a look," Josyff said quickly as he saw Esyal's jaw tightening. "You might pick up some ideas." Then he turned an appeasing eye to Esyal. "If you're still working in there you might look out for anything else like this."

After the meal, Josyff left the common room to work on the readings he and Badr had taken that day. His earlier encounter with the instruments that Nyk had found had brought to the forefront of his mind just how much time and sheer brute calculation the modern equipment saved, and he was anticipating a quick and easy task. When Badr joined him a little later however, he was scowling and his fingers were tapping out an irritable tattoo on the table.

"What's the matter?"

Josyff growled. "Another damned closing error," he said, jabbing a finger into a paper covered with figures. "I thought yesterday's error might come out in the wash, but..." The tattoo did a final flourish culminating in a noisy slap. "I've been through these calculations three times, if I've been through them once—there's no mistake."

Badr was hesitant. "If it's not the calculations, it could be the equipment. Maybe the..."

Josyff cut across him. "No, there's nothing wrong with the equipment. If it's not the calculations—and it isn't—it's the readings. It's me. I've done something stupid, been careless."

"But..."

"Yes, I know—everything was checked and re-checked several times—routine practice etcetera etcetera, but I'm all that's left. It's not as if it's been a particularly normal time, has it? I've probably not been concentrating at some point."

Badr seemed set to disagree, but Josyff did not give him time.

"There's no way an error of this size should be occurring over these distances," he announced definitively. "But still, it has—and twice now." His brow furrowed. "I doubt it's of any practical significance in a place this size but I'm reluctant to continue until we've found out what's causing it." He pushed his chair back noisily and stood up. "Anyway, I've had enough for today. Whatever's happened has happened and I'm probably locked into a mistake somewhere." He tapped his head. "Tomorrow, we'll re-check what we did today. Bit of a nuisance but it shouldn't take too long—all the stations are established. And *you* can take the readings."

Badr shuffled awkwardly.

"Whatever you want," he said resignedly. "I suppose you're right. Better we spend a little time sorting it out now than have something really bad show up later."

Back in the common room they found Nyk and the others poring over the scrolls which Esyal had been persuaded to retrieve from the Archive.

"Anything interesting?" Josyff asked.

Nyk pulled a sour face. "Not at first glance. It's difficult to know what they were trying to do. It's very big—doesn't look like a temporary escape bridge for a few. I'll read through it in more detail tomorrow."

"And I'll see if there's anything else that might help," Esyal added.

There was a little desultory conversation after that but with Nyk engrossed in the scrolls and, despite his best efforts, Josyff troubled by the error in his work, the travails of the day made themselves felt and the group broke up.

Josyff lay in bed gazing up at the ceiling. Physically he was tired. As was normal in his profession he had walked a long way during the day and his body was relishing the prospect of sleep. His mind however, was awash with thoughts which forbade that.

Leave them be, he kept instructing himself, there's no logic to what's happening. It's enough the others know about it, enough that it's not just me.

But the thoughts persisted—almost as though they were being sifted through by something outside him.

He swore and turned over on to his side.

I never told them about the judging, he remembered, irritably.

Then he was falling...

CHAPTER 51

Falling, falling...

Josyff heard himself snatching in a deep breath. It was biting cold and full of terror.

But the very act of breathing seemed also to draw in the brightness that was around him and it filled every part of him. The fear receded.

His arms were extended to the side, his legs were splayed and a wind was buffeting him violently. Yet was he falling? Or was he floating—held aloft by a powerful wind? He looked about him but he could see nothing which would answer these questions. What he did see were birds, gliding and swooping all about him. He could hear them calling to one another. They were gulls, brilliant white against the sun-bright blueness of the sky. Unbidden, his hand went to the scar on his forehead and a shudder shook him as, momentarily, he relived his previous encounter with such birds: the clock's relentless tolling rang in his ears and he felt again the powerful beating of their wings, like the spirit of night itself, surging towards him.

The moment passed, for here he sensed none of the malice that had pervaded that happening.

Then he noticed that his involuntary response seemed to have shaken everything around him, sending an unseen ripple through this new world that flurried and briefly scattered the gulls like the unexpected appearance of a dangerous predator.

"*We can touch you only through your strangeness so it can only be of your own creating. We are learning—we are all learning. As the chaos mounts so we find the courage—and the skill—to ride it. So must you."*

The words of the figure—the First Comer—returned to him.

This is mine? he thought. This is *my* creation?

"This is our *creation."*

The voice—or was it voices—was close by. He turned.

Abruptly, all was still. The buffeting wind had stopped as had the chatter of the gulls, though there was an ululating hint of it somewhere at the edges of his awareness.

"What you (see? feel? sense?) we cannot know. That is yours. It's reshaping is ours—(a bridge? a way?) to reach you."

Josyff looked around to locate the speaker but could see no one. And he was no longer falling. He was standing on something, though he could not see what. There was a hint of a wall about him shimmering uncertainly in the blueness and mingling unsteadily with the now slow-moving images of the gulls.

Even as he watched, the walls became clearer and more solid until he saw that they were those of the Common Room. But they were distorted in some way that he could not immediately fathom and he could feel his eyes straining uncomfortably as they struggled unsuccessfully to bring them into focus. Then he sensed an intention. It was a good intention, but it alarmed him.

"No!" he cried out. "Not there, nor anywhere that's part of my normal life. I'm forced to accept your existence, and your wanting—needing—something of me, but it is difficult and I don't want it confused with images from the real world—I must keep you apart."

There was a brief stillness, then:

"It is understood, Measurer. It is not easy for any of us."

A sensation of bewilderment and disorientation swept through Josyff. It felt as though part of it were not his, but it was gone before he could reflect on it. Nevertheless there was a lingering impression—it was as though a switch had been thrown...

Machine...

Were these First Comers using a machine of some kind to reach him? Equipment that mapped and measured his 'strangeness' so that they might better use it, just as he did with buildings and landscapes?

He was uncertain how he should respond to the idea. He felt an unexpected frisson of fellow feeling for whoever was striving to encompass and define the complex terrain of the mind of this alien "Measurer" with its innumerable ever-dividing highways and byways. Yet too, he felt alarmed and, a tad pompously, he noted, a little indignant at being reduced to a laboratory specimen.

But he had time to consider neither. Without any sense of change he was suddenly standing in the bright blueness as he had before. Gulls were all around him again, swooping and gliding. But still they held no menace. Nor was he falling.

A little more at ease than he had been, he gazed around only to discover that the scene was the same in every direction. As he returned to his original position however, it was to see a figure standing some way in front of him. Though it offered no immediate threat, he tensed. Then, recovering, he leaned forward slightly and peered at it intently. It was the figure he had seen before: an old man, robed, like a monk, though this time his features were clearer. Lean-faced with sharp blue eyes, white, slightly unkempt hair, and a short white beard, he looked familiar.

From my own mind, Josyff reminded himself as his memory inevitably began searching for the source of the familiarity. Someone he had seen once? Someone he had read about and imagined? An amalgam of several people such as might shimmer through a dream? No answer came.

"*This (image? contact? impression?) disturbs you?*" said the figure. The voice was again vaguely familiar. It was measured and cultured though it rose and fell slightly as if a wind were carrying part of it away, and some words and phrases seemed to blur into several meanings. There was also an echoing hint at times of more than one person speaking.

"No, no. Not at all," Josyff said hurriedly, raising a placatory hand. "I was just trying to think where I'd seen... heard... you, but..." He gave up. "It doesn't matter. I suppose it's because not all parts of my... strangeness... are readily available to me when I want them."

"*No,*" said the figure, without a pause. "*They will not be. They cannot be. It is their—and your—nature. This much we know.*"

The certainty in the man's tone intrigued Josyff but his predominant concern was to find out why he had been brought to this place, wherever it was. He was about to voice it when the memory of his contact with the Diirredyn intruded.

"You were there," he said with some force, anger mounting. "You were there when those... things... those creatures... held me and 'judged' me. You watched and listened and did nothing to help."

The figure nodded slowly, but it was a movement without meaning. It was almost as though the manoeuvre was being tested.

"*Yes, that is true. We were with you during the examination.*"

"And you did nothing to help."

"*That too is true. But you did not need help. Besides, it was not possible.*"

"I don't understand. What if their... judgement... had been against me? What would have happened then?"

"*The judgement could not have been against you. You are the Measurer. This we knew. It is not a matter for debate or conjecture.*"

"You're not answering my question. What if?"

"The question has no meaning. Were you not the Measurer they could not have reached you as they did. What they did was not necessary. Why they did it is a mystery, as are many things they do. Do not concern yourself."

Josyff scowled at what he took to be this casual treatment of his concerns.

"But you *were* there," he repeated as a final reproach.

"Yes. While there is much we know about our enemy's intentions, there is much that we do not. They are not given to rationality, but they are cunning and treacherous and it was important we study their actions."

"Study? You mean you used me to spy on them?"

"We used what they had done to you. We initiated nothing, nor would we have without your word—this, we sense, is important to you. But, yes, we were spying on them."

The stark honesty of the answer defused much of Josyff's anger.

"And did you learn anything?" he asked after a short pause.

"We confirmed what we already knew. What you do—your work—is of the utmost importance—you are pivotal. Also you are nearer the Heart than you were—the disturbance is already considerable."

"Disturbance?"

"In your strangeness."

Josyff shook his head. "I don't understand any of this."

"No. You could not. That you are—that you exist—is a great revelation—you are so (inadequate, curtailed, incomplete)—such a life-form has not been thought possible."

Josyff bridled at the description he sensed in the unclear words, then...

"You bring great hope."

Again his anger evaporated.

"What do you want?" he asked with a mixture of irritation and resignation.

There was a pause. The figure shimmered slightly.

"This is difficult. We know there can be no true mutual understanding between us, but though you are... (strange? paradoxical? anomalous?)... you are, and you are sentient, within the bounds of your (sphere? world? life-fold?), and we sense you need some measure of what is happening if you are to do what must be done."

"Yes. That is true, for sure."

There was another pause.

"We will try. We can lead you through a (reflection? shadow? echo?) of our world from what we find in your strangeness. Do you wish this?"

Josyff hesitated, then nodded.

"Yes."

The figure held out his hand. Josyff reached out and took it.

CHAPTER 52

The gulls scattered out of Josyff's awareness like dead leaves caught in a bustling autumn breeze. They wheeled and vanished into the distance as though into a vortex, drawing the bright blueness of the sky after them. As it stretched and swirled it became a myriad rainbow colours which began to flow about Josyff, spinning and turning, now graceful, dancing, now giddying.

As he watched, Josyff thought he could make out familiar shapes but none was still long enough for him to identify it. They had the elusive quality of a sidelong glimpse into a place not accessible to the normal senses.

All around him too were sounds, equally familiar and elusive. They rose and fell in harmony with this subtle confusion...

And, without any sense of transition, he was gazing up into a blue sky again. A gentle breeze was blowing, the sun was warm on his face and a few white clouds were floating lazily by. He looked down to find that he was standing on top of a grassy rise, part of an undulating country landscape. Fields littered with hedgerows and trees carried his gaze to the horizon which was lined with mountains. Bare but unforbidding in the bright sunlight, they ran majestically in both directions for as far as Josyff could see.

The word 'beautiful' did not so much form in his mind as suffuse his entire body as he drew in a deep summer-scented breath.

"*Indeed,*" came an unsought agreement. "*This is as we were.*"

Josyff experienced no surprise as he turned to the robed figure standing on his right. He noted that he was a similar height and build to himself. But older—patriarchal, almost.

"*Look.*"

The figure was pointing—a long, sinewy hand extended.

Josyff followed its direction. In a dip between two large peaks something glittered, bright as a morning star. Josyff screwed his eyes tight to dim this solitary light, but to little effect though he thought he could make out a building behind and above it.

"Is that your home?" he asked.

"*In a manner of speaking,*" the figure replied, not without a hint of amusement, Josyff thought. "*It is where you would place us.*"

Like Josyff, the figure was also gazing about as though he had found himself in a strange place. "*There is much beauty in your strangeness, Measurer. I would not have thought it possible with so (limited? incomplete? inadequate?) a resource.*" He became pensive. "*You are indeed mysterious creatures. It is salutary to come upon such things from time to time. To learn the value—the necessity—of humility.*"

He turned and looked directly at Josyff. "*Each hesitant step we take into your strangeness divides and divides, leading into mystery and complexity far beyond our ability to (know? see? encompass?).*"

He raised a hand as if to touch Josyff's face as one might touch a wondrous carving or painting. Josyff flinched slightly and the hand stopped. It remained motionless in mid air as though forgotten as the figure continued, still pensive, half talking to himself.

"It is almost as though the Universe decrees that you must have capabilities beyond ours to compensate for the restraints it has placed on you. Some need for deeper balance perhaps? Balance across all the (spaces? worlds? facets?). Fascinating. Fascinating." Then he straightened, as though recollecting himself. Josyff noted that even as he was speaking, his movements were becoming more natural—as if he were learning continually. *"Still, those are conjectures for another time—a more peaceful time—if we ever achieve it. Let me..."*

"Why am I not afraid?" Josyff asked abruptly, his own thoughts suddenly disrupted by this question. "Why am I not bewildered, disorientated, even fearing for my sanity, finding myself in this place, talking to..." He shrugged. "Who are you, anyway? Come to that, *what* are you?"

The figure looked intently at Josyff. He still had the manner of someone examining a specimen, though his eyes were those of someone experiencing not merely something new, but something startlingly new, and something changing.

"Knowledge grows on knowledge, faster and faster," he said. *"For a (span of ages?) your very existence was thought impossible. You were the obscure study of a few... (academics...mages...) idly testing the limits of what was known. Now..."* He made an expansive gesture. *"Now, with your coming to this place..."* Josyff briefly sensed the Keep, oppressive, all about them. *"...and the Destroyer—and the Warrior—coupled with the urgency of the increasingly terrible nature of our circumstances, understanding of you—of everything—has expanded beyond all belief."* The voice became unexpectedly agitated. Josyff clearly detected the excitement of a man enjoying his work. *"And continues to do so. With each moment that passes it grows and while each new piece of learning opens a myriad other questions, our knowledge, our ability to (speak? contact? reach?) you grows ever more familiar and secure. As to who I am, I am how you would perceive a First Comer. Amongst my own I am..."* Part sound, part vision, the sensation that washed over and through Josyff was like a mixture of rolling waves and buffeting winds. Though it in no way threatened or hurt him, he found himself stepping back in the face of this turmoil. Then, floating in its midst he caught, *"Amrassian."*

"Amrassian," he echoed. "That is your name—or your title?"

Confusion filled the figure's face. *"It is what I am,"* he replied. Then another hint of humour. *"Or it will suffice, at least."*

"Inadequate?" Josyff offered.

"Yes and no," came the reply. *"It is a measure of part of what I am, but it is all you could envision and it is adequate for our purposes."*

Josyff did not pursue the matter. He was beginning to realize that no insult was intended in the constant referring to him as inadequate.

"It's what I'll call you then," he said, adding with a slight smile and a gesture towards the figure, "This part of you, anyway."

They were walking slowly in the direction of the mountains. The grass was soft under Josyff's feet and littered with wild flowers.

Like stars, Josyff thought.

"*Aah.*"

The soft exclamation was full of realization but Amrassian offered no explanation and they continued walking side by side in silence.

"All this is my own, reshaped by you?" Josyff asked after a little while, extending an arm across the scene.

"*It is.*"

"It's unsettling. So real. A measure of your increasing understanding?"

"*A measure of our increased understanding of your aspect of reality, yes.*"

"And you see more of reality than we do?" Josyff felt defensive, almost in spite of himself. Amrassian's response was unexpected.

"*It feels so, and I would have said so without a doubt until very recently. Now, though, having discovered you and your kind, having touched on your wild and mysterious strangeness, I am less certain, less...*" Amrassian paused.

"Arrogant?" Josyff offered, in wary humour.

Amrassian bowed his head. "*Complacent would be a kinder word, but yes, arrogant. What is complacency but a form of arrogance?*"

Josyff's defensiveness evaporated. He felt the need to change the subject.

"The other things we all of us experienced over the last few days—the noises, the visions, the dreams—were they you also—learning?"

Amrassian stopped and looked apologetic. "*Not all, but much, yes. Fumbling and blundering as much as learning, though,*" he said. "*Was hurt done?*"

"A little," Josyff replied, rubbing his forehead. "Nothing serious. But the shaking you made caused great alarm, and the closing of the drawbridge could have done terrible harm—could have killed someone. Why did you do that? Didn't you realize?"

Amrassian became very still for a moment, as though the shell of his body had been vacated, then he was present again. "*This is no simple matter, no...*" He faltered for a moment then gently extended his hand as though pushing something. "*No readily calculable push and move—cause and effect. I will show. Do not be afraid.*"

Before Josyff could question this remark he felt the ground shift under his feet and a howling wind began tugging at him violently. He looked down to see that he was standing on a narrow walkway, high above a river in full and tumultuous spate through a shear-sided gorge. He swayed and his hands flailed out wildly to catch his balance. As they did so, the walkway rocked unsteadily...

His cry of terror had barely reached his throat when he was back standing by Amrassian in the sunlit field. Nevertheless, he reached out and seized the man's arm for support.

"What was that?" he exclaimed as he recovered his breath.

"That is where we are. As I thought you might best understand it. Great disturbance, great flux, tenuous balance and stability."

"A vivid demonstration," Josyff said, still badly shaken. He released Amrassian's arm. "I'd be grateful if you didn't give me another one."

"Was hurt done?"

Despite his still present alarm, Josyff could do no other than give a relieved snort of a laugh at this apparently automatic repetition of Amrassian's concern.

"No, no hurt was done—you just frightened the life out of me. And I still don't understand what you're trying to tell me."

"I will try with your... words," Amrassian said, setting off walking again. *"We do not know if your all coming together in the place—you, the Destroyer, the Warrior—is mere chance or part of a deeper pattern, but whichever it is, it is an opportunity which may not come again in many ages."*

"An opportunity for what?"

Amrassian stopped and looked about him. Once again, Josyff felt the presence of the Keep all around, oppressive, immovable, intrusive, an infinitely heavy burden.

"To be free. To be free of this."

There was such pain and desperation in his voice that Josyff winced.

"You mean the Keep?" he said in a mixture of bewilderment and exasperation. "But it's only a building—stones, mortar, timbers—how can it possibly bind you? It's me and the others you've locked in. You're..." He waved his arms vaguely. "You're... somewhere else."

Amrassian looked at him squarely. His expression made Josyff feel like both a profoundly stupid pupil and someone watching helplessly as another drowned.

"In your (world? space? facet?) this place may be as you say—innocuous, harmless." He gave a sour chuckle. *"Indeed it couldn't be otherwise. But you are part of a greater whole. You are both a shadow, a reflection, and an illumination. Our every action affects you, but in turn your every action affects us. Some—most—dwindle into nothingness almost immediately, others diverge, expand and dissipate, but some move outwards endlessly, incalculably."* He made a broad encompassing gesture. *"And the making of this place was one such."*

"And it harmed you—is harming you still?"

"Yes. Grievously."

Josyff anticipated. "It would be pointless to ask how this could be, I presume?"

"It reached... (across? through? into?). But you presume correctly," Amrassian replied, adding, with a hint of weariness. *"You would be wise indeed if you understood that. As would we."*

Josyff suddenly felt a great empathy for this robed figure, this familiar yet unfamiliar creation compounded somehow from his own imaginings. Whoever and wherever this individual was, he was a rational creature struggling to find solutions to problems of a kind he had never faced before, and the only guidance his experience could offer was the fact that he had solved intractable problems before.

It was neither guarantee nor solace.

It's he who's falling through the sky, Josyff thought. And he's reaching out to me.

"So we move on in ignorance and hope, do we?" he said. "Not something new to either of us, I suspect. I will help you if I can, but tell me why you took such risks with us to hold us here."

"I have told you. Your coming together may not happen again for many ages. Your separating, scattering, could not be risked."

"But our lives could be."

Amrassian was silent for some time.

"This is a war, Measurer. Things must be done which would not be countenanced in quieter times—fine and difficult judgements made. But we took great care—to have made you or the Warrior no more would have been disastrous for us all. What our calculations did not—could not—account for was your own interference with what we did."

"The damage in the Gatehouse was *our* fault?" Josyff said, with some indignation.

"Gatehouse..." There was a pause. *"Ah yes... I see. Fault? No, there was no fault. You responded in an unforeseen way and there were consequences. They were not what was expected but you were not at fault—you could not know. Fault—blame—lies with the war itself—it is its nature."*

"It is you who make war, not us," Josyff said.

There was anger in the reply. *"I am not a fighter by choice, Measurer. I do what I do because of where I find myself. Do you not also?"*

It was a reproach Josyff could find no convincing answer to.

"I fight—we all fight—to prevent a great darkness overwhelming us—one that would have appalling consequences for your kind also."

"I've no choice but to accept you word for that. From my brief encounter with your enemies I can't see them bringing anything other than ill to whoever they encounter. But why do you fight? When did this begin, and over what?"

There was another pause—longer this time.

"*It is an ancient war.*"

The reply was heavy with uncertainty and... shame?

CHAPTER 53

A terrible realization formed in Josyff's mind.

"You don't know why you are fighting!" he said. The disbelief in his voice seemed to send a tremor through the entire landscape. Amrassian looked at him sharply, but almost immediately Josyff felt again that the body he was looking at had momentarily been deserted. Then it was alive again.

"*Do not seek to judge us, Measurer.*"

Josyff did not feel inclined to accept any rebuke. He almost shouted. "I was not judging you. I asked you why do you fight? When did all this begin, and over what? Given that you dragged me into this, they're not unreasonable questions. And 'It's an ancient war' isn't an answer."

Amrassian looked at Josyff intently, though this time there was a searching presence behind the eyes.

"*You are right, Measurer,*" he said eventually. "*They are reasonable questions. But I have no answer to them.*"

Josyff opened his arms in a despairing gesture. "You must have. Wars don't just happen, like bad weather, they're made—by people! There must have been a cause."

"*It has always been so.*"

Josyff tipped into exasperation. "Continual war? No, no, no. Continual destruction, death, turmoil. I don't believe you. Your society couldn't have survived."

"*There have been long spans of... quietness. But always they return—seeking to overthrow, to dominate all.*"

"They? The Diiredyn—those who claim 'to have been forever'—like you, the 'First Comers'?"

"*Yes.*"

"Don't you ever... talk to them—make peace overtures—try to find out what they want—come to some kind of an accommodation?"

"*It is not possible.*"

Josyff's frustration was mounting. "How can it not be possible? If you fight, if you have fought *forever*—you've met on the battlefield if nowhere else—surely there is the occasional truce—for the exchanging of prisoners."

"*Prisoners?*"

"Enemy soldiers who have surrendered."

"Soldiers? Surrendered?"

Josyff put his hand to his forehead.

"Soldiers—those of you who do the actual fighting—the young, the strong. They surrender when their position becomes impossible, when they cannot hope to win, when to continue would just be to die for no reason."

Amrassian leaned forward slightly, once again scrutinizing Josyff intently.

"This is how it is in your world?"

"Yes. Although, fortunately, my country hasn't been involved in a war for a long time."

"It is difficult to understand, your world, your ways."

Josyff was about to reciprocate the comment but Amrassian continued.

"We have no... soldiers. We each of us fight as we must. We do not... surrender... nor do the enemy. If we are defeated we become the enemy, the darkness. If we are victorious, they are transfigured into the light."

"They become one of you?" Josyff anticipated.

"Yes. How could it be otherwise?"

Josyff gave up. "I... I can't begin to understand you. What kind of creatures are you?"

"It is your incompleteness that makes your conflicts thus. Your understanding is not necessary. Indeed, it is impossible. What you must understand is the importance of your part in our conflict. The extremes of chance have brought you into this and all outcomes are beyond calculation. All that is known is that the Heart of this Abomination binds both us and our enemies and must be destroyed if we—and you with us—are not all to sink into stagnation and oblivion. You must complete your work. The Warrior will..."

Amrassian stopped abruptly and drew in a sharp breath. Josyff looked at him equally sharply, only to see an all-too-human expression of fear and disbelief rapidly being hidden behind a mask of confidence. It occurred to him that whatever means Amrassian was using to speak with him in this form it was becoming increasingly more subtle almost by the minute. Where was this all leading? The realization was vivid, but he did not dwell on it. Instead he followed Amrassian's gaze.

In the distance, dense black clouds were gathering over the mountains. Except that they were not behaving as clouds did. Rather they were like billowing smoke, growing with improbable speed and shifting and changing as though impelled by some inner force. As they rose higher and higher into the sky they seemed to drain all colour out of it.

And they were flickering, shimmering...

Like a vast flock of great birds...

As he gazed spellbound into the looming darkness, Josyff felt that, like the sky and now the landscape, he too was being drained into it—drawn to the luring rhythm of an unheard drum. Then Amrassian's voice, distant and urgent, reached through to him.

"Measurer, we are attacked. I (we?) must flee (fight?)."

Briefly the voice became unfocused and clamorous—many voices raised in confusion—then Amrassian's voice came again, full of forced calmness.

"This meeting (joining? touching?) has been good. We shall speak again. We..." Josyff leaned forward into the sudden silence, then, *"Go to the Warrior, she..."*

The voice ended as if severed.

Without any sense of transition, Josyff was in his room again, lying on his bed. Hastily he switched on the light. He felt a brief frisson of panic as it did not light immediately, but then it emerged, dim and strained, like a distant, sour moon, as though it were trapped behind a dark, shifting gauze. Josyff watched as it seemed to struggle to force the darkness aside. He willed it on and slowly it grew in intensity until, almost with a flourish, it finally scattered the shadows to their natural hiding places. It was a strange illusion and Josyff shook his head as if it might have been of his own making.

"Go to the Warrior..."

Amrassian's words crackled through his concern, dispelling it just as the light had dispelled the shadows. Propelled by their urgency, Josyff swung off the bed and snatched up his dressing gown, only a small part of him objecting that he was risking making a peculiar fool of himself knocking on Esyal's bedroom door in the middle of the night.

Within moments, a little breathless, he was outside her room. He was about to knock when his discretion finally caught up with him and his hand stopped in mid-air. His bare feet, chilled by the Keep's stone floors and stairs, also began to make themselves felt, helping to distance him from his encounter with Amrassian and tempting him with the thought of pending folly and the warm bed he had just abandoned. He hesitated and half turned to leave but as he did so he became aware of the noise coming from Esyal's room. Hidden at first by the sound of his own breathing he had not noticed it, but now he held his breath and pressed his ear against the door. The sound needed no identification. Faint, but quite distinct, it was the chilling clamour of the Diirredyn, larded with the screeching hate and fury that had filled his mind as he had plummeted out of their judging.

"Go to the Warrior..."

Amrassian's words rose up to urge him on and, without thinking, he pushed the door violently.

His effort rebounded on him, pushing him back. The door was locked.

She would have bolted it from the inside, of course, especially with her increased concern about Adroyan.

He rested his hands on the door, leaning on it. It would not be possible for him to force it open—like everything else in the Keep it was nothing if not robust.

Should he go for Nyk—fetch tools to break down the door?

Even as he was thinking this, the sound of the Diirredyn seemed to grow louder—and more triumphant.

Whatever other objections there might be to rousing Nyk, there would not be enough time, he knew—something bad was happened to Esyal right now.

And he was the only one who could help her.

He stepped back and glanced up and down the corridor, as if searching for inspiration. Then, none coming, he began beating the door and shouting Esyal's name. The sound of the Diirredyn filled the reverberations, mocking him and the pain in his fists as they struck the solid door.

Suddenly, he was ablaze with anger—anger at being drawn into this whole insane situation, anger at the New Order and its creeping insidiousness, at Adroyan, Amrassian, the builders of the Keep, at Esyal for her psychotic meddling in politics, and, not least, himself for being so helpless.

"Draw the bolts, Esyal!" he roared, now kicking the door. "Draw the damn bolts! Move yourself! Get to the door! Let me in!"

His voice mingled with his hammering blows and the Diirredyn's scornful chorus, and his thoughts began to spin and spin until they threatened to become an uncontrollable maelstrom. Then something was reaching out to him, hesitant, fearful even, of being taken and swept away by this mounting frenzy. With it came Amrassian's voice, distant and broken, as though he was gasping for breath.

"Your need, Measurer. What is your need?"

Josyff paused in his onslaught and slumped forward with his forehead against the door. He made no effort to restrain his anger as he replied. "To get through this door—what do you think?"

As he spoke, the image of the bolts holding the door shut came to him—solid, well-fitting, silent in use—a small tribute to Nyk's meticulous maintenance of the building. Esyal's need for security against Adroyan had turned her room from a fortress into a prison, perhaps even a killing ground.

"I understand." There was a pause. *"The danger is great. We must try, or..."* There was another pause. Then, with determination: *"Do not be afraid, Measurer. Do what you must."*

Before he could respond to this, Josyff felt an overwhelming disorientation—a giddying distancing from himself such as he might experience in the face of a pending accident—something that was recognized for what it was, but inevitable. He seemed to see himself simultaneously not only

267

from many different directions but strangely distorted. He could feel his brain struggling to bring together the images his eyes were receiving and he partly closed them in an attempt to quieten it. It did not help. Tactile confusion replaced the visual confusion. His hands and fingers—indeed, every part of his entire body—echoed the distortions he had seen—they were not where they should be. Worse, they were in places that could not be and moving in directions that could not be. It was as though the boundaries of reality had collapsed.

Yet even through this confusion, he sensed a unifying pattern—an elusive logic. Not that this tiny spark of insight and curiosity offered him any stability against the turmoil flooding his mind. A terrified cry formed somewhere inside him—whatever 'inside' meant here—but before it found voice, Amrassian was speaking again. His tone was full of both awe and urgency.

"Yes, this should not be. The abomination makes this possible. Do not be afraid. You are what you are—unchanged—but you (see? feel? are?) now your (our?) totality."

The words meant nothing to Josyff as he struggled with the sensations pervading him.

Then, powerfully urgent this time. *"Measurer, your need! What is your need?"*

An image of the door bolts returned to Josyff, distant and vague as though it was being offered as a reminder. Instinctively he corrected it, recapturing their solidity and purpose. Then, as though following his will, his hand moved to take one of the bolts. There were so many perspectives that he watched as though it were not his. He both saw and felt his hand close about the bolt—the cold hard touch of the metal was familiar but oddly blurred as if it too had many perspectives. Then he turned and drew it, feeling it click into its open position. Immediately he drew the second one.

And with a stunning jolt, all confusion and disorientation was gone. He was himself again, leaning heavily against the door.

It opened.

CHAPTER 54

Unbalanced, Josyff stumbled into the room.

Where before the sound of the Diirredyn had been distant, it now washed over him like an appalling flood. The din was deafening, but he had little time to consider it, for he found himself careening forward into a broiling darkness.

He was running downhill!

Even as his mind registered the fact, his arms were flailing and his heels were digging into the floor in an attempt to stop this desperate flight. It had some effect but still he was travelling at a terrifying speed.

And the texture of the floor had changed. No longer was it the carpeted boarding or stone of the Keep's bedrooms, it was...

Grass?

His foot slipped and he tumbled over backwards. A fairly heavy fall winded him a little and he noted, incongruously, that is *was* grass, but his predominant response was relief that he had not been injured and that his forward momentum had been radically reduced.

It had not been stopped completely however; his frighteningly long strides had become an undignified slither.

He was still driving his heels and his elbows into the ground when he stopped abruptly. The noise had changed. There was still a background roar, but it was clearer, and over-topping it were cries—cries of rage, of pain, of triumph, of terror. And just as the sound had become focused, so too had the shifting darkness. He blinked to clear his vision. Overhead, dense black clouds tinged with red were streaming purposefully across a grim grey sky while circling him at a wary distance was silhouetted...

A crowd...

And...

Weapons?

Yes, weapons. Edges and point glinted in the troubled light.

Josyff gaped.

"Get up!"

The voice was familiar but it was harsh with vicious urgency.

"Get up!"

A foot against his backside—part kick, part push—emphasized the instruction. It galvanized Josyff and he began levering himself up off the ground. A powerful and none-too-gentle hand helped him.

He was about to turn to his unknown helper and attacker when something gripped his ankle. Before he could look to see what it was, there was an oath, a blur of movement and a thud and the grip disappeared.

"And stay dead."

He recognized the voice—it was Esyal's.

"Guard my back!"

"What?"

"Guard my back, damn you! I don't know where you came from or what the hell's going on but you're here now. Grab a sword and learn to fight—quickly."

"A sword?" Josyff echoed vaguely.

"Take his—the one who just grabbed you."

Josyff looked down. There was a body at his feet, and all around, between him and the milling crowd, there were more bodies. Some were moving sluggishly—crawling away, he noted—but mainly they were still—and showing signs of horrific injuries. He had never seen anything like it and his knees started to buckle at the horror of it.

There was another oath, then, "Here!"

Esyal's voice shook him. She seized his hand and thrust something into it. He looked down at it vacantly—it was a sword.

"Wake up, or we're going to die!"

Esyal's brutal injunction was accompanied by a smart slap across the face which cut through his bewilderment and prompted an unexpected surge of anger which made him reach out towards her throat.

She avoided his hand and stepped closer to him.

"Guard my back," she said again. The look in her eyes was deeply unnerving and Josyff turned away from it, at the same time nodding.

"Yes," he said. "I will."

And, as if their brief exchange had held both the crowd and the noise at bay, the uproar suddenly increased and some of the individuals at the front of the crowd began to edge forward. Esyal quickly moved around Josyff and placed her back against his. She held a sword in her right hand and a knife in her left and her posture was not one of crouching defence but was upright and challenging. It gave the impression that at any moment she might stride forward and scatter this crowd like a wind scattering dead leaves.

Josyff, by contrast, the shaking in his knees now pervading his whole body, was holding his sword with two hands and swinging it jerkily from side to side, a picture of fear and uncertainty.

"*Go to the Warrior,*" Amrassian had said, he recalled distantly, amongst a teeming confusion of other thoughts, but what earthly use could he be in this nightmare?

Inwardly he screamed out to Amrassian, "End this insanity! Get us out of here!"

But he remembered too, Amrassian's other words:

"*We are attacked.*"

And the tone of them...

A coldness inside him told him that whatever was happening, however nightmarish and improbable it might seem, there was great and real danger here and he could expect no rescue from Amrassian. As this bleak certainty seeped through him his fear began to be consumed by rage—not the near-petulance he had felt as he pounded on Esyal's bedroom door, but a deeper thing—purposeful, determined, and murderous...

But necessary...

Even as this happened there was a ripple of hesitation in the crowd facing him. It was as if they had sensed this change in him. Josyff tightened his grip on the sword—the grey sky with its red-tinged clouds reflected in it.

Then someone—something?—was screaming behind him.

With it came a stern command from Esyal.

"Watch your front, Surveyor."

And she was gone.

Despite her instruction, Josyff risked a quick glance over his shoulder. He saw nothing but a confusion of rapid movement. The screaming ended in an almost incongruous squeal and Esyal was at his back again. In his peripheral vision, Josyff saw something rolling away. He did not turn to see what it was.

"One more less," Esyal said.

"I can't use this thing," Josyff said, shaking the sword.

"I can see," Esyal said. "Imagine you're swishing the heads off weeds with a long stick. A big sweep, back and forth. Don't aim too high or they'll duck. And don't hit me with your back-swing either!"

"But they're not weeds, they're..."

"They're what? People? I don't know—maybe, maybe not, it's difficult to see in this light. But whatever they are, they've been trying to kill me for... since I found myself here. Now they'll probably be trying to kill both of us, I..."

She stopped as a raucous voice in the crowd shouted some kind of command. It was followed by a massive roar and the crowd began to move forward. Josyff noticed however, that the advance had markedly less enthusiasm than the shouting, though it gave him little consolation. It was still an advance!

He followed Esyal's advice and began swinging the sword as he had indeed swung a stick in the fields as a child, decapitating too proud thistles and cutting swathes through long grasses. He did not notice but his arms and shoulders relaxed, his reach increased and the tip of the sword began to hiss through the gloomy air. Esyal, by contrast, moved body, sword and searching vision, through a slower arc.

"I want to try something," Esyal said.

Josyff grunted.

"Move forward."

"What!"

"Move forward—move towards them!"

"But..."

"Do it!"

This command was accompanied by a vigorous push which made Josyff almost stumble forward. He quickly recovered his balance and was about to protest when Esyal snapped out another order.

271

"And again! Just keep waving the sword and walk forward—right towards them. I'll be protecting your back."

She did not push him this time but kept a relentless pressure on his back which forced him to keep moving forward. Briefly he tried to resist but, despite his superior size and weight, it was to no avail.

"What are you doing?" he asked in some desperation after a few paces.

"What are *they* doing?" came the response.

"What do you mean?"

There was irritation in the reply. "What are they doing—that armed crowd in front of you?"

"They're..." Still moving reluctantly forward, Josyff squinted through the gloomy air. "They're retreating—moving back."

There was a brief pause then suddenly Esyal moved and an arm wrapped itself around Josyff's neck and tightened brutally. He tried to struggle but he was being kept off-balance and could find no purchase.

"Be still!" Esyal hissed in his ear. "Or I'll hurt you."

Josyff dropped his sword and reached up to grab the arm holding him. It was quite slender and should have been weak but not only did it not yield, it tightened.

"End this! End this now! Or I'll kill him. I'll kill the Measurer."

Esyal's voice bellowed into Josyff's ear. Its intensity made him wince. Then the meaning tipped him towards panic.

"Be still, damn you!" Esyal hissed again, urgent.

Josyff felt something under his chin. Something sharp.

Then, loud, commanding and menacing. "I'll drive this through his brain if you don't let us go."

Josyff vaguely sensed a change in the noise from the surrounding crowd. A movement from Esyal drew him further off-balance backwards, heightening his panic. The sharpness under his chin followed him...

CHAPTER 55

Josyff struggled to move away from the knife under his chin, but it remained purposefully constant—and the pressure of the arm around his throat increased. His pulse began to pound in his ears, merging with the din of the surrounding crowd and then overtopping it.

Then there was a brief maelstrom of whirling blackness and abruptly he was free.

He was lying unsteadily on... something?

Abuse came from under him and the something pushed him violently to one side. As he rolled over awkwardly, the light came on. Blinking, he saw that he was in the Keep again. Nearby, Esyal was clambering to her feet. She had her knife in her hand.

"What's happening? What in God's name is happening?" he burst out, his voice hoarse from both Esyal's choke and the fear it had induced. He staggered towards her as he levered himself to his feet. Instantly the knife was extended towards him. It glinted menacingly in the light, but it was her eyes that disturbed him more—focused and intent, they seemed to search right into him and he realized that much of her was still on the battlefield and that she was more than capable of killing him.

He raised his hands in both defence and denial and quickly retreated a pace. "It's all right, it's all right," he said. "We're back, we're back. You got us back. Somehow. I just lost my balance—my legs are still shaking—all of me is shaking. What was that? Where was it?"

Slowly the coldness seeped out of Esyal's eyes but she did not lower the knife.

"Don't ask *me*. I just went to bed and the next thing I'm there, in the middle of that... army... a sword in my hand and hacking at anything that comes near." She frowned. "And full of fighting knowledge." To Josyff's relief she laid the knife down on a nearby table. She put her hands to her temples. "Things I've never learned. Cold, frightening things. I still have them now. How can..." She shook her head and a look of despair passed over her face.

"There's no point asking you, is there? You're no wiser than I am. We're like corks in the water, the two of us. Bobbing and helpless. These... creatures... can do what they want with us."

"Hardly helpless, the way you were wielding that sword," Josyff offered. He massaged his neck. His hand was still unsteady. "And you're stronger than you know."

But Esyal's despairing expression had already gone. It had been replaced by one of anger and grim resolution.

"You know what I mean," she retorted sharply.

Josyff nodded and continued rubbing his neck. It felt bruised—Esyal was indeed much stronger than her comparatively slight frame indicated. Her tactic had badly frightened him but now, with the familiarity of the Keep about him again, it intrigued him. He wrapped an arm about his neck in imitation of her grip.

"Why this?" he asked. "Did you think I wasn't frightened enough as it was?"

"Did I cut you?" Esyal said, ignoring the question. Her expression was partly compassionate, partly coldly assessing.

Josyff wiped his hand under his chin and examined his fingers. They were clean.

"No."

"Hmm. Good. The way you were wriggling..." She left the conclusion hanging, then answered his question.

"It felt like the right thing to do. That crowd, that army... whatever it was, changed when you appeared—became less aggressive—confused, even. It obviously wasn't because of your fighting skills, but you meant something to them, probably something important. I thought, 'let's find out.'"

Part of Josyff rebelled at this easy dismissal of his fighting prowess but it was only a small part. He looked down at his hands, remembering how alien the sword had felt. Could he have used it? Swung it down on the head of some advancing foe with all that that meant? He hoped so, given the extremity...

But they weren't thistles and grasses...

Esyal was probably right. Perhaps he was only an armchair warrior.

Had Amrassian known that too, with his deep access into his 'strangeness'? Had he deliberately thrown him to the enemy in the knowledge that they would not harm him and to give Esyal precisely the opportunity she had taken?

There was no way of knowing, of course, but Josyff quietly resolved to interrogate him if—when—they met again.

Esyal was concluding her explanation. "And you did." She clapped her hands, an almost incongruous girlish action. "Mean something, that is."

Josyff sat down. "Well, I'm the Measurer—whatever that is. I'm charged by both sides with 'finding the Heart' of this place. What it is, where it is and what happens to me... to us... to this place, and, not least, their damned war, when I find it, God only knows."

"Or if you don't find it?" Esyal said.

Josyff looked at her bleakly. "I've a feeling that's not an option. I think just doing what I do will bring me to it in some way."

Esyal leaned forward, intent now. "But if you don't—if we can get away from here before your work is finished?"

Josyff shrugged. "That's up to Nyk and Henk..." He paused. "And Adroyan."

Esyal's lip curled unpleasantly. "Your murderous employer?" She was caustic. "He can't *make* you work."

"No, but he can make sure I don't work again, if I just walk away from here because I was frightened by a few... dreams."

"Dreams? Dreams! For Heaven's sake man, what do you think just happened to us both? That was no dream! You *do* understand that we could've died there—wherever it was—and none too pleasantly?"

"Yes—no—I don't know," Josyff spluttered. He extended a hand before Esyal could pounce on his uncertainty. "I've answered the question about leaving before. I'll keep on doing my job here until it's finished or until Nyk finds a way out of here. If we're not finished by then I'll decide then." He took the initiative. "What *you* can do is help Nyk and Henk as you offered. They've known one another a long time. Each knows how the other thinks, but that's not necessarily an advantage with a problem that's so far off their beaten track. You being there might well spark something off. And..." His manner softened. "By the way, I haven't thanked you for saving my..." He rubbed this throat again, ruefully. "I was going to say, saving my neck, but thanks for saving my life."

Esyal looked both surprised and somewhat embarrassed, far from certain how to deal with this.

"I... it was... nothing," she managed eventually, adding brusquely, "I think we were just lucky."

"Maybe, maybe not. Your instinct was true. Perhaps we aren't the corks you take us for."

"Perhaps," Esyal agreed reluctantly. "We've still got our wits, I suppose, but..."

She left the comment unfinished and flopped down on the edge of the bed. "More to the point, what shall we do now? Tell the others what's just happened?"

Almost to his own surprise, Josyff was unequivocal. "Yes. We said we would and we must. We're all stuck in here and we're better being open about what's happening, however insane it seems, than trying to pretend everything's perfectly normal bar a little problem with an early winter and a jammed gate. Besides, things seem to be getting worse. It could even be that Badr or any of the others might be drawn into something themselves, and knowing what's happened to us might be important to them."

"You think that's possible?"

"It seems *anything* is," Josyff replied. "But yes, I think it's quite possible. I'm beginning to think the Keep picks those it can use."

Esyal eyed him warily. "You make it sound as though it's alive."

Josyff wrinkled his nose and shook his head. "Bad choice of phrase. It's no more aware of what it's doing than a magnet drawing pieces of metal to it. But it's some kind of magnet nevertheless."

"Drawing us to what?"

"Me and you... and Adroyan... to war, apparently. The others... who can say. But they're entitled to know what we know, however little it might be."

"Tell them we do, then." Esyal let out a noisy breath. "Breakfast should be even more interesting than today's."

The reminder of their daily routines made Josyff glance at the clock. It was the same as in his own room, he noted, and briefly it brought back to him his nightmare of tumbling into it—if nightmare it had been. With it came the thought, "where was I falling to?" and an image of clocks throughout the Keep all joined in some dark and complex network. He turned away from both quickly.

"It's a long time to dawn," he said a little too briskly.

Esyal resolved his uncertainty before he voiced it.

"Go back to bed," she said resolutely. "I think they've finished with us for the night."

Josyff was less certain.

"You might be right. But even so I'm not sure I'd be able to sleep."

She gave him a sour smile. "Don't worry about it. Just try lying awake and see what happens."

"I'm not sure I *want* to sleep."

Esyal looked at him, intent again. "Understand this, Surveyor. These First Comers... and their enemies... seem to be able to move us wherever they want and, to some extent, whenever they want, and there's nothing we can do about it—not yet, anyway. You're older than me, but take some advice: time spent fretting about this is time wasted and energy lost—it corrodes—rots you from the inside—it could even be fatal. Like it or not, given no choice, as here, you must accept whatever happens as quickly as you can and deal with it *as it is—especially* if its violent. Don't encumber yourself with causes and consequences. They're for afterwards—worry about them at the wrong time and there'll *be* no afterwards! Trust me, it's the only way you'll get through all this."

Josyff found it hard to hold her gaze. Her eyes were not those of a young woman. They had a darkly ancient cast to them.

Hunter's eyes—warrior's eyes.

Time spent with the Rhanen, he realized—not only outside the law but outside all the normal ways of society. Who could say what that would bring to the surface?

His thoughts drifted on to an unexpected conclusion. It was almost as if she'd been deliberately prepared for what was now happening.

Before he could reject the idea, it developed and a flurry of questions clattered unbidden into his mind.

What have *I* been prepared for? What is the Measurer? What does he do that's so important to these warring creatures? What was so important that his mere presence was enough to make the Diirredyn abandon the killing of Esyal, for presumably it was their army he had been plunged into? And how had that affected whatever assault had been launched on Amrassian?

He dragged himself back to Esyal's comments.

"I understand what you say, but I don't know that I can. Causes and consequences are intrinsic parts of my work. Not to mention the fact that weighing them carefully has helped me survive this far under the New Order. As for dealing with violence..." He gave a helpless shrug. "I'm not like you. You're an..." He searched for a word. "An outlaw. I'm not. I live an ordinary life—one I want to keep and one I can deal with. It's full of things that are important to me."

Esyal nodded, her face a brief mixture of impatience and painful loss. "Nevertheless," she said. "Just remember what I've said. You're not stupid; you know I'm right. You'll find a way. I did, and you can, I've no doubts about that. Worry about your... attachments... cling to them, and you may well lose both them and everything else."

Her matter-of-fact tone chilled Josyff more than any amount of apocalyptic rhetoric could have done.

"I'll try..."

"No! Don't try—do! Just do it. When it doesn't work, do something else. You're not rehearsing for some future event. There are no rules in a fight—you do what you have to. If you feel bad afterwards, hard luck—you survived—the other guy didn't."

The force in her voice made Josyff step back a pace, but Esyal pressed on, though a little more conciliatory.

"Besides, you did better than you think. You kept your wits about you— listened—did as you were told—took the sword and prepared to defend yourself. I was damn glad to have you there. You guarded my back well enough..."

Josyff raised his eyebrows. "Until you decided to stab me in mine."

Esyal closed her eyes and her grim face vanished as a laugh burst out of her.

"Yes. Well. Think yourself lucky. If that hadn't worked I'd have done something else. Now clear off!" She waved him away and lay back on the bed.

"I'll see you at breakfast, then," Josyff retorted.

CHAPTER 56

Back in his own room again, Josyff clambered into bed quite undisturbed by the reservations about sleeping he had touched on to Esyal. Somewhere they had faded away. Suddenly very tired he fell asleep almost as soon as he turned out the light.

When he woke he was wide awake. His memory of the previous night was sharp and clear but for some reason it did not trouble him. Nor did the prospect of telling the others. He was working out how and when he might begin the tale as he opened his bedroom door.

Facing him, hand poised to knock, was Adroyan.

Josyff started. It seemed to him that Adroyan's black eyes were windows through which he could see the tormented sky that had over-topped the battlefield where he and Esyal had stood. Then he realized the Adroyan was speaking. Reflexes long honed in dealing with the New Order brought Josyff's everyday world surging back to the forefront of his concerns.

"I'm sorry, sir," he said, looking suitably confused and slapping his hand to his chest. "You startled me. I'm barely awake."

"I asked if you were well," Adroyan said, leaning forward slightly.

The dark vision in his eyes had gone but they were still disconcerting in their searching intensity, though it was the look of someone concerned about losing something important to their needs rather than concerned for a friend, as the words tried to affect.

"I am, sir, thank you, kind of you to ask," Josyff replied, risking an element of surprise in his tone. He blustered on, wilfully normal. "Slept well, actually. I must be acclimatizing to the place at last. And it probably helps that the work's well under way now." He motioned that they should walk along the corridor towards the stairs. It allowed him to avoid Adroyan's direct gaze without appearing either rude or ill-at-ease. "We've a little checking to do—a minor difficulty that cropped up yesterday in the plotting—but I don't envisage any serious problems and we should make good progress today. Badr and I are working well; he was a good choice."

Adroyan seemed slightly unbalanced by this almost hearty reply, but he recovered quickly and, taking Josyff's arm, stopped him.

"You were not disturbed last night—threatened in some way?"

A tangle of possibilities flooded into Josyff's mind. Should he tell the truth and oblige Adroyan to tell him about the conflict between his 'Ancients'—the Diirredyn—and Amrassian's First Comers—something he had assiduously avoided mentioning when they had spoken after the judging? Or should he just lie and reiterate his claim to a good night's sleep?

What does he know? Do the Diirredyn come to him like Amrassian comes to me? Is he transported to their world, to receive their instructions?

No, he decided. Twice Adroyan had referred to him as being 'blessed' because he had been drawn into the presence of the Diirredyn, and his manner had been almost awestricken—even, to some degree, envious. He did not speak directly to these creatures! Whatever contact he had with them it was not like his with Amrassian. It was something vague and uncertain.

Josyff was torn. On the one hand he was more than curious to know how Adroyan would explain the war. On the other, exposing him as being less than candid about the Diirredyn might have difficult consequences, not to mention the fact that he might inadvertently reveal his own contact with Amrassian.

Though it went against his nature he decided to opt for the lie. With the decision came a small frisson of triumph. Let Adroyan doubt what his masters had told him. Let the Diirredyn's agent in this place be subtly undermined. The response surprised him, but did not change his mind.

"Threatened, sir? What do you mean? What could threaten me here? Was there another earth tremor in the night?" He resumed his walk towards the stairs. "As I said, I slept well; I think I could have slept through a substantial commotion."

As he had anticipated, this reply unsettled Adroyan who hesitated for a moment before striding out to catch up with him. Josyff glanced at him as he fell in by his side. He did not stare but he noticed clearly enough the mixture of emotions on Adroyan's face—confusion, bewilderment and irritation verging on anger. Some impulse pushed Josyff forward.

"Are *you* well, sir?" he asked. "You seem a little ill-at-ease." He lowered his voice and became confidential. "Regarding the events of yesterday morning, sir, if it'll put your mind at ease, I've taken your advice to heart." He gestured. "They're matters quite beyond me. I've pushed them from my mind. All that matters for me now is the work. Let's get it finished—to your satisfaction—everyone's satisfaction—and get away from here. Everything else is... nothing to do with me."

"Very wise," Adroyan replied, though his tone was distant and it was obvious that his thoughts were elsewhere. He pressed. "You are *certain* you experienced nothing unusual last night?"

They were moving down the stairs. The sound of activity in the Common Room and kitchen rose up to meet them.

"The only unusual thing, sir, was that I slept particularly well..."

Adroyan stopped abruptly. "Tell Qualto I will eat in my room." He looked at Josyff intently again. "It is important that you take care, Surveyor. Let nothing divert you from the decision you have made. Your work is pivotal. And you *must* advise me if anything... untoward... happens."

"I understand, sir."

Adroyan turned without any further comment and walked away quickly. Josyff watched him go. Though he could not have said why, he knew that lying about the previous night had been the wisest thing to do. To have done otherwise would surely have brought down intensive scrutiny and he had no desire to be working with Adroyan breathing down his neck, still less to be interrogated about Amrassian and the First Comers! As it was, he had little doubt that Adroyan's concern for him would last only until he had 'found the Heart' of this place, whatever that meant. After that, he would be... expendable. Indeed, Adroyan's very dependence on him now might make him the focus of some future reproach. Whatever the man's intentions and ambitions were, gratitude seemed unlikely. It was a bad thought. Josyff sensed only great harm coming—great harm extending far beyond himself. Somehow, through Adroyan and the New Order, the influence of the Diirredyn would flow into this everyday world, perhaps even come to dominate it, either for their own amusement or as part of their war against the First Comers. As if to emphasize this last, an image of an army making an overwhelming flanking attack on an enemy passed fleetingly through his mind.

Yet, even as he watched the retreating figure, he was struck by its very ordinariness. Here was a man like himself, heir presumably to all the same weaknesses and follies, far from home, snowbound amongst strangers in this bizarre place, wrestling day by day with the problems and vicissitudes of his life—some of his own making, some thrust upon him by circumstances.

The obvious dawned on Josyff: that all human monsters—dictators, warlords, tyrants, the whole range of them down through to the schoolyard bully—were like that. They carried no distinguishing aura that marked them apart from the herd—they were prosaic, mundane. Yet this realization somehow made things worse—a reminder in those familiar, commonplace trappings, that such people were only a little different from the rest of us.

And then came the corollary.

What would it take to make me like that?

The question carried him back to the battlefield again.

Would he have used that sword?

And what would he have become, if he had?

Esyal had used hers and she was still Esyal. But too, she was subtly changed—older in some way—there was something in her eyes.

Unthinkingly his hand drifted to his throat. It was still a little tender to the touch and the dull pain combined with this thought brought back the memory of Esyal's iron-like grip. Such strength she had! He was bigger than her and, he would have imagined, stronger, but he had not been able to free himself, and he knew that she could have killed him had she wished. At the touch of that dark recollection, the confidence he had just brought to bear on Adroyan evaporated. His body began to tremble and fear flooded through him, threatening to overwhelm him, to reduce him to a plaintive shivering remnant of a man, begging to be left alone. It took him some effort to regain control.

Breakfast proved to be an odd affair. The tension of avoided subjects hung in the air, and such talk as there was—and there was not much—was casual and occupied with their various intentions for the day.

"You didn't tell them," Esyal reproached Josyff afterwards.

"It... there... there didn't seem to be a suitable opportunity," Josyff managed uncomfortably. Then he turned the accusation back to her. "Nor did you, I notice," with a petulance he had not intended. He went on hastily. "We'll tell them this evening. I might tell Badr through the day... if..."

"A suitable opportunity presents itself," Esyal concluded for him, an edge to her voice.

"Yes," Josyff conceded sourly. "Are you going to help Nyk and Henk?"

"I certainly am. Whether they want it or not."

They parted without further comment.

As on the previous day, Josyff found the familiar routines of his work comforting. They enabled him to set aside, for long spells at a time, all thoughts of the Diirredyn and the First Comers, their eerie war and his involvement in it. With Badr on the instrument, they spent the first part of the morning checking their previous day's work. As all their stations were established, it did not take them long and they compared the two sets of readings when Badr had finished.

"They're identical, save a spit," Badr said, shaking his head. "And that's not nearly enough to account for the closing error you got. I'll be damned. It makes no sense. I was hoping for some nice conventional misreading—transposed figures or some such."

"Me too."

"Maybe it's the plotter."

"No. The first thing I checked. It's fine."

Badr puffed out his cheeks. "What should we do?"

"I don't think we've much choice," Josyff said. "It might be a big error by our lights, but we won't be extrapolating over the countryside, and in absolute terms it's not much—not enough to seriously impair our final plot of the place. We'll have to press on and keep an eye on it. Maybe it'll come out in the wash."

Badr looked doubtful.

Josyff grimaced. "Yes, well, it's still all we can do. If it turns into a big problem we'll just have to... work something out."

So they continued. Steadily their network of invisible lines threaded its way through the Keep, building up the skeleton from which would be hung its corridors and stairways, its rooms and halls. The two men worked well together, making good progress and, despite the fact that the Keep was both much larger than it appeared to be from the outside and unusually complex, Josyff felt his grasp of it was becoming more sure—the place was beginning to take shape. As they neared late afternoon he found he was looking forward to plotting the day's work. It would be interesting to see how the plotted result compared with his impressions. And he was intrigued to know what had happened to the closing error. Would it 'come out in the wash' after all, would it remain constant, or would it have grown as the work had spread? When they finally finished, his enthusiasm got the better of him and while Badr went his own ways, he began plotting the work.

He jumped as Esyal came into the room. She was carrying a tray of food.

"Oops, sorry," she said. "Qualto's compliments. Badr said you'd probably be engrossed in your work after today." She looked at him narrowly. "I gather a 'suitable opportunity' didn't arise," she said, pointedly.

Josyff grasped the tray firmly just before she placed it on some important papers. The food smelled good. He hadn't realized how hungry he was—he glanced at the clock—or how long he'd been here. He had indeed been engrossed.

"That's kind of Qualto," he said. "I must remember to thank him. And no, an opportunity didn't arise." He made an airy gesture. "We'll tell them tomorrow, definitely," he promised.

"Together with whatever happens tonight?"

Josyff's hand stopped halfway to his mouth and he glowered at her.

She gave a disclaiming shrug, sat down and swung her feet up on to a nearby chair. "How's the work coming on?" she asked, lolling back.

Josyff began eating again. "Fine," he said, speaking with his mouth full. "A couple more days like this and we'll really see something."

Esyal sat up and leaned forward, squinting at the plotter.

"Doesn't look like anything to me," she announced. "Just a mass of lines— if they weren't straight I'd say it's a tree drawn by a kid—badly drawn."

Josyff could not avoid smiling at the combination of curiosity and disdain.

"It's a kind of a tree, I suppose," he said. "And, for your information, it's well drawn. It..."

"What's that red circle?" she interrupted, pointing.

Josyff pursed his lips irritably. "That's a closing error," he said flatly.

This time it was Esyal who smiled. "Ooo," she exclaimed mockingly. Her hand ran over the plotted work. "An error. You did all this and it's *wrong*?"

"It's not wrong," Josyff protested, immediately cursing himself for the defensiveness in his tone. It seemed that Esyal's every reaction was to attack. "You come back to where you started so all the lengths back and forth, left and right, up and down should come to zero." He ran his forefinger along the table in demonstration.

"But they didn't," Esyal said accusingly.

"They never do," Josyff said with forced calmness. "It's an imperfect world. Tiny errors in the readings, slight inaccuracies in the equipment, always add up to give a closing error."

Esyal seemed partly mollified.

"And what do you do with it when you've got it?"

"Well, if it's too big, you check you've entered the correct figures and, if needs be, the calculations, the fieldwork, blah blah. It can be frustrating, to put it mildly."

"And if it's not too big?"

"It's distributed throughout the whole survey—so every part is a little out."

Esyal nodded sagely. She was staring at the plotter intently.

"Ah, brush it under the carpet, eh?" she said, adding quickly, before Josyff could respond, "How big's too big?"

"This big," Josyff replied without thinking and indicating the red circle.

"Oops." Esyal's eyes widened. "How serious is it?"

Josyff pulled an unhappy face. "It's serious and not serious. Not serious in that it won't materially affect the accuracy of any plans drawn for building work, if that's what's intended. Serious in that it just shouldn't be *that* big. It makes no sense. It's a mystery."

"What isn't around here?" she retorted.

"Yes, that's true. But these are simple measurements, simple straight lines, simple geometry. They should add up properly."

Esyal wrinkled her nose. "Well, leave it for the night. You might be staring right at the problem and not seeing it."

"Good advice," Josyff agreed. "I'd normally follow it. But it's stuck in here." He tapped his head. "And I'd be poor company for anyone."

Esyal nodded and stood up to leave. "We've still got to tell them," she said accusingly, pausing in the doorway.

"Yes," Josyff replied flatly.

I never asked how she got on with Nyk and Henk, he thought, when she had left. He toyed with the idea of going after her but the momentum of his concerns about the closing error was already reasserting itself—obviously no spectacular progress had been made or she would have told him without being asked.

He ate the meal, but scarcely noticed it—his eyes fixed on the plotter and his notes, and his mind turning over figures and ideas. What was holding him there—and aggravating him, he knew—was the feeling of an answer teetering on the edge of revealing itself.

In the end, however, it was the room's clock that forced its will on him, its chime jerking him into wakefulness.

CHAPTER 57

Josyff swore as he grabbed the edge of his chair to prevent himself from tumbling off. It took him a moment or two to bring his consciousness from wherever it had been drifting back-to the Keep and the present.

He stood up, stretched, and reached to turn off the plotter. Before he did so he could not resist making the network of straight lines rotate through several different angles, using the red circle of the closing error as centre. Although there was very little detail on the image, in his mind he could see the main features of the Keep that they had surveyed so far draped about this skeletal structure. And, despite the distraction of the error, there was a hint of order about the whole that intrigued him. Somewhat to his surprise he found he was anticipating the following day's work with some enthusiasm. It would be fascinating to see this place encapsulated, its complexities clearly laid out—to be marvelled at, he was beginning to suspect. Of course it would also facilitate any changes that the New Order might want to make, but he could do nothing about that.

The thought of the New Order slightly soured his brief euphoria about the project and he flicked the plotter off.

Even so, its final image stayed with him and while he was walking to his room, it was dancing through his thoughts—turning and twisting—taunting him, it seemed.

He shrugged the problem off with a grunt. Better get to bed, he was going to do nothing worthwhile now. Maybe tomorrow might...

He yawned, noisily.

"You'll sleep the sleep of the just, tonight."

Josyff jumped.

It was Qualto. He also jumped.

"I'm sorry, I'm sorry, I didn't mean to startle you," he said, hands fluttering.

"Not so much startled as frightened me half to death," Josyff replied, though with a smile. "I was miles away."

Qualto looked at him knowingly.

"I don't think so," he said. "I think you were right here."

Josyff raised his hands in mock surrender. "You have me there, Qualto. Surveying places like this isn't the kind of work that turns off when the plotter's turned off."

Qualto looked around. They were at a junction of five passages, all of which were lit for some way before disappearing into darkness. Their arched ceilings came together in an elegant if asymmetrical pattern of deceptive simplicity.

"I can imagine," he said. "Trying to capture something as complicated as this place on paper has got to be... engrossing." His face became concerned. "Even so, it's late to be working—are there difficulties? Badr seemed to think you'd had a good day."

"We have," Josyff confirmed. "We've met a small problem—well, more of a puzzle than a real problem—but we've made some worthwhile progress. A few days in the same vein and we should be very well on our way. Which will be no small relief after everything that's happened." He looked at Qualto significantly. "Speaking of which, how did Nyk and Henk get on today with finding a way out?"

"Ah—you mean Nyk, Henk and *Esyal*," Qualto corrected. "Quite well, though not too happily, I suspect. I think they're finding our *warrior* girl a bit of a handful." He laughed at the thought. "Though I had no problem with her in the kitchen. She seems to be very capable; willing to help, willing to learn—quite refreshing. Still, as far as I can tell it's been mainly head scratching and wandering about scavenging materials."

"No real ideas, yet, then?"

"No. But if anyone can find a way, it'll be Nyk. He never lets go until a problem's solved—worries them to death in the end. He's very... resolute... when he's taxed in some way. And meticulous."

"I'm sure he is," Josyff said. "Judging from the way this place has been maintained."

"And you, Surveyor..." Qualto's gaze fixed him. "Your work having gone well, I gather that you've had no more... strange encounters?"

Josyff hesitated, suddenly transfixed—caught between two opposing desires. The work's going well, keep silent about last night's events—it'll only create questions, confusion, doubts. On the other hand, he did not imagine that this grotesque nightmare was finished, that it would simply fade away, and the others needed to be at least forewarned. And in this vein, he *had* promised to be open about all such events—sought safety in numbers, as it were.

"Is anything wrong?"

Qualto's concerned voice reached through to him.

That promise had been the right one—only prey runs away and tries to hide.

"No, no," he replied quickly, though at the same time he raised a hand in a 'listen' gesture. "Last night..." And, without pausing to order his thoughts he was telling Qualto about everything that had happened the previous night.

His listener was wide-eyed and open-mouthed when he finished with an uncertain "and here we are" shrug. Qualto was obviously struggling.

"It's very frightening, Surveyor," he said eventually.

Josyff tested the water directly. "The tale I'm telling, or being trapped here with a lunatic surveyor?"

"Beautiful landscapes, mysterious guide, wobbling bridges, unlocking bolted doors, then tumbling into a room to face an army. It's a lunatic tale all right, but I don't think it's a lunatic telling it. With everything that's happened round here these past few days, try as I might, I can't see you— or Esyal—as mad, or even eccentric, for that matter. Like it or not, I don't seem to have much choice in what to believe."

He straightened up and his coat opened. Josyff noticed a kitchen knife in his belt. He looked at it conspicuously and raised an eyebrow.

"I see you made some kind of a choice earlier," he said.

Qualto patted the knife. "Just felt the need," he said. "Can't say why, really. I'm a cook, surveyor—always have been. Not a fighting man. I'm not even quarrelsome—indeed I'm probably too easy-going for my own good. But I've worked in some odd places and I've learned that I have to be prepared to look after myself if need arises." He patted the knife again. "Does this bother you?"

"No. It just surprised me a little, but no, it doesn't bother me. In fact, somehow, it's reassuring—telling me I'm not alone. I think you're right to follow your judgement."

Qualto leaned forward. "Would you like one?" he asked earnestly. "I've got plenty—amuses me—kitchens are always full of them—edged weapons—for cutting meat." He grinned mischievously and made a sawing action with his hand.

Josyff was taken aback by the request and his immediate reaction was to refuse the offer. He was a civilized man living in a civilized society—he had no need for weapons, still less carrying them. The thoughts came to him readily—almost as though they had been put there by someone else rather than evolved for his own reasoning. As indeed they had, he realized with vivid clarity. They stank of the New Order. 'We will protect you.' One of the many devices they used to increase their power—subtly undermining the independence, the self-reliance, and thus the whole worth of the individual. And part of the protective cover he had adopted to survive under the New Order was pretending to accept such insidious deceit...

He swore inwardly.

He had thought himself outside such transparent deceit, but he had fallen into line—in pretending to acquiesce, he *had* acquiesced—like the rest of the sheep...

...Prey.

For what kind of predator?

He swore again.

Time to change, he thought. He too was working in an 'odd place' now. He must set his own standards of civilization here and that included being able to defend them. Time to learn—re-learn?—from cooks, handymen, young women, from anyone and anything—even Adroyan.

"Yes, if you don't mind, I think I would," he replied.

Qualto took his arm and, turning him round, led him purposefully towards the kitchen.

"Are you hungry?" Qualto asked as they entered.

Josyff could not restrain the soft laugh that burst out of him at this abrupt reversion from armourer to thoughtful host.

"No thanks." He slapped his stomach. "The meal you sent round was excellent, and more than enough. For which, my thanks."

Qualto gave a nod and a satisfied chuckle by way of acknowledgement. He was rooting noisily through various drawers.

"Ah—I thought so. This will do."

Josyff half expected to see a large carving knife appear, but Qualto was holding a folding pocket knife. A notch in the handle and a stub on the blade enabled it to be opened with one hand. Qualto demonstrated. The blade clicked into place. It glinted in the bright kitchen lights. Josyff found his eyes drawn to its clean lines and pristine surface. It was beautiful. The response surprised him—it was a knife, for crying out loud, a working tool, maybe a weapon, not a work of art. Yet work of art it was too, he thought. And its simple elegance radiated efficiency, with all that that meant. The paradox was uncomfortable...

...the curve of its cutting edge seemed to be resonating somewhere deep inside him—an odd, elusive sensation.

Qualto picked up a sharpening steel and offered the blade to it. Then he paused, put the steel down and tested the blade.

"No. Can't improve on that," he said after a brief hesitation. "I'd forgotten how well this held its edge." He nodded reflectively.

"That's no kitchen knife," Josyff said, in a gentle taunt.

Qualto smile broadly. "No, it isn't," he agreed. "It's just one I acquired on the way." Deftly, he opened and closed it again. "It's a fine knife. And you're welcome to it." He held it out.

Josyff was reluctant. "It's also not a cheap one, I imagine," he said.

"No, it isn't," Qualto replied. "But it's long bought and paid for and it's doing nothing here. It'll only deteriorate, which would be a shame. Please accept it. A good knife is always useful. And under the present circumstances..."

He left the remark hovering.

Josyff yielded, took the knife and thanked him. With some awkwardness he opened it. Qualto watched him anxiously.

"It's very sharp," he said, paternally. "Probably sharper than anything you've encountered before." He raised an admonitory finger. "Be cautious—show it some respect."

Josyff looked at him quizzically.

"Respect, surveyor. As you would a cliff edge. If you don't, you won't feel it cutting you, and it will cut deep."

"You're starting to make me feel nervous," Josyff said.

"That's a good place to start," Qualto retorted, slapping him gently on the arm. Then, cook again: "You're sure you don't want anything to eat?"

Back in his own room, Josyff examined his gift more closely, opening and closing it several times before leaving it on the table by his bedside.

Beautiful and lethal, the paradox was still there but he did not fret about it.

His body was pleasantly tired from his day's work—surveying invariably involved a great deal of walking—but his mind was wide awake. His encounter with Qualto had been unusual but in no way unsettling. Indeed, the man's concern had been oddly touching—and, as he had told him, reassuring—indicating depths in him beyond the immediate impression of his jovial exterior.

Josyff reflected on Amrassian's remarks about the interactions between their two worlds, the mutual, apparently incalculable, cause and effect.

What strange and subtle geometry was at work there? And what allies might it have made for him? Or enemies?

He picked up the knife again, opened it, and, tongue protruding slightly, tentatively tested its edge on his thumb. The thin grey line of cut outer skin that appeared, even though, as Qualto had said, he felt no pressure, made him bare his teeth in an animal rictus. Qualto was right, he had never handled anything as sharp as this, short of a razor, and he began to understand what he had meant by "respect."

He took a final admiring look at the shining, polished blade then closed it and returned it to the table.

As he lay back, thoughts of the work he and Badr had done that day rolled inexorably back into his mind. It was as clear and precise to him as it had been displayed on the plotter, in fact it was more so, because as he walked mentally through it he was able to linger in the corridors, rooms, halls, stairways, that would be measured and plotted in due course. The error intruded, inevitably, an uneasy red mismatch, a twisted and improbable knot, but he did not dwell on it. At best, it would resolve itself, at worst it would be no great impediment to finalizing the work.

Then, as he began to drift into sleep, the knife was there. Bright and shining, its keen edge was cutting through his work, scattering his precisely angled lines so that they fell in all directions. He reached out in dismay to catch them. Some flipped away from his closing hand as though caught in an otherwise unfelt breeze, others disintegrated at his touch, shattering into dark clouds of twittering numbers, while yet others fell about his feet and cracked like well-dried kindling as he walked through them. Then one was improbably heavy, over-balancing him and dragging his hand down. At the same time it wrapped itself about his wrist—almost as though it had a will of its own. As he struggled to unwind it, he felt those about his feet tangling him. Then he was falling...

He woke with a violent jolt...

...and a growling oath.

Muscle spasms!!

Wide awake now, he rolled over noisily and pulled the sheets tight about him.

Someone knocked on the door.

CHAPTER 58

It took Josyff a moment to identify the sound, tangled as it was with the frayed residue of his dream and his abrupt awakening.

The light had come on and he found himself looking at the bolts on his door, briefly fearful that a hand would appear from some mysterious direction and draw them. He shook off the image and swung out of bed. Halfway to the door and struggling into his dressing gown he caught sight of the knife on the table by his bed.

Some warrior, you, he thought ruefully. Ever prepared! He dithered for a moment, debating whether to continue to the door or return for the knife before the normal etiquettes of his life prevailed and he stepped to the door and opened it.

Henk looked down at him with beady unease.

"You must come. You must see this," he said, before Josyff could speak. At the same time he took Josyff's arm urgently. Josyff yanked it free angrily.

"Henk, what the devil..."

He stopped in mid-exclamation as Henk's expression was suddenly pleading.

"You must come. You must see this," Henk repeated, with almost child-like urgency.

"It's the middle of the night," Josyff protested, though it was more the reflex of the newly-wakened than something said in serious expectation of getting rid of his visitor.

As if in confirmation of this, Henk looked down and said, "Put your shoes on. And a coat. It's cold."

It took Josyff some effort to keep the irritation from his face but his shoulders were raised and tense as he yielded to this advice. Slipping on his coat, his gaze went to the knife again and, without a moment's thought or hesitation, he snatched it up and dropped it comfortingly into his pocket.

Henk was already moving along the corridor as Josyff closed the door. He had to trot to catch up with him.

"What in God's name is the matter?" he demanded as he reached him. "Has there been an accident or something?"

Henk's striding pace did not falter as he shook his head.

"You'll see it," he said. "You'll see it. It's been going on for months. I showed Badr—and Qualto—but they didn't believe me. Badr, fair enough, but Qualto should've..."

"See what?" Josyff interrupted.

Henk put his hands to his head.

"I can feel it changing—bending, twisting, branching. This place is in my head. I think it always has been..."

"You've a headache?" Josyff asked, realizing it was the wrong thing to say even as he said it.

Henk scowled. "No," he exclaimed irritably. "I'd settle for a headache if it would get rid of this." He slapped the side of his head.

Josyff resisted the temptation to ask him what 'this' was and tried to drag the conversation to more prosaic matters.

"Did you make any progress towards getting us out of here?" he asked.

"Some—I think," Henk replied unhelpfully. "Nyk's the one who does the real thinking when it comes to sorting out things like that. Can't help much, really. I'm just the labourer."

"Was Esyal a help?"

Henk's pace faltered.

"She's willing enough," came a grudging concession. "But she's a city girl. Bright enough in a way, I suppose, but not very practical."

"She can fetch and carry, though," Josyff offered.

"Mmm."

"I think you'll find she's a quick learner."

"Mmm."

Josyff decided to give up.

Then they were entering the Great Hall. The lights high above them flickered on as Henk strode into the centre and stopped. As ever, the place was cold, and, with a shiver, Josyff pulled his coat tight about him. Not that the shiver was entirely due to the cold. From the beginning he had found this place unsettling. Now the lighting, untempered by any sunlight, seemed baleful and, in addition to the gaping mouths and staring eyes of the many carvings that protruded from the walls, the two rows of balconies had a looming, intimidating aspect, almost as though there were an invisible and repellent audience craning forward to watch.

Josyff frowned at the thought, but it refused to be dismissed. As he looked up he tried to pull his already tight coat even tighter.

"You can feel it too."

Henk's words sounded unnaturally loud.

"F-feel what?" Josyff stammered, stamping his feet as though to blame the cold for this wavering.

"Something else here—something..." He seemed to be forcing the words out. "Something with us—all around us." A broad gesture encompassed the entire hall.

Josyff opted for rough reassurance. "It's cold and the middle of the night," he said, as breezily as he could. "And this place isn't the cheeriest even when the sun's shining."

But he could hear the hollowness in his own words.

Henk simply shrugged by way of reply. He pointed.

"There. Look."

Josyff followed his extended hand. It was pointing to an arched doorway at the far end of the hall. There did not appear to be anything unusual about it though even as he was thinking this, Josyff knew that something was wrong—something was out of place—and glaringly so, though what it was eluded him. Like a long-familiar name abruptly forgotten, it at once clamoured for attention and refused to reveal itself. He forced his mind to silence and focused on the doorway. There *was* nothing unusual about it. It was typical of the Keep in every way. At the same time, another part of him, methodical and professional, was running through the work he and Badr had completed.

It stopped with a jarring suddenness and he became aware of his mouth dropping open in shock.

The doorway had not been there when they surveyed the Hall!

The conflict between what he was seeing and what his long and well-trained memory was telling him momentarily paralysed him.

He found he was breathing heavily when his reasoning mind finally broke the deadlock. Vividly he recalled Badr's somewhat eyebrow-raised account of his long and uneasy trek through the Keep with Henk and Qualto during which Henk had claimed such things were happening. It was not something either of them had given any serious credence to and even though much had happened since then, Josyff had given it little further thought. This, however, was real and directly in front of him. A solid archway, and a partly lit passage leading from it. And it had not been there before.

Forcing himself to slowness, Josyff looked around the Hall to check that tiredness and the general strangeness of events had not played some trick of orientation on him.

But no, there was no confusion about where he was and where he was looking—or what he was seeing.

The door *was* there and it should not have been.

Nevertheless, despite his faith in the accuracy of his memory, the improbability of what was happening demanded final verification.

Without speaking, he turned and walked towards the room which he and Badr had commandeered as the base for their work. Henk watched him then moved after him.

Josyff turned on the plotter and began scanning through the work. He and Badr had not begun plotting details yet but all the passages leading off the Great Hall had been used as the legs of their traversing framework. He straightened up and gazed at the result. It was exactly as he had remembered: there had been no doorway there. He pointed at the plotter for the benefit of Henk who was standing to one side and slightly behind him, his eyes shifting alternately from the plotter to Josyff.

"That's the Great Hall," Josyff said, tracing out the lines. "And that's us, here."

His hand stopped at a gap in one line.

"That..." His other hand pointed through the open door of the room and indicated an archway at the far end of the hall. "...is that opening there. And this... is that one."

He indicated another.

Then he tapped the plotter where the new archway should have been. The line was unbroken

"Nothing. There was nothing there when we did this work."

His voice was flat and neutral as though the absence of emotion might make things other than they were.

Henk was almost excited. "I knew this was happening. I said so, didn't I? And no one believed." His emphasising hand was trembling. "Never mind it didn't make sense—wasn't possible—I *knew* it. And now *you've* seen it— seen it! And it's in your notes—and on your machine here. You wouldn't have missed a doorway there, would you?" His tone was part plea, part accusation.

"No," Josyff replied, his voice still flat. He found he was driving his fingernails into his palms. His mind was in turmoil. Henk was horrifically right and he could feel slender threads that he had not realized were sustaining him, snapping: maybe, just maybe, the closing and jamming of the drawbridge had some rational explanation; maybe, just maybe, his strange transportations too could be explained as some kind of delusion. But this was no delusion. This was a manifest and unequivocal change in the all-too-tangible fabric of the Keep.

Henk let out a triumphant growl and left the room. Josyff watched him absently, but it was the plotter that was holding his attention. The red circle marking the closing error took his eye away from where the new archway should have been. Fringed by the lines unevenly radiating from it, it seemed to be taunting him still, hinting at a pattern which a little effort might reveal.

Then Henk's progress at the edge of his vision snapped his attention sharply back to the Great Hall.

Where was he going?

The lank figure was striding purposefully towards the archway. Josyff turned off the plotter and ran after him.

"What are you doing?" he demanded, alarmed. He placed himself in front of Henk just as he was about to enter the passage.

"Seeing where it goes to," Henk replied, matter-of-fact.

Early memories flooded in on Josyff. Like most in his profession, he had been lost while wandering about unfamiliar buildings, and had had ill-hung doors close behind him, locking him in. But such incidents merely served to prompt a mildly obsessive caution in the future. Here, Josyff felt an almost paralysing fear at the thought of venturing into this passage.

"This... thing... came from nowhere. What if it... goes back... moves... closes, while you're in there?"

Henk's reply was unexpected.

"It's part of the Keep. It won't."

Josyff gaped, then spluttered. "What do you mean, 'It's part of the Keep. It won't.'?"

"It won't. They don't."

"*They?*"

"I told you. There've been others. I've walked along them—there's no problem. I took Qualto and your friend down one the other day but Qualto didn't seem to notice. Good cook, Qualto, but doesn't get about much." His brow furrowed then a glint of amusement came into his eyes. "Seems like the place is... unfolding... emerging. You might have to hurry with your measuring if you want to keep up."

And with a self-satisfied nod at this conclusion he stepped around Josyff and walked off down the passage.

Josyff stood for a moment, unable to move as Henk's comments sent his mind whirling.

By the time he regained some of his composure and turned to question him, Henk was some way down the passage. The lights were clicking on ahead of him around a sweeping bend. Josyff stretched out his arm and leaned heavily on the wall. He wanted to go after him, find out more about these 'new' passages that he seemed to be so familiar with. But fear—primitive and overwhelming—held him at the entrance, only his fingers, curling around the edge of the corner, venturing into this unknown region.

His other hand slipped unknowingly into his pocket and wrapped itself about the knife. Its touch mocked him.

Warrior indeed, he thought. Too frightened to walk along a passage. His eyes took in the archway and the passage. Nothing about either was strange—as he had noted at the first, it was typical Keep construction in every way and it had the typical long-built appearance of everything else in the place. But his fear still held sway.

Henk had disappeared around the bend...

Josyff tightened his grip about the knife, took a deep breath, and strode forward.

CHAPTER 59

To help keep his fear at bay, Josyff broke into a jog trot. He found he was clutching the knife, nervously twisting it round in his hand.

He swore inwardly. Childish, childish. Then he called out.

"Henk!"

There was no reply save a faint echo of his own voice. He reached the bend and could not stop himself from looking back over his shoulder towards the Great Hall. He had a disconcerting impression that such of the carvings as he could make out were staring after him. He took another deep, unsteady breath.

The passage was clean and airy and without any sense of menace, but his fear still clung to him. He saw Henk ahead and he called out again. Henk stopped, turned, gave an acknowledging wave and turned off down a side passage.

When Josyff reached where he had been standing, he found that there were four passages meeting there. All were lit for some way before tapering into darkness. He hesitated. In addition to struggling to keep at bay the frenzy of his rational mind as it tried to make sense of what had happened, there came now another practical concern—regardless of how this could all have come about, if there was one junction, then there could be others, and to go careening recklessly after Henk would be to risk failing to note these and becoming lost—perhaps irretrievably, in this madness. Out of habit he reached into his pocket for a piece of chalk which he routinely carried for precisely such eventualities but he encountered only the knife again...

It plunged him into a debate with himself.

What, in the name of sanity, was he doing running about this place in the middle of the night in his dressing gown? The incongruity of what he was doing leavened its disturbing nature.

And it was cold!

He should go back and get changed into something more appropriate for this kind of exploring.

But Henk would be far ahead by then...

He already is...

And what are you going to do when you catch up with him? Keep following him? Wandering about in this...

What...?

Keep within a Keep.

The thought made no sense, but then, almost explosively, an alarming vision unfurled in his mind: a many-layered building, full of impossible perspectives, and a confusion of endlessly shifting visual echoes that tangled and folded about themselves in increasingly complex patterns into an over-arching and unknowable distance. Disorientated, Josyff was vaguely aware of someone gasping nearby and it took him a moment to realize that it was himself. He could do no other than marvel at this manifestation, but as he sought to cling on to it, to hold it fast while he studied it, it began to shift and fade. He almost cried out as it finally melted into nothingness and slipped away from him, like leaf smoke in an autumn breeze.

Even as it vanished however, he sensed, woven through it, the pattern of the lines that had marked out the closing error on the plotter. It formed a focus of some kind but, like the vision itself, it too slipped away.

He found he was leaning on the wall for support—the experience had left him oddly drained.

Tiredness, he diagnosed, straightening up and putting his hands to his head. That, and terror in the face of such unreason. He looked into the darkness where Henk had been. It would be madness to go after him now, but in any event, he could feel every part of his body refusing to move forward. Get back, it was demanding urgently. Back to the Great Hall. Quickly. You've seen what Henk wanted you to. However insane the appearance of this passage was, either it would be here in the morning, in which case it could be surveyed with everything else—or it wouldn't. And Henk? He too would either be here in the morning... or not.

He rebelled only slightly at the callousness of this conclusion. The stark reality was that if Henk was in danger there was nothing he could do for him—save get lost.

And if this place vanished as mysteriously as it had come...?

Josyff drove his fingernails into his palms at the thought and turned back the way he had come. As he walked he passed two adjoining passages. He was far from certain that they had been there before, but they confirmed the rightness of his decision to abandon his pursuit of Henk: if they had been there, then his tiredness had made him miss them and if they hadn't then this... whatever it was... was still continuing—growing. The thought lengthened his stride, and he was more than a little relieved when he came round the bend and saw the Great Hall through the archway ahead. It seemed to him however, that it was further away than it had been before and he had a frisson of nightmare fear that it might begin to retreat as he moved towards it, dwindling, smaller and smaller like an image seen through the wrong end of a telescope. He tried to reject the idea, but his stride lengthened further and then became a run.

He was out of breath when he finally emerged into the Great Hall, but his euphoria was temporary, for the sense of being watched in this place that he had had before was many times worse now. It hung in the strained lighting like a miasma, clinging, almost tangible. At the edge of his vision he felt he could see the carvings craning after him, while in the balconies there was a dark mobility, cloudlike and diffuse. Nothing untoward was to be seen when he turned to look directly but the impression persisted— intrusions from an unknowable direction.

And was there a noise, too? Sibilant and full of meaning?

He fought down a powerful urge to flee and instead cursed, gritted his teeth and marched towards his work room.

Minutes later, with dogged professionalism, he had set up the equipment and taken a series of readings locating the new archway. Then he made chalk marks on the wall either side of it.

"Right," he announced into the empty passage when he had finished. "Stay, go, do what the Hell you like. At least we'll know where you were!"

* * * *

Esyal rolled on to her back with a noisy growl of irritation and stared up at her bedroom ceiling. She was having difficulty getting to sleep. She had welcomed the opportunity to help Nyk and Henk with their efforts to find a way out of the Keep. Indeed, watching and listening to Nyk at work had been no small revelation. Sharp, intelligent and, despite a fair amount of ritual grumbling, unflaggingly positive in his outlook, he had risen in her estimation considerably. There was indeed hope that they would get out of here before they were drawn too irrevocably into this mysterious conflict between the Diirredyn and the First Comers.

But it would be no easy task. The moat was too wide to be spanned by any of the timbers that they had found and painstakingly gathered in the snow-covered courtyard, and even if it had not been, it would have been no easy task to thrust one over the wall to rest on the far side.

She had lost track of Nyk's detailed reasoning as the day progressed, but quite a lot of the time he was talking out loud to himself as much as to his companions.

The scene shown on the scrolls in the Archive came back to her and she resolved to take it to Nyk the following day. Possibly there were ideas to be found in it...

Even though it fell down? She prepared to ignore the anticipated taunt.

Whatever those people in the past had been trying to achieve, their efforts had been far more grandiose than anything that Nyk was contemplating. He would succeed where they failed, she was sure, and following her confidence, her thoughts turned to being free of this place.

She frowned as a maze of future possibilities opened before her. Would she be discovered for what she was before she could reach the city and quietly disappear? *Would* she be able to disappear? Would her network of old friends and new allies still be there? What had happened there in these last few interminable days? For all she knew, the attack on her group in the mountains might have been the result of a betrayal, and if so, what treachery might be elsewhere?

About which you can do precisely nothing, a cold voice within her cut across the burgeoning concern.

Her immediate and ready acceptance of this conclusion disturbed her. Not simply because of its harshness, but because it was unlike her. It was part of the new knowledge that had filled her mind when she was suddenly on that dark battlefield. Throughout the day she had kept thoughts about this learning at bay by engrossing herself in the work that Nyk and Henk were doing. But it had been with her nevertheless—a dark shadow at her shoulder. Now it could not be gainsaid.

Where had it come from? And who had put it there? The Diirredyn? Or the First Comers? Or had her transportation to that place opened some deep and grim recess in her own mind? Amrassian had said that he (they?)

reached her and Josyff only through what lay in their 'strangeness'—their minds. But this new knowledge did not feel like anything she had ever known, although, with an irony that almost made her smile, its brutal clarity dissipated her concern that her mind was being interfered with. It is what it is, and you can see it, it told her bluntly. What you do with it is *your* decision. You can't unlearn it. Adding, finally, anyway, perhaps it's out of Josyff's mind not yours.

Which brought her to *why* it had happened. What purpose was it meant to serve? More tellingly, *whose* purpose was it meant to serve?

Then she *did* begin to feel afraid. Somehow she had survived that battlefield, but it was no place she wished to return to, with or without this new knowledge, and she had no idea how she had come there. How, therefore, was such a thing to be prevented? What could she do?

Just get out of here as soon as possible, was her immediate answer. But, chillingly, came the thought in its wake: that might not be enough. Maybe this contact between her everyday reality and that of the First Comers and their enemies was not confined to the Keep. Maybe it was a function of her mind rather than her location. And what would be the consequences of a sudden translation into their world—or wherever it was—while she was trekking through the snowbound mountains as opposed to lying in her bed? Could it be that she was in two places at the same time—part of her in some bizarre conflict, while another froze to death in the snow?

Her thoughts began to circle, unable to find anything solid to cling to.

She cut through them ruthlessly. They were serving no useful purpose. She was where she was. Whether leaving the building would protect her or not was irrelevant. An escape route had to be found for everyone just from practical considerations of the here and now, but at the moment it was not possible. Nor could any action on her part make it so save doing what she was doing: listening to Nyk, thinking, and helping where she could. Nor could she do anything to prevent herself from being whisked into some strange other world. As she had learned with the Rhanen, the wisest policy was to accept what was happening as quickly as possible, and deal with it for what it was rather than waste her strength on pointless denial. Perhaps this new knowledge was hers after all—something that her opposition to the New Order had quietly built up in the darker reaches of her mind and which the machinations of the First Comers or the Diirredyn had merely brought to the surface.

And if she was the puppet of these creatures, she had edged weapons both in her belt and in her mind, and once she saw the strings...

She smiled. She did not relish being where she was, but it was no different from constantly having to evade the New Order's police—the memory of their grey uniforms and the mockery of the gentle White Dove insignia turned her smile into a vicious sneer. In reality, she was safer, warmer and better fed now than she had been for a long time, and it felt good.

This assessment and acceptance of her position helped her to relax and she began to feel pleasantly drowsy. Yet foremost in her mind as she drifted towards sleep was a renewed and colder than ever determination to kill Adroyan. She would not break her word to Josyff unless circumstances demanded—Adroyan *was* set on killing her, she was certain—but kill him she would, sooner or later. More significant than any personal threat he was to her, she knew now that the New Order, oppressive and intolerant though it was, was merely a reflection of something far more foul and dangerous, and that Adroyan lay near to the heart of it.

Though she conceded that no strict logic informed this conclusion, it seemed to have a peculiar assuredness, a solidity that it had lacked before, as though a special link, a bridge had been made from somewhere...

The image rose to dominate her drowsing thoughts, a great road tapering into a bright, obscuring distance and drawing her along.

Amrassian was there, some way ahead, beckoning her.

CHAPTER 60

Josyff opened his eyes cautiously, uncertain where he might find himself.

But all was normal. The clock clucked by way of greeting and snow brightness lit his room. Further, he felt well and refreshed. No dreams had disturbed him, still less any mysterious translations into the world—or worlds—of the First Comers. And even as the insanity of the previous night's events returned to him, they brought no great sense of shock or dismay. He had seen what he had seen and done what he had done, now it was a matter of seeing how events had played themselves out. Rather guiltily, he noted that he felt no great concern for Henk, but somehow he sensed that he would be well and unharmed.

Nevertheless, he made a detour on his way to the Common Room to look at the Great Hall. There was none of the uneasiness that had suffused it the night before when he arrived, though it was still cold. The equipment was where he had left it and, he checked, it had not been moved. The new archway was still there, looking as though it had been there always, and it still bore the small chalk marks he had made. He peered along the passage. That too seemed to be unchanged and still quite typical of the Keep, unremarkable and unthreatening. Briefly, Josyff recalled his ambivalent feelings as he had noted the banal ordinariness of the retreating figure of Adroyan the previous day. It was a salutary reminder, he reflected. True danger is rarely dramatic.

He looked at the balconies and the watching carvings, but here again there was no sense of anything untoward—nothing more than usual, that is, it was always a somewhat unsettling place. Then he left to go to the Common Room. As he walked along, he remembered Esyal's reproach and resolved to tell the others about the battle he and Esyal had been pitched into. And now he could add the appearance of the new passage.

Unless Henk had already told them.

If Henk was there...

He forced himself not to dwell on what this might imply and began to work out just how he was going to broach the explaining of his transportation to a battlefield—somewhere. He could see the expressions he would encounter and he gritted his teeth at the prospect.

But it *had* happened and he had to be faithful to his promise to tell all. It was what they had all agreed on and it was the only way to maintain any semblance of sanity. Besides, he reaffirmed, they *did* need to know what was happening. It would be extreme arrogance on his part to assume that he alone, or he and Esyal alone, were the only ones to be playing some part in this increasingly disturbing saga.

He paused at the entrance to the Common Room and took a deep breath. Still far from clear how he was going to begin, he knew this meant he would just have to start and see what developed. He stepped through the open door.

Badr and Nyk were sitting at opposite sides of the table. Nyk was leaning forward and making a point about something. Badr was nodding. Qualto was flurrying around, setting their breakfasts.

"Good morning," Josyff said. He took a guess at the topic of conversation. "Discussing how to get out of here?" he asked.

"Yes," Badr replied. "Nyk has some interesting ideas. Perhaps we can talk about them before we start work."

Qualto brushed past Josyff. "Good morning, surveyor, your breakfast is ready. I'll get it for you."

Josyff gave an acknowledging nod then glanced around the room.

"Where are Esyal and Henk?"

He felt a chill in his stomach.

Qualto paused in the doorway and answered a question that had not been asked. "Adroyan's in his room—he's not having breakfast." Though his tone was mildly caustic, there was concern there, too. "He eats very little—I hope he's all right. This is neither the time nor the place to be ill." He returned to Josyff's question with a shrug. "Henk and Esyal? No idea."

The chill in Josyff's stomach worsened.

"I'll check their rooms," he said after a momentary hesitation.

Both Badr and Nyk sat back and looked at him.

"Is something wrong?" Badr asked.

Josyff hesitated again. "Yes... no... I don't know, but... things... have happened. I'll tell you when I get back."

Badr pushed his chair back and was rising but Josyff held out a hand to stop him.

"No, stay there. Finish your meal. I might be fussing about nothing. They've probably overslept."

"Henk doesn't oversleep," Nyk said. "But then again he doesn't always have breakfast."

"I won't be long."

For all his attempt at a lack of concern, Josyff could not help breaking into a run as soon as he was away from the Common Room. Reaching Henk's room he knocked on the door more loudly than he had intended. It opened immediately, making him jump, and he was looking up into Henk's long and saturnine face.

"Are you all right?" he asked.

"I will be when we get out of here," came the reply, without any preamble.

"I was concerned about you after last night."

There was a faint hint of weary patience in Henk's eye.

"I told you. The place is growing. Getting bigger, not smaller. Sort of unfolding. I came across all sorts of places last night—endless new passages, rooms, halls, stairways." Then he shuddered and seemed to struggle to control himself.

Josyff thought better of pressing him for an explanation. "But..." He floundered. "I'd have thought after that thing chased you the other night you'd have wanted to stay in... familiar... places, near to the rest of us, not go wandering off into new ones. Come to that, what were you doing in the Great Hall at that time of night?"

Henk looked as if he was about to close the door but merely turned his head away from Josyff's inquiring gaze.

"I don't know. I can't think straight. I can't sleep—don't want to sleep, anyway."

Josyff was torn between compassion for this man who had been pursued through a place that he knew so well by some terrifying manifestation of the Diirredyn's intent, and an unexpected irritation at a cringing note in his voice. The two responses tempered one another into a slightly paternal briskness. Nothing was to be gained and perhaps much was to be lost by venting his own fears on Henk.

"Well, it's morning now, and there's a day ahead for helping Nyk find a way out. Who knows what it'll bring. Come on, get something to eat. That, and some company, will make you feel better." He motioned him forward. "I just want to check on Esyal."

Henk was closing the door. He stopped and asked Badr's question. "Has something happened?"

Josyff gave a different answer. "I don't know. I don't think so. It's just that she wasn't at breakfast, and..." He let the sentence fade into an awkward silence.

Henk gave him a narrow look.

"I'll come with you."

At Esyal's door, Josyff paused and held up an unnecessary hand for silence. He craned forward, his ear close to the door, but no sound was to be heard coming from inside. Henk reached over him and knocked on the door but again there was no sound. He knocked again, more loudly, and Josyff called out her name.

The answering silence seemed to deepen about them and after a brief glance at Henk, as if seeking permission, Josyff turned the handle and pushed the door.

It was unbolted.

That alone made him pause as it swung open. Esyal bolted her door, he knew; the memory of how he had unbolted it the previous night flitted uncomfortably by. Tentatively, he stepped inside, speaking her name quite loudly, more than a little concerned that he might receive a chair over his head, or worse, for his pains.

No attack came but, for an instant, he was teetering on the edge of the vast bird-filled blue void he had experienced before. Even as he registered it however, it began to swirl giddyingly and spin away from him, shrinking into a vertiginous distance. He clutched at the door frame to prevent himself from tumbling forward.

"Steady," he heard Henk asking somewhere in an echoing distance, but his attention was on Esyal—if it was Esyal, for the figure in front of him was at the confused heart of the retreating vision and as he blinked in a futile attempt to bring it into focus, it shifted, becoming first Esyal and then... Amrassian, was it?

Before he could decide, the twisting confusion had vanished, taking with it the part of the figure that might have been Amrassian and leaving only Esyal.

She was swaying slightly and her eyes were distant and glazed.

For a moment he thought she was going to collapse and he moved forward to catch her, but she turned towards him, hand outstretched to stop him. Her eyes were disconcerting: almost completely black, he thought, though they were partly closed and the light was casting an awkward shadow. When she spoke, however, he froze, for it was Amrassian's voice that he heard coming from all about him. It was faint and laboured, as though the speaker was exhausted, but it was clear enough.

And urgent.

"*Listen, Measurer, listen—while I can speak thus. Terrible things are afoot— things such as never have happened before.*" There was both disbelief and horror in the voice. "*They are so numerous, so strong. We are facing defeat...*"

For an instant, Josyff's mind was filled with a scorched and blasted landscape, alive with the movement of a dark and gathering army. Black spear points rent the air and sword edges glinted in the red flickering glare of the sky—flickering because it was filled with black carrion birds, swooping and screaming.

"No!" Josyff cried out in denial as he forced the images aside. "Is that how things are? Is that of my making? Is my very thinking bringing this upon you?"

"*No... such things are... constructs... to enable us to reach...*" He faltered. Then there was despair in his voice. "*I do not know. I do not know. All certainty has gone. The chaos of your strangeness is... overwhelming. I can no longer separate cause and effect, nor even your bounded and limited world from the real one. We could have done no other than search for you but we had not realized how terrible the danger—not defeat—it cannot be happening...*"

"What is this danger? And what is your defeat to us?"

"*The danger is total. The instability that will come from the means they will use will destroy everything.*"

"Everything? What do you mean?"

There was a hint of both anger and hysteria in the reply.

"*All things!—our world and with it yours—they will cease to be.*"

Josyff could only echo again. "Cease to be? You mean destroyed— destroyed completely? What are you talking about? Why would anyone—even your enemies—do such a thing?"

Amrassian's voice was suddenly loud, the hinted anger now full blown. "*They do not know. They do not understand. Reason is not their way. They think...*" There was an almost vicious scorn in the word. "*...they will control these things, but it cannot be. They seek to use... are using... the... (breach, tear, intrusion)...*" Josyff could not make out the word. "*...of the Keep—that which binds—to be free so that they can move against us so that we cannot resist, but it will destroy us all.*"

An insight filled Josyff. It was extra-ordinarily clear, though it seemed to be shot through more with the spirit of Esyal than a revelation of his own. He did not question its source however, but shouted out immediately, partly as a reflex response to Amrassian's raised voice and partly in frustration and anger.

"This is madness. Madness! You and they are sides of the same coin. You both come from the Sundering of the Silence, whatever that was! What they can do, you can do! If you cannot reason with them, attack them— attack them as they'd attack you, and before they do."

Abruptly, the room was very still. Josyff stood motionless, held by the feeling that to move would be to disturb some vast and delicate balance.

Then Amrassian's voice was back, full of both doubt and finality.

"No, no! It isn't possible. To do thus would be to become them, to precipitate the destruction ourselves."

"I don't understand."

"No... no, you cannot. We are beyond you."

There were so many meanings in 'beyond'.

Josyff frowned, seeking a simple way.

"Why do you come to me then? What do you want? How can I help if I don't understand?"

"We must try to seal the (breach, tear, intrusion)..." Again Josyff could not make out the word, though complex, shifting images of the Keep hung about it. *"Do your work, Measurer. Find the Heart."*

Josyff was about to protest his ignorance again, but Amrassian was gone.

Esyal's eyes cleared and she blinked for a moment to bring them into focus.

"What just happened?" she demanded. "And what the hell are you two doing here?"

Josyff explained.

Esyal put her hands to her head. Her face became tense with concentration. "Yes. He called me. Took me somewhere. Told me things..." She swore. "It's like a damned dream—bits and pieces, coming and going." She turned from side to side, like a trapped animal, then began pacing the room.

"They're terrified," she said. "I remember that much. Something really bad is happening—or about to happen."

"Presumably this pending attack."

Instead of replying, Esyal's eyes opened wide and she stared past Josyff. At the same time there was a cry from Henk behind him.

Josyff spun round.

CHAPTER 61

Two men were standing beside Henk holding his arms and looking at him closely.

Josyff recognized the grey uniforms and white dove insignia immediately. Although the sudden appearance of the two men startled him, and despite his uneasiness about the New Order's police cum army, Josyff experienced an overwhelming sense of relief.

"The drawbridge is down," he said, to no one in particular. "It's down. It's down! We're free!" He turned back to Esyal. "We can get out of here."

But Esyal was shaking her head.

"No. Something's wrong," she said, still staring intently at the two figures.

Josyff's eyes followed hers and he saw it. The two men were identical. And there was something lifeless about their faces. The word 'ill-formed' came to him, but he had little time to consider it, for they had apparently finished their examination of Henk and were turning their attention to the room. Without speaking, both of them abandoned Henk and moved towards Josyff, their movements making them look like hunting animals. His hand came up automatically to ward them off as they came too close.

He had been about to ask how they had come here, but the question faded as he looked into the two identical faces now scrutinizing him. They were like masks, except for the eyes which were horrifically alive. Though he could not have said how, Josyff could feel the will of the Diirredyn peering through them.

Then they spoke. Their mouths moved simultaneously, but the words that Josyff heard did not match the lip movements and seemed to be all around him. This was alarming and disorientating in itself, but was nothing compared to the voice—voices?

{"Measurer, you are to come with us. The Heart is near—come, you must find it."}

Josyff made to speak, but his mouth was dry and he could not. Powerful hands seized his arms and began dragging him towards the door. Then a buffeting blow broke him free and sent him tottering to one side. Even as he struggled to regain his balance he was aware of Esyal turning to face the two men, eyes black as night and terrifying, and her hand drawing her knife. Words of protest began to form, but they were slow and lumbering against the speed of her movement. They rumbled futilely in his mind as she made one blurring slash across the throats of the two men. She had stabbed both of them again by the time Josyff had recovered both his balance and his voice.

"In the name of God, what..."

"They're their creatures," Esyal burst out. "Look! Look!" She was pointing as she moved to put herself between the two men and Josyff. Numbed by this explosive and shocking burst of violence, Josyff could do no other than follow her urging. Eerily, the two men were swaying but were otherwise motionless.

And they were not bleeding.

"Their creatures," Esyal said again, this time her voice almost a whisper as though she needed a soft reassurance. Josyff noticed distantly that her hand holding the knife was shaking.

For a seemingly interminable time, there was nothing but silence and stillness in the room. Then, Josyff became aware of a distant insect buzzing. Even as he turned his attention to it, it rose to a high-pitched shriek. It was emanating from the two swaying figures and was beyond doubt the cry of something living, but it was not human—it was feral and horrifying.

Josyff's flesh crawled at its touch and he clamped his hands over his ears in a vain attempt to shut it out. Esyal, by contrast, brought her knife forward in anticipation of an attack. Her eyes narrowed and she crouched slightly, her legs flexing ready for sudden movement.

And indeed the two men were moving towards her. Josyff could not take his gaze from their faces. They were still blank and masklike despite the dreadful injuries that Esyal had inflicted, but their eyes were more alive than ever: black, storm-filled and boiling with malice and rage. As were the gashes in their throats. It was as though Esyal had sliced open the very fabric of reality to reveal the fearful world of the Diirredyn. Josyff had a momentary vision of them bursting through, a monstrous black tide overwhelming everything. He felt sick and light-headed. His whole body was shaking.

Then he was aware of Henk moving back into the room, his long face pale and fearful but also determined. It was evident that he was not prepared to let Esyal stand alone again. As she had done when she protected him, he reached for the nearest weapon—a chair. He had barely grasped it however, when the shrieking began to diminish and the two figures to falter. Both of them reached out clawing hands in identical gestures towards Esyal, but they were...

...falling...?

...shrinking...?

...fading...?

Josyff could not determine *what* was happening. It was as though his mind could not accept what his eyes were seeing. Around the two men was a shimmering haze of distortion, twisting and dancing like the air above an open fire, but more complex by far, and all sense of distance and position was gone—were they near, far, up, down?

Josyff reached back and placed a hand against the wall to steady himself, and Esyal too, took an uncertain step back. She gave a curt nod as Josyff put his other hand gently on her shoulder to support her.

The shrieking reasserted itself briefly, and then, abruptly, it was gone. As were the two men. The distortion surrounding them had buckled and twisted, growing smaller and smaller as it fell in upon itself with each movement, until, silently, it vanished.

No one moved for some time but the normality that slowly seeped back into the room was fraught. Esyal stepped forward hesitantly and crouched down to examine the floor where the two men had stood, but there was no trace of what they had been or where they had gone. She brushed the carpet with her hand—an oddly female gesture, Josyff thought—unexpectedly reassuring. But there was nothing reassuring or feminine about her expression when she stood up.

Henk was about to blurt out a question when she answered it with the two words she had spoken before. "Their creatures. They're through, they're through." She put a hand to her head and her face contorted with effort. "I can't remember. He told me things—important things—and I can't remember. It was so clear, now it's all slipped away."

Her anger and distress gave Josyff a mundane focus that further helped him recover some semblance of composure.

"It'll be there, Esyal," he said, tapping his own head. "Whatever he's told you, it'll still be there. It's just... buried... for the moment. Don't chase after it..."

"I know!" Esyal snapped. "It's..." She stopped and gave a short bitter laugh. "When I pretended I'd lost my memory I remembered everything, especially pretending that I couldn't remember. Now..."

Henk finally found his voice. Whatever questions Esyal and Josyff had about the mysterious manifestation they had just witnessed, his was simple, clear, and consistent.

"Is the drawbridge really down...?"

Josyff felt a twinge of irritation but he managed to keep it from his face.

"No. At least I doubt it. You can go and look if you want, but I agree with Esyal, those... things... were *their* creatures. They probably came in the same way that thing that chased you did, maybe your new passages did too..." He stopped as a cold thought came to him. "Perhaps that's what they are, these new passages—a way in for them—a way in for their... army."

He looked at Esyal but there was no answering revelation in her face. "I don't know," she said. "I don't know anything about passages. All I can remember is that they're coming and..." She paused as if on the point of recollecting something then shook her head. "Just that they're coming... and a vague cloud of impressions and instincts..."

Though she showed no outward emotion, Josyff could sense tension amounting almost to desperation. He pointed vaguely to where the two men had disappeared.

"What should we do then?"

Esyal made a visible effort to collect herself.

"Do what we've been doing," she said a little too briskly. "It's all we can do." She looked at Henk. "You and Nyk carry on trying to find a way out." Then Josyff. "You carry on surveying. This... war... seems to be going badly for Amrassian's side but whatever that means for us and whatever it is that *you* are doing, it seems that both sides still want it." She looked earnestly at Josyff. "I don't suppose you know what it is you're doing, do you?"

Josyff shook his head. "Not for them, no. I'm just doing what I've always done—surveying, that's all. All this business about the Heart of the place, means nothing to me. I've no idea what it is, where it is, or what the devil I'm supposed to do with it."

Esyal shrugged.

"What are you going to do?" Josyff asked.

"Try not to think about what I'm turning into," she replied. Pain showed through. "But right now I'm going to the kitchen to find some bigger and better weapons." She patted the knife in her belt. "Whatever these creatures are, sharp edges seem to work well enough on them." She glanced at Henk. "I don't suppose there's anything like an armoury in this place is there?"

"No," he said as though this lack might be his fault.

Esyal breathed out noisily. "Splendid," she said, sourly. "Caught in the middle of a war and hardly a weapon in sight."

"Speak to Nyk—he's got all sorts of things in his workshops," Henk said. "I will."

"But we tell the others about all this before any of us does anything."

It proved to be an interesting telling, the Common Room oscillating between angry pandemonium and impenetrable silence. Ironically it was Henk's testimony that tilted the balance of the doubt. Whatever concerns Qualto and Nyk might have had about the guests that had been foisted on them, they knew and trusted Henk.

Esyal, subtly dominating now, re-issued her instructions as soon as the debate began to circle. Badr glanced at Josyff for confirmation. He nodded. "And if we come across more of these... soldiers... trying to... kidnap you?" His rational mind in direct conflict with everything he was being told, Badr only managed to ask the question by directing it to Esyal and larding it with an uneasy irony.

Esyal replied simply. "Run away if you can. I've no idea what they are, what they want or what they can do." She became cautionary. "But it's more than likely that whoever's sending them will have learned something from what's just happened. They've been learning all the time—we're presumably as strange to them as they are to us. This whole business started with noises in the night and the drawbridge opening and shutting itself. Now look what's happening. Yes, run away." She looked at her audience then added, "That said, arm yourselves anyway, all of you. And be prepared to defend yourselves." She looked to Nyk and Qualto. "Whatever you've got that's practical, please."

"And what will you be doing?" Nyk asked, a hint of indignation in his voice.

"I've half a mind to go after Adroyan. He's their man and there's no saying what part he's playing in all this."

"No, you agreed..."

Esyal's hand silenced Josyff's protest. "But I won't. Precisely because we *don't* know enough about him." She grimaced. "I'll—we'll—just have to watch him. But if he goes for me, I'll do whatever I have to."

She was not asking permission and Josyff did not argue.

"You spoke to him earlier, Qualto. How did he seem?" he asked.

Qualto pulled a sour face. "Cold, distant, same as usual."

"You sensed nothing out of the ordinary? Nothing at all?" Esyal pressed.

"No. Nothing."

The answer did not seem to satisfy Esyal but she did not pursue the topic.

"I'll come with you to pick some weapons, before you start on your work, if I may," she said to Nyk, adding to Josyff and Badr. "And I'll track you down with whatever I find."

The group broke up without any further discussion.

Badr maintained an uncomfortable silence as he and Josyff walked to the Great Hall. Josyff was content not to disturb it. Badr's concerns would be obvious, more than reasonable, and difficult for him to voice. He found himself paradoxically offering up a small prayer that the new passageway in the Hall had not disappeared.

It had not.

Badr walked straight to it and stared bleakly along it.

Uncharacteristically he stammered as he echoed Josyff's own thoughts. "I don't know what to say. I don't know whether I'm glad or sorry to see this."

His face betrayed his mixed responses and some pain. "I'm sorry. I didn't mean I didn't believe you... I... I meant no offence."

"None taken," Josyff said. "God knows, this whole business defies all reason—or any kind of reason we've been brought up to." He slapped the edge of the archway. "But this thing *is* what it is. I took its position last night and nothing's changed."

There was a brief silence, then Josyff said, "All we can do is what we came here for, measure the place and..." He shrugged. "Measure the place."

Which they did for the remainder of that day, using their work as they had done the previous day to still the churning questions that both of them knew could not be answered.

They were interrupted only by Qualto bringing them food—"You take some finding, but I'm beginning to understand the marks you make."— and Esyal, who tipped out a bagful of clattering hardware at their feet.

"Spoilt for choice, really," she said. "There mightn't be an armoury in this place, but I don't think anyone's thrown out a tool or a kitchen knife since it was built. And Nyk's a compulsive hoarder—the stuff he's got. 'Might come in handy, might come in handy," she mimicked before giving a rueful smile. "I shouldn't mock, I suppose, he's probably right."

Badr offered a small protest as he looked down distastefully at a machete she gave him. "What am I supposed to do with this?" he asked, with a pained scowl. "This is all... ridiculous."

"No it's not." Esyal and Josyff spoke at the same time and ended Badr's tentative rebellion.

"You hit people with it if you have to," Esyal added, answering his question. "Thus." She demonstrated. Badr met her gaze but could not hold it.

"I managed to find some sheaths as well," she went on, releasing him. "Hardly perfect but they'll save you having to carry them around."

Badr's reluctance continued, but he said nothing and duly threaded the sheath for his machete on to his belt. He let out a noisy breath when she had gone. "She's... changing. She's frightening."

"Indeed she is," Josyff agreed. He was about to concede that everything that was happening was frightening, but decided against it. Nothing was to be gained by stating the obvious. "But she's on our side and I for one am glad of it."

Even though they did a great deal of cautious checking and re-checking, they worked well that day, moving with silent and increasing efficiency. Both were glad of the opportunity to immerse themselves in familiarity.

"Excellent," Josyff exclaimed, stretching noisily as they returned to the Great Hall in the late afternoon. "Let's get this plotted."

His satisfaction faded, however, as, a little later, he stared at the results of the day's work.

"I don't understand it," Badr said looking over his shoulder. "What the devil's happening? That error's getting *bigger*."

"Yes," Josyff agreed flatly.

"The instruments are fine, and it's not possible that both of us would make so consistent a set of mistakes, day in, day out."

"No," Josyff agreed again.

Badr let out an angry snort of frustration and slapped the table noisily, but any further discussion was cut short by the arrival of Nyk. There was an uncharacteristic agitation about him.

"I think you should look at this, gentlemen," he said.

CHAPTER 62

Nyk offered nothing further by way of explanation other than to motion them to follow him until they were climbing up a narrow winding stairway.

"It started snowing again," he said over his shoulder. "I thought, light the beacon again. Don't know why, really. We can't help any lost souls who follow it, can we? Maybe some vague idea that there might be help out there—people looking for Adroyan, perhaps. Maybe just a change from banging my head against the wall all day trying to get us out of here—I don't know. Anyway, it doesn't really matter now."

They had reached the top of the stair—a wide circular landing. There was a single solid door set deep into the wall and the stone floor in front of it was wet with recent traffic. Nyk pulled it open. A blast of cold air laden with scurrying snowflakes engulfed the party. Josyff shivered and wrapped his jacket tight about him.

"Look at this," Nyk said. He stepped outside and the others followed.

They were on a high balcony traversing one of the Keep's randomly placed towers. Nyk leaned over the wall and pointed downwards.

"There's the Beacon. Probably wouldn't have noticed if it hadn't been snowing—showing up the beam."

Josyff and Badr stood either side of him, following his extended hand.

"I'm sorry," Josyff said after a moment. "What's the matter? I can't see anything unusual."

"Just look at the beam," Nyk said.

Josyff did as he was asked. Then he screwed up his eyes and leaned further forward as though that might make his vision clearer.

"It's... it's..." This time he rubbed his eyes.

"It's bending," Badr said. His voice was almost a whisper, as though the very mentioning of such an idea were a fearful heresy, but a gust of wind suddenly filled the beam with bright flaring snowflakes to confirm this revelation beyond all doubt.

Josyff felt his hands trembling. Something stirred inside him.

"There's more."

The voice jolted both Josyff and Badr out of the eerie silence that the sight had thrust them into. It was Esyal, standing behind them.

"Come round here," she said forcefully before either of them could speak.

She led them round the balcony to the far side of the tower. Lights clicked on to illuminate their way but she extinguished some of them to deepen the darkness. "We just came up here for a better view of the light—couldn't make it out properly down below. And I spotted this." She pointed.

Josyff peered out into the falling snow lit by the balcony lights. Esyal extinguished another.

"Do you see it now?"

But Josyff had already seen it. A solitary star hanging where he knew there should only have been darkness. That it shifted and danced like a star would be due to the falling snow.

"No, there isn't anything out there," Nyk said, answering his question before he asked it. "Just mountains. Keep watching."

He moved off round the balcony and, after a moment, Josyff heard him shouting. The light faltered and then vanished. There was more shouting and it reappeared. As did Nyk.

"It went out and came on again?" As much statement as question.

Josyff had some difficulty in speaking. "It's the Beacon?" Also as much statement as question.

"Yes."

"That can't be possible."

It was Badr and there was an edge to his voice. Josyff too found that it took some effort to keep his own voice steady as he asked Nyk, "You've checked this, haven't you?"

"Oh yes," Nyk replied flatly. "More than once. Turned it off, turned it on, half covered it—moved it, such as we can. There's no debate. Whatever's happening..." He pointed. "*That's* the Beacon."

"How can such a thing happen?" Badr asked no one in particular.

The soft hissing of the falling snow was all the reply he received.

"Go back inside. We've seen what we've seen and this is no place to discuss it."

Nyk was unexpectedly commanding. Josyff found he had to tear his gaze away from the hypnotic lure of the distant Beacon—and all that it meant...

But what *did* it mean...?

As Nyk shepherded them back through the door, he became oddly paternal. "And mind the stairs—the top ones are wet and slippery."

The sound of the door being closed echoed dully around the landing. To Josyff it brought at once a sense of homely security and fearful confinement—a disturbing confusion of sensations. The sound of the bolts being shot home, by contrast, almost released an hysterical laughter. Bolts on a door at the top of a tower! Who were they supposed to keep out? And what benefit would they be against the enemy already inside? He left the questions unasked.

By an unspoken consent, they headed for the Common Room—frightened animals scurrying back to their familiar den, Josyff thought. When they arrived, Henk and Qualto were already there, red-faced and damp from their second trip to light the Beacon. They looked expectantly at Josyff who avoided their gaze.

"It's some freakish weather condition," Badr attempted.

Josyff dropped into a chair by the fire and stared into it. A burning coal fell, releasing a small swirling cloud of sparks which fled up the chimney. Briefly, in their dance, Josyff saw the bright snowflakes marking out the slow sweeping curve of the Beacon light. It seemed to bite deep into his mind and he closed his eyes in an attempt to dismiss it. He had to force himself back to Badr's comment.

"It's freakish all right," he said. "But it's not the weather—that's no rainbow, no mirage!—I wish it were. It's some manifestation from *their* world. The First Comers and the Diirredyn." He turned towards his listeners and became explanatory. "Every... vision... encounter... I've had with them has been full of impossible perspectives. And they keep calling us deficient in some way. In their eyes, we lack something—we're... inadequate. I think their world..." He waved his hand vaguely. "...somehow has more dimensions than the three we know. And now it seems to be... leaking into ours."

"It's not leaking," Esyal said. "The Diirredyn are deliberately breaking through—something they've never been able to do before—never even thought possible before."

"You know this?"

Esyal shrugged. "Apparently. And that it's this place that's *making* it possible."

Josyff glanced around. "This place and perhaps me," he said.

"Perhaps you, perhaps me, perhaps all of us; *that* I don't know." Esyal was brusque. "But it doesn't matter. We..."

"What does it mean—the light from the Beacon bending round like that?"

It was Henk. He was looking earnestly at Josyff, but it was Nyk who answered. "That's the tenth time you've asked that and the surveyor doesn't know any more than me or Qualto." Henk bridled at his tone, but Nyk struck first. "I'll tell you what I think it means. I think it means that if we do manage to get over that damned moat somehow, it'll do us no good—I think we'll trek off into the snow and come right back here. Assuming we don't go over the edge of somewhere."

"No, no. It makes no sense. It's not possible."

Nyk's tone became sympathetic. "You're right—it doesn't make any sense. Neither does the light from the Beacon bending. Neither does everything else that's happening here! But we've still seen what we've seen, haven't we? There's no argument, no doubt, about it. And anyway, you're the one who's been telling us that something's wrong with the place for months now."

Henk's natural slouch became even deeper and he sat down slowly by the table. Qualto fidgeted.

Josyff opted not to interfere in this family dispute.

"Which leaves us with, what are we going to do?" he said instead. He looked at each of the others in turn, ending with Esyal. She turned away from him sharply then stiffened and twisted from one side to the other. Like a trapped animal, he thought.

She stopped abruptly. "We should kill Adroyan—kill him now," she said starkly. "Cut this whole business off at the source."

"*You* know the source of this?" Josyff's tone was angry. It provoked an equally angry response.

"They told us to kill him at the beginning—make him no more —remember?"

Josyff agreed unhappily. "Yes, I do." He hesitated. "But they haven't mentioned it since." Despite all that had happened, a part of him clung to a hope that things might somehow resolve themselves peacefully and shedding blood would shatter this beyond repair.

"*Since!*" She was scornful. "Since, they've been pre-occupied—busy losing." Her eyes were wide and her jaw set. "We can't sit around doing nothing. Aside from whatever they want us for, *we're* in danger. You saw those... men things... those creatures. They were coming for you, you might recall." She was gathering momentum. "And you've seen that damned light." She pointed. "They're through—they're here—they're twisting the very fabric of our world, our reality, as part of their war. God knows what they'll send next—what if it's that army we faced? Want to face that running about the place? We were lucky last time. And when you've done what you have to—whatever *that* is—when you're no longer needed—what then?" She let the question hang in what was now a cowed silence. "If we don't stop all this while we can, we'll be... gone." She snapped her fingers and puffed out a noisy breath. "Like so many sorry candles in that snow storm out there."

Josyff wanted to deny what she was saying but he could not. Nevertheless, killing was killing—irrevocable—and his whole being rebelled against it. The things Esyal had done on that dark battlefield and to the two men—or whatever they were—who had come for him, were still hung about with a faint aura of unreality, but murdering Adroyan was unequivocally real. His brief vision of the ordinariness of the man returned to him as if to emphasize the point. It made him look down at his own hands. They were slightly soiled from the balcony wall and the handrail to the tower stairs. He was vaguely aware of Nyk and the others listening with some horror to this grim conversation.

"No," he said, in flat denial. "I won't allow it."

He felt both the emptiness and the folly of his words even as he spoke them.

"What?" Esyal's response was inevitable but its tone still made him wince. "*You* won't allow *me*? Have you forgotten who's been doing the fighting around here? Who's saved your neck twice already?"

"I meant..."

"I don't care what you meant." She swore and then became suddenly quiet. "I've been fighting so long now, I can hardly remember a time when I wasn't. I didn't want to be like this—I *don't* want to be like this—I'd rather be..." She floundered. "Buying dresses, having a normal life..." She scowled and waved an arm as if to brush the thoughts aside. "But some things you can't run away from. A line has to be drawn—and held, with all that that means. The New Order was always foul..." She made a grasping gesture and grimaced. "Quietly gathering power to itself—for our own good, by the way—and most people too stupid or too lazy to notice—or care. But I never dreamt what it was really like—not in my wildest. Couldn't have dreamt. A vanguard for these... nightmare creatures? Never!" Her intensity held the others silent, then she looked round as if assessing the quality of allies. "You're all here for reasons you know and understand, but why am

I here?" The question was patently rhetorical. "So many outlandish coin-cidences. But I *am* here. I wasn't caught by whoever attacked our party. I didn't die out there in the snow huddled up in that tiny cave. I got another chance. Maybe there's some deep mysterious purpose behind it all, maybe it was just plain good luck." She shrugged. "But whatever it was, this is where I must stand." Her tone became emphatic. "This is where *we* must stand, given we're all trapped here. We can't let them in. They'll destroy everything we know if they come into this world to fight their war—not least, us."

"And you think killing Adroyan—one man—will do this—stop them?" Josyff said.

"He's *their* man," Esyal responded immediately. "*You*, above all, know that. He *is* here for some purpose—like you. These creatures might call us... insignificant... but they need us for something—something important—and if we cut off their contact here..." She made a slashing gesture with her hand.

"By that reasoning you could do the same by killing me," Josyff said. "Both sides seem to need me for something."

Esyal looked at him and for an instant there was a cold calculation in her eyes that chilled and horrified him almost as much as his contact with the Diirredyn had done.

Nor did her response reassure him.

"Maybe," she said flatly. "Maybe."

"Whoa!" It was Qualto. His voice was uncharacteristically resolute and he stepped forward and held out a restraining hand towards Esyal. "Enough of that." As he watched this unexpected interruption, Josyff realized that his hand was in his pocket, wrapped tightly about the knife Qualto had given him. He released it awkwardly. His fingers ached.

Esyal looked at Qualto and her head tilted to one side slightly as though listening to something faint and distant.

"Enough indeed," she echoed, adding, almost apologetically, "I'm think-ing very strangely of late." She turned back to Josyff. "But I haven't forgotten who saved my life. Nor will I. Besides, as you say, both sides appear to need you. You seem to be at the very heart of all this somehow, so..."

{*"He is indeed."*}

It was Adroyan.

CHAPTER 63

Adroyan's voice, loaded with the sound of the Diirredyn, filled the room like an icy wind.

Everyone turned towards him, startled.

Everyone except Esyal who, in one single move, swept up a long knife that was lying on the table, and moved straight towards him. Her response was so swift that Josyff had no chance to remonstrate with her, although, somewhat to his surprise, bewilderment filled him.

What was she doing? Whatever else he might be, Adroyan was a big man, and he carried himself well. Hurt him, Esyal might well, but kill him? Unlikely with such a full-frontal and seemingly reckless charge.

And indeed Adroyan made no attempt to avoid her. Instead he extended his arm and hissed, {*"Stay where you are, Warrior!"*}

The venom and disdain in the word "warrior" made Josyff's flesh crawl and it brought Esyal to an abrupt halt.

{*"If you make this... vessel... no more, it will avail you nothing. Those you would defend are doomed. The Ways are opening, our Final Victory is inevitable..."*} Then it was Adroyan speaking, though his manner was strained as if he were having to concentrate intensely.

"Besides, you will not kill me—make me no more. You have neither the skill nor the power. If you choose to assail me, I will kill you." He snapped his fingers, though that too appeared to take some effort.

Unexpectedly, Esyal relaxed and stepped back a pace though still keeping the knife extended. Her eyes narrowed searchingly as she looked at him.

"Possibly, possibly not," she said. "Though I think you overestimate yourself. One of the perils of wielding power—hubris." As she spoke she reached behind herself and unhurriedly drew out another knife.

Josyff tensed, expecting a sudden burst of violent movement and bloody destruction, but Esyal remained still, keeping the second knife hanging innocuously by her side.

"But either way, *they* don't care, do they? Your masters. You're just a voice for them—an empty vessel—ringing to their rhythm. I see you're having trouble keeping them at bay as we speak. Anxious to get here, are they? To use you more fully?" She leaned forward a little and spoke to him almost maternally. "Didn't you realize how it would be? Didn't they explain it to you? That you're expendable. Or that you won't be needed whatever the outcome of their damned war?" Then she was taunting. "What did they offer you? Sorry, foolish question. It was power, of course—which you now have. They were true to their word too, weren't they—helped you with your New Order—drew you in. But what else was there? What else could there be for the likes of you? Only more of the same, I imagine. Draw you in further. But what was it? Power over the lands beyond this? Our neighbours? Perhaps even further." She made an expansive gesture. The light caught the curving path of her knife blade. "And absolute rule, naturally. You would have to be free from the restraints of the Ordrans—the doting monkeys you needed to help you this far, First Member?"

Adroyan made no immediate response. He seemed to be unaffected by her needling tone, but Josyff winced inwardly at it. She was obviously testing the man in some way, but what was she trying to do? Josyff felt that he should intervene, try at least to forestall what seemed to be pending—instigate rational debate and perhaps reconciliation. Even as the thought came to him he recognized it for what it was—just an old habit—a valuable attribute for most of his life, but worse than useless here. It would not affect the warring parties save perhaps to mark him as weak and confused. He had touched and been touched by the Diirredyn. What were to him daily commonplaces—co-operation, compromise, a deep-rooted tolerance for the thoughts and ways of others—were meaningless against such alien horror. Even Amrassian had not seemed to understand. He wondered how the First Comers and the Diirredyn had come to be the way they were, but he did not dwell on it. He was here, now, and here, as Esyal had said, a line had to be drawn. What was needed now was simple clarity, like the cut from a fine sword—clean, unmarred, made with both precision and unfaltering ease. Though he accepted the validity of his own logic, the image unsettled him with its brutal implications.

It was, however, a different, stranger problem that was preventing him for interrupting Esyal.

When he had peered out over the balcony and seen swirling snowflakes dancing in the light of the Beacon—dancing in a bright arc that curved out through the darkness—something had happened to him—something in his mind—deep in his mind—beyond the shock that might reasonably follow such a sight. And it had persisted, rising and falling to its own rhythm as he had returned to the Common Room. Now, though he could have described no outward sensations, he felt like a man in an earthquake. What should have been solid and supporting, that to which he was rooted, was shifting. Vertigo threatened. He gripped the arms of his chair and drew in a long slow breath and the threat receded. But not its cause. Though he struggled to listen to Esyal—to focus on what was undoubtedly a dangerous here and now—images kept forcing their way into his thinking—images from the Plotter—images centred about the lines that drew together to form the closing error. Like will-o'-the-wisp lights to night travellers they lured him on and, almost in spite of himself, he found he was trying to make some sense of them.

It's more than instrument error—or human error, they said. There's something important here. It was as though his normal problem-solving technique was in reverse. Instead of being let go, to drop into the deeps of his mind, thoughts were surging upwards, demanding attention. Yet at the same time they shifted and slid, almost wilfully elusive.

But, unsettling though this was, Josyff knew he had to bring his full concentration on to what was passing between Esyal and Adroyan. They were the visible protagonists of this war and, for the moment, he presumed, it would be him they were fighting over, even though he still had no indication of what his part in all this was.

He glanced at Adroyan. Why had he come here, to the Common Room? Especially as his manner was little short of triumphant. The Diirredyn had sent their chilling message directly through him.

{*"The Ways are opening; our Final Victory is inevitable..."*}

Why had he not simply waited until the Diirredyn's forces had made their way from wherever to wherever and swept to this long-awaited victory? The tiny vanguard that Esyal had killed or despatched back to their own world showed that a way was indeed open to them and, dangerous though she might be, surely she could be overcome by weight of numbers—Josyff doubted the Diirredyn would stop at freely expending any number of their own kind to win what they wanted.

Adroyan glanced at him briefly and, out of nowhere, came the stark thought—he's come for me!

Just like those two... soldiers.

Josyff's throat went dry and his heart began to pound.

It dawned on him brutally that he had been taking solace from the fact that both sides in this conflict had been asking the same of him...

"Do your work."

It had given him an unspoken sense of neutrality, detachment, of mutual protection. He had felt safe.

But that was now gone—as if it had never been. If the Diirredyn wanted him kept within their physical control, then his role might—must—be more partisan than he had imagined. Could it be that while doing what both these enemies wanted he might be able to affect the outcome in some way?

He found his hand closing about Qualto's knife again as a sense of helplessness threatened to turn into hopelessness. Somehow, this small measure of his ability to defend himself, however futilely, kept it at bay and his thoughts swung back quickly to his new revelation.

Although his ignorance of his role was as profound as ever, he had no reservations about whom he would help if circumstances allowed. But what choice might he have if he was held by the Diirredyn? What compulsions could they bring to bear?

Esyal was about to continue her icy tirade but Adroyan spoke first.

"You are mired in ignorance, child. Ignorance bolstered by the fortuitous outcome of some minor confrontations. But they were simply to test your strength." He paused. "And it has been found wanting. You are a sorry remnant of the Warriors that were." Josyff saw Esyal's eyes narrow slightly at the hint of patronizing amusement in Adroyan's voice. "But even the greatest could not have prevailed against what is now happening. You can forget utterly any notion of effecting a victory or even of offering serious opposition. However, you are not totally without value, and you must turn your mind to the choice you now have. You may continue as you are, and die eventually, doubtless ingloriously, unless..." He hesitated. "unless... they take you for a... plaything. They are looking forward to diverting themselves on humanity's more unusable or troublesome creatures... they seem particularly to relish our... terror... it..." His voice had become increasingly distant. Now it faltered and faded and the sentence hung unfinished leaving Josyff with the vivid impression that he had inadvertently ventured on to something he had not wished to, something that disturbed even him. He recovered quickly and leaned forward, paternal now. "Or you can set aside your foolishness and join me in the glory that is to come." He extended his hand.

Esyal did not respond well to this offer of seeming friendship.

"If you bring that a fraction closer I'll cut if off," she said with a softness that heightened the menace of the threat.

Josyff saw Adroyan's jaw stiffen and for a moment thought that he was about to test Esyal's challenge. Instead his fingers curled slowly, first into a claw and then into a fist, then the hand was withdrawn completely.

"Your choice, child. Your value is not *that* great." His too-dismissive manner revealed a tension in him. "You have little time," he added as he took a short pace backwards and turned to Josyff.

"Measurer—surveyor—you too have choices." Then, part commanding, part pleading, "Come with me—now. Your work is nearing completion—great rewards could be yours. But if you stay with this... deluded creature... you will be led astray and destroyed in what is to come..."

"The glory will destroy him?" Esyal sniped.

"The glory is for those who accept the will of the Old Ones."

"And the others—those who do not?"

"All will be given the choice."

"And those who do not?" Esyal pressed.

Rage boiled briefly in Adroyan's eyes at this interrogation, but he controlled it.

"The war will come this way—that is beyond anything any of us can do to change. And even though victory is certain, there will be great changes—there will be casualties amongst those who do not have our protection."

"There will be mayhem and slaughter for those who do not fall down and worship," Esyal interpreted.

Adroyan's reply hissed out furiously. "These are our creators, child. Our masters. Superior beyond imagining. Without them neither we nor this whole world would be. They are not to be questioned. They come now to take sovereignty over what is properly theirs."

Esyal's lip curled in disdain.

"Masters! You've been deceived, First Member," she said, laying a sneering emphasis on his title. "They might well be *your* masters but they're nothing to do with us, still less this world. They stumbled on us by the purest chance and they're so blinded by hate that all they see is an insane opportunity to destroy their old enemies. They care nothing for us or our worship, and they certainly care nothing for you, whatever they've promised. Listen to them more carefully, you'll hear them laughing. Laughing at you, First Member. You're a pawn, a cypher, a useful idiot."

Adroyan flinched before this onslaught.

"Enough!" he burst out furiously, but Esyal continued, her contempt changing into challenging rage.

"What they're going to do will bring more than 'great changes', it'll rend the very fabric of reality—all realities—ours *and* theirs and God knows who else's. They'll destroy everything, including themselves, but they're too obsessed to see it."

Once again Josyff feared that Adroyan was about to attack Esyal, but despite his patent rage he made no move. The sound of his angry shout, however, seemed to be hanging in the air, mingling with Esyal's. The two voices echoed and overlapped over and over until they became like a living thing, dancing and jigging through his mind, wrapping about the whirling thoughts that he had barely suppressed in his efforts to pay attention to Esyal and Adroyan. He put his hand to his head in an attempt to clear it, but to no avail. Then he was gripping the arms of the chair tightly.

"How can you know all this?" he forced himself to ask Esyal, snatching for a distraction.

Esyal looked at him sharply, her brow furrowing anxiously. Her expression briefly became a mixture of doubt and triumph as some inner conflict between fighter and young woman struggled to the surface. When she spoke she stammered slightly, though it was more the ordering of thoughts than uncertainty.

"It's... it's... in my head," she said. "They've put it there somehow—along with all the other stuff. Or shown it to me—opened something—as though it's always been there. It's everything that took me into the Rhanen to fight creatures like him." She gesticulated contemptuously towards Adroyan. "And now it's led me here—to finish the work."

Adroyan had regained control of himself, though his dark eyes were fearsome.

"No, child," he said. "It is you who have been deceived, you the cypher, and it is I who am to finish the work—the work barely started by the New Order—the work of the Masters. Spin whatever lies you wish, this cannot now be hindered by any fumbling doubts you might place in the ear of even someone as important as the Measurer. You are a mere irritation." A gesture dismissed her and he began speaking directly to Josyff. His voice was suddenly deep and persuasive, rumbling softly into Josyff's mind, suffusing him with the sense of a concerned father speaking gently and seriously to a wayward son. It stilled his tumbling thoughts and promised relief, even escape from all this insanity. He leaned forward to listen more intently but as he did so he heard Esyal's voice protesting.

"No!"

It was distorted and distant, but it cut through the aura surrounding Adroyan's words like jagged lightning across a night sky, and the wild confusion of images that had been tormenting him since he came down from the tower returned with even greater force, their claims now irresistible...

Scarcely knowing what he was doing, Josyff levered himself to his feet. He was vaguely aware of both Adroyan and Esyal moving towards him—trying to restrain him?—but then he was running down the corridor...

CHAPTER 64

Josyff felt strangely isolated. Although he knew he was running he felt more as if he were motionless and the corridor was moving past him, almost as though his feet were turning the entire world like a frantic animal in a caged wheel. He could not have stopped if he had wanted to; the swirling thoughts consuming him were carrying him along like a river in spate towards some inevitable destination.

Accompanying his eerie detachment was an almost total absence of fear and an oddly heightened awareness. He knew that Esyal and Adroyan were pursuing him, urgent ripples in the dark, shadowing confusion of his wake: Esyal, younger and fitter, the nearest, Adroyan further back but grim and purposeful.

But they would not catch him—could not catch him.

And when he got where he was going...?

...It would not matter...?

He was running through the Great Hall, its statues like leering spectators on the banks of this flood, seemingly urging him on. A reverberation shook him which he identified as the door to the temporary plotting room slamming behind him.

He saw his hand turning on the plotter...

There, central, was the familiar pattern of lines that had surreptitiously come to dominate his work here—the closing error.

Esyal opened the door. She was flushed and breathing heavily and she was still carrying the two knives. She extended one slightly and couched the other by her side as Adroyan caught up with her.

"Stay where you are!"

The instruction was unnecessary. Adroyan had begun slowing even as he entered the Hall and he stopped some distance from her. Briefly they stared at one another, then, as if he had heard something, Adroyan straightened and looked up. Slowly he began moving his head from side to side, like a hunting animal testing the air. Then, his head still turning, searching, he was walking away from her—moving slowly towards the centre of the Hall, his arms extended sideways as if in greeting.

Esyal watched him closely but made no effort to follow, moving only to keep herself between him and Josyff. She frowned and her eyes narrowed—the far end of the Hall seemed to be distorted. She did not dwell on it, assuming it as an after-effect of her explosive pursuit of Josyff.

Still concentrating on Adroyan she gave Josyff a quick glance.

"What was all that about?" she demanded of him. "And what the hell's here that's suddenly so important?"

Josyff did not reply.

"Damn you, Josyff, answer me! I'm supposed to be protecting you, but how can I if you're going to do things like that? Tell me what's happening. I need to know."

But although he heard the plea, Josyff was not listening. His hands were manipulating the images on the plotter, working as though they belonged to someone else. All the work that he and Badr had done over the previous days was appearing: corridors, stairways and rooms reduced to a complex interlinked web of unsymmetrical and seemingly patternless lines. It was no unfamiliar sight—it was a routine precursor to the conclusion of almost every job he had ever done: buildings, places, reduced to shapes on paper, three dimensions strangely translated into two, so that clients, owners, could ponder and reflect and make decisions that in their turn would blossom out into solid, tangible change.

The word 'owners' stuck in his mind. The New Order as property owners, even as a powerful political group, seemed almost incongruous now, the merest reflection of some darker truth. And the goal of reducing the Keep to drawings too, seemed trivial. Yet these considerations were at the fringes of his thoughts, as was the paradoxical recognition that the turmoil currently driving him was his own mind intensely pursuing this latter end. The quiet relentlessness that had carried him through problem after problem during his professional life was now rampant: feral and furious in its determination. It unnerved and excited him at the same time. Two conflicting responses: let's see what all this is about, and, let's get this over with as quickly as possible. Unexpectedly, a brief vision of his old life—his home, his wife, began to form...

How long ago had that been...?

But, with an equally brief frisson of guilt and no small effort, he turned it away. It would sustain him at some level, he knew—he hoped—but it would be dangerous and destructive if it were allowed to distract him now. It could plunge him into mewling self-pity and while he had no idea what the consequences of this would be he had little doubt that they would be disastrous.

His eyes were flicking between the shifting shape in front of him, turning and twisting as he manipulated it through different viewpoints, and the rows and columns of figures which defined it—good figures, accurate figures, figures well checked and balanced... except for that damned error—that elusive error. The red circle marking it remained static, pivotal, throughout all the changes he was ringing. It was hypnotic in its stillness amid all the movement—like a watching eye—a taunting eye...

Badr joined Esyal in the doorway followed by Nyk and then a red-faced Qualto. They were all breathing heavily.

"Where's Henk?" Esyal asked.

Nyk shrugged then asked, "What's happening?"

But he was not looking at Josyff, immobile, save for his dancing fingers, in front of the glowing plotter. He was looking at Adroyan still standing in the middle of the Hall, his arms extended sideways.

"That's how Henk said he found him the other day," Qualto said, whispering, and pausing from patting his chest to tentatively mimicking the gesture. "When he'd passed out—remember?"

But Nyk's attention had moved. His eyes narrowed as though he was having difficulty focusing and he began to crane forward. So engrossed was he that he eventually staggered and Esyal had to catch hold of him.

"Careful."

"My eyes have gone... funny," Nyk replied, alternately opening them wide and screwing them tight shut. "Must be the running."

"I don't think it's your eyes," Esyal said, following his gaze. "Look again."

The distortion of the end of the Hall which she too had attributed to her sudden dash after Josyff, was still there—clear and distinct.

"Everything's... out of shape." It was Qualto, his voice far from steady. "Like looking through the bottom of a glass. Wh... what is it? Some kind of optical illusion?"

Esyal stared critically at the far end of the Hall. There was no blurring or fuzziness—no shimmering unsteadiness to show that Qualto's suggestion might be right, and so gradually did it develop from where they were standing that it was not possible to see exactly where the change began. A few days ago such a sight would have been deeply unnerving, but the events of those same few days had changed her radically and now she noted the development with a kind of cold detachment. It was what it was. The 'why?' and the 'how?' were, for the moment, irrelevant.

Yet for no reason that she could fathom, save that it must be part of the knowledge imparted to her by Amrassian and the First Comers, she knew what it was—it was their world, moving in a way that should not be possible. Drawn there by the machinations of its Diirredyn, aided doubtless by Adroyan and his acolytes, it was swelling into this world like an obscene pregnancy. Soon it would yield its burden and their army would emerge on its way to destroy their ancient enemy...

And everything else...

Desperation, bewilderment and anger shared equally in the question that followed inexorably—how could they be so blind not to see what they were going to do?

Yet, in part, she knew the answer. She could feel the Diirredyn's frenzied hatred, their obsessive, manic determination not merely to defeat but to eradicate utterly the First Comers—it was pressing in on her mind, just as their world was pressing in on the Great Hall.

All reason was gone.

The knowledge of how they could have come to such a pass was denied her. She could not avoid the suspicion that the cause of this conflict was not merely ancient, it was long-forgotten—by both sides.

Then again, perhaps I might not be so willing to fight for you if I knew the truth, she thought bleakly in her one-sided discourse with Amrassian. In either case it did not matter. She was where she was and effectively without choice. The moralizing was over and the decision made.

Kill or be killed.

Now there must be only sharp-edged focus, unclouded by past or future, or all would definitely be lost. It helped that no considered, steepling-fingered debate was needed to gauge the nature of the Diirredyn.

"What is it?" Qualto pressed his question, cutting across her wandering thoughts and returning her attention to the distortion at the end of the Hall.

She told him, and what was about to happen.

"How do you know?"

Esyal shook her head. "I just do," she said flatly.

Qualto gave her a narrow look but left the question for another.

"And what happens when this... army... comes through? What happens to us?"

A parade of easy lies filed through Esyal's mind but she opted for the truth.

"*That* I *don't* know. But if it *does* come through, Amrassian said that everything... *everything*—will be destroyed."

"Everything?" Qualto queried.

"Everything," Esyal confirmed. "Us, them, our world, their world."

"You *know* this too?" Qualto said, part jibe, part nervous inquiry.

"I know Amrassian believes it. As far as I can judge, he's struggling to avoid being overwhelmed by sheer panic. And I *do* know the Diirredyn are demented enough."

Part of Esyal noted that Qualto was taking this grim tale remarkably calmly.

Probably doesn't believe it, she thought. *Can't say I blame him.*

"What are we to do?" he asked.

Esyal could not keep the surprise from her face.

Good question, she thought. Amrassian had been frank when she had asked the same question—he did not know. "*Your world is your world, what you will see (hear, feel, sense?) is beyond us to understand—all comes from your strangeness.*"

"We're supposed to stop it happening," she replied. "But don't bother asking me how."

She glanced at Josyff, still staring at the images he was manipulating on the plotter.

Qualto followed her gaze. "And the surveyor?"

Esyal shook her head slowly. "Both sides want him to do something, but he's no idea what." She paused and continued watching Josyff. "I imagine what he's doing now is part of it, but..." She fell silent for a moment, then shrugged, and looked back to Qualto. "I think we're just going to have to make this up as we go along."

Qualto pursed his lips and nodded. "It's not a bad way—I cook like that all the time."

An ungainly splutter of a laugh snorted out of Esyal as Qualto's manner reached through her guard and touched something vital. It brought an odd sense of release—including, not least, a reminder not to be afraid to be afraid. Fear was an ancient resource, she knew—it could be transmuted into a powerful ally which would protect her both mentally and physically if she let it.

If...

She found herself moved, humbled even, as she took in what Qualto was. It was her consistent experience that the best people to help and support her in her long fight against the New Order had always been not the noisily indignant, the blusteringly self-righteous, but those who had quietly, and quite unannounced, appeared by her side when things had to be done. It was a good omen.

"You said *if* this army comes through, before," Qualto said. "Was it just a manner of speaking?"

Just as his unexpected humour had reached deep into her, so did this question, reinforcing her new-found opinion of him.

"If?" she echoed, half to herself. Why had she said 'if'?

She felt a way forward forming, albeit vague and elusive.

The Diirredyn had already made sorties into this world, all very different, and, though she had known nothing about them, she had defeated them. Something in her thinking changed abruptly—everything was the same but different. By virtue of the seemingly impossible things they had done—the sealing of the drawbridge, the transporting of her into the thick of an army, the manifestation of the two New Order soldiers—she had unwittingly invested them with godlike characteristics. But they were not gods, fundamentally they were not gods! How could she have thought that? They were just different—as were the First Comers—though both demonstrated all too human traits—bad and good. And in *this* world, they were floundering. Amrassian had more or less conceded this and would have done for sure had she had the wit to ask him outright. But the Diirredyn, consumed by hatred and arrogance, were oblivious. What they had achieved here had probably been as much by blind chance as calculation, but they accepted it as a measure of their ability. Both blundering and vicious, she doubted they learned much.

"*We* are just as unknown to them as they are to us," she said, voicing the thoughts as they came to her. "We're unknowable, incalculable. They reach us, using something in the way we think—our 'strangeness' as they call it. We can't stop them doing that—but they don't really know what they're doing—they're banging on a wall to find a way through, oblivious to the fact that it might fall on them."

"Which means?" Qualto prompted caustically.

Esyal tapped her head. "Which means that we have the advantage here. We must be able to use our minds too, once their power comes into this world."

Qualto's brow wrinkled. "So when this army of theirs appears, we imagine a bigger one of our own and then let them fight it out?" His raised eyebrows and bantering manner made Esyal smile.

"No harm in hoping I suppose, but I doubt it. Can't speak for you, of course, but I've never been that lucky. It's what goes on beneath our thoughts, that they use—everything we know, everything we have in here..." She tapped her head again. "It just comes when it's needed—like from a huge library—but it's not constantly in our thoughts. Somehow it must reach into their world. It mightn't even be the thoughts themselves, the knowledge we have, it might be to do with the way we keep it, store it."

A hint of realization came into her eyes. "That's what he's done—Amrassian—he's put stuff into my mind—where he could—deep down somewhere. That's why I keep remembering things I know I've never learned." The realization deepened. "It's all he can do—or all he dares do. The First Comers know that if they do what the Diirredyn are going to do—enter this world, to fight them on *their* terms, *they'll*..." She paused.

"Destroy everything." Qualto finished her sentence.

"Yes," she confirmed. "So he said. Don't know what that means, though—how it'll happen."

"I don't suppose it matters really."

"I don't suppose it does."

"More to the point..." Qualto looked significantly at her head. "Did he put enough in there to tell you what to do?"

"I doubt it," Esyal replied. "I think if he'd had a clear winning strategy, he'd have told me directly."

Qualto looked thoughtful.

"Unless, of course, knowing about it consciously might actually prevent your 'strangeness' from using it," he offered.

Esyal's eyes narrowed and her mouth tightened as her reasoning began to circle in on itself. "I don't think this is helping," she said tartly, cutting through it.

"Well then, just do what you've been doing," Qualto said, unexpectedly firm. "Trust your judgement."

Esyal looked doubtful. "Like your cooking?" she asked. The words came out a little more harshly than she had intended.

"You have a *choice*?" Qualto retorted sharply, adding defensively. "Anyway, I've never been out of a job and I've not poisoned anyone yet, so, yes, like my cooking."

Esyal nodded and returned to glowering at Adroyan, still motionless at the centre of the Hall, somehow the focus of the distortion all around him.

She was torn. Should she act now, rush in quickly, kill him, or, at the least, injure him—reduce his effectiveness? Or should she await developments? Nyk, a silent observer so far, shifted impatiently. A machete he was carrying caught the lights of the Hall.

No, Esyal decided, this isn't going to get better. Once the breach is made, God knows what's going to happen. Do it now.

With only eye contact by way of a request, she took the machete from Nyk.

She hefted it then took a deep breath and braced herself for a charge across the Hall.

Josyff let out a cry.

CHAPTER 65

Josyff had felt increasingly like a passenger in his own body since he had seen the light of the Beacon curving through the falling snow. Something had been set in motion and its momentum was beyond his control. He sensed a slender shifting thread of action and reaction dwindling back to his laboured arrival at the Keep, perhaps even beyond that, like a soft breeze that disturbs the dust and pebbles as precursor to a great avalanche. He did not, *could not*, pursue the thought however, as almost his every mental resource was occupied in riding an avalanche of his own.

His mind was leaping from thought to thought as they cascaded by—grasping and assessing, then moving on, lest too detailed a consideration would see him swept away.

He was elated. A small, still, part of him revelled in the coming together of seemingly disparate and disconnected parts, to form a patterned whole. This was no new experience for him—a solution was emerging, though, and this *was* new, he had no idea to what. Further, the sheer magnitude and intensity of this was beyond anything he had ever known.

Numbers, made familiar by the previous days' fretting and testing, became alive as he manipulated them both in his head and on the plotter. They drew with them the lines and shapes that he and Badr had so meticulously mapped and, both improbably and tantalizingly, the circle that had marked the closing error began to shrink.

But with the elation came also apprehension. Something was approaching. Something presaged by a feeling akin to vertigo, faintly reminiscent of what he had felt when he had unbolted Esyal's door. It was as though, dreamlike, he was not only sitting in front of the plotter, but hovering at some unguessable vantage over the Great Hall and its occupants. Indeed he felt he was hovering over the Keep itself, its towers and turrets stark and solid against the dark snowlit mountains, reduced now to vagueness and unreality like a badly painted backdrop. Even stranger, he seemed to be hovering in time over everything that had happened recently, both watching and part of an eerie shifting kaleidoscope of the past days, merged somehow into a single event.

The fear was slight at first, but it increased in intensity rapidly until he felt it was going to paralyse him.

A knowledge, perhaps his own, perhaps not, told him that this would be disastrous—great harm would follow, though he did not know what. The phrase "Let go" floated through the frenzy, bringing with it the memory of falling through a blue sky, surrounded by wheeling birds. Was that what he had to do somehow? Even as he pondered the question, he could feel mental calculations piling up like raging floodwater behind an obstruction. He had precious little choice but to let go—whatever that meant—he certainly couldn't stop and think! But it was curiosity that took him forward, though curiosity was barely the word describe such an intense need. A great edifice of numbers and shapes had formed in his mind, a slow revelation built up from the familiarity of endless repetition and who could say what past experience. It was the Keep, but not the Keep. Hazy and unsteady, it teetered in and out of his awareness—now clear, albeit incomplete, now gone, as though a turbulent swirling fog kept snatching it from view.

Working almost totally by instinct, Josyff found himself strangely divided. His sole function, it seemed, was to maintain a balance between the control needed to preserve and extend this eerie fabrication, and a driving frenzy that was demanding to see it in its completed entirety.

Was this a reflection of the needs—the desires—of the Diirredyn and the First Comers?

Like others, the thought came and went before it could be considered, tossed roughly aside in the swirling mayhem.

Then, unheralded, it was there...

Massive and obvious. As though, head bowed, intently looking for something, he had taken a fretful step back to see that it had been in front of him all the time.

But what was it?

And who—what—was he to be seeing it thus?

It was indeed the Keep, without a doubt, but it was no human vision he had of it.

That he saw how it had come about offered no explanation. The reasoning of his deeper mind had solved the problem of the closing error. That glaring, red-eyed circle that had marked it had gone now from the plotter, as had the unsettling instability it indicated from the inner scene filling his mind.

But the perspectives—perspectives of both time and distance...

How could they be?

Each of the lines—line-of-sight, razor-straight, light-borne lines that framed the skeleton of the Keep—was curved.

No... it wasn't possible...

But it was so—that same precision and accuracy guaranteed it absolutely, and the mathematics that sustained the consequences could not be gainsaid.

No similar logic took him to his next thinking though he knew it was correct—a subtle touch of Amrassian, he wondered, briefly. Something in the shaping of the Keep—something rare and improbable—had reached through to touch, to join with, the world of the Diirredyn and the First Comers. He thought of Adroyan mistaking another mountain for the site of the Keep on their journey back from meeting him with his guides. Perhaps there was a fortuitous quality in this whole region that drew the worlds together, one that found its focus in this particular peak and which the builders of the Keep inadvertently responded to, fashioning in ever more refined detail the makings of a unique key that could open a rare and mysterious door. Or, perhaps peculiarly sensitive individuals—Adroyan's forebears?—had wilfully and with malevolent intent formed the Keep thus. Either way, the deed was done, and the door was there, a door which, had it been in an ancient myth, would have carried the traditional injunction that it not be opened on pain of fearful retribution.

But this was no thing of vicarious menace in the fireside story-telling safety of myth; it was no allegory. It was real.

And somewhere, somehow, in the depths of his mind—that place that so disturbed Amrassian—his strangeness—the door had been made manifest and the final refinement of the key had taken place.

Yet even as these images formed Josyff rejected the analogy of the door. The Keep—the Keep he now saw, vivid in his imagination, was far stranger than a simple opening between two separate and distinct places. It was as solid and robust as he had come to know it, but, at the same time, it was ephemeral, shifting, changing—an uncertain coinciding of two deeply intermingled worlds.

Then the euphoria of discovery began to fade, eroded by the grimmer remembrance that this conclusion was what had been sought by both the Diirredyn and the First Comers. But for what end? What would happen now and what would be his part in it?

As these reflections came to him, so did both renewed fear and his awareness of the Great Hall and Esyal and the others: Adroyan, surrounded by and... guiding?... feeding?... a dark and ominous presence; Esyal, watchful and alert, seeing far more than she realized and about to do something precipitate; Nyk, Qualto and Badr, uncertain and shadowy, threaded peculiarly through events. And Henk. Where was Henk? Josyff sensed him, away from this troubled centre, part of the pattern and not part of it, following a stern purpose of his own. Notwithstanding these eerie insights, a mixture of concern for his companions and a primitive need to be with others of his own kind at such a time made Josyff push his chair back so that he could stand up. But something was wrong. His movements seemed to be extending far beyond his body, as if he were suddenly the wrong shape—and bigger, much bigger. And the effects of his attempted movement were rippling ever outwards. It was a giddying sensation and he had to grip the edge of the table to steady himself. It's just the dash from the Common Room, and then sitting too still, too long, too engrossed, at the plotter, he managed to rationalize, but he knew that that was not the case. He was not outside the vision of the Keep that was still clear and impossible in his mind, he was part of it.

Gritting his teeth, he tightened his grip on the edge of the table, then pushed his chair again. The effort seemed to draw power in upon him from the surroundings, and abruptly, he was falling. He let out a cry.

Esyal spun round, wide-eyed. Despite everything that was happening, the Great Hall had been silent and Josyff's cry had cut through it harshly. Further, there was a peculiar quality to it. It was echoing—and dwindling— almost as though he were hurtling away from her at great speed. Even as she turned she was vaguely aware of a ripple running through the distortion at the far end of the Hall in response to it.

Prosaically, however, her immediate thought was that he had tumbled off his chair. But he was still sitting in front of the plotter, the only sign of change being that his hands were no longer operating it but holding the edge of the table.

"What's the matter?" she asked, but Josyff did not reply.

"Josyff! What's the matter?" she repeated, louder.

Still no reply.

"Watch him. Tell me if he does anything," she instructed Nyk and Qualto, levelling the machete at Adroyan. Despite this command, she spared Josyff only a couple of brief glances as she began to edge cautiously into the room. Her gaze remained focused intently on Adroyan, for fear that a momentary lapse of concentration would see him slip from view, surreptitiously vanishing into the bizarre landscape being formed by the slowly changing distortion. Reaching Josyff, she placed a hand on his shoulder and, whispering his name urgently, gently shook him. There was no response. She squatted down beside him so that she could see both him and Adroyan.

Josyff's eyes were open, but not focused.

"You must protect what remains here, Warrior."

It was Amrassian, his voice faint and distant. Esyal stood up quickly and looked around but there was no one else in the room.

The voice went on. *"We have sent (folded? turned? translated?) the greater part of the Measurer into his strangeness."*

"What?"

Amrassian repeated himself, adding, *"It is our faith (belief? trust? hope?) that he will find the Way."*

"Faith? Faith! What are you talking about?" Esyal began to flounder as anger rose up within her. She menaced the empty room with the machete. "I don't understand. What have you done to him? What's happening? What am I supposed to do?"

"It is your world; I (we?) cannot help. Do what you must."

"Wh... what!" Esyal exclaimed, stammering with rage now.

"We cannot help..."

"I heard that! Damn you. You..." She stopped, her jaw tense with effort and her eyes blazing. "We'll talk about that in a moment," she went on, through clenched teeth. "For now, what the hell have you done to Josyff?"

"The greater part of him is in his strangeness..."

"I heard that too! What's it supposed to mean?"

Amrassian's voice faded even further. *"We are... sorely pressed. You must protect him, or we are all lo..."*

And he was gone.

Esyal jerked upright as if she had been slapped, his disappearance was so abrupt. The room felt peculiarly empty. A stream of obscenities were gathering to be launched after him, but, as though a wind had dispersed a clinging mist, her mind was suddenly sharp and clear and they transmuted themselves almost immediately into a more purposeful intent. Nothing was to be gained by seeking after this elusive... ally—she formed the word reluctantly—and much might well be lost—time, certainly.

"My world," she muttered. "*My* world."

In a glance, she took in the distortion slowly twisting the Great Hall into something surreal and nightmarish with Adroyan as its seemingly still centre. She took in, too, Badr, who had moved into the room and was looking at the plotter over Josyff's head, while Nyk and Qualto were standing like bewildered spectators.

Bewildered spectators looking at *her*, she realized with a jolt. Looking at her and *to* her—for leadership. A grim humour surfaced from somewhere. From rescued waif to champion. She had no idea what to do—but it was more than they had. Was that the way it was with all leaders? She let the thought go.

"What's the matter with him?" Qualto asked from the open doorway.

Esyal raised a hand for silence. She had become aware of a sound— unsteady and unclear. Her brow furrowed in concentration—improbably, it sounded like an animal howling, though whether in pain or triumph she could not tell.

"Can you hear that?" she asked.

Qualto tilted his head, then frowned. "Yes, what is it?" Then, without waiting for an answer. "I think we should go. Get out of here. Right now. This is all... insane."

Nyk nodded in agreement.

Badr was shaking his head, though whether at this suggestion or something else was not clear.

Esyal was briefly torn between raging at Qualto and pleading with him. In the end she said calmly, "We can't leave the surveyor. I don't know what's happened to him but he's in some kind of trance. Besides, you're forgetting we're locked in here. And judging from that Beacon, it's probably just as insane outside, plus its freezing cold."

She looked at each in turn then once again at Adroyan and finally at the machete she was still tightly clenching. Then she took the knife from her belt in the other hand.

"Look after the surveyor—keep him safe. I'm going to try to end this right now."

Even as she spoke, the distant sound grew in nerve-jangling intensity. Insofar as she could identify it, it sounded like a mixture of triumphant screaming and a thousand brazen trumpets raised in discordant fanfare. The distortion rippled to its broken rhythm, waves of movement passing through it, making the end of the Hall quiver obscenely. Those carvings so far caught in it twisted and turned, now looking at her, wild-eyed, now looking at each other as though whispering and plotting.

And from their gaping mouths, into the chaotic tumult, came the sound of hunting animals, baying.

CHAPTER 66

Once again Josyff found himself falling through a world of swooping gulls and twisting, dancing, golden lines. That it was no new experience did little to assuage his terror, still less did the fact that the sunlit blueness surrounding him was riven with black, fire-tinted clouds—some looming far above him in massive thunderheads, streaked with baleful lightning, others pulsing and billowing with an unseen energy as though rising from a great conflagration.

It found immediate voice.

"Amrassian!"

The blueness and all about him seemed to shiver briefly, but whatever he had expected from this cry, it was not what he heard. Faint and distant came the chilling reply.

"God (hope? chance? fortune?) speed and guide you, Measurer. Seek the Way. It is there—in your strangeness." There was terrible doubt—guilt?—in the fading voice. *"Forgive us, you... you... are... our... only..."*

And, as though severed by a sharp blade, it was gone. In its place were the mingled cries of the gulls and Josyff's own rising roar as terror became rage at the implications of Amrassian's words.

Wherever he was, and whatever part Amrassian had played in bringing him here, he had been abandoned. Though no logic of events told him this, he knew it for a certainty.

Was he simply expendable? Was his translation to this place necessary for Amrassian's end—perhaps to deprive the Diirredyn of access to his peculiar skills—whatever they were. Or had Amrassian sent him here in a last desperate effort to seek an answer to the Diirredyn's manic intentions?

It felt more like the latter. The great skyscape he was tumbling through was no limbo, no quiet place of neglect and abandonment—it was surely a reflection of a great conflict somewhere.

Either way, he was alone, an innocent bystander dragged unasked into all this. A hapless pawn? Or worse, more than a pawn—a piece of unknown power capable of being used by both opponents, blundering about in a game whose rules he did not know, and for ends far beyond his understanding. And yet a piece whose actions might be pivotal.

And on whose behalf *was* he fighting?

The Diirredyn will destroy everything, Amrassian had told him, and he had no reason to doubt that, even though such an action defied all reason.

Amrassian had always seemed... human... humane even, troubled by doubts and fears. The Diirredyn, by contrast, from his limited contact with them, seemed to be terrifyingly insane—a nightmare come true.

All of which told him little. His instinct was to help the First Comers but he did not even know how to help himself, which was his immediate concern. Indeed, he did not even know where he was! Was he hurtling towards the ground and a violent death? He noted that the question brought no clutching fear to his insides, which in itself must be telling him something. He had worked on tall buildings and while he had no morbid fear of heights he had respect for them, not to mention two vivid memories of carelessness that had brought him sharply to the then present with his heart racing. As it always did, his grip tightened as he recalled them.

Then he turned his face into the buffeting wind. There was nothing but blueness ahead of him. Whatever danger was here, it was not a crushing collision with the ground.

He sensed his mind about to drift off into a vast bifurcating tangle of probabilities, but a pain in his hands drew his attention back. Looking at them he saw they were still tightly clenched, driving his nails into his palms. He opened them, flexed them and held them up to the cooling wind.

This place is some fabrication of my own, he reminded himself, with an effort. Compounded from the contents of my... strangeness—that place where Amrassian dared not go. Clouds, birds, dancing golden lines— they're shadows on the wall, shaped by my imagination.

What is *any* reality except what my mind—my brain—makes of it?

The question came from nowhere and he shied away from it as though stung, some deeper knowledge telling him immediately that it was profoundly dangerous to him now. Whatever the true reality behind it, this vast display around him was all his mind could conjure out of it. Remember how you just saw the Keep? he thought. Humans cannot see or think like that—but you did.

Briefly, hesitant questions about his own sanity began to re-emerge, twitching nervously at the edges of his thoughts, but they were swept away by his increasing sense of urgency. Whatever the nature of this reality and whatever his mental state, there was a danger here sufficiently "real" to kill him and he had to deal with it!

Think about what you're doing—focus. Accept all this at its face value. It's just another problem to be solved. Except this time, if Amrassian's to be believed, you're in the place where they're normally solved. It was a conclusion he found neither helpful nor reassuring, but...

"It's all I've got!" he shouted into the blue sky.

His voice rolled away from him, echoing and re-echoing. The birds about him scattered as though at an alarm call, and the clouds themselves seemed to tremble as the words reached them.

Josyff noted this effect and, clutching at the immediately obvious, closed his eyes and willed himself to stop falling. He was not surprised however, when nothing happened. The easy way was always worth a try, but problems that easily solved don't come to this place.

As he opened his eyes and dismissed this whimsy, he noticed that he was now falling towards a layer of cloud. He felt a frisson of alarm as he could not recall having seen it before, but it stretched as far as he could see in every direction. He had scarcely registered it however, when he was falling through it. A damp, penetrating cold enfolded him and he became aware of the faint smell of something burning—something unpleasant.

Then he was through it, though now he was falling through a drizzling rain. The strange golden lines were still waving and dancing about him, seemingly brighter in the gloomier light, but the birds had gone.

Probably prefer the finer weather.

The incongruity and irrelevance of the thought made him smile, though his amusement faded rapidly as he saw below him an unusual patterning—a vaguely familiar and ominous patterning.

The creator of countless plans and maps, it did not take him long to identify it.

It was the ground! Different in many ways from the lined simplicity and clarity of a map, but unmistakable nevertheless. He took it in at a glance—fields, rivers, forests, snow-capped mountains.

The tentative complacency he had been sustaining since his translation to this place was replaced instantly by terror and panic. Whingeing plaints about the injustice of what was happening, flimsy assurances telling him that he was protected and privileged in some way, that this was his place and he could think his way out of it, disappeared under the primeval scream that rose to take possession of him. Eyes closed, he kicked and flailed and tumbled, all semblance of civilized man gone. Then, momentarily, he was falling through the interior of the bedroom clock again, bells and rattling chains all about him. Something brushed against his hands and, driven by instinct, he snatched at it. As he did, his eyes snapped open. Despite the rainy gloom, everything seemed to be almost unbearably bright. Brightest of all was the golden line immediately in front of him. He could not tell how far away it was, still less what it was, but he could feel his hands closing about something. Again, by instinct, he drew his hands tight to his chest.

The golden line came with them, broadening until it filled his entire vision.

Then he was not falling...

Esyal froze at the sound, half expecting to see the wavering carvings take life and emerge from the walls in full cry. The response was visceral, the sound speaking directly to some ancient part of her, but it did not fare long against the almost equally ancient fighting anger she had built up.

"Stay where you are!" she bellowed at the three men beside her, setting her own voice in direct challenge to that of the enemy.

"You said it—where would we go?" It was Qualto, affecting a defiance that his foot shuffling indicated he did not feel.

Esyal gave him an appreciative nod then glanced at the door to the room where Josyff was sitting. It was thick and robust. But what would that mean to creatures who seemed to be able to twist and bend stone walls?

It was an unanswerable question. She looked down at the weapons she was still holding. They glittered in the wavering light of the Hall. Then, each in turn, she looked along their edges. Qualto's influence showed itself. Very sharp. The finest of lines.

Unsettling but defiant images came to her. Length without width, she thought. Bend and twist what you like, you won't avoid the danger these hold for you. No matter how alien your world, these will be the same in all parts of it. If you're alive as we are, these will cut you, separate you, kill you—make you no more.

She looked at her companions. Badr still had the machete in its sheath hanging from his belt, and Nyk and Qualto had the knives stuck in their belts that she had thrust upon them earlier. There was no sense of incongruity now save that they were a sorry little group to be pitched against what appeared to be such overwhelming odds.

But they weren't overwhelming yet, were they? she reminded herself forcefully. A lot of noise, a lot of disorientating movement, but no threat. Nothing even like the two New Order 'soldiers' she had dealt with so easily, and certainly nothing like the army she had found herself in the middle of with Josyff. Just Adroyan—somehow the focus of all this disturbance—the Diirredyn's key to this place. Just Adroyan—heart of the New Order—its First Member—her enemy then and her enemy now—everyone's enemy now.

"And delivered to me," she muttered.

She reiterated her earlier instruction. "Guard the Measurer—the surveyor. Anything comes that's not me..." She paused. "Or Henk... kill it."

Then she turned and walked towards the motionless figure of Adroyan.

CHAPTER 67

The sudden halt to his falling made Josyff stagger and automatically he reached out to steady himself. At the same time his eyes jerked open despite a faltering concern about the dazzling brightness of the golden light that had enfolded him. It was gone however, replaced by...

By what? The light was not bright but it took his eyes a moment to focus...

He was in a passageway, his hand resting on the wall.

Disorientated by the abrupt change, he turned and leaned his full weight against the wall, mentally enjoining himself to calm down. He was trembling and his heart was pounding so violently that it was some time before it slowed sufficiently for him to become unconcerned about it. Then he was examining this new mystery that Amrassian had brought him to.

If it was Amrassian...

He decided gradually that it probably wasn't. There was a peculiarly empty place in him where, he was beginning to realize, Amrassian had been. And too, there were his last words, "...*seek the Way... forgive us...*"

They were parting words.

As for 'forgive us...'

He was on his own. Cast adrift in this place. A world of his own making, or a world made by others from the unknowable recesses of his mind—his strangeness?

It did not matter. Whatever it was—wherever it was—he knew, by the very nature of the place, that he had no direct and conscious control over it.

And no way of returning to the Keep.

He did not dwell on that. It would serve no useful purpose save to disturb him further, he knew. He must focus on the here and now to survive, take these events one step at a time, however bizarre. And slowly, as he continued to adjust to his new circumstances—certainly less fantastical than falling through a bird-strewn sky—more prosaic, though no less alarming thoughts began to come to him. How was he going to find food here—or water? Might he die of starvation, or worse, thirst?

Not in my own place, surely, came the semblance of a reply, though it was rooted more in hope than anything truly convincing.

Then these concerns were ousted by others. Was the enemy in this place too, cast perhaps in human form like the two ostensible soldiers that Esyal had... killed... made no more? His hand groped around in his pocket until it found the knife that Qualto had given him. Two or three times he opened it a little way then closed it. It felt very reassuring. Thinking about what it meant as a weapon he remembered vividly how Esyal had used her knife—fast, direct, without hesitation—without a *flicker* of hesitation—it was more frightening now than it had been then. He understood the tactical logic of this response—in combat, ancient survival mechanisms ruled, coupled with chaos and, once committed, the least faltering might mean death.

Whether he could do such a thing himself—assess a situation and key himself to such a massive and awful response—he did not know, but he strongly doubted it. He wondered briefly how Esyal had found it in herself to do what she had done. Was it one of the things that Amrassian had given her, or had he simply released something that was already there? Or perhaps it was nothing to do with Amrassian; perhaps it was a trait born in her and honed by the time she had spent fighting the New Order, a trait that made Amrassian call her Warrior.

And you, Measurer, what is your trait, clutching your knife for comfort like a child clutches a toy, and lounging against a wall like a beggar?

He responded to his own barb by standing up and looking round at his new surroundings.

His solution to the closing error, that bringing together of complex shapes into a unified, albeit apparently impossible whole, was still with him—and with him triumphantly. He smiled. That's *my* trait, he thought—persistence and an aptitude for manipulating shapes in his mind, though what conceivable relevance it had to this conflict he had been drawn into he could not imagine.

Nor will I find out, just standing here, he concluded ruefully.

He turned his attention to a more careful scrutiny of the passageway.

In size and shape it reminded him of the Keep, but it was very different. It was brighter, for one thing. There was no gloom in the tapering distance where the lights had not lit. Indeed, he noted, with some surprise, there were no lights.

How the devil is it lit, then?

He was tempted to ferret around in search of an answer to this but his more urgent preoccupations stopped him. It did not matter how the place was lit, for pity's sake! It was beyond the world he belonged to, something formed from his own imagination and knowledge. Who could say what physical laws applied here, if any? He knew he was not dreaming, but this place would doubtless have dreamlike qualities.

He looked one way then the next. The passage curved slightly in both directions, eventually disappearing from view and giving him no indication of which might be the best way to go. So he set off.

He opted to stroll rather than to stride out—vaguely concerned that he was trespassing in some way and that heavy footfalls might draw attention. Besides, where was he going in any hurry? And too, he wanted to get the feel of this place.

As he walked, old habits reasserted themselves and abandoning his grip on the knife he rooted around in his pockets to retrieve a piece of chalk. Not that he had encountered any branch passages or doorways yet, but still...

Idly he made to draw a line on the wall. It did not take very well, prompting him to run his hand over the surface. Despite appearing to have a rough texture, it was very smooth—glassy almost. And—he leaned forward to examine it more closely—it seemed to be faintly translucent. *That* was where the light was coming from, or at least finding its way into the passage. Precisely *where* it was coming from was another matter. He knelt down to find that the floor was similarly constructed.

"Move on," he muttered to himself, ignoring the further questions that this discovery released. He stood up and continued walking.

After some time, just as the monotony of the passage was beginning to impinge on him, he found himself in a large hall. He came on it with unexpected suddenness, particularly as the walls and ceiling of the passage flared out into it rather than forming a clear-cut doorway.

Drifting off, not paying attention, he decided as he stopped and looked across the open space. Its perspective seemed peculiar though he could not see why immediately. And he thought he could detect the waving golden lines that he had seen as he had been falling, though they were very elusive, vanishing when he looked straight at them. He rubbed his eyes but it made no difference.

It was grasping one of those—or apparently grasping one—that had brought him here, he recalled.

Quickly he reached out sideways towards where he thought he saw one at the edge of his vision. But, closing his hand, there was nothing there—nothing to see—nothing to feel...

He completed his recollection. It was grasping one of those *in a moment of abject terror* that had brought him here!

Which meant...?

The question made him feel very uneasy and he let it go and returned to his study of the hall.

Several passages opened into it. Some, like the one he had just come along, opened gradually, while others formed conventional clear-edged intersections—some archways, some doorways. There were no windows.

His eyes drifted upwards and he gave a soft exclamation of surprise. The walls gradually tapered together to form a single steep-sided dome high above him. Again though, something about the perspective was unsettling, giving him the impression that if he reached up, he could touch the crown itself. Tentatively, his hand moved as if to test this, but he let it fall back awkwardly.

Turning, he looked back at the entrance he had just come through. There were others identical to it and he was about to attempt another chalk mark to identify it when the pointlessness of what he was intending dawned on him.

"You'll be wanting to get back to where, precisely?" he asked himself, not without some humour. "It's not as if you know where you are, is it?"

He dropped the chalk back into his pocket and began walking round the edge of the hall. The first entrance he came to had a door. Cautiously he turned the handle and pushed. It opened silently, but revealed only another passage, as did the next and the next. The one after that, however, opened on to a landing in a stair well. Leaning forward, but still with his hand on the door, the only door on the landing, he listened intently. There was only silence. Not even that low susurration that often echoes softly through large buildings. A plain metal handrail protected the edge of the landing and, checking that the door had no tendency to close on its own, he stepped across to it.

It was smooth and cold to the touch, all too real, although, as with the stonework of the walls, he was uncertain whether this was a reassurance or not.

He leaned forward and peered over the handrail and his grip tightened immediately. The stairs tapered giddyingly down into the depths, a square spiral shrinking and shrinking until it was just a dark point.

He found he was holding his breath as well as the handrail and it took him some effort to release both.

This wasn't possible! No building could be so high!

Hesitantly he leaned back and forced himself to look upwards.

The sight was the same.

"What in God's name *is* this place?" he whispered.

He stood for a moment, peculiarly numb. Then, without consciously making the decision, he was walking up the stairs.

The well was not big and the flights of stairs were quite short—nine steps, he counted—and after seven flights he was on another landing, his legs aching. Like the one he had left, it had a single doorway. Looking down the well he could not quite see the door to the hall but he knew it was in the same position.

He frowned. This made no sense. He had not come up very far—certainly nothing like the height of the hall. This door would open out partway up the wall! Could it be some kind of a trap such as might be found in an old castle, designed to pitch invaders headlong on to the floor of the hall? It seemed improbable, even incongruous. But the door was where it was, that couldn't be denied. And he had seen no high openings when he had been in the hall.

He abandoned any further speculation in favour of simple action. Leaning back slightly in anticipation of the appearance of a dangerous drop, he turned the handle and gently pushed the door.

It opened smoothly and silently.

To reveal... the hall?

Holding on to the door he hesitantly swung one leg forward and tapped the floor with his foot, half fearing that he was the victim of an optical illusion, some distortion in perspective that was making the floor seem higher than it was. But it was solid. Still cautious, and testing his footfalls, he stepped through the door and gazed around.

This wasn't possible. There had been something strange about the perspective of the hall below, but not *this* strange! He edged back through the door then ran down the seven flights to the landing he had started from. The door was still open and, entering the hall, he turned to examine the wall where the other door should have been. There was no sign of it.

He found himself almost willing one, childlike, to appear, but then he reminded himself again that this was not a world like his own. Be it one of his making, or something drawn from him by Amrassian, or both, or even neither, but a world in its own right that circumstances had allowed him to enter, what he had to do now was survive in it, and then escape from it— get back to *his* world—the real world?

Focus, he instructed himself. Focus—think—learn.

And Amrassian's need? Perhaps *everyone's* need—the need to prevent the Diirredyn prosecuting their war through the Keep, destroying Esyal and the others? Having not the least measure of how to achieve this he could do nothing—save flounder.

I'm a loose cannon, he thought, ruefully. That was what Amrassian had done with him—released him as an unknown, unknowing, weapon into his damned war.

The thought became a revelation and Josyff found himself drawing deep, cold breaths.

Had it been an act of faith or one of desperation?

Was there a difference?

It was irrelevant. He was where he was—without knowledge of any kind for guidance. Given that, it did not matter what he did.

Anger suddenly welled up inside him, black and manic, displacing all other emotions and concerns. He understood Esyal's murderous actions now—he could and would do whatever he had to, to survive. With his passing from his own world so had passed all restraint from him.

His hand closed about Qualto's knife and he took it out of his pocket and eased the blade open.

It glinted in the diffuse but bright lighting as he stared at the distorted reflections of the hall in it.

And as he looked at the image of one of the open archways, something moved.

CHAPTER 68

"Kill it?" exclaimed Badr after the retreating figure of Esyal.

Esyal turned and shouted the answer to a different question above the howling din coming from the swaying carvings.

"None of us want to be here, Badr, but we are, and we've no choices left." She motioned over her shoulder towards Adroyan. "That's an enemy that'll kill us all without a thought, and he..." The hand came back over the shoulder and pointed the knife in it towards Josyff's inert form. "Is important. Guard him as if your lives depend on him—because they probably do. And, yes, if anything comes that's not me or Henk—kill the damn thing—it won't be human."

"I... I can't kill anything."

"Then learn or die."

And Esyal was striding out towards Adroyan again.

Badr bared his teeth and clenched his fists in frustration but avoided the gaze of his companions.

Qualto shuddered conspicuously and cast an uneasy glance at Nyk. He fumbled with the knife in his belt.

"We can't let her do this alone," he said unenthusiastically.

Nyk looked torn, glancing unhappily between Esyal and Josyff. "I'm not sure we'd be any help," he said, his voice unsteady. "Whatever's happened to her, she's not the bewildered thing we found in that cave. She's some part of all this—whatever the hell it is." His look encompassed the entire Hall. "I think... I think we should do what she says—look after the surveyor here." He made a visible effort to become more practical. "Badr, what do you think?"

He had to call his name again before Badr jerked out of his dark reverie, and then he had to repeat the question.

Badr squinted after Esyal as if considering renewing their last exchange. But though she was still striding out she appeared scarcely to have moved—she seemed to be both ploughing through, and part of, the distortion now clearly centred about the motionless figure of Adroyan. The sight unsettled him in ways he did not begin to understand, primitive ways, and he nodded to Nyk.

"Yes. You're right. Let's get him away from here. Let's all get away from here."

The prospect galvanized the three men and for a little while there was a flurry of purposeful confusion as they hoisted Josyff's unconscious and unhelpful form from its seat in front of the plotter. Eventually he was suspended between Nyk and Badr, his arms draped about their shoulders and his feet dragging on the floor as they made their way across the Great Hall. Qualto brought up an awkward rearguard.

"Where shall we go?" Badr asked.

"The main door," Nyk replied, after a moment's thought. "Henk's got a few supplies stacked there and we can get out quickly if we have to."

"It's winter out there, you know," Badr said.

"And it's madness in here—take your pick," Nyk retorted sharply. "We can shelter in the Gatehouse if we have to, and... and maybe the Gate's open now." He stopped and looked at Badr squarely. "I don't know—but we can't stay here, can we?"

"You're right. I'm sorry," Badr said, adjusting Josyff's inert body across his shoulders. They set off again.

As they moved from the Great Hall into a passage, the baying and roaring changed character, becoming shriller and more menacing. They all glanced back as though this signalled some kind of pursuit but nothing different could be seen. The end of the Hall was still a swimming region of distortion and Esyal was still moving forward without seemingly making progress.

If they had been hoping that leaving the Great Hall would take them away from the noise, they were disappointed, for it echoed off the walls and the floor and the arched stone ceiling as though the passage were a great organ pipe. The sound became all-pervasive and without direction. All three bowed their heads as though battling against a bitter wind.

While her intent was focused completely on Adroyan, Esyal's eyes were everywhere as she strode forward—searching for any telltale break in the pattern of movement about her that might indicate the emergence of an attack.

She was aware that she had passed into that part of the Hall that was distorting, although she could not have identified exactly where it began. And immediately where she was, where she trod, all was solid and still.

Adroyan, his arms still extended, as if in ecstatic worship, was some way in front of her, seemingly defenceless.

Part of her was debating how she would kill this man. A smaller part was debating *could* she kill him? She had had no difficulty striking down the shadowy enemies that had circled her and Josyff on the dark battlefield they had both been translated to, nor any in attacking the two creatures that had appeared as New Order soldiers. But whatever else Adroyan might be, he was still human: he had carried her through the snow, perhaps even saved her life by so doing; they had eaten and talked together, albeit in mutual distrust and enmity. There was something repellent about the idea of coldly destroying him, not least as he appeared to be quite oblivious to her approach.

Her harder nature prevailed. He is the cause of all this—it is his power that sustained the New Order and corroded your country's ancient ways to hold it in subtle, cringing thrall—turned you from young woman to... to what? She hefted the machete unconsciously by way of reply, but let the question hang. All this was bad enough in its own right, but now it seemed it was simply to further some greater ambition, some perverse and obscene ambition. He was an abomination. He *had* to be destroyed. And no one else could do it except her. Whatever destiny, whatever interminable chain of cause and effect had brought her here, it was what it was, and beyond any changing. Might as well flee screaming in terror as show him the merest hint of pity.

...And it won't be as easy as you think...

This reminder came like iced water in her face and ended all debate.

A salutary warning.

Focus, she reminded herself grimly. This was a dangerous place and all that mattered was the destruction of her enemy. Any thoughts or actions not dedicated totally to this would be fatal to her—and probably to Josyff and the others—and, if Amrassian was to be believed, would have consequences far beyond the Keep. And the warning *was* apt—despite the appearance of helplessness, it was beyond belief that Adroyan would be truly defenceless in this place.

She shook her head slightly but briskly to clear the last remnants of doubt and debate—she needed to be here, now.

It was as she pressed on that it came to her she had been walking towards Adroyan for longer than it should have taken her to traverse half the length of the Hall. She paused and cursed herself for dreaming, all senses now sharp and alert. She looked at Adroyan intently for a moment, and then cautiously risked a couple of swift backward glances.

As she had half expected, what she saw was distorted and wavering, but she took in Nyk and Badr carrying Josyff out of the Hall, with Qualto walking behind them, his eyes everywhere.

Good, she thought, with an unexpected sense of relief—good allies—automatically doing what she would have told them to. Get away from here—make for the main door—better the winter snows than being drawn into what was happening here.

At the same time she noted that they were indeed a long way away—certainly further than the length of the Hall.

Her gaze returned quickly to Adroyan, taking in as it did the increasingly mobile carvings. Perhaps it was just an illusion but she fancied that they were torn between watching her and watching Josyff being removed from the Hall. It was an impression heightened by the noise all about her—a high pitched hint of desperation just tainting its otherwise triumphant, hate-filled fury.

"Howl while you can," she shouted into the din. "Your way to this place is about to die." But even as she shouted, the Hall fell still and quiet and her last words rang out almost incongruously.

For no reason that she could fathom she spun round and bellowed, "Nyk, Badr—run!" Then she was facing Adroyan again.

Something was different about him. It was almost as though he were both here and not here—as though part of him were moving in a different place. But it was something she sensed rather than saw.

More immediately, what she did see was him staring at her intently. His black eyes were mobile and disturbing, eerie windows into that very place beyond.

"Put down your weapons, child," he said. His voice was soft but all-pervading and, briefly, she was filled with a comforting vision of all this being over, a vision of a return to a life of peace and safety and normality—so much that she wanted, and so badly.

Like a dog obeying its master's call, her hands began to open of their own accord.

But even as the weapons began to slip from her, another part of her shrieked out a piercing inner cry of denial and warning. It mingled jaggedly with the jarring clatter of the weapons landing on the stone floor and brought her to a sharp and intense wakefulness. As her hands had opened unbidden to Adroyan's call, so her legs bent to her own inner call and she was scooping up the weapons almost before she realized she had dropped them.

"Put them down," Adroyan said again, his voice still alluring. "You have no need of them. Why would you wish to hurt me? I mean you no harm—I would have you as my ally. You have greatness within you. You are worthy of far better than the life of a skulking and ineffectual rebel. A rebel for a hopeless—indeed, a bad cause, at that. A new millennium is coming and you can join me in its creation. It will bring order and prosperity to our whole land..."

"And beyond," Esyal interjected as she rose slowly to her feet, the machete levelled at Adroyan.

"And beyond," he conceded, though his tone indicated that he was merely stating the obvious. "Far beyond. It will be..."

Abruptly Esyal banged the knife and machete together. The rasping note made Adroyan start and he seemed to shimmer, the only movement in the now still Hall.

"No! You're insane. It will *not* be," Esyal declaimed. "Your masters were stopped the last time they tried to come, and they'll be stopped now. And you're wasting your lies on me, First Member." She laid a scornful emphasis on the last two words. "I know *you* from your own deeds—your silent, slithering tyranny quietly choking the life out of people. And now I know the creatures you serve. Better than you, it seems. You swallow their lies as our people swallowed yours. There'll be no victory if they pass through this world. It'll destroy everything—including them—including *you*." Despite herself, a note almost of plaintiveness crept briefly into her voice. "Can you truly not see what they are like? Are you *so* blinded by your own miserable ambitions, your own mindless lust for power?"

Adroyan looked at her in silence for a long time, as though holding an inner debate.

"What is coming is coming, child," he said eventually. "And there is nothing you... or anyone... can do about it. I'll waste no further time with you—you have made your choice and the loss is yours, not ours. You are not needed. Stand aside."

The voice now was harsh, overtones of the voices of the Diirredyn edging it, but it still spoke directly to her body and it took her some effort to prevent her legs from obeying its instruction.

It helped that she immediately saw the command for what it was...

A weakness!

He could not do what he wanted while she stood in front of him—in remaining where she was she was opposing both his intention and his will. She gave no outward sign of this revelation but took a small step forward—not in petulant defiance but slowly, as a quiet demonstration of *her* unyielding intention. She would stand her ground.

"Take a weapon to no one unless you are prepared to kill them—and prepared to be killed," someone had once told her. She accepted the grim simplicity of the advice at a deep level now. She was very afraid, but it did not matter—it would strengthen her. Amongst other things, it told her she was still rational and in control.

She kept moving slightly both to put the trembling that was pervading her to some use and to prevent it from showing. Adroyan was bigger than her and undoubtedly far stronger, and it would be a mistake to assume he could not move quickly. But he was apparently unarmed, and she had two keen-edged weapons which could do great harm very quickly while she was beyond his reach.

Stay calm, breathe easy, she instructed herself, as she became aware of her heart pounding faster and faster. Make no plans, move as he moves...

"Stand aside," he said again, though this time his voice was like the hiss of a many-thonged whip and seemed to scar even the air it passed through. Esyal felt the response in her limbs again but now it was easily mastered.

She was about to reply when he leapt forward.

CHAPTER 69

The movement in the midst of such silent stillness made Josyff jump and, uncertain which opening he had been looking at in the reflection in the knife blade, he spun almost completely round as he scanned the hall. But there was nothing there. Whatever he had seen, there was no sign of it now—just a cluster of the waving golden lines trembling uncertainly. They were there long enough this time for him to be sure they were no illusion, but not long enough for him to study them.

Clutching at one of them had brought him to this place—saved his life, he reminded himself, with some gratitude—but had perhaps someone else come here in the same way?

Or something...

And if so, where was it?

It would have to have been demonically fast to flee the hall in the time it took him to turn around, and he had heard no racing footsteps, as surely he must have done in this silence. He blinked deliberately as though that might retrospectively make clear what he had seen.

His senses heightened by alarm, he became more aware of the golden lines drifting through the place. Though they still avoided direct inspection, he sensed as much as saw that there was a... disjointing... effect about them, as though they were dividing? folding? separating? something.

What the devil were they? And were they here or in his mind?

Even as the questions formed, one drifted, as ever, into the edge of his sight. For fear that the least movement might cause it to vanish like startled prey, he held his breath and kept his eyes firmly forward while concentrating on his peripheral vision. The line wavered gracefully. Very slowly he raised his eyes in the hope that he might see how high it reached. Then, equally slowly, he risked craning his head back.

Would these things continue upwards to converge in the high dome of this place or would they just sway like so many tall grasses? Either way, he reflected, perspective alone should bring more of them within his field of view and perhaps give him an opportunity to discreetly examine them.

Then a conspicuous movement caught his eye, breaking his carefully balanced concentration, and the line vanished from both his sight and his thoughts.

The movement came from some way above him—a shimmering danced there. It was not unlike the air above a blazing fire, except that it was quite localized and had no apparent cause. He could not judge either its height or size and he was briefly disorientated, instinctively taking a cautious step backwards. This brought him neither information nor reassurance however. The disturbance, though transparent, flickered with an unsettling, even unhealthy, light, and shifted uneasily from side to side as though it were searching for something. Further, those parts of the hall that Josyff could see through it were subtly changed—almost as if they belonged to a different building—a darker, more ill-used one, with erratic shadows flitting to and fro.

He felt an almost overwhelming urge to flee. Yet at the same time a sterner part of him determined to stand firm. Whether this thing was hostile, friendly, or just a passing phenomenon, it might hold answers. Besides, if it was dangerous, running away might well draw it after him.

And where could you run to anyway in this bizarre place? he concluded.

"What are you?" he called out. "Where've you come from?"

His voice echoed in a way that seemed at odds with the shape of the hall—almost as though the walls were testing his words.

The disturbance drifted downwards. Josyff watched it warily, then began slowly circling about it, at the same time casting about for something that might serve as a weapon he could use without coming within arm's reach of this thing.

There was nothing. Reaching into his pockets he retrieved a couple of coins. Their solid link to his old familiar world felt peculiar—they were so irrelevant now, utterly valueless—save perhaps as missiles. He jangled them idly for a moment, debating whether to throw one into the apparition to see what happened, but it felt like a childishly ineffective gesture. Then, as if prompted by the worthlessness of the money, a driving reckless-ness suddenly took possession of him and, dropping the coins back into his pocket, he strode forward and walked directly towards the disturbance. As he reached it, it changed, becoming cloudy and turbulent. A hesitation shook him but he was too close and walking too quickly to stop and he was abruptly surrounded by a stormy greyness. He had little time for alarm however, for just as he had passed quickly through the clouds when he had been falling, now he passed quickly through this. Yet though he had taken perhaps only two paces, when he emerged he had a powerful memory of having travelled down a long road, lined on either side by a silent, watch-ing crowd, consisting of likenesses of himself. Each stood whole and solid yet impossibly close to his neighbour as though wafer thin, and behind them stood line upon echoing line of like images retreating into an end-less distance. A flurrying confusion of waving golden lines had ended this vision and Josyff found himself standing on an uneven rocky surface, a cold wind tugging at him.

He pulled his jacket about him automatically and, blinking, gazed around at this new place without taking anything in. It was not that it was brighter than the hall he had just left, but that it was very different. It had a yellowish, unwholesome tint to it that made him grimace with distaste.

It took some effort, but he resolved not to be bewildered by this further, unaccountable change. He had been cast adrift into his own psyche, or some creation from his psyche. How it had happened would be beyond him, and the reason for it would probably neither enlighten nor encourage him. He half-closed his eyes in concentration. Above all he must focus on surviving in these strange places and at the same time discover what he was supposed to do here. Briefly, fretful thoughts troubled him about how he was going to get back to the Keep, but even as he was dismissing them, something told him that the Keep was all about him, that he had not left it.

All I have to do is truly see that, he thought, not without some dark amusement.

He opened his eyes fully to study this new landscape. He was standing on a rocky prominence, looking out over valleys and mountains. Like the hall which he had just left, there were hints of the golden lines waving through it, and a subtle unease about its perspective which he could not identify. This was less concerning however, than the sense of menace that seemed to pervade everywhere. Dark and jagged mountains hunched over and about him, and narrow steep-sided valleys wove reluctantly between them. Immediately below him an angry-looking river foamed along one valley, twisting and turning, its noise mingling with the wind to surround him with a faint, echoing susurration.

Thoughts of his personal survival returned to him, lost and alone as he was in this bleak and precipitous terrain, but he did not dwell on them. He turned to look up the mountain on which he was standing. Rising from the summit, like a watching sentry, was a building. It took him a moment to recover from a brief inclination to hide, then he made himself study the building. It reminded him in some ways of the Keep, or how the Keep might have had it been fashioned by a more malevolent mind. For where the Keep seemed to grow naturally from its surroundings, this was not unlike a mailed fist, clenched and menacing, that had punched its way through the top of the mountain, skirted as it was by a fringe of tumbled and broken rocks. Sharp towers stood stark against the sallow sky like knuckle spikes. He wondered whether it housed the equivalents of Nyk and Henk and Quattro, and what kind of reception he might expect from them if it did.

He did not relish the prospect of discovering the answer to this, but the logic of his position left him no alternative. He could stay where he was and do nothing, or he could wander off aimlessly into this dire and dangerous landscape. The building it would have to be. He gave it a sour glance then set off towards it.

He had not gone far when he came across a semblance of a path. The light threw awkward shadows making him particularly cautious about where he put his feet, but he made steady, if uncomfortable, progress. Occasionally the path took the building from his sight but eventually, again, as with the Keep, he was on a final steep ascent. Unlike the Keep, there was no chasm to serve as a moat and the gates of the arched entrance stood open. He paused as he reached it, both to catch his breath and to examine the outside of the place more closely.

It exuded a massive solidity—like something from another age, even a mythical age, he reflected.

He looked around. There was nothing but mountains in every direction and professional habits tempted him to conjecture how such a place might have been built, until he reminded himself that, despite its appearance, its very reality was questionable.

Cautiously he walked through the deep gateway. It led him to a paved courtyard. Like the hall he had just left, it was silent and still—the walls keeping out the wind and even the sound of the river below. And it had a subtle aura of neglect, as though nothing had happened here for a very long time.

Several doors opened on to the courtyard, but he went to the largest, directly in front of the main gate. Heavy iron studs dotted it, all deeply rusted, as was the large handle. Nevertheless, he took hold of it and pulled. Somewhat to his surprise, the door yielded, albeit grudgingly and with a slow squeal of disapproval from its hinges.

If there *is* a Nyk here, he's markedly less conscientious than the one I know, he thought wryly, as he stepped inside. Lights came on, as they did in the Keep, though more slowly and unsteadily, and with some conspicuously noisy cluckings and buzzings.

He found himself in a large, semi-circular foyer served by four doors, heavy with bolt heads and iron bands, and three passageways. Its heavy undecorated stonework was both oppressive and sinister, and there was a grittiness under his feet that served to heighten the feeling of disuse and neglect about the place.

"Is there anyone here?" he shouted.

The returning silence carried no surprise for him.

He tried each of the doors in turn. They were all unlocked but they were all stiff and reluctant. The rooms they opened into were cheerless and sparsely furnished and gave no indication of what they had been used for with the exception of one which was a work room or store of some kind. Cupboards, shelves and well-used benches lined the walls, all cluttered with tools, randomly heaped boxes of all sizes and conditions, and a wide variety of bottles and glass jars filled with an even wider variety of liquids and bits and pieces of hardware. Spread through these was a range of eccentrically-shaped paper parcels and several bundles of dog-eared documents tied with coarse string. Various artefacts hung from hooks in the ceiling and in the few spaces between the benches, piles of timber, masonry and other building materials mouldered. There was no sense of order about the place, though doubtless someone at some time had 'known where everything was', and the whole was covered in dust. The sight brought Nyk to mind again—not the disorder, but the apparent reluctance to part with anything that 'might come in handy'.

Josyff surveyed the scene for a moment, then one of the lights buzzed and clucked noisily, startling him. It prompted a search. Nose wrinkled against the dust he was stirring up, Josyff began moving items to see if he could find a light of any kind. He had never grown fully used to the apparently autonomous lighting in the Keep, especially in its long straight corridors where a moving darkness both followed behind and retreated ahead, but at least it had been consistent and reliable. The lighting here, by contrast, felt distinctly frailer and he had no desire to find himself plunged into pitch darkness due to ancient neglect.

Peering into a cardboard box he came across a large ball of fine twine. Blowing the dust from it, he studied it thoughtfully. He could fasten this to the main door and play it out as he explored the building.

"You're losing your nerve and your wits," he said, interrupting his own thoughts. Why would he want to return to the main door? Nothing that he could see tied him to where he had come from, the Keep. There was no marked way back.

"You're lost wherever you are in this place—any of these places," he said out loud.

You have to let go.

A more mundane, if somewhat acid, reproach concluded his thinking. And since when do you need a piece of string to find your way around a building, surveyor?

He dropped the string back into the box.

A light of some kind, however, was a different matter—no amount of experience could help him see in the dark. He started on a systematic search of the room. The clear, if small purpose, made him feel more relaxed as he worked methodically through the cupboards, even though he knew that it was merely a substitute for the greater purpose of discovering what he was supposed to be doing here.

During the course of his search he came across a rusted machete. The sight of it reminded him of those being carried by Nyk and the others and it made him smile. Considering there appeared to be only a fairly small and orderly garden at the Keep and absolutely nothing approaching undergrowth for probably miles around both the Keep and, he assumed, this place, these things were remarkably ubiquitous!

He hefted it and made a few tentative swings. It had precious little edge but it felt good—it was heavy and well-balanced and certainly capable of doing a great deal of harm. It gave him an unexpected feeling of confidence and he used it to rattle gently through the dark interior of the deep cupboard he had found it in. He was rewarded by the warning clink of glass. Shading his eyes, he peered in. There was a lamp.

It was an old-fashioned thing and, like everything else here, it bore the scars of both usage and neglect. It was intact however. He shook it. It gave only a rusty rattle but he had already noted a large drum which had contributed a characteristic smell to the whole room. To some surprise on his part, the drum proved to be well over half full and with a functioning tap. A few moments later, the lamp too was full. Tongue protruding slightly he worked the striker. It felt a little creaky but after a couple of attempts the flame took and the lamp flared brightly. It was an oddly hopeful and cheering sight and for a little while he just stared at it.

Then, recollecting himself, he tucked the machete into his belt, took up the lamp and returned to the foyer. He was about to extinguish the lamp, but instead opted for turning the flame low. If indeed he were suddenly plunged into darkness he would simply have to turn it up rather than grope about for the striker.

Then he set off along one of the passageways.

CHAPTER 70

As Adroyan moved, countless fading images trailed behind him like a wake—as though time was overlapping itself—one moment unable to move freely to the next. An eerie sight, it distracted Esyal with almost fatal consequences for Adroyan was indeed armed. Older and wiser reflexes jerked Esyal back a step and tumbled her on to the floor. As she fell, she saw a brief bright arc of flashing steel pass over her, and both heard and felt the hiss of the air fleeing its lethal passage. The sensation vibrated through her and heightened her already intense focus into an unbearable sharpness. At once willed by her mind and yet ahead of it, she pivoted rapidly on her back to follow Adroyan's movement and both her legs straightened in a powerful kick to his knees. It did not connect fully but it delivered sufficient impact to prevent Adroyan pursuing any further attack and it enabled her to roll rapidly away from him. She snatched up her dropped knife as she used the momentum of her roll to bring herself to her feet. The machete she had somehow retained.

Teeth bared, she took in the totality of Adroyan. He was staggering slightly as he regained his balance, after-images lingering about his every movement. A tension in him and a slight leaning to one side told her that he was making a deliberate effort not to massage the knee she had struck.

I win that exchange then, she deduced. Better to end it with one single blow, but, failing that, each minor injury drained and weakened him and in so doing, strengthened her.

She saw also the weapon that had nearly killed her. It was a long knife like the one she had snatched up in the kitchen when the mysterious cry had interrupted her uneasy debate with Adroyan. She recalled the pains she had gone to subsequently to dispel any suspicions that this might have prompted. All irrelevant now. And was that so recent? It might have been another lifetime, things had changed so.

She did not dwell on the memory. Already Adroyan had recovered sufficiently for it to be too risky for her to simply charge in and finish him. Nevertheless, the sight of the improvised weapon told her that he had learned something from the incident in the kitchen. It told her something else as well.

Like the rest of us—having to make it up as you go along, she thought. Long, long, scheming and planning has brought you here, I imagine, but now, at the culmination, everything branches and branches—consequences vanish in a cloud of confusion—chaos is here—great matters will turn on the least thing. There was a bitter but heartening relish in the thought, then...

Keep moving, she reminded herself harshly in case this revelation became a digression. Keep moving. Keep attacking. On and on, without conscience or pity until you are safe.

She began walking towards him. There was a simple consideration—though Adroyan was bigger than her, the machete still gave her a longer reach. And she had her knife also.

She was briefly tempted to wave the machete menacingly in front of her but she resisted it. Do nothing that was not necessary—such pointless posturing would almost certainly tell him something. Better to let him learn what he needed to know when it was too late—when she was striking directly to her target. She straightened and continued forward, slowly, purposefully, taking in everything around her, but focused intently on where she was going to attack.

Adroyan seemingly met her gaze, but his black eyes were dead and told her nothing. Then he took two long strides backwards, turned, and ran towards the passage that Nyk and the others had taken. Esyal stopped at this sudden movement, then swore and ran after him. Almost immediately she found herself in the wake of the fading after-images that were marking his movement. They did not impinge on her in any way, though she could not stop herself from lifting her arm to sweep them away. As she did so she saw that similar images were trailing from her own body too. In spite of herself she stopped briefly to test this disturbing phenomenon, then a deeper urgency pushed her forward again.

What did he want Josyff for?

It didn't matter. It would be no good thing for any of them. He had to be stopped—destroyed.

Adroyan was running unexpectedly quickly and was already some way ahead of her as she reached the passage. He stopped momentarily at a junction, lifted his head back and turned it from side to side, like a hunting animal, then he was off again.

Nearing the junction, Esyal was set to follow him when a note of caution brought her to a frustrated halt. He could be lying in ambush for her. She flattened herself against the opposite wall then side-stepped quickly into the junction, knife and machete extended—just in time to see Adroyan turning at another junction some way ahead, swirling images following him. She grimaced—she would have to pause at every turning, and with each pause he would increase his lead.

"Stay where you are!" she bellowed, scarcely knowing why. Her voice echoed off the arched stone roof—a sound tinged, she thought, with the mocking screeching of the Diirredyn. She moved round the next junction as cautiously as she had the first but this time Adroyan was nowhere to be seen.

She let out an angry hiss then set off running again, this time faster. She would have to take a chance on his laying in wait for her and rely on her speed to at least lessen his advantage.

Besides, he had not chosen to confront her in the Hall...

Nevertheless she had to pause and turn in the middle of the next junction to look for him or to listen for any sounds of his flight. She was momentarily startled by the sight of the images that she, like Adroyan, appeared to be creating, surging towards and around her before vanishing.

What madness were these creatures loosing into this world?

She let the question go—for all practical purposes it was answered in her use of the word 'madness'.

The lights in the passages on either side were only just blinking into life, indicating that Adroyan had not gone that way.

She was running again.

She had little doubt that Adroyan would be following the way in which Nyk and the others had taken Josyff, but where *were* they taking him?

This passage went past the Common Room and the Kitchen and thence on to the main entrance, which heartened her. There would be risks outside but more hiding places.

Then, a memory of Qualto, unexpectedly tactical, testing her knife, floated into her mind.

He would direct them to the kitchen! Apart from the luring sense of security in the familiar, there was food, water, even fire there—not to mention plenty of impromptu weapons. As good a place as any to defend, and to make a stand if needed. Yes, it would be the kitchen.

One more junction—swift but cautious—then...

There he was, as she had guessed. Still with the long knife in his hand, Adroyan was standing at the door to the kitchen, facing it and swaying backwards and forwards. Shifting images danced after him, marking the serpentine path of his movement.

Though Esyal had been moving silently, Adroyan stopped and slowly turned to look at her. Briefly, an almost overwhelming fear threatened to master her, but again she forced herself to move forward.

She curled her lip and sneered both in defiance and in an attempt to draw him away from the kitchen.

"Your Glorious Destiny slipping away from you, First Member? Your Great Scheme foundering on a kitchen door and the wits of a cook, a handyman and a surveyor..." She hesitated mockingly. "And, of course, me?"

When Adroyan replied, his voice was shot through with the sound of the Diirredyn. It gave it a nerve-jangling quality.

"You could have been of value, child, but you chose otherwise. Now you are a mere irritation. What you do is of no concern to us but if you interfere further you will die."

Despite the quiet coldness of the words, there was also anger in his voice, something that Esyal found she had not expected. It was good in that it showed him to be unsettled and gave the lie to his airy protestations of easy and imminent victory—it could lead him into error. It was bad in that it would undoubtedly increase his resolution and make him more dangerous.

"I've not many choices then, have I?" she replied, still slowly moving forward against the almost tangible force of his will. "Do nothing and die, along with everyone else—and you, of course—as these creatures tear into this world. Or do something and be killed by you..." She paused. "Or not." Again she sneered. "What would you advise, First Member?" She stopped and raised a hand, palm forward, in a mock placating gesture. The knife, supported only by her thumb, glinted, as did her eyes. "No, no, don't answer—don't answer." She was taunting again. "Just for my curiosity, tell me instead what's gone wrong with your great plan—why are your masters scrabbling at the doors of our world like incontinent dogs instead of surging on to glory? Didn't the surveyor do his job right? Has he missed something out? Personally I thought he was quite conscientious—seemed to know what he was doing—and worked hard, didn't he? Or did Amrassian just... send him to sleep... before he was finished?"

This time, a black and awful anger showed on Adroyan's face. He made to take a step towards her but something seemed to be pulling him back to his station at the door.

"Still dancing to their tune, eh? Puppet master become puppet? I like the irony."

She laughed coldly, still taunting.

The images reflecting Adroyan's movements shuddered.

"Well, answer me," Esyal pressed. "I'm entitled to know what I'm about to die for, aren't I?"

She had come quite close to him now. It was a finely judged distance. Two paces he would have to make if he wanted to attack her. Enough perhaps to tempt him into rashness, enough for her to observe and strike.

"You are nothing," Adroyan replied, as though forcing the words out. "Less than nothing. Your time has passed, as you will, soon."

"Your constant refrain, First Member. But it's so much windy rhetoric, isn't it? If I am so insignificant, why did you think it necessary to sneak into Qualto's kitchen and pilfer a knife to protect yourself? And why do you run away instead of using it? I'll tell you why—because doubt is beginning to seep into your shrivelled soul. Let me deepen it for you." She leaned forward, eyes merciless and feral. "I don't know what I am. I've been changed—by the First Comers, I presume—there are things in my head—dark knowledge—that I've never learned, I'm sure. Now, though I never asked for it, I find I'm a made thing—like you, except that I'm aware of it. But you weren't warned about me, were you? You weren't warned of any opposition to your scheme. Whatever *you* might think of me, I strike fear into your masters." She paused briefly to watch the effects of her words. "Hasn't it occurred to you yet—as someone skilled in lies and treachery—that your masters are the same—that you are told only what they want you to know—that you are expendable—that your only worth to them is as a useful idiot?"

Even as she was voicing this last provocation, Esyal felt the attack coming.

CHAPTER 71

Henk was muttering to himself as he checked over the bundles he had stacked by the main door. Clothes, blankets, food, water, and various other items necessary for survival in the snow-filled mountains—they were survival caches. Together with a couple of tents, there were six in all, one for each of the Keep's occupants, except Adroyan. He being in some way at the dark heart of events, he could fend for himself. Henk did not pretend to understand what was happening or concern himself with what was to be done about it—that matters were becoming dangerous was all too obvious and so was the solution—flight. Let the others chase after the surveyor; *he* would make sure that *all* of them would stand a chance if—when—everything went bad.

What disturbed Henk most was the Keep itself. Though it had never bothered him particularly, it had always had for him a watching, waiting atmosphere, one that often chimed with something deep within himself, though he would not have expressed it in those terms. The changes in its further reaches that had been happening recently however, were a different matter—they *did* bother him. It felt as though the place was waking up, though he had not pressed this with Nyk and Qualto, anticipating blank-eyed looks or raised eyebrows, or perhaps worse. Shut up here for months on end, good, easy relations with each other superseded most other concerns. Even when the seemingly impossible had happened and new passages had appeared he had found it oddly difficult to raise the matter. It did not help that these passages had some degree of familiarity about them, as though they had been there all the time but he had never noticed them—the thought, unfurling, like a flower, used to come to him. In his kinder moments, he excused Nyk and Qualto's indifference, not to say, disbelief, with their being too engrossed in their daily routines to be bothered about mysterious events far off their beaten tracks, though he regretted now that he had not persisted in his efforts to make them realize that something deeply strange was happening.

He paused and reviewed this reproach and then exonerated himself. What could they have done, anyway?

Except leave sooner, of course.

He gave a shrug and a pained smile. It made his jaw ache. That was all water over the weir now. The arrival of these various strangers had acted like a stick poked into a beehive and the insanity now swarming through the place brutally dismissed all previous concerns.

He stepped back and cast a sergeant-majorly eye over the row of provisions. Everything that he could think of to keep them warm and well-nourished while trekking through the snow-filled mountains was there. It would be dangerous, necessarily, particularly if the weather turned really nasty, but staying here would be far more so, he was sure.

Of course, there was still one problem, as his rueful thought that they might have left earlier had reminded him.

He put on his coat, pulled it tight about him and opened the main door. A flurry of snowflakes flew in and a small drift that had been leaning on the door collapsed over his feet. He kicked the snow aside and stepped out, closing the door behind him.

Despite everything that was happening, the snow-covered courtyard and the falling snow dancing through the lights was a captivating sight and, for a moment, he just stared at it, cold air filling his lungs and emerging as frosted breath to be wafted into nothingness by the slight breeze.

The magic faded all too quickly however, as he forced himself to look across to the gateway. The Keep's lighting left him no opportunity for even the brief hope of confusion. The drawbridge was still closed.

Although it did not show in his stooped posture, he had to struggle with an urge to run raging across the courtyard and pound relentlessly on the implacable blank face of the drawbridge. A sudden sharp gust of wind whirled snowflakes in his face, making him step back. His momentary anger retreated at the same time. Before he indulged himself in mindless fury, he reminded himself caustically, he'd better check that the drawbridge was still being *held* shut!

As he walked across to the Gatehouse, stepping high through the deepening snow, he felt that there was something unusual about the courtyard, but didn't pause to search it out. Moments later he confirmed what he had suspected: the wheel controlling the drawbridge was as solid and immovable as ever. The drawbridge was still being held shut by some force—a massive force.

He allowed himself a brief growl of annoyance; then, his options closed, he became practical again. The Gatehouse was separate from the main body of the Keep. Maybe, just maybe, whatever was happening there might not extend to it. He was not sanguine about this slender speculation but better some hope than none. Also the drawbridge mechanism being here, they would know immediately if it was released.

It was where they should be. He would bring the supplies here.

He had made two trips across the courtyard before the strangeness he had sensed at the outset troubled him enough to make him stop and look around. Nothing seemed to be out of place, yet something was definitely wrong.

It was only when he looked up that he saw what was happening. The last time he had seen the Beacon, its beam had swept impossibly in a wide curve out into the mountain darkness. It had been a deeply unsettling sight. Now he could see, as the snowflakes jigged through it, that the curve of the beam was even greater. He closed his eyes and opened them again in the hope that perhaps it might be an optical illusion—something to do with the storm. But it was not. The curve of the beam was clearly visible, and it was the pale shadows that this distorted light was throwing into the court-yard that made it seem different.

Turn the damn thing off, came an abrupt and angry thought. This con-clusion was not derived from any chain of reasoning—it just seemed to be the right thing to do—perhaps wresting some small control from whoever was doing this.

"Yes," he muttered as he turned back to the door. "Yes."

It took him only a few minutes to move the remainder of the supplies and then, after another sour look at the curving, snow-filled light, he set off towards the narrow alley that would lead him to the Beacon.

For no reason that he could have explained, save that he felt a vague need for some kind of overview, Josyff chose to move upwards. He took the first flight of stairs he came to, making a chalk mark on the stone jamb—he half expected to find himself at the bottom again when he reached the top, as in the hall he had just been transported from. Although he tried not to ponder how such a thing could have happened, he sensed the question rumbling in the depths of his mind, mingling with the other unsettling insights that had given him the solution to the closing error. A doubt sprang from nowhere, had it been only a partial solution? He thrust that thought away *very* quickly.

Concentrate on where you are, he reprimanded himself. And who you are. With impossibility and insanity constantly baying at the horizons of everything that was happening, and fear pervading him to the core like a cloying miasma, his trust in himself and his grasp of immediate events were things he must protect at all costs. All other thoughts, even those of great value to him—his wife, his family, his job—could only hinder, probably endanger him here.

When he reached the first landing he examined the jamb. There was no mark. And indeed this floor, though having the same architecture as the one below, was different. He reflected for a moment, running through his mind his first view of the building. If he could take this place at face value, then—he looked around—*that* room should be against an external wall and should have a large window in it.

Which it did, set deep in the wall directly opposite him as he pushed open the stiff door. A quick glance through it showed him the courtyard and confirmed his assessment of where he was in the building. Beyond the courtyard wall, mountains disappeared into the jaundiced distance like a frozen, angry sea.

As he turned to leave the room, he glanced at the nondescript furniture. It all looked well-used. A couple of armchairs, a few wooden chairs around a plain wooden table, a chest of drawers—he opened one—it was empty, save for a few papers covered with doodles. He canted his head as he looked at one of them—the patterns were intricate and quite neatly drawn—intriguing. Whoever had made them had had a good hand—and quite an eye. He pushed it into his pocket without thinking and looked around the room again. There was a large clock—stopped, he noted. It reminded him of the one in his bedroom at the Keep.

How odd, he thought, that he should find a sense of reassurance in such a recent and not particularly pleasant memory, yet it felt almost as if he had known the bedroom clock with affection since his childhood.

Any familiar thread to cling to through all this, he knew he needed.

But the reminiscence prompted him to think again about this whole building, despite his best intentions. Its architecture was intimidating, both brutal and sinister, yet those rooms he had looked at so far were full of the banal remnants of ordinary human occupation. He recalled again watching Adroyan walking away from him—ordinary, unexceptional, all too human. Evil things should be more dramatic, more easily identified, more easily hated and destroyed. The humanity in them carried too many reminders of one's own failings. A different turning one day, a different aptitude, might you not ultimately have gone that way?

But I didn't, Josyff replied to himself with unexpected anger. There's always choice. He slammed the drawer shut and left the room.

He went up two more flights of stairs, on each floor encountering nothing unusual or even radically different. The building seemed to have none of the impossible perspectives that the previous one had had. He decided to examine this floor more closely. As he paused he became aware of a low and very soft background noise. It was the sound of an ordinary building, quietly responding to the outside world, another feature which made this place different from the hall he had left. But there were no other sounds— no distant hints of occupation. He was more relieved than concerned. Who could say what kind of people—creatures—he might find in this place?

He headed in the direction that he calculated would bring him to the far side of the building and eventually he came to a large double door. Theatrically he pushed both leaves open simultaneously only to find himself blinking in the brightness. It took a moment for his eyes to adjust; he had not realized how gloomy the corridors had been. He was in a large hall. A dining hall, was his first impression as he took in the many utilitarian tables and chairs. A glance to one end confirmed it by revealing a long counter and a wide, closed hatch.

More interesting, however, was the source of the light filling the room— a row of tall windows along the wall opposite the door. He walked straight towards them. The echoing sound of his footsteps drew his attention to the floor, which was timber rather than the stone he had found everywhere else.

He pushed a table to one side and rested his hands on the window sill. The sky beyond was still yellow and unhealthy looking—he wrinkled his nose in distaste. This place was surely not something compounded from his own imagination—but...

The question—or reproach?—vanished as he looked downwards.

CHAPTER 72

As he had in the Great Hall, Adroyan moved forward not only without warning but very quickly. This time however, Esyal was prepared. She made no wild swings with either of her weapons but simply stepped forwards and sideways, away from the arcing line of the slashing attack and towards her opponent. At the same time she extended the machete straight towards his throat—simple, direct and deadly.

Except that this time it was Adroyan's wiser reflexes that saved him. His head jerked back violently, but the rest of him was still travelling forward and he crashed backwards heavily on to the floor in a whirling confusion of after-images. Esyal's intense focus cut clean through them, the machete leaving its own trail, like a silver spear, moving unerringly towards his throat. It was not deflected by any great skill on Adroyan's part but by his arms flailing wildly as he struggled to recover. The blow upset Esyal's balance but not her intent and she spent no time bewailing the failed attack but moved immediately to another.

The encounter had reversed their positions, leaving her standing by the door and facing down the passage she had just come along. A movement caught her attention, snatching her eyes briefly away from her victim. The pause, albeit only momentary, was sufficient for Adroyan to roll frantically out of immediate harm's way. Esyal noted his escape but her fury and self-reproach at this were tempered by an almost overwhelming sense of despair. For the movement that had distracted her came from a group of figures moving along the passage towards her. She knew them to be creations of the Diirredyn, just as she had known the two New Order 'soldiers' had been, but this time there were many of them—a great many. The after-images that lingered and swirled behind them mingled into a livid mass like the one that had driven Henk to seek shelter in her room. Except that here it had more the semblance of some monstrous living creature, profligately spawning its blank-eyed manlike children to serve its obscene will.

Esyal took courage from the fact that she had defeated everything that had come against her so far. But she did not know how, and now, facing who could say how many of these creatures, doubt began to erode her assurance.

Still they came...

So many... there seemed to be more than the passage could possibly hold.

Esyal screwed her eyes to clear her vision but the image was unchanged. The figures were carrying something with them of the distortion she had seen in the Great Hall.

And Adroyan was rising to his feet to greet them. He faced them with extended arms and they paused. Esyal could not hear what was said, or even *if* anything was said, though something passed between them she was certain, for Adroyan turned towards her and pointed. Her fear was growing, but still part of her was coldly assessing her tactical position. She clung to it, though it held little comfort.

Whether or not these new arrivals were as slow and ineffectual as the two she had dispatched previously was of little import—there were too many of them. Sheer weight of numbers would surely overwhelm here no matter how many she 'killed'. A grotesque image of her sheltering behind a barricade of fallen bodies came to her briefly until she recalled that the two 'soldiers' had simply vanished.

His silent peroration apparently over, Adroyan was stepping to one side. He pointed to her again and the crowd resumed its advance.

Esyal swore. She could flee down the passage but that would leave Josyff defended solely by kitchen door and whatever resistance Nyk and the others could muster. She banged on the door with the butt of the machete.

"Let me in!"

She heard a voice replying but it was muffled by the thick door.

"I can't hear you," she shouted back. "For God's sake, let me in!"

The first of the Diirredyn's creations were nearly on her—two of them. There was something peculiarly horrible about the way they moved—human, but not human.

And they were carrying knives!

Panic and rage battled for control of her.

"Help me!" she screamed, at the same time as she dropped low and swung the machete across the thighs of the two attackers. The cold part of her noted that however the Diirredyn made these creatures they were human enough to collapse immediately at this brutal destruction of their supporting system. It noted too that the wounds, unlike those she had inflicted on the two 'soldiers', bled a little before becoming gaping black gashes.

The two tumbling figures tripped up a third close behind them and Esyal ran him—it—clean through as she stood upright again. Its eyes were ghastly. With her hand on its chest, she simultaneously pushed it away as she withdrew the machete. Its collapse further impeded those following.

Then there was a mindless blurring of all Esyal's senses save a diamond hard focus that followed her two blades: choosing and attacking targets without even the briefest moment of either anticipation or encumbering recall—unremitting and relentless. Past and future were gone. Time was no more, though threading through this frenzy was an increasing chorus of high-pitched shrieking as her victims, in whatever passed for their death throes, shimmered into a whirling confusion and then slipped into nothingness.

Abruptly, she felt her arms pinioned from behind. Before she could react she was dragged violently backwards and thrown down. The force of the assault was so great that she slid some way along the floor before screaming reflexes rolled her over and brought her to her feet, both blades extended. So heightened were her senses that she took in what was happening so quickly that time itself seemed to be slowed almost to stillness. Badr and Nyk were slamming the kitchen door, apparently against some resistance, while Qualto was rapidly abandoning an attempt to help her up and was retreating, wide-eyed with his hands raised.

Both gratitude and relief swept through her, yet at the same time came the now almost inexorable inner commentary on what had just happened to her. A simple but biting reproach, this time with scorn in its last word: "Guard your back, warrior."

Qualto's emerging cry of alarm and the sound of the door bolts being thrown helped her senses back to a more normal reality.

"Careful, careful," Qualto was shouting at her, almost falling over as he continued his retreat. "It's us. Don't..."

A surge of sound drowned the rest of his plea. Badr and Nyk backed away from the door as sharply as Qualto had from Esyal. It was a massive cry of rage and frustration, so loud that it filled the room like a crushing force, echoing and re-echoing until it came from every direction. All four could do no other than cover their ears.

As the noise faded, it transformed itself into a mixture of pounding blows on the door and a frantic animal scrabbling.

"Like rats," Qualto said, his lips curling in both distaste and fear.

"No rats here," Nyk said, oddly practical.

"Barricade the door!" Esyal shouted.

"With what?" Badr shouted in return, waving an arm across the kitchen. Esyal took in his concern. Except for a few chairs and a table, everything was fastened to the walls.

"Is there any other way out of here?" she asked Qualto, knowing the answer even as he shook his head. She looked at the windows, but Qualto shook his head even more resolutely.

"*Big* drop," he said, pointing downwards.

Esyal scowled as she turned her attention back to the door.

"Look to the surveyor," Nyk said to her, sharply. "You two give me a hand with these."

He was examining the doors to a tall cupboard. Then a screwdriver appeared from one of his several pockets and he was unscrewing the hinges.

Esyal hesitated for a moment then did as he had instructed.

Josyff was sitting—had been dumped—in a chair and was slumped across the table like a sated drunk. Esyal checked his pulse and breathing. His pulse was strong and steady but she could not hear his breathing above the din filling the room. She placed her knife by his mouth and it misted convincingly. Whatever was the matter with him, there was no immediate threat to his life.

She thought back to his collapse and Amrassian's voice seeping through her mind.

"*We have sent the greater part of the Measurer into his strangeness.*" What in the name of sanity did that mean? And it wasn't 'sent' was it? It was something subtly elusive, something that a single word could not encompass.

And he had not been reassuring.

"*It is our faith that he will find the Way.*"

Faith! Ye gods, is that all they could offer? She had been angry then and the memory made her angrier now. They had taken part of Josyff's mind to some other place—left him totally helpless here—to find an answer to their problems *as an act of blind hope!*

Damn them to hell!

As for her... even less reassurance.

"*You must protect what remains here, Warrior—we cannot help you. Do what you must.*"

We cannot help you—*that*, at least, had been unequivocal.

She drew up a chair and leant on the table alongside the Surveyor.

"Where are you, Josyff?" she hissed at him. "Where have they sent you? What the devil's happening? These... creatures... are getting into our world—they... die... easily enough, but they're changing—all the time they seem to be learning. And they're armed now—and there's so many—more than I can deal with—more than all of us can deal with. They're bound to get through that door eventually and I... I can't protect you."

A rending crash brought her sharply upright, heart pounding, but it was only Nyk and the others setting about the cupboard door with their feet and a machete. Looking at the trio, she swallowed an oath and opted instead to utter a silent prayer of thanks for them. To some extent she had chosen this way, but these were three ordinary people plunged into this insanity through no doing of their own. They could have been running round like headless chickens, but they were dealing with what was happening and doing something. Something useful, too, if she was any judge of Nyk.

She returned her attention to Josyff, reaching out and shaking him. He made no response.

"How is he?" Badr called out.

Esyal shrugged. "He's all right... I presume. He's breathing—his heart's beating—he's just... not here. They've..." She hesitated. "They've... sent... him somewhere."

"Sent?"

Esyal shrugged. "I don't think there's anything we can do for him except watch him. Whatever they've done, they've done. He's special to them in some way—I'm sure they know what they're doing."

Badr's expression showed distinct disbelief but before he could voice it, Esyal asked Nyk, "What are you doing?"

"What I can to strengthen this door," he replied without stopping in his work. He was rough-hewing short lengths of the destroyed cupboard door. Then he was issuing curt instructions to Qualto and Badr and using the hilt of his machete to hammer the pieces tightly between the joints in the deep stone reveals to the door recess. A zigzag pattern began to emerge.

"It won't last long," he said. "But it's better than nothing."

Esyal was impressed. Like every other door in the Keep, the kitchen door was thick, heavily hinged and heavily bolted. Further, it opened inwards, which meant that if the attackers smashed it—and there was not enough space in the passage to wield any kind of a decent ram—they would not be able to drag it out of the way to give themselves a clear way through. Nyk had understated his achievement. His reinforcement might well not last long against a determined assault, but it was a damned sight better than nothing. It would give them far more time than they would have had otherwise.

Time...

Not a good word right now.

How much...?

Leave it. *Leave it!* We must fight the battle we find ourselves in. Whatever Josyff's doing—if anything—whatever Amrassian was doing, whatever had happened to Henk—were all irrelevant. She and the three men were where they were. The importance of Josyff to what was happening, and thus their need to protect him, was manifest in the pounding din filling the kitchen. Esyal allowed herself a brief regret—she should have killed Adroyan when she had the chance—struck him down—to hell with the consequences. The fact that in that world at that time it had not been a realistic option gave her little solace.

Badr and Qualto were removing the last long cupboard door.

"Use it to barricade the door," Esyal shouted to Nyk. "Wedge it in as tight as you can—just leave a gap at the top so we can attack anyone—anything—that gets that far." She brushed a pile of splintered timbers with her foot. "And find some long pieces—pieces we can sharpen up—use as spears."

There was not much left of the doors but they managed to find four good lengths which Qualto sharpened with a few deft blows from a cleaver. Then he was throwing every edged implement in the kitchen on to the table and his sharpening steel was flashing to and fro like the blade of a master swordsman. Esyal met his gaze. She could not read it but she knew there was great danger there.

What is waking here? she thought.

And, as if in reply, Qualto spun a long heavy-bladed carving knife into the air and caught it.

Nyk cried out.

Esyal turned quickly.

He was pointing.

Sticking through the door was the tip of a spear.

CHAPTER 73

Josyff stared in amazement at the view. He was still on a high vantage, but the mountains which had swept to the far distance on the other side of the building were here tapering rapidly into a vast undulating plain.

It was broken by slow, meandering rivers and ragged stretches of weary forest and, where the many greens of a wild landscape might have been expected, were the browns and yellows of decaying and dead vegetation.

What has blighted this place? Josyff thought, not without an unexpected twinge of guilt, as though it might in some way be his fault. After all, every-thing here was supposed to have been derived from his own thoughts.

Then again, even if that were so, he was not its creator.

All of which was irrelevant, of course. What was happening was beyond any reasoning he could aspire to. Somewhere in these bizarre worlds he was being transported between, lay something that Amrassian and the First Comers needed to win their war against the Diirredyn, the Old Ones. But what? And where was he to find it? Earlier concerns returned to fret at him. He could starve to death in this place, even, conceivably, die of thirst—or something worse if he drank from any of the rivers he could see—always assuming he could reach them.

"Your faith in me is faith indeed," he said, his breath briefly steaming the window in front of him. "Rooted deep in blind hope."

He wondered what was happening in Amrassian's world, wherever and whatever such a place could be? And what kind of battles could be being fought there—battles where not only were no prisoners taken, but the whole concept of taking prisoners was apparently beyond them? And too, what would be happening to Esyal and the others? He looked down at his hands as if to judge their reality. Had he just vanished from the Keep or was he somehow both here and there as he had been in his other... trans-formations? Even as he was thinking of his companions a sense of dark menace suddenly pervaded him and he felt himself surrounded by a great commotion and a clamorous pounding. He spun round, heart racing, half expecting to find some enemy closing on him, but half knowing that this uproar was within himself. The big room was unchanged—still, silent, and mundane—as far in character from a battlefield as could be imagined.

As though startled by his movement, both the din and the menace dwin-dled. But they did not disappear, they became a low, shifting rumbling, not so much diminished in character as moved far away.

Hold on to this, came an unexpected—and urgent—thought. It's important.

The image of a narrow bridge flitted through his mind.

Still unsettled, he turned back to the window.

The landscape was subtly different. Something now was wrong with its perspective, and there were faltering hints of the golden lines permeating it. As usual, they defied direct examination.

Then he realized that though he was looking at the horizon, he was cran-ing his head back. He shook it and brought his gaze back to the immediate terrain then slowly followed a particular river into the distance. It made no difference. Though he could see nothing unusual along its route, he found he was looking upwards again. There was a claustrophobic quality about what was happening.

Curving, curving, curving, everything folding in on itself, like the light from the Beacon. What could cause such a thing? What did it mean? There was something in what he was looking at—something to do with the solution he had found to the closing error—something further—a refinement...?

But how could there be. It was complete, surely...?

And what did it have to do with anything, anyway, least of all his present predicament?

Everything! It brought you here, didn't it?

He swore softly both at this conclusion and the simultaneous return of his chronic irritation at the obduracy of the closing error.

He found he had little choice but to yield to it for the moment.

The solution was an artefact of numbers—numbers from measurements. They were accurate enough for the requirements of his work, but necessarily they would be inaccurate in absolute terms.

He leaned forward, pressing his hands on the window sill and his head against the window. This doesn't matter, he insisted to himself angrily. He needed to find out why he was here—and how to get back, how to end all this—not to be fretting about what were now unimportant aspects of his work. But his appeal was to no avail. The numbers had somehow come together and they had manifested the solution, for the most part visually— he could see it now, with its impossible curves and shapes. And he could see that, elegant and beautiful though it might be, it was indeed *not* perfect. It was a hint of where the numbers were leading.

The revelation filled him with a mixture of anger and ravening curiosity.

He screwed his eyes tight and then opened them wide in the hope that this might dispatch this unwanted intrusion, but it did not. Worse, as he looked out towards the high horizon again, it was to see that the jaundiced sky was now scarred by storm clouds—black and ominous but shot through with flickering flamelight.

Approaching storm clouds.

Fear began to twist his stomach, telling him that this was the enemy.

But how had they come here? Hadn't he been sent here precisely because it was somewhere the Diirredyn could not reach? Or was that just another part of Amrassian's blind faith?

The fear increased. Perhaps the First Comers had fallen. Perhaps the Diirredyn were even now sweeping through the Keep and setting in train the destruction of all things that Amrassian had foretold.

In the mental numbness that followed this, the faint commotion and sense of menace he had felt before, swelled a little. It was still distant, but unequivocally it was there. Like the gathering clouds, it was disturbing, but, unlike the clouds, it was also peculiarly reassuring. It told him in some way that his concern about defeat was premature—battle might well have been engaged but it was not over yet.

Then he realized he was trembling, and, abruptly, as if released by his awareness of this, a bitter eruption of both terror and rage swept through him. A torrent of savage reproach against everything that had brought him to this place surged out of him uncontrollably, like vomit. There was neither order nor logic in it and he found himself roaring incoherently into the hall, his passion mocked by his voice falling flat amid the audience of empty chairs and tables. Mingling with this upheaval was an almost overwhelming urge to flee, to hide, even to throw himself on the mercy of these vile invaders, anything to have this all finished—to be out of this place, out of these mountains, back in *his* world, with familiarity all about him, with his wife beside him, safe and secure again.

Gradually the flood eased and some semblance of normality seeped over him as his innate realism reasserted itself. There was nowhere to run and nowhere to hide, and not just for the obvious reason that he had no idea where he was. Things always had to be faced and dealt with—always! Nor would he be truly safe if he were back in his 'normal' world. No one was safe under the New Order, that chilling reflection of this greater evil. He had merely been skilful and lucky. As for negotiations with the Diirredyn! The memory of their touching him was still vivid and awful and it was as alien as it was foul. There was not a vestige of either reason or humanity about them. He was just some instrument of war to them—something to be used and discarded—or worse.

His trembling lessened and almost vanished as these thoughts paraded themselves. Though he was still afraid, the outburst had been cathartic and the fear was now more a goad to his resolution than a burden—indeed it was turning into a dark anger. The return to his old life would necessarily be his goal but, he reminded himself, too-anxious thoughts of it now would hinder not help. He must be completely focused here. He turned back to the window and looked out again at the darkening sky.

The bleak landscape was fading in the shadow of the clouds and, somewhat to his relief, it was no longer possible to see the high arching horizon. Then a brilliant flash made him jump.

Lightning?

Unbidden, an old habit had him counting the seconds to the thunderclap to find out how far away the storm was. But the count soon became improbable, telling him that there was only going to be silence. Lightning without thunder—just another unsettling aspect of this place.

Even as he decided this, there was a second flash. This made him not merely jump but turn his gaze away and step back in alarm. There had been no forking lights rending the darkness as they danced to and from the ground. Instead, the entire sky had been illuminated. The flash was so bright that it left repellent green after-images lingering in his vision, and although it had lasted for the merest heart-beat, what he had seen had burnt itself into his mind. For just as when Adroyan had held him motionless for the scrutiny of his masters, so now Josyff knew he had peered again into the world of the Diirredyn. It was as though a huge veil had been momentarily lifted. Those same searching eyes were there, feral and awful, some blood-red, some glistening black. The same clawing hands were there too—if hands they were—reaching out towards him in lust and fury. And the whole was carried to him through the eerie perspectives of these strange other worlds and seen through the impossible—inhuman—vision he had possessed when he saw the solution to the closing error. Images were at once close to him and far away, part of a vast, sweeping worldscape alive and seething with frenzied activity. More disturbing than these, however, was the hatred and malice that came too, all the worse because it was deeply alien in character. It hung about him like an acrid cloud and, once again, fear threatened to take control of him.

He managed to fight it down. It would unman him completely now. If these things were coming, they were coming, and he could do nothing to stop them. All that was left for him was to fight his ground. Whatever was happening to the others back in the Keep and to Amrassian and his... people... he must do what he could to engage this enemy and make it pay as high a price as he could manage.

You're pictures in the sky, he told himself. If you want to take me then you must manifest yourself more than that. The thought brought back the memory of the two New Order 'soldiers' who had come for him, and Esyal's swift and brutal dispatch of them. Could he do that? Could he find that ruthless clarity of purpose within himself?

You'll have no choice, came one reply.

It neither informed nor comforted him, but a booming concussion filled the room and ended his conjecture. It was so violent that he had to steady himself against a table. He turned back to the windows. Gone was the landscape, gone was the darkening sky, both replaced by a foaming blackness surging to and fro as if seeking a way in. For an instant it seemed to Josyff that all the windows were bellying in towards him and, instinctively, he closed his eyes and raised a hand to protect himself from shattering glass. But none came. When he cautiously opened his eyes, the windows were intact. But they were creaking...

Or *was* it creaking?

And a sound like fingernails being drawn down the glass began to fill the room. It made his flesh crawl.

Snatching up his lamp, he fled.

CHAPTER 74

Henk held the lantern high as he picked his way along the narrow alley that led to the courtyard over which the Beacon shone—the Keep's lighting did not extend along the alley and the ground was uneven. Grunting to himself, he rehearsed the old complaints about the access to the Beacon, but it was simply a habit—something familiar for him to cling to amid all this confusion—all this... fear.

When he emerged into the courtyard he looked up. Enough snow was falling to mark the bright line of the light from the Beacon and even within the limited confines of the small courtyard he could see that it was curving.

It was a sight that unsettled him in ways he could not begin to find words for. The response it invoked felt ancient, primitive. The one word that did come was 'madness', all madness. And yet it was there, in front of him...

He would shut the damn thing off!

That would not put an end to whatever was bending the light, of course, but...

His thoughts came to a halt. There was nowhere for them to go. Reasoning would only go full circle, like the damned beam...

So he was just responding...

...Just turn it off...

Henk blinked. The thought expressed both his intention and his feelings, but it was almost as if it had come from somewhere else. Further, he found his legs responding unbidden to the command and he had to force himself to stop after two or three steps.

Brow furrowed, he looked around the courtyard, half expecting to see someone there waving him to get on with the job.

He shook his head in self-reproach for such foolishness and walked over to the stairs that led to the Beacon. They were awkward to manage at the best of times, but he set off up them quite briskly. Indeed, he set off at the even brisker pace than he adopted whenever Qualto, hesitant and uncertain, and ripe for gentle taunting, was with him. Now however, the snow had made the stairs particularly treacherous and, after his foot slipped for the second time, he seized the handrail tightly and came to a wilful halt, breathing heavily and with his heart thumping.

What are you doing? he rebuked himself angrily. Fall down these, here, now, and the least that will happen is something broken. He had a brief vision of dragging himself back to the main courtyard...

And then where...?

Just slow down. He hesitated. Was he doing the right thing? After all, this thing doesn't *need* to be turned off, does it?

But even as he tried to dismiss his intention as a mere whim and fancy, the sense of deep wrongness in the curving light beam came to him again.

Turn it off!

The thought seemed to echo through his mind.

He started up the stairs again, though this time much more cautiously, particularly along the narrow platform that joined the two flights.

Then he was there, standing by the Beacon, one hand resting on it proprietorially. As was invariably the case when he came here, and despite the circumstances, he felt a distinct frisson of pleasure as he looked at it. With its sharp-cut facets, glistening surfaces and clear, steady light, it had an aura of perfection about it. The response soon soured as he looked out into the night along the bright, snow-filled beam. Clear and steady it still was, save for the dancing of the snowflakes caught by it, but where it should have cut through the dark like a sword blade, it curved. Not only that, it was curving far more than it had only...

Only hours ago...?

Had it only been a few hours since they had discovered this?

He recalled the simple tests that he, Nyk and Esyal had performed to determine that the light was indeed bending and that it was not some illusion brought on by the weather. Nyk's ruthless pragmatism was usually reassuring, but here it had proved to be deeply unnerving, not least because it left no room for anything but acceptance.

The recollection of Nyk's attitude made him wonder what he would see if he was up on the tower balcony now. Would the Beacon no longer be a distant point of light—a star, perhaps? a benighted traveller?—but closer and brighter, more obviously itself? Would the vaguely illuminated mass of the Keep, veiled in the billowing snow, be visible in the background, hovering over the deep valley? Might he not even see himself, peering out into the darkness? Henk shuddered, more than the winter cold was striking through to him. He found himself gripping the Beacon tightly for support.

Turn it off!

There it was again. Shriller than before and still like something from outside himself. It vibrated and echoed to and fro, as though trapped by great walls and vaulted ceilings, chiming with a sense of claustrophobia he realized had been growing for some time. He found himself reaching up, self-consciously, half-afraid he might touch something.

But there was nothing, save the chill of a few snowflakes falling on his upturned palm. Yet the question had been asked and others tumbled after it. If the Beacon's light was bending more and more, where would it end? Was it being brought about by the same crushing force that was holding the drawbridge closed? What was happening to the mountains and valleys hereabouts?

And would his turning off the light stop it?

That did not come from outside him. Nor was the answer difficult. He had no doubt that the drawbridge was jammed shut whether it was seen or not, so whatever was bending the light would presumably still be there also—and still tightening. He patted the Beacon nervously, suddenly uncertain as to why he was there. The curving beam of light arcing out before him was as disturbing as ever, but just turning it off seemed now to be a much less enticing prospect than before.

What were the others doing? They had gone chasing after Adroyan and the surveyor. God knows what was happening to them now...

He frowned. For all his concern, he was loath to go back into the Keep to find out. Indeed he was loath even to leave the Beacon.

Still, at least he had prepared a survival plan of sorts as far as he was able...

Yet he should do more.

But what?

He looked again at the curving beam.

Circling, circling...

Tightening...?

Perhaps... perhaps, if he moved the Beacon...?

After all, it *did* move. Although it was always left in its present position, for reasons unknown, it could be moved to sweep the light through wide arcs both vertically and horizontally. And Nyk always tested this as part of his routine maintenance.

Henk felt defiant. Yes, let's see what this damned light does when its source moves! See how it copes with being dragged across the nearby peaks and valleys!

And too, perhaps if someone *is* out there...

Faint hints of rescue from outside stirred in Henk's mind but he let them fade. Anyone out there would probably need rescuing themselves. Besides, why would anyone be coming to rescue them?

He loosened the latches securing the Beacon.

Like the drawbridge, the Beacon, though large and heavy, was both well designed and well engineered and could be moved with very little effort. This, coupled with the particularly fine graduations on the scales that marked its movement, ensured that it could be positioned with almost absurd accuracy.

He took hold of one of the manoeuvring handles and pushed it gently, anticipating the usual easy movement. But it did not happen. There was no massive, arm-jolting resistance such as the wheel controlling the drawbridge had exhibited, but more a sensation of inertia, as though he were pushing it uphill. And as if in confirmation of this, the Beacon quietly returned to its original position when he released it.

He pushed again, a little harder, and the same thing happened. His immediate reaction was to look around the Beacon to see if anything was caught in the turning mechanism. But even as he was looking he knew he would find nothing. The rollers and bearings were sheltered from the snow and there were no branches or dead leaves up here to clog them. Nor did he or Nyk casually leave cleaning cloths and tools lying about.

He pushed again, this time watching what happened to the light beam.

It did not respond immediately and when it did, the movement rippled along it like a reluctant whiplash, as if it, too, were struggling against something. Henk thought he heard a faint hissing.

As he was gradually becoming used to what he was seeing, Henk's curiosity began to dominate. He moved the Beacon to shine the beam upwards. Again he felt the resistance, and again the beam responded slowly, though this time it curved not only horizontally but vertically as well, rising for some way, then dipping elegantly downwards, like a moonlit rainbow, until it was lost from view. He stared at it for a moment then let the Beacon return to its original position. Then he pushed as hard as he could. The Beacon moved as before, but the resistance increased both dramatically and rapidly, soon bringing him to a halt. The light trembled with the effort he was making, tiny stuttering shimmers running to and fro along it, but he could not move it further.

This time though, he definitely heard something. It was not a pleasant sound—like a distant and angry commotion. And it was vaguely familiar. He gave a final grunt of effort before releasing the Beacon again. As it rolled back so the sound faded, though it lingered for a short while, menacingly.

Henk listened to it intently as it dwindled until it was lost in the soft hissing of the falling snow. Slowly the familiarity it carried formed itself into a memory. It was the noise of that... thing... the cloud... that had pursued him through the Keep and which Esyal had fought off.

The terror of the incident returned, unexpectedly snatching his breath away and making him gasp. He glanced frantically from side to side, for any sign that the abomination might be returning. But nothing had changed. He found his hand was on the long knife that Esyal had thrust on him. He drew it and hefted it. It had an edge honed by Qualto and that gave him some reassurance. He might not know what these creatures were, but he knew they could be defeated. All he had to do was show the courage that Esyal had...

His bravado faded. Slight, Esyal might be, but she was no lost child of the storm. She was brave and she could fight. She was as frightening in some ways as... them. But *he* was no warrior. All he wanted to do was run and run—get away from here—get back... home. It was an odd thought, the Keep being perhaps more home to him than where he came from— as indeed it was for all of them. He glanced in the direction of the closed drawbridge, then at the snow-filled light beam circling into the darkness. What he wanted and what he could achieve were two different things. The reality was that he had no choice but to deal with whatever was happening. He wanted to bellow, "Why me?" into the winter night, but the very uselessness of the question stopped him and instead he snarled in frustration and struck the Beacon with the side of his fist.

A tremor ran along the beam in response, and the distant hissing rose up again.

Henk's eyes narrowed.

Was that a hint of alarm, even fear, he detected?

CHAPTER 75

An odd stillness filled Esyal as she looked at the spear tip protruding through the door. Was this the beginning of the end? The gradual, inevitable chipping away of the Keep's defences?

Even as anger at this weakness was rising, she became aware of a movement beside her. It was Qualto. He was striding across the kitchen carrying a heavy pan. Before Esyal realized what he intended, he had reached over their rough barricade, and struck two almighty blows. When he stood back, the spear tip was bent at right angles wedging it in the door. It waggled feebly. The sight was both dramatic and incongruous and Esyal could not forbear both applauding and laughing. Nyk and Badr joined in and Qualto raised his pan in triumph.

There was a sudden lull in the enemy's clamour and the silence carried the four listeners with it. But it was short-lived and the din returned with equal suddenness.

"Any more that come through, do the same," Esyal shouted above it, similarly returning to her role. "Every one that's stuck there will get in their way."

Qualto hefted his pan. "My thinking exactly."

"But they must get through eventually," Badr said.

Esyal snarled. "The world will end *eventually*. Sooner rather than later if these creatures get the surveyor. We deal with the here and now. We protect him as long as we can and..."

She paused.

"And what?" Badr pressed, though almost reluctantly.

"And, and," Esyal echoed. "All ifs, buts, ands and maybes just ended. We fight. That's all. We fight. We win. We defeat them." She pointed to the door. "Look. It doesn't matter how many there are, unless they find a way of coming through the walls or the windows, that's the only way in. Their numbers are no use if they can only get in two at a time." Her lip curled. "They've brought their own barricade. We'll block the door with their dead..."

Their conversation was interrupted by another spear tip piercing the door. Qualto flattened it with the same gusto as before.

Badr did not look wholly convinced by Esyal's prognosis but her manner forbade any further debate. He just said, "I wonder where Henk is."

"Still trying to find a way out of the place, I'd think," Nyk said. "But doing something useful somewhere, you can rest assured."

"Out there? With that lot?" Badr said.

Nyk stopped sharpening a wooden stake. "He knows this place better than any of us. And don't confuse his... off-handedness... with stupidity."

Badr bridled a little then gave a curt nod to acknowledge the rebuke, but another sound vibrated through the kitchen before he could speak.

"Axes," Nyk diagnosed bleakly.

"The sooner they get in, the sooner they start dying," Esyal countered. She straightened, took a deep breath and looked round at the others.

"Thank you for your hospitality and kindness, gentlemen. And thank you not least for saving my life. It's been a privilege to know you." There was a pause as all eyes returned her gaze with both uncertainty and mounting alarm, then she bared her teeth in a malevolent rictus. "And it'll be an even greater privilege to get to know you better when we get out of here. You're all armed?"

It was a rhetorical question—keen edges and sharpened points abounded. Now, thanks to her ever more commanding manner, so did determination.

Qualto looked down at the pan he was carrying then looked up sharply and snapped his fingers.

"Dangerous places, kitchens," he said, as much to himself as anyone else, and he was scurrying about lighting oven rings, and rooting out bottles and jars and emptying them into pans. Esyal watched him, but he was moving with such purpose that she did not question him. Instead she went up to the pounding door.

"You creatures out there, fetch Adroyan!" she shouted. "Fetch him now, before you start dying for no purpose."

The noise faltered, and in the comparative silence she spoke softly to her companions. "Anything that gives us time is to the good, I'm sure. Time maybe for the surveyor to waken, or do... whatever it is he has to do... wherever he is." She looked over at Josyff's still form slumped across the table and it took her some effort to keep her doubts from her face. "Time maybe for Henk to do something."

"Child?"

Adroyan's voice was unmistakable even though it was more than ever permeated by the equally unmistakable sound of the Diirredyn. Reaching into the room, it set Esyal's teeth on edge.

374

"You cannot win this," Esyal said. "We're too well protected. Your people will die by the score."

{*"Die? We cannot die."*}

Not Adroyan this time.

"Where you belong, perhaps, but you are in a strange land—a land where you do *not* belong—a land where your very presence defies the rightful order of things. Venture further into it and you *will* die... you will become no more."

{*"It is you who will... die... if you stand in our way, child—as will your companions. Nothing can keep us from the Measurer—we are numbered beyond your imagining."*}

Esyal sneered. "You are few and desperate, sustained in this reality by the sorry creature you've made your vessel. I've injured him twice already. He will fail you and you will dwindle into screaming nothingness when I finally kill him. Did you think to intrude into our world without consequence?"

There was a brief but incoherent outburst in response to this, out of which emerged Adroyan again, "Rhetoric, child. Brave noises to hide behind—to hide from the truth. Open the door and you and your companions will be spared."

Esyal leaned against the makeshift barricade and reflected briefly. Her immediate reaction was to shout fighting defiance, but the others were conscripts, drawn into this by a combination of circumstances and her forcefulness. *Her* judgement about what was happening was vividly clear. Years of opposing the New Order made her think routinely to the heart of matters more than most, but she knew, too, that some of her knowledge had been put there by Amrassian. And while this had a powerful aura of truth about it, reinforced by every contact with the Diirredyn, the others did not have this advantage.

It seems there's more to leadership than just the simplicity of wielding a knife, she reflected with grim ruefulness.

"What will happen to us?" she asked, affecting an interest she did not feel and unnecessarily holding out a hand for silence.

"You will be spared."

"That wasn't my question. Will we be allowed to walk free and unharmed from here—back to our lives—if we give you the surveyor?"

The pause that followed, she knew, would give the others a measure of the worth of the reply.

"...Yes."

"And where will we go in this world when your masters have passed through it?"

Another pause.

"All will be well. You have been deceived."

Her pretence fell away.

"No, First Member. We've had this conversation. It's you who've been deceived. Look around you—look at them! Ask yourself, do these creatures belong here? They might look human, but they're not, are they? They're fabrications from our minds. Grotesque—obscene—artefacts. And do you have any control over them? Will you—or our whole world—be anything other than expendable when they have what they want?"

There was another pause.

"You have been deceived."

Esyal turned and looked at the others. "You heard the offer. If you want to leave, now's the time—no reproach."

"He's lying. Him being New Order is enough to guarantee that, without all this insanity," Badr said, unexpectedly outspoken. Qualto nodded. "But in any case we can't just... hand over the surveyor... Josyff. God knows what they'll do to him, but I doubt it'll be for his good."

Nyk also nodded his agreement.

There was unanimity. Esyal had not expected anything other, but she was relieved nevertheless.

"What are you going to tell him?" Badr asked.

"Nothing," Esyal replied after a moment's consideration. "Let him stew a while. As I said, anything that draws things out—gains us time—will be to the good."

Silence filled the room, save for the hiss of Qualto's oven rings and the bubbling of pans. As though fearful of disturbing this brief calm, Qualto was tip-toeing round his charges inspecting and adjusting them as required.

Prompted by the lull, Esyal's curiosity came to the fore. She spoke softly.

"What are you doing?"

"Dangerous places, kitchens," Qualto said, as he had before. "Not only things that cut." He patted the machete in his belt. "But things that burn and scald. Very nasty things." He paused. "Never thought of it before."

Esyal patted his arm in sympathy. "Never had the need," she said, adding, "I'd rather be out shopping myself. But we're here, albeit through none of our own seeking. So none of us can have what we want and your kitchen becomes a battlefield."

"Child."

Adroyan's voice intruded.

"What is your decision?"

"Sorry—didn't hear you," Esyal shouted back, returning to the barricade.

Adroyan repeated his question, Esyal noting with some satisfaction the impatience in his voice.

"We're still talking about it," she replied.

"There is no more time."

"Your masters have been planning this for time without measure," Esyal said. "A little time now will not make any difference, surely? We need to know if we'll be given food and clothes for our journey through the moun..."

"There is no more time."

Esyal echoed the words silently with a vicious curl of her mouth.

Then the onslaught began again, more violent than ever.

CHAPTER 76

Josyff banged his thigh against the corner of a table as he dashed for the door. The pain both slowed him and calmed him to some extent, reminding him that whatever was going to happen, and whatever he thought about it, panicking was unlikely to help.

He reached the doors with an ungainly, half-hopping step and pushed them open with his shoulder and body weight. They swung to behind him as he staggered across the passageway to lean against the wall. He rubbed his leg and looked up and down the passage. Which way should be go? His mind whirled. Telling himself not to panic was one thing, actually doing it was another, not least given that the screeching was seeping through the doors like clinging fog.

His legs made the decision for him, pushing him away from the wall, turning him to the right and setting off at a lumpy trot. He gave no thought to stopping. He knew that his instincts could usually be trusted when his mind was at an impasse.

Go upwards...

Yes, go upwards.

Rise to face this thing.

As this somewhat unexpected resolution came to him, he emerged into a broad circular hallway. There were several wide openings spaced evenly around the circumference, and a low wall around the centre which, he discovered as he peered over it, was protecting an open well. He presumed that it reached right down through the building, but he could not confirm this as, like the Keep, the lighting extended only some way from him and the view disappeared into darkness after a few floors. It was the same when he looked upwards.

Then the screeching was on him again. It grew rapidly louder and began to echo around the circular walls like a hunting animal seeking him out. Immediately he headed for an opening through which he could see stairs leading upwards.

The stairs were wide and airy, leading round in a sweeping arc, and he set off up them two at a time. He noted that at each landing the stairs narrowed a little but he could not have said how many floors he had risen through before eventually he was forced to stop to catch his breath. Leaning forward with his hands on his knees, he strove to listen above the sound of his pumping heart and laboured breathing for any indication of pursuit. And it was there. Faint but unequivocal. Straightening up he looked at the next flight of stairs. They continued the pattern of narrowing but they were gloomier than those below—and steeper. The overall impression they gave was of being older than the other stairs.

Slow down, he instructed himself, and he straightened up and took several deep breaths. It's only a noise. Unpleasant, but hardly likely to be fatal. He would surely have heard if they had broken those great windows in the dining hall. Still, they would get in sooner or later, presumably, and all he could do—given that flight was not possible—was find the best ground to fight on. A negotiator by both nature and experience, the thought felt alien to him but he forced himself to hang on to it. There *was* no alternative. Somewhat self-consciously he patted the machete in his belt, then checked the lamp. Despite his hectic flight, it was still burning with a low steady flame. He adjusted it and, for a moment, it shone brightly, then he lowered it again, and set off up the stairs.

They *were* steeper, he found, and, strangely, they were pervaded with a feeling not merely of being older, but of being ancient.

Old built on top of new? He left the question.

The makings of a strategy began to form.

He could not run for ever. The instinct that had led him upwards where he must inevitably be trapped was to be trusted, he saw now. To have gone down would have left him the choice of going outside into whatever mayhem was happening there, or being pursued around the rambling lower floors of this place.

His alternatives were falling away—tapering to just one, simple and clear.

And when these stairs are narrow enough, I'll stop, he thought. These creatures, whatever they are, don't seem to fight well and numbers are no use to them if only one at a time can come at him. It was an echo of Esyal's thinking, albeit more reluctant. He could already touch both walls without straightening his arms. He took out the machete and swung a few crisscrossing blows. Too wide would obviously see him overwhelmed, but too narrow would see him hampered by the walls. A little narrower would be ideal, he judged.

Ideal! The word gave him an unexpected frisson of distaste. Ideal: the highest and the best! The highest and the best for slaughter—what an abuse of the language...

He crushed the brief intrusion. I have to be like Esyal. I have to focus totally on destroying my enemies until I am safe. I have to forget everything I value and everyone I love—to do less will be to lose them all for sure. Part of him was appalled by this conclusion but it dwindled and faded in the glare of its grim logic.

"I will kill every one of you," he muttered between clenched teeth. "You've meddled with our world for generations, it seems. Now you drag me from my life and assail my sanity—lose me in God knows what limbo for God knows what vile ends. I'm no warrior, but I'll do my damnedest to make sure whatever you want from me will carry a terrible price."

He tapped the machete on each wall. The next flight of stairs would probably be just right.

But that option proved to be unavailable. There were no more stairs. A few steps further on around the curve of the stairs and he found himself facing a door. He was about to push it open when caution intervened and he stopped and held his ear close to it. Nothing was to be heard, but nevertheless he held the machete ready as he silently lifted the latch. Then, taking a deep breath, he flung the door open, ready to face...

Nothing. There was no one there. He was standing on a circular landing, with the underside of a fluted conical roof rising above him. On the far side was another door. Opening to the outside, he judged, looking at its robust construction and heavy bolts and hinges. Either on to a high balcony, or perhaps a walkway to another tower—the former, he felt, though he had little sense of where he was by now.

He looked back down the stairs and at the open door then he glanced around the landing. It was quite empty—there was nothing that might be used to secure the door.

This is where I stand then, he concluded bleakly. At least he had the high ground—and only the width of the door to defend. He swung the door to and fro. It moved easily. With his foot behind it, it might serve as a shield to some extent, further narrowing the space for his pursuers. Also, his first response could be to slam it squarely in the face of the first arrival. Could be very effective against someone running up the stairs. And it would slow down anyone following him.

Still he would have preferred to secure the door in some way.

Then a thought occurred to him and, taking careful aim, he swung the machete down the edge of the door. It took several hard blows and some wrenching but he eventually succeeded in separating two large pieces of wood, crudely triangular. Wedges. They'd secure the door! He closed it and pushed one wedge into the gap at the top and the other under the bottom edge. He drove them in as far as he could with the butt of the machete. Then he kicked the bottom one home with some relish.

As he stepped back from this exertion, he suddenly felt the small room closing about him.

He was trapped.

He forced himself into a debate to keep at bay the fear he felt returning.

What else could I have done?

You've only bought a little time.

Same rejoinder. What else could I have done? Every second I can delay these creatures could perhaps give Amrassian and the others an advantage.

You hope...

Yes, I hope.

And if their war's already lost?

Here he was certain.

It isn't—I'd know, I'm sure. And that's why they're still pursuing me.

Weakness threatened.

What the devil do they want?

But the question consumed itself and any lapse towards panic ended before it began.

He started pacing the floor, pondering practicalities.

How long was it going to be before they found him? Would they be searching the place methodically, logically, or could they scent him out in some way, like hunting animals?

And what would they be like? Would they be like the blank-eyed New Order soldiers that Esyal had... dispatched? Or like the menacing turbulence that had pursued Henk?

It doesn't matter. I'll find out when they get here. Then I'll deal with them as best I can.

He took Qualto's knife from his pocket and opened and closed it several times nervously. Then he made a few awkward passes with the knife in one hand and the machete in the other. He had never thought of himself as a fighter, other than in brief flights of foolish male fantasy, and he had never confused these with reality. Just as well, he mused. The reality of the violence he had seen since he came here—Esyal's—was horribly different from any fantasy. Full of uneasy and contradictory responses—responses that lingered long after the deed. And its horror was heightened by its very ordinariness. Again he recalled the same impression as he had watched Adroyan walking away from him—a monster—and an ordinary man. Just as he was—using his wits to avoid trouble and to survive wherever he found himself.

And where've your wits brought you now? The caustic observation made him smile, then chuckle unexpectedly.

"No," he said to the empty room. "Not my fault. Couldn't have foreseen anything like this in my wildest imaginings."

But then, though we live it as if it did, life doesn't go in straight lines, does it? Never! He knew that—God knows, he knew that! But all this...!

So deal with it.

He looked down at his two weapons and tightened his grip on them.

I will.

Then he bellowed out a furious challenge to his unseen assailants.

A thunderous percussion shook the room.

CHAPTER 77

Henk struck the Beacon again, and this time listened carefully as ripples ran along the beam. The sound he had heard before rose up again and it was definitely shot through with anger and alarm. It was as though he were disturbing a wasp's nest.

It was also an uneasy analogy—what would happen to him if he disturbed it too much?

Then again, what would happen if he did nothing?

And what would happen if he turned the light off?

He had a momentary impression of darkness crashing in upon him, sweeping all before it like a great wave. Unbidden, the fist that had struck the Beacon became a hand, patting as if to reassure.

Then came another question: where had the idea that he should turn off the Beacon come from? There were more important things he should be doing. Could it have been them—these... things—seeping into the place from God knows where? Were they seeping into him as well? After all, he was the one who knew the Keep best, the one who had sensed and then discovered its changes months ago.

He looked at the curving beam of light. What *would* happen if he turned it off? Should he risk it? The image of the surging darkness returned. Would he be able to turn it on again, or would he have done something irreparable? He was patting the Beacon again. He looked at it—as much to take his gaze from the curving light as for any other reason. It was a fine piece of work—efficient and elegant, and with a fine purpose: to shine out across the mountains to guide benighted travellers to safety. Surely such a thing could not be used to bring harm?

Let it be, he decided finally. Let it shine.

He pushed it gently and watched as the snow-laden beam responded to the movement before settling back to its original position.

Something inside him seemed to shift—as though the beam itself had shone into him.

The light is resisting what's happening, he thought. It didn't want to be twisted thus. It wanted to soar out over the mountains, and beyond—for ever—on and on, unhindered. The very act of constraining it to this unnatural distortion was evidence enough of the ill intent of those doing it.

He must help.

But what could he do? He was just a caretaker, nothing special. He had no professional training like the surveyor and Badr, or frightening skills and passions like Esyal. He was not even special amongst his peers. Nyk was the thinker, the organizer, the problem-solver. Qualto kept them alive and civilized. He just plodded and did what he was told.

Did it well, though, he thought, seeking some solace amid this self-denigration. No one ever complained about his work, or even needed to explain things twice—most of the time. And he got things done. Besides, what was happening here was beyond everyone's experience anyway. The surveyor, with Badr in his wake, seemed, if not downright bewildered, far from certain, while Nyk and Qualto were just following Esyal.

There was nothing in Henk's past to help him now. Ahead of him lay only darkness. He peered out into the night and slumped a little as his thoughts ground to a halt, foundering on this conclusion.

He could not have said how long he stood there, but eventually something in the darkness itself began to impinge on him. He screwed his eyes tight and leaned forward. It was as though he could see through to the other side of the falling snow, to a blackness that was deeper than the mere night. And the beam seemed to be curving more than when he had arrived.

Something was closing in...

Tightening its grip...

He tightened his own on the Beacon in response.

Where would all this end?

Do something...

What?

In the absence of any answer to this, he pushed the Beacon again, first side to side and then up and down. It was harder to move and the beam wavered and thrashed like a live thing trying to shake off a restraint. And the hissing anger came again, far louder now, echoing and re-echoing off the walls, pressing in on him, menacing him.

Part of him still wanted to cower before it, or flee as he had when he had been pursued through the Keep. But he was schooling himself to a new way of thinking. His previous flight had won him nothing, save the fear and humiliation of the hunted. Esyal's standing and fighting had turned the predators into prey. Having seen that—having *seen* it—how could he do less?

A misquotation came to him.

"Better to die on your feet than on your knees."

He snarled and swore and shouted out his own version.

"Better not to die at all!"

These creatures had trapped him in this place for their own ends, left him no opportunity to fly, let them take the consequences.

And seizing the handles of the Beacon, he began wrenching it violently to and fro.

CHAPTER 78

Despite herself, Esyal jumped back as the pounding on the door began again, so sudden and violent was it. The hammering, accompanied by the scratching, renewed now with even greater ferocity, seemed to shake the whole room. Weaving through its brutal rhythm came the sound of innumerable voices, wordless but flesh-crawling, rising and falling like some demonic musical instrument.

Qualto paused from his collection of bottles and pans. "It seems you've upset him," he said, unexpectedly ironic.

"It's a good start," Esyal retorted. She hefted her machete. "As soon as I can I'll upset his head from his shoulders."

"I doubt you'll get the chance," Badr said, affecting a calm he did not feel. "I don't think he's the type to lead from the front."

"Then he'll be last man standing," Esyal replied.

There was a quietness in her manner more frightening than any warlike bluster and Badr looked at her nervously. She turned and met his gaze. He found he could not look away.

"Don't misunderstand," she said. "There'll be us four—and him—on his own."

She released him, but he had no rejoinder for her.

Qualto flattened two more spear points. Then the thin edge of an axe appeared. Qualto faltered briefly then smacked it ferociously with the pan. As he stepped away from the door he looked ruefully at the bottom of the pan. "It's been a damn good pan, that," he said.

"Casualty of war," Esyal retorted, giving him a knowing look. "We'll bury it with honours."

Qualto tapped the base of the pan and held it to the light, then he returned Esyal's look and this time it was she who could not look away.

"We'll cook a victory feast in it... Commander," he said.

A change in the noise filling the kitchen made all four turn back sharply to the door. A long ragged hole had appeared. An axe head was working its way free, widening the hole as it did. A spear flew through the hole making them all duck. Another followed it.

Simultaneously, Esyal swept up the two spears and Qualto seized a steaming pan from one of his stoves. Before anyone else could react he had run to the door and hurled the contents over the barricade and through the opening with remarkable accuracy.

The general din was fragmented by screams.

"Dangerous places, kitchens," Qualto said again as he retreated to a sink to refill the pan.

Nyk tried to do the same but much of the boiling water missed the hole and splashed against the door. He jumped back, swearing and hastily wiping himself down. Esyal noted Qualto's jaw stiffening at this waste of his resources and she intervened before he could speak.

"Leave that to Qualto, Nyk, he throws better than you. You and Badr pick up those." She pointed to the lengths of wood they had rough-hewn into spears. "Protect him. Anything shows itself in the opening..." She made a thrusting gesture.

The screaming was dwindling but it was being replaced by the sound of axes being vigorously applied. A head appeared in the opening but disappeared almost immediately as Badr thrust his makeshift spear at it.

Esyal noted the response. Whatever these creatures are, they feel pain and they value whatever passes for their lives, she thought. Their human characteristics are more than superficial—we're not dealing with completely mindless puppets. An unpleasant afterthought came as she watched Qualto hurl another panful of boiling water through the relentlessly widening gap—would their cunning and viciousness be human as well?

"I can throw this faster than I can boil it," Qualto said as he withdrew again.

"Don't fill them so full," Esyal said. "Little and often while we can. Look out!"

The warning was accompanied by a violent push which sent Qualto staggering—a spear passed between them. It hit the far wall and clattered to the floor.

"Don't turn your back on them!" she shouted angrily, at the same time moving to steady Qualto. "Any of you. Stay alert—stay alive."

She picked up the spear and looked at it. It was ornately decorated and it glinted in the light.

"This the Keep's?" she asked Nyk.

He shot the spear a quick glance and shook his head. "Nothing like that round here."

Esyal frowned. It was not relevant to what was happening but she could not help asking herself, "why would they make... create... something like this—so elaborate?"

She did not pursue the thought as another head appeared in the opening and, without thinking, she hurled the spear at it.

And hit it, in the mouth. Frantic hands came up to pull it free and the head dropped out of sight, dragging the spear with it. Esyal pushed past Badr and Nyk, leapt up and swung on the end of the spear before it disappeared. Her weight pulled it free and Badr caught her as, unbalanced, she tottered backwards. The point of the spear was covered in blood.

Qualto was about to launch another pan full of boiling water through the gap when it filled with thrusting spear points. Nyk snatched up a chair and swung it at them. For a while it tangled them in confusion but it was eventually shaken off to clatter down behind the barricade.

"Again, Nyk," Esyal shouted. "Again. Keep them busy."

While they were futilely attacking the gap with their spears they shouldn't be able to hack at the door. The same realization soon dawned on the enemy however, and the spear points disappeared to be replaced by even more vigorous chopping than before. The gap was soon extended out of sight, below the top of the barricade.

"Put the lights out, Qualto," she said. He looked at her, puzzled.

"Put them out!" she repeated forcefully. "We'll see them better if they're in the light and we're in the dark."

Qualto did as he was told, leaving the kitchen lit by the light coming in through the gap in the door, the purple flames of his various stoves, and a faint snow-tinted glow coming through the window from the lights in the courtyard beyond.

Esyal continued urgently.

"Nyk, Badr, that table there, that table there—in the corner—on its side. Qualto, get the surveyor behind it." Her instructions placed one table behind the barricade and another in the corner of the room with Josyff slumped behind it—a final defensive enclave.

"No change?" she asked Qualto as he was manipulating Josyff's body into what he hoped would be a comfortable posture.

"No change," he confirmed.

Then Esyal was on the table by the barricade, spear in hand.

She felt a powerful frisson of fear as she saw the size of the gap in the door, but she saw also the men wielding the axes and the fear became a cold rage, a pitiless focus. Part of her was appalled by it, but it stayed silent, knowing that this was not its time.

Two thrusts dispatched the two men with an explosive violence. Esyal noted her strength, accuracy and speed but did not question where they came from—she knew that this was as it should be, and that was enough.

There was a brief lull in the activity at the door, then a figure dashed in front of the gap and lunged at her with a spear. In one move Esyal released the spear she was holding, twisted to avoid the attack and seized the shaft as it passed her. Continuing the turn sharply she tore the spear from the attacker's grasp then twisted back in the opposite direction, driving the butt end at his head. There was a thud that made both Badr and Nyk wince, and the attacker disappeared. Esyal spun the spear to bring it point foremost, ready to impale anything that came within sight.

Then the chopping began again, though this time more hesitantly, the axe-wielders keeping well to the side of the door.

"Take your time!" Esyal shouted. "Make the most of what you've got. The sooner you get in the sooner you die. I don't know how you creatures die, but I know you do and I know you don't like it. And look at your great leader—he's one of us not one of you. Ask him why it has to be you, here, dying in this alien place."

Somewhat to her surprise there was a lull in the chopping and a slight change in the tone of the clamouring voices. The lull did not last for long, however. She could just make out Adroyan's voice, raised and angry, through the din, then the destruction of the door began again, as vigorously as before.

Several figures scuttled past the gap quicker than she could react. Then suddenly two dashed into view, preparing to throw. Instantly she lunged at them, swinging the head of her spear in a short arc as she did so. It struck neither but it fouled the throw of one who tripped and fell as he dodged the blow. The second evaded her attack more skilfully and threw. Esyal just managed to duck and swing her weapon up defensively. It caught the spear on the underside and deflected it upwards. Even without looking, she knew what she had done, almost feeling the trajectory of the spear as it flew across the kitchen to strike the window and, as she turned and dropped below the level of the barricade, she heard the glass breaking. She had an instant vision of great flurries of snow and splintering glass cascading into the room carried on the bitter wind as though dashing to safety. Qualto's stoves flared briefly in retaliation, and... there was something strange about the light beyond the window.

Then Qualto was dashing through the storm, brush in hand, hurriedly sweeping up the glass.

Esyal could not forbear. "What the devil are you doing!" she shouted. "We don't need to have..."

"I can use the glass." Qualto cut across her, his tone brooking no further debate.

Esyal hesitated for a moment then turned her attention to Nyk and Badr.

"Up here, now!" she said.

Even as the two men were clambering on to the table to join her, Esyal was turning back to the door. To her horror a figure was struggling through the widened gap.

"Leave us alone," she screamed. "Go back where you came from." At the same time she thrust the spear clean through him, turning it so that its point was driven deep into the undamaged part of the door, wedging him there.

"Adroyan," she bellowed furiously. "You madman. Who do you think you're dealing with? Send these creatures back! We'll kill them all—choke this door—this entire passage—with your stinking dead. You will not get in here. *You will not get the surveyor!*"

There was no reply except a redoubling of the din. She had expected nothing. The outburst had been for her own, and the others' benefit.

The body in the door jerked obscenely as unseen hands struggled to pull it free.

"This is what you've been sent here for," Esyal shouted. "To die, like this one. To die at the whim of a madman. To die for nothing."

Again there was no response, but again she had expected none. It needed no great insight to realize that Adroyan's troops were beyond all reason. Whatever power drove them cared nothing for their lives and had inspired them to care nothing for themselves. Once they broke through, she and the others would be killed without a thought.

She made a silent vow to kill Josyff when all else was lost.

CHAPTER 79

Josyff stepped back as the noise resonated around the room. It echoed all about him, pressing in on him, making him feel as though he were the source of it.

His mind clutched for explanations. What could have struck the door like that? It was no peevish blow of the fist, nor even a hammer blow. Yet there was no room on the stairs for anything bigger—and whatever made that noise, was big!

There was a second blow. He placed a hand on the wall to steady himself. It was shaking with the impact.

This was not possible—not in thick stone walls like these.

Unless the whole tower was moving! But that couldn't be, surely?

A brief vision of being crushed by this room as it collapsed and tumbled through the rooftops below made him glance round quickly, looking for cracks appearing in the walls. But there were none—of course—he knew well enough that his body was far more sensitive to vibration than any building! This rationalization, however, did not stop him jumping when a third blow shook the room.

He became aware of his heart thumping and his breathing becoming rapid and noisy.

He tightened his grip on the machete, partly to stop his hands from trembling.

"Come on, come on, damn you," he muttered through clenched teeth. "Show yourselves. Let's get to this."

Then the familiar screeching of the Diirredyn was gibbering about him again, unintelligible but coherent and full at once of both malice and triumph.

Josyff focused grimly on the door, waiting for the sounds of an attack on it.

But there were no such sounds—just the ghastly din of Diirredyn. And then, pulsing to its rhythm, the door began to change shape. Josyff screwed his eyes tight shut and then opened them, but the effect was still the same. Not only was the door changing shape, but so was the frame... and all the stonework around it. It was a terrifying sight—and it was spreading. He had seen it before—it was like the distortion he had seen in the Great Hall—just before Esyal moved towards it—just before he... came here.

Instinct more than reason told him abruptly that while Amrassian might have thrown him into some abyss of unknowing where neither the Diirredyn nor he could reach him, that would not stop them trying and that though they could not indeed enter this world to seize him, they could perhaps encompass it, change it—bend it to their will until it became nothing more than a prison cell for him—like an insect trapped in amber. What this would avail them he did not pause to consider, so frightening was the idea.

The distortion continued to spread, bellying the door and the wall towards him. He moved back, at the same time tentatively prodding the door with his machete. The contact felt solid and real—he had half-expected the machete to pass through it. He cast a hasty glance over his shoulder. The far side of the room and the outer door—his only way out—were unaffected. But what was beyond it? That turbulent darkness he had just fled from? Still the distortion grew. He thrust the machete against the door and leaned on it in the faint hope that somehow this might stop its advance. But it had no effect. Instead, the end of the machete twisted to follow the surreal lines of the door. He withdrew it hastily and it was normal again.

But what would happen to him if the distortion reached *him*?

The room was by now conspicuously smaller and claustrophobia began to make itself felt, turning his stomach solid and cold, making his breathing shallow and harsh.

He waved the machete vaguely in front of him and shouted.

"Stop this. Show yourselves." Then, desperately, "If you kill me, you'll have nothing." But even as he spoke he remembered that perhaps his real self—whatever that might be—could well be still in the Keep, in the charge of Esyal and the others. Although he felt all too solid and whole in this place, it might be—it *was*—no more than a construct taken from the depths of his mind by...?

And what would it mean to the Diirredyn, to Amrassian, to the real world of the Keep if he perished here?

Perhaps nothing?

Would this body, this consciousness, just be an inadvertent casualty of a greater battle elsewhere?

The thoughts did not reassure. He thrust the machete into his belt and, despite himself, reached out and pushed on the nearing door. A ripple ran through it and out through the whole distorted region. The door did not feel any different, but, just as had happened with the machete, his hand changed shape, the fingers extending and twisting, the palm spreading obscenely, the whole alive with tiny rippling movements. He gazed at it for a moment, horrified, then snatched it back. As he did so he had the feeling that he was drawing part of the Diirredyn's will with it—acid and clinging. He opened and closed his hand several times to dispel the sensation, at the same time examining it minutely. It did not appear to be injured but it felt contaminated, as if he had been marked in some way, like a hunting lure. His concern about this vanished however, as his gaze returned to the distortion, its expansion continuing, seemingly enlivened by his touch.

He felt his control slipping away. Struggle with it as he might, his claustrophobia was growing. He looked round frantically as though some mode of escape might miraculously have appeared—something that would whisk him into another world as had happened before. But there was nothing.

Only the door behind him.

He took a further step backward as the screeching of the Diirredyn grew louder, rising and falling, part breaking waves, part religious chant, all foul.

He was in the alcove of the outer door. Under other circumstances, such a place would have afforded shelter and protection, but here it became an inevitable trap as the distortion touched the wall.

And still it advanced.

He had to breathe!

Heart pounding, gasping for breath... for a moment, Josyff was gone. Something else that shared his body, older by far than he, emerged to turn him round, drive back the bolts on the door and push it open.

It was he who slammed it after he staggered through however, as much in defiance as in any hope that it might achieve anything. Turning as he retreated, he collided with a stone parapet wall. Glancing round quickly he saw he was on a narrow balcony running around a circular tower. A vertical ladder by the door ran up to and along a steep conical roof that terminated in a slender metal spike. But all this he noted merely in passing. What dominated his vision was the sky—if sky it could be called any more. For wherever he looked, all he could see was fire. Baleful flames roared high into the heavens amid billowing clouds of livid smoke that tumbled over themselves in their haste, like a panicking crowd. Josyff clutched the stone parapet in despair, then, searching for a perspective, he looked over it. But there was no patchwork of roofs and courtyards below. Instead, the tower disappeared into a swirling sea of molten rock. As he watched, a breaker, lurid red and so bright that he had to half close his eyes, crashed against the stonework. He felt the impact through the stonework, and the scrabbling urgency as it reached up the wall towards him like a manic climber searching for a handhold, before it tumbled back in a shower of arcing sparks.

The earth ablaze, the sky ablaze, Josyff could do no other than turn back to the door. It took his eyes a moment to recover after the brightness filling everywhere, but he knew what he was looking at even before he could see it clearly. The distortion that had outflanked his impromptu defences at the top of the stairs and forced him out into this nightmare was shimmering in the coarse grain of the wood. Long held at bay, panic now surged through him. He turned round several times, looking frantically in every direction and slapping his hands against the parapet wall, against the wall of the tower, against himself, as if this might push this appalling world away. A juddering vibration shook the tower as another breaker struck it and the distortion in the door trembled and edged forward. The movement drove the last vestiges of coherent thought from Josyff. He lurched forward, and, in imitation of the breakers below, clambered up the ladder.

It was the briefest of scrabbling journeys to the top of the tower.

He stood there, one foot on the top rung of the ladder, the other pressed against the steep roof, and his right hand clutching the spike that rose from the peak of the tower. The molten sea boiling at its base stretched out and out, but there was no horizon. Imperceptibly it became part of the blazing sky that arched high above him.

If this place is mine, he found himself thinking, almost praying, let it be otherwise.

The tower shook again and a surge of flame-lit smoke briefly darkened part of the sky.

The spike he was holding felt secure and safe, homely almost. He tightened his grip about it for comfort.

Let it be otherwise!

Like a child.

Childish...

No!

No!

This is my end...

How did I come here?

Step by step...

Consequences...

All unforeseeable...

Briefly, an image of his wife...

I am so sorry...

So sorry...

So much not done...

No! No! Not whimpering. Not like a child.

The tower shook again.

Both terror and rage surged through him and he raised a fist to the burning sky and cursed the Diirredyn and the First Comers equally.

Then he took a deep breath and, roaring, he clattered wildly down the sloping ladder and launched himself out into the void.

CHAPTER 80

Esyal did not have time to ponder her brutal decision to kill Josyff if he could no longer be defended—what it meant—what she had become. The kitchen—Qualto's orderly world—had become another place—a nightmare maelstrom. Dense snow, driven by a battering wind, was pouring in through the broken window. Lit by the wildly dancing lights from Qualto's roaring stoves, and the shadows of the figures fighting in the doorway, it twisted and surged around the room as if searching for an escape, before lapsing into incongruously graceful drifts, transforming the scene into a shifting and bitterly cold landscape.

Esyal, Nyk and Badr were taking a toll of the attackers with their machetes and captured spears, but, despite the losses, the assault against the door was being redoubled and with each increase in the width of the gap it became more difficult to defend.

In between tending something on one of his stoves, Qualto had wrapped Josyff in a mixture of tablecloths and towels in an attempt to protect him from the deepening cold.

As he was returning to one of his stoves again, a rending screech cut through the din of the Diirredyn and the curses of the defenders. A large part of the door had been prised loose.

"Get ready to fall back and protect Josyff," Esyal shouted.

Qualto stumbled to the table. He was carrying a heavy pan.

"Help me up!"

Esyal hesitated.

"Help me up, damn you, this is dangerous."

Hands reached down and hauled him on to the table.

Esyal crouched low to question him but Qualto jabbed a finger towards Josyff.

"Go now—right now!"

Again Esyal hesitated, but Qualto cast a knowing glance at the pan he was holding. Even in the wind that was shaking the room, a pungent smell and curls of smoke were issuing from it, and snowflakes landing on it hissed into nothingness.

Esyal shouted to the others.

"Now! Get down! Protect Josyff!"

As Badr and Nyk clambered off the table, Qualto stood up and hurled the pan through the door in a single move. He followed it immediately with two bottles hastily retrieved from his pockets then dropped down below the barricade with a speed few would have thought him capable of. Esyal took the hint and did the same. There was a low concussion and a flare of yellow light from the corridor. Something struck the top of the door opening and clattered on to the table in front of Esyal, then black smoking flames were reaching greedily through the gap in the door. Fed by dreadful screams from the corridor they had an urgency which seemed to mimic that of the snow blowing in through the window.

Esyal picked up what had fallen on to the table. It was a long sliver of glass, streaky with grease and soot. She looked at the broken window and then at Qualto, now scuttling across the floor to join the others by Josyff.

Kitchens are dangerous places, eh? she thought grimly as she tossed the shard back over the barricade. Not a fraction as dangerous as you though, Qualto, not a fraction.

She was about to stand up to make a final defence of the door before retreating when a violent impact shook the barricade and tumbled her off the table. The door had finally yielded. As it collapsed into the room it took with it most of Nyk's makeshift barricade. Esyal rolled to her feet just as a figure lurched uncontrollably through the debris. Without a pause in her movement, she swung the machete and severed the man's neck with a single blow. The carcase staggered on for a couple of steps before sprawling forward on the snow-covered floor, its spraying blood briefly reddening the whirling snow. Two other figures paused momentarily in the doorway at the sight of this sudden and massive destruction, and died immediately for their pains—as did a third, tripping over their falling bodies.

The wind howled as though in triumph and Esyal had to steady herself against its blast as snow streamed past her horizontally, sweeping out through the doorway.

Abruptly, a bowman appeared, standing against the far side of the corridor. This time it was Esyal who hesitated, torn between her instinct to attack and destroy, and her tactical reasoning which saw that he was too far away to be reached without exposing herself to attack from the side. She saw his eyes narrowing against the wind as he raised and drew the bow, but just as she was preparing to drop to one side, a long spear passed by her and thrust clear through her would-be attacker. His arrow skittered harmlessly across the floor as he fell and Qualto seized Esyal's arm.

"Defend the surveyor!" he shouted to her, dragging her away from the door.

She managed a slap of gratitude on his shoulder as she recovered her balance, then she pushed him towards the table that was sheltering the others and roared, "Machete!" at them. Badr lofted one to her which she caught with her free hand. Using the momentum of the catch she turned to face the doorway, arms crossed and extended.

Only moments ago she had threatened to block it with the enemy dead. Now, circumstance presented her with the opportunity, for several men were struggling to get through the tangle of debris and bodies. They were armed and armoured in a variety of ways, she noted—no uniformity, not even consistency—a bizarrely random collection for an army. Out of the depths of our minds, she thought, briefly. Not that it mattered. It was sufficient now that they could be killed and, with her two machetes arcing out in wide destructive swathes, she set about making good her threat. By a dark irony, the door, cleared of the barricade, proved easier to defend than before. Wide enough to give her room to manoeuvre, it was too narrow for the attackers to push through in force. And they paid a fearful price. Only an occasional slip by Esyal on the blood-slicked snow-covered floor gave them any respite. Then, unasked and unsought, Badr, Qualto and Nyk were by her side, long spears and missiles harassing.

For an instant she was in another time, another place. Long ranks of levelled pikes buckled and swayed, but held against a vast and murderous enemy. Clouds of arrows darkened a bright blue cloudless sky and the air was full of the screams of the dying and the roars of fighters. Then, even as her mind reached out to touch these images, it curled in upon itself and, in the blink of an eye, she was in ten thousand such battles. She felt the very depths of what she was, of what made her, spiralling back, spanning ages and places beyond knowing—eternally holding the line against those who would enslave and destroy. This was the source of her new knowledge—not taught or given to her by Amrassian, but already there—not new but *ancient* knowledge. Revealed to her, perhaps, through Amrassian's strange vantage, but hers already, nevertheless.

Then there was silence. So sudden was it that she almost lurched forward, the vivid immediacy of her revelation gone as quickly as it had come.

And so deep the silence...

Strange vantage...

All these creatures had it, she reflected bitterly. What could they see that she couldn't? How could they move in their worlds?

And something *was* moving. She could feel it—far below her awareness...

Something bad...

Her skin crawled.

393

Then the wind, powerful and icy on her back, shivered her back to where she was.

"Have they gone? Is it over?" Nyk whispered tentatively through its howling.

Esyal shook her head and raised a hand for silence. Her body was alive with warnings.

"Get ready," she said, leaning forward slightly and raising her two weapons.

"What fo..."

Nyk did not finish his question. The stack of bodies engorging the doorway suddenly swelled towards them, then overtopping itself like a breaking wave, it burst into the room, corpses given a brief return to life as they tumbled and sprawled across the snow-covered floor.

The wind screamed.

"Get back! Get back!" Esyal was shouting unnecessarily as all of them jumped back to avoid this awful flood.

Nyk slipped and tumbled over backwards but Badr caught him and dragged him to the last remnant of shelter behind the table were Josyff sat propped upright like an unstrung marionette.

Esyal recovered from the destruction of their second barricade as quickly as she recovered her balance. Stepping over the bodies, she moved forward towards the door in anticipation of a further attack. Qualto stood by her, his spear swaying unsteadily from side to side across the now open doorway. The snow was covering their backs even as they waited.

One of the stoves flared momentarily, filling the room with an angry light and throwing the shadows of the two defenders on to the snow rushing past them. As it faded, Esyal blinked and then retreated a pace as though trying to bring something into focus. Qualto followed her.

Then Esyal leaned over to Qualto and said, quietly, "Go to the others."

Qualto hesitated.

"Go now," Esyal insisted urgently, though still speaking softly. "Something's coming you can't help me with. Guard the surveyor as best you can." She looked at him significantly. "Whatever happens, don't let them take him alive."

He returned her look.

"This is... awful," he said after a difficult silence.

"Yes," Esyal replied. "It is. It's also not the time for such thoughts. We're where we are. We do what we must to survive." She nodded through the storm towards the far corner. "Now go."

Qualto retreated reluctantly.

"And thank you."

Esyal turned back to the doorway.

Something had changed. Everything was subtly different. There would be no more reckless charges, she knew. Whatever motivated these creatures, she and the others had somehow made that approach too expensive for them. She felt no sense of victory however, no elation. This was not over yet. Her enemy still lived.

She peered narrowly into the tunnel formed by the converging streaks of snow surging past her and through the doorway. In the distance, she thought she saw a fire-fly light bobbing and dancing.

Distance?

Where was the far wall of the passage? Why wasn't snow piling against it as it was even now against her legs.

They're doing what they do, came the thought. Coming from a direction, from somewhere, you cannot even comprehend.

Esyal refused the fear and doubt being offered.

But they must come where I *can* comprehend if they're to reach the Surveyor.

But what will they bring?

Esyal's lip curled as she crushed this, too.

And what will *I* bring?

The light was definitely there. And it was growing—or nearing?—she could not tell which. It changed and shifted as though she were looking at it through the bottom of a cracked glass. It was profoundly disorientating and she instinctively raised a machete defensively.

Then, as though he had been there all the time and reality itself had simply unfolded to reveal him, he was there. Adroyan. The same but different. He shimmered as though standing in the flames of a great fire. Fading after-images swept from him as he moved, just as they had when he had run from the Great Hall. Esyal levelled the machete at him. It, too, left after-images as it moved. They were no less disconcerting than they had been before but she did not allow them to distract her. Dimly she was aware that she had perhaps already answered the question about what they were—the Diirredyn must come to where *she* could comprehend if they were to reach the Surveyor, but they did not fit into this world—*could* not fit into this world—any more than she could see both sides of a coin at the same time or an eye could see itself. It defied some deep natural order. Yet, in their frenzy, they *were* coming—distorting this order with a force that must increase exponentially as they drew nearer, squeezing time itself and the events it carried into the now. She was appalled by her sense of the destruction that would come—how could they not see it?

But she let the question and all its implications float by her unhindered and unhindering, for she also sensed that she and Adroyan would be pivotal in either allowing or preventing this. She felt a brief understanding and pity for Amrassian. Whatever kind of creatures he and his kind were, they were floundering against such intentions. Their ancient enemy, seemingly infected with a suicidal insanity, must have stunned them into disbelief and denial. Reaching out into some vague and dangerous realm must have been an act of desperation, and touching her and Josyff must have been as much terrifying as it was reassuring. At the same time, she could not avoid a degree of scorn. For a race fighting a seemingly eternal war, had they not learned yet that to defeat an enemy you must be at least as bad as they? Only then might you survive—marred but perhaps wiser—your only shreds of comfort subsequently being that you did not start the conflict and you stopped when you were safe. Then again, perhaps they had—they had found and somehow primed their weapon in her—an alien creature—unpredictably dangerous—and expendable—pivots can be crushed.

She cursed them, but not without some grim irony as her scorn tilted back towards respect.

Then there was only Adroyan.

"You should have come sooner," she said. "Spared your soldiers their dismal fate."

"They served their purpose," Adroyan replied. His voice still resonated with the chilling sound of the Diirredyn, but the callous indifference in it was all-too-human.

"And when you have served yours?" Esyal taunted.

"I will be as *they* are. Lord of all this world as it is transformed—as it transcends—into their realm—as all that is transcends into their realm."

Esyal staggered slightly as a violent gust of wind buffeted her. She found the chill on her back oddly heartening—a touch of normality in the face of the unsettling view of Adroyan, seemingly there and not there at the same time.

Almost despite herself, she let her anger spill out. "You're insane. Your masters will destroy 'all that is.'" She sneered the phrase. "Can't you see that? Can't you feel it—all around you—in everything they do? And why would you want such power? What can you do with it? Have you even given it a moment's thought?"

The wind howled into the ensuing silence. Adroyan neither moved nor replied. Esyal gestured to the bodies lying at their feet.

"You've seen the way they treat their own. Do you honestly think they'll reward *you*—a feeble... alien... creature from a... lesser... world?"

Try as she might, she could not read his face, shadowy in the flickering, snow-filled light. She tried an appeal, a small part of her still clinging to avoiding a conflict.

"Turn back. Turn back now. You've been used and deceived." She was about to call him "a useful idiot" again but, with an effort, she did not.

"The surveyor is needed," Adroyan said, as though she had not spoken.

Esyal's faint hope guttered out.

"I *will* kill you if you come nearer."

Adroyan tipped his head forward as though listening to something. Then, his voice steady and cold, he said, "Yes. Quite the blood-soaked slaughterer, aren't you, murderess? Quite the fitting champion for our vicious and poisonous race. But you cannot harm me—I am beyond your reach. Stay and perish, or stand aside and spare yourself—and your sorry companions; it's of no import. The surveyor is found, he is ours already. No place could hide him from our seeing. All that remains is to retrieve his frame here to plumb the depths within him."

"There is one place hidden from your seeing."

Adroyan inclined his head questioningly.

"Death. We will kill him before we allow you to take him."

Adroyan turned and looked directly at her. He was silent for a moment, then, "You, perhaps, might—but not the others. They will be too slow, too hesitant."

"They..."

Adroyan caught her while she was still speaking. His move was so fast that she was sliding across the floor, her body ringing with the impact, before she realized what was happening.

Consciousness was slipping away from her as she saw Adroyan enter the room, flame-lit after-images flaring about him, as though his very presence was tearing reality to admit the Diirredyn themselves.

CHAPTER 81

Henk did not question what he was doing. Whatever the creatures were that had caused all this mess, they were affected in some way by the snow-lit beam of light curving out from the Beacon and that was enough. He still sensed the beam's opposition to the forces that were distorting it into this unnatural pathway, and he could do no other than join with it.

"Move, move!" he grunted as he levered on the Beacon's handles, exhorting both himself and the light to battle on relentlessly. Ripples of his efforts trembled along the beam occasionally accumulating and running to and fro as though in search of a way to break free, only to dissipate and vanish like waves retreating down a sea shore.

Henk's long, wiry frame had a strength and a stamina which was deceptive, and though he could feel the resistance to his efforts growing, it served only to make him even more determined. As did the mounting cacophony about him, gibbering to the rhythms of the dancing beam. He found himself listening for some clue about what caused the most angry response but no easy pattern emerged.

Eventually he began to tire. The Beacon was becoming heavier to move as the beam's curvature increased, and it was snapping back to its original position with increasing violence. Soon he would not be able to move it at all and then what would happen? He would have to do something else. But what? Turning it off would be disastrous, he was sure now, nor could he wedge it to shine along some other trajectory even if he had been able to move it.

He had no choice but to stop briefly to catch his breath. The beacon juddered into stillness and the sound of the wind impinged on him again. He slapped his hand against the Beacon in frustration as he gazed out along the curving beam. How long could this go on for? Would it eventually be forced into a full circle, to mark the enveloping of the Keep with a glittering noose? He had a fleeting, choking vision of a sphere of darkness—nothingness—shrinking and shrinking, bending the towers of the Keep inwards, then the ramparts of its higher walls, then...

His grip tightened on the handles of the Beacon as if for reassurance, but none was to be found. What did come was the unwanted knowledge that during this brief pause the Beacon had become too heavy to move. The discovery sent his mood oscillating between rage and deep fatalism and it was some time before he gained control of himself. Then in a gesture like a parent brushing something from a troubled child's face he ran a hand down the lens of the Beacon. The touch of the light on his hand felt strange—it was as though something was flowing around it at great speed.

His gesture dislodged some melting snowflakes and they smeared into rainbow streaks before they vanished, unexpected colour in this eerie landscape of glaring brightness and encroaching darkness. Equally unexpected, the image hung in his mind. It was like a lure, and he felt something stirring, being drawn from the depths—remnants of long-forgotten learning, struggling to reassert themselves.

Colours...

Colours splitting, fragmenting...

For the merest instant he was a child leaning forward at a worn but familiar desk, watching in wonder as a thin beam of bright white light was shone into a thick wedge of glass and splintered into those same colours across a white screen.

So long ago... an odd, aching recollection... reaching across his life...

Just as the Beacon's light reached across the mountains and valleys, he thought.

Or used to!

Anger displaced the memory and he looked out into the darkness again. Colours were there too, following his brief glance almost directly into the Beacon's light—dancing and jigging until his eyes adjusted.

A cursory tug at the handles confirmed that the Beacon was now immobile—held there by forces beyond anything he could oppose.

But, as if opened by that shaft of memory, his mind was somehow freer, ranging across possibilities. One drew him on.

He might no longer be able to move the Beacon, but he could move the lens.

The idea shook him. It had an element almost of sacrilege about it. Doing anything to the lens was Nyk's job and *only* Nyk's job on the rare occasions when it was decided that a special cleaning was needed. The lens was quite fragile, its alignment critical and its adjustment difficult. Qualto and he kept a dutiful watching distance away when Nyk was working on it and did *exactly* what he told them if he asked for help. Henk found himself holding his breath in remembrance.

But that was long ago now, he thought as he breathed out—in a time before the world had gone insane. His idea developed.

The lens was large but not heavy, and if he loosened it he would be able to manipulate it and shine at least some part of the beam in different directions. What precise good that might do he could not have said, nor did he consider—it was sufficient that movement of the beam seemed to disturb *them*.

And it was all he could do.

Even so, he still felt a frisson of unease as he looked at the ring of polished hand screws that secured the lens. It was these that had to be handled with care, having to be tightened not only gently but in a certain order to avoid damaging or distorting the lens.

"But I'm only unscrewing them," he muttered, as though explaining directly to Nyk. "There's no harm in that, surely? It's not as though I'm likely to drop the lens, is it?"

His justification made in this one-sided discourse, he set about loosening the screws.

After the experience of the light—or something—passing through his hand, he was reluctant to step directly in front of the Beacon. He had the vague feeling that this same... something... might not only pass through him but carry away some part, perhaps even all of him, sending it hurtling along the beam to... wherever it went.

However, it was not possible to get to the other side of the Beacon round the back, so he was driven to stretching across it to reach the screws on the far side. The higher ones presented no great problem but he soon found that those further round could not be reached like this. Whether he wanted to or not, he would have to step through the beam.

He paused for a moment, torn. Then impatience spurred him on.

He was probably frightened about nothing. How can light do any hurt? All he had to do was step through it quickly. He would be in the light for the briefest of moments.

As though testing the temperature of a bath he waved his hand through the beam, first rapidly then more slowly. The strange effect was still there but it passed as soon as his hand was clear of the light and, as before, seemed to have done no harm.

"Come on, move yourself," he said.

Then, gripping one of the hand screws for support, he took a long stride in front of the Beacon and reached for a screw on the far side. As the light swept over him he felt a sensation somewhere between juddering goose-flesh and stepping from cool shadows into warm sunlight. He had little time to reflect on it however, for the snow had made the platform slippery and his over-extended foot skidded away from him as soon as he put his weight on it. Automatically he released the hand screw he was holding and seized the one he had been reaching for. It saved him from a heavy fall but, as he struggled to regain his balance, he could not avoid putting most of his weight on it.

And it turned.

As it did so, Henk became a spectator in a long, slow nightmare.

He could hear the creaking of the reality all about him as it was being forced ever inwards. He could hear the desperate rush of the light from the Beacon. He could hear the grating of the minor imperfections in the screw.

And he could hear the straining of the lens as the screw tightened.

Then, deafeningly, louder than a thunderclap, he heard the lens cracking.

CHAPTER 82

Josyff was falling.

Falling, falling...

He made no sound now, though his mind was screaming, trailing behind him and cutting through the din of the Diirredyn like the sharpest of blades. Burning brightness boiled and surged before him like the face of the sun, growing ever nearer...

But no impact came...

When he had hurled himself, terrified and demented, from the tower, he had had the tremulous, desperate thought of an explosive but brief pain before a welcome oblivion. But it had not happened.

The inexorable calculator in him emerged.

It was mere heartbeats to that dreadful boiling sea. But he was still falling...

Patterns were forming in the chaos of the brightness before him. Ornate strings necklaced with images of themselves filled his vision, curling and twisting like fantastic plants.

An insight emerged—patterns within patterns—subtle and elusive. Patterns where lay the Way that the Diirredyn were searching for—the Way that would bring them upon their enemies from a direction they could not defend...

But it was a Way that could not be.

The patterns would go on forever. Smaller and smaller but never ending—and never meeting.

Forever...

And *there* was Amrassian's fear—the resources needed to follow this were infinite—gathering them could fracture not only their reality but much more beyond.

Then came a more personal and more immediately frightening realization. He would not stop falling! He would not come to some brutal but swift and crushing end. He too would go on forever, falling down and down through this endlessly shrinking complexity, until...

Until what?

A different terror replaced that which had thrown him from the tower.

He must die in this place, just as surely as if he had fallen into that molten sea. But when? And how? What was this body he was in? What was time and decay in this place? Or would he perhaps become insane first? And if he did, what of this place then, this place formed from his mind? Would it, too, disintegrate, vanish like smoke in the wind? And what of the other part of him, still in the Keep?

But he was alive!

And he wanted to live!

Abruptly, every part of him roared out in a massive declamation of fury and defiance.

The patterns trembled at its touch, their colours shifting and changing.

Then it came to him that there were not two parts to him, one here and some other back in the Keep. They were just different aspects of an entirety—himself, his mind, his world—as they existed across many planes of reality. Planes which were strangely folded and normally unknowable and inaccessible.

Something at the heart of what he was must have placed the deeper reaches of his perception near the edges of these other planes—left him lying in the tidal flats of their shifts and changes, to be found by the Diirredyn, driven to searching in extremities in their war-lust.

Esyal and Adroyan must be the same, presumably. His kin, in a way, blessed, or cursed, with this same arbitrary gift brought down through time; drawn to fill their roles as inexorably as the weight of the world draws water downhill...

Drawn...

As was the Keep, clearly in his mind now. The work he and Badr had done merged with his new insights to reveal its part in these events. Though it was tantalisingly incomplete, he knew now that it was its shape and its coincidence with shapes in the realm of the Diirredyn and Amrassian that had brought these places together, nothing more.

Pure chance or some subtle influence from the Diirredyn?

It was irrelevant.

He had a brief frisson of black humour. What, in any event, could be relevant to a man falling through eternity?

Unexpectedly a reply came.

Survival!

But...

This is a place of the mind—your mind. Use it!

But...

USE IT!

He realized he was shouting. It did not matter that he understood nothing of what was happening. He had faced and overcome intractable problems all his life. Why should he stop now?

He closed his eyes and turned to his inner view of the Keep.

It was beautiful. Glittering and many-faceted, it was shot through with subtle patterns of symmetries and planes of being, and it shimmered with countless movements and rhythms. It was a vision he knew he could not see in his 'normal' world—there, its unseen, unseeable, splendour was reduced to stone and timber and the fussy clutter of numbers that marked out the extent of the Diirredyn's interference, yielding that intractable closing error.

But it was changing. Changing in response to that same interference. The Diirredyn's relentless pressure was forcing it into shapes that could not be sustained. He saw where his place in it would be. *He* was the Heart of the Keep. A final key, a final bridge. The ever narrowing focus would move into the depths of his mind. Except that he knew now what Amrassian had known, there was no end, there was no point of final focus. And what would happen if that aspect of him in the Keep were taken by Adroyan— himself presumably a portal for the Diirredyn? Would they be able to seek him out here, where his conscious mind was?

He *must* find a way back! Whatever reason Amrassian had for throwing him into this place, he was helpless here and it could soon become a trap. He *had* to be on ground that he knew and understood. Ground on which he could at least attempt to fight. Ground on which Esyal might be better able to protect him.

Then something caught his attention. Something moving rapidly through the constantly changing vista of the Keep. A bright thread of light was whiplashing to and fro as though trying to escape. Suddenly, and very briefly, it arced beyond the Keep and a bright sliver flew free.

He could feel it luring him and, too, the will of the Diirredyn opposing it, striving to crush it. Then he sensed something he had not expected to feel again—a human presence—opposing the Diirredyn's opposition, willing the light into movement. It felt almost alien, so long did it seem since he had run from the Common Room—and people.

It was Henk!

His presence was unmistakeable. Almost in spite of himself, hope and excitement filled him.

Whatever you're doing, Henk, keep doing it—keep doing it!

The light burst free again. It hovered momentarily and something in Josyff reached out to it.

And took it!

CHAPTER 83

Esyal struggled with both pain and despair. Pain from the blow that had sent her across the room and despair at the sight of what Adroyan had become. The after-images that followed his every move were now far more intense, full of blazing turbulence and seeming to have a life of their own. They reached back to the shattered door and beyond, into...

Don't look!

Esyal closed her eyes and jerked her head away. The briefest glimpse had told her that this was the world of the Diirredyn and, warrior though she might be, to stare directly into it was to take her despair beyond any chance of recovery. That place and its denizens were Amrassian's problem. Hers was Adroyan. She was the doorkeeper. Her task was to deal with the Diirredyn's vanguard into this world, this solitary intruder.

Not that her thoughts were so ordered. They clattered piecemeal through her efforts to stay conscious. Every part of her seemed to have taken the impact of Adroyan's blow and the urge to curl up and sink into darkness was almost irresistible. She clenched her fist in a brief spasm of determination and found it tightening about something. Despite the power and speed of Adroyan's blow, some instinct had maintained her grip on her machete. It helped her to gather her scattered wits.

As did the snow covering the floor. It was cold on her cheek and the bitter wind was blowing flakes into her mouth and nose.

Adroyan was moving towards Josyff, still slumped in the corner and hesitantly protected by Nyk, Qualto and Badr, oddly shadowed in the turbulent light.

They would not even slow him, she knew. Better they abandon Josyff and flee than die fruitlessly, facing this thing that Adroyan had become.

But even if she had been able to shout a warning, it was unlikely it would be heard above the howling wind and the shrieking chorus of the Diirredyn.

"You can still move" came an angry thought. "Pain never hurt anyone—do something!"

Using the machete for support and breathing deeply to clear her mind, she began to lever herself up. The wind buffeted her as she stood and she lurched awkwardly into a nearby table.

Her eyes were fixed on Adroyan. His back was to her and he did not appear to have noticed this small movement in all the uproar.

Just as well, she thought. Not only was she weaker, but whatever attributes the Diirredyn had imbued him with, he was radically different from the man she had bested at every meeting so far. She had not seen even a hint of the blow that had felled her—and he had struck her while she was talking.

Serve me right, she reflected, with a reluctant hint of admiration at the tactic. Took you for granted, didn't I? But it won't happen again.

Then, she realized that Adroyan had not seized Josyff. Surely he was not afraid of the three defenders?

Snow was flying past her, almost horizontally, converging—but on what? Where was it going? She found she had lost all sense of distance. At one moment, Adroyan was far, then near, now surrounded by the blizzard, now surrounded by the boiling flames sweeping from his every movement. The images flowed to and fro like a bad dream—a complex maelstrom such as she had seen in the Great Hall. Only Josyff and the others seemed normal—unchanging, oddly detached spectators.

And Adroyan was moving with peculiar slowness, as though he were struggling against something.

The wind?

No. Something more than that. Indeed, as she tried to make sense of what she was seeing, the flames and the snow-laden wind themselves appeared to be struggling, one with the other, yet somehow unable to reach each other. She had a sense of conflict happening beyond her ability to see. The battlefield of the Diirredyn and the First Comers?

It did not matter. She could only deal with what she could see and that was Adroyan. Struggling he might be, but he was still moving forward and he would reach Josyff soon enough. Once that happened, she realized sharply, then the flames and the snow *would* meet and this seemingly eternal battle would break through into this world carrying total destruction with it.

He had to be stopped.

With his back still towards her, a variety of killing and disabling strokes were open to her, but the difficulty she was having in judging distance made her hesitant to charge in. And too, how heightened was his fighting skill now? That he had not killed her when she was down might have been ineptitude on his part, but then perhaps it might have simply been contempt—she was no longer a threat. Similarly, was his back being turned to her a sign of folly or disdain, or a feint, a trap to lure her into recklessness? She cut through her own speculation. One thing was not in doubt; she had no time to debate such niceties.

She tapped her hand on the table she had steadied herself against, then paused and looked down at it. She gave it a gentle push and it moved quite easily. Any noise it made could not be heard over the general din.

The floor under her feet was slippery, but there was nothing else for it!

A bright light suddenly filled the room. It turned the streaking snow black and the flames dull and grey, but it was gone as quickly as it had come.

In the brief interval of its illumination however, the distorting perspectives had vanished and the room was normal again. It acted like a signal to Esyal. Still clutching the machete and holding that momentary image in her mind, she began to push the table towards where Adroyan had been. Her feet slithered on the snow-covered floor but she used her stumbling instability to push the table harder and faster. She sensed after-images peeling off from it—and herself—as cold and white as Adroyan's were blazing, but she ignored them.

Adroyan had reached Josyff and was bending forward, his arms extended to take him. Nyk, Qualto and Badr all had their weapons extended and their hands raised as though to protect their eyes against something, but their defence was vague and unfocused as if they could not actually see Adroyan.

Esyal was moving so quickly now that she felt she was falling, but Adroyan seemed almost to be moving with her, so slowly was she nearing him.

She heard herself screaming in fury and frustration as Adroyan completed his long, slow movement and placed his hands either side of Josyff's head.

Josyff was floating—being carried by this fragment of light. But to where? Would it dance off and continue him on his hurtling journey further and further into the unending depths? Or would it be folded back into the Keep? And had he any choice about what it did?

There were no answers. The Keep was still there—both in his mind and in what his eyes were seeing. He *had* to get back to it... get away from this place...

Had to...

The light flickered for a moment and once again Josyff sensed the presence of Henk. He reached out for it—touched it—felt it falter...

A noise, sharp, whip-crack short, sent a shimmer through him and everything about him.

The bright white light changed.

Josyff's eyes opened.

He was staring directly into Adroyan's face. Eyes like black pits stared back. Josyff's widened in terror. He tried to turn his head away but Adroyan's grip was too strong. He was helpless. He had returned to the Keep as he had wished but it was not the familiar ground he had expected, somewhere where reason and tactics and cunning might be used. Behind the looming bulk of Adroyan all was turmoil and confusion as flames and blinding snow combated.

He could make out Adroyan's mouth moving.

{"You are ours now, Measurer."} The voices of the Diirredyn filled his head, hideously clear now. *{"Your strangeness has opened the Way. We shall pass through this... place... and on to the annihilation of our enemies—to our final victory."}*

Josyff managed to tear his gaze away for a moment and glance sideways. He could see Esyal, her mouth wide, her eyes blazing, moving towards Adroyan, pushing something, white echoes of her movements flaring out behind her. But everything about her was painfully slow. She would not be able to help him.

"Look at me!" It was Adroyan's voice this time, though resonating with the sound of the Diirredyn.

Josyff's eyes snapped to the front again. From somewhere he found a spark of resistance.

"Don't do this. Don't go to that place." His voice was faint and distant even to himself. "There is no Way! It cannot be! Everything will be destroyed!"

"You are a vessel, Measurer. The entire power of the Ancients has been dedicated to this great coming together—this sacred moment. It is far beyond your understanding. You have served your purpose. Be proud as you die that you have been the means to the creation of this new world. Your name will be honoured down all eternity."

The word 'die' rang in Josyff's ears like a clanging tocsin, the focus of all that he was and his denial of Adroyan's intention. A vague and a distant sound began to crystallize about the word also, but surging into his mind came the memory of Qualto's knife. Even as it did he realized that his hand was closing about it in his pocket. It was solid and comforting and any qualms he might have had about what he was going to do with it were gone utterly. He drew the knife, thumbed open the blade and made a slashing diagonal lunge.

He had scarcely moved when a massive blow struck the back of his hand and knocked the knife from it. The reflexes that had drawn the knife however, were still in play, and immediately his hand clawed and returned to its lunge toward Adroyan's throat.

But just as effortlessly as he had disarmed him, so now Adroyan seized Josyff's wrist. It was a powerful, irresistible grip.

There was weary contempt in Adroyan's voice. "There is nothing you can do, Measurer. It is over for you."

Josyff's defiance again found voice, though this time in a mindless scream of rage and frustration. It ended with the cry, "Esyal!" triggered by a glimpse of her still moving towards him with terrifying slowness.

There was an all too human scorn in Adroyan's reply. "Your Warrior is a broken reed, Measurer. Like you, she had her choice. Like you she chose wrongly. Now she is in a place where she cannot reach us. It is over for her too."

Though Josyff did not notice the change, Adroyan had released his hands and was again holding his head.

Then the sound he had heard began to intrude on him. A groaning, straining sound as of something reluctantly yielding. As it grew in intensity so it rose in pitch to a tortured shrieking, and with it, as if they were bound together, Josyff could sense Esyal drawing nearer... faster and faster.

Trailing from her, following her, carrying her? was a dazzling iridescence.

It filled everywhere, pervading both the flames and the hurtling snow with its countless colours. The shrieking, now almost unbearable, ended abruptly in a sharp, but thunderous, crash, which made Josyff, belatedly, raise his hands to cover his ears. At the same time, there was a violent impact and Adroyan's grip on his head was gone.

As was Adroyan...

But where? Indeed, where had *everything* gone?

For all about Josyff now was awash with swirling colours.

Is this how it is to be? Is this the result of the Diirredyn's folly? Is this the end of all things?

The thought took him completely by surprise, as did the curiosity that came with it when he might reasonably have expected fear.

But then it did not feel like the end of anything. Rather, it was like the lancing of a long-festering sore—a release. He lifted a hand and the colours swirled about it as though the air itself had become visible. And shapes began to form in it—coherent shapes. At first he could not identify them, then...

There was... Esyal... shimmering—standing with her back to him...

And Adroyan, rising to face her...

She had downed him!

But he was an appalling sight—demonic almost—radiating both malice and great power.

Josyff struggled to his feet—he must help—Esyal was in great danger—she could not be left to face this thing alone.

Yet even as he made to step forward, he knew he could not help her. This might once have been Qualto's kitchen, a simple, functional room inside the Keep, but now it was awash with the golden lines—a boiling confusion of different realities coming together as great forces gathered. The perspectives his eyes allowed him showed him far less than his many other new senses recognized. Adroyan and Esyal might seem to be near to him but parts of them were in other places. She was the Warrior—the manifestation of Amrassian's people here, guarding this impossible by-way that the Diirredyn were seeking. If she fell, then he would not be able to stand against Adroyan. His inner knowledge would be won by the Diirredyn and *all* things would fall.

But the realization made no difference. He still could not help her.

What then was his role now? Surely not that of passive, helpless spectator? He, who had been the focus of all this horror and madness, was to stand and wait the outcome of another's battle?

That could not be. He must not allow it to be.

His mind raced faster and faster, reason battling against increasing terror and frustration. He raised his clenched fists. Again, rainbow colours eddied in the wake of this movement, at once beautiful and a measure of the deep mystery of the world he was occupying...

A world being squeezed and distorted by the Diirredyn.

He moved his hand again and watched the colours washing from it.

Then as his hand turned, some of them merged briefly into glittering bright white threads before parting again, and from somewhere he understood what it was.

This was the light that had carried him back to this world!

The white light he had seen breaking free from the confines of the Keep!

From the Diirredyn's influence!

Somehow it had been shattered into its component parts...

Released...

Was it that that had brought him back to this world?

It did not matter—he could feel the light... feel it! Working still against the Diirredyn's will, and their efforts to find a way into this world in search of victory.

He looked again at Adroyan, fearsome and powerful, and Esyal, watchful and afraid but unwavering.

All about them was screaming confusion, blood red glaring and ice blizzard white, laced with frenzied golden lines struggling as though to escape a great wind.

So much coming together—such an alignment.

And the Diirredyn—ravening for victory.

And he was pivotal...

...

Pivotal

...

Thoughts came to him as though suddenly released from bondage.

He had little doubt now that the Diirredyn, and the First Comers, were not ancient progenitors to humanity—still less creators or old gods. They were simply aspects of it, existing in some normally inaccessible dimensions. Whatever passed for reason amongst them was all too human—and deeply flawed.

Then, ludicrous and ordinary, two words burst into his thoughts like a blow.

Closing error.

They left him momentarily stunned.

It wasn't possible... surely...?

Yet...

Closing error.

Josyff swore violently in both wide-eyed incredulity and trembling rage at the folly and tawdriness this dreadful insight revealed. Blinded by who could say what hatreds, the Diirredyn must have wilfully ignored the true conclusion of their own reasoning—that what they were attempting was impossible.

He felt nauseous. It *was* all too human. Horrifically human, for there was nothing mundane or ordinary about the forces they had marshalled to achieve this monstrous and impossible folly. Who could say how long their will had been reaching across the unbridgeable gap, resonating where their forms could not go—shaping, twisting, then manipulating as their knowledge grew—minds, thoughts, objects—anything they could touch? And who could say how far their influence had spread in their pursuit of this monstrous folly? Now, just as a loud cry might bring down an avalanche, so could their ever-mounting efforts bring destruction into this world.

As if for relief from this stark conclusion, Josyff's attention returned to Adroyan and Esyal, and the seemingly motionless figures of Nyk and the others. Briefly he thought he sensed Amrassian's touch.

This must not happen.

His immediate fury had passed. It had changed, and a deep anger, cold and unstoppable, began to spread through him.

It brought with it a great clarity.

I must not let this happen.

I *will* not let this happen.

CHAPTER 84

Esyal had come to the verge of despair as she had seen Adroyan take hold of Josyff. Every part of her cried out with effort, but she had been unable to reach him in time. Then, heralded by a sound, short and fierce, like the cracking of a great whip, had come a tidal wave of colours. It washed over her, at once beautiful and terrifying, and abruptly, the eerie stretching of distance that was keeping her from Adroyan was gone. She could hear her own voice again, screaming with rage, feel the slithering floor under her feet, feel the weight of the heavy wooden table skidding across it...

...And the impact of it striking Adroyan, breaking him free from Josyff and sending him sprawling.

Swirling rainbow colours mingled with the flames that marked his passage but Esyal had no eye for such things, nor thoughts for any of the insane confusion all about her. Her focus was total. Here was the cause. Here was her enemy. Here he must be destroyed and destroyed quickly. To think of anything else, however fleetingly, would be to blur the great clarity of this intention and precipitate failure. She sprang on to the table, took one stride across it then jumped over the far edge, intending to land on him and strike him down. But even as she was descending, she saw him roll away and begin swinging to his feet—she noted the speed at which he moved. Shifting her balance, she dropped low as her feet hit the ground, both to absorb the impact and to bring her below any attack. At the same time she swung her machete in a sweeping horizontal arc. It struck nothing, but she used the momentum of the movement to bring it over her head and swing it vertically downwards.

It should have cleaved Adroyan's head but he calmly leaned back to avoid the blow—again, Esyal noted the speed of his response.

She must not give him the least fraction of an advantage.

But even as this resolve formed, Adroyan was speaking.

"Too late, *Warrior*." The word was full of triumphant scorn. "Too late. The merest hair's breadth now lies between the worlds. In their splendour they are coming."

Esyal hesitated. Although Adroyan's manner showed almost overwhelming confidence, something was amiss. Something had disturbed him but she had no inkling what it might be. It was not her attack, she was sure. His confidence in his physical ability was well-placed, she knew. Nevertheless...

Kill him! Kill him now!

Her driving imperative pushed this momentary digression aside, but she remained motionless, her strategy changed. Given that she could not now destroy him quickly, she must be defensive—watch, wait, strike him when he committed himself to an attack—as he must now if he wanted Josyff.

She risked a quick glance over her shoulder but she could see little through the snow driving into her face save vague, grey silhouettes, presumably Qualto and the others, apparently motionless.

The sound of the Diirredyn stopped abruptly. So abruptly in fact that she almost lurched forward. The comparative normality of the shattered kitchen closed about her. Lit by the still-flickering stoves and buffeted by the snow-laden wind blowing through the broken window, it seemed incongruous, at once comforting and claustrophobic.

But there was nothing incongruous about Adroyan as he turned towards her. She felt her knees shaking under the intensity and malevolence of his gaze.

"The power of the Gods is mine now, Warrior," Adroyan said, curling his lip disdainfully at the last word. He glanced upwards as though looking at something in the far distance. "And the moment is come. Time to end this."

Like her, he was carrying a machete. She returned his sneer with one of her own.

"A pity your gods—your puppet masters—did not give you something a little more fitting to fight with. Mind you don't cut your strings with it."

She risked a brief, mocking, tip-toe marionette pose, dangling her own machete at him ineptly. As she recovered she casually rested her other hand on the top of a nearby chair. The movement had freed her body from the tension that had built up as she had stood watching him, and she could use the chair to entangle his legs when he advanced. She would not be able to match his strength so she must use her agility and speed. Above all, she must take his balance.

He did not respond to the jibe other than to narrow his eyes slightly. Even so, it seemed to Esyal for an instant that through them shone the baleful light of the Diirredyn's world. She fought down an unexpectedly powerful urge to charge forward and attack him.

There was a noise behind her, unsteady footsteps in the debris. She flung her arm back urgently in a signal to stop. Nyk and the others could not help her now; they would only get in the way—and probably be killed for their efforts.

Then Adroyan straightened up and inclined his head forward, looking past her. Esyal frowned, suspecting a trick.

Then Josyff was standing by her.

Somewhere, the forces of the Diirredyn and the First Comers were gathered. The former, in their blind fury, set to bring about great destruction for something that could not be; the latter, waiting.

For what?

Unknown creatures, unknown consciousness, unknown aspects of

411

humanity. Here and in presences across unknowable spaces, Adroyan and Esyal disputed the Way that was not a Way. Both set to kill or die for something that could not be.

Josyff breathed slowly.

His strength did not lie in the fierce fighting skills that Esyal had drawn on to protect him so far. It lay in the very depths of his mind, the realm of dreams and nightmares and who knew what ancient skills and knowledge.

His thoughts were calm and clear. He touched the screaming will of the Diirredyn.

Your prying, your searching, has brought you thus far. I will take you to the end now. I will *lead* you into the Heart itself. But know this. Where we go is mine and has guided me truly always. You will learn what it is you have sought for, what the Heart really is. And you will learn what it is you have unleashed. This ends now! Expect justice!

He closed his eyes and felt his many selves begin to walk through the totality of the Keep. They carried his trust, he must not hinder them. With them went his cold, determined anger and the myriad threading colours of the searching light.

He could not do anything about the solid and massive building of this reality...

But elsewhere the fabric was different.

And in the wake of his many passings came change. Twisting and folding, regions of the Keep, distant and alien, became other than they had been.

On and on.

Change upon change.

Making a Way of his own.

...

Silence...

...

Then he was on a high vantage.

Below him was icy fury and blazing tumult separated by a void, black with a frightening emptiness.

Again he sensed the touch of Amrassian, though reaching out to him this time, and laden with aching, almost unbearable insights.

Such terrible wrongness. This (we?) should not be. Must not be.

Was it an absolution—a blessing even?

Words came unbidden.

"Be as you once were," he said.

And even as his voice echoed through the many soaring spaces he occupied, his thoughts were plunging towards the dreadful gulf, both carrying and being carried by the light. It leapt ahead like a predator finally within reach of its prey, surging down into the void, spreading across it, bridging it, many coloured and brilliant.

Beautiful, thought Josyff. A healing.

There was the sound of a great rushing—a coming together...

A high-pitched hissing filled Josyff's head.

It was a long, timeless moment before he recognized it as a sharp intake of breath—his own.

He heard Esyal give a slight cry and felt her brace herself.

Then came a dull thud.

Slowly his vision cleared.

Sprawled dismally on the floor in the wreck of Qualto's kitchen, lay Adroyan.

CHAPTER 85

Henk burst into the room, uncharacteristically agitated—arms waving, eyes wide and mouth agape.

He lumbered to an ungainly halt as he took in the scene and his agitation increased.

After several unsuccessful tries he managed a string of "Wha, wha, wha," before reaching, "What's happened?" followed immediately, bursting out, by, "They've gone, all gone, the place is normal again. I broke the lens on the Beacon—Nyk, I'm sorry, I'm sorry, I didn't know what to do. I... What happened?"

"That's a good question."

It was Qualto. He had moved to Josyff's side and was looking at him intently. Josyff put a hand on his shoulder, partly for support, partly to reassure. He turned to look at Nyk and Badr.

"Are you all right?" he asked

He had to ask again before he got a reply.

"Yes." The two men spoke almost simultaneously. Nyk extended an unsteady hand towards the motionless form of Adroyan.

"He's dead," Esyal said. Despite the certainty in her voice however, she carefully kicked the machete from his hand and kept her own levelled and purposeful as she bent down to drag him over onto his back.

"He looks pathetic somehow," she said as she checked his pulse.

"Yes," Josyff agreed. "He is now. But he wasn't. He was insane and murderously dangerous."

Esyal nodded. "I didn't touch him," she said. It was a simple statement, not a plea.

"What happened?" Badr echoed Henk's question.

"What did you see?" Josyff asked in return. He looked at each of them in turn.

It was Nyk who answered. "We were fighting—holding them back. But when the door went and... he..." He indicated Adroyan. "...came in, I thought 'we're all going to die here'—I've never been so..." He faltered and cleared his throat. "But at the end it was just..." He shrugged. "Terrible noise—rumblings, shrieking—lights everywhere." He shook his head as if to clear it. "I couldn't see anything, hear anything. Just uproar and confusion... dreadful. Then..." He snapped his fingers. "It was all gone. Just stopped, vanished." There was general nodding from Qualto and Badr.

A cold gust of wind blew a flurry of snow through the broken window. It stirred the brief silence that had followed Nyk's account.

"I'll get that patched up," Nyk said, stepping towards the door, suddenly anxious to be practical. Josyff reached out to stop him but Qualto intervened.

"They *have* gone, haven't they?" he asked earnestly.

"Yes." It was Henk. "Completely, utterly gone. The place is clean again—fresh." He patted the wall. "It's not been like this for... years."

"You'll not be leaving, then?" Qualto pulled a gentle irony from somewhere.

"Oh no," Henk replied, still patting the wall. "Oh no, I belong here. We all belong here. Let's get this mess sorted out. It's going to be a good winter."

Henk's unexpected enthusiasm marked, for Josyff, the real end to the Diirredyn's desperate intrusion. It seemed to trigger almost a rush back to normality.

In the immediate aftermath, Nyk, Henk and Qualto busied themselves restoring Qualto's ruined kitchen—Qualto using the opportunity to make some long pestered-for improvements, prompting at times a dangerous degree of eye-narrowing from Nyk. Josyff and Badr, after a brief debate, continued their survey of the place. Esyal fiddled with the archives and moved between the two groups. Sometimes she had a lost and haunted look.

It surprised Josyff that none of them reported any serious after-effects—nightmares or visions. Indeed, he himself slept very well, and even began to develop a degree of affection for his dacoit clock. He remarked on it one evening in the common room.

It was Henk—now, on occasions, almost jovial—who replied. "Remember that scroll? Who can say how long those things were meddling, twisting our minds, even twisting the building itself? Or how far they reached? Now, they've just—gone—vanished. We're free of them. It's... wonderful."

There was general agreement around the firelit room, although familiar questions about what Josyff had actually done came in its wake.

"I've no idea," he replied. "I'm sorry. I just panicked at first—thought I was going insane—hoped it would go away. You all protected me. In the end..." He shrugged. "Something deep inside me—something *they'd* been using—said 'enough'. I remember anger... terrible anger." He fell silent. Then he grimaced and shook his head. "It stopped me running and cowering—gave me my mind back—let... parts... of me move through other manifestations of the Keep and change them—led me to the place between their armies. As for how that... bridge... came to be..." He shrugged. "All those colours... beautiful." His voice faded and his eyes became distant.

"It still makes no sense," Esyal said into the silence.

"No," Josyff agreed. "It doesn't. But it *did* happen, didn't it?"

Esyal scowled and persisted. "But what were they? *Where* were they? Are you sure they've gone? What's to stop them coming again—with their damned war?"

Josyff lifted his hands defensively. "I've told you, I've no idea," he protested. "We all saw things like human beings, but then they were made from my mind—our minds—weren't they? I think both the Diirredyn and the First Comers were some manifestation of ourselves—perhaps of everyone—in other dimensions. I'm certain the Keep, and the mountains hereabouts, and perhaps even things beyond, far beyond—acted as... a wedge, a lightning rod, a focus, a bridge—god knows, I certainly don't. But the Keep is changed now. It can't happen again."

He became thoughtful. "I think when that bridge was made, their dimension folded in on itself, an imbalance was corrected. Somehow they annihilated one another—became no more, as Amrassian said. But... it's all speculation... guesswork. Our instincts got us through this and I'm happy to keep trusting mine. They're truly gone."

"It still makes no sense," Esyal repeated, growling and fidgeting. "How can there be all these different... dimensions? Where are they?" Her lip curled and she waved her hands vaguely.

Josyff looked at her, then picked up a piece of paper. He ran his finger along two edges, counting. "One, two." Then he gripped it between his thumb and forefinger. "Three. Can you see it?"

Before Esyal could reply, he tore off a strip, twisted it, clipped the ends together and thrust it in her hand. "When you've decided how many sides this piece of paper has, let me know how many edges it has." Esyal eyed him suspiciously but he merely raised a challenging eyebrow. Badr chuckled softly.

By common consent it was agreed that nothing was to be served, save accusations of insanity, by spreading the tale abroad. There had been no signs of violence on Adroyan's body. Whatever thrall the Diirredyn had held him in, its sudden withdrawal had cost him the ultimate price.

"He just collapsed," Josyff suggested, looking significantly at everyone. "Heart, maybe—we're not doctors, are we? There wasn't a flicker of life in him when we checked him, was there? Nothing we could do."

His body was placed in the Keep's morgue, the existence of which caused an exchange of significant looks between Josyff and Badr, but no questions.

One bright afternoon, Josyff came across Esyal standing on the drawbridge and looking out at the snow-covered mountains.

"I think you'll find the New Order isn't what it was," he said as he joined her. "The leader's gone and whatever influence the Diirredyn had on his followers, his acolytes, will have gone too."

Esyal pulled a face. Her eyes shone with tears though she didn't weep. "And me?" she asked. "I don't think I want to be what I've become."

Josyff was blunt. "Oh. You mean someone who puts life and limb on the line to protect others?"

Esyal faltered. "No... I... I..."

Josyff cut her short. "I'm a lot older than you, used to carrying responsibility, exercising authority over others. But when this started, I floundered, dithered like a dead leaf in the wind—useless. You didn't. You held the line. That's what warriors do. Look the truth in the eye. Stand between the weak and harm. None of the rest of us—none of us—could have dealt with Adroyan and those... things... he was bringing across. And before that you stood against the New Order, so whatever you used to be was no bad thing. Now you've been tempered into something better—stronger, wiser. Be proud of that, be glad of it. You'll find plenty of good use for it, trust me. The remains of the New Order won't disappear overnight and their like are always with us."

She looked at him enigmatically, making him clear his throat self-consciously. He became prosaic. "Which reminds me," he said. "We need to think about the tale you're going to tell when spring comes and we get back to the city. It won't be hard, but we do need to work it out. And you *do* know I... we... will help you in any way we can, don't you? I..."

A burst of laughter across the courtyard interrupted him. It came from Qualto and Badr emerging from the main door. Henk and Nyk were behind them, Henk laughing, Nyk gesticulating and shaking his head ruefully.

"Come on," said Josyff, motioning Esyal forward. "Let's see what they've been up to."

As they set off, Josyff looked up. He breathed in the cold mountain air deeply and it seemed to him that not only the courtyard but the whole bright, clear sky arching high above him was filled with the echoing laughter of his friends' voices.

About the author

Roger Taylor was born in Heywood, Lancashire, and now lives in the Wirral. He is a chartered civil and structural engineer, a pistol, rifle and shotgun shooter, instructor/student in aikido, and an enthusiastic and loud but bone-jarringly inaccurate piano player.

He wrote four books between 1983 and 1986 and built up a handsome rejection file before the third was accepted by Headline to become the first two books of the Chronicles of Hawklan.

Also by Roger Taylor

The Call of the Sword
The Fall of Fyorlund
The Waking of Orthlund
Into Narsindal
Dream Finder
Farnor
Valderen
Whistler
Ibryen
Arash-Felloren
Caddoran
The Return of the Sword

All titles are also available as ebooks from from
www.mushroom-ebooks.com